Players of the Game

by

Saji Anthony

Bloomington, IN authorHOUSE® Milton Keynes, UK

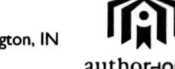

AuthorHouse™
1663 Liberty Drive, Suite 200
Bloomington, IN 47403
www.authorhouse.com
Phone: 1-800-839-8640

AuthorHouse™ UK Ltd.
500 Avebury Boulevard
Central Milton Keynes, MK9 2BE
www.authorhouse.co.uk
Phone: 08001974150

© 2007 Saji Anthony. All rights reserved.

No part of this book may be reproduced, stored in a retrieval system, or transmitted by any means without the written permission of the author.

First published by AuthorHouse 9/24/2007

ISBN: 978-1-4343-1029-3 (sc)

Library of Congress Control Number: 2007902882

Printed in the United States of America
Bloomington, Indiana

This book is printed on acid-free paper.

Chapter One

Beverly Hills, California, present day...

Anna tripped and nearly broke her neck coming through the front door of her house or *Le Chateau* as her best friend Hector liked to refer to it. She looked down to see what had nearly ended her life—a pair of Monolo Blahnik flats. Size eight. She sighed and rolled her eyes. Meena—her fifteen-year-old Belizean adopted daughter—had once again kicked off her shoes the minute she got through the front door. She snatched them up, one in each hand, and waved them in the air as she called her daughter's name.

"Meena! Meena! Come here! Right now!"

After a minute or so, a tall, black haired, slender girl with the bronze skin of her Mayan and Mestizo ancestors came sauntering into the living room where a riled Anna stood. Her skin glistened with pool water. Anna waved one of the shoes under Meena's nose.

"What did I tell you about leaving your shoes in the middle of the hallway, right in front of the door, at that? I nearly broke my neck tripping over these."

"Sorry, Mom. I forgot. I was so hot, I just went straight to the pool the minute I got home from school," Meena said, not really looking that sorry at all. Her long black hair was dripping water all over the carpet.

Anna let out a long puff of air and brushed her relaxed, long, shoulder-length, hair, back with a weep of one hand. She then eyed her daughter's bikini. It was so tiny that it left all but nothing to the imagination. Anna scowled.

"Where did you get the piece of dental floss?" she asked, pointing an accusing finger at the offending swimwear. "Not from me, I know."

Meena began to shuffle on her feet and look every which way but at Anna.

"Well, who bought it for you?" Anna asked, impatiently. Damn, she was hungry. She wondered what Elsa, her aunt who was visiting for the week, was going to prepare for dinner. For all the snobbish uppity behavior that her aunt Elsa exuded, no one would believe that the woman was such a whiz in the kitchen. One would think that such a domestic task would be beneath such a woman as Elsa, but cooking and baking were her passion. What was even more contradictory was the fact that her aunt was as lithe as a whip despite all the time spent in the kitchen with good food.

Meena looked down and mumbled something.

"What was that?" Anna said, extra loud.

"Tessa bought it for me. I saw it Neiman Marcus and I liked it."

Anna's face twisted up even further. Leave it to her sister Tessa not to see anything wrong with the fact that her fourteen-year-old niece was walking around with a scrap of cloth that barely covered her privates. Although Anna hardly had anything to do with her older sister, she didn't discourage a relationship between her and the children.

"I want you never to wear that thing again. Take it back and we'll exchange for another one," Anna commanded, handing Meena her shoes.

"But, Mom…I like it," Meena said, thrusting her full lips out in a pout.

"Yeah, well we can't get everything we want in this day an age. I'm sure a lot of people wish that they could walk around free in the buff, but that would be indecent and besides, and you'll be asking for a lot of trouble."

Meena wasn't going to give up easily. "What if I were to wear it just in the back, just in our pool."

Anna narrowed her eyes at her daughter's stubbornness. "And you think the neighbors have no eyes? They can see you."

"So what."

Anna raised an eyebrow. "So what? Who knows what kind of perverts we have surrounding us."

Meena chuckled. "You mean that old man Mr. Romaldi? He's like a grandfather. His wife invites us over for dinner."

"They're not the only neighbors that we have, you know. We're not friendly with everyone. Even if we were, it wouldn't make a difference," Anna pointed out. "Besides, any ole' one can just pass by one day and see you."

"Mom! We have a high fence surrounding the back plus security cameras. Our place isn't exactly open to the public," Meena exclaimed, not believing her mother's outlandish remarks.

Anna walked up to her daughter. Her daughter was a tall girl—5'9" to be exact, but Anna, at 5'7" was only two inches shorter.

Meena opened her eyes at her mother. "So now you're trying to intimidate me?" Her mother was unbelievable.

"No, I'm just getting a little closer, because I don't think you were quite hearing me good enough from where I was standing before." She put her hands on her slim hips. "Get rid of the bathing suit, please. We'll exchange it. Tomorrow, if you like."

Meena gave her mother a fierce look with her deep brown eyes and stalked from the room, and up the stairs. Her model thin body swaying as she walked.

Anna looked after her with disapproval. How did she manage to foster such a spoilt child? And where was that sweet little girl that Meena had once been? Gone with the wind and there was not a thing she could do about it.

Suddenly her cell phone rang. She sighed and answered it, already knowing who it was.

"Hello, Miss. Senghor? This is Mrs. Hamel."

Anna closed her eyes and prepared for the worst. "What has he done this time?"

"Well…Brian has gotten into some sort of confrontation with another student at the bus stop."

"What is he doing at the bus stop? He doesn't even take the bus… Oh yes, I forgot, his car's in the shop."

"Well, apparently, their meeting there was prearranged. They got into an argument in class earlier on. The teacher had stopped it and thought that was that. But apparently, unbeknownst to the teacher, they decided to take it further."

Stupid people. Why would they think that it would end there? Don't they know that kids took their fights out of the classroom and into the streets? They certainly should have had enough experience with that. She snatched up her car keys.

"I'm coming down there to get him now," she blasted into the phone and hung up before the woman could say another word.

Anna huffed and stalked out of the house raging mad. As she flounced her way to her Mercedes, she imagined what her neighbors would be saying if they could see her now. She forced herself into control and managed to walk normally, the rest of the way to the car.

As she drove to the school to pick up her wayward nephew, her mind drifted back to her past.

Anna grew up in Arizona with her older brother Malik, her older sister Tessa (who was the eldest), and her youngest sister Kati. Their father, Muhammad Senghor, was a former Senegalese government worker, who had retired and opened some small businesses and their mother was a pharmacist from Liverpool. Her mother's parents immigrated to England from the Caribbean island nation of Barbados. Their father, although Muslim by religion, didn't push Islam on his children. Growing up, they were exposed to both Christianity and Islam. They would celebrate holidays unique to both religions.They would go to their mother's Baptist church on Sundays and pray at their father's mosque on Fridays. They grew up speaking both English and Wolof—their father's native African language. It was a nice arrangement. The only thing was that their father wanted unquestioned obedience from all his children. Tessa, after applying and getting accepted to a college clear across the country on the east coast, escaped her father's clutches, and was only seen on holidays. The remaining three younger children, reacted each in their own way to their father. Anna, being the astute, good, people-pleasing person that she was while growing up, obeyed her father concerning everything. The oldest son, Malik, spoilt as he was, was indifferent to his father's commands. He followed them only when they were convenient for him. If not, he didn't bother. Lucky for him, he often got away with it. Anna knew that it was because he was a boy. Kati on the other hand, refused to do anything. Point blank. She marched to her own drumbeat at all times, no matter how out of sequence it was. From the time that Anna could remember, her little sister had a rebellious streak in her that couldn't be thwarted. Her father and her mother tried almost all methods of punishment, from spankings to grounding. Nothing worked. She was as wild as a horse. Or an African Buffalo , as her father would say.

The family home was a large and spacious Spanish styled compound with beautiful gardens surrounding it. In fact, the grounds were so large, that her father would hire Mexican gardeners to tend to the vegetation. Her father also hired a housekeeper that would come in five times a week and a nanny that took care of them from the time they were babies. The nanny's name was Kadejah—a Muslim woman from Aswan, Egypt. Anna remembered the nanny well, and was very fond of her. Kadejah was a middle-aged woman with dark chocolate skin and frizzled hair. Her eyes were wide and bright, her cheekbones high and sculpted. She was always very kind to them, and treated Anna and her siblings as if they were her own. She would make all kinds of exotic Nubian and Arabic foods. And many a time, though she knew that she could be fired, she would cover up for them if they did anything bad. She even taught them a little Nubian. Anna still remembered some words.

Anna still remembers the day that her father hired Romel Rivera as a gardener. Romel was of medium height, around 5'10", but this was tall compared with the others. He had glowing bronze skin and was well muscled. His face was handsome with dark sweltering eyes, full lips, and black glossy hair that hung down to his shoulders. Anna was 20 at the time and still living at home, going to a nearby university full time. Her brother had long since moved out and was working as an accountant at a major firm. Kati was 16 years old at the time and just as unruly as ever. At the moment, her mother and father were sending her to a Catholic school, thinking that it would settle her down, but she had been there two years, and the change had yet to come. She had been caught drinking, smoking pot, and cigarettes by both parents. Anna had even once caught her giving head to some boy from her school in one of the upstairs bathrooms at home. Anna had come home from her classes early because of a function going on at her school. She went upstairs to one of the bathrooms and there was her little sister, knees to the tiles, head down at the crotch of a standing boy whose blue eyes were rolling with pleasure in his head. Anna had grabbed her sister's hair in one hand and pulled her away. The boy, shocked and afraid, was speechless as Anna took both of her hands and gripped the back of his white, uniform shirt. She began to drag him from out of the bathroom.

"What are you doing?" The teenaged boy shrieked, twisting, and writhing like an eel as he was pulled through the hallway and down the stairs. Despite being a good three or so inches taller than Anna, he was finding it difficult to disengage her hand lock on him.

"I'm getting you out of my house!" Anna responded, heatedly.

Anna dragged him by the back of his white shirt, down the stairs and she was headed towards the front door. As soon as he began to realize this, he began to pull frantically at his pants, which were down around his ankles. His attempts were unsuccessful to say the least.

Finally, Anna shoved him through the front door and slammed the door shut behind him. The boy was left embarrassed and blushing on the front porch. Now that he wasn't moving, he now as quickly as he could, pulled up his pants and underwear. But not before the group of gardeners got a peek at him.

The gardeners had a good laugh at the boy and chattered to one another in Spanish. Then they began to call out to him.

The boy, obviously suffering from shock, stood frozen in the midst of his tormentors.

"Aye, where your *pantalones*, *chico*?" one yelled out to him

"Hah, your *culo* and *cajones* were all hanging out!" another laughed aloud.

The teenager, having now regained his composure, quickly fled down the block and disappeared around a corner. Anna chuckled, as she watched from the front window. The workers would have something interesting to discuss over the dinner table when they got home tonight. Anna's face turned grim again as she went back into the house to deal with her Kati. Her sister was where she had left her, in the hallway upstairs.

"Please don't tell Mom and Dad. Please," Kati begged.

"What the hell is wrong with you, coming up here doing things like that? What if it were Mom or Dad that came and saw you? Your ass would be grass right now," Anna yelled, enraged at her sister's sluttish behavior.

Anna gave her sister a look over. She was too developed for her age. Hell, at 36 C her sister's chest was bigger than hers had ever been at sixteen.

"I'm sorry—I like him. I wanted to do it. I don't know what I was thinking!" her sister pleaded.

Anna had let it go, not telling their parents a thing about it. But she promised that if she saw anything like it again, she would.

Then one day, a few weeks later, Kati was gone. Just like that. As was Romel Rivera, so they noticed. At first, they didn't see the connection, but eventually they suspected it, and then much to Muhammad Senghor's amazement and anger, it was confirmed. Kati had run away with the 23 year old, Mexican, gardener. No one saw it coming. It happened just like that.

"When I get my hands on that wetback's neck," he had proclaimed, fist in the air, as if making an oath to God, "I will snap it like a piece of chicken bone!" Anna had swallowed hard, glad that she wasn't in his position, or her sister's for that matter.

He had instantly called the police. And so the search began. Her mother was more sad than angry that her daughter had done such a thing. She would silently mope around the house for days while sighing deeply from time to time. Anna was angry that her sister could be so selfish.

While her brother, wanting to flex a little muscle, would come over, strut around, tormenting and intimidating the gardeners. If one was in his path while he was outside his parents' house, he would push them out of the way. He would yell at them over mistakes that only he could see and call them all types of names imaginable. Anna didn't know why the lot of them wouldn't fight back, she was sure that her brother would run for cover—many of them being more robust and stronger than he. By the end of the month, the vast majority of them had quit. This infuriated her father even more. Also, the fact that Kati still hadn't been found didn't help matters.

Finally, her father made the wise decision to eject his big-mouthed son from his premises and demanded Malik to go home after he had managed to cause the last few gardeners that were left, to quit. Anna was secretly glad. Her brother was a pain in the ass. Always had been.

Finally, after five months, they got the worst news that they could hear. Kati and Romel were possibly in Mexico. There wasn't much that the authorities could do. Mexico was a lawless land, the FBI had told them. And they could be anywhere. Besides, they weren't too eager to go after a run-away. Finally, her parents had hired a PI. Within another month, he had found them. He had pictures of them from all over the place. Kati in the marketplace bartering for food. Kati and Romel, holding hands in front of a house…Kati and Romel kissing intimately…the list went on. Her father was furious. Ranting, raving, mad.

"Can you get them?" This was more of a command than a question.

The PI, with his hazel eyes and thin lips had looked at him, thinking what a crazy man this is. "I can't just snatch her."

"Can you get the both of them and bring them here?" her father asked, loudly, not comprehending.

Why is this guy shouting like this? the PI asked himself. He looked over at the older girl Anna. She gave him a pleading look. He felt embarrassed for her—that this nut was her father.

"I can't do that. It's illegal. All I can do it bring back information for you. If you want her back, you'll have to be the one to go down there and get her."

"Are you suggesting that I don't want my daughter back?" Muhammad asked, suspiciously.

The PI stared at him, incredulous. "I'm not suggesting anything. I'm just saying I can only collect info."

"What good is that?" Muhammad exclaimed, waving his hands crazily in the air.

"Look. That's the most I could do." the PI said, calmly. He took a cigarette from his pants pocket and proceeded to light it.

Anna looked at her father. His face turned a bright purple—red for a dark skinned black man.

He snatched the cigarette out of the startled man's mouth, flung it on the ground, and ground his heel into to. "No smoking in my house!"

"You are one crazy mutherfucker," the man yelled, enraged. That was his last one! "We're not even in your house, we're outside!"

"Get out!" Muhammad yelled, advancing upon the PI with purpose.

The PI, anticipating bodily harm, made a quick escape. Cursing and yelling all the way to his black Jaguar, he got in, zoomd off down the road, and disappeared into the sunset.

And that was that.

Ψ

Anna, snapping out of her reminiscing, came back to the present. She hurriedly parked her Mercedes in the parking lot of the highschool and jumped out of the car. Anna came marching into the school that her daughter, her nephew, and her niece attended. This was it. Next year all of them were going to private school, she didn't care how loudly they complained!

The office secretary caught sight of her and immediately came over. The woman pushed her glasses up from her nose and cleared her throat. Her brown eyes held a sympathetic look in them. Anna almost snorted aloud, the last thing she needed was this woman's sympathy. She gave the woman a once over from the top of her head with her half relaxed-half not hair, to the cheap Wallmart shoes on her feet. This woman needed to save all her sympathy for herself—she needed all the sympathy that she could get by the looks of it. Anna would have loved to give her a makeover, but the woman would probably be insulted if she mentioned it, so she decided to keep her mouth shut for as far as that went.

"Brian is in the office right now. Unfortunately, the principal is in a meeting right now and won't be out for another hour. Brian's being suspended for a week. I'm really sorry about this."

What's really sorry is that appalling shade of red lipstick that you're wearing, woman. "It's okay, I'll deal with it," Anna said, aloud.

The woman led Anna into the office where a miserable looking Brian was propped up in one of the upholstered chairs. He had a busted lip and a big bruise on his cheek. He turned mournful eyes to Anna when he saw her walk into the room.

"What is wrong with you getting into fights with people at school?" Anna demanded.

"He started it Anna, I swear," Brian said, standing up and running a hand through his curly hair. His copper colored skin glowed under the lights.

"Perhaps I can suggest some counseling. We have a very good councilor at this school, her name is Mrs. Grayson," the women piped.

Anna stared her into silence, allowing the hush to linger in the air until a ruffled and uncomfortable Mrs. Hamel had the sense to see herself out of the room.

Anna eyed Brian's hair critically. When was the boy going to cut his hair? It was a mass of curls and waves.

"Come on. We'll discuss this when we reach home," Anna said, bustling her nephew out the door, and past the meddlesome secretary now perched cautiously behind her desk.

Once they were out at the car, Anna began questioning him.

"What do you mean he started it? Someone's always starting with you, aren't they?"

"Well it's true. I was sitting in pre-calculus, minding my business. The teacher asked a question on some of the homework. I gave my answer, and the stupid jerk kept saying that I was wrong, even though I was right.

Anna smiled a little. One thing about Brian, he was a math whiz. For as long as Brian had been going to school, he got straight A's in all his math classes. He was good with numbers and figures. Math was his favorite subject, but he couldn't stand English class or anything like that. Writing wasn't one of his strong points.

Brian continued. "But he kept going on, saying that it was the wrong answer, like I was dumb or something so I asked him if he had a problem. He said yeah, so I asked him if he wanted to solve it with me."

"I assume not by talking it out," Anna said, sighing.

"Nah. What kinda punk would I be? I said we could fight it out after school. So we met at the back of the school near the parking lot and we started fighting. I was getting him good until a bunch the teachers jumped in and stopped us," Brian said, regretfully.

"Fighting is not okay!" Anna exclaimed, trying to sound convincing. "You cannot solve your problems by battling with fists."

"Yeah, maybe next time I'll bring a bat," Brian said, rather seriously.

Anna glanced at her nephew, appalled. What was she going to do with him? He was out of control; there was no denying it. Anna had given her niece and nephew everything they ever wanted, while growing up. Maybe that was the problem—they were spoilt and used to things going their way.

Chapter Two

Anna had met Hector, her long time best friend, while they were in University. She still remembered that day. It was during orientation.

"Your hair is to diiiiiiiie for...who did it?" A voice screeched behind her. Simultaneously, she felt a hand pull gently at her cornrows.

Anna twirled around to face a tall, good-looking, well-tanned boy with a Roman nose and shoulder length, curling hair. His light brown eyes sparkled with delight. He wore a Duran Duran concert tee shirt and fitted sand blasted jeans over well-toned legs.

"Do I know you?" Anna asked, testily, patting her head—a nervous habit that she had picked up years ago.

The young man laughed and shook his head, his loose dark curls bouncing. "I just saw your hair from way over there, and I thought to myself, I just had to find out who had such a creative style." He shrugged his shoulders. "I love hair. I think that hair is the most interesting thing that we possess."

Anna nodded, thinking that this guy was crazy. The last thing she needed was an outrageous white boy on her case. She tried to discreetly back away. But there was no getting rid of him. He was right in her face.

"What's your name?" he asked, grinning from ear to ear.

"Anna."

"My name's Hector." He smiled as they shook hands. "So...where are you from?" he asked her, shaking his mane of hair.

"Sedona," Anna answered, realizing that Hector wasn't going anywhere anytime soon.

"Ah...a local girl. I'm from California. Santa Monica to be exact."

Anna nodded, not sure what to say in response to this piece of information. She supposed that it must be pretty boring around here for him, in comparison.

Some guy with a megaphone pushed himself to the front of the crowd and hopped onto the stage. The sun was beating down on him, and he was as red as a lobster. He looked like he was in a certain amount of pain.

"Okay, everyone partner up. We're gonna do some races!" he exclaimed in a false show of excitement.

"What are we, in grade school or something?" someone cried indignantly from the crowd of newly accepted students.

"Hey. I just do what they tell me to, all right?" the redfaced guy with the megaphone responded, testily. "It's all a part of orientation. Just pretend you're having fun."

A loud groan rose from the crowd of newly admitted students. It was too damn hot for all of that activity. Anna hoped that someone would pass out from a heatstroke to put a halt on things, but there was no such luck.

Hector automatically grabbed onto her elbow. "Lucky we found each other!" he exclaimed.

Anna was slowly developing a headache. Heck, she wished that she would pass out right now.

The students half-heartedly shuffled their way around until they were all paired up except for a few. A chubby black guy waddled over to where Anna and Hector stood.

"Can we be partners?" he asked Anna, completely ignoring Hector.

Before Anna could say anything in response, Hector chimed in, "She's my partner. Can't you see us standing here together?"

The fat boy cast a disdainful look at Hector before he waddled away.

"Fat fryer," Hector muttered.

Anna couldn't help but laugh. This guy was a trip!

Anna and Hector managed to win the first two races, thanks to Hector's over-zealous competitiveness.

"Go Anna, Go, Go, GO!" Hector yelled from the sidelines.

Anna wished that he would shut the fuck up. She was getting lightheaded and the sun seemed to be burning her eyes right out of the sockets. Her vision began to spin. Before she knew it, she had plopped bottom first on the grass.

Hector came rushing over, the first in the line of others. People began closing in around her, more curious bystanders than helpful ones.

"Get back!" Hector exclaimed, shoving people back with his sinewy arms, "She needs air to breathe!" Hector was causing quite a scene.

Anna was reasonably embarrassed. Things couldn't get any worse. But she did ask to pass out, didn't she? At least she didn't have to run around in the heat anymore, she thought to herself as she fell back into the grass.

She woke up under white sheets in a room with white walls. A face was hovering above her. Light brown eyes peered worriedly down at her alongside two more pairs of eyes that were darker in color.

"Honey, are you okay?" her mother asked her, a worried expression on her toffee colored face.

"I'm fine Mom," Anna answered.

"Good," her father answered quickly. "The university called us and told us that you passed out. What kind of idiots would have these children running around in 97 degree weather?" her father exploded.

"Now, now, Muhammad," her mother said, resting a calming hand on her husband. He cooled down immediately.

"That's what I thought," Hector jumped in, always ready to offer his viewpoint, "this is not the weather to be out in. My hair is a frizzy mess."

Muhammad eyed Hector quizzically, *who was this kid?* he asked himself, noting the hand on the hip and other effeminate body language with slight unease.

Anna tried to rise from the bed, sensing the tension in the room.

"Oh, no dear, don't get up," her mother said, in her very proper British accent.

"Mom, I'm fine," Anna said, continuing to rise. "Can I have some water?"

"Here you go," the nurse said, stepping forward and handing her a glass of water. Anna drank thirstily. She put the glass on the bedside table. "Mom, Dad, I'm fine. You can go home now." Anna rose from the hospital bed and stood up. "I'll go back to the campus, it's only ten minutes away."

"We might want to go back with you and look around the campus a little bit," the mother countered, suspecting dismissal.

Anna shrugged, she could never win with her parents. It was best to just let them do as they wanted.

"Are you going to be staying on campus?" Hector asked, grasping her arm and leading her away from her parents who were currently talking to each other and not paying them any attention, and then out of the room.

"No. I'll be commuting. I only live about twenty minutes away. Are you staying on campus?" Anna asked, feeling a bond between them.

"Hell no. I have my own apartment off campus. I wouldn't live in those dorms if they bull whipped me," Hector avowed, his hand pressed dramatically to his chest.

Anna laughed. "I'm hungry."

"So am I. Let's get out of here. There's a good Greek restaurant down the street from here," Hector informed, excited at the prospect of escaping the morbid orientation process.

"Don't we have to go back to campus?" Anna asked, not wanting any trouble.

"Puuuleeeeze. They won't even notice that we're gone. It's not like they've put trackers on us."

"I don't have any money with me."

Hector flipped his hand. "No problem. It's on me." He linked his arm through hers. "Let us go my little *agapitos*."

Anna gave him a strange look, "What does that mean?"

"It's Greek for dear," he answered, leading her off towards the parking lot.

"I'm beginning to suspect that you're Greek," Anna commented.

"You would be half right *koritsi*," Hector said, as they approached a bright red Corvette convertible.

"What do you mean?" Anna asked, not getting him at all. "Nice car," she commented. She sat in the passenger seat.

"Thank you!" Hector said, pleased with the compliment. He took great pride in his car.

Hector hopped in and started the engine. "My father's Greek. He was born in Cyprus. But his parents are originally from Athens."

"What about your mom?"

"My mom is Bahraini."

"She's Arab?" Anna asked, liking the feel of the wind blowing in her face as they sped down the road.

"Yep," he affirmed.

"Oh," Anna responded. "Can I ask you a question?"

"You can ask me anything, hon."

"Well…I don't think that you're trying to pick me up or anything…"

Hector chuckled. "No darling."

"Are you…gay?" Anna asked, tentatively, not wanting to offend him.

"As can be!" Hector exclaimed, not the least bit ashamed.

Anna made a crooked smile. She suspected as much. "I'm guessing that your parents didn't take it too well."

"I told them when I was in last year of high school. They threatened to send me off to boarding school in Switzerland. I threatened to run away. They put me into therapy. After two sessions, the psychologist told them that there was nothing at all wrong with me. And that his sexual orientation cannot be helped. My father was pissed to no end. He alternated between threatening me and pleading with me to become straight."

"What about your mother?"

"Surprisingly, she was more accepting than my father. She eventually tolerated it. My father has yet to adopt that attitude."

"Are you the only child?"

"Of course not," he said, as if she should know, "I have one younger brother and a younger sister. Her name's Amani and she's a freshman in high school. You know how they are at that age—full of hormones. She's getting to be quite saucy; I have to keep an eye on her. The other day I took her to the mall and I caught her making eyes with some guy behind the counter while we were ordering pizza," Hector said, nodding.

"Also, about a week before that incident, my mother told me that Amani went out with some friends and didn't come back until one in the morning. My parents were practically tearing their hair out. My sister is getting to be a handful and then some."

Anna laughed. "She sounds like my sister Kati."

"Let me tell you, if your little sister is anything like mine, I give you my condolences," Hector stated looking rather sincere.

And there began a nineteen year old relationship as tight as a brother's and sister's, and occasionally, just as unpleasant.

Anna's parent's anxiously stood by and watched a striving, growing friendship between Hector and Anna as time passed in college. And much to Muhammed's annoyance, he saw an obedient, obliging Anna slowly being transformed into a sassy, brazen, young lady with much mouth. Pretty soon, he couldn't tell her anything without her yapping back. This was undoubtedly not a good way for a daughter to be, Muhammad decided. Hector had certainly brought her out of her shell—often kicking and screaming—during their time in college. By the time her four years in college were up, she was a changed person. She lived her own life in a way that suited her. She imagined that if she was the same person that she was nineteen years ago, she surely would have gotten crushed underfoot like an insect by now. It took a backbone of steel and a mind as sharp as nails to do what she did everyday. Many people would be astonished to hear the amount of crap that came in her direction on a daily basis as president of a record label. A cushy job always comes with pins in the cushion. Pins that stuck right in the ass and caused a good amount of discomfort. Ah well. Who was she to complain? She could definitely have done worse for herself.

Chapter Three

"God! If I have to put up with that little bastard for another minute, I'm gonna tear him a new asshole," a much harried looking Franklin said, as he came bustling into Anna's office.

Anna stared at her vice president of A&R sitting across from her, looking very tired and bothered. A shock of salt and pepper hair was standing on end and his complexion was flushed.

"Don't let them get under your skin, Frank. I try to discourage any physical violence against our artists," Anna said, with a smirk. Franklin had been working with her for about five years and been with the company for almost twenty years. Anna liked him a lot. He had a lot of gusto and got things done. He did an excellent job as head of the Artist Development department. He took good care of the various music artists that were signed to their label. He handled the most difficult divas and demanding rappers and singers with equal efficiency. He made sure that the artists were well promoted and publicized. He was also a good friend to her. Anna had been the label's president for five years now. Of course, this was not unanimously accepted. She knew there were quite a few people in the different departments who were bitter that they were now working for a woman and, to add insult to injury, a black woman. Many were not above letting their bitterness be known, but Franklin had supported her all the way. "Don't let the assess get to ya," he was fond of telling her.

Anna was a little surprised that she was chosen to replace Hanson Lake as the next president of *Eden's Apple*. She had been working as vice president of the marketing department before her promotion. She was sure that one of the older more experienced presidents from another department was going to get the position, but Walter Damon, the CEO and owner of *Entourage Productions* Records—one of the hottest and most successful recording companies in the country, which owned two labels (*Eden's Apple* and *Krystel Klare Productions*)—had appointed her.

"I think that ye can really make things move hereaboot. Those olde blokes won't do anything but what Andrew's has been doing for a donkey's years. That's fine, but it's not stonking. We wanna shake and move!" Walter had told her, his East End London cockney coming out in full throttle as he spoke excitedly. So here she was, five years later. Things were certainly shaking and moving. She had managed to sign a bunch of artists within the past five years and she had brought the company from good to top rate, prime level. Walter Damon was proud of her and he showed it with the lavish pay she received—more than Hanson was ever paid, she knew. Not only that, her position brought her a lot of perks and advantages. She was invited to all the best parties and events.

"The *Prince*," Franklin said, referring to Duke and emphasizing it with dripping sarcasm, "now tells us that the hotel that we have booked for him isn't good enough."

Anna was shocked. "But it's a five star hotel! All the stars go there when they stop in New York City. It has the best service, top of the line. Besides, you don't really have to deal with that, do you?"

"No, but it infuriates me none-the-less to hear it. According to him, he found another hotel that is even better and of course, more expensive. He says the environment at this one is more therapeutic and will help him perform better," Franklin said, in a mocking, singsong voice.

Anna shook her head in disbelief. Duke was a relatively new artist to the label. This particular talent was a rap artist that had been discovered wiping tables at a restaurant in Little Rock, Arkansas…

Ψ

Delvair Bello, the top and most well paid A&R agent, was a natural at finding talent. He was so good at sniffing out new talent that in fact, that he was nicknamed "*The Weasel.*"

On this particular afternoon, Delvair had decided to eat out at one of his most favorite restaurants. It was a restaurant he liked to go to when he was visiting his homestate, Arkansas. Despite his miserable start in Little Rock, he still bought a condo in the affluent part of the city and stayed there on the weekends that he wished to get away from the materialism and shallowness that permeated a good portion of LA (particularly in Beverly Hills, where he lived). Also, he couldn't help

Players of the Game

but admit, it gave him a certain amount of satisfaction and pleasure to bump into old neighbours from his childhood and see the look of shock and amazement when they saw him driving a luxury car and wearing designer clothes. He would stop and chat with them, while condescendingly and pointedly looking at his Cartier watch, as if he was rushed for time as he benevolently graced them with his attentions. As snobbish as he knew his behavior was, he didn't care. These were all people had that thought Delvair would never make it out of the projects, much more become a great sucess. After finishing, Delvair tipped the waiter handsomely. For a good meal and for looking *so* good. The waiter gladly accepted the tip and gave Delvair a wink as he thought to himself, why not give the little fag a thrill.

When Delvair got to the parking lot he noticed a gaggle of busboys. Delvair, being the curious person that he was, decided to get a little closer to see what was going on. Growing up in a rough neighborhood made one afraid of almost nothing.

Somebody began rapping. Being that Delvair was short in stature, he could barely see over the shoulders of the boys. He couldn't see the person's face yet. He listened some more. This young man had talent. His lyrics were flawless and his style was unique. Delvair noted the unusual way that he had of rapping rapidly one minute and slowing down the next, and then speeding it all up again. It gave the effect of going on a roller coaster, Delvair thought. It all sounded very good, he hadn't heard anything like it before.

He tried to push himself past the broad, sturdy shoulders of the young black men. One of them turned around, not appreciating being forced aside.

"What are you doing, dwarf! Step your short nigga ass back," he commented harshly.

Delvair puffed up with disdain at this insult. He then launched into a tirade, "I am an agent at *Eden's Apple*. If this man is going to go anywhere with his talent, I would be the one to bring him there. Now let me through," he sniffed. Four years of undergrad at Berkeley and two subsequent years at Harvard Business school had certainly covered up the street slang and talk of his youth nicely.

The young men wordlessly stepped aside for him. They parted like the red sea. Delvair was feeling quite important at this point. He came to the tall young man in the center. *Nice looking.* Delvair thought and tried to keep his mind on the business at hand.

"What is your name?" Delvair asked, taking charge.

"C-man...," he drawled.

Delvair fought down the excitement that he got from the young man's lazy bedroom eyes and from what he thought was a very sexy southern drawl.

"Do you have a real name?" Delvair asked, in a controlled voice. He mustn't let his attractions get the most of him.

"Terrance Philips," he answered.

"How old are you?"

"Sixteen."

Hmmm. Jailbait. He had better not even consider it. Better to keep things strictly business.

"Let's say we go and get some coffee and discuss a few things," Delvair offered. He didn't like standing in the middle of a crowd of spectators. They were making him nervous.

"You payin'?" he asked.

Talk about in your face, Delvair thought. "Yes."

"I don't drink no coffee. How about Dairy Queen? Buy me some ice cream?"

"Whatever you wish...," Delvair trailed off. This boy was certainly demanding.

The boy squinted at him. "You ain't tryin' to pick me up are ya? You one of them sissies?"

"I am not!" he said, indignantly. Better not to scare him away.

"Cool, and you got a Audi? Damn , you livin' it large, huh. Maybe I could cop me one of those one day."

Once they had settled down, each of them with their ice cream sundaes, Delvair decided to get down to business.

"I heard you back there. You were pretty good." He was damn good, but Delvair thought it best not to pump his head up.

"Really, you think so? I been rappin' a long time. Ever since I was way little, man."

"Yeah. I think you're good enough to get a deal. I would be glad to represent you."

Players of the Game

Living the ghetto had taught Terrance little trust. He squinted in suspicion. "How I know you ain't just playing me. How do I know you fo' real?"

Delvair dug into the pockets or his Armani slacks and pulled out a card. He handed it to Terrance. Terrence took it from him and eyed it closely, looking for any telltale signs of underhandedness. Seeing none, he pocketed the card.

"So you from Eden's Apple! Man, that is *the* record label!"

"Yes, it is," Delvair said, proudly.

They talked some more, for about another forty-five minutes. And after Terrance agreed to call Delvair tomorrow evening, around one (Delvair *did not* get up earlier than ten), they left. Delvair dropped him in front of a dilapidated duplex that Terrance pointed out to him.

"Yep. That's my home," Terrance announced.

Delvair shuddered, remembering his own wretchedly humble beginnings. He stepped on the gas the minute Terrance hopped out of the car and shut the door.

Delvair zoomed down the road, the graffiti filled streets gradually changing to the polished streets and neighborhoods of the upper class. He signed with relief as the valet took his car keys . Back to his beautiful condo that overlooked the city with a doorman and round the clock security—back to the present.

Ψ

Hector walked around the large ballroom of the twelve-bedroom mansion, surveying the decorations and the setups to be sure that all was going well. His employees flurried around him, fixing up the room to perfection—setting up the tables and arranging the seating.

"Mr. Minatos…you did say to use the ivory silk table cloth, am I correct?" Tanya, one of his employees, asked.

"Yes, I did. But remember to only use the royal blue table clothes on the tables that are in the periphery. We want the inner tables to have the ivory table cloths," Hector answered briskly. He was sure that he had gone over this with her before.

"Well, I do remember you saying that…but I was thinking…"

Tanya was a master at "beating around the bush," if there ever was one.

"Yeeeesss?" Hector asked, impatiently

"I want to show you something…"

Hector hesitantly followed her to where the tables were.

"I think that it would look better if we were to put the blue on the ten inner tables and the ivory on the outer tables. Look at the wall decorations. I think that the royal blue would clash with them a little if they were so close."

Hector considered her observation. There was actually truth to what she was saying. It *would* look a little better if the ivory were on the tables closest to the walls.

"Tanya, you are absolutely right. Good that you picked up on that! Cause this has to be perfect. This is one of the biggest events that we have done this month! We cannot mess this up in the least. Absolute perfection is a must!" Hector exclaimed emphatically, wagging a finger.

Tanya nodded and ran a hand over her short hair currently dyed a bright shocking auburn. She needed a touch up relaxer and a shape up at the back near her neck. She blinked her eyes, which shone luminously in her deep mahogany skin. She liked working for Hector Minatos. Although he could be moody at times, he was fair and he never talked down to his employees and gave credit where it was due. He was also fun to work with. One never knew what would happen from day to day. Things were always interesting.

"Moving on!" Hector exclaimed, brushing past Tanya and into the kitchen. Time to check up on the food and the staff handling it.

The large kitchen was packed with chef assistants and servers. Commands and orders could be heard all over the place. Most of the orders and commands were coming from Comete, The Traveling Chef, as they called him. He was trying to get his assistant to place the food the way he wanted and was giving some direction on what more to add in the mixture of some recipe.

Hector walked up to Comete, a dashing Portuguese man with black curling hair, coal black eyes, swarthy skin, and full lips. He was a small man—around five eight— with a slight-built body. He was 42, but looked at least a decade younger.

He was also Hector's lover.

Hector had met Comete, three years ago, at a social gathering that Anna had invited him to. At the time, Hector had been just getting over a breakup of a long-term relationship. Those were the only type of relationships that Hector had, he wasn't the type to hop in and out of beds. He believed in love and commitment. Unfortunately, his last lover, Chris, hadn't.

Chris was a dashing, blue eyed, blond haired dreamboat with devastatingly good looks. He had been the valet that parked his car at an event that he had attended. Chris had very soon made his way from the parking lot and into Hector's house.

Hector had supported him in every way—bought him clothes, and everything else that he wanted and was glad to do it. He was in love. Chris didn't even have to work. The relationship had lasted for eight years. Hector had suspected a few indiscretions on Chris's part, but there was never any real hard evidence, so Hector had let it go but then one day Hector had come home to catch Chris fervently making out with the pool boy in a lounge chair on the deck. Hector had been broken hearted, but had promptly thrown Chris out of his sprawling six-bedroom house that very night. When something had to be done, Hector wasn't one to dally. He got right down to it.

Of course, Chris by now, being used to living in luxury and comfort, had been bewildered at all of it suddenly being taken away. Chris had foolishly gotten a lawyer, in an attempt to make claim to some of Hector's possessions, with the excuse that they had been living together for eight long years. He deserved something. They were more-or-less in a common law relationship. Well that hadn't worked. Hector's lawyers had decimated Chris in court. Shame faced, Chris had left town within a few days afterwards and Hector hadn't heard from him since. Good riddance. It was a long time before Hector had been able to even look at a blond haired man without the horrible memories of Chris flooding his head.

Anna had dragged him out to the birthday party of one of her agents at the company.

"It'll be fun. Get your mind off of your misery."

"I don't know…," Hector had said, miserably.

"Come on. You can't sit here and pine after Chris forever," she pounced, sensing his weakening.

So he had gone. Rarely was he able to withstand Anna nagging and wheedling. She was a very persuasive individual.

Comete had been sitting at their table.

"Hector, this is Comete. Comete, this is Hector," Anna said, casually.

It was a clear set up. Hector decided to go along with it, what else was he to do?

"Niiize to meet you," Comete had responded, extending an elegant hand towards Hector.

He had a charming little accent. And he was easy on the eyes, he thought noting Comete's dark good looks.

"Nice to meet you too," Hector had responded, taking his hand. Comete had a nice, firm handshake. Hector was surprisingly impressed.

At first, Hector had thought that Comete might be a little younger than him, but in fact, Comete was 38, four years older than Hector was. Hector was surprised that they got along well and at the end of the night they had exchanged numbers. Pretty soon, they were in a relationship.

"I want you to a know, Hector," Comete had told him in a deadly serious tone one morning a after a night of passionate lovemaking, "I do not tolerate cheating…no other menzzz…you and I alone." Hector was very relieved. Comete wanted commitment too. There were not a lot that had that thought in mind.

Three happily blissful years had gone by, and Hector knew that he was in love.

He never thought he would find love again, after Chris. But he had. And he was happy that the love wasn't a one-way street. Comete loved him as well, and it showed.

Hector gave Comete a swift kiss on the cheek. Comete turned around, smiled at his significant other, and then turned back the task at hand, which happened to be telling a fresh-faced assistant exactly how much butter to add to a recipe.

"So how is it going in these parts?" Hector asked, eyeing a shrimp salad that an Asian girl was carrying on the tray.

"I am, as they a say, 'holding up de forte'," Comete said, and chuckled. Then his expression turned troubled. He then loudly rapped the wooden spoon that he had in his hand on the counter.

In an instant, the kitchen that was once bustling with activity, was as silent and as still as a tomb.

"No! No! Do not poot anymore sugar in dare!" Comete yelled frantically to a dough-faced white chap with slicked back red hair.

"But it wasn't sweet enough," the young man muttered.

Comete shook his head briskly—Hector was sure his head was going to fly off.

"It izzzz...sweet enough! No more! Deees is not your kitchen ok? I see zat you live off of de s sugar!" Comete said, giving the young man's fleshy middle an indignant poke with his wooden spoon. The young man frowned, unamused.

"Just put deeee amount dat I tell you, k?" Comete shrilled.

The young man nodded quickly, and ambled off, embarrassed. One of the most famous and bestchefs in the country had just shamed him. He was sure that he would never live it down.

"Okey-dokie, I continue!" Comete said, unfazed. "You go back to da oderr teeengs...k?" he said, giving Hector a sneaking pat on the ass.

Hector giggled, "Behave!" Hector said, and wagged a playful finger at Comete as he walked away.

Hector took a deep breath and looked around. Everything was going to be great tonight, he was sure of that.

Chapter Four

Meena waited impatiently by her locker. There was no sign of her friend Xander. *Well, I'mgonna leave by myself.* She caught sight of a teacher walking down the hallway. She quickly rushed into the bathroom and stayed there until she heard the teacher pass. When she came back out, she finally saw her friend walking down the empty hallways.

He rushed up to her, his orange dyed, frizzled hair standing on end. "I told Mr. Timmel that I was using the bathroom."

"It took you that long to ask him to use the bathroom?" Meena asked, starting to walk towards the doors of the school.

"Well, you know he doesn't like to be interrupted when he's talking, "Xander said, pushing his tinted shades up on his nose. He pulled at one of the numerous piercing on his ears.

Meena rolled her eyes. "Come on. They're not going to stay there at the mall forever. We gotta get over there before they leave. We have to be there by eleven." Meena grabbed his wrist and pulled him along.

"But we have until three. So we don't need to be all stuffy about it."

Meena shook her head. "I —want —to —be —one of the first people there."

"Man you are going to be a model if it's the last thing that you do, huh," Xander commented as he was being pulled along.

They caught the bus and arrived at the mall by 11:10. Meena and Xander found the area where they were holding the competition. It was not hard to miss. The turnout was large. People were there for acting, modeling, and commercials. The tryouts were going on until three. Meena was ready to go. She walked right up to the table. Xander stood back and eyed a cute black girl in tight jeans and a big chest.

"I'm here about the modeling," Meena blurted out to a dark skinned black man sitting at the table.

The man gave her a lazy look. These pretty girls and pretty boys had been coming through all day, and frankly, he was getting tired of them. "You can go sign up at that table over there," he said, pointing at a table where a white woman with unnaturally red hair sat with a clipboard.

"Thank you," Meena said, before heading toward the redhead..

At least this one was polite, the man thought before turning to the next young potential starlet.

"Sign in here," the woman said, dryly. She slid the clipboard over to Meena. Meena carefully signed her name.

"You can speed it up. This isn't a writing contest," the woman said, acidly. "Now go stand over there." She flicked her wrist in the general direction of a line of young people, ranging from around twelve to around twenty-five.

Meena began to look around, where was Xander? He was nowhere to be seen. His shock of bright orange hair was nowhere in sight. Meena went to the very back of the line. Suddenly the girl in front of her turned around. She had light brown hair and green eyes. She was short and a little chubby, but attractively so.

"Hi, so what are you here for?"

Meena really wasn't in the mood for small talk, but seeing that she was going to be in the line for a while, she decided to answer.

"Modeling," Meena responded.

"Cool!" the girl commented. She was waiting for Meena to ask her the same question, but saw that she didn't so she decided to take it upon herself to inform her.

"I'm here for acting."

"That's nice...," Meena commented absently. Where was Xander?

"I think you would make a great model. You're gorgeous and you have the perfect body. You're so tall and thin. You look so exotic!" the girl gushed.

"Thanks....look, do you think you can hold my place in line? I have to go find my friend.... Looks like he's lost."

"Sure, no problem!" the girl nodded her head enthusiastically.

Meena wandered into the crowd. She spotted Xander talking to some girl in jeans that looked as if they were painted on. She had dark velvety skin—the girl was gorgeous and obviously older. She looked about seventeen—three years Xander's senior.

Meena walked up to Xander. "Hey. I was looking for you."

Xander turned towards her, not looking thrilled with her sudden appearance. "I bin' over here all along

The older girl looked hard at her, thinking this pretty Latina girl was moving in on her turf.

Xander sighed in resignation. "This is my friend Meena. Meena, this is Monique.

"Charmed," the girl said, not sounding so at all.

Meena gave her a crooked grin then turned back to Xander. "Well, I'm going to be over there waiting in line. Come on over when you're ready."

Meena walked back towards the line, hoping all the while that the girl hadn't given up her spot. She spotted the light haired girl in the line and rushed over. The girl smiled and gestured for her to come in front of her. The guy directly behind her chubby friend gave Meena a dirty look. She ignored it.

"Thank you so much," Meena said, flicking her long black hair over her shoulders.

Finally she reached the front of the line where a pencil thin black woman and two men—one Asian and one white—sat at a table.

"You can step forward," the black woman told her.

And so she did.

The Asian man gave her a once over, taking in the Fendi handbag, the fitted capri pants, the off shoulder top and the strappy Dolce &Gabanna sandals, and decided that this girl had style.

The white guy checked her out and saw that she had a wonderful figure. She looked perfect for modeling. And she was a good height for it.

"How tall are you?" the white man asked.

"Five foot nine inches and one fourth of an inch," Meena answered thinking that the extra height would give her an advantage.

"How much do you weigh?" the woman asked.

"120 pounds," Meena answered. She took exactly ten pounds off her true weight, thinking that 130 sounded too heavy.

"Turn around for me," the woman commanded.

Meena did a full circle, slowly.

The woman nodded. "You have a wonderful figure."

The Asian man nodded in agreement. "Why don't you walk over to the far wall over there and then back? I just want to get a sense of you."

Meena started walking a sexy walk, swinging her hips. The white man protested.

"Just be natural with yourself. Relax. None of that stripper stuff."

Players of the Game

Meena took a deep breath and began walking again. This time she let herself relax and let her confidence shine through.

"You're pretty good," the Asian man told her when she came back to her spot, "You need some work, but it's not drastic. Do you have a portfolio?"

Damn! Xander had it in his shoulder bag. He could be anywhere.

Meena saw a toffee colored hand slide a folder onto the table. Meena looked up. It was Xander. He gave her a smile. Meena smiled back. Xander was pretty much reliable. She could count on him for almost anything.

The woman took up the folder and opened it. She looked at the pictures and then passed them down to the others to look at. Finally, they all looked up at her.

"We're interested," the white man said, nodding his head.

Meena's heart pounded heavily in her chest, this was it! This was her opportunity!

"We want you to meet us at our office tomorrow around four. By no means do we want you to skip school as you have done today," the white man said, with a little grin.

Meena blushed at this comment as she took the business card from the woman's elegant fingers.

Meena squealed with delight and fell into her friend's arms once they had left the table of model agents.

"You made it! This calls for celebration. Let's go get something to eat," Xander said, truly happy for his friend.

"Sure... where?" Meena asked, hesitantly as they walked towards the exit of the mall.

"What about at *Surgio's*. We can get a pepperoni pizza with Italian sausage. Your favorite."

"Ummm...maybe I shouldn't."

"Whadayah mean?" he asked, confused

"Well...now that I'm a model I can't be eating all of that fattening stuff. Maybe I should get something with less fat," Meena said, shrugging her shoulders, trying to look nonchalant.

"First of all, they only said that they were interested and told you to come to their office tomorrow. Technically, you're not a model yet."

"Yeah, but I will be!" Meena said, with a defiant look in her eyes and a raised chin.

"But…even if you were…I can't see you giving up pizza and ice cream and all that stuff. You eat it all the time!"

"Yeah, but I can't eat it anymore. I'll get fat!" Meena cried out.

"You've never gotten fat before, why would you now?" Xander asked, grumpily. He didn't like all this fussy behavior coming from Meena. It wasn't like her at all.

Meena shrugged her shoulders. What did he know? He was a guy—guys didn't have to worry about food and weight and stuff like that. Nobody cared if a guy was a few pounds heavier than he should be. But let a girl be an extra pound or two, they would put the screws to her. The world was unfair.

Well…maybe they could go to Sugio's after all.

"Surgio's has salads…don't they?" Meena pondered out loud.

Ψ

"Okay, get off me! That's enough!" Nadina shrieked as she shooed the two pesky hair stylists a away from her. They were straightening her hair to death. If they kept it up, she figured, there wouldn't be any hair left to style.

"It isn't straight enough!" Jacque cried out in annoyance, as he shook his blond frosted locks.

Nadina turned around and faced him, a truculent expression on her beautiful cinnamon colored face. "Well this will have to do." She ran her fingers through her medium shoulder length hair. "Believe me. It is good enough."

"But, Meeez Nadina…your hair will stand on eeend!" the other one, Philippe, exclaimed defiantly.

What is it with these people? Why were they trying to straighten her hair to death like a white girl's? She wasn't white, not now or ever, nor did she ever wish to be. She was black woman. She was proud of her textured locks, but in this business, you did what the people wanted. If they wanted her hair straight and blowing in the wind in the music video, then…they would get their way. Nadina didn't wish to argue with them all the time.

Nadina gave the two French nags a churlish glare and turned back around. They immediately advanced back upon her hair with delight. The battle was over for now. They had won.

By the time her hairdressers were done styling and her makeup was artfully applied, she didn't recognize herself, as usual. They had added light brown hair extensions (weave! Nadina knew, but they liked to call it extensions) that went past the middle of her back.

"You look beautiful!" her makeup artist Gina cooed.

The two French nags nodded in agreement. Even Nadina had to admit to herself that she looked exotically stunning and beautiful.

"Luckily, we don't have to work hard, you're already a gorgeous girl!" her wardrobe designer piped in, walking up to the group of admirers.

Nadina was growing tired of the fluffy compliments. "Okay John, let's get me into my clothes. And I hardly qualify as being a girl, considering that I'm 31," she said, as she hopped down from her chair.

The two nags gasped in shock and horror at the blatant mention of her age.

Unlike many in the entertainment industry, Nadina didn't mind revealing her age. Hey, everyone gets along in years; it was a part of life. Besides, she wasn't really old.

Nadina followed John to the wardrobe section of the set.

"Look at this. I think you would look great in it. It's for the first part of the video, when you're speeding down the road." He pulled out a fitted Donna Karen top with a plunging neckline and matching skirt. Nadina smiled in agreement.

"You like?" he asked, his dark face smiling broadly.

"I like very much," Nadina said, truthfully. John was always picking tasteful things for her music videos and performances. She didn't know what she would do without him. He then showed her the rest of the clothes that she would be wearing through the video. She approved of all of them. John smiled at her. Suddenly he got a little nervous, and began to shift on his feet. *Oh gosh, he's about to ask me out Nadina* thought with alarm.

"Umm...Nadina, you know I was wondering if you were doing..."

Suddenly, Nadina's assistant Moko was rushing up to them, her mane of black hair with blond streaks flying wildly, her red spiked designer heels clicking on the floor as she walked. Nadina breathed a sigh of relief.

"Nadina! You've got to get back on the set. They're ready to shoot!"

Nadina hooked her arm through the young Japanese girl's arm. Nadina liked her and didn't regret for a moment the day that she had hired her a year ago after her last assistant Angelo had been caught selling footage of her taking showers and baths in her Beverly Hill's mansion. There was even footage of her…in bed. What a scandal *that* had been. Luckily, with the help of good lawyers and good connections, the messy situation had been cleaned up. With a little grin, she thought, Angelo must have really regretted the day that he did that.

Nadina got on the set. The first scene was the balcony scene. Instantly, people began touching up her make-up and then the cameras began to run.

Showtime.

Ψ

"Maaan! These towels are hard. Can't I get some new ones?" Duke complained over the phone.

Delvair counted to five before he answered. "But, you told me that the towels were Turkish spun cotton. That should be very comfortable," he said, trying to hide his irritation.

"Yeah, well, ain't they got Egyptian cotton? That's the one I be hearing all about!"

At this point, Delvair had slipped off his reading glasses and was slowly messaging his temples. This kid was a real pain, demanding and nagging from the very beginning.

"For the hundredth time, I am your agent, not your personal assistant. You want something concerning things like towels and room service you talk to Mike. I am not the one to call. On the other hand, you have questions concerning your bookings and things like that, you contact me. There is a difference. Do you understand?"

"Awight, awight, tinkerbell," Duke muttered

Delvair resisted the urge to curse. How he hated that name that Duke called him! A name Duke had taken to after he had found out that he, his agent, was gay. But he put up with it. After all, Duke was giving him fifteen percent of his paycheck.

"And Duke. Make suuure that you are ready for your seven o'clock performance. We have to—"

Delvair heard the dial tone. Duke had hung up on him. *Damn that kid*, Delvair though furiously as he slammed the phone down.

Once off the phone, Duke called room service to bring up some food. He was hungry as hell. He hadn't eaten since he got off the plane, six hours ago.

"Bring me up a steak with all the trimmings. Put some potato wedges on the side. Make sure everything's well done and my wedges are crispy. I want a coke and cut me a nice slice of carrot cake with icing," Duke demanded from the person on the other end of the phone.

The young man on the other side of the phone was quite impressed. This rap star was a serious eater, but how lucky for him that he would get to be the one to bring up his food!

"It will be up in a short while, Duke," the man said, gushingly

"Awwiiight," Duke drawled. "Tell me, they're any cute girls around here that I can hit up?" Duke asked him.

"Excuse me?" the man asked, confused.

"Man, what's wrong witchew. I mean some cute girls I can kick it wit' have some fun wit', know what I mean? Where can I get me some girls like that."

"I-I'm not sure about that," the man stuttered. He didn't like the turn that the conversation was taking.

"Just bring up my food," Duke snapped, impatiently then hung up the phone.

The man was only too happy to oblige.

Ψ

Duke loved the rush that he got from the crowd. There were thousands of admirers there to see him perform. He loved how they shouted his name; he loved the grasping hands that thrust out towards him, desperate for a touch from The Great Duke. Bodyguards surrounded him from all sides as he walked from the stage after his performance.

"I LOVE YOU DUKE!" a girl screamed as she jumped out in his path. One of the bodyguards rushed from his side, and tried to ward the girl off with a large hand. But she was not to be put off that easily. She tried to worm her way past the two guards that were now in front of Duke. Getting fed up, they each gripped an arm, elevated her above ground level, and carried her away between them, her feet swaying and kicking in protest.

"Get off me, you muscle heads, Damn you! You big apes!" she snarled like a vicious dog.

Later on that night, Duke dismissed his masseuse. He was getting tired and had had enough messaging for the night. Besides, he had to get up early in the morning for an interview.

"You can leave now," he said, to the tall muscled Scandinavian man with the long blond hair and the tight white pants.

"You are sure you do not want anyteeeng else?" the man asked, giving him a pointed look, his eyes full of open lust.

Duke's heart dropped in his stomach. He felt the remains of his meal from earlier on creeping up into his throat.

"Nah man, I'm fine," he said, not wanting to get the man angry. He was a lot bigger than Duke was. Who knew what he would do?

"Okaaaayy…because I could give you some more serviiiice…if you would like…you would find pleasure," the man offered again, sure that he could get this young, sturdy, scrumptious, chocolate, delight.

Duke shook his head vigorously. "Nah, the massage was enough, dude. You kin leave. Peace, out."

"Whatever you wish," the man said, accepting defeat. He walked slowly to the door. Duke followed after him to make sure he found his way out.

Just before he opened the door, the man turned around and faced him. Duke felt his heart slam into his chest.

"Y-yo man. What's up wit you?" Duke asked, nervously.

"I juzzz wanted to say, yuh, If you, aye…change a your mind…give me a call." He opened the door and walked out.

Duke shut the door firmly behind him. Gosh, these homos were all over the place! This country was full of them. Especially back home in sunny LA. The city was creeping with them. Everywhere he turned, they were in his face.

After making sure the door was locked, he made his way back to the bed. He turned down the smooth silk sheets and got in.

Duke was just about to drift asleep when he heard a tap that sounded like it was on a window. He looked around and realized that it was coming from the glass sliding door in the other bedroom of his suite. He walked into the other room and pulled back the drapes. Standing there was the white, brown haired girl from earlier on that his bodyguards had carried off. She was in a tight jean jumpsuit zipped up at the front.

Duke was shocked. How did she get up there? He didn't quite know what to do. Let her in?

"I just want to talk to you. I swear I won't hurt you," the girl yelled from behind the glass.

Against his better judgment, Duke opened the door and let her in.

The girl rushed in, happy to be granted entrance.

The girl took a seat on one of the plush chairs without being asked.

"I just wanted to tell you how much I like you…I mean, you are so cute and so talented, and you are so hot!"

Duke looked at her. She looked around eighteen. Not bad looking, I would do her, he thought as he eyed her body. He usually preferred black girls for their curves and sometimes a Puerto Rican or two, but this white girl was stacked.

Duke smiled, "Thanks, ma. I appreciate the support."

The girl stood up. "I think that I can support you in other ways too…" The girl slipped down the zipper of her jumpsuit and stepped out of it. She was only wearing a red lace thong! Duke was instantly excited.

Duke licked his lips. He was no longer tired. "Why don't you step into my room and show me, little ma."

The girl threw him a sexy smile and walked into the other room. Duke followed her in and shut the door behind them.

Ψ

"I banged on the door for like an hour. He won't let me in!" Mike the assistant cried to Delvair over the phone the next morning.

"You know he sleeps like a rock. Just open the door with the spare key and get his ass up," Delvair said, with vexation.

"I don't have a key," Mike responded, sounding sorrowful

"Well get one from the front desk!"

"They won't give me one!"

"I'll be up there in thirty minutes," Delvair snapped, and hung up the phone. Gosh. Did he have to do everything himself? He was acting as this boy's agent, as well as his personal assistant.

When he arrived, he came to Duke's door, where a despondent Mike stood grasping the unyielding door handle.

He shoved past him and inserted the key that he had threatened the man at the front desk for, into the lock. He swung open the door.

"Terrance! Get up! You know you have an interview with *Shout Magazine* this morning," he called, as he went from room to room. This place was like a maze, a bit much for a single person. It was no wonder Duke couldn't hear them. His room was probably located in the depths of the earth.

Finally, he stumbled upon the bedroom where Duke was sleeping peacefully in bed. Only he wasn't alone. A girl was sprawled there too, her arms fanned out, her breasts exposed to the air. She too was in deep sleep.

Mike ogled at her.

Delvair's caramel face grew red in anger.

"Why don't you wait outside for a moment, Mike."

"But I-"

"Wait outside until I call you back in!" Delvair snapped.

Mike scuttled out.

Delvair grasped one of Duke's shoulders and shook him vigorously. Duke finally stirred and sat up in the bed.

"What's da deal..." Duke muttered, sleepily.

The girl in the bed stirred, but did not wake up.

"The deal is," Delvair snapped, "that you have to get up at this moment and get ready for an interview that you have in an hour. Get this little tramp," he said, waving a hand in the direction of the girl, "out of your bed. Get rid of her. We need to get moving."

"Yo!" Duke said, poking at the girl. "YO, MAN!" Duke yelled. The girl woke up.

"Hello..." she cooed at Duke and proceeded to nibble on his ear. Duke shrunk back. She looked around the room realizing that the two of them were not alone. "Who is he?" she asked, pointing a finger at caramel skinned, black man that was standing over the bed.

Delvair gave her a nasty look.

"Get outta here," Duke said, getting up and wrapping the sheet around his slim hips.

Delvair tried to keep his eyes off of Terrence's lovely form. But allowed himself a few serendipitous glances.

"Already? Why don't we have breakfast? We can talk—"

"Nah. Get the fuck out. I gotta leave now," Duke snapped cutting her off. He walked towards the bathroom. Soon the rushing water of the shower could be heard.

Delvair gave her a haughty look. She turned and glared at him, believing that this was his entire fault.

"Well, I'll leave my number on the dresser and you can call me later..." the girl yelled at the closed bathroom door.

The girl was walking around buck-ass naked, Delvair noted in disgust.

"Believe me, he won't be calling you," Delvair said, bitchily.

"What do you know, you little queen," she snarled.

"Believe me, I know. You little tramp. Now that he's had his round, why don't you leave before you cause yourself further embarrassment?" Delvair said, smoothly.

The girl angrily pulled on her underwear and then her jumpsuit.

"You probably want him for yourself!" the girl screamed at Delvair, as she zipped up the suit.

"The door is that way," Delvair sniffed, pointing a disdainful finger to his left.

The girl stalked up the hall and out of the suite. The door slammed angrily behind her.

Finally, Duke came out of the shower with a towel wrapped around his sinewy hips, his long lithe legs sticking out beneath. Delvair took in the sight with greedy eyes.

Snapping out of it, Delvair said, "Hurry up and get dressed. We are going to be late. Let's make sure that we are only fashionably late and not kill-your-career late," he said, indignantly and left the room.

Once Delvair was in the other room, he took out his Xanax and popped a pill in his mouth.

Without the pills, he was sure, he would have had a nervous breakdown a long time ago.

Chapter Five

As a finale, Maria did a back flip and then a backhand spring off the balance beam and landed on the padded mat. Despite her effort, one foot stepped unsteadily backwards. Darn! She had been working on that finish for the entire week and she had yet to get it perfectly right. If it wasn't her coordination, it was her landing getting messed up. She waited for the unavoidable reproach from her gymnastics coach Darlene.

"Steady, Rivera! You have to think before you land. Land with control!" she barked.

Maria cringed. The woman could be so abrasive. After being in the Marines for nine years, straight out of college, Darlene had become a gymnastics coach—returning to the sport of her youth. To the gymnasts that she coached, it appeared that Darlene had forgotten that she was no longer in the service. She barked out commands and orders and held such a tight fist over the gymnasium that the gymnasts had a sense that they were in boot camp instead of gymnastics.

Darlene appearance went right along with the image of a commanding officer in the Marines. She was a tall, well muscled and toned. One look at her, and anyone could tell that she was one not to be messed with. She looked like she could bend a steel bar.

The woman rarely cracked a smile. Her ruddy face with it angular features and piercing blue eyes was almost always set in a scowl of disapproval. She rarely praised her gymnasts for a job well done. She was a staunch believer in the saying that there is always room of improvement. Therefore, why compliment when it could have been done better?

Maria groaned in exasperation. "I keep stepping back!"

"I can see that," Darlene said, with a twinge of sarcasm, "You have to keep both feet firm, in one spot when you land. Try it again. I know you can do it."

Maria nodded slightly and got back on the beam.

Concentrate, Maria. Concentrate.

Maria got through the routine smoothly, without mistake. Her landing was perfect.

Darlene nodded in approval. It was the closest that she would come to a compliment unless it was something truly amazing.

"Okay. Let's go through the uneven bars. The competition is next week Thursday. You have to have everything down pat."

Maria hoped that her aunt Anna had remembered about the competition. She had promised to be there—said she wouldn't miss it for the world.

Maria got through the uneven bar routine the first time perfectly—except for her landing. It was a bit shaky.

"Again," Darlene said, simply.

Maria got back on the bar. She went thought the routine. She landed in one spot with no stumbling.

"Okay. Not bad. But you are a bit hesitant when you switch bars. You might not think that people can notice, and most people can't. But the judges will see it. And so will all the other people that know what to look for."

Man! She felt like she was never good enough. Maria breathed in.

"Do you want me to do it again?"

"Do you want to?" Darlene countered.

Maria sighed and got back up on the bars.

Ψ

"You did what?" Anna asked her daughter for the second time, not believing what she was being told.

"Yeah, I skipped afternoon classes. But it was worth it because now I have an opportunity to do modeling…they were interested in me, Mom."

"But you skipped school. That is inexcusable," Anna snapped. God, what was wrong with these kids?

"But just think, I might not even need school if I become a model!"

"Are you kidding me?" Anna asked, flabbergasted at her daughter's words. "Modeling doesn't last forever, you know. After modeling, then what? And if modeling doesn't work out for you, what will you do?

And if modeling does work out for you and unfortunate circumstances happen for which you have to leave, then what will you do?"

Meena looked at Anna blankly. It was clear that she hadn't considered those possibilities.

"Well Mom, I won't skip school again. But please, please, let me go to the agency tomorrow evening. Pleeeeze!"

Anna looked at her daughter, not sure what decision to make. Against her better judgment, she decided to allow it.

"Fine. But there are strings attached. For one, I will come with you tomorrow. You are still a minor. Secondly, if I see a drop in any of your grades, you will be out of it so fast, your head will spin."

Meena smiled, overjoyed. "I promise Mom! I won't disappoint you!"

Now where had she heard *that* before?

Ψ

March, 1988...

"I swear that this is the third time that he's walked past this table," Pamela said, and sipped her iced tea.

"And he seems to be looking at you," Hector said regrettably, wishing that the handsome stranger was looking at him instead. Too bad. He was such a good-looking man.

"Cut it out, you guys," Anna said dismissively, and shoved a spoonful of pasta in her mouth.

"Seriously. The man is definitely checking you out. Look at him over there by the bar," Pamela said, as she tossed her thick black hair over her shoulders.

"Oh, puleezzz," Anna said, disbelievingly. But she couldn't help but sneak a peak. A white man with green eyes stared back at her. Intensely. Anna felt her face grow warm.

"And he's an older man. Ummm. Those are often the best!" Hector said, knowingly.

Anna gave him a weird look.

Suddenly a waiter came up to their table and facing Anna he said, "Madame, some wine, complements of the gentleman sitting at the bar."

Anna looked over at the handsome older man again. He raised a glass of drink at her, winked, and took a sip.

"Oh Gosh!" Pamela shrieked. "This is the most expensive wine in this restaurant! He's got to be loaded."

"Go over to him," Hector urged, already cracking the bottle open.

"Did I say you could open it?" Anna asked her friend, eyebrow raised.

"Well, you can't finish it all off by yourself," Hector retorted smartly.

Anna gave him a vicious look.

"Hello," a deep voice drawled.

Anna looked up. It was the man that had given her the champagne. His gorgeous eyes bored into her's.

"H-hi. Thanks for the wine," Anna said. What a stupid first thing to say, she thought to herself.

"It was my pleasure. My name's Winston Hurst.

"My name's Anna. Anna Senghor," she responded, shaking his hand.

"Would you mind if we were to have a drink together?" The handsome stranger asked.

Anna noted the southern accent. It sounded very genteel and smooth.

"She would love to take a drink with you!" Hector responded, fingers gripped firmly around the bottle of wine. He was already going through his second glass.

"I'll buy us two more glasses," the man said, with an understanding smile. He saw that the ostentatious young man wasn't about to relinquish the bottle without a battle.

He held out his hand to help her up. When Anna stood, she really saw how tall he was. And he was so big! His shoulders were big and broad.

"How tall are you?" Anna asked, as they made their way to the bar.

6'4" he responded, gently.

Once at the bar, he settled his large form on one of the barstool. Anna sat down beside him.

"What would you like? Some of the same champagne?" he asked, politely. His eyes were full of interest and attraction. Anna's face was getting hotter by the minute.

"Sure...umm...

"What about some Dom Perignon?"

"That would be fine." Anna responded, as calmly as she could.

Once they had the wine, they got to talking.

"So where are you from?" Anna asked, languidly sipping her wine.

"I was born in Chicago. But spent most of my years in Texas. Lived there practically all my live. I just got here two days ago. I've started a new sector in my business over here in LA and I'm opening a new building for my oil and gas company. I wanted to come and see it off."

"Oh, ok. So you own your own business, huh, and you're a Southern boy."

The man smiled brilliantly. "Yes and yes."

"Do you get to travel a lot in your business?"

"Oh yes, my dear." He sat back. "Let's see…I've been to Nigeria, Egypt, Saudi Arabia, Pakistan, Indonesia, Singapore, China, Japan… the list goes on. My business has ties in half of those countries. In fact, about five months ago, I just came back from training oil workers in Nigeria."

"Oh, wow," Anna remarked.

"Well, enough about me. I'm sure you don't want to hear me gabble on about business…so are you from LA?"

"No. I was born and raised in Arizona. I came out here after I graduated," Anna answered.

"Oh, okay. So what do you do?" he asked, politely.

"Well, I just graduated with a double degree in business and communications."

"That's an interesting combination," he said nodding his head.

Anna shifted, feeling slightly uncomfortable. "I don't have a job yet…but I'm looking for one. Luckily, I have some savings to live on. My friend Hector and I decided to move out here. He got a job down here, so I moved with him. We share a condo."

"And you chose LA?" he asked, with a little smile

Anna laughed. "Yeah, but you know…I thought it would be interesting out here," she said, and shrugged her shoulders. He laughed. "You're an enchanting woman. But you must know that already."

Anna's face grew hot with the compliment. He was so good looking that Anna felt that she would melt right there. But he did look to be older than her.

"So do you usually date black women?" Anna asked, cutting to the chase. Once the words left her mouth, she thought they sounded stupid.

"Well, I've dated a black woman once," he answered. "That was about five years ago. After that, I never really had the opportunity. I don't really have an absolute preference when it comes to women. As long as I'm attracted to them...but I must say. I find black women rather enchanting."

"How old are you?" she asked, boldly.

"36," he responded. He sat back in his chair and looked at her, with admiration in his eyes. "You're a very attractive woman. Your face is lovely, and those cheekbones...I'm sorry."

"It's okay," Anna said, and smiled.

"So, how old are you?" he asked. "I know you're younger than me."

"Yes, I am. I'm 21," Anna responded, and took a long swallow of her drink.

The man smiled softly. "Besides the way you look, I wouldn't be able to tell. You carry yourself very well, and you have a brilliant, mature mind."

"Thank you," Anna said, softly, feeling a little embarrassed.

"I would love to take you out for dinner one day. Would you object to that?" he asked, his eyes studying her. He spread his hands out on the countertop. They were big and strong looking. Anna suppressed a shiver.

"I wouldn't mind. Actually, I would like that," Anna said, staring at him. He was gorgeous with his green- brown eyes, his thick, dark chestnut hair, and his defined jaw line.

And so the courtship began.

Anna was enthralled and totally taken with him. He took her to fine restaurants, bought her expensive gifts, bought her jewelry.

It had been three months since they had started seeing each other. Not once had he tried to get her to sleep with him. He never tried to seduce her.

"I can wait. When you are ready, you will tell me. But until then…I am enjoying just being with you. I am satisfied just having you in my arms."

Anna was a little surprised. The few guys that she had gone out with had always tried to get her to sleep with them.

But she never did.

She was still a virgin. Only she didn't tell Winston, thinking that he would he put off by that.

Then one day, he said that he wanted her to meet his father. Anna was a little hesitant to do so.

"Are you sure that's a good idea?" she asked, scratching her head.

Winston laughed, "You do that every time that you're nervous."

"What?"

"Scratch your head."

"I don't know…he might not approve…you know how southerners can be."

"I don't need anyone's approval, for one. A father's approval is nice, but if it's at the cost of my happiness, it is not crucial. Secondly, do you think that I would invite you to meet somebody that is unpleasant? I love my father very much and he is a kind and decent man. I notice that you tend to generalize white southerners as all being of one type. Believe me, we're all not rednecks that are out to lynch black people."

Anna's face went hot with shame. "I didn't say that—"

"You didn't, but you were thinking it," Winston quipped with a smile. "But it's okay." He kissed her on her forehead. "Come on. You won't regret it. I've already told my father all about you. He's anxious to meet you."

"Okay. But this isn't going to be a family turn out will it? Do I have to be scrutinized by your sister and your brothers as well?"

Winston laughed. "No, my sweet. It'll be only the three of us. Just as cozy as can be."

Winston's father wasn't exactly as she expected him to be.

The minute Winston's father had set eyes on her he said, "Why don't you make me a very happy man by dumping my son and then marrying me?" He had a twinkle in his eyes and he wore a mischievous grin. He kissed Anna's hand gallantly. "Nice to meet you my dear. You can call me Earnest. Of course, I already know your name, Anna, from my son constantly talking about you. Now I can see why!"

Anna blushed. Winston laughed, obviously used to his father's far out humor. Anna was a little taken aback to see their many physical similarities. They had the same green eyes, although Earnest didn't have the brown flecks in them, they also had the same smile and the same handsome facial features—only Winston was a little darker in complexion.

"You'll have to excuse my father, he doesn't know how to behave in the presence of a beautiful woman," Winston joked, and gave his father a hug.

"And how are you my boy?" he asked, holding his son back at arm's length.

"I'm fine, Dad. What about you?" he asked, concern flickering in his eyes.

His father dropped his eyes, in avoidance, and quickly looked up at Anna with a smile. "Of course I'm fine. You two are here. Come on in. Josef will take your bags upstairs," he said, indicating the bored looking Slavic man standing nearby.

"Come, come," Earnest said, excitedly, "let me show you around the place. Bernice's in the kitchen cooking up a storm! You'll love her cooking as much as you'll like her!" he said, bubbly.

The house was beautiful. Antique furnishings and beautiful artwork decorated the house.

The outside was even more impressive. It was a gigantic ranch with a lot of land.

"Them horses over there are my babies. I raise them. Breed them. Then I deal a lot of them. But I keep some of them for myself, sometimes you grow extra attached to one or two, once in a while," he said, in reference to the horses that roamed the expensive green pastures, "Bill and Emilio over there, take care of the horses for me. They also deal with their training, breeding, and other such things."

Anna's eyes lit up. She loved horses. She had gone horseback riding a few times and loved it.

Earnest noticed her interest. "You like horses, huh. My Angela used to love the horses. She would ride them every time she came down… always keepin' up on them…" Earnest got a far away look in his eyes.

Anna looked at Winston and saw the worry mixed with fear that quickly flashed in his eyes. His face was tense.

"Well, I don't have a lot of experience," Anna commented, trying to break the discomfort.

"Well, you can ride while you're here! Winston can teach you all the proper techniques and all, he's been riding since he could walk!" Earnest chuckled.

Winston grinned. "I wouldn't mind teaching you at all."

Anna smiled. This weekend was going to be great.

"Well kids!" Earnest said, clapping his hands together, "I do believe that we should be getting back to the house now. Bernice should be just about done."

They walked back to the house. The dinning room table was set very nicely. A tall, plump, black, middle-aged woman came from the kitchen and greeted them.

A nice fat black woman in the kitchen, fits southern image doesn't it. Anna thought sarcastically.

"Is supper ready my dear?" he asked the woman, with a twinkle in his eyes.

"It sure is Earnest. Nice and ready for you and the young folk over here," she said, with a gentle smile.

"Thank you, my dear," Earnest said, with a smile. "Why don't we all sit down. It is time to partake!"

And partake they did.

That very night she heard the crying. Soft pitiful mewling that was mournful and chilled her to her bones.

Anna looked over at the digital clock on her nightstand. It was one in the morning. She and Winston had asked for separate rooms, to which Winston's father had replied, "Come on now, I'm not that old fashioned, I ain't got a problem with you two doin' it under my roof. Ya'll can holler and scream all you want! I won't hear ya! When I'm asleep, I sleep like a rock in a pond!"

Winston's face had turned a deep red. "Dad. We still would like separate rooms. We haven't been dating for that long."

Earnest had given them a queer look. "Eight months is long enough, ain't it?" he said with a smile, but he acquiesced.

Anna quietly left her room. She was curious to see where the noise was coming from. When she stood outside her bedroom door, she thought that it was coming from down the hall. She slowly walked in that direction. The soft crying got louder as she advanced. She then turned the corner and saw a door right ahead of her. She tiptoed to the door and put her ear to it. The weeping went on for a few more seconds and then it ceased. It became dead silent. Suddenly Anna was afraid. She wanted to just go back to her room. She would be so embarrassed if someone were to catch her here, sneaking around.

She slowly made her way back to her room, barely breathing because she was afraid that it would keep too much noise. When she got into the bedroom and closed the door, she let out a sigh of relief. She felt dizzy and her heart was pounding crazily in her chest.

She walked carefully back to her bed, climbed in and pulled the covers up over her head. She tried to calm herself down, slow her speeding heart.

Finally, she drifted to into a restless sleep.

The next morning, Anna woke up and pulled back the curtains. The Saturday morning sun shone in brightly. A bright morning could always chase away the fears of the night. Looking through the window, she almost forgot about how afraid she was last night and the odd crying that she heard in the dead of the night.

It was pushed even further to the back of her mind when she came down for breakfast. Earnest was at the table and greeted her with a bright smile, his green eyes sparkling.

"Morning gorgeous. I hope you slept well?"

"I did," Anna lied.

"Good. Good. Cause you're in for a treat! Bernice's made her Belgian waffles this mornin' the best you've tasted I can guarantee," he said, brightly. "And there's my sleepy headed son."

Anna turned around to see a dazed looking Winston walk through the door and take a seat at the table. He rubbed his eyes and yawned.

Anna smiled softly at him, feeling her heart flutter. He looked like a little boy that had been dragged up to go to school.

"Here's some orange juice." Anna poured him a glass from the jug sitting on the table.

"Thanks," Winston said, and smiled. He put his hand over hers and rubbed it with his thumb. Anna felt like firecrackers were going off up and down her spine.

Earnest gave them a knowing look.

"Here ya go, a nice hot plate of homemade waffles for ya," Bernice said, as she came breezing into the dinning room. She placed the waffle piled plate in the center of the table. Then she went back on got the rest of the condiments.

"These are fresh strawberries and blackberries. Picked from right off this land. Same goes for the blue berries and the raspberries," Winston said, as he scooped a little of each onto his plate. He then put three waffles on his plate and added a glob of whip cream to each one. He poured strawberry sauce over them and sprinkled on the fruit.

Anna took two from the plate, added what she wanted, and began to eat. It was really good. As she ate, her mind wondered back to the events of last night. She was still curious about the crying in the middle of the night, but she didn't feel that it was her place to ask.

Amidst much joyful talking, playful bantering, and memory sharing, they ate and finished their breakfast.

"Well, kiddies," Earnest began, wiping his mouth with a napkin and rising from his chair, "I have to go into town and visit with a prospective buyer for my Lizzie. A thoroughbred, black Arabian. Fine horse, my Lizzie is. But it's time for she and I to part," he finished.

"He always names his horses. Even the ones that he's going to sell," Winston said to Anna with a little smile.

"I'll see you kids later on. Go on and have fun. There's lots to do here. And you know Josef will take you into town if ya'll feel like it. Or you can take my Lincoln and drive it yourselves. I'll be takin' the Bronco," he smiled. And with that, he left them.

"So how 'bout we go out and take a ride on those horses?" Winston beamed at Anna, his face bright and his dimples appeared in his handsome face, making him even more attractive.

"Sure, I'll love to," Anna responded.

After riding the horses, they bathed and got ready. "Let's go into town," Winston suggested.

They went into the different stores and looked around. Anna noticed that people were openly staring at them as they walked in the streets.

"I wish they'd stop staring at us like that," Anna commented, annoyed.

Winston stopped and kissed her on the tip of her nose. "They can't help it. It's because you're so beautiful."

They held on to each other's hands even tighter.

They went into a jewelry store and looked around.

"This necklace is beautiful," Anna said in awe, as she looked at a small pendant made of gold.

Winston came over and looked at it. He smiled. "It would look beautiful on you." He looked up at the woman eyeing them suspiciously as she stood behind the counter . "How much does this here pendant cost?"

"Seven hundred," the woman responded.

"I'll buy it. No need to wrap it up, miss." He said, as he gave the woman his credit card.

He wrapped the necklace around Anna's neck and fastened it at the back. "You look lovely," he whispered in her ear.

The woman scowled at them.

"You didn't have to buy this. I didn't say I liked it so that you could get it for me," Anna said, seriously.

"I know you didn't darling. I wanted to get it for you." He grasped her hand and led her out of the shop.

Once they were outside, they realized how late it had gotten. The sun was just setting in the sky.

"Are you hungry, Sugar?" he asked.

"I sure am," Anna laughed, "Hungry enough to eat a horse."

"Well, we got a lot of horses back home, but they're not for the eating," Winston said, jokingly,

"Really? Well then I'll settle for a meal at one of these here restaurants."

"Good. That was exactly what I was thinking," Winston said with a grin.

It seemed as if the whole restaurant froze and looked at them the moment they stepped in. A sea of white faces, curiously eyeing them. Some whispering was going on.

The maître d' seated them after a moment's hesitation.

People at the tables beside them stared openly. Anna looked at Winston. His face was stony.

Anna swallowed the lump forming in her throat. "So what are you ordering?" she asked, in a forced, cheery voice.

Winston cleared his throat and smiled at her, "Let's see. I haven't been here for a while…I think I'll get the ribs. Nothing like Texas barbecued ribs."

Anna nodded, her smile wavering. She looked down at her menu and tried to focus on what was on it.

Finally, a waiter came to their table. With a guarded expression, he asked them if they wanted some refreshments.

"I'll have a coke," Winston said.

"I'll have some water. Spring water, please," Anna said, looking up at the waiter. His dark eyes avoided eye contact with her. Instead, he looked back at Winston, addressing him. "Well, I'll be back in a second to take your order." Then he was off without another word.

There was a moment of uncomfortable silence at the table.

"Well, I think I'll have the grilled chicken and the Spanish rice," Anna said, and closed her menu.

"Sounds good," Winston said.

The waiter was back in a second. He placed a glass of coke in front of Winston and a glass of water in front of Anna

"I'll have the grilled chicken with rice. But please. I don't want any of the gravy on the rice. The vegetables are enough," Anna said.

The waiter wrote that down hurriedly and turned to face Winston. "And what would you be having, Sir.

Winston stared at the waiter, glanced at Anna and looked back at the waiter. "I'll have the steak and the mashed potatoes with sour cream and chives," he said, slowly.

The waiter nodded at him, turned and left.

"He didn't even look at me once," Anna muttered, sipping her water.

"I've noticed," Winston said, stiffly.

Minutes later the food was out. Anna's rice was soaked in gravy.

"Ah, excuse me," Anna said, stopping the waiter before he turned away again.

"Yes?" he said, not looking directly in her face, but at a spot behind her head.

"Do you think you can look me in the face for a second? Don't worry, I don't bite," she said, wryly.

The waiter's brown eyes zeroed in on hers, a challenging look within them.

"Thank-you. Now," Anna began, folding her hand neatly on the table, "I specifically asked you *not* to put gravy on my rice. I think I said it more than once. In fact, I thought that was what you were writing down on that pad of paper of yours. But I understand that it is really busy, and you might have forgotten. So please, just send this back and get me another one without any gravy like I asked. Thank you."

The young man gave her a fierce look. "I didn't hear you ask for no gravy," he drawled. "Seems like you lookin' to stir some trouble in'ere."

"I heard her ask for no gravy. And I'm sure that any one of these people here in the tables beside us can vouch for that, seeing that they've been keeping a close eye and ear on us ever since we came in," Winston said, crisply.

Their neighbors turned away, embarrassed.

"Lookit. I din' hear her ask fa no gravy," he said, growing red in the face, "You two come up in here looking for trouble. Walkin' in here like you two the most naturalist thing in da world. I think it's just sick."

Anna looked at Winston, appalled at the man's words. Winston's face was red as a beet. His eyes glittered with pure ferocity. His hands clamped into fists on the tabletop.

"Look here, you little hick. I don't know which woods you crawled out of. You can barely speak English, yet you're here having the nerve to criticize us. For off, it is none of your goddamned business what we do. Our relationship is not your concern. Your concern is to take our take our orders right and to bring our food to us. That's all. I don't give a damn what your opinion is."

The man opened his mouth to say something, but Winston cut him off again.

"Now. You take her food back and then I want you to call your manager and bring him right here. We didn't come in here for anything else but to eat. But seeing that you're asking for it, you're going to get it."

The young man retreated with her plate, his face pallid and pinched.

Soon the manager was at their table. His expression was sorrowful. They told him about the waiter. The manager's face grew redder and redder as the story advanced.

"Tim! Git your ass over here!" The manager called to the waiter. He came shuffling over.

"You damned fool. Treating the customers like that. You ain't got no right, I tell you. Furthermore, do you know who this man is?"

"No," the young man mumbled

"Huh?" the manager yelled.

"No," the waiter said a little louder, sensing impending doom.

"This here's Winston Hurst. Earnest Hurst's son. You know, Hurst Stables?"

The man blushed in shame. He looked down to the floor and said a barely audible, "Yes."

"Go on. Git boy. You're ass is outta here. Don't bother to come in the rest of next week. After that, I'll decide if I want you working here ever again."

The young man hurried off.

The manager turned to them, all smiles.

"The meals are on the house. So is dessert. Heck. I'll even send ya two home with a whole sweet potato pie tonight."

The manager turned to Anna and looked at her. "I'm really, and truly sorry for all this. It ain't right. This is a small Texas town and people round here still stuck like it was years ago, ya know? It's all nonsense."

"It's not okay, but it is. Thank you for your apology," Anna said, giving him a tentative smile.

The man smiled back. "What about a nice bottle of wine? We have some Chianti. Think you'll like that?" the manager asked them.

"We'll love it," Winston answered with a nod.

The manager breathed a sigh of relief, obviously glad that he had gotten the situation under control. He turned to get the items for them.

As they stepped outside into the night, Anna clutching the bottle of wine, Winston holding the pie in one hand and slinging the other hand around Anna's shoulder, Winston said, "How do you like Texas so far?" he asked, with a little smirk.

Anna gave him a wry look. She didn't bother to answer.

Ψ

When they hit the Los Angeles Airport, Anna was elated. She was back home, back to the familiarities of the West coast, *or the non-South*, she bitterly thought.

Winston was almost as happy and even relieved to be out of Texas.

"How does a trip to Italy sound," he commented casually to her one day in the car as they were driving into town one day.

"You're going to Italy?" Anna asked him.

"I would like for *us* to go to Italy. How does that sound? I have a few things that I have tie up business wise, down there. I would love it if you were to come with me. We'll be going to Naples. I have a beautiful house down by the Tyrrhenian Sea. Of course, I'll pay for the flight and everything. We'll be leaving next Tuesday."

"I would love to come. But I can pay for myself," Anna said, excitedly. Italy! She had been to a few countries in Europe to which her dad had occasionally dragged the family while on business, but she never been to Italy. This was going to be fun

Winston shook his head. "I know you can afford it, but it's my treat. I'll pay."

"I'll pay for my flight," Anna said, stubbornly.

"Fine. You pay for the flight, but that's it," Winston said, sternly.

Winston's handsome face cracked into a smile. "You are one headstrong lady. I like that. A woman with spirit."

They arrived in Italy at around six in the evening.

In Italian, Winston gave the driver directions to their residence.

"I didn't know you spoke Italian," Anna said, impressed.

"Yes, I do. I took courses in college. Then I was an exchange student in Rome for two semesters. I picked the language up pretty fast. When you throw yourself in the culture, you have no choice but to learn the language," he responded.

The house by the beach was beautiful. It had sandstone columns on the front and beautiful gardens surrounding it. It looked like a hideaway from ancient Roman era.

The trip to Italy was marvelous. They went out to eat every night and during the first part of the day, when Winston would be out at his business meetings, Anna would walk on the nearby beach and relax around the house. After Winston would come back, they would go to see the sights and all the things that Naples, Italy had to offer.

Anna found herself falling in love with him. He was a remarkable man. They did everything together, and they would pass the night away in each other's arms talking about any and everything. Nothing more. She was very happy with him.

One day, he came back around five o'clock which was later than usual.

"I got held up at work. We had some new employees that needed training schedules prepared for them. Get ready. We'll go out for dinner tonight. I found this new restaurant in the village. Very quaint. You'll love it."

They talked, they laughed, they joked, and they shared their meals—eating off each other's plate. Time seemed to fly as they ate their delicious meals.

Winston grasped her hand across the table and looked deeply into her eyes. His face was suddenly serious and pensive. Anna got worried.

"What's the matter, Win?" she asked, scared that he was about to give her bad news.

He shook his head. "There's nothing wrong. Nothing at all. Everything is right—you and me, our relationship. You are a remarkable woman and you have shown me how very true that is this past week."

Anna smiled. "I feel the same way. I want to stay like this forever."

"I love you Anna," he said, suddenly.

Anna stared at him. She could tell that he was being serious and in her heart, Anna knew that she loved him too.

"I just wanted you to know that. You don't have to say it back," he said.

"I love you too, Winston," Anna said, softly.

"Anna, you don't have to—"

"No. I really do. I love you. You make me happy, you make me smile." Anna rubbed her thumb across the back of his hand. "I love you."

Winston smiled at her, his eyes full of love.

"Let's leave," Anna said, quietly.

"But you're not finished—"

"I know. It's okay. I want to leave now...I think that we should."

Understanding dawned on him.

"If that's what you want, Anna."

Anna nodded, looking down. "It is exactly what I want. I want to be with you tonight."

Winston smiled softly. "And so do I."

They paid for the bill and then they were off. They went back to his suite. Once they were inside, his took off his jacket and hung it up.

"Do you want something to drink?" he asked, rising to go to the mini bar.

"No, I'm fine. I don't think either of us should drink tonight."

Winston smiled and pulled her into his arms. He raised her chin and kissed her gently. Anna stared into his eyes.

"I've never slept with a man before," Anna told him softly. She closed her eyes, not wanting to see his expression. "I'm a virgin."

"I had a feeling that you were. It's okay, Honey, I think that is part of your appeal. You have this innocence about you, this purity." He kissed the tip of her nose and then her forehead.

"I want to make love to you, Winston. Tonight," she said, firmly, yet gently.

"I don't want you to regret it," he said, running his hands through her hair. "I want you to be sure about this."

"I am very sure," Anna said. She held his face and drew his lips back down to hers. He embraced her fully, pulling her body right up to his.

Ψ

They woke up to the bright sun shining through the window on them. When they woke, they didn't get up straightway. They lounged in the bed, lazily and languorously in each other's arms. Then they made love again. Softly, gently and slowly.

Finally, hunger pulled them from the bed.

"I know what. We'll cook breakfast together. Anna said, growing excited. We can go to the market and get all the stuff that we need."

Winston grinned. "I'm so glad that you could cook, cause I could barely fry an egg."

They laughed.

Soon, it was almost time for them to leave Italy and go back home.

"Tonight, I have something special planned for our dinner," Winston announced over the phone to her, "I'll be home soon."

"What is it?" Anna asked, curiously.

"I'm not going to tell you," he said, laughing. "It's a surprise."

Soon he was home, around four. The doorbell sounded soon afterwards.

"Who's that? Are you expecting someone?" Anna asked him curiously.

He only winked at her and went to answer the door. Anna saw a man in the chef's outfit followed by two people carrying in cooking supplies.

Anna grinned. "You brought people in to cook for us?" she asked, incredulously.

He grinned mischievously. "Sure did."

The chef worked away in the kitchen as they sat sipping wine and talking. The doorbell chimed again.

"Who is it this time?"

Winston, once again without answering, got up to answer the door. Four men in black suits—two holding a violin one holding a harmonica and the other with nothing—came into the room.

"And here are our singers," Winston said, enjoying the look of rapture that came over Anna face.

They sang mostly in Italian, beautiful folk songs. Winston roughly translated for her. Then they sang some songs in English. It was beautiful. They continued to play and to sing as they ate the wonderful meal that the Napoli chef had prepared for them.

"Anna. I need to have you in my life."

"I am in your life," Anna responded.

"But I want to make it a sure thing. I want it to be certain," he said, looking very serious. He then said, "My friends and family always ask me why I'm not married yet and I know its because I've been waiting for the right person."

"What are you talking about?" Anna asked, although she had a feeling about where it was leading.

Winston reached into his pocket and pulled out a crimson velvet box.

Anna gasped. Winston opened the box. A diamond solitaire sat inside. The impossibly large stone shone in the light coming from the dinning room's chandelier. It was beautiful.

"I know that it seems so soon…we've been together for almost nine months now, but it seems that we've been together for an eternity. I want you, Anna." Winston got down on one knee. "I need you. I am sure of this. Will you make me a very happy man and be my wife?"

Anna was speechless for a moment. But she soon caught her voice.

"Yes, Winston. I'll marry you," her voice cracked with emotion.

The musicians and the singer cheered and congratulated them. But they didn't stay for long. Soon Anna and Winston were alone in the house, with the silence of the beautiful night around them.

"Let's go to bed, my sweetheart," Winston said, his eyes full of longing desire.

They went upstairs.

And they made love, in the silver light of the moon that spilled across their bed from the window.

They did not sleep. And all was well.

Ψ

Anna wasn't looking forward to Winston meeting her father. She knew that Muhammad would give him a hard time.

Anna's mother had planned a Sunday family dinner in order to do the introductions.

"We're getting married Mom," Anna had told her mother one morning over the breakfast table as the two of them were sipping tea. She had spent the night over at her parents' house.

She showed her mom the ring.

"That's a big rock," her mother remarked, looking impressed. "You'd better not tell your father just yet. He'll have a fit."

Anna proceeded to inform her mother how old Winston was and that he was a white man from the South.

"Now, you'd better not tell your father *that*. Tell me dear. Why is it that you never told us all this before? You're so secretive, Anna."

"I told you that I was dating someone," Anna responded, feeling a little guilty.

"But it's only now that we get to meet him," Candace said. "And now you're getting married all of a sudden.

"It's not all of a sudden," Anna muttered

"It is," her mother firmly said.

"I didn't want you guys to scare him away," Anna responded. "Especially dad. He doesn't even want me to date. If it was up to him I would be living in seclusion somewhere."

"Anna, you can be quite dramatic at times. Your father's a Muslim, and yes, Muslims are more protective of their women but, but you must admit, your father is a lot better than most. Nevertheless, he has to know eventually."

"He'll find out on Sunday, anyways," Anna reasoned.

"Well, we should wait until then. Hold it of till the last minute, I'm telling you. It's better that way," her mother said nodding. *Muhammad was going to commit murder*, she thought.

Finally, Sunday was upon them. Anna felt slightly sick as she dressed and got ready to go to her parent's house. Winston was going to pick her up in a little while.

Anna had just finished dressing as the doorbell rang. She ran to open it. It was Winston.

"Hi, sugar. Are you ready?" He asked, kissing her.

"You look very nice," Anna said, taking in his khaki colored designer slacks, his cable knit cream sweater, and his expensive leather Italian loafers. He looked absolutely handsome and somewhat boyish with his sparkling green eyes and dimples.

"And you…look stunningly beautiful as always," he said, with admiration and pride in his eyes. He kissed her tenderly on the forehead.

"Are those for me?" Anna asked, noticing the bouquet of flowers that he held in his hands.

"No, no sugar pie. These are for your mother," he said, with a smile.

They rang the doorbell. Candace answered the door. Muhammad stood behind his wife with a stony expression on his face.

"Hi Mom. Hi Dad," Anna said, giving her mother and father kisses on their cheeks. "This is Winston."

"Come on in!" Candace exclaimed, obviously impressed with his appearance. Muhammad only raised a cynical eyebrow, which was less than what Anna expected.

"I'm glad to meet you. You're just as beautiful as your daughter," Winston said, kissing the hand of Anna's mother. Candace laughed, delighted.

"These are for you, Mrs. Senghor," He said, handing her the flowers.

"Thank you, Winston. Please call me Candace though."

Muhammad shot his wife a look that she failed to take notice of. But Anna saw it. She was amused.

"Hello, Mr. Senghor. I am delighted to finally meet you," Winston said, walking up to Muhammad with his hand extended in greeting.

Muhammad reluctantly shook his hand. He looked Winston up and down. He was looking for a flaw with which he could use to pick the interloper apart but apparently, he found none. He grunted back a greeting.

Winston was not put off. He gave Muhammad a winning smile.

"And this is my sister, Tessa," Anna said, trying to hustle the introductions along.

"I'm so glad to meet you," Tessa beamed, as she shook his hand.

"And this," Anna said, pausing with a burdened sigh, "is my brother Malik."

Malik, like his father, was not pleased with the fact that Anna had chosen this white man as a husband. He fixed Winston with a piercing look that was not at all friendly. But he shook his hand, silently.

"Well, shall we all go and sit at the dinner table? The meal is ready," Candace announced.

They went into the dinning room and sat down.

"I almost forgot the wine glasses. I'll be right back," Candace said, getting up.

"I'll help you," Anna said, quickly getting up.

Once they were in the kitchen and out of earshot, Anna commented, "I thought that Dad would have a worse reaction than that when he saw Winston. He didn't look too surprised,

"Well, I decided to tell your father after all. We wouldn't have wanted anything crazy to occur. You know how your father could be."

"Yes, I do. That's why I hope that you told Dad to behave himself," Anna said, reaching for the crystal wine glasses.

"As best I could. Your father is very stubborn. But I think that he's talking it quite well."

The dinner didn't go as badly as Anna thought it would. In fact, it seemed that in the end, Muhammad grudgingly accepted Winston. He was even impressed when Winston told him about his businesses. Only Malik sat through supper in silence, refusing to participate in any conversation as he stared menacingly at Winston. But Winston totally ignored that. He continued to be respectful and friendly throughout the meal.

"Well that didn't go so bad. I even think that your dad likes me," Winston said, as they drove away.

"Yeah. Wasn't as bad as I thought it would be," Anna said, settling back.

Chapter Six

After much prodding from Hector, Anna had agreed to let him do the decorations for the hall, where the reception was being held. Anna had to admit that it was a job well done, and when she had told Hector as much, he had responded, with a sniff, that it should come as no surprise.

They honeymooned in the Canary Islands (Anna's choice) for a week and a half. Anna wanted to stay longer, but Winston had to get back to work. After all, he had a company that needed him.

And Anna was eager to go into the workforce.

"I think I want to get a job at a television station or something," Anna told Winston one day, as they were sitting down over breakfast.

"You don't have to work, you know Anna," Winston had responded, as picked up the Wall Street Journal to read.

"Yeah, I know. But I want to. I don't just want to sit around and do nothing," Anna said.

"You wouldn't be sitting around doing nothing. You have this house to decorate, for example. You can see to that. We have furniture to buy. You can go and choose that out. You can have this household to run, if you want to. That is a job in itself. Plus you could have the days to do whatever you wish."

"You know I love decorating and I would love to do that. But I thought that we were going to choose things out for the house together. I mean, wouldn't that be more fun than me doing that alone?" Anna asked him.

Winston tore his eyes away from the paper. "Yes. It would be fun to do all that together. But, I'm so tied up at work and all…it would be kind of hard."

"But you don't work all the time. We could go on a weekend that you're off. Something like that."

"Of course baby. If that's what you want," Winston said, distractedly.

Ψ

Anna had found out that *DJ Play*, one of the major, most popular music television stations, was looking for a associate producer. She faxed them her resume and crossed her fingers. She wasn't really expecting to get a call back. After all, she hadn't much experience out in the workplace in that field, although she did have an internship at a news broadcasting station.

A week later, she received a call. No one had been home at the time of the call, but she received a message. They wanted her to come in for an interview the next morning at eight-thirty. Anna jumped up and down in joy. She decided that she wouldn't tell Winston until she had actually gotten the job. If she did get the job.

The next morning, she was up bright and early to get ready for the job interview.

"You're up early," Winston groaned from under the linen sheets, barely awake. "Where are you going?"

"I have an interview, for a job," Anna replied.

"Huh? You never told me that before."

"Really?" Anna replied innocently, "I thought that I had told you yesterday. That was when they called me. They told me to come in the next morning, today."

Winston rolled his eyes and turned away from her in the bed. "When are you coming home?" he asked.

"I should be home by noon," Anna responded. She grabbed her purse, walked over to her husband, and kissed him on his cheek goodbye.

"Is that the best that you can do?" he mumbled and pulled her back down, kissing her fully on the lips. His hand slid up to her breasts. Anna playfully slapped them away.

"No time for that, my dear. I have to get going."

"Fine, fine, go. But when I see you again this evening…I'm going to jump your bones, little lady."

Ψ

The attractive, buxom, middle-aged brunette sat behind the desk and peered at Anna, closely scrutinizing her. She was dressed in a nicely cut navy skirt suit and strappy high-heeled sandals. Her nameplate read *Celeste Packard*.

"Well you're fresh out of school. But your credentials are good."

"I'm a hard worker and I learn fast," Anna said.

"You have to be, by looking at your grades. You graduated in the top ten percentile of your class." The woman put down Anna's folder and sat back. "Plus, you had an internship with one of the leading stations in this state. This job is no piece of cake, but a lot of people find it enjoyable. You will generate and oversee content research, you will help with locating and booking guests and artists. You have to perform interviews, you have to help come up with show topics and help arrange the shows for each day. that means finding stories. Basically, you will be doing a lot of organizing."

"I can handle that," Anna said, with confidence.

"Okay. In that case you're hired," the woman said, quickly.

"What? Just like that?" Anna asked, surprised

"Yes. You have had the biggest impact on me out of all the people that came for this job interview. I think that you will be just right for the job." She leaned forward, her gray eyes boring into Anna's. "When can you start?"

"I can start right now," Anna said, excitedly.

"Come in tomorrow. Ten in the morning sharp. I don't take well to tardiness, but I think that you would find me to be a very fair person. Welcome aboard, Mrs. Hurst."

"Thank you so much, you won't be disappointed," Anna said, rising from her chair.

"I certainly hope not," Celeste quipped.

Ψ

Anna checked her watch. She was ten minutes late. The traffic had been terrible on that street and what was normally a twenty minute drive had turned into a twenty-five minute drive. She rushed into the building.

"You're late," Celeste said, dryly.

"I know, but I could explain—"

"Let me guess, the traffic was terrible."

"Yes, actually it was."

"I'll take that excuse for today, Anna. But you only get to make one first impression," Celeste said, matter-of-factly.

Anna's face burned with embarrassment. This was not a good start for the day.

Celeste motioned to a young black man with a jerry curl and tight, faded, stonewash jeans. He excused himself from the woman that he was talking to and came walking over.

"Anna, I want you to meet Ramón. He is our Senior Promotion Producer.

You, as well as some others, will be working with him."

"Nice to meet you dear," the man greeted with a smile. He extended a limp hand towards her. Anna smiled and shook his hand. She noticed that he had a slight accent.

"I'm so glad that she found a replacement. Things were starting to get a little hectic," he said, loudly.

"Well, Ramón. I'm giving her to you. Teach her all she needs to learn," Celeste told him.

"Fantastic, new clay to mold! This is going to be most enjoyable!" Ramón linked his arm through Anna's. Anna smiled. He reminded her so much of Hector. She felt instantly at ease.

He led her into a large office with a big table in the middle. It was covered with files and papers. The walls were covered with pictures, most of them autographed, of famous groups and artists. Among the pictures she saw Boy George from the Culture Club, his eyes heavily lined with makeup, his mouth upturned in a sardonic grin. She also saw Queen, Eurhythmics, Michael Jackson, Billy Ocean, Bonnie Tyler, Elton John, Rod Stewart, Mick Jagger, the studly George Michael...and it went on and on. Anna was enthralled.

"Come on girl, snap out of it. You will see people this famous in the flesh many a time during your time working here," he said, with a wry smile and a sweep of his hands.

"You look really young. How old are you?" asked Ramon.

"21. I'll be 22 in a few months though," Anna responded.

"Ah, a spring chicken," he said, brightly.

"You have a little bit of an accent..." Anna started

"Yes. I'm from Brazil. Rio de Janeiro. I've been here for almost ten years. I'm 26 now."

"Wow. I've been to Brazil before, but that was a long time ago. It was a family vacation," Anna responded.

"Brazil can be both beautiful and ugly at the same time. But, enough about that. It's time to get to work," he said, in a serious tone. "The first thing I want you to do is to go over the schedule for tomorrow. We have LL Cool J on tomorrow."

"Oh, he's hot!" Anna exclaimed.

"Don't I know it!" Ramón cried with intensity. "Anyways," he continued, "I want you to make sure that he has all the things that he is requesting during the break. Ritz crackers, Pepsi—"

"Are you serious?"

"Very!" Ramón quipped. "That is his request. It is to be fulfilled." Ramón shuffled some papers together and put them into a pile. "In the future, you will actually help with the booking of the guests and you and some other producers, which I will introduce you to later, will be organizing the show format. Seeing that we already have the rest of the week and next week's shows already planned, you're in the clear for the rest of the week as far as that's concerned. Okay, chop chop. Please make sure that all those things are in Mr. Cool J's break room!"

Anna gave him an amused grin and went to carry out his orders. This was definitely going to be an interesting job.

Chapter Seven

October 1988

When Winston had suggested that the two of them fly out there, to Texas, for the weekend Anna had hesitated.

"I don't know. I still have to finalize the plans for next Friday's show with some co-workers and then meet with Ramón later. It has to be done by tomorrow."

"Well, bring your work with you," Winston said, dismissively.

"I can't bring it with me. I have to meet up with my co-workers. I can't do that from over there," Anna responded as she wondered if Winston was paying any attention to what she was saying.

Winston gave her an impatient look. "We haven't been away for a while. We need to do something together"

"I agree…but this weekend is going to be hard for me."

"Why don't you meet up with Ramón today and tell him that you can't meet this weekend. Then we can leave tomorrow," he said, with more than a touch of irritation.

"Fine. I'll call him and see if he can."

Ψ

"You know this is really last minute. I was right in the middle of a facial when you called," Ramón said, mournfully.

"I know, but I'm going away this weekend. Winston really wanted me to do something this weekend. I'm sorry."

"Fine. But what about all those times that you wanted to go away, but he said no because of his job? I don't remember him ever giving work the brush off for you," Ramón pointed out cattily.

Anna couldn't argue with that. It was true.

Ψ

When they arrived at the ranch, Anna was instantly glad that they had come. It looked beautiful in the fall—the leaves were changing colors and the autumn afternoon sun was golden and enticing. She had only seen it in the summer time and to her, it seemed more beautiful at this time in the year.

"Glad we came out now?" Winston asked, noticing her enthrallment.

Anna nodded with a slight, lopsided smile.

Their driver took their bags from the car and carried them indoors.

"Hello Mr. and Mrs. Hurst." the housekeeper greeted.

"Hi Bernice, how are you today?"

"I'm just lovely," she said, kindly, "And how are the two of you doing?"

"Just great," Winston answered, "now that we're here."

They followed Bernice into the kitchen. "I've just finished making lunch, why don't you two come into the dinning room. Oh, and Winston, your father is coming home this evening. He heard that you two were coming and he wanted to be here."

"Oh, okay," Winston responded, with a smile and a small shrug, "I have an idea. Bernice, could you pack that food into a basket? I think my lady and I are going to have a picnic down by the lake. How does that sound, Hun?"

Anna's face lit up, "It sounds great."

The lake was lovely and crystal clear. Ripples sparkled across the translucent water. The grass around it was bright green and healthy, the sky was an endless stretch of bright blue punctuated with fluffy globs of white.

Anna and Winston chose an area about ten feet away from the lake and set up their picnic there.

"It is so beautiful out here," Anna sighed, joyously. She slipped off her slippers and settled down on the blanket.

Winston took out the food from the basket one by one, "Hmmm.... Bernice's macaroni and cheese...collard greens...mince meat pie... Caesar salad...biscuits....and a sweet potato pie!"

"Hmmm...I love southern cooking!" Anna exclaimed as she took a serving of each. Winston took his share and they sat back and began chatting.

"So, tell me about your mother, Winston," Anna said, as she took a bite of the flaky, buttery biscuit.

"What do you want to know?" Winston carefully asked, as he pilled his plate with a second serving of macaroni.

"Well…anything. You never talk about her. Let's see…was she born in Texas?"

Winston paused before answering her. He looked past her, towards the trees in the background. "No. She was born in Chicago," he replied.

"Oh, okay, the Midwest," Anna said, unnecessarily.

Winston nodded, still not looking at her.

"Do you still miss her?" Anna asked.

"Of course I do," Winston said quickly. "She died so suddenly, on a boating accident…." Winston looked at her now, directly. "She didn't deserve to die. She was so full of life and vitality. She was the one who taught us how to ride. She was so patient with the four of us. She would take us on walks…name the different trees for us…tell us stories…my mother was a wonderful woman."

"I'm sorry," Anna commented, swallowing hard.

"So am I. But that was twenty years ago, such a long time…I have to move on. But it's been harder for some of us," Winston said with a dark look.

Anna stared at him in puzzlement, but his look didn't last long. He gave her a tentative smile. "Well, let's say we each have us a slice of this here sweet potato pie."

Earnest made it home just as they were finished eating dinner.

"Man, I missed all the good stuff," Earnest said, with a smile.

"You sure did. Bernice cooked us a feast."

"Don't worry, Earnest. I got a plate fixed for ya. All I gotta do is ta warm it up," Bernice said, with a smile.

"That's okay, Bernice. I had me something to eat along the way. I'll just get some hot tea and take it with me to bed, if that's just dandy with you."

"Of course, Earnest. I'll fix you a nice hot cup of Chamomile tea. That'll put you right ta sleep."

"Thank you," Earnest said, with a smile. He turned to Anna, greeted her with a kiss and a hug, and then greeted his son.

"So, you kids ready to go upstairs? I am, I'm beat."

"Yeah. We're exhausted too," Anna admitted.

Players of the Game

That night Anna heard the crying, like she did those months before when they first came here.

Anna carefully climbed out of bed, making sure not to wake Winston. Then she left out of the room, glancing at the clock before she left—1:10 A.M. Anna remembered it being around the same time that it was when she heard the crying the first time she visited the ranch.

She snuck out of the room and down the hallway. Soon she was in front of the door from which the crying was issuing. She put her ear to the door. The wailing could be heard clearly now, almost as if she were in the same room. It sounded so mournful and full of sadness. A feeling of malaise instantly formed in the pit of Anna's stomach. What should she do? Should she knock to make sure that the person was alright? It sounded like the person was suffering terribly. The person might even be in trouble. Anna decided to knock on the door. Before she could back down in fear, she gave the door a tentative knock with her knuckles. The crying halted instantly.

Anna hesitated. "Is everything okay?" she asked, worriedly, her voice barely above a whisper. There was no reply. She swallowed the lump in her throat.

It was deathly silent now. Anna almost felt as if she had imagined the whole thing.

"I just wanted to make sure that everything was okay. I wasn't trying to intrude or anything. Okay. I'm going now, back to bed."

There was still no response as Anna moved away from the door and back into the main hallway. She couldn't remember the hallway being this dark. She moved past the other door as quickly as she could with as much silence as possible. She glanced behind her and as she was about to turn back around, she bumped into something hard and solid. Her mouth opened up, ready to shriek, but before any sound could issue forth, a large hand clamped over her mouth, instantly silencing her.

"What are you doing out here?" a voice that Anna recognized to be Winston's hissed angrily.

His hand was still over her mouth, so she could give no answer. Anna was in shock. What was he doing? Anna's heart pounded in fear. Her breathing became labored in panic.

With his hand still over her mouth, he dragged her to their bedroom door, pulled her into the room, and shut the door firmly behind her. Only then did he remove his hand from her mouth.

Anna spun angrily around. "What are you doing?"

"I should be asking you what you were doing out there in the middle of the night!" Winston spat. In a flash, he gripped her wrist tightly in his hand. "What were you doing out there?" he asked, angrily.

"Stop it, you're hurting me!" Anna exclaimed.

He didn't pay her any mind. He grabbed her upper arms and shook her, his face set in a vicious mask of anger.

For the first time that she had known Winston, she feared for her life.

"What did you do?"

"I heard crying, I was worried that someone was hurt—"

"Bullshit!" he snapped, and shoved her roughly to the carpeted floor. Her cheekbone hit the ground. A flash of pain went through her. Anna crawled backwards away from him until she was backed up against the cool wall—she felt the coldness seep through her thin nightdress and into her back.

Winston stared down at her ferociously. Anna began to cry—her sobbing was frantic and breathless. "I-I-I just went up to the d—door to hear what was happening, to ask if they were okay—" she stuttered.

Winston eyed her, his face still set. He jerked her up by her arm. Anna let out a little shriek as she heard a little pop come from shoulder. Winston pulled her close, grabbed her face, and pushed it up to look at him, as tears streamed down her face.

"That is none of your concern. Don't you ever go out there in the middle of the night again. Do you understand me?" It was more of a demand than a question. Anna nodded her head quickly as she cried.

"Good." He let her go and left the bedroom without another word, slamming the door behind him.

Anna stood in the center of the room, shaking like a leaf on a tree during a storm. She slowly made her way over to the bed and sat down on the edge. She tentatively touched her shoulder. She could feel a bone slightly sticking unnaturally out underneath her skin. It was dislocated, she guessed. But she felt no pain—it was numb.

She could barely believe what had just happened. Who was that man who had just manhandled her so brutally? She never thought that Winston would be capable of such violence towards her. Such fury and viciousness had shone in those green eyes of his tonight. Those were the same green eyes that would shine and sparkle at her with love and affection. She didn't deserve that treatment. Right? She hadn't done anything wrong. But then why did she feel so guilty? No, no. She had just wanted to help. Winston hadn't understood her purpose. It was just a misunderstanding…but still. His actions towards her just a moment ago were intolerable. She should call and tell somebody about it. They might be able to tell her what to do. Better yet, they could come and get her out of this weird place.

Anna picked up the phone and began to dial her sister Tessa's number. But by the time she got halfway through the number, she had lost her confidence and her will. She felt so guilty…the guilt was like a cloud hanging over her. Maybe it was her fault. Next time, she wouldn't be so nosy and eager to get into things that didn't concern her. Maybe Winston was right.

Anna replaced the receiver.

Anna stayed in the room long after the sun had risen in the sky. She was afraid to leave the bedroom. She looked over at the bedside clock. It was nine in the morning. For eight sleepless hours, she had stayed in this room. During that time, Winston had not come in once.

Anna winced as she rose from the bed. Her shoulder was killing her now. The pain had started about four hours ago, and was now steady and constant.

Suddenly, she heard a soft knock at the door, and then it opened. Winston stood there with a sheepish expression on his face. Anna cringed, but said nothing.

"I'm sorry, Anna, for the way that I behaved last night. That was unacceptable." His eyes darted around the room. "Do you mind if I come in?"

Anna continued to stare at him. She felt a rush of emotions, guilt, affection, anger, and fear. She automatically shrugged her shoulder. Of course, this sent a spike of pain through her. She gasped.

Winston came rushing over. "What is the matter, darling. Are you hurt?"

"I think my shoulder is dislocated. Either that, or it's broken," she said, dully.

Winston looked extremely apologetic and appropriately guilty. "That's from me, I guess."

He looked at her shoulder, his face grim when he saw it. "Well, we'd better get you to the doctor. Dr. Carslie's right in town. He has his own office at his house. He has been our family doctor for years."

They called before they left. When they got there, the doctor was waiting for them on the porch. He had snow-white flyaway hair and a matching handlebar mustache. His eyes were a soft brown that sparkled when he greeted them. He was short and robust with a barrel chest. He dressed casually in jeans and button up shirt, under his lab coat.

"Well, it is dislocated. But that's nothing that we can't fix here." He smiled and patted her hand. "How'd ya manage ta do that little lady?"

Anna glanced at her husband. He stood nervously behind the doctor. His eyes pleaded with hers.

"I was horseback riding and I fell off." Anna said, at last. It was better not to let others know their business. Plus, she was too ashamed to tell him what really happened.

The grandfatherly doctor smiled at her. "You gotta be careful riding them horses over there at that ranch missy." He gently pushed her to lie down on the examination table, face up. "Now, this is gonna hurt a little missus. Come on over here, Winston, and hold your wife's hand."

Winston came immediately over and held Anna's hand. She tolerated the contact in silence.

"Grit your teeth, girly, her I go!"

"Ahhhhhgh!" Anna yelled out. The pain was intense. She squeezed Winston's hand until it turned white as snow. Winston shuddered, but didn't complain.

"There ya go. All set. But you gotta be easy with it for the rest of next week. It's a little swelled and tender now," Dr. Carslie said, as he took off his glasses and wiped them.

"If the pain gets too intense you can take some Tylenol. You shouldn't need anything stronger than that."

"Thank you, Doc," Winston said, looking relieved.

Anna got up from the table and made an attempt at a smile.

They were in the Lincoln now. Winston was driving them back to the ranch.

"I want to go home," Anna said, blandly.

"Okay. If that's what you want. We can leave tomorrow morning," Winston said, nodding.

"I want to leave today. Right now, if possible," Anna said, shortly.

"Fine," he said. Then there was a long stretch of silence. Then finally, he started to speak again.

"I'm sorry Anna. I really am…that won't happen again. I got out of hand."

Anna didn't answer him. She looked out of the window in silence.

"It's just that my father…" he continued, "It was him that you heard. I might as well tell you now. He's a very unhappy man, Anna. Ever since my mother died. He blames himself for her death and he punishes himself over it. He won't let her go, he won't let her rest in peace."

Anna tuned to him now, her curiosity overcoming her sullenness. "Why does he blame himself?"

"My mother died in a boating accident. He just thinks that he could have prevented it some way…and he's angry with that. Since my mother died, he can't sleep at night. This has been going on for years. He has sleeping pills, but most of the time when he doesn't take them, he's awake and he cries for her. I want him to get some…psychological help, but he doesn't listen. He's not well, Anna. I just didn't want you see him like that. I just wanted you to see him for the man that he is underneath all of that. He's a good man, Anna."

"I know that," Anna said, softly. "I never questioned that and I don't question that now." Anna paused. "And I don't want you to think that I was being malicious by trying to find out what was happening. I just wanted to make sure that no one was hurting—"

"I know Anna. I know your intent was good. I overreacted. It's just that it upsets me so much…I love you Anna. I love you so much."

"I understand," Anna said, and held his hand. "I love you too." They drove in comfortable silence for the rest of the ride back to the ranch.

Chapter Eight

November, 1988

Hector looked up from the list just as his boss Toby came strutting in. Hector had been working for the renowned Toby Li for over a year, but Hector never ceased to be amazed by him and his fashion sense, or lack thereof.

Today, the slightly built Taiwanese-American man was togged up in an expensively cut lavender sports jacket over a pale pink silk button down shirt. The first two buttons were undone, revealing the beginnings of a smooth, hairless chest. His lower torso was encased in fitted black pants that hardly left anything to the imagination and a pair of brightly shined Armani mules adorned his feet.

Everyday Toby looked as if he was ready to march in the gay pride parade. He flaunted his sexuality with loud, bright blinkers. There was no mistaking him. From the well manicured nails and pedicured toenails to the perfectly styled hair he was…flashy. While this was not exactly Hector's style. (Hector had become a little more subtle over the years when it came to displaying his sexuality.) He respected the man none-the-less. After all, this man was the one to go to if one needed anything from interior designing to decorating and event planning. The *Home and Beyond* magazine, which was the bible of the interior decorating, often featured him in it. *Everybody* knew who Toby Li was. And if you didn't, you were nobody.

"So how does the list look?" Toby asked, his dark eyes studying him with intensity. Hector cleared his throat.

"Looking good. I don't think that Mrs. Hansen can squeeze in anymore people." Hector commented with a shake of his head.

Toby pursed his lips. "But she wants twenty more people for her party! We must fit them in," he said, with finality. He wore a determined expression on his face.

Hector looked at him bewildered. Then he thought about how effeminate the man's face looked. He would look good as a drag queen, he though. "But there's no more space. If we're going to hold it in the dinning room area…"

"Then we will move it outside!" Toby announced, triumphantly. He clapped his small hands together.

Hector began to panic; a sensation of strangulation began to form in his throat.

"But that would mean—everything—"

"Almost everything would have to be redone…," Toby finished for him. "We will use the same decorations and setting that we ordered, but we will have to set it outside. We will order a platform to be set up for the dancing area, we'll make a food buffet, we'll order a *gigantic* canopy …" Toby grinned as he imagined it, "I *do* hope that Mrs. Hansen warms to the idea…"

"I guess I'll be the one to inform her," Hector said, a little sarcastically.

"Thank *you* for offering! You are just divine!" Toby cooed with a sparkle in his black eyes.

Hector suspected that Toby had a thing for him. But he stayed clear of *that*. There was no way that he was going to become one of Mr. Li's playthings. Hector may be young but he definitely wasn't dumb. He needed Toby Li for one thing and one thing only. Experience. Experience so that he could one day open his own business in events planning, decorating, and design. But he knew Mr. Li wouldn't take too kindly to a potential rival, so he kept his future plans carefully hidden from his boss.

Later on that day, Hector met Anna for dinner. They went to a new restaurant that specialized in Indian cuisine. It had opened not to long ago and they had been dying to try it out.

"So you made it back from Texas with all you skin and unlynched," Hector said, deprecatingly. He paused to eye a brown-skinned East Indian waiter that passed their table. Not bad, he thought.

"Not likely that you would get his attention…I don't think that's exactly their style," Anna said, with a grin, noticing his stare.

Hector's face contorted in derision. "A lot you know." He poked at the basmati rice in his plate. "Remember Amir in college?"

Anna paused, thinking. "You mean that exchange student from Pakistan?"

"That's the one," Winston quipped. "He wasn't exactly your run-of-the-mill pious Muslim."

"But you went to the Mosque with him once, didn't you? But you're not even Muslim."

"Tut-tut, Anna," Hector said, mockingly, wagging his finger at her in mock reprimand, "you must ask yourself for what purpose did they go to the mosque…"

Anna nearly choked on her food. "You didn't!" she gasped

Hector gave her a sneaky look, "We did…right in the basement."

"I can't believe that."

"I was his first," He scoffed.

"Unbelievable. I would have never suspected."

"Believe it, my dear. He went back to Pakistan a changed man! So there. You must eat your words!" Hector said, feeling quite proud of himself.

Anna shook her head slowly. Hector was something else all together.

"Your cheek looks swollen," Hector commented, pointing his finger at it, "What happened?"

"I fell off a horse," She instantly replied, concentrating on her food.

She said that a little too quickly, Hector thought.

"Are you *sure?*"

"Of course I am," Anna said, looking him fully in the face now. She forced her eyes to look straight into his tan colored ones.

"Me and Winston were riding in the fields. The horse that I was on flipped out. I fell off, practically on my face." Anna shook her head, as if in remembrance of the horrible event. "It was quite painful."

"I can imagine," Hector responded, fully believing her now.

They said nothing more on the subject.

Ψ

November 1989

"Do you know what an *ass*hole your husband is?" Celeste said, stressing the 'ass' part of the word with a drawn out hiss. She stared down at Anna who was sitting in the workroom going over the schedule for the next week. Anna had just finished booking the hotels for the guests and making the last minute checks with each prospective star's agent.

She looked up at Celeste, a sorrowful expression already beginning to form on her face, "I'm sorry, I—"

"That man knows that we have a deadline here. You and Ramón have a shitload of work to do, yet he keeps calling here for you every minute. And then he cops an attitude with me, when I tell him this." Celeste cocked her head in contemplation. "Tell me. What exactly *is* your husband's problem?"

Anna gave her a pleading look.

Celeste sighed in defeat. "Go on ahead. But I want you to know that I'm getting tired of this."

Anna picked up the phone in the other room. "What is it this time, Winston?"

"Anna, Can't you come home a little earlier from work? I swear, this flu is just getting worse." He paused, waiting for her response, getting none, he plunged into the full details of his malady, "My chest is all clogged up and hurting, my throat feels like I just swallowed a bucketful of sand and I can barely breathe. I'm so weak. I need your help," He complained.

Anna squeezed her eyes shut. She was developing a serious headache. Winston had a caught the flu a few days ago and all of today and yesterday he had been calling her five, six, seven, times a day. Today was worse than yesterday. It was around one and he had already called her four times during the past five hours. Four more hours to go. She was sure that he would be calling non-stop to the very end.

"Winston. I can't get home early today. I have a deadline. I left soup and everything for you to warm up until I come home…"

"But I can barely get up," He moaned.

"I'll be home soon. Hold on until then. Please Winston. Don't cause me to lose my job. Bye now." Anna hung up before he could say anything else.

Ramón watched her as she came back into the office. He had a strange look on his face.

"What is it?" Anna mumbled as she picked up her checklist.

He shook his head and sighed. "That man has a chain around your neck. And I don't mean the good kind," He said, with a frown. "It's not healthy."

Anna rolled her eyes. "Come off it. He's not getting on any worse than any other man does when they get sick. You all get on like babies." Anna cringed as she leaned back up. Her side was still hurting her, five days after Winston had thrown her to the ground in a fit of rage and kicked her. He had carefully avoided her stomach. She ran a hand over it. It was still flat, but not for much longer, she knew.

"Is something wrong?" Ramón asked, his jerry curled hair gleaming in the lights of the room. "You have the thousand-yard-stare going on.."

"I am perfectly fine, thank you," Anna said, quickly. "Let's get back to work."

Ramón appraised her. "You know, you've done a lot of growing up since you first got here."

Did she have a choice?

In two weeks, Winston was completely cured. But then it was Ramón down with the flu.

"The flu is spreading around here like fire on dry wood!" Celeste intoned, not happy at all with many of her employees being out sick.

Anna was left to do most of the legwork and the planning by her own. It was definitely not an easy job.

Another two weeks had passed and Ramón was still out sick. Anna suspected that he was faking it, just to get out of work and get a paid vacation. She had called him earlier that week and he had not sounded *so* bad…at least to her. She ended up having to work late hours, far into the night in order to formulate shows, make schedules and to keep the show plans running smooth as silk. It was definitely getting to her.

One night she was in the office working, long past everyone else had gone home. She was getting extremely tired. Her lids were weighted down. I'll just take a little nap, she told herself, and then wake right up and work again. She glanced at the clock. It read 8:15. *I'll sleep till nine,* she told herself.

When Anna opened her eyes, it was one thirty in the morning.

"Shit!" She exclaimed. Winston was going to kill her. She looked down at her hands and realized that she was shaking. She grabbed up her stuff and left the building in a rush.

She arrived home at one-forty five. Five minutes earlier than it usually took her to get home. She had driven home in her little Beemer at top speed.

When she walked through the door, Winston was waiting for her with an angry glare.

"Where the hell were you? It's fuckin' two in the morning," he spat.

Anna's eyes began to pool with tears. She forced them back. "I was at the office working. But I fell asleep at the desk and when I woke up it was so late—"

"That's a load of crap," he snapped cutting her off. His tall, toned frame slowly ambled over to where she was in large living room. "So who were you seeing?"

Anna wasn't surprised at this accusation. He was always accusing her of having an affair, even though it was far from the truth. She loved him and didn't want to be with any other man.

"I wasn't with anyone," Anna said firmly. She met his eyes boldly, but inside she was terrified..

Bam! Winston socked her on the side her face. Anna tumbled back. Then he hit her in the other side of her face. This time she fell to the floor in a heap. She instinctively curled herself into a ball.

"You little whore!" Kick. Kick. Kick, "Who are you fuckin', huh? Who is it?" Punch. Kick, Kick. "Goddamned slut. Your bitch ass is probably out fucking all over the place."

His words hurt just as much as the physical pain that he was dealing out to her in full force. She felt as if she was falling to pieces inside. It was as if her heart was the lump that she was currently feeling her throat, and at any moment her heart would slide from her throat to her mouth and then out of her mouth to see it in little pieces on the richly carpeted floors of the living room. Oh, the emotional pain and mental anguish was just as brutal as each kick and each punch that he gave her.

He was out of control. He didn't even bother to aim away from her stomach, which was steadily growing with their child inside for the past two months. Anna squeezed her eyes shut just before his foot came and kicked her in her face. She felt blood gush. But she kept her eyes closed. All she could think about was the baby. Please, not the baby…

Exhausted, he finally left her. He left the house with a slam of the door. Anna didn't open her eyes until she heard the engine of his car turn on and he zoomed off into the night.

Then she slowly got up, to her knees first and then to her feet. Her blood was all over the carpet. Luckily, the carpet was dark, so it didn't show up that badly. She gingerly touched her face. Her hand came away with blood. She almost stumbled back to the floor. She willed herself to be steady.

She ended up back on the floor anyways. She crawled into the kitchen. She pulled out a bottle of water from the pantry and drank from it. That helped a little bit. She didn't feel like anything was broken. She felt a little stronger. She had to clean up the mess. All this blood...

She listened for his footsteps as she cleaned, slowly making progress despite her weakness. Afterwards, she climbed up the lavishly winding staircase and into bed. She was so exhausted.

She woke up in a cold sweat at four A.M. Cramps assailed her as she gripped her stomach. The pain was incredible. Her eyes began to tear. It felt as if a giant hand was squeezing her middle, getting tighter and tighter with each squeeze.

She had felt this before. Oh God, she was losing the baby.

Anna sobbed as she stumbled to the bathroom. She looked down and saw a bloodstain forming on her jeans. Once she was in the bathroom, she peeled off her jeans, and her underpants and sat down on the toilet with the little bit of strength that she had left. It was then that the blood came gushing out into the toilet. Anna moaned and clutched her tummy.

Soon everything began to swim before her eyes and blackness was creeping up into her vision.

She slid down from the toilet and writhed on the floor for a little. She was getting weaker and weaker. She closed her eyes and allowed the darkness to come.

Anna opened her eyes to find herself lying on the floor of the bathroom. Her cheek rested against the cold tiles of the floor. She raised her head a little and saw that it was light outside. She looked at the clock on the bathroom counter. It was almost eleven. She had been knocked out for almost seven hours. She slowly stood up, although her body begged for her to stay down. She was so weak. She looked around at the bathroom. There wasn't really a mess. Then she looked down at herself. Her clothes were covered in blood. If someone were to look at her, they would think that she had murdered someone. She had to clean herself up. She made her way over to the bath and ran the water as hot as it could get. She added bath salts and bubble bath. Then she slid in and bathed. When she came out, she put on some clean clothes and threw the clothes that she was wearing before into the garbage. There was no way she was going to wear those clothes again. She flushed the toilet and walked slowly into the bedroom. Winston wasn't there. In fact, the house had the distinct feeling of no one being there beside herself. She had to call someone.

Before she could even pick up the phone call someone, the phone rang shrilly, piercing the ominous silence of the morning. Fear instantly gripped her. She didn't want to speak to Winston. She let the phone ring and ring until the answering machine picked up.

Hector's voice came over loud and clear, "This message is for Anna. This is Hector. I was wondering if....

Anna quickly picked up the phone. "Hello?" she called into the mouthpiece. It was barely above a whisper.

"Hey, hon. I thought you were still asleep. I was wondering if you wanted to go with me to the Vanity Fair fashion show. Toby gave me two tickets…I know how much you like stuff like that. I know it's kinda last minute, but Toby just gave them to me today. I wanted to call you as early as possible in so that you had time to get prepared, that is, if you want to go—Anna are you alright?"

Anna was sobbing now. The tears were rolling down her face, unchecked.

"Honey…what is it?" Hector demanded, worried. "What happened? Did he do something to you?"

"N-n-no…"Anna lied.

"I'm coming over there right now," Hector said, with finality, "You just hold on, I'll be there in fifteen minutes."

Hector rang on the doorbell over and over until Anna swung the door open.

Hector took one look at her, and his face turned into a mask of shock and horror.

"My gosh. You look like you've been in a bar fight." Hector came into the room and closed the door behind him. He gently reached up and touched her face.

"He did this. That bastard," Hector spat out, his brown eyes blazing in anger. "Is he here?" he asked, cracking his knuckles.

"No he isn't," Anna answered truthfully with relief. Hector would be a worthy opponent for Winston. Though he wasn't as tall as Winston, Hector was still tall at 6'2" and he was well built and strong.

"No, no, Hector. You will not lay a hand on him," Anna said, quickly, sensing his intent.

Hector's eyes blazed like fire. They were gorgeous eyes, Anna noted.

"Why not? The little shit has no problem hitting a woman. Let him come and hit a man. Let's see how he stands up to me," Hector said, sounding slightly uncertain.

"Take me to the hospital," Anna said, hollowly.

"Did he break anything?" Hector shrieked

"No!" Anna exclaimed a little too loudly. "No," she repeated in a softer tone. "I don't think so."

"Well, you should go anyways. Pack some stuff. You'll be staying with me for a while. There's no way you're coming back to this house," Hector said, bridging no argument.

They went upstairs and threw some clothes into a bag. Or rather, Hector did. Anna just stood numbly by and watched him rush around the room sticking different articles of clothing into a suitcase.

"Come on," he said, gripping her hand. "We're on our way to the hospital, Hun."

After she was settled into a room, the doctor came to examine her.

Dr. Mead was a middle aged, balding, black man with chestnut colored skin and piercing black eyes.

Anna glanced at Hector, who made no move to leave the room.

"I want him to stay," Anna said, afraid to let Hector out of her sight.

"If that's what you want," the doctor said, carefully keeping a blank expression on his face as he said it. So the woman wanted her gay friend in the room with her while she was being examined, who was he to argue?

He questioned her as he examined her. "How old are you?"

"Twenty-two"

"These lacerations on your face and your arms. How did they happen?" he asked, already knowing the answer. He wasn't born yesterday. He had seen many women with similar injuries. The doctor looked at Hector, standing there so stoically, with a grim expression on his face. The young man's jaw was tight with tension and deep love for this young woman, underlying the look of anger and fierce protectiveness that shone from his eyes. The doctor sensed this strongly. If this man wasn't gay—well, he wasn't dead sure that the man was gay, but having often come across them over his many years of living in Los Angeles he was sure that he was—he would have argued that he was in love with her. But that was ridiculous. He decided to test the young man with the dark, loose curls that hung to his shoulders.

"Did you do this?" The doctor asked, in a low voice. He was now testing Anna's reflexes with a little hammer. Finding the appropriate response, he went on to test her blood pressure. He wrapped the machine around her upper arm.

The young man's face turned red under his bronze skin. His eyes blazed with fury. "I did not! It was that bast—"

"He didn't do this," Anna said, quickly before Hector could say anything else. She glanced at Hector. He was staring the doctor with vicious looks. It looked like he wanted to kill him. "No one did this. I fell."

"From what?" The doctor asked, testily. So she was going to cover for the bugger, whoever it was.

"My patio stairs," Anna answered quickly. She had been thinking up answers to possible questions on the ride over.

Hector let out a loud sound of anger and frustration. The doctor looked at the attractive young man with the small bump on the bridge of his nose. Very Mediterranean looking. Italian? He knew Italian men could be very macho, even the gay ones. He knew what happened. It was obvious that the young woman wasn't telling the truth.

"Those must be a really tall flight of stairs that you had to fall down from in order for all this damage to be done," the doctor said, with a note of surprise. She was going to carry the lie to the very end.

Anna shrugged. Hector, once again, let out a frustrated sigh.

"If you don't tell him anything, I will." Hector faced the doctor, staring him straight in his shining brown eyes.

"Her bastard of a husband did this to her. That was who."

"Shut up Hector!" Anna yelled

"He beats her! I keep telling her to leave him. I never liked him, I swear it," Hector spewed. He was on a roll now. He was not to be stopped. "The next time he does it, I'll kill him," He promised with a nod.

"Hector, stop it!" Anna cried.

The doctor observed them in silence. Sometimes it was best to shut up and just let others talk. Things often came out easier that way. People liked to hear themselves speak—a fact that he learned over the years.

Suddenly Hector's eyes bulged open wide. His jaw dropped. "What about the baby Anna?"

Anna's face burned. She looked down at her toes.

"He killed it?" Hector exclaimed. "Is it dead? He killed the others too, didn't he? You didn't just miscarry; he beat them out of you!"

Suddenly with a cry of rage, Anna leapt up from the examining table and charged right for Hector. Quick as a flash, she had her hands around her friend's throat before the doctor could even register what was going on.

By the time the doctor had called for the help of some nurses and staff, Hector had managed to peel her hands off and restrain her. She began to kick out at him with her feet. Hector attempted to shield his groin area from her thrusting feet with one hand, while at the same time, he attempted to hold her arms down with his other hand. It was not an easy task to accomplish. Finally, she made her mark with an upward thrust of her right knee—right in Hector's balls. He howled in pain and instantly let go of her. She took the little opportunity to further attack him. But the orderly, one doctor, two nurses and one security man were soon upon her and dragged her over to the hospital bed..

She was a wild woman now. Screaming, grunting, and wailing. Hectors eyes opened wide in fear.

"I think you'd better leave," one of the nurses said over her shoulders as she strapped one arm down. "You're making her more upset."

Hector was reluctant to leave her. He hesitated at the door until the doctor called out, "Leave now!"

Zombie-like, Hector left the hospital room, drifted to the nearest waiting room and sat down down. He was as stiff as a board and just as unfeeling. Suddenly a little Asian girl was in front of him. She grinned and handed out her doll to him. Hector noticed her only when she said, "Do you want to hold her? Her name's Natalie."

Hector turned his glazed eyes to the pretty child. He looked around. The only Asian woman in the room was sitting across from him with her head in her hands, unaware of her daughter, who was now standing in front of Hector.

Hector tried to smile. "No thanks. But she's very nice looking."

"Mister. Why are you crying?" the little girl asked, quizzically, pointing a finger at his face.

Shocked, Hector raised a hand to his face. Sure enough, it came away wet, wet with his tears. He hadn't even noticed he was crying.

The doctors had tranquilized Anna and ran a D&C on her to clear out any possible dead tissue from the fetus. They ran some more tests on her, finding her mostly fine, besides the bruised and the cuts. They wheeled her into a recovery room. Hector wanted to come in. But the doctors wouldn't let him. Dr. Mead came out to talk with him.

"Who knows how she's going to react when she gets up. She might be still angry with you. We don't want her getting upset."

"Are you going to keep her overnight?" Hector asked, twisting his hands.

"Yes, we would like to in order to observe her." The doctor squinted at Hector, studying the young man. "So, her husband did this to her."

"Yes." Hector answered quickly.

"How long has this been happening?"

"I'm not exactly sure. She managed to cover it up really well for a long time. I suspected a few times that something was amiss, but she would always tell me that I was being ridiculous...I would just believe her. I guess you could say that I really started to see definite evidence of abuse starting from about a month ago. I confronted her about it, she tried to avoid it. I even called the police on him a couple of times, but nothing happened. He got arrested once, and they took him down to the station, but he was home that same day because Anna refused to press charges" Hector paused. "Do you think you can get him arrested?"

The doctor admired the friend's loyalty. "We can't actually do anything unless Anna herself makes a statement and she has to press charges. If she is willing to do that, then we'll be onto something."

"And if she doesn't?"

The doctor shrugged his shoulders, trying to remain neutral. "Then there's nothing that can be done. We can't help someone that doesn't want to be helped."

Hector frowned. His brow creased in thought.

"Where are her parents?" he asked, trying a different route.

"They're in Arizona."

"Do they know about this abuse?"

Hector shook his head. "Anna never told them and she forbade me to tell them. She doesn't want them to know. She doesn't really speak to them a lot. Not anymore."

The doctor nodded knowingly. That was the usual pattern of abusers. Isolate the victim from family and friends. But the brute was obviously not successful with getting rid of this individual. It was obvious that this young man was here to stay.

The doctor left Hector. Hector tried to relax and sat down.

A nurse came out to where Hector was sitting. He was ready to drift off to sleep. She patted Hector on the shoulder softly. She smiled down at him. "Anna's awake now, she wants to see you."

Hector went into the room to find Anna propped up in bed. She gave Hector an apologetic smile as he entered. "I'm so sorry Hector. I'm sorry."

Suddenly her face crumpled and she started crying. "I hate myself. I'm just like him—how I attacked you like that. I'm just so fustrated and angry, I took it all out on you. Sorry."

Hector rushed over and held her in his arms. Anna leaned back on his broad chest. She listened to his heart beating steadily in his chest.

"It's okay Anna. You're not like him. You'll never be like him.

You weren't thinking straight. I'm sorry too. I shouldn't have blurted out those things." He kissed her head and ran his hand through her hair.

"Well, isn't this just a cozy sight," a voice drawled easily from behind them.

Both sets of eyes flashed to the door. There stood Winston. His face was calm and passive. He slowly walked into the room. Anna felt Hector's arms tighten around her.

"Why don't you step outside Hector. I gotta talk to my wife in private."

Hector gave him a vicious glare. "I'm not going anywhere. Not unless Anna wants me to."

Winston turned to his wife, his eyes burning into hers. "Well Anna? Gonna tell your little pet to leave?"

Hector was ready to spring. Anna gripped onto him, "Please Hector. Can you leave?"

"But Anna, he has nothing worthwhile to say to you!" he protested, getting up.

"Please, Hector, let me just listen to him, that's all."

"Don't listen to anything that he tells you." He stared straight at Winston as he said his next words, "I'll be waiting outside."

He brushed past Winston, barely resisting the urge to attack him. Hector walked slowly out the door. Winston slammed the door shut after him.

Winston started to walk towards the bed. Anna raised her hand in protest.

"Please stay where you are." She said, coldly.

"Fine." He pulled a long velvet box from his pocket and opened it towards her. "I bought you something."

Anna could see a sparkling necklace full of diamonds. She gasped.

"It's platinum. Ten carat diamonds…"

"I don't care. Why is it that you bring me something everything time you beat me?" Anna snapped, "It's not going to heal my wounds. And it won't bring back the baby that you killed."

Winston looked crestfallen. This was turning out to be harder than he thought it would be.

"What would this be...the third one of our children that you killed?" Anna spat out callously.

Winston swallowed hard. She could see his Adam's apple bobbing up and down.

"I'm sorry Anna. Please, believe me. I'm going to get help. We'll have babies, actual ones that'll be born..."

Suddenly the door opened. It was Dr. Mead. He glared at Winston, knowing fully who he was.

"So, you're the husband that enjoys beating up on his wife," He said, matter-of-factly.

Winston didn't say a thing. His face was unreadable.

"Now. If you would excuse me, I have to check up on her. The door is that way," The doctor said, tersely.

Winston hesitantly walked towards the door. He shut it behind him. He spotted Anna's fairy of a friend sitting in the waiting room, leafing through a magazine. An expression of rapt concentration was on Hector's face. Winston felt a swell of anger. He wanted to punch him to a pulp. The damn faggot was always interfering. The funny thing was that every time Winston tried to run him away, he was still always there sticking that damned nose into everything. It was high time that he had a chat with the queer.

He sat down across from Hector. Hector just noticed him as he sat down. He tensed visibly. He waited for Winston to speak, his brown eyes trained on him.

"Why don't you keep out of our business? What happens is between the two of us," Winston said, calmly.

Hector looked up at him, his face stony. "Anna *is* my business," He said, simply.

Winston's face turned red with rage. He said it with such calmness and ease. "No. She is not your business. You're not married to her. I am. Therefore, she is *my* business."

"Anna's my best friend, she's like a sister to me. I love her a lot. If anything happens to her, I deal with it too. I won't stand by and let anyone hurt her. You mess with her, you mess with me too," Hector said, his jaw set, obstinate. His eyes burned into Winston's.

Winston couldn't believe the nerve of him.

Behind the closed door, Dr. Mead just finished examining Anna. "Well, you appear to be doing fine now. But as I said earlier, we would still like to keep you until morning to watch over you."

"Okay, that's fine," Anna responded.

The doctor smiled. She reminded him of his own daughter. "Anna. You know that you don't deserve to be hit. No woman does."

Anna was silent.

The doctor continued, unperturbed. "Anna. I know he beat you. You can press charges."

"He's my husband," Anna whispered.

"It doesn't matter. You should end this…before it goes too far."

Anna was silent. She couldn't do it, as much as she hated him sometimes. He was her husband and that would be a great betrayal. Besides, it was embarrassing. She didn't want anyone to know what she endured. People would wonder how she could allow the beating to happen. People would think that she was weak. She didn't want people to think such things about her.

"So, do you want to press charges?"

"Would he go to jail?"

"Yes."

"For how long?" Anna asked, curious.

"I'm not sure. Not for a really long time, but he'll get a fair amount of time. He'll be charged with assault and battery. And then you can get a restraining order against him so that when he comes out, he wouldn't be able to come near you. If he violates this, he will be put back in jail."

"I can't do that," Anna said, softly. "I'm sorry."

"No. *I'm* sorry. Sorry that you feel that you have to protect your husband. A *real* man wouldn't lay his hands on a woman."

"I'm not pressing charges," She said, firmly.

"Fine. Your husband is still out there. Do you want me to ask him to leave?"

Anna thought for a moment. "Yes. I don't want to speak to him now."

"What about your friend?"

"I want him to stay. Can you call him in here?"

Dr. Mead stepped out of Anna's room. He walked into the waiting room. He saw that Hector and the husband were in deep conversation with each other.

They stopped, turned their heads towards him, and stood up.

"So, how is she?" the husband asked.

"She doesn't want to see you right now. So, it would be good if you were to leave," Dr. Mead said, instead of answering him.

"I'm not going anywhere," Winston retorted.

"That's fine. But you will not be going in her room. If you attempt to, you will be escorted off the premises," The doctor informed him, flatly.

Winston sneered at him. The doctor focused on Hector.

"Anna wants you to come in," the doctor said.

"What? There's no way that he's going in there before me. That's *my* wife!"

"I though we were clear on that. Your wife doesn't want to see you. You are not to enter her room. You need to leave," Dr. Mead said, keeping his face stern.

Winston stalked out of the waiting room and walked up to Anna's door. He flung it open.

"Call security!" Dr. Mead called out.

"What do you mean you don't want to speak to me? I said I was sorry!" Winston yelled, his face red.

Security was called. Before the uniformed enforcers could reach Winston, he sneered at Anna, spun on his heels, and walked away.

Hector went right in to see Anna. Her eyes were wide with fright. Hector came up to her and hugged her.

"It's okay, hon. You don't have to worry about him anymore. I won't let him hurt you."

Chapter Nine

Winter, 1989

It was the middle of December. Christmas was coming up and Anna still hadn't moved back in with her husband. She was living with Hector in his condo.

"You should just divorce him Anna. There's no sense you staying married to him."

Anna would always change the subject when the subject of her marriage was brought up. She wasn't ready to deal with that just yet.

Hector's parents had invited Hector and Anna to their Santa Barbara home for the Christmas holiday. Hector pestered Anna until she broke down and agreed to join him. The Minatos' home was a large and spacious seven-bedroom mansion with manicured lawns and a beautiful pool outback and a tennis court.

Demetrius Minatos was a tall, slightly overweight, robust man with olive skin and onyx colored eyes. He had a pencil thin mustache and thick headful of ink black hair beginning to gray at the temples. He had a serious manner and seldom smiled. But he was known for his wry sense of humor and he was always polite and always made people feel welcome. He was like a second father to Anna and so was Aisha Minatos. She was a striking woman with off-white, creamy skin, hazel colored eyes, and a mass of tightly curled dark brown hair. She was petite, around 5'3", and curvy—attractively filled out. She had full lips and high cheekbones that gave her an exotically aristocratic look. She was a quiet-spoken, intense woman. She was extremely warm and caring.

"Hello, Anna dear." Aisha leaned over and gave her a kiss on her cheek, a hug, and a warm smile. Demetrius leaned over and kissed her cheek as well. Aisha greeted her son in a similar manner. But not Demetrius.

Hector shifted nervously around on his feet. Demetrius looked everywhere but at his son, after an awkward moment, he said, "Well, everyone's here. Come on in."

"Hey!" Amani called as they stepped into the living room. She put an arm around both Anna and Hector at the same time. Hector gave her a kiss on the cheek and tickled her until she was on the floor giggling loudly. After she begged for mercy, he stopped.

"Come on, Hector. I'm seventeen, not seven," she said, sternly, although she was smiling. She was pretty girl with pitch-black curly hair, dark brown-almost black eyes, light olive skin, and full lips. She was also short like her mother, but with a lean, lithe body.

"Yeah, well you're still a little squirt to me," Hector joked. He turned to his brother who was sitting on the couch, "And come to think of it so are you."

Nicholas Minatos gave his older brother a twisted grin. "Yeah whatever. You're what. A year and a half older than me?"

"So what. I'm still older," Hector said, with a little laugh.

"I don't know why you deal with him," Nicholas said to Anna with a smile, "He must be a very irritating friend." Nicholas was a strikingly handsome young man at the age of 21 with wavy black hair and the same light brown eyes as his brother.

"You bet, but I still love him," Anna said, grinning.

After the small talk, they sat down and ate dinner. Anna enjoyed herself and each one of Hector's family members—Demetrius for his sarcastic, dry, wit, Aisha for her warm doting, Nicholas for his mischievousness and Amani for her playful teasing.

Mostly, all that Hector noticed was his father's coldness towards him the few times when he wasn't fully ignoring him. This both frustrated and pained Hector. He knew that his father had still never gotten over the fact that his eldest son wanted to be with men rather than women. And by the looks of it, Hector noted, he probably never would. It was funny. His father had been behaving like this towards him for four years—ever since he had confessed that he was gay, which had been about a month before going away to college.

Hector and Anna left Christmas evening. They had to get back to work tomorrow morning.

"Bye bye," Aisha said, with a kiss for each of them. She gave her husband a look that wasn't lost on either Anna or Hector. Demetrius ignored it. He gave Anna little smile and said a quick goodbye. He was obviously trying to avoid saying a goodbye to his son.

"He'll never get over me being gay. If it's been four years and he still isn't talking to me. He won't stop, believe me," Hector said, bitterly as they were driving back.

"Hector. You're his son and he loves you. I'm sure he'll eventually come around."

Hector snorted, "Not likely."

Anna said nothing. It was true and she couldn't deny it. It was clearly obvious that Demetrius Minatos was disgusted with his eldest son. She thought that it was a shame, but a fact nonetheless. And it hurt her to see how affected Hector was by it. She was sorry and her heart went out to him.

They arrived at Hector's apartment—which had been Anna's home for about three weeks now—at around twelve in the morning.

"I'm going to bed," Hector said, in defeat. He gave her a light kiss on the cheek.

"Yeah me too," Anna said, returning the kiss.

They both went their separate ways, each thinking about the Christmas holiday that they had just experienced before they drifted off to sleep.

Anna arrived at work to find her and Ramón's work office filled with long stem roses. Ramón was sitting amongst them, examining them curiously, as she walked in.

"Roses from your dear hubby!" he cried, mockingly. "He wants you back!"

Anna waved her hand in the air, "Throw them away."

Ramón pouted, his full lips sticking out in indignation. "Such a waste."

"Then you keep them," Anna snapped.

"Maybe I will," Ramón quipped, put out by her catty behavior. If he were in her position and someone sent *him* a bunch of roses, he would have been overjoyed.

"Help yourself," Anna said, wearily. "I can't work with them in here like this."

The roses were gotten rid of.

They began to work silently. There was tension in the air from this morning's matter concerning the roses. The silence was only punctuated with Ramón's coughing.

"Ramón, you've been outta work for like two weeks and you're still coughing," Anna replied, trying to make friendly talk because she felt sorry about snapping at him earlier.

"Why should you care?" Ramón retorted and let out a loud sniff. He was still upset with her.

"I'm sorry Ramón. Forgive me. I just don't want anything from that man." Anna said, stoically. In actuality, she was beginning to miss Winston badly and the sight of the roses in the room that morning had filled her with such joy that she had to make a lot of effort to keep her happiness concealed.

"Apology accepted," he said, with a smile. Then his face turned serious, "I don't know what's the matter. I've been feeling lousy for the past three weeks. This flu just won't let up. Even now, I feel like just crawling into bed. But I must work!" he declared.

And so they did.

Ψ

January, 1990

"Please Anna. I just want to talk to you. I swear," Winston pleaded over the phone. He had called non-stop for the five weeks that she had staying with Hector. Most of the time, Anna wouldn't take the calls. But sometimes she would. She would harden herself, her heart, as she listened to him implore for her forgiveness over the phone. He would show up at Hector's apartment a lot too. When Hector was home, he would never let Winston in or allow Anna to talk to him. 'You'd better not bring him in here when I'm not here' Hector had told her in a dead serious tone of voice. She never did, despite Winston's begging and pleading.

"I though I told you not to call here. Hector doesn't like you calling his house phone."

"I don't give a damn what that gaylord doesn't like!" Winston stormed, "I just want to speak to my wife. I want to work this out, Anna."

Suddenly tears came to her eyes. He hurt her so badly. She tried to feel indifferent to him, but she couldn't. He affected her so much. She loved him. She had never loved a man as much as she loved him.

"Why do you hit me?" she asked, quietly. "Why do you do it?"

"Because I was an idiot and I let my anger get out of hand. But all that's going to change I promise you. Please. Just meet me for lunch, let's say tomorrow if that's all right for you. We can talk this out." He paused, letting her take in the words. He then continued, "I miss you, baby. I can't stand living here when you're not around. I can't even sleep at night—I'm so used to having you beside me. I need you. Please baby."

"Baby...? You *killed* our baby," Anna whispered. "How could you?" she asked, fully crying now. She didn't care anymore, she couldn't hold it back.

"I'm sorry," he said, mournfully with tears in his voice. "I'm sorry...I wish I could bring it back...I want you to have my children, Anna. We'll make more." He paused, "Although we would never be able to replace the ones that you lost already." He added quickly.

"I don't know. I have to think about it," Anna responded, cautiously. She knew that if she met with him, she would crumble. She felt that it was bound to happen. That it was an inevitable. But she wanted to put it off for as long as she could.

"I'll call you tomorrow...if I decide yes," Anna said, softly. Gone was the first defense. It was only a matter of time. His dogged persistence would pay off.

"No it won't," she said, aloud, knowing fully that she was lying to herself.

"No what?" Winston asked, perplexed.

"I'll call you tomorrow," Anna responded, ignoring his question.

"If you don't call me, I'll call you," Winston promised her, persisting.

Anna hung up the phone without another word. She was sure that she heard footsteps in the hallway. Sure enough, there was jingling of keys. Hector opened the door and stepped in. He gave her a smile in greeting. He would have killed her if he knew that she was talking to Winston.

"Hey," Anna said, cheerily, "what's up?"

"Tired. That Toby has been working me non-stop," Hector complained as he went towards the kitchen. "I need a margarita!" he passionately exclaimed. "I'm going to fix some drinks. Do you want one Anna?"

"Yeah sure," Anna answered. She paused and then said, "Ramón has been out from work again, since Thursday, for two days. I think I'll visit after work. He's been sick. His cold just won't let up."

"It's been a rough winter," Hector offered. A rough winter in LA was weather that dipped below forty-five degrees Fahrenheit.

Anna nodded in agreement. She would definitely go and see Ramón tomorrow.

Ψ

Ramón lived in a nice condo in a nice area of the city. A sulky sounding Ramón buzzed her in and she was on her way up.

"Hello," Ramón greeted her with a wan smile and stepped aside to let her in. The condo was decorated stylishly in a modern manner. She sat down on the couch. He automatically brought over a pot of tea and poured a cup for her. She thanked him and took a sip. He poured a cup for himself and sat down across from her. "I have tea handy most of the time," he said listlessly.

"So, how are you doing?" she asked, although she already suspected what the answer would be. He looked pretty bad. He had lost a fair amount of weight and he looked extremely tired and worn. He let out a dry cough that rattled deep in his chest. He cringed in pain.

"Not good." He responded. His expression looked guarded. Anna frowned.

"Did you go to the doctor? You really should. Maybe he can give you some antibiotics or something."

A look flashed in Ramón's eyes and then it was gone. He looked as if he was struggling with something, with a thought perhaps. He finally spoke. "I *did* go to the doctor. Last week."

"So, what happened? What did he say?"

"He gave me a checkup. Said that he wasn't exactly sure what was the matter, my lymph nodes were a little swollen. But that happens when you have the flu. He decided to take some blood, to run some tests." He said, his voice becoming mechanical.

"So, did they find out what was the matter?" Anna asked, cautiously. Ramón's tension was beginning to rub off on her.

"Yes." He whispered.

"Is it bad?" Anna asked, swallowing hard.

"Yes." He responded. His eyes began to water. He fought to hold back the tears and to keep his voice strong. "I have HIV, Anna."

Anna felt as if someone had punched her in the stomach. "What?" she squeaked. This couldn't happen, not to her friend. She couldn't believe it. "It must be a mistake."

"It's no mistake," he said, bitterly, "It passed though my mind even before I got went to the doctor. I had a friend that died from AIDS six years ago when the disease was still new. It's still a new…disease. It's only been nine years. Damn. He had the same symptoms before he was diagnosed, that fatigue, chills, sweats, and the damned cold that would never go away. Anna, I'm going to die and there's not a thing I can do about it. There's not a thing anyone can do about it," he said, sullenly.

"But they have new drugs—"

"But not a cure. It's a losing battle, Anna. I'll eventually lose. My body can't fight forever, *I* can't fight forever."

"Do you…" Anna paused, not sure how to pose the question, "do you know who…"

"I haven't a clue who I got it from," he said, blandly, "What does it matter anyways? It won't change a thing."

Anna began to cry. She felt so helpless. It was as if one of her closest friends had just gotten a death sentence and in a sense, he had. This just added to her depression, to her pain over her estrangement from her husband. Then she began to think about the situation between Hector and his father forever eating away at him, and now this. There was so much sadness. Too much.

Ramón came over to her, put an arm around her, and pulled her close. He was crying too. They sat there and cried for a good while, letting everything out in a flood of tears like a salve to their broken hearts.

Anna knew she would never be the same again.

Ψ

Winston moved the last of Anna things from the car and into the house. He was elated that she came back to him. Anna wasn't exactly ecstatic but she did feel a kind of relief. She just felt that she belonged with him. The two-month separation had not been easy on her. Winston was such a part of her life, that during that time away from him, she felt pretty much lost. The fact that Anna felt that way scared her a little, but she was back home. This was where she needed to be.

Of course, Hector had been far from pleased about her decision and he had fought her and argued her down up to the last minute that she was in his apartment. "He's just going to beat you again. It's a really dumb move going back to him Anna, you're going to regret it."

And in the back of Anna's mind, Hector's words rang true, but she had felt compelled to leave. So like a robot, she had packed up all her stuff from around the apartment and placed them in a pile in the middle of the living room floor.

"Don't tell me that man is coming here to help you pick your stuff up!" Hector had huffed angrily.

"He won't come in," Anna had promised him.

"Then how are you going to get all the stuff to your car?" he had asked, in a shrieking tone of voice.

"I didn't bring a lot of stuff with me when I came here. I'll be fine. I'll bring it down to my car and to his."

"Fine. Whatever." And with that, he had stalked into his bedroom and slammed the door behind him. And by the time that Anna had gotten all her stuff into Winston's car, Hector he still had not come out of his room.

Two days had gone by since she had been back home with her husband and she hadn't heard from Hector, whom she usually talked to everyday. She missed him and she really felt bad about what happened.

"Forget him. He'll come around," Winston told her, while at the same time hoping that Hector wouldn't.

Much to Anna's delight at work the next day, she saw Ramón. He looked a lot better than he did when she saw him last week.

"Hey!" Anna said, enthused, "you look well."

Ramón gave her a smile. "Yeah. I'm feeling a lot better now." Ramón looked around to make sure that they were in their work office alone. "You won't believe the amount of pills that I have to take." His expression turned to a slight frown and his brow furrowed.

"I'm sorry Ramón," Anna said, sincerely, "I really am."

"Yeah, so am I. But I try to forget that I have it, you know? If I think about it all the time…I'll be so depressed." He hesitated, "And Anna?"

"Yes?"

"Can you keep...my condition between the both of us? I don't want everyone knowing. You know how people can be..."

"Of course, Ramón. You can trust me."

Ramón gave her a weak smile, and then clapped his hands together. "Well then, my dear, let's get to work! Guess who's our guest for this week?"

"Um, is—"

"Cher!" Ramón answered before she could get a chance. "I absolutely adore her!" he gushed.

"Yeah, and I want to get Public Enemy on for the following week. I'm working on it," Anna replied, happy to see that the old Ramón was back. She had missed him as he suffered though a month of deep depression. She was glad that he had come to terms with his situation and was trying to do the best that he could.

Every day, Winston came home with gifts for Anna—from expensive jewelry to flowers and candy.

"This is really extravagant," Anna commented as she examined the 24 K gold, anklet

"Nothing is too much for you," Winston said, with much intensity, "I love you Anna. And don't you ever forget it." He looked at her ankle after she had put it on. "It looks lovely on you, just as I thought. That was just what those beautiful slender ankles needed."

Anna's face got hot. He could still make her feel like a little schoolgirl with a crush. He had such a power over her...She just couldn't describe it or explain it.

He came to her now and gently held her hand. He kissed up her arm and then her neck. He softly held her face in his large hands. Anna felt herself grow weak with feeling for him. They kissed, delicately, almost cautiously at first. But soon their passion gave way and they were kissing with thirst and hunger, their tongues plunging, exploring, into each other's mouths. Their breathing quickened and two pairs of hands groped one another with great desire and need. Soon they were pulling at each other's clothes, right there in middle of the living room. Anna began to unbutton his shirt, but only got halfway. She pulled it over his head with impatience. Then she attacked his belt buckled and didn't stop until his pants were on the floor and he was in his boxers. Winston expertly and hastily ridded her of her clothes. Soon they were naked, exploring each other bodies earnestly—touching teasing, tasting. It was like they were getting to know each other for the first time. And then when they finally joined, it was pure sweetness. His strokes started out slow and probing and then increased in intensity and speed. Soon he was pounding away at her with abandon. "Ah yeah…who's are you?" he breathed out to Anna as she writhed in passion on the carpet. "Yours…," she whispered into his ears. "Say that you're mine," he commanded, almost reaching his peak, but waiting for her. "I'm yours," she gasped, just as she came. He came soon after. He collapsed on top of her, breathless.

"That was amazing," Anna managed to say, burying her head in the crook under his arm. They were still lying on the floor.

"I agree," he said, and kissed her on her forehead. He pulled her closer to his body. "I love you Anna."

"I love you Winston," Anna answered back softly. She kissed his chest, which was near her face.

She loved this man more than anything. He was her world. He was her life. He was her existence.

Chapter Ten

January, 1990

Anna ran her hand over her over grown middle. She felt the baby kick for the fourth time this day. She smiled. She was totally content. Not once had Winston been anything but kind, considerate and gentle towards her ever since she got back with him. And Hector had finally gotten over the fact that she and her husband were still together, well not totally, because he still refused to have anything to do with Winston, but he was getting there. When Hector had learned that she was pregnant, at first he was a little upset and worried, but then Anna's joy began to rub off on him. Soon, he was buying little gifts for the upcoming baby.

"Hello little dear, it's your Aunty Tessa!" her sister cooed as she rubbed Anna's stomach and then sat down across from Anna at their table at *The Addis Ababa*, a snazzy Ethiopian restaurant.

Anna rolled her eyes in humor. Her sister was always so overly dramatic, but she loved her.

Tessa was in town for the weekend, back from one of her wild trips as a journalist. She had just come back from covering a story in Indonesia where a Muslim extremist group had taken some Americans captive. The American government was now bartering for their return.

Anna looked at her sister, feeling a little envious. She was the eldest of all of them—a full ten years older than Anna, beautiful with her umber brown skin, large liquid eyes, and carefree with no husband or children. When Anna had told her that she was getting married, Tessa had fixed her with an odd look and asked, "Why you gonna do that for?" Tessa had sworn that she would never get married saying that married life was not the life for her. She wanted to be alone without having to worry about a husband and kids. She had a fantastic career that was interesting and led her on many adventures and travels.

"So, have you met any interesting men?" Anna asked, teasing her.

Tessa twisted up her face in disgust. "Are you kidding me? The only thing interesting about a man is what he has down his pants!" she said, and gave her sister a conspiratorial wink. Anna blushed deeply and looked around. It didn't seem that anyone heard her sister. Tessa could be so vulgar at times, that it was embarrassing.

"So what was it like in Indonesia?" Anna asked, desperately trying to change the subject.

"Hot and humid. The food was strange, but good. In most places, if I didn't buy bottled water, I had to boil it but I still got vicious diarrhea! But maybe that was because of the food," Tessa said, laughing.

Anna's face grew hot with embarrassment again.

"You know Anna, you need to relax," Tessa said, and took a sip of her wine, "You're too uptight. How's your sex life?"

"What?" Anna choked.

"Are you getting it on the regular? Is good ole' Winston putting out?" Tessa asked, boldly.

Anna couldn't believe her ears. She felt like sinking into the earth. "I'm pregnant." Anna muttered to curb her sister's topic.

Her sister plunged on, unperturbed by her sister's reluctance. "Yeah, but pregnant woman can still get some, you know. It's healthy!"

Anna took a long swig of her mango smoothie. It was going to be a long afternoon.

Ψ

"So, how did dinner with the sister go?" Ramón asked her the next day at work. He was a busy writing notes for the show.

"Like a roller coaster ride," Anna said, sitting down. She rubbed her belly.

Ramón looked at her. "I can't believe you're still working…you are a warrior."

Anna smiled at him and started working. A warrior she was. She had battled Winston all the way in order to continue working during her pregnancy. At first, he had staunchly refused to allow her to work. She was pregnant and she didn't need the stress, he said. There was no way he was going to allow his pregnant wife to slave away at a job and they were a far cry from needing any extra money. He was making a great amount of money with his oil and gas business. In fact, he was soon to go to Egypt to begin training of another group of employees. After that, he was going to Nigeria to stake out some prime land for a new oil pump and refinery. On top of all that, he was working on a contract with the government of Togo in order for its oil workers to implement his company's novel methods of oil and gas recovery, refinement and distribution.

But eventually, Anna had won, well somewhat. She had cut her work to about five hours a day, from eight in the morning until one in the afternoon. Winston had grudgingly agreed.

The labor pains had started at work when Anna was in the bathroom. She was washing her hands at the sink when her water broke. She waddled out of the office and got Ramón's attention. He had been talking to one of the co-workers. His eyes bugged out when he saw her. "W-what's going on?" he asked, nervously.

"I'm having the baby, Ramón…get me to the hospital, please!"

Ramón had hustled her into his Porsche as the coworkers looked on and wished her luck and he drove like the devil was on his tail.

"Red light!" Anna yelled, feeling like the baby was going to drop right there and then.

Ramón slammed on the break. The car screeched to a stop. He eyed her frantically. "Don't do that again! I *was* going to stop!"

On their way there, they had managed to call Winston. He arrived at the hospital soon afterwards. He went into the delivery room with Anna and held her hand as he helped her breathe. Anna's parents were also there as well as her brother. They waited in the waiting room with Ramón. Soon after, Hector came rushing in—Anna's mother had taken the liberty to tell him that Anna was in the hospital about to have the baby. "Did she have the baby yet?" Hector cried out hysterically once he saw them gathered.

"It's only been forty minutes," Muhammad had said, amused. Despite himself, he had grown to like Hector over the years. Muhammad mused at his excitement.

Finally, Anna had a baby girl ten hours later. A big baby, she weighed in at eight pounds, six ounces.

Finally, a nurse came and informed them that Anna was awake now. They could now go in and see her. They walked into the room where

Anna laid and Winston sat holding the baby with his face beaming with pride.

Muhammad took one look at his son-in-law and for an instant he felt as if someone had walked over his gave. Quite simply, he didn't like Winston. In fact, he despised him. The problem was that whenever Winston was around him and the rest of the family, he was nothing short of charming, polite and respectable. Winston was the model husband, always treating Anna with gentleness and kindness for as far as Muhammad could see. But something about him didn't sit right with Muhammad. He couldn't quite put his finger on it, but the feeling was there nonetheless.

"Muhammad," Winston said, ready to rise and greet his father-in-law. Muhammad motioned for him to stay seated. He didn't want him to get up and drop the baby or something like that.

Candace joined her husband at his side. The others followed suit. Winston handed the baby to the grandmother. Candace cooed over her for a while and then passed the baby on to Muhammad.

"How are you feeling Anna?" Candace asked her daughter as she sat down on the side of the bed. She looked her daughter over and of course, she looked exhausted.

"I feel a little better. Sleeping helped. But I feel so drained ," Anna said, tiredly. But her face was glowing with happiness. Candace smiled down at her daughter and smoothed her hair down. She was so proud of her. She looked over at Winston, he was watching them his face intense. Candace frowned a little and shifted uncomfortably. It seemed to her that Winston was always analyzing and evaluating with his penetrating stares. He made Candace somewhat uncomfortable. Not that there was any real reason for her discomfort, he was always so nice and charming, and that handsome face was always set in a smile whenever she saw him.

Winston expression changed from scrutiny to a warm smile. Candace smiled back, relieved. Muhammad noted his son-in-law smiling at his wife. Somehow, all the smiles, the charm, the allure, and the southern genteelness seemed forced, not natural, although it was very hard to tell. Winston was really good at his act, Muhammad had to admit. But Winston had made a mistake by being too perfect, too ideal. Muhammad looked over at Hector. The young man's face was stony as he watched Winston holding the child. He knew that Hector didn't like Winston, but he wasn't sure what his reasons were. Hector never would say, although sometimes he would mention things that Muhammad suspected had a double meaning to them if one were to look below the surface. But he never outwardly said anything against the man in Muhammad's presence, although it was clear that Winston wasn't one of Hector's favorite people.

"Where did Ramón go?" Anna asked, weakly.

"He had to go back to work," Hector responded. Hector had been eyeballing the attractive black Latino that had driven Anna to the hospital. He had made his interest known to the exotic Brazilian by striking up a conversation with him and then finally asking for his phone number. But Ramón had graciously declined, looking quite uncomfortable as he did so. *Ah well, you can't win them all*, Hector thought. Hector focused his attention on the little baby girl now being held by Anna's brother Malik. Hector scowled, there was another person that he could do without. Malik had made it clear that he was a homophobic from the first time that they had met five years ago. Malik treated Hector as if he was something that he could become contaminated with. He found Malik to be such a hateful person, so different from his sisters. He didn't know anything about the other youngest sister Kati except that she was in Mexico somewhere. Hector cut his eye at Malik.

Malik passed his niece over to her mother with a fair amount of discomfort. He wanted children one day, preferably sons that could carry on his name. But he did not feel comfortable with children and especially not babies. His wife would be handling all that—the crying, the dirty diapers, the feedings, the bathing, the fussing—he wanted no part of it. It never occurred to him that there was anything wrong with his reasoning. In his mind, it was a woman's job to raise the children and deal with all the gross stuff that came along with it. But it was up to him to teach his sons about things that really counted like money, relationships, women, things like that. And if there were any girls, his wife could handle them. Just the thought of having to deal with a female child made him uncomfortable. He squirmed a little. His eyes caught Hector's but he quickly flicked them away. He shuddered. That little faggot. He couldn't understand for the life of him what made him so interesting to Anna. He frowned. These gay freaks, out and about in the open. It was shameful. They behaved as if they were the norm, but they were the freaks of society. He wouldn't mind stuffing them all in a rocket and blasting them off to the moon or some distant planet…or doing away with them by some other method. But there were laws against that. They were society's burden, he thought balefully. He would have to put up with them, not matter how reluctantly. Then there was Winston. The damned redneck. His sister had to go and marry some white hick from the hills. Of course, Winston didn't get on like a hick…but Malik was sure that he was one none-the-less. Weren't all white southerners just that? They were all cut from the same cloth, as far as he was concerned. He probably had family members that were part of the KKK although Winston had vehemently denied this when Malik had first posed the idea to him. As if that were not enough, his damned sister had to go and have a baby by him. Some zebra kid that would most likely get teased and not know where it belonged. It was a shame, but not his problem.

Winston felt as if his face would crack from the constant smiling that he was doing. All of Anna's immediate family was here. Well not *all* of her immediate family, Tessa wasn't here—that sweet looking woman that exuded pure sexuality. Tessa was all flash and sparkle, so unlike Anna who despite her attractiveness, could just fade into the background like a wallflower. Winston felt a jolt of excitement and the beginning of an erection. Calm down ole boy, he told himself. Then his eyes crept over to Hector and that took care of that. All the excitement that had felt evaporated like water in Death Valley and the smile slipped from his face. Damn him, that little busy body. The fucking prick rod. Desert, camel-riding shepherd! Greek Freak…damn he hated him so much. Hector was a real meddler and he wished that he could find a way to shut him up. Of course, he could if he really wanted too…but that was pretty much out of the question. Hector was like a fly that kept buzzing in you ear and around your head. Even when swatted, it came back, louder than ever and twice as earnest. Winston caught Muhammad gazing at him, a curious expression on his face. Winston quickly painted on a smile—it wouldn't do to turn the in-laws against him.

Anna looked down at her little girl, her attention totally focused on the little bundle in her arms. It was at that moment that she knew she had nothing but love and devotion for her baby. Jackie. Her name would be Jackie. Jackie's eyes were opened and staring up at her. They were green, the same color as her father's eyes. Her dark waves stuck to her head. Her features were delicate. The baby wrapped her tiny hand around Anna's finger and grasped it tightly. Anna felt a tug of affection.

"What did you two decide to name her?" Candace asked, gazing down at her small granddaughter.

"Jackie," Anna answered instantly.

Winston looked at her and frowned. "I thought that we were going to name her after my mother, Angelina."

"That's what *you* wanted. But I want her name to be Jackie," Anna quipped. She wasn't going to back down on this one. Winston had always gotten his way with her. But not this time. She was sticking to this. "Her second name can be Angelina," she said, compromising.

Winston restrained himself from smacking her across the face and smiled instead.

"Whatever you want darling."

"Can I hold her?" Hector asked, moving closer to the bed and looking down at the baby.

"Of course you can," Anna responded, ignoring the dark look on Winston's face. She handed the baby over to Hector. He held her in wonder, delicately as if she were a piece of fine china. Anna laughed, "You have to hold her a little tighter than that, Hector, you don't want to drop her."

"I'll sit down," Hector said, quickly. He sat down in one of the straight back plastic chairs. She was so pretty, Hector thought as he let the little hand grasp his finger. So beautiful. He delicately smoothed down her soft hair. He could feel Winston's eyes boring into the side of his head. He ignored it.

Ψ

Anna lay in bed and flipped through the channels. The nanny came up to Anna with the baby in her arms.

"I'm going to take Jackie for a stroll in the park, Mrs. Hurst," Mae said, with a smile. She looked at the baby adoringly.

Mae was a nice Laotian woman with a lot of experience in taking care of small children. Anna had liked her instantly and hired her on the spot.

"That sounds great, Mae."

By the time that Mae came back, Anna was fast asleep. Winston found her like that when he came in later that evening from work. He kissed her forehead and went down the hallway to his home office to read the letter that he his secretary had given to him at his office today.

Once seated in his office, he looked down at the plain white envelope with no return address. Just his name on one side and the address of his office suite. He had known exactly what it was the moment he laid eyes on it. He sat down in his leather chair and opened the envelope. A single sentence, in bold typeface, was across the page. Although the sentence was only three words long, it held great meaning: *We found them*. He put the letter down on the top of his oak desk and stood up. He pulled out a small silver key from its secret hiding place. He went back to his desk and opened the bottom drawer with the key. After replacing the key, he dug his hand down past the old papers the envelopes. He pushed them aside when he felt the hard cool surface of it. He pulled it out and looked at the beautiful smiling face. The woman's face was a creamy olive complexion, her black hair was hanging down in waves. Her dark eyes sparkled with a look of excitement or anticipation. Her wide, full lips were curled up in a smile. Smile lines appeared and crow's feet were at the corner of her eyes, but this did nothing to diminish her offbeat attractiveness. Winston's was suddenly filled with anguish. And then rage like a red-hot fire overtook him. He knew what he had to do. He had no choice.

He gently ran a finger along the smiling face in the picture. He slowly brought the picture up to his face and kissed it lightly, affectionately, and tenderly.

He kissed the face of his mother.

His mind went back to all the memories and the times that he had with her. He remembered his mother lifting him on a pony at his father's ranch, when he was six. He remembered watching his mother painting a picture of his older sister, Antonia, outside in the field in their country home in Illinois. The sunlight from the sky would paint dark red highlights on her raven hair, as well as on his sister's. His mother's skin would turn mocha colored by the end of the day, his and his sister's skin a healthy tan, and they would walk into the house together and eat strawberry ice cream from straight out of the tub.

Then he remembered her laying cold in the mortuary. Her skin pale, her lips bloodless…

He placed the picture to stand up on his desk, a small representative of the woman that he believed was watching over him from her place in heaven. She would watch as he did his work tonight, carried out his business, his responsibility. She would watch and she would be proud. She would be very proud.

Chapter Eleven

Chicago, Illinois, January, 1936

Earnest lit his cigarette and took a long drag. Then he slowly let the smoke out through his mouth, the white wisps curled languidly in the darkness of the bedroom. He watched the shifting smoke with intensity until the last tendril had disappeared into the air. Only then did he take another drag. Julia watched him from the bed, her usually clear blue eyes were now misted in pleasure from their tryst in bed. "You always smoke afterward."

"You know that," Earnest said, softly, his subtle southern drawl rolling smoothly over his tongue. "It relaxes me."

Julia moved closer to him on the bed. She ran a manicured hand across his broad chest. He was a fine specimen of a man. "But don't I relax you?"

Earnest turned to her now, abandoning his cigarette smoking for the moment. Her straight, thick blond hair that usually hung neatly down to her collarbone was now tousled. Her soft, small lips were pursed in question. Her angular face with its high cheekbones, tapered jaw line, and high forehead was in an expression of slight concern. Her sky blue eyes bored into his. She was a beautiful woman, Earnest thought.

"Of course you do. But in bed, you drive me wild."

Julia blushed, pleased at this response. She rested her head against his chest.

"Mother's coming down this weekend," she said, softly.

Earnest leaned over and smashed out his cigarette in the ashtray on the side table. It was nothing but a stub now, anyways. "What for?" he asked, keeping his voice neutral.

"Well, you know…just to see how things are going," she answered breezily.

You mean to make sure that her daughter and I are still engaged. Earnest thought to himself. As much as he cared for Julia, her mother was like a thorn in his side. She was constantly sticking herself in business that didn't concern her. Always making suggestions, always probing and wanting information. Always offering her advice, which she believed, was as good as gold. She really got under his skin.

"She can't come this weekend," Earnest said firmly.

"Why not?" Julia asked with a pout.

"Because you can't just spring things like this on me, suddenly. I'm working this weekend. Better make it some other time, cause this weekend is definitely out of the question."

Julia's frown deepened.

Earnest didn't care.

He and Julia had met in high school. Earnest remembered seeing her tall, slender form across the cafeteria and asking about her. His friends had informed him that she had just moved from Georgia and she was a grade behind him.

As a football star, he had always had pretty girls coming after him, and he'd had his share of many of them. But they were old news and Julia was something new, something fresh for him to get into. When he saw her in math class the next day, he struck up a conversation with her and asked her on a date. She had agreed. So they went out and then some more after that. Eventually, they were *the* couple at the school. The most popular, most good-looking pair. Of course, now that Earnest was unavailable, girls threw themselves at him twice as often. Even one of Julia's friends had hit on him once. And at first, Earnest still saw other girls. But after a while, things got serious with him and Julia and he had stopped openly dating anyone else. He took her to his senior prom, leaving many girls jealous and in envy. He had met Julia's parents who were very well to do and came from an old, established southern family. Then Julia met his parents—his father being the co-owner of the main city bank and a reputable horse breeder and his mother a socialite from a moderately rich family that made its money from shipping. Then eventually, at a dinner after church, both sets of parents had met each other. After graduating with a 3.8 grade point average, Earnest had gotten accepted to his first choice of college—the University of Chicago. He was set to leave in about a month.

One day Earnest had come in late from hanging out with some friends to find his father in the front room waiting for him. His father gave him a friendly smile, his gray eyes sparkling. "Do you have a little time, Earnest?"

Earnest had nodded and sat down across from his father. He sat in wait of what he would say.

"You know, Julia is a very nice girl."

"Yes, she is," Earnest responded, wondering where this was all leading.

"She comes from a good family. A very well respected family with a good name and good breeding. It would be good for you to stick with her," her father said, casually as he lit up a cigar. "Your mother and I were talking today. Just how serious are you and Julia?"

Earnest frowned. So they were discussing him and his relationships behind his back. "We're pretty close," he responded, simply.

"How close? I mean, is this girl just a passing fancy? What are you going to do once you go away to college? Do you plan to still keep in contact with her?" his father asked, flicking his lighter on and off.

Earnest watched the flame each time, the light reflecting in his green eyes. "I guess…we haven't really talked about it as of yet."

"Well, I think that you two should begin to discuss it." The father looked at him with an increasingly intense look. "Son. Once you get out of college and start out in business, it pays to have a good start. That includes marrying well. Marrying Julia would be marrying well. Not only is she beautiful, her family has a name, connections, and money." His father's face softened a bit now, and he chuckled. "I might even say they are half a rung above us, but more-or-less on the same footing. Do you understand what I'm getting at?"

Earnest only nodded slowly, transfixed at his father's words. Marriage had never occurred to him. Further more, marrying Julia. He had never really thought of his future with Julia. He was just thinking of the here and now with her. He was enjoying her company now, and to him that was all that had mattered. He wasn't even sure if he loved her. He wasn't sure what his true feelings were concerning her beyond physical and sexual attraction.

His father stood up and stretched. "It's getting late. Why don't you get to bed? You can think about all this tomorrow, huh?"

Earnest stood up, bade his father goodnight, and climbed the stairs to bed. He thought about his father's words to him that night until he fell into a fitful sleep.

After a while and a many communications between Julia's parents and his own, it was understood that they were to be married, after Earnest was graduated college. So, Earnest thought it fitting to get her a ring.

His father found him a diamond solitaire. Earnest had presented it to Julia. She loved it. She had leapt into his arms when he had put it on her slender finger.

The night before he was leave for school in Chicago, they had driven up to his parents' cabin by the lake. They only went there during the summer, so it was abandoned now. After some passionate kissing and heavy petting, Earnest had attempted to unbutton her blouse. She pulled away.

"No, Earnest. We can't do that."

"Why not?" He had asked, frustrated. Just like a girl to get you all bothered and then leave you high and dry.

"I'm not ready to do that yet," she responded.

"But we've been together for almost two years. We're engaged. We're practically married, so what does it matter? I'm going to be gone for months," he said, running a hand through his dark, reddish-brown hair.

"Still…we aren't married yet. I wouldn't feel comfortable doing it. You understand, don't you?"

"No. I don't understand. I don't understand how you could agree to come here with me, kiss me like that, touch me like that, and then deny me. It doesn't make any sense to me," Earnest said, stubbornly. The other girls had been so easy. Why couldn't she be the same way?

Julia moved closer to him. She ran a hand down his chest. He tried to move away, but she only moved closer. "I'm not teasing you. Let me show you that."

Her hand slid from his chest and further down. She fumbled with his pants zipper and his belt. Once his pants were open, she pushed her hands eagerly through his fly and into his pants. She sighed as she felt his hard penis in her hands. "Yes," she said, softly. "Let me show you. I'll make it feel just as good as making love."

She slowly began to caress the length of him. Earnest groaned in pleasure. Her hand movements became more hurried, Earnest raised his hands to her small round breasts and gripped them, running his thumbs over her taut nipples. Julia plunged her tongue into his mouth, tasting him as she worked him with her hand.

Finally, with a drawn out moan of relief, Earnest came; spilling rivulets all over her delicate hand. He sighed and lay back, drained.

Julia smiled, looking at his seed on her hand. "I told you that it would feel as good as sex, didn't I?"

So Earnest had left the next day in a train headed for Chicago. He kissed his mother goodbye. She had tears in her green eyes. Her auburn hair was in a chignon

"Goodbye, Sir," he said, and shook his father's hand.

His farther gave him an affectionate pat on the back. "You go up there and make us proud son. Us Texans have a reputation to uphold."

Earnest nodded with a small smile. "I will Dad. And don't worry Mom. I'll see you for Christmas."

Earnest turned to Julia. His faced flushed slightly as he remembered the past night. She smiled up at him disarmingly. Her face was guileless, innocent and pure. There was no trace of the vixen of last night. She leaned over and kissed him on the cheek, he lips lingered near his ear. "I love you," she whispered. Only he heard her.

Flustered, he pulled back and retreated to the train. After one last farewell, he climbed in after giving his ticket to the conductor.

Once seated with the train pulling out of the station, he felt a tremendous sense of relief sweep over him. He could finally breathe.

The months passed quickly at school. Julia would come up to visit him every other weekend. She came up for Thanksgiving. She never once brought up the subject of love since that day that he had whispered those words in his ear before he boarded the train. He would take her out and show her around. His college friends were impressed with her beauty and her charisma, more impressed than he was, it seemed. During these visits, he didn't try to sleep with her, and she didn't offer. Finally, the semester was over and he came home for Christmas.

He and Julia had gone out to see a play at the theater. Actually, she had been the one that wanted to go so he indulged her. She didn't demand a lot from him, so he didn't mind.

Afterward, they had dinner at the Four Seasons Hotel restaurant. It was a nice elegant affair.

"Why don't we get a room for the night?" Earnest had suggested casually. He tensed, waiting for her answer. He decided that it was time.

"That sounds like a good idea," Julia said, easily. She continued to eat her food.

Earnest was shocked. He had expected her to protest. It was not that he was in lacking of sex. Chicago had a lot of sensual woman to offer. They found his southern accent sexy and charming. He was a southern gentleman, and they liked him. Some even loved him. But he didn't love any of them and made no pretense to. They seemed to accept this. Currently, back in Chicago, he was sleeping with a red-haired beauty called Mira.

That night, they had made love. Urgently and passionately. He had been pleased and somewhat amused to find that Julia was still a virgin. He didn't think that she would have held out much longer after he had left town. But she had, and this struck him with realization of just how deep her feelings were for him.

The vacation ended quickly and soon he was back at school, back to his studies. The next three years had passed by quickly. He had done well in school, never getting less that a 3.8. So finally, when he graduated with honors in 1935, he had received many job offers. Businesses were hunting him down. He knew that his father wanted him to return home and go into the family business of horse breeding or to take a position at the bank, although his father never said so directly. But Earnest didn't want to go home so soon. He decided that he wanted to stay in Chicago and see what was there to offer him. He had told his parents just as much, and they didn't take the news so well.

"Well, what about Julia?" his mother had asked him, "We thought that you two were getting married once you graduated."

"Well Mom, what's the rush? Julia still has another year of school left," Earnest had pointed out.

That response had been met with silence. As for Julia, although she had kept her feeling hidden quite well, she didn't seem too pleased that he wasn't coming back to Texas immediately after graduating.

"But we are still getting married, aren't we?" she had asked him, her cornflower eyes having shadow of doubt. Her rosebud lips were parted in question. At that moment, he had wanted to bed her. But they were in an upscale restaurant in downtown Chicago.

"It doesn't mean the wedding's off, I just want to see about some jobs over here."

"Are *we* going to live *here*?" she had asked, a look of shock flashing across her face.

Earnest had studied her and answered carefully. "I don't know."

Earnest's college friend Abner Bernstein had gotten him the job at his family's downtown department store as a floor manager.

"Excuse me, can I get some help here?" a loud female voice called out. Earnest turned around from the sales associate that he was talking to and found himself facing a short dark girl with big dark eyes and a poof of wavy black hair. His eyes swept over her, quickly taking in details, She was short with a lush body not concealed beneath the fitted cashmere sweater that clung to her full chest and the slim, pleated skirt that showed the gentle curve of her hips. Her small feet were encased in a pair of expensive dress heels that he recognized to be designer. His eyes went back up to her face. Her mouth was stretched wide, maybe a little too wide, but it was full. Her dark eyes were large, set in a creamy-light olive colored face with skin that looked soft to the touch. She was not beautiful, although she was passably pretty or so Earnest thought. She was at the very least, eye-catching. Exotically tantalizing. She looked really young—around eighteen or nineteen.

Earnest felt his heart jump to his throat and a rush of emotion that had never really experienced before

"Are you done looking?" the girl said, slyly, and allowed herself a toothy grin. She had a set of big white teeth. A bunch of girlish giggles followed.

Earnest tore his eyes from her form and looked around. It was only then that he saw the two other young women at either side of her. They, just like her, were dark haired and dark eyed—one was impossibly thin and tall and the other was shorter and quite plump. They also had the same olive complexions.

"I-I'm sorry. What can I do for you?" Earnest asked, feeling flustered. It wasn't even his job to be on the floor. He had his own office, for crying out loud. But instead of passing him off to his sales associate, he found himself wanting to aid her himself.

"I would like to purchase these items," the young woman said, depositing the array of expensive looking clothes on the counter. Her two friends did the same, emptying their arms of the items that they held. Earnest rang them up. The total came to 200 dollars. The girl whipped out her wallet without blinking an eye. Soon the three women were off, talking and giggling along the way. Earnest watched after them. He watched the dark hair of the girl in the middle until it disappeared from his sight.

Over the next three months, Earnest discovered that she was a regular customer at the department store. She would come in with the same two friends, shop up a storm, and then depart. As often as he could, Earnest would make sure that he was around when she was there. He had found out that her name was Angie from her friends calling her aloud, but that was all he knew about the dark haired girl. There was something so attractive about her, although he had seen woman that were far prettier than she was. She was lovely, that's what she was, and she took his breath away.

One day she came in by herself to shop. By the time she was done, it was clear that she was going to need help carrying her purchases.

"Would you like me to help you carry you things to the car?" Earnest asked. The floor person gave him an odd look. He was doing things that were beneath his position.

The girl seemed to hesitate, her large, sensual mouth pursed in thought.

"I guess it would be alright," she said, cautiously. He smiled at her, she gave him a nervous half smile.

He followed her out to a big, late modeled, black car. A young man stepped from the driver's side in a chauffeur's uniform. He hurriedly relieved Earnest of his burden, placed the packages in the back, and held the car door open, patiently waiting for the young woman to enter..

"Thank you," she said, politely and was about to turn away

"W-wait…ah…"

The young woman turned back around eyeing him curiously. "What is it?"

"W-what's your name?" he asked, although knowing the answer already.

"Why do you want to know that for?" she asked, suspiciously.

He flushed. "I was just asking. You're so pretty." Man, did that sound stupid. He looked at the ground. When he looked up again, the girl was smiling cynically. Then she let out a low throaty chuckle.

"My name's Angelina. Angie for short. You're Earnest, right?"

"Yep," he smiled, "I guess the name tag gave it away."

She allowed herself a full smile, her big white teeth flashing. Winston looked at her mouth and felt himself getting aroused. For sure, she was not on the same level of beauty that Julia processed, but to him, Angelina was *gorgeous* and had an aura and appeal about her that Julia lacked. And in his mind, that made Angelina ten times more attractive than Julia. He wanted to get to know this dark, mysterious, girl.

"Yeah, well, I gotta go now," Angelina said, choppily. "I guess I'll see you around."

"I hope to," Earnest said gently..

Angelina's lips twisted in a half smile. Without another word, she hopped into the car. Her driver shut the door after Angelina, tipped his black cap to Earnest, and got into the driver's side of the car

Earnest watched the car until it disappeared down the road.

Angelina watched Earnest from the back window until she could see him no longer.

Chapter Twelve

Feburary, 1936

"For the life of me, I can't imagine why you would choose this place," Julia complained as they sat down in small Cajun restaurant.

"What's wrong with it? I heard the food was good, so I think that we should try it out, but if you want to go somewhere else..."

"No, it's okay. If you heard it was good, then maybe it is."

They ordered their food and then finally it arrived.

"I was looking at some wedding dresses in the catalogues. I was thinking of getting it custom made...what do you think?" she asked him.

Earnest looked down at his food, shrugged his shoulders, and looked back up at her. "Whatever you want I'll be fine with it."

Julia nodded slowly. "You know, you've been getting on rather strangely since I came yesterday. Is there something the matter?" she asked him, her eyes probing his.

"Nothing. Why would you think a thing like that?"

"I don't know. Maybe I'm wrong," she said, absently.

They finished their dinner with strained conversation. Finally, they got up.

"I'm ready to go to bed, darling. I'm beginning to get a headache," Julia said, taking off her small cream hat and shaking loose her short blond hair. Earnest noticed that it came only to her jawbone.

"You cut your hair," he stated.

"Yes, I did. Short hair is very chic you know. I saw it on this girl in the magazine and she looked amazing, so I decided to try it myself. What do you think?"

"It looks nice," Earnest said, sticking to the expected response.

They walked back to the hotel. Julia climbed into bed. "Come join me sweetheart," she said, invitingly.

Earnest came over and kissed her, "I'm gonna go out for a walk. I want to check out the museum down the block. They're supposed to have gotten a new exhibit this week. I'll be back before nine, though."

"Oh," she pouted a little. "Why can't you stay here with me?"

"I'm a bit restless, you see? I want to go outside for a little. Nothing to do with you, just don't want to be indoors right now."

"Okay, fine," Julia said, coolly. She turned away from him and wrapped the covers around herself. Earnest slipped through the door. He knew that if he had stayed there, they would have ended up making love. At the moment, he didn't want that.

Earnest stopped in at the museum and looked over the new exhibit of Aztec Indian sculpture and art.

He was so engrossed in it that he almost didn't notice the person beside him. He looked over and saw the profile of a face framed with long dark hair. It was Angelina. She was so caught up in a sculpture that she didn't seem to be attuned to what was around her.

"Hello," he called softly

Angelina looked up at him in suprise, and recognition dawned on her face. "Hello. What are you doing over here?"

"Same thing you are—admiring the art."

Angelina turned back to the display. "I was looking at that sculpture. It looks so life like, doesn't it?"

"It sure does," Earnest said, eying it.

"So you like museums?" he asked her, casually.

"I love them. When I was a little girl, my father used to take me to them all the time. My two brothers and me. I used to enjoy that so much."

"I've been going to museums since I was young too. My mom used to take me."

She nodded her dark head slowly. There was a beat of silence.

"Look. I was wondering, if you would like to go out for coffee sometime…maybe dinner?" Earnest asked, before he could stop himself. What was he doing? He was an engaged man.

"I don't know…I—" Angelina hesitated; a trapped look came into her eyes.

"I'm sorry. I shouldn't have asked you. We barely know each other… that was presumptuous of me." He cleared his throat and looked around, "Look, I'd better be going now. It's getting late. Is there anywhere you would like me to walk you?" he asked her, politely.

She shook her head, "No. I'm fine."

"Okay then, I'll be seeing you around," he said, and was off.

He forced himself not to look back although he felt her eyes boring into the back of his head. He breathed only once he stepped out of the door and into the cool evening air.

On Julia's last night there in Chicago, He showed her the night of her life—he wined and dined her. He took her dancing. They went back to his apartment worn but at the same time fully energized. They never made it to the bedroom. They had sex right there on the floor of his hallway. Then they went to the bedroom and made love again on his large bed.

So it was here, after their lovemaking and during his smoking that Julia had began to question him and had informed him of another one of her mother's attempts to visit.

"So you're not going back tomorrow morning?" he asked, inhaling deeply.

"No. I told you that my mother is coming up," she said, a little impatiently.

"And again, I ask why? You never mentioned this before. Didn't I tell you about this last month? About springing things on me at the last moment?"

"I just found out," she said, vaguely, with a shrug.

Earnest looked at her, her blond head resting on his chest. He felt a flash of anger. He knew that she must have called her mother when he was out at the museum the other night, what else could it be? It was no coincidence that on both occasions's of Julia mentioning a visit from her mother, each time, they were in bed. The sneaky bitch.

Earnest ousted his second cigarette and turned slowly around until her head slid off of him.

"Hey! You're not mad are you?" Julia asked, sitting up.

"Good-night Julia," he said, before closing his eyes.

Ψ

Meredith Compton came down to Chicago on the eight A.M. train on a mission and that mission was to get her daughter married off to Earnest Hurst the minute she was graduated from college in three months..

The three of them went out to dinner at *The Rose Garden*, a five star restaurant in the heart of Chicago and of course, it was at Earnest's expense.

"So," the matronly woman began, folding her hands neatly on the table in front of her. "When you two are married, do you plan to live here? Or are you going to move back to Texas?"

Earnest downed his glass of champagne—expensive champagne that Meredith had ordered. He looked over at Julia who was studiously feeding her face.

"I'm not sure," Earnest finally answered.

Meredith's eyebrows rose in astonishment. "You mean, you haven't decided yet? Julia and I are already planning the wedding. She already had her wedding dress made. She decided to get it custom done. No store bought dresses for her."

Earnest looked at her, shocked. Julia had never told her this. She already had her wedding dress? She had told him that she was *considering* how she wanted her dress to be. *And* they were planning the wedding? *Behind his back?* This was too much for him. He took another swallow of champagne instead of answering.

"I think that I want to go to law school," Earnest told them

"What? Law?" Meredith asked, astonishment written all over her round face.

"Yes. I've been looking at a few law schools, and I think I want to go it."

"I thought you were going to be going into business for you father—" Julia started

"I'm not going to be spending my life only raising horses and selling them," He said, and took another swig of his champagne.

"But your father's business is very lucrative…" Meredith said, still in shock.

"It doesn't matter. I want to do something else. The law interests me. So, I want to do it," Earnest said, with finality.

No one else argued with him.

The lunch dragged on endlessly. By the end, Earnest was at his wits end. He felt ganged up on by the mother and daughter team that had clearly made their ambitions known.

That afternoon he was glad to see the both of them off at the train station. He would see them in May, in two months, when he was on vacation. Although he was sure that Julia would be coming in for her visits. Not once had it occurred to him to go and visit her. His job at the department store had consumed his life and now a dark haired beauty was consuming his thoughts.

He had applied for law school at the University of Georgia and got in. He was to start there this fall.

He didn't see Angelina for weeks. Finally, that the end of that month of March, he saw her come into the store. She quickly spotted him. She gave him a nervous smile and turned back to examining the shoes.

Earnest looked at her with longing. Her alluring face was set in concentration on the display of shoes before her. Earnest forced himself to stay away from her. Finally, she came to the checkout counter. She gave him a warm smile, much to Earnest's surprise.

"So how are you today?" Earnest asked, gently.

"I'm fine, and you?" she asked, softly.

Earnest shrugged, "I'm surviving."

She smiled at him with that big mouth of hers, her eyes bright. The smile died slowly from her lips. She looked past him. "You know I was thinking….If the offer still stands…"

"Yes?" Earnest asked, filling with excitement.

"Well…if you still want to go out someplace…I don't drink coffee though, so…"

"Then I can take you out for dinner," He said, quickly. "Wherever you want to go."

She smiled softly at him. "I would like that."

"So, when are you free?" he asked her, "What about tomorrow?"

She thought for a moment. "No…tomorrow's no good…what about Friday?"

"Sounds good to me. Shall I call you" he asked her, "or I can pick you up?

She appeared to consider this. "What about I meet you in front of the store, let's say around seven."

Earnest was a little surprised, but he guessed that she was probably one of the careful types. She didn't know him very well, although during the past year of him seeing her in and out of the department store, he felt like he knew her well.

"That's fine. Friday, at seven. Let's shake on it," He said, with a smile as he held out his hand.

She held out her small hands, with its slender, childlike fingers, and she placed them in his large hands. They shook on it.

They laughed a little. Earnest saw how ravishing her smile was. It seemed to be able to light up a room.

"Well, I'd better go. I'll see you on Friday," she called as she breezed away from him.

Earnest watched her as she walked away.

Ψ

They went out to a small French restaurant. They talked, laughed, and had a good time.

"So, what's it like in Texas?" Angelina asked, playing with the stem of the wine glass.

"Different from here," Earnest shrugged with a smile, "I live on a ranch. My father raises horses and breeds them."

Angelina contemplated this before speaking. "Well that's interesting. So what else does your family do?"

"Well, my father is also the co-owner of one of the biggest banks in Texas.. My mom…well, she's just my mom. She takes care of us all. I have an older sister, Vanessa. She's married with two kids and I have a younger brother, Henry. He's about to start college this year." He looked at her. "So what about you? Tell me about your family?"

Angelina shifted in her seat. "Well…let's see. I have an older brother and a twin brother…"

"You're a twin?" he asked, "That's amazing. How's that for you?" he said, jokingly.

Angelina laughed. "Well, It's always been, so he's just a part of me. We're very close, my brother and I. In fact, all three of us are close."

"Oh, and what about your parents?"

"What about them?" Angelina asked, guardedly.

"Tell me about them. I told you about mine."

Angelina's tense expression relaxed. "Well, my father's in business. My mom…she passed away when I was ten."

"I'm sorry to hear that," Earnest said, wishing he had never asked her. She looked so small and sad now. Almost as if she had shrunken even smaller than she already was.

"It's okay. I'm over it now, I think. Well, you never really get over it. It's more like I've accepted it," She said, with a little painful smile.

"So what kind of business does your father do? Is he in retail?" he asked. He thought that a lot of Jews were in that business and he guessed that she was Jewish, with her dark looks. Plus, it seemed like she had money to spare, with the amount of shopping that she did.

"Why would you think that?" she asked him, curiously.

"Well...," he suddenly felt flustered, thinking he had put his foot in his mouth, "I know that a lot of Jews go into retail business...and I..."

"You think that I'm Jewish?" she asked, calmly.

"Um...I was just guessing."

"First off just because you're Jewish doesn't mean that you have to be in the retail business, second of all...I'm not Jewish."

"Oh. I'm sorry, I didn't mean..."

"No offense taken," She snapped. "Why should I be offended?"

Earnest decided to shut his mouth for a while. He seemed to be getting himself into trouble. Why the hell had he just assumed that she was Jewish by the way that she looked and by her use of money? Then he goes and says that he didn't mean to offend her by saying she was Jewish...man oh man..

Angelina took a sip of her wine and looked at him. "How old are you?" she asked.

"23," he answered. "What about you?"

"17," she answered. "And I'm sorry for snapping at you."

"No problem. I think I deserved it."

She smiled at him, tentatively. "So what's it like living on a ranch with all those horses? I've been in the city all my life."

So he began talking more about his life, how he grew up and about his family and friends. Angelina would put in a few things about herself, although she was not very open. But all in all, they enjoyed themselves.

He drove her home that night, well, at least he thought he did. She told him to stop in front of a two-story house that had green hedges around the front.

"Thank you, I really had fun," She said, softly.

"I enjoyed your company as well…can I see you again?" he asked her.

She was still before she forced out a small jerky nod. She smiled impishly.

"Can I call you?" Earnest asked her.

"Why don't I call you?" she compromised.

So he gave her his number. That night when he drove home, he felt like he was on a cloud, floating to heaven.

Ψ

"Are you nuts man? You went out on a date with Angelina Gionelli?" Abner asked him after Earnest had told him about it. "That girl that always comes in here, that's Angela Gionelli."

"Gionelli? That's her last name? Actually, I've been on four dates with her so far," Earnest said, teasingly.

"Yes, Gionelli is her last name!" Abner responded. It was apparent that his friend wasn't making the connection.

"Angelina is the daughter of Rocco Gionelli. Her father is the head of one of the biggest crime families. Her mother's father, Giovanni DeMarco, was a *don*. She's part of a Mafia family, man, do I have to paint you a picture?"

"You've go to be kidding me…" Earnest responded, shocked at this revelation.

"It's no joke. Why do you think she's so secretive? The best thing to do is to leave her alone man, before you get yourself killed. Rocco Gionelli won't take it well if his daughter is seeing some WASP. Those Italians stick together, man."

Earnest went home that day from work with a lot on his mind. *Angelina Gionelli. The daughter of the Mafia. People who killed without mercy. Gangsters.* Just when Earnest was in bed, the telephone rang. He picked it up. "Hello."

"Hi Earnest," a soft voice answered.

It was Angelina. He took a big swallow. "How are you doing?"

"I'm doing fine. What about you?"

"I'm good. I just got into bed. It's been a busy day. I was surprised that I didn't see you at the store today. I thought that you would have come in to see me or something."

"Yeah, I was thinking about it. I wanted to, but I was really busy today," She said, haltingly.

"Okay. Do you still want to go see that musical tomorrow?"

"Yes. Of course," Angelina said, with a smile.

They chatted for a little longer. Earnest didn't bring up the subject concerning her alleged crime family.

"Well, it's getting late. I have classes tomorrow morning…"

"Really, what are you taking?" Earnest asked.

"Painting," She answered.

"You must be really good."

"I'm okay," she said, fully downplaying her talent.

"So, can I pick you up tomorrow at home?"

"How about we meet at *Joe's*? We can have a coffee before we go to the musical."

"I thought you hated coffee," He asked, easily.

"Well…I can have tea," She quipped.

Earnest smiled. She was good…he had to admit.

They got off the phone with the promise of seeing each other tomorrow. As Earnest lay in bed he thought about the mysterious girl that he had met. A girl that had turned out to be an Italian Mafia daughter. Well, he wasn't sure if it was so, but her secretive behavior was certainly giving credence to what Abner had told him earlier.

Angela replaced the receiver. She didn't hear her brother Anthony come up behind her.

"So who was that?" he asked, curiosity shining in his black eyes.

Angelina jumped. He had given her a fright. "Geeze, Tony. You don't have to sneak up on me like that," She said, trying to keep her tone light. Her twin brother was so nosey.

"I wasn't sneakin' up on you. You were just so wrapped up in your conversation that you didn't notice me," He retorted.

"Don't worry about it. Nobody important. It was just a friend," She answered quickly with the wave of her wrist. She walked into the library. Her brother followed her.

"A friend?"

"A friend," she said, irritated. "Why don't you just leave it alone, huh?"

Anthony's face softened. "I'm sorry Ange, I was just being nosey. You know that's how I am, how can I help it?" he said, giving her an impish grin. Her brother was so handsome. Better looking than she was, she thought. And he was tall, where she was short. She couldn't resist a smile back. "You're forgiven. I'm tired and I'm going to bed."

"Tired from what, all that shopping that you do with Renata and Francesca?"

Angelina swatted him playfully. "Don't forget I go to art school too."

"Yeah, I know. I was just kidding with you sis. Love ya to death, you know that."

Angelina smiled at her brother. "I love you too." Standing on the stairs, she was eyelevel with him. Quick as a flash, she gripped his head between her hands, with a hand on either cheek, and pulled his head towards her, and, she had planted a loud gushy kiss on his forehead. She laughed gleefully.

"Yuck. You slobbered all over me," he cried as he wiped at his forehead. He pretended to be cross, but he couldn't help but smile.

"Nite Tony, I'll see you tomorrow."

"Yeah, night Ange," Tony said, slipping on his coat.

"Where are you going?" Angela asked, from the middle of the stairs.

"I got a few things to do. Some business, you know," He said, quickly. "You go to bed now, sis."

"Don't you tell me what to do Tony, I'm older than you," Angela said, putting her hands on her full hips.

Tony looked at her, amused. "Yeah, by ten minutes. Big deal." He turned to open the door, "I'll see you tomorrow Ange," he called over his shoulder before he walked out the door.

Angela walked the rest of the way up the stairs and climbed into her big four-poster bed.

As she lay, her thoughts were on Earnest. She felt a shiver as she remembered how his hand met her's when he helped her up from her seat in the restaurant. He was so handsome with his thick reddish-brown hair and his deep green eyes.. He was tall and athletic, body shaped to male perfection. He was almost too good to be true, and she was cautious. Why would he want her? She was so plain, well at least she thought that she was. What would an Anglo Saxon Protestant want with her? A Catholic Italian. She remembered when she was young and was in grade school. She was always so different looking than the other girls in her class. Where their skin was a light white, her's was dusky. Their eyes were blue, green, hazel, or some other color. Hers was dark brown, almost black. Their hair was straight and light, her's was black and wavy. She remembered one day when she came home from school crying because some older boy had picked on her and called her a Guinea. Her father had reminded them of their rich heritage and culture. She reminded her that she had a lot to be proud of. She had felt better then.

The next day, her twin brother, her older brother and one other older male cousin, Vinny, had come up after classes and beat the boy up. The boy was out of school for weeks and when he finally came back, he had stayed clear of Angelina, not even daring to look at her.

Angela finally fell asleep with a lot on her mind.

Ψ

The musical was phenomenal. Angelina and Earnest left the theater chatting happily about the performance, arm in arm. They made a striking pair—Earnest tall and athletic with clear, porcelain colored skin, emerald colored eyes, and straight russet hair, Angela the complete opposite—short and curvy with ebony hair, dark eyes and beautiful olive skin.

They stopped at a restaurant with mainly Italian cuisine.

As they were eating, Earnest studied her. She was eating her food, neatly, but without the airs that girls that he had known, including Julia, often did when eating in front of a man. Her creamy olive complexion glowed in the lights of the restaurant. Her large, dark eyes sparkled mesmerizing, her nose was straight and slightly upturned. Her mouth was wide, some might argue a little too wide for her face, but Earnest found it appealing. Her lips were full and lush. Her ears stuck out a little bit. Her neck was slender and delicate. Overall, her face was a little pixie-like in appearance, and that to him, made her so appealing. She was not usual in appearance; she had a unique look about her that was so different and compelling for him. She had an unconventional attractiveness.

"What's wrong with you?" Angelina asked him.

"Nothing. I was just admiring your beauty. You are a very stunning woman, Angelina," He said, truly meaning it.

Angelina blushed, her face turning red. "No I'm not."

Earnest searched her expression. He could tell that she wasn't just fishing for compliments; she truly did not believe that she was attractive.

"You are. How can you not see that this is true? You're gorgeous and I mean it. You are exotically beautiful. You don't look like any other woman that you see on the street. You have a different look about you…it's attractive, Angelina, and it draws people in." Earnest leaned towards her. "You've drawn me in."

Angelina looked at him, her face expressionless. She was speechless and didn't know what to say. Finally, after some silence, Angelina said, softly, "If you think I'm gorgeous, if you saw my cousin Marianne, you would probably flip." She gave a deep throaty laugh.

Earnest stared at her, and that was when he knew that he was in love with her. And he was so sure of it. He had never felt these feelings towards any woman in her life. Woman had been in and out of his life. He had bedded most of them, dined some of them, and used others for a warm body at night. And not one had affected him the way that this young woman before him did, not even Julia. She made him weak. She was his obsession. By far, she was not the most beautiful girl that he had been with. In fact, he was used to being seen with women that were gorgeous by Anglo society's standard—tall, lithe, hanging hair, beautiful eyes, soft lips, and bright white skin, model like in appearance—like Julie. But Angelina was different. Something about her made him want her. Her personality was vibrant, her spirit was strong. She was feminine, yet at the same time so down to earth, and so real, so different from Julie. He found himself comparing her with Julie a lot. Then he thought about her father and her family and their alleged involvement with the Mafia. He just had to know.

"Angelina…"

"Call me Angie, please," She said, with a soft smile.

"Okay. Angie, I've heard some things about you…about your family."

"What?"

"Well..." Earnest began to squirm in his seat, "I've heard that Rocco Gionelli is your father."

Angelina stiffened in her seat, and her face got tense. He could see her lips pressed firmly together. She looked down at her small hands and looked back up at him.

"Well...is it true?" Earnest asked, gently. He had to know.

She gave a jerky nod, "But I guess you've known all along." Her face turned angry. "Guess it was a thrill for you, going out with the daughter of the Mafia. Did you tell all your friends?" she snapped.

Earnest shook his head. "I didn't know until a few days ago. I asked you out before I even knew. I asked you out because I liked you and I was attracted to you. And I still am."

She looked at him, cynicism in her eyes. "So what now? I suppose that you will have nothing more to do with me."

Earnest made a bold move by reaching across the table and clamping her hands into his. He rubbed his thumb across the top of her hand. "No way is that going to happen. Angelina...you have me already. I can't get you out of my mind. You're constantly in my thoughts...I dream about you...I want you. And I think I love you. No, no, I don't think. I do love you," He said, shaking his head. "It may get me killed," Earnest chuckled mirthlessly. "But I am going to do everything and anything within my power to keep you in my life and to have you for myself...I want you to be mine."

Angelina's already big eyes got even larger. "You don't mean that."

"I do," Earnest said, simply.

"Then I don't know what to say..."

Earnest reached up a hand across the table and took a tendril of her black, shiny hair between his fingers, and touched it. It was as smooth and as soft as he imagined.

"Then don't say anything at all," Earnest murmured, tucking the hair behind her dainty ears. "Just believe me."

Chapter Thirteen

May, 1936

 Anthony Gionelli knew his twin like the back of his hand. He knew the way she thought, the way she responded to things, her behaviors, and often her thoughts. That was why he knew that she was lying two weeks ago on that night when he had come in and saw her having a conversation on the phone and she had told him that it was a friend. It was a lie. He knew it. His father was too busy to have picked up on anything and his older brother Sal—married with a kid and a mistress— was away from the family house and too busy to notice anything like that. He could tell, because ever since that night two weeks ago, she had been going around the house with a gratified smile on her face and she had been going out in the evenings a lot. She would tell them she was going out with her friends, and while it was true that she would often go out with her friends, he knew that these times, it wasn't with one of her girlfriends.

 His sister had met a man.

 But Anthony had no idea who this man was, what he looked like, or what his name was.

 So he had decided to follow her tonight on one of her excursions to go and meet 'friends'. He had followed her up to the restaurant where the taxi dropped her off. He watched as his sister tucked her long jacket around her small frame as she walked to the door or the restaurant, her heels clicking on the pavement. She spoke for a while with a man at the door. He nodded, smiled, and held the restaurant door open for her. She walked through the doors of the restaurant.

 Anthony got out of the car. He dropped the cigarette that he was smoking and smashed it with the heel of his two- toned spectator wing tips. He walked up to the door of the restaurant. The man at the door stared him in the face with no expression.

 "Can you let me in?" Anthony asked him, running a hand through his black hair.

"I can if you got a reservation, which would mean that your name would have to be on this here list that I have. What's your name buddy?"

"Look. I ain't got no reservation. Do you think you can do me a favor...just let me in, huh? I'll make it worth your while if ya do?"

The man's face turned mocking. "Oh, really? Don't give me that. I don't have the time for this. Why don't you hit the road, buddy."

Anthony stepped forwards and gave the man a hard punch in the stomach before he knew what hit him. The man doubled over in pain. He fell to his knees.

"How's that for ya? The next time I ask you nicely, you oblige. Don't talk to me like I'm stupid or something. I don't appreciate that. You never know who you're messing with. *Chou.*"

Anthony stepped past him, went through the restaurant doors, and closed the door behind him. His quick brown eyes scanned the restaurant. He saw his sister sitting at a table by herself. She was sipping at a glass of water and lucky for him, was looking in the other direction.

Anthony was led to a table. The table that the waiter was leading him too was a little too close to his sister's table.

"Can you give me a table near the wall or something? I don't like to be on the left side or the middle. It's a little quirk I've got."

The waiter looked at him and shrugged. "Sure." He didn't question him. He had had stranger requests than this before. He led him to a table near the wall.

"Would you like anything, Sir?" the waiter asked.

"Yeah, could you get me a Scotch on the rocks?"

The waiter went off to get his drink. Anthony looked over towards his sister. She was still sitting by herself. Maybe he was just imagining things...maybe his sister wasn't sneaking around with a man after all. He felt a little relieved.

He began to look around the restaurant, his eyes studying people. He liked to imagine what people were talking about, what different couples were saying to each other. His eyes wandered to the front of the restaurant. A tall man, that looked to be around his mid twenties, had just come into the restaurant. The man was handsome. His hair was a deep reddish brown or auburn and he was very well dressed in a long navy trench coat and expensive polished-to-a-shine leather shoes. He handed his coat to the person at the door. Underneath he was wearing a white button down shirt on top of a white cable cardigan and black trousers. Anthony noticed him for a while and his eyes turned back to his sister who was still sitting alone. Only now, her face was lit up in happiness. He followed her gaze.

It was pretty apparent that she was looking right at the russet haired man that had just walked through the door.

Anthony looked back at the tall man. He was smiling now, as well. And he was staring straight and Angelina. Sure enough, he walked right up to the table. Much to Anthony's shock and bemusement, his sister stood up and gave the man a hug. They sat down across from each other.

He looked at them as their mouths moved in conversation. His sister's face was lit up in adoration. The little bit of the man's face showing reflected similar emotions. Anthony couldn't believe this.

"Here you go, Sir," the waiter said, placing the drink on the table.

"Thanks," Anthony responded, his eyes still on his sister's table and the people sitting there.

After finishing their drinks, his sister and the man got up. She looped an arm through his and they walked towards the door of the restaurant and out the door.

After a while, Anthony got up and left as well, leaving the waiter a hefty tip.

He got out just as his sister was getting into the car, the man holding the door open for her. He shut the door firmly after she had gotten in. The man went around to the driver's side and got in. He started the engine, and they were off.

"Follow them. Be discreet about it, huh? Keep about two cars behind them."

"Yes, Sir," the chauffer responded.

And they were off.

Ψ

Four hours later, Anthony made sure that he made it home after his sister. He sat in the car for about thirty minutes after he saw Angelina go through the door of the house.

"Hey, sis," he called casually, as the doorman took his coat. His sister was sitting in the living room curled up on the couch, reading a book.

She looked up. "Hey Anthony. How was your day?"

"It was all right. Busy as always. What about you? What did you do today?"

Angela looked around the room quickly, her dark eyes flashing. "Umm...let's see." Her face was an expression of deep concentration. "Well, I was here for most of the morning. Then I went out with the girls for lunch...then we went over to see that new movie playing. Then I dropped them home and came back here," she said, smiling.

Anthony lit a cigarette. His sister was pretty good at lying. If he hadn't followed her that afternoon, he would almost believe her story. It was plausible.

"Really? Because I called Francesca and Maria and their parents said that they were away for the weekend."

Angelina laughed nervously. "That's because I was with Gretchen."

"Get off it, Ange. You went to meet a guy."

Angelina's face turned bright red under the olive. "You were following me?" she asked, testily.

"I was in town and I saw you with him," Anthony lied. "How was I to know that you were going to be sneaking around with lover boy today? Next time give me some warning," he snapped back.

Angelina gave him a fierce look, but Anthony could see the fear underneath.

"Who is he Angelina?" he asked, softly.

Angelina pursed her lips. A look of extreme anguish came over her face. She didn't answer.

"Tell me Angelina," he pressed, "who is he? How did you meet him?"

"Don't hurt him—"

Anthony scowled, "I'm not going to hurt him. And I'm not going to tell Dad, but I don't want my sister sneaking around town with a man that the family knows nothing about. It's inappropriate."

Angelina began to cry, tears slid down her face. "I met him downtown in the shopping center." She stared him in the eyes, her brown-black eyes wet with tears. "He's not Italian, but it doesn't matter. He's a good man, he's polite and kind, and…I love him."

"You what?" Anthony asked, not sure if he was hearing correctly.

"He loves me and I love him."

"Bring him home and let us meet him, and we'll decide that."

Angelina looked terrified. "Why?"

"Don't worry, we ain't gonna crucify him. I think that Dad should know if you gonna be seeing him and you got feeling for him like that, don't you?"

Angelina nodded slowly, she was still looking down. Anthony came over to his sister on the couch, sat down, and put an arm around her small shoulders. "Look. I'm your brother. I'm on your side. I ain't gonna do nothing that would hurt you, you know that. It just ain't right a young lady running around on the sly…you know what I'm sayin'? How about on Sunday. Why don't you invite you friend over for dinner?"

"Okay," Angelina said, and relaxed in her brother's arms.

Good. This Sunday they would check this guy out and see if he was all right. He wasn't Italian, and that was the first problem. But we'll see. If the guy was a creep, they would just send him packing. It was as simple as that.

Ψ

"Sure. Just tell me what time to be there," Earnest told her easily when she had telephoned him and told him about meeting her family. His calm tone was not really how he felt. Inside, his stomach was churning. They wanted to meet him. Did he really have a choice?

The minute he got off the phone with Angela, the phone rang. He picked it up. "Hello?"

"Hey darling," a smooth voice greeted. It was Julia.

Earnest ran his hand through his hair before answering. "Hello, Julia. How are you doing?"

"I should be asking you that. I haven't heard from you for a week. Is everything all right?"

"Yes. Of course."

"Then I guess you're all packed and ready for coming up here," Julia said.

"What do you mean?" Earnest asked, confused.

"Thursday's my graduation, Earnest, don't tell me you forgot. You are coming up here, aren't you?" She asked, testily.

"Of course I am. I haven't forgotten," Earnest said, with mock disgust. He had totally forgotten about it. It was Monday night. He would have to leave town this evening if he was to get to Texas in time.

"Well, what time is your train coming in so that we can pick you up?" Julia asked him.

"Well, I'm not sure about the time yet. Let me call you back in an hour and tell you. I'll know by then," he said, quickly.

"Okay, fine," Julia said, wearily. "Be sure that you do. And don't forget."

"How could I?" Earnest said, and forced a laugh. "I'll talk to you soon."

"Earnest?"

"Yes?"

"I love you," Julia said, softly. "And I can't wait for us to be married."

"I know," Earnest whispered. There was some silence. Obviously, Julia was waiting for him to say more, but there was nothing more for him to say on the issue. "I'll call you back. Wait by the phone," he said, finally before hanging up.

Julia hung up the phone after listening to the dial tone for about thirty seconds. Her heart felt heavy and sad. She knew something was wrong between Earnest and her but she just wasn't sure what it was. She had tried to be the best she could with Earnest and it seemed as if all her efforts were in vain. For the first time in her life Julia felt afraid and helpless.

Earnest arrived at the station in Texas at five, Thursay morning. He had booked a train leaving that same day to go back to Chicago. He wasn't about to miss the meeting with Angelina and her family. He knew that Julia was expecting him to stay the weekend and would not like that he was leaving the same day of her graduation, but there was nothing that he could do about it—well at least that's what he told himself.

Julia, her parents, and his parents were there to greet him at the station. Julia looked lovely in a form fitting floral dress. Her short blond hair was done in a bob and her clear blue eyes were sparkling. She looked phenomenal and any other man would have been glad to have her, but the sight of her didn't excite nor warm Earnest. So he knew that he was truly over her, if there had ever been anything to get over in the first place. He wasn't sure that he had ever loved her. He was sure that he didn't love her now. That was when he knew that he couldn't go through with the marriage. It just wouldn't be right. He would have to tell her. But not now. Now wasn't the right time.

The graduation was a nice affair. Julia had graduated with honors. He was happy for her. Afterwards the six of them had gone out to lunch at a small restaurant in town.

"I'm going back this evening. I'm taking the seven o'clock train," Earnest told them as they sat down eating their food.

There was an awkward silence.

His mother blinked her eyes and looked around the table. Everyone exchanged glances. Finally, Belinda, his mother, asked him, "What do you mean? You just got here. We thought you were staying the weekend."

"I have to get back to work. They're going to be really busy this weekend with one of the managers gone. They need me. I was lucky that I got off these past three days," he said, easily. "I'm sorry about that."

He looked at Julia and saw that her face had turned bright red. She was embarrassed. The two sets of parents looked at her sympathetically.

"Are you sure that you can't stay until tomorrow morning at least?" Mr. Compton asked.

Hadn't he just said that he had to work this weekend? Well it wasn't true, but that was what he had told them. Angelina's dinner wasn't until Sunday evening at six, anyway. He supposed that he could stay.

"Fine. I'll do that," he said, nodding. "I'll just have to make up the hours on Monday," he said, as if he were making a sacrifice for Julia.

Julia had smiled at him gratefully, "Good. I'm so glad that you could stay longer."

"So son, do you still have your mind set on law school?" Harris asked his son.

"I got accepted into the University of Georgia Law. So, I'll be starting this fall."

His father looked at him, his face turning red, "I thought you wanted to come back and go into business back at the ranch."

"Maybe later, perhaps, but really, Dad, that was all *you* ever talked about, not *me*. But I want to do law. I've decided that. And don't worry father, I'll be paying for it myself."

There was an uncomfortable silence. Harris finally spoke again. "Fine. You want to do law, I'm glad that you know that you will be paying for it."

"I know very well, Sir."

Unavoidably, the conversation went on to wedding plans and such.

"So, let's plan a date for the wedding so that we can get everything organized." Belinda said, trying to break the tension.

So the woman began to chatter about it. Earnest stayed quiet. His father cast him a few careful glances, but said nothing to him.

Later on that night, Earnest and his father were sitting out on the porch smoking cigars.

"Is there something that you want to tell me Earnest?" his father had asked him cautiously.

"What do you mean?"

"You were awfully quiet when the subject of the wedding came up. And I would have thought that you would want to stay here longer."

"I am staying longer, I changed the time."

"You wouldn't have if we hadn't asked you."

Earnest didn't respond. He breathed out the smoke, through his lips.

"You don't want to marry Julia, do you," his father stated, a little sadly.

Earnest was still for a moment before he shook his head. "No, I don't."

"Why?"

Earnest didn't respond. He looked out at the stars in the sky and at the moon. The sky was very clear tonight. The air was warm, yet not too much so.

"You've met someone else, haven't you," his father said, a little sadly.

"I have," Earnest admitted.

His father took a deep breath. "Who is she?"

"A girl that I met in Chicago. Her name is Angie. I've been seeing her for about six months now."

"Do you love her?"

"I do. I love her very much," Earnest said, honestly.

"Do you want to marry her?" his father asked.

"I think so. I haven't given that much thought," Earnest said, nodding. "If I get married, it would be to her."

"I see," the father said, simply. What was he to do? If his son was in love with another person and didn't want to get married, there was nothing that he could do about it. He was a grown man.

"You know you're going to have to tell Julia before this gets too far," the father said, matter-of-factly.

"I know. And I will. Please, let me do it. But not yet."

"Okay," the father said, hesitantly. "But hurry."

"I'll try," Earnest responded.

"No. You have to."

Ψ

Earnest slowed his Cadillac in front of the large house, set way back from the street with the tall hedges. A short dark man in a suit stood by the entrance to the driveway, which was between the hedges. He motioned for Earnest to come in.

Earnest drove the car through and up black pavement of the driveway. Finally, he parked the car and stepped out. The man was waiting for him.

"Follow me please."

Earnest was getting even more nervous than he already was. Obviously, this was a man of few words.

"My name's Earnest," he offered.

"I know that already," the man said, politely.

"What's your name?" Earnest asked, trying to be friendly.

"You can call me Gino," he said, shortly, but not unfriendly like.

Earnest guessed that probably wasn't his real name. Ah, well. He had more important things to focus on like how to impress Rocco Gionelli and the rest of his family. This felt so surreal to him. Never in his life would he have thought that he would be going to have supper with a Mafia family. It was so astounding that it almost blew his breath away just thinking about it. And for a second he asked himself, *what am I getting myself into?*

But he loved Angelina and he would do anything for her. And if it meant meeting her family, then so be it. He was in knee deep because he was head over heals. There were a lot of body parts involved, he joked to himself.

Finally, they stepped through the doors. There was a doorman waiting.

"Sam will take your coat," Gino said, "and you can follow me into the drawing room".

After the doorman had taken his coat, he followed Gino.

"Mr. Gionelli, Mr. Hurst is here," Gino called through the door that he had cracked slightly and stuck his head through.

"Send him in," a heavily accented voice called.

Gino opened the door wider and stepped back for Earnest to enter. Earnest hesitated a little and slowly went in. Once he was in the room, Gino shut the door behind him.

A handsome, slim, middle-aged, dark haired man with light bronze tinged skin and black olive eyes was sitting in a high back plush, leather chair. He was wearing an expensive looking charcoal colored suit. He wore black and white wing tips that were polished to a high shine. The man's face was pleasant as he examined Earnest in an equal amount of curiosity.

"Hello, I am Angelina's father, Rocco," he said, not getting up from his seat. Earnest walked over to shake his hand. "Glad to meet you, Sir."

"Please sit down. Would you like something to drink?"

"Some water would be nice," Earnest said.

Rocco got up and walked to the little bar on the side of the room. "Would you like some lemon in the water?"

"Yes, please," Earnest answered.

Rocco came back over to where Earnest sat and handed him a glass of ice water with a lemon slice on the side of the glass.

"Thank you," Earnest said, as he took his drink.

Rocco nodded and sat back in his chair with his own drink, which was a glass of brandy.

"So tell me a little about yourself. Not that Angelina hasn't been going on and on about you," Rocco said, smiling. "But I would like to hear a little from you."

Earnest took a gulp of his water and set it on the coaster on the little table beside him.

"Well, I was born in Texas, and raised there. My father owns a horse ranch. He raises horses, breeds them, and sells them. It's a family business. His father passed it down to him and his father's father passed it down to his father and so on. My father is also the co-owner at the main bank back in Texas."

"So, you graduated from the University of Chicago, my daughter tells me."

"Yes. I graduated about a year ago with a business degree. I'm going into law school at the University of Georgia in the fall."

"Hmmm…going back south? That's a far way from here," Rocco said, stroking his eyebrows.

"Yeah, it is. But nothing is written in stone. I got accepted to another law school that is just in the next state over, about five hours from here. I might go there," Earnest said, quickly. He took another sip of his water. At the moment, his throat felt so dry.

Rocco just nodded and sipped his drink. He swirled the liquid around in his glass. The tinkling sound of the ice against the glass was very clear in the room.

"Do you have any brothers and sisters?" Rocco asked, politely.

"I have an older sister who's married. She has two boys. I also have a younger brother that's in college now."

Rocco nodded and said, "I have two brothers and one sister. But my sister died when he was ten. She had consumption. When I was 22, I moved to the states from Sicily. Most of my family still lives back in Sicily—they have no desire to leave. It wasn't easy for me. America is not very nice to Italian immigrants."

Earnest shifted in his seat, somehow feeling guilty. "I know. That's not fair."

Rocco smiled. "But of course that is not your fault. So, you say that you are going into law. Do you know what kind that you want to specialize in?"

"I'm not sure as of yet," Earnest said. "Whatever I feel most drawn to do when I get there."

Suddenly, there was a soft knock at the door.

"Papa?" a voice that Earnest recognized to be Angelina's, called from behind the closed the door.

"Come in my dear," Rocco called.

Angelina came through the door. Earnest's heart fluttered at the sight of her. Her dark wavy hair was pulled back from her face with two silver clips and she wore a filmy material, cream-colored dress that complemented her complexion. Her small feet wore laved up wedge shoes. She looked beautiful. Earnest felt like he was going to melt.

Rocco noticed his daughter's blush and the look of adoration that came into the young man's eyes when he saw his daughter. There was no mistaking it. There were some very strong feelings here. He hoped that he wouldn't have to get rid of the kid.

In the dining room, Earnest was introduced to Anthony—Angelina's twin brother, Her older brother Sal, his wife Marie and their four-year-old son.

"You're in for a treat. You're going to have some of the best tasting Italian food that you have ever tasted," Rocco said to Earnest, with a smile.

And so it was. The food was delightful and Earnest enjoyed every minute of it despite the cleverly concealed grilling that he received at the dinner table. Angelina, who was seated across from him, gave him reassuring smiles. This, he was sure, gave him the strength to endure. Finally, the dinner was over. The men went into the library to smoke cigars. Earnest began to relax with them; despite their cultural differences.

Finally, it was time to leave. Rocco nodded at him and said, "Despite the fact that you aren't Italian...I think that you're a good man. Treat my daughter right. I don't want you jerking her around or anything," he warned.

"I won't. I love your daughter, Mr. Gionelli," Winston said, seriously.

"Do you now?" He mused.

"I do," he said, firmly.

Rocco nodded slowly, seeming ingesting this information, but not saying anything more.

Angelina walked him to his car.

"See. It wasn't so bad. I think my family likes you," she said, when they stopped in front of his car.

"I sure hope so. Cause I plan on spending a lot of time with you. And if knew for sure that your father and or brothers were not watching from the windows, I would kiss you."

Angelina blushed. Earnest's heart skipped a beat. She had such a devastatingly strong affect on him.

"I'll see you tomorrow. Stop by the store around six when I get off and we'll go see a movie and grab something to eat," Earnest said, softly.

She smiled up at him, her girlish looks so evident especially now. "Okay," she stood on her tiptoes and wrapped her arms around his neck. Her lips were close to his ears.

"I love you," she whispered.

Earnest felt a faint feel of déjà vu. A year ago, before he left Texas, Julia had whispered the very same words into his ears. But this time it was different. This time, he had a response.

"I love you too," he whispered back. And he meant every word of it.

Chapter Fourteen

July, 1936

Julia had graduated two months ago and yetEarnest had remained silent on the subject of their marriage. She was also hearing less and less from him. Most of the time, she would be doing the calling and when she called and spoke to him he always sounded so far away and distracted. He would tell her he'll call the next day, and he never would.

Then finally, the day came when she thought that her world was going to fall apart at the seams. It was a phone call from Earnest.

"Julia, we need to talk."

"What about?" Julia had asked, nervously as she tried to keep her voice light.

"This is something that can't be discussed over the phone. It is better if we are face to face," he answered.

"This has to do with you and me, doesn't it?" Julia asked, in the choked voice.

There was silence on the other end and then finally he answered, softly. "Yes."

Then there was more silence as Julia contemplated Earnest's words. She knew what they meant. He was going to break up with her. She definitely knew that something was up. And her woman's intuition told her that this something was another woman. She was sickened at just the thought of it, but what else could it be?

"I'm not free this weekend or the next, but the following weekend, I am free. I know that it's some time away, but that can't be helped. I have a full work schedule for this week and the next. I would come sooner if I could, believe me. So I'll book a train and arrive in Texas on Saturday afternoon. We'll talk then."

"Okay," Julia whispered.

"Well, I'll talk to you later…I have so much to do. Have a good night. Goodbye Julia," he said, so formally.

"Goodnight," she said, trying not to cry as she hung up the phone. She sat very still on the chair in her bedroom. That was when she had decided that she was going to go to Chicago this weekend. Except that Earnest wouldn't know it. She would do a little investigating.

Julia found a hotel near the apartment building that Earnest lived in. The next day she followed him to work. She knew that he got off at around five, so she went home, and came back at that time, and followed him home in the car that she rented. He went straight home. Julia went back to her room and fell asleep. When she woke up, it was eight in the evening. She rushed over to the window that faced her fiancé's apartment building. His Cadillac was not parked in its usual position at the front. He was gone, had left when she was sleeping.

Anxiously, she got into her rented car and started driving around the city hoping to catch a glimpse of his car. Finally, just when she was about to give up, she saw a Cadillac that looked to be Earnest's pass by her. She looked at the license plate when it passed. It was Earnest's car. She couldn't believe her luck. She followed it.

Finally, his car stopped in front of an opera theater. She parked across the road from it and watched his car.

Earnest stepped out of his car, smartly dressed in a black tuxedo and shoes. He came around to the other side and opened the passenger side door. A small dark girl in a long, fox fur coat stepped out. The girl was beaming as she looked up into Earnest's face. The girl looped her arm through his and together they walked up to the large double doors. Those were the only physical details that she could make out.

Julia thought that she was going to die. So he was seeing another woman. She felt as if a dark cloud was above her. Suddenly the clear night looked less inviting and invigorating than it looked threatening and bleak.

She drove back to her hotel in a deep depression. Once again, the feeling of helplessness came over. She felt as if the perfect life that she envisioned for herself was slowly sinking down the drain, out of sight and out of her reach. Her existence was being threatened and she didn't know what to do about it.

Julia unlocked her hotel door and went straight to the bathroom. She began to run a bath. Yes, a nice hot bath was exactly what she needed right now. She needed to relax and think things through.

As she sunk into the super warm bath water and let the bubbles float all around her body, she began to think. And as she thought, she began to grow angry. She began to realize that this was a battle. If she was going to have Earnest, she would have to fight for him. She was not going to let that little woman get him so easily, not after everything that she had done for Earnest. And all the things they had gone through together and all the things that she had been through because of him. This unnamed, unknown woman was an enemy to be chased away and vanquished.

Julia sunk lower into the bathwater. Her sore muscles were soothed by the warmness, but her heart was beating in her chest with her thoughts. To begin with, she had to find out who this woman was. Put a name to the person. Then she would talk to her. She would at least give her a chance to hear that Earnest was an engaged man. She was sure the woman didn't know this. But if she did, it was obvious that this was not an issue for her, and there would be an even bigger problem. And if this was the case, Julia would have to fight dirty. She wasn't afraid to fight for the man that she loved, nor was she ashamed. But that bridge would be crossed when she got there. First things first, find out who this woman is and meet with her. She would do all this tomorrow.

Julia found out that the young woman liked to frequent the downtown shopping center where Earnest worked. She also noticed that she would come in at lunchtime. There, she would meet with Earnest and they would go out to lunch together. After a week of watching this routine, she decided to make her move.

She came in inconspicuously by the clothing section. She was wearing a pair of black glasses. She wore a red wig over her own blond hair. And over this wig, she wore a hat. She wore a black mink fir coat. There was no way that Earnest would recognize her right away. Not unless he looked really close. But she wasn't going to get close enough for him to look at her really close. She watched as Earnest and his lady friend walked out the store and she was filled with rage. She had to tell herself to calm down and to focus on the task on hand.

Her eyes flicked to the counter, where a floor person stood. She went over there. The young woman looked at the tall red haired woman in obvious awe. To her, the statuesque woman in high heels looked like a movie star with her dark frames and her fur coat. Though the girl couldn't see her eyes because of the frames, she could tell that the woman was beautiful.

"Can I help you?" the mousy sales girl asked, her voice a small squeak.

Julia smiled down at her, patronizingly. "Of course, darling. I was standing way back there…" Julia said, pointing to the clothing section. "when I saw that small, dark haired girl standing over there. Now. If I was not mistaken, I could have sworn that was my little cousin… although of course I'm not sure…do you happen to know who that was?" Julia asked, in a breathy voice.

The young skinny woman was obviously impressed with Julia, who seemed to reek of Hollywood.

"I have no idea, Ma'am. I'm sorry, but she comes in here a lot to see Mr. Hurst. So, maybe if you were—"

"Francine, why don't you go and do the inventory. I'll finish helping this woman out," Abner Bernstein told his employee.

"Of course, Mr. Bernstein, I'll get on it right away." And with one last fascinated look at the red haired woman, she scurried off to do her work.

Abner smiled at her. "How can I help you today?"

Julia got a little flustered. "Well, I was just asking the young lady about a young woman that came in here a lot, she looks like my cousin, but I wasn't sure…do you think you can help me? It is very important that I find her…she's been estranged from the family for so long…this simply cannot go on much longer."

"You mean that woman that comes in here to see Earnest?" Abner asked her.

"I don't know who Earnest is…but your girl just told me that she did come in here to see him. And I was told by her that she comes in here a lot…but I might just be confusing her…"

"Well, not unless your cousin's name in Angelina Gionelli. Is that your cousin?" he asked, his eyes squinting.

Somehow, Julia felt that she had better say no. She made a mental note of the name.

"No, no its not. I'm so sorry. She looks quite similar to my cousin Suzanne Marshall. But never mind. I'm sorry to have caused you trouble…"

"No trouble at all." He looked at her with interest. "So are you new in town?"

"No, I'm just visiting for the week," Julia said, quickly, trying to back away from the situation.

"Well, why don't I show you around town? I'll take you out for dinner, dancing, whatever you like," he said, cheerfully. In his eyes, Julia could read open interest—she had grown accustomed to seeing this and could recognize it immediately.

"Well, you see that might be a problem. I'm staying with my uncle and his wife. They have a load of things planned for me...I don't know if I'll find the time..."

"Well, how bout you give me your number and I'll call you sometime? We could chat," Abner offered.

Boy, he was insistent. This one was not going to back down easily.

"Well...my uncle wouldn't like strange men calling his house for his niece," she said, playfully. "He's so old fashioned. What about you give me your number and I'll call you? I'll tell you when I'm free."

"Well, that sounds good." Abner gave her his card, "You can reach me here at work with that number. I wrote my home phone on the back. You have a nice stay in town and I hope to see you again," he said, pointedly so there was no mistaking his intentions.

"Thank you Abner," she said, reading his nametag, "and I hope to see you before I go back to Florida." She slid his card in her purse.

"I knew I heard a southern accent," he said, pleased.

"Bye-bye now...," Julia said, beginning to turn away,

"What's your name?" Abner asked, stopping her.

"Corrine," she said, quickly. That was the name of a restaurant that she saw when she stopped in Alabama on the way over.

"That's a beautiful name," he said, adoration in his eyes.

"Thank you. Now I really must be leaving." She made a quick exit and breathed a sigh of relief once she was out the door. She wrote the mystery girl's name down the minute she got out the door before she could forget it.

When Julia came back to the hotel room, she called the operator and asked for the number of Gionelli. After getting a number, she thanked the operator and hung up. She was feeling a little better now. She would call the girl later and have a little chat with her.

Ψ

After having her art classes then going out to lunch with Earnest, Angelina finally came home with the intent of relaxing. When she came in her brother called out.

"Ange, that you?"

"Yeah, it's me," she answered as she shut the door behind her.

"You're just in time. There's somebody on the phone for you," Anthony called from upstairs.

"Who is it?" Angelina asked, as the butler took her jacket and hung it up.

"I dunno. It some woman who says she's a friend," he answered.

Angela ran up the large carpeted stairway and down the hall into the library. Her brother was there. He held out the phone for her.

"Ask her if she's got a boyfriend. She sounds cute," he said, with an impish grin.

Angelina rolled her eyes at her twin and took the phone from him. He left the room.

"Hello?" She called into the receiver, breathless from her run up the stairs.

"Hello," a voice answered coolly. "Is this Angelina Gionelli?"

"Yes it is," Angelina answered, a little wary now, "Who is this?"

"A friend," the voice said, crisply. "A friend that is trying to educate you before you make any stupid moves."

"What do you mean?" Angelina asked, getting a little frightened.

"I mean, I have a little information that you might find quite interesting. This concerns Earnest. I'm sure you know him," the voice said, tersely.

"Yes," Angelina answered in a small voice. "But I don't understand…"

"Why don't we meet for lunch somewhere tomorrow and I'll clear everything up. This is a sympathy meeting, darling. I think that a woman should know things about a man before she even considers becoming seriously involved with him."

Angelina thought for a while. This has to be some sort of joke, but what if it wasn't? She got scared, but she decided that it would be best to hear what this woman had to say.

"We can meet at the Olive Grove at noon. That's the only time that I'm free." Angelina said. She would make an excuse to miss lunch with Earnest tomorrow. She'll tell him that she had to go see a family member or something.

"That's fine. I guess I shall see you then," the voice said.

"How will I know who you are?" Angelina asked.

"I'll know who you are. Just sit tight."

Then with that, the person hung up. Angelina was left holding the receiver in her hand. She hung up after a while. What could possibly be wrong when everything was going so great?

Ψ

Angelina came in to the restaurant the next afternoon.

"Hello, can I have a table please. If someone asks for me, tell them that Angelina Gionelli is seated already."

"Of course, Ma'am," the man said, getting flustered. This was the daughter of Rocco Gionelli.

He got her a table near the front, which was where the important people sat. A waiter came to her table right away and asked her if she would like anything.

She sat down and asked the waiter for a glass of water.

Angelina studied the door, watching people as they came out, singling out the women. So far, nobody had come to her table.

A tall blond woman came through the door. She spoke to the host at the door. He pointed the woman in the direction of Angelina. The woman's cold blue eyes locked on Angelina. She came walking over, causing many heads to turn as she did so. The woman was absolutely beautiful, Angelina thought to herself.

Julia came and sat down from across her with a nod of her head in greeting. The waiter came over. She ordered a cup of coffee.

When the waiter had walked away, she gave the small woman across from her a good look over.

But this woman who was now commanding all of Earnest's attention was not even her equal, she thought. She definitely wasn't as good-looking as herself, Julia thought. The girl wasn't any competition to her in the looks department. She was short, her mouth, from where Julia sat, looked a little too wide stretched, if one were to ask her. Her nose was too small and upturned and her ears stuck out a little bit. But the girl's eyes were large, dark and bright and her hair luxuriantly dark and thick. Her body was small and curvy. She looked almost like a life size doll.

And of all people, Earnest had to choose an Italian. They were almost as bad as Negroes with their weird accents, weird clothes and olive skin, she thought disgustedly. Being a woman from the 1930's South, Julia didn't see anything wrong with her judgements and prejudices. She was a product of her time.

The darker woman studied Julia just as intently. "Who are you?" Angelina asked, firmly.

"My name is Julia. I'm Earnest's fiancé," she said, primly.

Angelina almost choked on her water. "What do you mean?"

"I mean that me and Earnest are about to be married, my dear. We have been engaged for four years now."

Angelina stared back at her numbly, not saying a word.

"Then I suppose he hasn't mentioned me," Julia shook her head slowly, "That's Earnest. It is so like him. I guess he wanted a little affair before he gets shackled down," she said, and chuckled softly. "I'm sorry that it's at your expense. He shouldn't play with young girls like you. How old are you, sixteen?"

"I'm 17," she answered softly. She felt as if her heart was falling out and a deep sorrow washed over her. How could he do this to her?

"My, you do look much younger. I myself am 22."

Angelina's eyes filled up with tears despite her efforts not to cry.

Julia frowned. "There, there. I didn't tell you this to be spiteful. I told you this to warn you as a fellow woman. I understand how hurt you are and I wouldn't want him to hurt you any further."

Angelina wiped her eyes. "I had no idea. He never mentioned anything like that. I'm so embarrassed," she whispered.

"No need to be. Just stay clear of him, darling. Fortunately for you, I'll be the one to have to deal with him. You wouldn't believe how awful it was for me, to find out about all his…women he had here in Chicago when I was back home in Texas, slaving away at school and planning a wedding. But I love him, Angelina. That's what keeps me from leaving him. That's what keeps me going."

"I have to go now," Angelina said, in a tight voice, already rising from her seat.

"Yeah, well so do I. I'll not waste anymore of your time. Do take care of yourself dear. If we don't take care of ourselves, we cannot expect a man to," Julia said, pushing her chair in.

Angelina walked past the awful woman and out the door. She stepped into her Lincoln and told the driver to take her home.

Angelina looked out the back window at the woman standing on the curb outside the restaurant. The woman's face, devoid of expression, stared back at her.

Julia allowed herself a smile when the car was out of sight. She went back to her room and gave Earnest a call.

"Hello, Julia, how are you doing?" Earnest asked, formally.

"You don't have to sound so business-like, Earnest. You can be a little warmer," she whined.

"Julia, what is it? I don't have the time for your complaints right now," he said, impatiently.

"I just wanted to see how you were doing…I was about to leave for the weekend for the country." Room service came with the spring water that she had ordered. "You can put that right there," she said to the man.

"What was that?" Earnest asked.

"Nothing, dear." She peeled off a one dollar bill and gave it to the server. He thanked her and left

"That's nice," Earnest said, not really caring. "Have a nice trip."

"Thank you Earnest. I will." They said goodbye and hung up.

She felt better already. He would come back to her if it was the last thing he did.

Ψ

For seven days, Earnest hadn't see hide nor hair of Angelina. She would always come into the store to meet him for lunch, but he hadn't seen her since last Thursday and he had last spoken to her on Friday when she had called in the morning to cancel their lunch date because she had to go and see her aunt in the next town. He had tried to call her the following week, and each time he would get the message that she wasn't there or she was busy and she would call back. Now it was Friday, and as the lunch hour drew near, he knew that she wouldn't be there, yet again.

Earnest was scared. Through his mind, he went through the last day that they had went out to lunch to think if he had done anything that might have been offensive or if there was any strange behavior on her part. He could come up with nothing.

Finally, on Saturday, he got up the nerve to go to her house.

He got out his car and looked at the house. He was sure that he saw a curtain move. He walked to the great Tudor doors and rang the big brass knocker. After a while, a thin, balding man in a black suit, who Earnest recognized to be the butler, answered the door.

"Can I help you?" the man asked, looking him over.

"Is Angelina here?" he asked, feeling a little anxious.

"Let him in, Sam," a man's voice called from behind him, somewhere in the house.

The man opened the door wide, allowing Earnest entrance. Earnest nodded his head and stepped past the man who was now staring at him stonily.

Suddenly a man came out walking down the large, wide staircase. The man looked to be around thirty with black hair slicked back, light olive skin and dark brown eyes. He was wearing a pair of black slacks and a black silk vest over a white shirt. He recognized the man to be Sal, Angelina's older brother

The man's face did not look pleasant. He came and stood face to face with Earnest. Sal was almost as tall as him.

"You know, I ought to blow your head off, you lousy bastard for messing with my little sister," he spat out.

Earnest's felt a prickling sensation at the back of his neck. "What do you mean?"

The man's attractive features twisted up in anger. "What do I mean? You asking me that? I oughta kill you."

"I don't understand—"

"You got a fiancé back in Texas, huh. Did you think my sister was just something to past the time away?" The man hauled back and punched Earnest in the face, catching him totally unaware.

Earnest doubled over, holding his nose. A gush of blood flowed out.

"You lousy little prick. You think you're better than us, don't you? You bastard," he said, and kicked him to the floor.

"Stop!" A woman's voice screamed, "Stop it Sal."

Earnest was on the floor now, his ribs were killing him from where the kick was put. He recognized Angelina's voice. He struggled to his feet.

He saw Angelina clutching her brother's arm. Her face was a frightened mask. She let go of her brother and came over to Earnest.

"Come into the kitchen. I'll clean you up."

"Don't bring that bastard in here, do you hear?"

"Shut up, Sal." Angelina snapped. "Just stop it, please. You had no right to hit him."

Angelina led him to the kitchen where she got a damp cloth and wiped off his face.

Earnest stared at her, her small face set in concentration. She looked like an angel in his eyes.

"Angelina I—"

"Don't say a thing. You shouldn't have come here. They would like nothing better than to kill you. I had to beg them to leave you alone. They think that you made a fool of them by coming here making yourself seem...so perfect. You have a fiancé. Why did you lie to me Earnest?" Angelina asked, her face angry.

"Please, I was going to end it with her. I don't love her, Angelina. I was going to go and see her next weekend to tell her. You have to believe me. I have a ticket to go to Texas this weekend. I made the reservations with Amtrak last week."

"You're a liar. I don't believe a word you're saying," she said, and threw down the cloth. "It's not broken," she said referring to his nose.

"Please believe me...Angelina," Earnest said getting up. He felt dizzy and sat back down. Angelina helped him to his feet.

"You'd better leave now, Earnest. I don't think that we should see each other anymore."

"I love you, Angelina. I love *you*. Not her. *Not* Julia. Doesn't that mean anything at all?" he asked, when he was standing out on her front porch.

"Goodbye Earnest. Have a nice life." With that, she shut the door firmly in his face.

Angelina ran up the stairs to her room and shed the tears that she had been holding back the whole time.

Sal walked up the stairs and put his ears to his sister's door. He heard her sobbing, and he was filled with rage. He wasn't able to protect his sister from this pain. There was nothing that he could do. Well, maybe there was…

Ψ

When Earnest got home, he made an ice pack, put it to his nose he laid down in bed, but he didn't go to sleep. He thought. How did Angelina find out about Julia? How could she have known? Angelina hadn't mentioned anything about how she found out and he was hesitant to speak to her anymore at the moment, until he got this situation straightened out.

Suddenly, something hit him. The phone call that he had gotten from Julia two Fridays ago. From where had she made the call? She had said that she was at home, preparing to leave for the country. But there was something about that conversation that was nagging him. But he could think what.

Come on, think he told himself. It was something that she said. Then he remembered something. He could have sworn that she was telling someone to put something down. And then she heard a man say, "Thank you, Ma'am," in the background. She could have been in a restaurant…but people usually don't tell a waiter to put the food right here. The waiters put it down, automatically, right in front of a person.

Then he thought of something else. He thought back to the weekend, two years ago, at a hotel that they had stayed in during a trip to Las Vegas. Julia had ordered up some wine for them. When the server came, she had said similar, if not those exact same words that she had heard over the phone. "You can put that right over there." Then when Julia had given him a tip, the server had said, "thank you Ma'am." Julia's maid at home didn't say "thank you Ma'am," because there was no reason to. It wasn't like Julia tipped the maid. So she could have been in a hotel. But where and why, if that was the case?

He called the operator.

"Hello, can I help you?" the female voice rang out.

"Yes, I was wondering if you could trace a call for me that I received on this line around…five on Friday the 19th. That was my sister and she had forgotten to give me the number where she was staying. You see, out mother is sick in the hospital, and now I have no idea where she is…"

"Of course, Sir," the voice said sympathetically. "We usually don't do this, but in your case I'll make an exception. Hold on please."

Earnest waited on the phone for about ten minutes. Finally, the voice came back on.

"Okay. We connected a woman to this line from The Madison, in Chicago, Illinois at 5:35 p.m. The number of that line is CHIcago 2569."

Earnest felt cold fingers creeping up his spine. Suddenly, he knew.

"Thank you so much. I appreciate that."

"Not a problem. I hope your mother gets better."

"Thank you," Earnest said feeling a little guilty for lying.

So, Julia had called him from the Madison. The hotel across the street from his building. She had been down here and it was clear to him that she had told Angelina. She must have sensed that he was going to come down this weekend to break it off with her, because that was precisely what he had been planning to do.

Earnest telephoned his father.

"Hello son," Harry said joyously when he heard his son's voice.

"Hi Dad," he greeted.

"Is something the matter?" his father asked, sensing something amiss.

"Dad. Julia came down here behind my back and told Angelina that we were engaged. Dad, you know that I was planning to come up this weekend to break things off with her."

His parents had yet to meet Angelina, although he talked a lot about her. He had to admit that he was a little nervous as to how they would respond to her. Although his parents were not outright bigots, there was still an unspoken understanding, as it was all over the community, as to what was "acceptable" and what wasn't. He had no idea how they would react if they knew that she was Italian.

"I know that son. You shouldn't have waited so long," Harry said sadly, "So what has happened?"

"Angelina won't speak to me. And her family…is upset," he said reminiscing on the punch that he had received from Angelina's brother Sal.

"Well, you can't rightly blame them. So, what are you going to do? Are you still coming down this weekend?"

"Yes. I think that I'd better do that. I'll confront Julia about what she did. Not a word to her, Dad."

"Fine. I wish you luck son," his father said.

"Where's Mom?"

"She's out in town. She'll be back in a few hours."

They talked a while longer about smaller things, and then got off the phone. Earnest went to his kitchen and made some tea. He sat at the little table and sipped at it.

He wasn't sure that he would be able to sleep tonight.

Chapter Fifteen

It wasn't hard for them to find information on Earnest Hurst. They found out that his parents lived in a small town of Texas. They found out the home address, unbeknownst to Angelina.

Wednesday morning, bright and early, Sal and Anthony Gionelli caught the train to go to Texas.

They booked themselves into a small, neat looking motel where the man at the front desk gave them a look of open curiosity. They didn't fit into the small town look with their dark, expensive suits and slicked back hair.

"You men from the city?" the old man had asked.

"Yeah. Can you get us a room? The best you got," Sal answered hurriedly.

"Sure thing," he held out a key. "I see the Texas sun has already gotten to yah," he said with a chuckle.

Anthony snatched the key from his hand and gave the old man a hard look. The old man, growing frightened, had retreated towards the back office, "Have a nice stay, Sirs," he said, inching away.

The next morning, they had rented a car and located the residence of Harry and Belinda Hurst.

"Well, they're well off," Sal said, noting the large house and the vast land surrounding it.

"Time to pay Mr. Hurst's parents a visit."

They went up to the door and knocked. Finally, a woman in an apron answered the door.

"Can I help you?" the woman asked, with a strong European accent.

"Yes. Is Mr. or Mrs. Hurst here?"

"And who are you?"

"I'm Sal and this is my brother Anthony. We're Angelina's brothers."

"Hold on a moment please." She closed the door softly. After a while, she came back and ushered them inside.

"They're in the living room. Follow me."

When they came in, a tall, attractive older man that looked to be in his late fifties with brown hair and a suit told them to sit down. A pretty, older woman with red hair and wide green eyes, whom they assumed to be Mrs. Hurst, was standing beside him. She looked at them wide eyed.

"So, why are you here?" Mr. Hurst asked, cutting to the chase.

"We're here about our sister Angelina. We just want to know what's going on. She's hurt, you know. She told us that your son was already engaged to Julia. But he's been seeing her. Did you know about it?" Sal asked.

"Yes I did. About three months ago, my son told me that he didn't love Julia. He said that he was in love with another woman that he had met in Chicago. He told me that he name was Angie. I'm assuming that this is the Angelina that you're talking about." He paused. "You came all the way to Texas to talk with us?" Mr. Hurst asked, a little incredulously.

"Yes. We care a lot about our sister," Anthony answered shortly.

"Well, anyways, I told him that he should tell Julia soon that he wasn't going to marry her. You see, he didn't quite know how to go about it. Instead of telling her anything, he gave Julia the cold shoulder, you see. Finally, he's decided to tell her."

"What do you mean?" Sal asked.

"Well, this weekend, he is coming down to talk to Julia. He's going to break off the engagement. He told me from early last week

"So your son wasn't going to marry Julia?"

"He has no intention to," the red-haired woman answered, speaking for the first time, "I guess I've noticed for a while that he wasn't really passionate about Julia, but I just ignored it. My son loves your sister," the woman said with a little smile, "He wants to marry her, he told us that much. He talks about her all the time."

The two brothers exchanged looks of astonishment. They had come here expecting to hear that Earnest was getting married to the woman Julia and they had expected the parents to know little, if anything at all, about their sister. Obviously, this was not' the case.

"My son is broken up over the whole issue. He called me in obvious distress. He wants to make things right with your sister. He loves her and doesn't want to lose her. I hope that you will tell her this…" Mrs. Hurst said trailing off.

"We will," Sal answered, getting up, "And thank you for your time. I'm glad that were able to clear the air."

They left to go back to the motel. There was no reason to stay here any longer. They had learned what they needed to. They would go back to Chicago tomorrow. But they wouldn't tell their sister about this meeting. What was done was done. She would get over Earnest.

After the two young men had left through the door, Earnest's parents sat in the living room, astonished that Angelina's brothers would come all the way from Chicago to talk with them concerning Angelina and Earnest.

Unbeknownst to Mr. And Mrs. Hurst, they had just saved their son's life.

Ψ

"How could you do that Julia? Interfere in my life like that," Earnest asked.

"You never told her. You should have, it's not my fault," Julia answered, petulantly.

"It doesn't matter anyways. You didn't accomplish anything except drive away the woman I love. We're over, Julia. Whether or not I'm with Angie. We've been over for a long time."

"Earnest, please don't say this—"

"No, we're finished. Goodbye. The day after I get home, I'll be leaving for law school in Georgia."

Earnest stood up from the table and put on his hat. There was nothing more to say to her.

"Please don't leave!" Julia cried, getting up. "After everything…"

Earnest started to walk away.

Julia followed him. "After everything I've done for you! Damn you, Earnest!" she screamed.

A waiter rushed up to her. "Ma'am, could you keep it down."

"Get off me! I'm leaving. Can't you see me walking towards the door?" she asked shoving the hand off from her shoulder.

She followed Earnest out into the street, cursing and screaming behind him all the way. He didn't say a single word. He hailed a taxi, and took off down the road.

That was the last time Earnest ever saw Julia again.

Chapter Sixteen

Fall, 1936

"Well, that's all for today. It's a nice day, I'm sure you guys have some trouble to get into," the professor said.

There was laughter in the crowd of students. Earnest looked over at his friend Abner. Both of them had decided to go to law school. They had decided to do a dual study program—J.D and M.B.A.—with the thoughts of going into coporate law once their studies were completed.

"Well, that's it for the day. So what shall we have tonight, dear friend," Abner said putting an arm around Earnest's shoulder, "Macaroni and cheese or macaroni and cheese?"

Earnest laughed. "Why don't we go grocery shopping today? The fridge and the cupboard are bare."

"Sure thing," Abner said as they climbed into his Thunderbird.

Abner stopped at a red light with a screech.

"What's the matter with you?" Earnest asked. "Are you trying to kill us?"

"No, just you," Abner said jokingly, "Kidding, I thought I could get through the yellow light…"

Earnest looked around. His eyes fastened onto a dark haired girl with waves down her back passing by the car. She reminded him of Angelina.

"Look at her. Doesn't she look like Angie?" Earnest asked, softly.

Abner gave him a weird look. "Yeah ,she has dark hair like her. But that's about it. Come on. Forget about the mob princess. It's been six months since you left. You've written her letters and she hasn't written back. Let it go, there's lots of pretty girls here."

Earnest looked away as the car rolled off. His friend would never understand.

Ψ

April, 1938

Angelina's usually lush body with its generous curves was now gaunt and skinny. Her eyes, which used to be wide and bright, where flat and lusterless. Her hair, having not been cut, was now very long, flowing down to her waist. She barely spoke, only when it was necessary and she refused to leave the house, and had dropped out of her art class. Her brothers and her father were worried sick about her. They were sure that she was about to commit suicide at any moment.

"We should tell Papa about the meeting we had with Earnest's parents," Anthony told his brother. "Papa'll know what to do."

"I thought we agreed that it was best that Earnest was outta her life. Why do you think we intercepted all those letters that he mailed to her?"

"Yeah but look at her. She's depressed. This has been going on for months. I'm afraid for her, Sal. We have to do something."

When Rocco heard about the meeting, he was upset with his sons. "Why didn't you tell me anything about it?"

Sal shrugged, "We didn't think there was a reason to. It was no big deal."

"We can't let her go on this way. We thought that she would get over it…maybe she will, but it's been a while now. We have to tell her," Anthony said, worried about his twin.

"We should get him here." Rocco went over to his desk and dialed a number.

"Yeah, Pete. He goes to Georgia Law. Find him. Tell him that Angelina wants to see him…its really important. Yeah, buy him a ticket if he could get up here." Rocco hung up the phone and turned to look at his sons.

"Okay. Let's see where this goes."

Anthony balked at his father. "Whaddaya mean? Do you mean to get the two of them together?"

Rocco lit a cigarette and took a long drag before answering. "Maybe. That might not be such a bad idea."

"Papa, what are you talking about? You want that they should get married or something?"

Rocco shrugged his shoulders. "Angelina loves him. He loves her. That's a good thing. Look at her getting all sick over him. Besides, he might become a useful member of this family."

"How so?" Anthony demanded in a surly manner.

"He's a smart guy. He's gonna be a lawyer and besides that, which is the most important, he's an outsider. He's one of them. A part of the Anglo society. He could be a bridge between them to us, you know. That could help us out a lot. He could be a big help, you know."

"Who says he's gonna wanna help us?" Sal asked, more than a little ticked off because it seemed that his father was siding with someone whom he considered the enemy.

"He will. You just watch and see," Rocco said scratching his jaw. "Just think of this as a business arrangement, boys."

Anthony and Sal exchanged looks. They weren't sure what to say.

Ψ

"I've had enough studying for the night," Abner said as he closed his textbook shut, "I'm gonna go and get some sleep. These finals are going to be a killer. Are you coming?"

"Not yet. I'll be home in a while. I still want to do a little more work on these case files," Earnest said, glancing up.

"All right. I'll see you later," Abner said shrugging into his coat. He walked out of the library.

After about an hour, finally Earnest had had enough. He looked up at the clock on the wall. It was one fifteen in the morning. It was time for him to get some rest. He had classes early tomorrow.

He noted that it was deathly quiet in the library as he walked towards the door. Outside, he could hear the chirping of the crickets, but besides that, there was nothing. No one was around and shadows were everywhere. He walked briskly towards his Cadillac. As he got closer and closer to his car, he could see that a dark haired man was leaning against it smoking a cigarette. Winston was alarmed. His first instinct was to run, but he realized that wouldn't solve anything. Also, it was apparent that the man had already seen him. So he decided to just continue walking and see what the man wanted. Whatever it was, he would face it like a man.

Players of the Game

Earnest walked up to the car, the man's dark eyes followed him. "Earnest, am I right?"

"Who's asking?" Earnest responded belligerently, sure that he was about to get mugged. His eyes darted around him, expecting to see others come from the shadows.

"I ain't here to do nothing to ya. I got a message for you from Mr. Rocco Gionelli."

Earnest looked at the man warily. The man stared back at him, revealing nothing in his rather bland, pale looking face. Earnest said nothing.

"Rocco wants to know if you can come up to Chicago this weekend. He wants to speak with you."

Earnest's face turned hostile. "Why? So he can get rid of me?" Earnest stalked up to his car door and opened it, "Do you think I'm an idiot or something?" he asked, before he went into his car and shut the door.

The man came up to the open window. "This ain't about whacking you or nothing. He wants to *see* you. It's about Angelina. There's no need to be afraid for ya well bein'. This is a totally amicable meetin' Mr. Hurst. Mr. Gionelli is willing to pay for your train going and coming. And you can stay at the house, or if you feel more comfortable, he'll pay for a hotel."

Earnest stared at him. He didn't know whether to believe this man or not.

The man reached into his coat and pulled out a train ticket. He gave it to Earnest. "Use it if you could come. Mr. Gionelli'll call you tomorrow evening, so you know that it's legit." The man backed away from the car. "Well, nice meeting you Mr. Hurst. But I gotta get outta here. Have a good night."

And with that, the man walked away until he disappeared into the shadows of the night.

Earnest stared down at the train ticket in his hand. Angelina. Her name made his heart speed up at the mention of it. He still missed her and loved her. Not a day had gone by that he never thought about her. Since being in law school, he hadn't even looked at another woman. All the others seemed to pale in comparison to Angelina. She was his flower, his jewel.

He decided that he would go. No matter what was waiting for him in Chicago, he was going to go. And if he was to be blown away, at least he would get to see Angelina before he went to meet his maker.

Ψ

When Earnest saw Angelina, he couldn't believe his eyes. She was almost all skin and bones. Her eyes, which were always so large and black, dominated her face even more, giving her haunted, desperate look. Earnest felt his heart plunge to his feet. A lump filled his throat.

"My darling Angelina," he whispered. He slowly held out his arms, "My darling, my love."

Angelina looked at him, her eyes full of pain. She looked at her brother and her father who stood nearby observing. Rocco nodded at his daughter. She looked back at Earnest and walked slowly into his arms. She rested her head against his chest and began to cry. Earnest held her small body, swaying as he did so. He kissed her on the top of her dark head. He didn't care that they were watching. It was like he and Angelina were the only ones in the room. Finally, they were together again. Oh, how he loved her. He didn't want anyone else, just her. He knew what he had to do.

Earnest gently removed himself from Angelina's grasp and moved away. He turned to look at Sal, his expression was neutral. Earnest then turned towards Rocco who was looking at his daughter with an expression of relief. "Mr. Gionelli. I love your daughter Angelina and she is one of the best things that happened to me. And it would be my honor if you would grant my request for your permission to ask for her hand in marriage."

Ψ

Earnest's friends and family had protested loudly against his engagement to Angelina. Earnest was disappointed to find out that his parents were against the marriage, saying that if they had known that she was Italian, they wouldn't have supported the relationship.

"A Catholic?!" Earnest's mother had exclaimed. "You must be out of your mind. And an Italian…those people are so different from us, Earnest. It would never work."

Fortunately, they didn't know anything about her being the daughter of a mob boss. That of course, would have only made things worse. But he knew that it was only a matter of time before they got word of it. Some of Earnest's family, who knew a few details about the situation, were calling it a shotgun wedding. But Earnest didn't pay that any attention. There were also some outcries coming from Angelina's side. Family members and friends thought it was crazy for her to be marrying a non-Catholic and even worse, a non-Italian They though that Rocco Gionelli was crazy, allowing this wedding to take place. What would a non-Italian know about their customs and heritage? Nothing at all, they thought bitterly. But despite that, Earnest and Angelina were married that fall on September 1st, 1938. Abner stood as his best man. He had been one of the loudest protesters, knowing fully about her family's involvements, but in the end, he had been there for Earnest anyway. He knew that his friend was marrying Angelina for all the right reasons—he was in love with her, and she with him.

It was decided that Angelina would stay in Chicago for the rest of the year to finish up her art classes and come back down with him to Georgia after the winter holidays and their honeymoon In another two years, he would be done law school and business school. Rocco didn't much like the idea of his daughter going down to the south to live, but she was a married woman now and he believed that she had to follow her husband, no matter where that might be. Besides, he comforted himself with the fact that he had some family living in Atlanta.

So rather reluctantly, Rocco had bought them a big spacious house down in the city of Atlanta, Georgia. He also bought them a new Lincoln. Earnest moved into the house when he went back down to start his fall semester on September 6. Both he and Angelina knew that a honeymoon at the moment would be impossible. They decided that they would go on one after the Christmas day.

"You ever need somebody when you're down there, you can call my cousin Frankie. He got a nice family, wife and kids and all. I told them all about you, so don't be surprised if they ask you over for dinner or something. Don't forget, you're family now. And I hope your folks will come around, I know they aren't taking this well at all," Rocco had told him before he left.

Yeah, that was to say the least. His parents were taking his marriage to Angelina very badly. As if though it was a funeral. In fact, he got a sense of how badly it was when he got a call later on the next week from his mother.

"How could you? Are you crazy? This on top of everything else," she had shrieked into his ears the moment he picked up the phone.

Earnest sighed, knowing that he was in for it now. "What is it, Mom?"

"I know about that Italian girl you married. I know about her family! How could you marry into the mob? You married a mob princess!" his mom screeched. "Your father's sick, Earnest." Then she began to sob.

"What do you mean Dad's sick?" Earnest asked, with fear.

"He had a heart attack. He's in the hospital."

"I'll come down this weekend and see him," Earnest said hurriedly

"Don't bother. You'll only upset him more," she snapped. "After this marriage of yours to that gangster's daughter, everything has gone down hill."

"Who told you this?" Earnest asked, softly. "About her father being a gangster?"

"The whole town's talking about it, Earnest," she wailed.

"Mom, how would they know about what's happening in Chicago that all the way down in Texas?"

"I don't know, but they do! Word travels Earnest. You've hurt me so bad. How could you do this?"

"What makes you so sure that it's true?" Earnest asked, getting defensive.

"Then tell me it's a lie! Tell me!" his mother yelled hysterically.

Earnest didn't answer.

"I should have known. A Dego. A damn Guinea."

"Don't say that Mom. You're talking about my wife," he snapped, anger seeping in.

"Maybe I could have gotten past that, but your father and I will not accept the fact that she has family in the mob. And if you stay married to her, I guess you could pretty much stop speaking to us. We can't be a part of that way of life."

"Mom, please. Don't do this. You can't believe everything you hear...Angelina has nothing to do with it. She can't help what her family does. Try to understand. Please, let me come see father."

"I'm sorry Earnest, but I can't. This is a very foolish thing for you to have gotten into. You know where we are, but we will not be getting involved. And I don't want you to come down here. This whole situation with you and this Angelina is what's gotten your father in this position to begin with. Goodbye." And with that, she hung up the phone.

Earnest replaced the receiver, his mind heavy with thought. His mother had more or less given him an ultimatum between his wife and his parents. She had also said that he was the reason that his father was sick. He was the one killing his father. He loved his parents and he loved his wife. The only difference was that he had a responsibility towards his wife, so he had to choose her. This was his life now, his parents would have to accept it. He was sure that they would come around eventually.

The next Friday after classes, Earnest got a phone call.

"Hey, Earnest. This is Frankie Arnone. How are you doing?"

Earnest was a little taken aback. He didn't expect to be getting a call from Frankie, Although Rocco had told him about him.

"Hello. I'm fine, and how are you?" Earnest responded, sitting down in an armchair.

"I'm great. Listen, my cousin told me that you were here in town, and my wife and I would like if you were to come over for dinner. Introduce you to the family and all that."

"That sounds great. I'm free this weekend...I'm not too sure about next week..."

"Well, what about you come this Sunday? Isabella will cook a meal the likes of which you've never tasted before!" he promised with a chuckle.

Earnest couldn't help but laugh. "That sounds great. What time shall I be there?"

"How about around one. That seems like a good enough time."

"Okay, sounds good," Earnest said making a mental note.

"Great. Then it's set," there was a beat, "and welcome to the family, Earnest. My cousin tells me that you're a good guy."

"Thank you, Sir, I appreciate that," Earnest said sincerely.

"All right, all right, I'll see you on Sunday. And none of that 'Sir' stuff. Call me Frankie, son. You have a good day and if you need anything, feel free to give us a call. Don't even hesitate, do you hear?" Frankie said intently.

"Thank you...Frankie. I will," Earnest said. "What is it that you would like me to bring?"

"Whatcha mean?" he asked, befuddled.

"I mean, for the dinner. A dish or something."

"Nah, nah. I don't want you to bring me no dish no bowl or whatever," he said jokingly. "Just bring yourself, alright?"

"All right," Earnest said with a smile. He already liked the man.

After they hung up the phone, Earnest went to bed thinking that he would bring some wine over there on Sunday despite what Frankie said. He didn't like going to anyone's dinner empty handed. That was something that his mother always taught him.

Before he went over to the Arnone's house, he swung by the store and picked up a bottle of good white wine. He got to the house about five minutes to one. A young girl, that looked to be around sixteen, with light brown hair and green eyes answered the door. She smiled at him.

"Are you Earnest?" she asked, looking at him curiously.

Earnest smiled, "Yes I am."

"So you're the one that my cousin married."

"That's right."

"You're in law school, right?" she asked.

"Yes I am," Earnest answered with a smile.

"Where are you from again?" the girl asked.

"Deena, let him in, huh? Go help your mother in the kitchen and quit interrogating him," a voice boomed from behind her.

The girl turned around and scowled. "Aww, Dad. I was just asking him a few questions."

"Yeah, yeah," said a husky, middle-aged man approaching from behind. He shooed Deena away. "Go on now. Why you got to pester everybody that comes to this house? That's why we ain't got a lot of guests," he said with a laugh.

Deena reluctantly left, disappearing into the house.

Frankie held the door open. "Why don't you come on in? Sorry about my daughter, she's too nosey for her own good," he said with a laugh.

"Well, no problem there. She has the right to be curious about me. After all, I married her cousin."

Frankie smiled, revealing a row of perfect white teeth. His light brown eyes shone. "Well, I guess we can't blame her too much. Come on, let me introduce you to the family."

Earnest followed him into the large airy kitchen where a woman with light, wavy hair stood in an apron, mixing something in a bowl. She looked up and smiled when she saw them come in.

"Hello. You must be Earnest," she said wiping off her hands. She came over, Earnest held out his hand. She pulled him in and gave him a hug instead and patted him on the cheek.

"I don't give handshakes to family and friends," she said with a smile.

"This is my darling Isabella. The most beautiful Florentine anyone could find."

Isabella blushed and flicked a hand at him. "Oh, cut it out Frankie," she said obviously pleased with her husband's compliment. "Anyways. Dinner should be ready soon. I just have a few things to tie up."

"No problem baby. Where's Michael and Donovan?" Frankie asked his wife.

"They're outside in the back. I hope they're not running around out there, I don't want them to mess up what they have on," she fussed.

"Odds are, hon, they probably already have," Frankie said with a smirk. "Ah well. They can change into something else if they're too messed up," Frankie turned to Earnest. "Come on, I want you to meet my sons."

Earnest followed him through the house. "You have a very nice house, Frankie," Earnest commented looking around.

"Thank you."

Finally, they were outside. Earnest could see two boys chasing each other around and screaming in the spacious backyard. They had dark hair and they looked to be around four years in age. He saw that Deena was sitting in a chair reading on the patio.

"Don and Mikey. Get over here and say hi to your new cousin Earnest," he boomed.

The boys stopped and looked up.

"Come on over, huh? Humor your father," Frankie said waving his hands.

The boys looked at each other and came over, curiosity finally bringing them over.

"Are they twins?" Earnest asked, although they didn't look exactly alike.

"They are, but they ain't identical," Frankie answered and then said, "come on and say hello to your cousin Earnest."

The two little boys came up to them.

"All right," Frankie said putting his hand on the small shoulder of one boy with green eyes, "this here's Mikey. Say hi."

The boy waved and said, "Hello."

Frankie put his hand on the other little boy with the same light brown eyes as his father, "And this here's Don."

Don said, "Hello," and then, "Can we go and play now?"

"Yeah, yeah. Get outta here," he said ruffling their hair, "Just don't get your clothes are dirtied up before dinner."

"Okay, Daddy!" they called as they rushed back to their play.

"Now that you've met the family," Frankie said as they stepped into the house, "Why don't we go into the library from some before dinner drinks. Well, let me ask you first, do you drink?"

"I sure do," Earnest replied, and then seeing the raised eyebrow from Frankie after that comment, he quickly added "In moderation of course. I'm not a drunk or anything like that."

Frankie chuckled. "I didn't think that you were. Come on sit down. What would you like?"

Earnest sat down in a plush leather chair. "I'll have a scotch on the rocks."

"Coming right up," Frankie said heading off to mix the drinks.

They sat back and chatted about various topics. Frankie was thinking to himself that here was a bright young man. They were pretty much as ease with each other by the time that Isabella called them for dinner.

The dinner was wonderful. Earnest couldn't remember the last time that he had so much good food. When he finished off the first plate of food, Mrs. Arnone was piling on some more. He was thinking that these Italians sure could cook and if Angelina was half the cook that Mrs. Arnone was, he would be a very happy man indeed.

"Eat, Eat, Earnest. You need to keep your strength up, young man!" Isabella would exclaim as spoonfuls of pasta, meat, and sauces was heaped upon his plate.

And Earnest ate every bit of it and then some. By the time he was done, he was stuffed to the gills and could barely move. Afterwards, they went out in the backyard and sat down as they drank cool lemonade. Earnest drank half a glass and couldn't take in anymore. He was sure that he was going to explode.

Finally, it was time for him to go home.

"You drop by anytime you want, Earnest, consider this your home," Mrs. Arnone told him as she gave him a kiss on the cheek.

"That's right. Come over anytime and you don't gotta worry about calling us beforehand, all right?" Frankie added, patting him on the back.

"Thank you," Earnest responded, with a smile.

"No problem. I know you got studying to do and all."

"Yeah, I sure do. But thank you for the meal."

"No problem at all," Frankie said. "Later this week, I'll send Deena over with some food, huh?"

"Sure, sounds good. It'll be a change from my usual diet of canned food," Earnest said jokingly.

Later that week, true to his word, he had food sent to his house. But instead of Deena, it was Mrs. Arnone that showed up at the door. She gave him a smile. "I have some *Arancine* here for you. I think you'll like it and some *Caponata*, which is a sort of salad. And I brought some dessert for you…some *Cannoli*!"

Earnest had put the food in the fridge after Mrs. Arnone left. It sure looked good. He would have some later for dinner.

Later that day, Abner came over to the house to study for their end of the semester exam. They studied for a while and then took a break to eat. Winston took out the food that Isabella brought over for him.

Abner eyed the food with interest. "What's all this? I see your getting into the ethnic food now," he remarked.

"Isabella, Rocco's cousin's wife, brought it over for me," Winston told him as he brought down some plates.

"Well, it can't be as good as Jewish food, but I'll try it anyways," Abner sniffed.

Winston laughed at his friend. "You would say that, wouldn't you."

Abner grinned in response. They ate the food and talked.

"So, you say that Angelina is coming up here in January?" Abner asked, eating a *cannoli*.

"Yep. She'll be up here in January. You know, I miss her so much."

"Even though you go down every other weekend to see her?" Abner teased.

"Of course. She's my wife. I'll only be completely satisfied when she's here beside me next month," Winston said.

"Speaking of that, so what's it like being a married man?" Abner asked.

Winston shrugged. "Well, It's pretty good. As long as you like who you're married to."

They both laughed heartily and finished their meal. Afterwards they studied far into the night.

Chapter Seventeen

After their honeymoon in Greece, all expenses paid by Rocco, Angelina moved her things into the Georgia house and they began their life together. Earnest was extremely happy. He felt as if he were dreaming. He had has dream woman, a sweet sensitive, loving woman that was all his and he loved her dearly.

"I'm so glad that you're here with me now. I missed you," Angelina said, leaning on his chest. They were sitting on the couch in the living room

Earnest wrapped his arms around her small frame and kissed the top of her dark head. "Even though I came up there to see you every other weekend?" he asked, smiling.

"Still. I missed you when you weren't there," she answered, her eyes closed.

Earnest smiled. "I missed you too," he held her chin and tipped her face up towards his.

"We had a nice honeymoon, didn't we," he said softly. It was beautiful. A week and a half of relaxation. Making love to Angelina who was fresh and inexperienced was like a dream. It was a pleasure teaching her and having her beautiful lush body with the large, taunt breasts and smooth curving hips and nicely rounded thighs. He loved the way that she stared at him adoringly with her dark eyes.

Angelina flushed and turned her eyes downward. Earnest smiled. She was so innocent and he loved that.

"Don't be ashamed, darling, I'm your husband, and you're my wife," Earnest said softly.

She turned her eyes back up to him. He leaned in and kissed her passionately and deeply. The kiss went on and became more urgent and hungry. Earnest loosened her hair and laid her back on the couch. Her dark hair was spread out like curtain.

"You are so beautiful," he whispered as he undid the first button on her shirt.

And that was how they spent the first evening together at their house.

Ψ

Fall, 1939

Earnest was about to begin his last year in law school when he realized that he was going to be in some serious financial problems he wasn't careful. He was in debt from all the loans that he had taken out for law school and he had no idea how he was going to pay for this last year. He had just recently, and quite unexpectedly, been laid of from a fairly good paying job as a floor manager at a retail store. He had then scrabbled in search for a job and just two weeks ago, he managed to land a job as a clerk at the post office. But this job was considerably less in pay, and it wasn't going to cut it. He couldn't pay the leftover school fee that his loan didn't cover, *plus* the household bills with this current job. He couldn't go to his parents, because he wasn't on good terms with them and he didn't want to ask his father-in-law for any money. Somehow he felt, that if he did, in a way, Rocco would then own him. He didn't want to owe him anything. Although he was his wife's father, Earnest knew the type of things that Rocco was involved in and he wanted no part of it. That was his biggest reason for not asking for help. . Secondly, It would be a definite stab to his pride. Rocco had given him and Angelina a car and a house. That was more than enough. What kind of man would he be if he couldn't take care of his family? Finally, he made the decision to postpone going the last year until he had enough money.

Angelina and he were sitting down over dinner when Earnest announced to her that he would be working this fall instead of going to law school.

Angelina looked at him with shock in her face. "Why are you doing that?"

"Well, I want to take a break and work for a while. I think a need a breather," Earnest said, putting a forkful of fettuccine in his mouth.

Angelina looked at him speculatively. "Why do you think that you need a break?"

"Well, I'm getting a little tired going to school and stuff. I want to get out into the working world for a while."

Players of the Game

"Are you sure?" Angelina said not fully believing him.

"Yeah I'm sure. Now come on and let's finished eating in peace," Earnest said with a touch of testiness.

And so they did.

Ψ

Angelina didn't believe a word of what Earnest told her over the dinner table yesterday evening. The next morning, the first thing she did was to call the University of Georgia Law School. She called the extension for the financial office. A woman answered the phone and identified herself as Mrs. Dresco.

"Hello. I want to make an inquiry concerning a student called Earnest Hurst."

"What is that you want to know?" The woman asked her.

"Well, can you find out if he has made his payment for the fall?" Angelina asked.

"First of all, may I ask who this is?" the woman questioned.

"My name is Angelina. I am his wife and he asked me to check up on this," she responded, trying to keep all the confidence in her voice.

"Okay. Let me just check here…well, no he hasn't. He hasn't made a payment since…January 15. That was payment for the past semester that has just passed. The next payment for fall would have been due, under normal circumstances, on May 23. But Winston has come in and discussed his situation with me. He said that he lost his job. He found a new one, but it doesn't pay enough. He wouldn't be able to pay for school.. As a result of that, he told us that he decided to take that last year off and finish off at a later date. He's such a good student, that we agreed to this. He could come back when he is ready and only take the remaining credits that he needs. But I'm sure you've heard all of this before, has he come up with a means to pay? Is that why he asked you to call?" the woman inquired.

"Oh, yes. We actually did find a way to do it. Will it be all right if we were to make the payment on Monday next week?" Angelina asked.

"Oh, that would be fine. Even thought it would be late. It is July."

"Yeah I know," Angelina said quickly. Of course, she knew it was past the due date. She didn't need this woman telling her that.

Angelina hung up the phone and digested the information that she had just learned. So Earnest had lied to her. He never told her that he was in any sort of financial problems concerning school. And secondly, he never told her that he lost his job as a floor manager Macey's. She decided that she would confront him.

"Why didn't you tell me that you were having problems paying for school?"

Earnest looked at her with unconcealed shock. "What do you mean?"

"I know about you loosing your job at Macey's and you not being able to finish off law school," she countered. "Why didn't you tell me?"

Earnest's face turned red. "How did you find out about that? Did you go snooping around?" he demanded

"Earnest, I wanted to know what was going on. You weren't telling me anything. So I called your school—"

"I can't believe you did that!" he shrieked. Angelina stepped back, a little frightened. He looked so enraged. "I can't believe my wife was sneaking around my back, getting into all my affairs as if though I am a little child. How dare you!"

Angelina was hurt, she only wanted to help him. "But we're married. Don't you think that we should confide in each other? Tell each other everything?"

"That's no excuse! I had my reasons for not saying anything. It has nothing to do with you," he boomed, fist clenched at his sides. He stepped back and sat down heavily on the couch. He put his face in his hands, rubbed his face, and looked up at her.

"I don't want to talk about this anymore. You had no right to do what you did," Earnest said, his green eyes dark.

"Can't you use your trust fund money?" Angelina asked him.

"Are you kidding me? I don't get to touch that money until I'm thirty five," Earnest said derisively.

"Well, can't you ask your parents for a loan?" Angelina questioned.

Earnest looked at her as if she were a remedial child. "You've got to be joking. Come crawling back to them? Hell no! nothing would give my father more satisfaction than to see me fall flat on my face with this law school thing. I won't do it," he said with finality.

"Well Earnest, maybe my father could help you—"

"No!" Earnest snapped. "I'm not taking any money from your father. Who do you think I am?"

"My husband. And I love you. I just want to help you. I'm sure my father wouldn't mind Earnest.'

"There's no way," Earnest said chopping the air with his hand, "What kind of man do you think I am? He's already bought us this house, a car…now you want me to ask him to give me some more? There's no way in hell."

"But—"

"No!" Earnest rumbled. "That's it! I don't want to hear another word about it. I'll work for a year and save. Then I'll go back and finish. End of discussion," he said before he stalked from the room.

But for Angelina, it wasn't over.

Ψ

The next day when Earnest came back from work, He noticed that the house was empty. He called out Angelina's name and didn't get a response. Finally, he saw a note on the dinner table from her.

I went to Frankie's house for a while to pick up some food that Aunt Isabella has made for us. I'll be back in a little bit. Love Angelia.

Earnest sat down and switched on the radio. He listened to an announcement discussing how America was aiding the British in their fight against Germany. The Americans were doing almost everything to help them, except getting into the war themselves. The newscaster discussed the passing of a peacetime draft bill. Earnest wasn't too surprised. There was only so much that we could do to stay out of the war. He was sure that pretty soon America would be entering the war.

When Angelina came home that evening, she didn't look happy.

"What's the matter?" Earnest asked, coming over to her.

"Did you hear about the peacetime draft?" she asked, taking off her jacket. She was holding a dish of food. She didn't know why it was so cold today considering it was only September.

"Yeah, I heard about it," Earnest said uneasily.

"What if you get drafted for that?" Angelina asked, in an accusing tone.

"So what. It's only a peacetime draft. It's not as if we're going to war," Earnest replied.

Angelina pressed her lips together tightly. She walked past him and into the kitchen. Earnest turned around and watched her retreating back.

"What's the matter?" Earnest asked. "Why are you so mad?"

Angelina placed the dish down on the counter turned around and faced him, her face a frozen expressionless mask,

"I'm going to go and make dinner. You do want to eat dinner, don't you?"

Ψ

In October, 1941, Angelina found out that she was pregnant. She paid close attention to all the strife building up in Europe. She was terrified. Terrified that at any moment America would go to war. This meant that Earnest would go away and she might never see him again. Every time she thought about this, it made her sick.

It had been over a year since Earnest had dropped out of law school and began to work full time. Angelina had finally realized that Earnest was not backing down. He still refused to take any money for help to go to school.

"I almost have enough. By next year, I'll have enough to go back to school," Earnest told her.

"By then a war might break out here!" Angelina cried out to him. She had just gotten home from the doctor's office and had yet to tell her husband the news of her pregnancy.

"It's not going to happen so soon. Believe me," Earnest said, trying to calm her down.

"But Earnest, look at what's been going on! Germany invading the Soviet, Germany seizing Leningrad…gosh that Hitler is crazy! He could do anything," Angelina cried out frantically.

Earnest had had enough his wife's bickering mood, he turned on her with ferocity. "What the hell's that matter with you? Why are you pestering me today, huh?" he yelled, his face red with rage.

Angelina closed her mouth and stared at him. Her eyes filled up with tears. "I love you Earnest. I don't want anything to happen to you... and especially not now."

He looked at her confused. "What do you mean?"

"I'm pregnant, Earnest. I just found out today," she said barely above a whisper.

Earnest plopped down on the sofa, his head in his hands. He didn't say anything.

Angelina sat beside him and placed a hand on his shoulder. "Earnest, talk to me. Please don't do this."

His face was covered with his hands. He didn't move or say a thing.

"Honey you're scaring me," Angelina said, her eyes wide with alarm. "Please say something."

Earnest slowly raised his head. "If we declare war, I'll be called Angelina. There's no doubt about it. I had to register for the peacetime draft and I'll definitely be going to war if we have one," Earnest said slowly.

Angelina began to cry. "But the baby. Please Earnest. If you'll only ask—

Earnest shot up from the sofa. "No way are we going to rehash that again. I'm not going to ask your father for the money to go to school. Don't bring that up again. It's a dead end, trust me. Besides, school or no school, I'd still have to go to war."

Angelina stood up and came beside him. She tried to touch his face, he jerked away. "But baby...

"Cut it out, Angelina. You're only getting me mad. You don't know when to give up."

Suddenly Angelina was filled with rage. She picked up a vase resting on the table. It was a Waterford vase that a cousin had given them for their wedding. She hurled it at the wall in fury. It shattered loudly and the pieces fell all over the floor. Earnest looked at the broken pieces and then at her in stunned silence.

"Damn it!" she screamed. "You won't even listen to me. This isn't about you, this is about out child! We're going to have a baby! I don't want her father dead! I don't want to raise her by myself," she wailed, her hair wild and crazy, just like her eyes.

Earnest looked at his wife, her large chest heaving in anger. "How do you know it's a girl?"

She sat down in the couch. "I can feel it. I just do…I can't really explain it," she said softly. She looked up at him, her eyes suddenly soft, "Can you imagine her? Maybe she'll have your green eyes, my dark hair or even your auburn hair…she'll be beautiful. Don't you want to see that?"

Suddenly it seemed as if the room changed and he was in another world. He could almost see her standing there. Her hair russet, her eyes the dark liquid pools of her mother. Her small arms opened wide, asking for a hug from him, from her father. She was beautiful.

Earnest began to cry, tears fell from his eyes. He abruptly turned and walked towards the door. Angelina followed after him in alarm,

"Where are you going?" she asked, her small arms pulling at his shirt. "Please, don't leave. I'm sorry baby. I'm so sorry."

He tugged himself from her grasp and when she latched on again, he tugged away, once again.

"Are you coming back!" she shrieked. She began to cry loudly, "Don't go—" she could barely speak as the sobs racked her body.

He pulled her hands off one last time before he was through the door. He closed it behind him.

He was barely up the driveway before she came out, standing on the porch. She screamed at him, her eyes wild and her appearance disheveled.

"Damn you, Earnest! Come back ,you coward! You're not a man! What man walks away from his pregnant wife?!" she shrieked loudly. The whole neighborhood could hear. He could see a few faces peeking from behind curtains.

He walked swiftly back to where his wife stood at the porch, her eyes popped wide open in alarm. He gripped her upper arm.

"Please. I'm sorry Earnest," she cried as she struggled against him. He was pulling her back into the house, "Stop!" she screamed. "Please!" she sobbed. She began to wail.

"Shut the fuck up!" He whispered harshly, "You will *not* embarrass me in front of the neighbors. I know you're probably used to scenes, but I won't have it," he said jerking her through the door.

He slammed the door behind them. He then turned around and gripped both of her upper arms. She struggled. "No, no!" she cried in a high pitch wail.

Earnest pushed her onto the sofa and just stared at her. Her hair was tumbled across her face, she looked terrified.

Suddenly, the wind had gone out his sail. He stepped back and looked at her in sorrow. He turned and walked towards the door. He left, slamming the door behind him.

This time Angelina didn't follow him

Ψ

Earnest stayed in the bar for as long as he could. He drank beer after beer, drink after drink until the world swirled around him.

The bartender, a small Irish man with brown hair and blue eyes finally came up to where he sat slumped on a stool.

"Come on, partner, it's high time you got out of here," the man said calmly, not wanting any trouble.

"Says who?" Earnest slurred.

"Says I," the man responded, smartly.

"Yeah?" Earnest slobbered, his eyes bugged open in mockery, "Well, I don't give a fuck, you little leprechaun."

Before the man could open up his mouth for a response, a hand clamped down firmly on Earnest's shoulder. Earnest turned around and looked up. The face hovering above him looked a little blurry. He squinted and saw the face of Frankie.

"Come on kid, let's get you home," Frankie said gently pulling on his arm.

Earnest shook his head. "I don't wanna. I think I wanna stay here," he said and turned around to face the bartender, "with my little friend here. You know, my mom's mother has a sprinkling of Irish in her," he slurred.

The bartender looked at him, shook his head, and walked off to the other end of the bar to attend to the other customers. He was sure that whoever the other guy was, he would take care of the drunken bum.

"Come on. We're going home right now," Frankie said, trying to pull him up.

Earnest shrugged. "I guess I could," he looked at the bartender on the other end of the bar. "I don't think he likes me too much."

"Frankly Earnest, I don't like you too much right now," Frankie boomed. "Now let's get you up."

Earnest gave him a sloppy nod and attempted to rise. He lost his balance and tumbled over. Frankie reached out to try and catch him, but missed. The side of Earnest's head connected with the edge of a table before he hit the floor.

There were gasps as Frankie and the others in the bar crowded around him. Earnest shifted on the floor. Frankie stooped down and touched his shoulder. "Are you all right?" he asked.

Earnest slowly sat up and held his head. It was bleeding heavily. "I think my head is going to explode," Earnest said with pain.

"Hey, can one of yous bring me a towel or something and stopping standing here gaping at him," Frankie snapped.

People scattered. They didn't know who this man was, but his voice sounded like he was a man that didn't take any kind of nonsense.

The bartender brought them a towel. Frankie thanked him and put it against the side of Earnest's head.

"Here, hold it," Frankie said as he looped an arm around Earnest's waist. The bartender came over and helped Frankie bring Earnest up.

"Thanks. Can you help me bring him out to the car?" Frankie asked the short man.

"Yes, of course."

The two men brought him to the car and once he was seated in the passenger side, they shut the door.

"Here, let me give you this," Frankie said, pulling some money out of his wallet.

The bartender automatically shook his head. "No need for that, mate."

"No, no. Just take it. For all the trouble. Thanks for the help. This is my cousin's husband, you know. He usually doesn't get on like this…but they been going through something so…"

The bartender nodded his head knowingly. "I understand. Just keep the money. I don't want it."

"Here," Frankie said stuffing it into the man's apron pocket. "I want you to have it." He turned away before the man could protest any further.

Frankie started the car and looked over at Earnest who as sullenly sitting down in silence.

"You got to hold the towel a little tighter than that," he said before backing up and driving off.

Earnest shakily held it tighter to his head. This was definitely not a good night.

Earnest ended up with 16 stitches in his head. It was two o'clock in the morning before he arrived home, via Frankie's driving.

The house was as silent as a tomb.

"Angie!" Earnest called out. There was no response. Earnest turned around and looked at Frankie.

"She's not here. She's over at my house," Frankie explained.

"Why?" Earnest asked, astounded.

"Well, she came over earlier asking me to look for you. She's still over there," Frankie told him. "Why don't you go to bed and sleep it off. We'll deal with this in the morning. Now come on, let me help you the stairs."

"Are you gonna stay here?" Earnest asked, his voice still slurred.

"Yeah, I'll stay the night. We'll get up and talk in the morning," he responded.

"What we got to talk about?" Earnest asked, his eyes closed. His head was killing him and he felt so sick in his stomach.

"We got lots to discuss," Frankie said assuredly.

Suddenly, Earnest's stomach lurched, he rushed to the bathroom where he emptied the contents of his stomach into the porcelain bowl of the toilet. Frankie stood that the door and watched him.

"You all right, kid?" he asked, coming over.

"Yeah," Earnest gasped, lifting his face. He sat back and leaned against the cool tile walls of the bathroom.

"Come on. Let's go to the kitchen. I'll make you some coffee."

Ψ

Later on the next day, Angelina and Earnest were talking things out.

"I love you, Angie, but I want you to understand that I will not be taking any money from your father. I almost have the money that I need to go back." He touched her face. "And don't worry. Nothing's going to happen. We'll be fine."

Angelina just nodded and snuggled in her husband's arms, feeling safe for the moment.

"Mom, Angie's pregnant," Earnest said to his mom over the phone.

He and his parents had kept a cold distance from each other ever since his marriage to Angelina three years ago. But he decided that it was at least fair to let her know about the pregnancy.

His mother didn't say anything for a while. "Angelina's pregnant?" she asked, quietly.

"Yes Mom. I just thought that you should know. After all, it will be your grandchild," he answered.

"Your father died, Earnest," his mother whispered. "He passed away two days ago," she said and broke into sobs.

Earnest's heart dropped. He sat down, suddenly weak. His head was spinning. "Oh God. Mother, are you serious?"

"Of course I am! Why would I say something like that if it wasn't true?"

"Why didn't you call me?" Earnest asked as a lump in his throat formed.

His mother was silent on the other end for a moment before she began to cry.

They cried together on the phone. Finally, his mother spoke.

"We're trying to plan the funeral. Your sister and your brother are coming in. Are you going to come?"

"Yes. I'll come up this weekend. Is it okay if I bring Angelina?"

The mother was silent for a moment. "Please. Is there a way that she could stay there? I'm not ready for her...yet. Please Earnest, understand."

"I just can't leave here. She's my wife," Earnest said firmly

Another silence. "Is she doing okay?" his mother asked, gently.

"Yes, she is."

"How far along is she?" his mother asked, fully interested now.

"About a month and a half," he answered.

"I see." Then a pause. "Thank you for telling me Earnest," his mother said. She paused again, "I have to think—a little," his mother said haltingly.

"Okay Mom, I'll talk to you later," he said, a little sadly.

"All right. Be safe, bye Earnest," she said before she hung up.

Ψ

"You've got to go to your father's funeral, Earnest. If you don't you'll regret it," Angelina told him.

Earnest shook his head firmly. "No. I'm not leaving you here. I'm not leaving my pregnant wife home alone."

Angelina came up to him and placed a gentle hand on him. "Listen. I won't be alone. I'll have Isabella and Frankie. If I need anything, I'll call them. I'll even go and stay with them, for the time that your gone if that makes you feel better."

"No. Angelina, I can't—"

"No, you listen to me. You've had your way this whole time, I bent to you over everything…Earnest, now you listen to me. You've got to go. It wouldn't be right if you didn't. Please…do this for me."

"I'll go, but I'm bringing you with me," he said sternly

Angelina shook her head. "No. Now is not the time for me to be there with them."

Earnest looked into her eyes, seeing her heart. "Okay. I'll go."

Chapter Eighteen

Over at Frankie's house, Angelina and the family were gathered around the radio listening to the same thing.

Yesterday, the Japanese had bombed Pearl harbor. It was December 8, 1941. America would not stand idly by, they had to take action. So America declared war on Japan. America had officially entered the war.

Angelina watched in horror. This meant that soon they would be recruiting men. And that meant Earnest. He was a perfect candidate. He was young and strong and in perfect physical condition.

"Darling, are you all right?" Isabella asked, seeing Angelina's face go pale.

"I-I'm fine. I was just thinking, now that we're in the war…soon they would be drafting people." Angelina ran her hand over her stomach, which was still flat but would soon be swelling with a child.

There was silence all around as they contemplated this.

"Yes…I suppose they would," Frankie answered hesitantly.

Angelina let out a cry and plopped down on her chair. She held her face in her hands. "That means Earnest can be drafted. He might be called to go to war…Oh, God!"

Isabella came up to her and knelt before her. "But honey, Earnest is in school. As long as he's there, he can't be drafted," she said assuring her.

"Not so," Frankie said shaking his head. "They can still call him."

"But he's not even in school anymore, Isabella," Angelina cried. "He's not going back in the fall. He's going to work."

"Why?" Frankie asked, surprised, "It's his last year!"

"He doesn't have the money to finish right now. And he doesn't want to ask his parents for a loan and he wouldn't hear of me asking my father for some help."

"Well, I could understand him wanting to be independent. You know a man doesn't want to have to depend on anyone. He wants to be able to take care of himself and his family by himself," Frankie pointed out.

"I know," Angelina howled. "But do you think that you can talk to him for me? Maybe my father could do something to stop him from being called in…"

Frankie shook his slowly. "I don't know about that, Angelina."

"Please! I don't want him to go off to war and get killed."

Frankie held up his hand. "Okay, okay. I'll try. But don't get your hopes up. You better go talk to your father. Why don't you do that instead?"

"I don't want to talk to my father until Earnest agrees to it. If I do he'll think that I was meddling again and he'll he even more angry with me."

"Okay, okay, fine. I'll talk to him. But I ain't making no promises."

Ψ

"I won't do it Frankie. I have to work this out my own way," Earnest told him.

"You do know that this means you can go to war? Do you want to do that being just married and all?" Frankie asked, putting it to him another way

Earnest looked at him and quickly flicked his eyes away. He hadn't really thought of it that way. But his pride got the better of him. He turned to Frankie with his face set. "If it means that, then that's what will happen. Besides, it's our job to protect out country."

Frankie shrugged his shoulders in defeat. At least Angelina couldn't say that he did nothing. "Let me tell ya. You're making a big mistake."

Ψ

It was about a month's time before the letter arrived stating that Earnest was being drafted for the war. Earnest got to it first. His heart fell as he read it. He had been preparing himself for this, yet when it actually did come, he couldn't hold back his trepidation. Up to this point, Angelina had been begging and pleading with him to let her talk to Rocco. She kept telling him that Rocco might be able to help him stay out of the war. But he had staunchly refused. It was hard for him to do so, seeing the hurt in her eyes, but he had to. If they were going to survive by themselves, they couldn't lean on her father or anyone else. Now here he was holding the draft notice, asking him to report to Camp Wheeler at nine A.M. next Monday morning. He had to find a way to break it to Angelina. Thinking of her reaction made him sicker than the thought of going to war. To go over seas where the chances were high that he wouldn't make it back home alive.

The next day, Earnest was still trying to think of a way to break it to his wife. He came home from work to find her sitting listening to the news on the radio in the den.

She turned to face him, her dark eyes large in her face.

"People are being drafted everyday." She looked so small and frightened. "It's so horrible. Anthony was drafted," she said, her voice flat and devoid of emotion. "He wants to go. Maybe Daddy could have gotten him out of it, but he wouldn't hear of it."

Earnest felt a lump forming in his throat. He had to tell her. On top of all this. Her brother…and now him. Earnest came slowly to her side. He sat down beside her.

Angelina looked at him suspiciously. "What is it?"

Earnest cleared his throat. He was dying inside. A wave of sorrow coursed through his body. His wife's face was blurred before his eyes. He opened his mouth to speak, but no sound came out.

Angelina gasped, her hand moving to her mouth. "Don't say anything, please," she cried. "Just hold me, Earnest please…don't say it." Tears coursed down her face. "Just hold me," she whispered.

So he didn't. He drew her into his arms and held her. They clung to each other for the longest time.

Ψ

Tuesday, July the 14th, 1942 at approximately seven fifteen A.M., Angelina Hurst stood helplessly by as she watched her husband leave her on a train headed to Camp McCain in Grenada, Mississippi. There, he would receive basic training. Isabella and Frankie came along to see Earnest off.

Before Earnest got on the train, he held his wife's face in between his hands.

"Please don't worry, my darling," he said quietly. He pushed a stray strand of black hair away from her face and tucked it behind her ears.

"I can't help it," Angelina sobbed. "I can't help but worry, Earnest."

"I'll be fine honey. I'll be back in no time," Earnest said trying to convince himself as well as her. He couldn't let her see how much going to war was affecting him.

Earnest lovingly put his hands on Angelina's swelling stomach. She was eight months pregnant. He wouldn't be home to see the birth of his child.

He raised her face until she was looking up at him. He slowly swept his eyes over every contour of her face, taking in her watery, dark eyes, her small upturned nose, and her wide generous mouth. A mouth that he had kissed many times. A face that he loved dearly. He had to take in every detail of her and burn it into his mind to hold with him until he came back to her. He didn't know when he would see her again face to face. A bitter taste rose in his mouth.

"Why are you looking at me like that, Earnest?" Angelina asked, plaintively.

Earnest kissed her full on the lips, and said, "No other reason than that I love you." He ran his hand through her long dark hair.

A man in uniform came up behind them and cleared his throat, hating to break up the goodbye.

"Hurst, we're all ready to board. We'll be leaving in about five."

Earnest nodded his head at the corporal and turned back to his wife.

"Well, you'd better get going," Angelina said, trying to make her voice light.

"Yeah," he said regretfully. He turned to Frankie and Isabella who were standing behind them all the while. They walked up to him.

"We will miss you. You just go and fight a good war over there," Isabella said embracing him and giving him a kiss on the cheek."Yeah, you bring yourself back to us all in one piece and that's an order, do you hear me?" Frankie said gruffly. Frankie's eyes were watering and the tears were threatening to break loose. He felt really bad about Earnest going off to war. He had come to think of Earnest as a younger brother or even a son. He wished all the best for him and would be distressed if anything were to happen to him.

Earnest pulled him into a hug. Frankie kissed him on both his cheeks and held him at arms length. "You be good now."

Earnest merely nodded, not trusting himself to speak. He was afraid that if he did, he would fall apart.

He went up to Angelina and gave her one last kiss, holding her small body close to his.

"I love you and don't you ever forget it. No matter what happens," Earnest whispered to her.

Angelina nodded her head, her tears were flowing freely now. Both her twin brother and her husband were going to war and she wasn't sure that she would ever see them again.

The three of them watched as Earnest boarded the train. He kept looking back, but he couldn't help it. Finally, the train began to move. He watched as Angelina stood on the platform, her face a mask of misery. Her dark eyes stared at him, never moving. He stared back. He couldn't even raise his arm to wave. His body felt as if it were made of lead.

He watched her figure until it was just a blur,
And then she disappeared.

Ψ

As the bus pulled into the camp, Earnest looked out the window and took notice of all the men that were dressed in fatigues. Men were in training in the field and there was not one person with a smile. They all looked grim. Some of the men in the field looked over at the bus and shook their heads slowly and sadly. Earnest thought that he heard somebody say to another, "Fresh meat to break down." From that point on, Earnest turned away from the widows and stared straight ahead.

Finally, the bus came to a stop. The bus doors opened and a young man with brown hair and eyes hopped up onto the bus. His dark eyes swept over the bus full of new army recruits.

"All right. My name is Private Brimley. Welcome to Camp McCain," he drawled. But on his face was not an expression of welcome or any goodwill. "Ya'll boys got a long nine weeks ahead of ya . You'll be issued clothing and supplies. After that, you will be assigned to your bunks.

After *that*, you boys have the pleasure of having a free haircut, courtesy of the United Sates Army." He gave them a lopsided grin. "All right men. Get on up and follow me."

Earnest stepped of the bus, following the train of young men. There were mutters and some grunts as they followed the cocky young private that walked with a swagger. Earnest looked around him. Supposedly, Anthony was supposed to be at this camp. He wondered if he was here yet.

Soon they arrived at a building filled with others that had just arrived as well.

He was given a stack of clean clothing that looked a little worn, a scrub brush, some soap, a bucket, and a clothesline. When he got to the very end, a man gave him a rubber stamp that had his name on it. "You're to stamp your name on your belongings. Do it if you don't want to lose your stuff. You'll lose enough stuff as it is."

He thought that the examination he had endured back in Georgia was enough, but apparently, there was more to come. He suffered through yet another extensive physical and numerous shots, some to the behind. It was not pleasant at all. By the time all of that was done, he was pretty miserable. But come to find out that there was still more to go for this day. He and the others were given buzz haircuts. Afterwards, they were given their fatigues, brand new boondockers, and helmets.

Then began the torture.

They were hustled into the field, yelled and screamed at and ordered to stand in a line stretching across the field.

A tall man with ropey muscles, blond peach fuzz hair, and icy blue eyes came before them. He sneered at them and spat on the ground.

"My name's Sergeant Kirkland. I am not here to be your mama or your papa. If you came here expecting to be coddled, let me tell you shit straight right now. This will be one of the worst experiences of your life. Consider this hell, boys. And consider me the gatekeeper. I'm here to whip your boys into shape and to strengthen your mind. Prepare you for battle against the fuckin' Huns and the Japs. I'll do anything to achieve that, even if I have to break you," he said in a deadly serious tone of voice.

Earnest knew this man wasn't lying. Sergeant Kirkland meant business.

Ψ

"Hey, Earnest! Hey!"

It was early morning the next day and Earnest was sitting in the mess hall eating breakfast. It was packed wall to wall with soldiers and noisy conversation was going on all around him. He was sitting across from a young man named Jeremy Hicks and beside him was another young man named Larry Goldsmith.

Jeremy was a short slender man with sandy hair and sparkling gray eyes. He was from Minnesota. Larry was a tall, handsome, gangly young man with black hair, hazel eyes, and well defined features. He was from Boston Massachusetts.

The three of them had been just in the middle of a discussion concerning one of the sergeants, when Earnest heard the calling of his name. He turned around and saw a dark haired, olive complected young man approaching him with a smile on his face. He pushed his way through the crowd of people.

It was his brother-in-law Anthony. Earnest smiled in greeting. "Hey Tony. I was looking for you yesterday. Sit down with us."

Earnest made a space beside him and Anthony sat down. He made introductions.

"Anthony, this is Jeremy and Larry. They're my bunkmates. You guys, this is my wife's brother, Anthony."

They all said hi to each other. They talked as they ate, about their families and friends. Each of them had varying backgrounds. Back in Boston, Larry was up and coming investor. Jeremy was an agriculturist from Nebraska and ran a large farm with his father.

"So, what do you do Anthony?" Larry asked.

Anthony hesitated. "Well, I went to school for business and right now…I'm in construction," he answered vaguely.

"Oh, okay. What company do you work for? Or have you opened your own business?" Jeremy asked.

"Well, the company's kinda new…I don't think you've heard of it. What about you? What kind of farming do you do?" Anthony asked, desperately trying to direct the conversation elsewhere.

"Oh, I do quite a few. My specialty though is Barley and Flaxseed. Before I left, we were starting to grow Canola," Jeremy said proudly.

"I see,." Larry said nodding. "I have a cousin that has a dairy farm out in upstate New York. It's going quite well," he added.

"Are you guys married or anything?" Anthony asked the two men.

"I'm engaged," Larry answered with a slight smile. "Do you want to see a picture of her? I keep it on me all the time." He pulled it out of his pocket.

They all leaned over to look at it. "She's gorgeous," Anthony commented, looking at the handsome, dark haired woman in the photo.

"Thank you. Her name's Rebecca," Larry told them with obvious pride.

"I'm not married or even engaged, but I am seeing someone. I plan to ask her to marry me as soon as I get back. Her name's Heather," Jeremy said with a smile. He showed them the picture of a blond woman with cool good looks and green eyes.

When Earnest saw the picture, his stomach lurched. Jeremy's woman reminded him of Julia. He took a long swallow of his water.

In that brief moment, memories of her came flooding back to him.

Memories that he wanted to forget.

"Hey, Jewboy!" a voice yelled.

The four men turned to see where the yell was coming from.

A ginger haired man with a sprinkling of freckles, was staring down at a young, dark blond haired man at another table. The man with ginger hair had a face red with anger.

"You're in my seat!" the ginger haired man shouted.

The dark blond haired man stood up and scowled at the other young man.

"I don't see any names on the seats," the blond man said, his hazel eyes flashing.

"To hell with that, you kike. You'd better sit with your own or something."

Earnest's stomach lurched. He glanced at Lenny. Lenny's face was red with anger. He stood up.

"Wait a minute Lenny—" Jeremy began, putting a hand on his arm.

Lenny ignored it and walked towards where the two men were standing. The ginger haired man turned to face him. He grinned nastily at Lenny.

"Oh so what do you want now, come to defend your own?"

"You're nothing but a prick. Why don't you scat and find something to do instead of harassing people?" Lenny said, trying to remain calm.

"I will. Why don't you get your friend up and bring him over to where you're sitting at the Jew table?"

At that comment, Anthony and Earnest stood up. They walked over to where Lenny was.

The mess hall was totally silent now as the soldiers watched the scene unfolding before their eyes.

"You've got a real chip on your shoulders, don't you," Earnest stated calmly.

"Screw off and stay out of it, Jew lover" the red haired man said.

"I'm not staying out of anything," Earnest said easily.

"Why don't you just leave this guy alone and let him sit where he wants, like everyone else is doing?" Anthony asked, glancing around.

"Screw off! Besides, what are you…a Guinea? I'd know one of you guys anywhere."

With that, Anthony leaned back and administered a punch that glanced off the ginger haired man's face. The young man stumbled backwards.

"What the hell is going on in here?" Sergeant Kirkland asked, appearing at the door of the mess hall.

"This motherfucker just punched me!" the ginger headed man gasped as he held the side of his face.

Anthony sneered at the bloodied face. "Yeah, well he was harassing people calling them Jewboy and trying to tell them where they should sit."

Sergeant Kirkland stared at Anthony. "Who the hell'd he call a Jewboy?"

Anthony pointed at the dark-blond haired man who was standing up beside them.

Sergeant Kirkland turned to him. "Are you a Jew?" he asked.

The young man glanced quickly around and nodded his head.

"And are you a boy or a girl?"

"I'm a man, Sir" the young man responded, stiffly.

"Okay then," Kirkland continued, completely ignoring his response. "You're a Jew and a boy. Jewboy. I don't see what the big deal is. Another outbreak like this, you all will be in some serious shit."

The young man's face turned red with rage, as did Earnest, Lenny, and Anthony's faces. But they said nothing.

Sergeant Kirkland turned on his heels and walked out.

Chapter Nineteen

Angelina was shocked to see Earnest's mother, Belinda Hurst, standing at her doorway.

"Mrs. Hurst," Angelina said with surprise. She stood there, too shocked to move. She looked down and saw that her mother-in-law was carrying a suitcase.

Belinda smiled tentatively. "Hello. Can I come in?" she asked.

"Of course you can," Angelina said, stepping back and holding the door open.

Belinda stepped in nervously. "May I sit down?"

"Of course you can. Do you want some tea?" Angelina asked, snapping out of it.

"That would be nice, if it's not too much trouble, Angie," she responded, folding her hands.

With one last look, she went to the kitchen and put some water into the pot.

"Would you like some cake? Or something else to eat?" Angelina called out.

"No thank you. Just the tea would be nice," Belinda called.

After the water had boiled, Angelina served the tea. The two women sat down at the table to drink.

"I guess you're wondering why I'm here...Angelina, I want to make peace. I just feel like everything's falling apart. Earnest's father is gone, my two sons are off at war...I want to bury the hatchet. Angelina, can you forgive me?" Belinda pleaded.

Angelina looked into her mother-in-law's green eyes. She had been dreaming for this moment to happen.

"Of course I forgive you. And I want to apologize on my part if I have done anything to hurt you," Angelina said reaching across the table and taking Belinda's hand.

"Thank you so much, Angelina. Now on to another topic, how are you feeling? And my son's been gone for months, and you and the baby are here alone."

Players of the Game

Angelina nodded. "I know. I was going to go and stay with my cousin and his family. My father wants me to come to Chicago, but I don't want to travel all the way over there with Antonia."

Belinda frowned. "I understand." Then there was some silence as she appeared to be thinking about something. Suddenly her face lit up, "Why don't I stay here with you until Earnest comes home?" she suggested, excited by the idea.

Angelina's eyes flicked to the suitcase resting on the foor near Belinda's feet and then back to Belinda's face.

Angelina smiled broadly. "I love that idea. That will give us a chance to get to know each other better."

"I'm so glad I came," Belinda said with tears in her eyes, "Thank you for giving me this chance."

Ψ

In October, 1942, the 1st Division landed in the port city of Oran in North Africa. Unfortunately, after the battle in Oran was through, the division did not stay together, as their commander so wanted them to. The troops were divided up and sent to other units. Earnest, Anthony, Jeremy, and Larry along with a bunch of other men were sent to the British brigade. They were on the Tunisian front. The battling was intense. The air was smoking and resounding with the sounds of explosions and gunfire. As they made their way, Earnest watched as a man from his unit was blown into pieces from a bomb exploding. He had gotten used to such sights, but the first time that he saw something like that, he was sick to his stomach.

"How you holding up?" he screamed over to Larry, who was a few feet away from him.

"I'm fine, at least I think I am," he yelled back. Larry's face was caked with dirt and grime, as was his own, Earnest supposed.

The winter was harsh in Tunisia. It was Christmas day and the war for Longstop Hill raged on. Earnest thought about the picture of his three-month-old daughter, Antonia, that had been sent to him through the mail by Angelina. He felt a swell of pride as he thought of her. He had to make it home alive. His child needed him.

After this battle was over, Earnest along with the others were more-or-less stuck in the hills of Medjez. The Germans had strong fortifications, so it was so hard for the Allied unit to go any farther.

Then in February of 1943, Rommel, the German General, attacked Kasserine Pass. They fought with all their might, but every day, more and more soldiers on the Allied Forces were dying.

"Jeremy!" Earnest screamed, "Move!"

Jeremy turned wild eyes to Earnest and looked down at the grenade that had been thrown near his feet. He ran like a bat out of hell. Fast enough not to get the full brunt of the explosion, but not fast enough to be entirely free of its effects.

With a scream of intense pain, Earnest saw Jeremy go down hard. He rushed over to where Jeremy was. Anthony and Larry, who where never too far away, caught sight of the situation and came immediately over.

"Help me get him up!" Earnest called out unnecessarily to them, considering that they were already automatically going to Jeremy's side.

Earnest looked down and saw a bleeding stub where Jeremy's left leg was supposed to be. Jeremy squinted in pain and small cries of pain were issuing from between his lips. His brow was beaded with sweat. Earnest looked up at the others and they exchanged looks of alarm. Well, at least he was still alive, but he wouldn't be for much longer if they didn't get him out of there.

Finally, the army medics got to him and they took him away. Days later they learned that he had been sent back home.

By the time the battle of Kasserine Pass was over, almost 6,200 troops were dead. But the withdrawal of the Germans had begun. They were finally making headway. Disastrous assaults were made on the German units who were set on fighting to the very last of their men.

Days later, the Germans gave up over 250,000 of their men to the Allies in North Africa. The Allied forces were victorious.

Ψ

"I never thought that I'd get to see my parents' homeland under these conditions," Anthony said when they arrived on the island of Sicily. It was July 9, 1943 at two-thirty in the morning. They had been planning and training for weeks before in North Africa before they arrived on Gela Beach to attack the Germans.

After hours of small arms fighting and the American Navy firing inland at the German tanks from the gulf of Gela, the Germans had retreated, for the time being.

But then the Germans began attacking from the air at the Allied troops. Soon the American forces were being overwhelmed. General Allen desperately requested for more naval gunfire and air support.

Soon the Germans had broken through General Roosevelt's forces, and were advancing towards the edge of the beach. The American troops were ordered to stand strong.

Earnest along with other men hid in foxholes. When the German tanks came within shooting range, the troops would jump out of the holes and shoot at the tank. This did serious damage to the tanks. But this was not good enough. They were still being overrun.

Another regiment hurried to meet these German tanks that had gotten through. The German tanks ended up retreating. And although the Germans tried again later on in the afternoon, they were not victorious. The America Navy was ready for them. Earnest's first division was commanded to further attack and push back the Germans at midnight.

It was at the battle of Troina that German resistance was destroyed. Again, another victory for the Allies.

Earnest felt as if this was never going to end. Despite the victories that they had achieved, he had the depressing feeling that he was never going to see home again. Since Jeremy got injured and was sent home, Anthony, Larry and himself had been sticking together even tighter than ever. The 1st Infantry arrived on the shores of France at approximately 6:30 in the morning on June 1944. Almost immediately, they were being attacked. Only a few squads managed to get off the beach. Finally, they were able to shove through and get behind the enemy positions. This gave coverage to the beach, and the other troops were able to get up the beachhead.

They suffered 3000 casualties. Earnest was extremely saddened at the death of so many of his fellow troops. But he was also happy to be alive. Soon after this, Earnest along with Larry and Anthony were transferred to the 6th Armored Division.

On April, 11, 1945 they liberated the Buchenwald concentration camp. The British and American troops were horrified as they saw the condition that the people were in. Emaciated bodies littered the dirt floor. There was a pile of dead bodies at another end-inside and out of the camp. Bony people in tattered rags with hollowed out eyes stared vacantly, barely able to move let alone speak. The troops immediately searched the ground and incarcerated any SS soldiers in sight. But most had fled to the woods.

Larry was instantly sick. He rushed off to the side and expelled the contents of his stomach. He stooped down and began to sob bitterly. Earnest and Anthony rushed to his side. Earnest too felt the urge to throw up. He couldn't believe what his eyes were taking in. He could barely believe that humans could be treated in this way.

"Look at this! My God!" Larry sobbed, uncontrollably now. He turned watery eyes to the both of them, "These are my people. Look what happened to them. I heard stories, but I never knew that it was this bad."

Earnest put a comforting arm around Larry. Anthony patted his back.

They didn't know what to say.

Soon, there was food circulating around the camp. The food was given out in proper portions, enough that the malnourished people could take in at a time. They were not used to such rich foods after being starved. They were also under constant medical care.

That night, their troops set up camp inside the concentration camp.

They had been discussing the situation at hand when gunfire broke out in the darkness.

The troops were immediately on alert. "What the hell is this!" Anthony exclaimed as a bullet that just barely missed him zoomed by.

They got their guns in hand and ran for cover. They had no idea how many people were out there shooting at them. They were sure that they were some SS soldiers that had escaped the rounding up from earlier on. Or soldiers that had made a run for it at the first indication that the British and American troops were coming.

Earnest saw a figure dash across one building and go behind another one. Earnest shot at him, but missed.

Because they were not sure how many there were, they had to be extremely careful. The troops divided up and sneaked behind and around the buildings with their arms in tow.

Suddenly a barrage of machine gun shots rang out.

"Ahhh!" Larry cried as he was hit. Anthony was instantly at his side. He looked around and spotted Earnest along with two other troops. He yelled to them. "Larry's down! I need help over here." They rushed over. Anthony held Larry's head in his lap.

There was so much blood. The blood was soaking through Larry's clothing and into Anthony's. Anthony's hands were covered with blood as he undid the buttons of Larry's shirt. He was shot in the stomach and in the chest. Larry was weak and in an incredible amount of pain.

The night air was lighted up with the gunshots. All around them, the Allies continued to fight against the faceless enemy. They had managed to take down two, but there were still more. How many? They didn't know.

They carried Larry into the building serving as the medical room. The doctor, Moche Liberman, rushed over the minute they brought him in. The doctor was attempting to thwart the bleeding.

Anthony and Earnest stood right by his side, through the moments that Larry's breathing became more and more labored.

"Anthony," Larry called out softly.

Anthony came closer to him, putting his ear near the dying man's mouth. "What is it Larry?" he asked, tears falling from his eyes. Anthony and Larry had become especially close during the three years that they had served together.

"Please...I want you to go into my pack. Look in the inner pocket and get out a small envelope. Can you please give that to Rebecca?" He paused, a tear sliding down his face. "And tell her that I love her. Always."

Anthony shook his head, his tears running freely. Earnest was also crying.

"You can give it to her yourself, Larry," Anthony said.

"I won't be able to Anthony. I know this. I'm not going to get out of here alive." He gave a little weak chuckle. The blood in his lungs bubbled as he did so. "Funny. I thought I would be killed off the first year. But now that we've made it all the way to the end, I get killed now." Larry reached his hands out to both Earnest and Anthony. He waited for them to put their hands into his. They did.

The three of them held hands as they listened to the gunfire around them outside.

They held his hand as Moche Liberman recited the *Vidui*, Lenny being too weak to join in the confession.

They held Larry Goldsmith's hand until it was limp and there was no more life in it and only then did they let go when the white sheet was raised over his head and face.

Outside, the shooting had ceased. The wayward SS soldiers had been captured.

Buchenwald was once again free.

They had thought that all four of them would be going home together.

But only two of them would be going home.

Ψ

Rebecca opened the letter slowly with a heavy heart. Her heart was thumping loudly in her chest. Her eyes focused on the lines that were written in Larry's distinct loopy script.

The thought that you are going to be my wife, still gives me chills of pleasure every time I think about it. I remember when we met, at that tender age of sixteen. I knew I was in love from the moment that I met you. And over the years, I have watched you grow even more and more beautiful.

When I asked you to marry me, I told you that I would find something befitting for you. A ring that would be unique and special, as you are. Nothing that I saw around me back home satisfied me. Everyone had them. They all looked more or-less the same. You're not the same as everybody else, so why should the symbol of my love for you be?

Now here in Sicily, we have been victorious against the Germans. We have liberated the Sicilians from the Germans force occupation of their nation.

As we went through the city, many people have come out to greet us. They touch us, smile and cheer for us in their Sicilian. There are tears in there eyes as they thank us.

Many of the citizens beg for us to take accommodations in their homes. I was accepted, along with two other soldiers into the home of an elderly couple.

I love the nights here. They are beautiful and calming, so that is when I walk. This particular night, with your picture in my pocket, near my heart as always, I leave the house of my hosts. I am careful not to disturb them. I don't go too far, there is some danger in that. But tonight, I go a little further that usual.

I did not realize that I was wandering into an area highly populated by Gypsies. They are outside around campfires. There are adults and small children and teenagers. Dressed colorfully. They spot me before I could turn around and retreat. A woman, with a large smile on her face, approaches me. She speaks to me in a language that I do not understand. It doesn't sound like the language of the native Sicilians. I know that it is the language of their people.

The woman draws me towards the other, gently. I know then that they mean me no harm. They take in my military uniform and smile at me in welcome.

"You are an American?" an elderly man asks in broken English. I only nod, I was feeling a little nervous at this point, you see.

"Please sit, we mean you no harm. My name is Louis," he says softly, "You have been good to us."

So I take a seat on a small wooden chair that is near the campfire. Some of them begin to dance and sing. Many of their movements reminding me of the natives in Northern India, from which their ancestors came..

Soon we begin to talk. And of course, the subject of you comes up. Forgive me darling, I cannot help but bring you up to everyone I meet. You are so precious and I want everyone to know of you. So I take out you picture for all of them to see.

The old man named Louis leans over and stares at the picture. As he stares, his eyes become more and more filled with tears. Soon they are spilling out. He wipes at his face and looks up at me. At this time I am alarmed at his reaction and I am wondering why he was become so upset by the sight of your picture.

"Forgive me," he says as he continues to wipe at his face, "it's just that she looks like my daughter, Julianna. My daughter died many years ago. She was murdered. Two men accosted her on the street and murdered her...oh

God. I am sorry. But she looks like her twin…I was moved by his story, "I'm sorry about that. I'll put the picture away. I' so sorry about your daughter. Did they ever catch who did it?" *I asked him.*

He shook his head. "No. They never did. It still haunts me. She was engaged, just like you are to your Rebecca."

Soon, it is time for me to leave. We have busy days ahead of us, as you can imagine. I need all the sleep that I can get.

The old man walks me to the edge of their camp. Then his eyes lit up suddenly, "Hold on for a moment please. I have something for you." *He rushes back to one of the caravans and disappears inside. Soon he is out again, and he walks back to where I stand.*

In is fist, he has something clutched. I look down in curiosity. "Hold up your hand," *he tells me. So I do. He puts the small object in my hand. It feels somewhat heavy and solid.*

In my palm lays a ring. And Rebecca, it is beautiful. It appears to be solid gold. A bright red stone is mounted in it. Even in the night, it sparkles. I was amazed. I looked over to him. "Are you giving me this?" *I asked.*

The old man nodded vigorously. "Yes. This was my Julianna's ring. Her mother and I gave it to her when we found out that she was engaged. We saved and we saved and had this ring made."

I couldn't take the ring. How could I keep this ring—the one thing that he had left from his daughter from so long ago? The ring was obviously worth a small fortune and I could only imagine the sacrifice that he went through to obtain it. "I can't take it, I won't," *I said stubbornly. I tried to put it back in his hand and said,* "But I thank you for giving me your time and I appreciate it. I wish you all the luck in the world."

Tears filled the old man's eyes. "I give you this, Larry. I give you this because I believe that my daughter's spirit lives on in your Rebecca. I feel it, Larry. By giving it to her, I feel that I am giving it to my Julianna. Look, see her picture," *Louis said as he pulled a picture out of his pocket.*

I looked at it and I was shocked.

He hadn't been lying.

It was you, Rebecca. I looked at that young gypsy woman and I saw you.

That was the only reason that I took the ring from the man, because he believed that his daughter was you. And at that point, I believed it too.

So here it is, Rebecca. The ring that had been given to that young gypsy woman so many years before. A woman no doubt as special, as spirited, and wonderful a person as you are. You are deserving of it.

By giving this to you, I am also giving that old gypsy man's daughter her ring, a ring that she no doubt deserved.

And whenever you look at this ring, through the years in our marriage, I want you to be reminded of my love for you and you will know that you are a special and precious individual.

And as the years go by, we will watch our children grow, we will see them have children of their own, and we will grow old together. There is no one else in this word that I would rather share my life with.

I love you forever and I'll see you when I come home.

Love, your Larry.

Her Larry was dead and she would never see him again. He was gone forever. None of her plans and dreams of a life that she would have with him would ever become reality.

Rebecca looked up from the letter with tears in her eyes and with blurred vision. She could hardly see the form of the handsome young soldier with the black hair and olive skin that stood somberly before her in an army uniform.

She felt as if her world had just come to an end.

Chapter Twenty

It was September 15, 1945 and Earnest was home from the war. On September 2 of that same year, the Japanese had surrendered. World War the second was over.

At first, it was a little odd and uncomfortable to be home again. Earnest was coming home to a daughter that he didn't know or hadn't seen except through photographs. She was three years old, and she didn't know him. He knew that her name was Antonia and that she had dark russet hair, only a few shades darker than his, dark hazel-green eyes and creamy skin slightly tinged with the olive of her mother's. She was beautiful and he couldn't wait to see her.

Fortunately, it wasn't hard for little Antonia to get used to her father. Her mother and Grandmother had told her about her father everyday, so it was almost as if she had known him herself. So after Antonia's initial shyness, she was fine and had warmed up to Earnest almost immediately. After a day or so, they were inseparable.

Earnest enrolled for his last year at the University of Georgia Law school and finished with flying colors. He was immediately offered jobs in some of the country's top law firms, including one very prestigious one in Georgia called Dunburke and Stone. As the offers kept rolling in, he decided that he was more interesting in criminal defense that in business law. Had he known that he would end up being a defense attorney rather than a coporate lawyer, he wouldn't have done the dual program (he could have shaved off one year of schooling, not to mention the unnecessary expense). But extra schooling never hurts, Earnest thought to himself..

Abner, who moved back to Chicago right efter law school, was barred in Illinois and was working at a firm in Chicago. He too had decided that becoming a criminal defense attorney was more to his liking.

Pretty soon, Abner was telling Earnest that he should move back up to Chicago and then take his bar exam.

"It's great here, Earnest. I think you're going to love it. We can open a practice up here," he had told him.

After some consideration and discussion, Earnest and Angelina decided to move back to Chicago. Angelina was more that happy to go because that was where most of her family was, including her father and her twin brother.

So they sold the house and moved.

After taking the bar exam, Earnest joined the lawfirm where Abner worked and for a while both he and Abber enjoyed their place of employment. But pretty soon, they grappled with the idea of opening up their own practice.

"We can do it, Earnest. Just imagine, we'll be handling our own cases. We won't be well known, if known at all, when we start. But soon, as we build up clientele and win cases, our reputation will spread and people would be busting down their doors to have us!" Abner said to him one day when they were out for lunch.

Earnest nodded his head. "I like the idea…but we're going to have to find an office and everything. We also will have to take out a loan."

Abner sat back in his chair. "Well, we shouldn't have to borrow too much money. I can put up a good amount towards it. And I'm sure that you can give some as well."

Earnest nodded. "Okay. So why don't we get this started?"

They found a nice office in downtown Chicago. At first business was slow, but within a year their establishment was doing pretty well for itself.

It was later on, in the winter of 1946 that Angelina told him that she was pregnant.

Nine months later, their son Dwight was born weighing in at seven pounds and six ounces. Angelina's father, her brothers, and Earnest's mother came down to greet the baby. It was also then that Rocco made a request of him.

Rocco and Earnest had been sitting around outside on the back patio of their house. Angelina and Earnest's mother were inside with the new baby.

"Earnest, I have a favor to ask you," Rocco had said calmly as he flicked the ashes off his cigarette.

Earnest sat up in the lounge chair. "What is it?"

"I have a friend…he's in a little bit of trouble. The lawyer that he has now isn't really used to handling the situation that's at hand…"

"What kind of trouble has he gotten into?" Earnest asked, suspiciously.

"Well…he had to deal with a guy that had been making some problems for him."

Earnest knew where this was leading. "What did he do?"

"He just roughed the guy up a little. That's all," Rocco answered.

"Did the man end up in the hospital?" Earnest asked him.

"Not for anything serious. The guy got a few stitches, that's all."

Earnest considered this for a moment in silence. He felt trapped. "What's his name?"

"Fredo. Fredo Ferrara," Rocco answered easily.

Finally, Earnest decided to come to the inevitable point. "Do you want me to represent him?"

Rocco took a long drag of his cigarette and exhaled before he answered.

"You're a damn good lawyer, Earnest and I know that you can get him off. He didn't do anything wrong. He was just doing what he had to do. It was nothing that was unnecessary."

There was no way out now. Earnest would do what his father-in-law wanted him to do.

Ψ

Within three months of meeting each other, Anthony and Rebecca Feldman were married. At the wedding, a rabbi performed the wedding. Initially, Rebecca parents were fuming when she told them that she would be marrying a Roman Catholic. But soon, realizing that It would take place none-the-less (they could see the determination in their daughter's face when she told them the news) they decided to just accept it. They loved their daughter too much to alienate her and that is exactly what would happen if they stood up against it.

For a little while, earlier on in the relationship, Anthony felt a little bad about having a relationship with the fiancé if his dead friend Larry, but as his feelings for Rebecca grew, he found that he couldn't help himself. He was in love with her. There was no doubt about it. Besides. Larry was gone and there was nothing that anyone could do about it.

He would want Rebecca to move on and who better a person to move on with than a good friend? He would take good care of her out of love for his dead friend and most of all, out of love for her.

They honeymooned in Europe. They spent three days on the Agapolus islands of Greece, three days in Paris and another three days in Naples.

Anthony didn't think he could be any happier.

Ψ

Matthew Hurst was born in July of 1948 after a twenty-eight hour labor. He was a healthy baby weighing in at seven pounds, ten ounces. Angelina was exhausted, but happy when the doctor placed her little boy in her arms.

Earnest was beaming. Rocco passed out cigars to the male family members that were waiting in the hospital lobby.

Two days after Angelina came back home with the baby, Earnest organized a little bash. Little Mathew was piled with gifts of all sorts from adoring family friends and family members. Earnest knew a lot of the people at the get together celebrating the birth of his second-born son, but there were also a considerable amount of people that he didn't know. But Rocco knew them. Most of the gifts were extremely expensive. Earnest noted that the most expensive gifts came from the friends of Rocco. Little five-year-old Antonia was also the life of the party. Completely un-shy, she was at her mother's side as she circled among the guests. Antonia smiled, coaxed, and flashed her big hazel eyes at the guests. She even chatted with them a little. Adoring guests watched as the pretty little auburn haired girl made her way around the room. Rocco was the most proud as he watched his little granddaughter.

"Definitely not the quiet type!" he announced to a circle of people as he proudly lifted his granddaughter onto his shoulders.

Rocco was equally proud of his newborn grandson whom he carried in his arms like precious cargo. *"Mio nipote prezioso,"* he would say as he cuddled the little bundle.

"What does that mean?" Earnest asked his wife after he overheard Rocco say this.

"It means my precious grandson," Angelina responded.

"I think it would be good for our children to know Italian," Earnest said nodding his head. He watched as his wife took a sip of the white wine. "I'm glad that you speak to them in Italian sometimes."

"Antonia already understands a lot," Angelina said and turned to look for her daughter who was standing near her uncle at the moment. She gestured for her to come over.

"*Antonia, lei può portarme quella piastra di formaggio?*"

"Okay mama." The little girl walked towards the refreshment table.

"I think I understood a little bit of that. You asked her to bring you something. I didn't get the next word," Earnest said.

Angelina smiled at her husband. "You're right. I asked her to bring that plate of cheese on the table over there."

Antonia came back with a small plate of cheese. She was smiling as she handed it to her mother.

"*Ringraziarla, caro*"

"*Lei è benvenuto*, mama," the little girl responded, and then sped away to play with her older twin cousins, Frankie's twin sons.

"It's amazing how well they get along with such a big age difference. They're eleven and she's five. You would think that they would find her to be a bother," Earnest commented with a smile.

Ψ

Fredo Ferrera was only the beginning of a long line of Rocco's friends that needed Earnest's legal aid. At first, Abner was against the whole deal.

"I know exactly what this is, and I want no part of it," Abner had told him the day that he said that he was representing Fredo Ferrera.

"Come on Abner. We're lawyers and it's our job to help others legally. No matter who that person is," Earnest had said.

"Get real Earnest," Abner retorted. "You know where this is going to lead. We agree to represent one person from Rocco's cronies then there's going to be more. Pretty soon, people will be calling us mob lawyers," Abner said fretfully.

"Look. We'll just do it this once. It's just that in this case, Rocco believed that we would be better for the job."

"But what about ethics and morals?" Abner retorted.

"What about them? We are doing an ethical thing. We are helping a man that is in need of it. I don't think that you can be any more moral than that. Fredo is a poor Italian immigrant. He has nothing. If we don't help him, he'll get torn to pieces in the courtroom. Can you honestly stand by and see something like that happen?"

Abner, at that point, sighed and sat down across from Earnest's desk.

"Fine. We'll do it. But just this once. We're becoming prestigious. The last thing we need is any connections to things like this to mess everything up."

So they had represented Fredo Ferrera and they had won. And just as Abner had predicted, Rocco slowly began directing a stream of clients in their direction. Soon Earnest and Abner were dealing with cases from property disputes to homicide. At first, Abner would complain about it but the large sums of money that they were receiving for their services, soon silenced him.

Abner and Earnest soon began to see that doing what they were doing also came with perks.

After a hard morning at the office, Earnest and Abner decided to go out to lunch at a restaurant. The moment the owner, a small Italian-American man, saw who they were, he directed them towards a table at the front and he gave them complimentary drinks 'on-the-house.' They also got a big discount on the price of their orders. Earnest and Abner left them a good tip.

"What do you suppose that was all about?" Abner asked, quite unnecessarily, once they were out of the restaurant. Earnest looked at him, but said nothing. They both knew full well what it was about. They were gaining a reputation and a name. Abner, who enjoyed power and wealth, was enjoying every moment of it even though he had been in staunch opposition at the beginning. They got invited to the best parties, they got invitations to go sailing, invitations to lunch, they got expensive gifts, invites to vacations, they got to meet important and famous people, and they had more beautiful women than they knew what to do with. Well Abner enjoyed the women, but Earnest having no interest in any other than Angelina, didn't partake.

"Aren't you ever going to get married? You know, settle down?" Earnest asked his long time friend one day.

Abner had smiled and said, "What? Tie myself down when I have all these beautiful woman around me? Not on your life. Variety is the spice of life."

"Well...don't you want some stability?" Earnest asked.

Abner scowled. "You sound like my mother. She always asking me Why I don't find a nice Jewish girl and settle down. I'll find someone like that when I'm ready. As of now...I want to enjoy myself. A new woman every night...you've forgotten what that was like, Earnest. It feels good."

"Well, I don't want that anymore. You find someone like Angelina, you'll know what I mean."

Abner shrugged his shoulders with indifference

Ψ

"You do realize that were almost like Rocco's advisors now? " Abner said one day after coming out of a meeting with Rocco and some other men.

"That's a bunch of crock and you know it," Earnest snapped.

"What do you mean? You know it as well as I do. He relies on us for financial advice and for legal advice and even other things." Abner shook his head slowly with a slight smile. "Man, if someone had ever told me before that I would have connections to the mob, I would have laughed in their face."

Earnest realized that what Abner was saying was right. But somehow, he couldn't bring himself to admit it or acknowledge that.

Somehow, Earnest thought that if he put it in the most remote area of his mind, he wouldn't have to think about it. That was all he wanted.

Ψ

Winston Hurst was born in Feburary, 11, 1952. He was a big baby, weighing in at eight pounds and twelve onces. Of the the babies so far, he was the most difficult. He would cry and cry for hours on end. Winston and Angelina were barely getting any sleep and they were very worried about him. They decided to take him to the doctor.

"He has colic. I'll give you some medication that should help," the doctor told them after an examination of the baby.

"Well thank God it's not anything more serious," Angelina said with a great amount of relief.

Ψ

"I want my cut out of the deal. Where the hell's my fuckin' money?" Anthony screamed into the man's ear as he held his head back by the hair.

"S-S-Sir, I'm gonna get it. It's just that, he took it man. He said he was gonna cut off my balls if I didn't give him a bigger percent."

"So, you gave him my part," Anthony hissed. "How smart was that?"

"I—I ain't had no choice."

"You coulda gave him your part," Anthony said. "Do you think that it's my problem that the man wanted to cut your balls off? Huh?"

"N-N-No Mr. Gionelli," the man stuttered

The dim lights of the warehouse shimmered on the thin film of sweat now coating the skin of Alexandre Zarkovski. Three big men stood in the shadows and coolly observed the scene in front of them. Ready to jump in when called or if needed.

"You fuckin Pollack. You'd better give me your part then, and maybe you'll get away with your life."

"I don't have it," he gasped

Anthony pulled a tighter grip on his hair. "What did you say Alex boy?"

"I don't got it. I spent it," he said softly, knowing that he had just sentenced himself to death or something far worse.

Before he knew what hit him, Anthony pulled out a box cutter from his back pocket and made a clean cut across Alexandre's throat from ear to ear.

Alexandre Zarkovski let out a blood-curdling scream that was quickly silenced as the blood drained out. The two men in the shadows came forward, knowing that they were needed. They held the young Polish-American man down as Anthony continued to slice away at the man's neck. Pretty soon, there was no need to hold him down.

The four of them quickly drained off all the blood from the body and using an electric saw cut the body into pieces. They put the pieces into a duffle bag and put it into the trunk of the car. Two of the men stayed behind to clean up. Anthony and the other man got into the car to dispose of the body.

Anthony and the other man drove to the clearing in the woods and took the bag out of the car. They dug a hole about six feet deep andthrew the duffle bag in. They then took a bottle of lye and poured it over the bags. They covered them up with dirt. The ground looked undisturbed. The cops weren't gonna find Alexandre Zarkovski that easily.

Ψ

Later on that night, when Anthony returned home, Rebecca noticed a spot on her husband's shirt.

"Is that blood, Anthony?" she asked, trying to get a closer look.

Anthony quickly looked down and saw what she was looking at. Shit. He missed a spot. He was usually so thorough about cleaning up after himself.

"Yeah. My nose was bleeding earlier on," he said quickly in response. Thank God for his quick thinking.

"Aww. It's all this dry, hot air that we've been getting lately. Are you okay now?" she asked him, as she came up to him and touched him on the cheek.

"Yeah I'm perfectly fine. Now that I'm back home here with you," Anthony said and gave her a kiss on the lips. He pulled off his jacket and hung it up. "I'm kinda hungry, did you cook anything for dinner?"

Ψ

"You look beautiful honey," Earnest said looking at his wife's reflection in the mirror. He was truly impressed.

Angelina was wearing a champagne colored chiffon, off the shoulder, Dior dress that fitted her small, curvy figure to perfection. It had only been a month since Angelina had given birth to Winston, but she was almost down to her usual weight. A diamond necklace was around her small throat, diamond earrings dangled from her ears and she wore a diamond tennis bracelet. Her make-up was flawless.

"You look handsome yourself," Angelina said when she turned around and faced her husband. "But then again, you always do."

Earnest smirked. "Please. Nothing compared to your beauty. Not me, not anyone." He pulled his wife into his arms and kissed her soundly on the lips. "Do you know how much I love and adore you?" he whispered into her ears.

Angelina stood on her toes and wrapped her arms around her husband, "Yes, as long as you know how much I love and adore you," she answered back.

Earnest chuckled, his face buried in her shoulder. He loved the smell of her, "Then it's settled. We both love and adore each other."

Angelina gently pushed her husband back. "Come on. We're going to be late. My father got us the best tickets in the house," she said excitedly, spraying on a last touch of some designer perfume that Earnest had gotten her in France a couple of months ago. "All the stars are going to be there! This is the event of the century!"

Earnest and Angelina were in Hollywood, California, to attend the award ceremony at the Pentages Theater. Rocco had gotten them tickets to the 1951Academy Awards, which were held March, 20, 1952. Rocco had also gotten them an invite to the after party where they would brush shoulders with all the greats.

Angelina picked up the phone in their hotel room. "I'm going to call Francine before we leave to make sure everything is okay back at home." Francine, a middle-aged, Portuguese woman, was the regular babysitter/nanny.

"How's everything over there?" Angelina asked Francine once she picked up the phone.

"Everything is fine, Mrs. Hurst. I have all the emergency numbers. Things are in order. Baby Winston and Matthew are here safe and sound Antonia is over at the Jennie Watson's house for a sleepover. And Dwight is over at friend's house. I have numbers for both places."

Angelina smiled."Thank you, Mrs. Corzas. I know I went over those things with you already. Thanks for being so patient."

"That's fine," Francine said with a chuckle. Angelina said bye and they hung up.

"All right. Let's get outta here," Earnest said with a smile.

Angelina and Earnest met Abner at the door. A tall, lithe, red headed woman with sculpted cheekbones and with an elegant (if not beautiful) face was clutched onto his arm.

"This is Dorothy Ashford," Abner said referring to the tall redhead. "Dorothy, this is my friend Earnest and his lovely wife, Angelina."

The bony redhead extended a waiflike hand in their direction, her slanted, icy blue eyes staring at them with great intensity. "Charmed," she simply said.

Earnest took her hand and planted a light kiss on the bony knuckles. Angelina smiled pleasantly at Dorothy. Dorothy did something with her face that Angelina supposed, could pass as a smile. Angelina was sure that this woman was going to be impossible to get along with.

The party of four took their seats near the front. As luck would have it, Angelina and Dorothy were seated in between the two men side by side. Soon the awards began.

"*Bride of the Gorilla.* What were they thinking?" Dorothy leaned over and whispered to Angelina when she caught sight of Gisela Werbisek—one of the actresses that played in the movie.

Angelina smiled in agreement. "That movie was a definite career killer for those actors."

Dorothy rolled her cerulean eyes in her head, "Don't I know it!"

Angelina smiled, Dorothy didn't seem to be such a hard person to get along with after all. She seemed to have a good sense of humor. Well, I'll never judge a book by its cover again, Angelina thought to herself.

The awards were very exciting. The award for Best Motion Picture was given to *An American in Paris* . The Best Actor award was given to Humphrey Bogart for his role in *The African Queen,*. Vivian Leigh got the best actress award for her role in *A Streetcar Named Desire.* The after party was phenomenal. They met many of the famous actors and actresses. Angelina and Earnest were having the time of their life. Angelina even got to see her favorite actress, Judy Garland.

Dorothy introduced them to many of the actors and actresses, many of whom she seemed to know on a personal level.

"How do you know all these people?" Angelina asked her, astounded.

A look of surprise flashed in Dorothy's eyes. "My father owns the Ashford Productions studio. Many of these actors and actresses have been or currently are under contract with my father."

Angelina's eyes widened. "Oh, how could I have been so foolish… your last name…I just didn't make the connection."

Dorothy linked a bony arm through Angelina's arm. "It's all right, darling. I'm sure there are enough people with the last name of Ashford around to fill a small country."

Ψ

Rocco sat and stared out the window of his office into the gardens below. He was lost in thought. Yesterday evening, he had gotten some very disturbing news and he was praying to the Virgin Mary that it wasn't so. Drugs. Prostitution. His own son involved in such shameful things. Things like that were a no-no that his men knew to stay away from. He would hate for anything like that to be traced back to The Family. His father-in-law would be turning in his grave if he knew of such goings-on. There were things that were beneath him, believe it or not. How could his son think that he wouldn't find out about it? He found out about most everything, sooner or later. He thought back to the article that came out almost a month ago about that missing Polish-American who was a well-known drug dealer. He frowned, thinking that he would be very disappointed if his son had anything to do with it. Not for the fact that the man was dead, but that indicated that if Anthony was involved with a man like Alexandre Zarkovski it likely meant that he was really involved in the drug sale. Also, people like Zarkovski worked in packs. If the killing was traced back to The Family, Zarkovski's cronies were likely to want to exact revenge, though it wouldn't be the brightest thing to do on their part, they wouldn't care. It was a matter of honor to them, although Rocco was sure that they hadn't the slightest idea what that was about. Well, Anthony did a good job getting rid of him and clearing any tracks that may lead back to him or the family. They were never able to find the young Polish-American or who might have done it. The cops weren't going to waste a lot of time looking for a drug pusher. To them, it was one less scumbag of the street that they had to deal with.

"Papa, you wanted to speak with me?"

Rocco turned around in his chair. His youngest son stood at the door. He was wearing a finely cut suit that could have only been Italian made and leather loafers on his feet. His thick black hair was combed back. His handsome face with the straight Roman nose and the chiseled jawbone wore an expression of concern. Looking at him, Rocco told himself, it couldn't be true. Not his handsome, bright *bambino*, his dear *figlio*.

"How is Rebecca?" Rocco asked, not in a hurry to get to the point.

"She's doing fine. Her back is giving her some real pain," Anthony answered as he fixed himself a drink from his father's mini bar.

"Well, that's a part of pregnancy. Your mother's ankles used to swell up pretty badly when she was pregnant with you and Angelina," he stated. He stared at his son, taking in the wide width of his back as he stood facing away from him towards the bar.

Anthony turned around and faced his father. "What's the matter, Papa? I knew something was wrong from the tone of your voice on the phone."

"Anthony, I want to ask you something and I want you to be totally honest with me."

Anthony gave his father a startled look. He gripped the glass of scotch tighter in his hand and took a sip. He took a seat in one of the velvet chairs. "What is it?

Rocco walked over to the window and pulled back the curtain. He could see the traffic going down the street. A man was rushing out of his car and walking swiftly towards one of the office buildings as he glanced at his watch. He was probably late for a meeting.

Anthony patiently waited for his father to speak. Rocco was never one to rush out with things. He took his time. He would talk when he was ready. Only thing was that Anthony was dying to know what this was all about.

"People have been telling me things, Anthony. Things that I don't like. Things about you," Rocco said, still facing the window.

Anthony sat back in his chair. "What things?" he asked, trying to keep his cool.

Rocco turned around and faced his son. "Answer me this, my *figlio*, have you become involved in things that we should have nothing to do with?"

"Like what?" Anthony asked, his heart beginning to pound strongly in his chest.

"Drugs, prostitution, anything like that?"

Players of the Game

Anthony was silent. He looked to the floor. He was afraid to speak.

"Answer me, Anthony. Tell me it is not true."

Anthony's mouth tensed into a thin line. He was never capable of lying to his father.

His son's silence told him all he needed to know. "Why would you do this Anthony?" Rocco asked, with his palms upturned in a beseeching manner, "You have everything you need; you're managing the hotel here in Chicago and you're doing other things. I give you lots to do. You make good money. What would make you want to deal with drugs and prostitution?"

Anthony sneered, "Yeah, good money. But not good enough. I want to bring in the big bucks, Papa, just like you do."

Rocco walked up to is son, a worried frown creasing his face. "But everything I have is yours, you know this. It took me years to build myself up to where I am today. Many years from that penniless young man that came from Sicily thirty years ago. I didn't get here by dealing drugs and being involved with prostitution."

"Yeah, like everything you did is legal and legit," Anthony retorted.

Rocco hit the desk with his fist. Anthony involuntarily jumped in his chair. "But there are lines, Anthony. Lines that we do not cross and boundaries that we do not bridge. You know this!"

"Yeah, but I heard the Poggioreale family is getting into the prostitution. They have a section of the town where they—"

"I don't care!" Rocco said slamming his fist in his hand. The smack of skin against skin resounded through the room.

"They can do what they want, that is none of our business. You don't get into things like that and remain unharmed, they will come to their own downfall eventually." Rocco moved around from behind his desk and sat down across from Anthony. He was inches away from his face. "Don't you dare bring something like that into this family, do you hear me? Do you understand?"

"Yes," Anthony mumbled, looking down at his shuffling feet.

"Good," Rocco said nodding his head. "And I have one last question. Did you have to do with the killing of that man Alexandre Zarkovski?" Rocco asked, already full well knowing the answer.

"Yes," Anthony responded, stonily. "He shorted me on money from a sale."

"I trust that you disposed of the body properly."

"Yes. We did."

"Don't let me find you involved in anything like this again."

"Of course not Papa."

Chapter Twenty-one

The marriage of Abner Bernstein and Dorothy Ashford in June 1953 hit the headlines of the papers. It was the event of the year and everybody who was everybody showed up at the wedding and after-party—celebrities, high profile people, and not to mention friends and family.

If anything, the wedding gifts were even more extraordinary that the guests. One of the most expensive gifts was a brand-new Bentley given to Abner and Dorothy by Rocco.

A day later, the happy couple was off to their honeymoon in Aruba.

"That was a very beautiful wedding, wasn't it?" Angelina commented the next day as they were sitting in the family room. Angelina was bouncing one-year-old Winston on her knees, while Antonia and Matthew were playing with their toys on the floor beside them.

"Mother, father, it is okay if I were to go over to Jennie's house?" Antonia asked, as she stood up from the carpeted floor.

Earnest looked at her daughter—the dark flowing hair, the clear luminous hazel-green eyes, similar to his own. The porcelain skin with a slight tinge of bronze. She was growing into a remarkable beauty.

"Of course you can dear, if it's okay with your mother," Earnest answered as he looked towards his wife.

"It would be perfectly fine. Are they coming to pick you up?" Angelina asked.

"I'll call her. I'm sure that Mr. Watson will come and get me," she responded, happily.

Angelina and Earnest smiled. The Watsons were close family friends and Jennie and Antonia were the best of friends.

"Okay. Well, how about I give Mr. Watson a call and ask him if it would be okay."

Pretty soon, the ivory white Cadillac rolled up in front of the house.

"Mr. Watson and Jennie are here!" Angelina called to her daughter.

After kissing her father and her mother goodbye, she was out the door.

Angelina sat on the arm of the armchair that Winston was sitting in. He wrapped his arm around her waist.

"They look so happy together, Abner and Dorothy," Angelina commented, "I never thought that Abner would ever settle down and get married. But it seems like they're a perfect match. She'll be the one to tame him."

Earnest nodded with a slight smile. "I never thought I'll see the day either. His parents wanted him to marry a nice Jewish girl…Dorothy is neither!"

Angelina playfully swatted him on the arm. "Dorothy's a wonderful person. I admit, at first I didn't like her but she turned out to be such a caring individual, in her own way of course. I wouldn't trade her for the world. She has a heart of gold."

"I know darling," Earnest said and kissed her on the cheek, "but you, my dear, she cannot hold a candle to."

"She's so elegant and worldly. Such class and charm. I feel like such a little girl compared to her."

"Honestly darling. You are all woman," Earnest said and kissed her passionately.

"Mommy and Daddy are kissing!" Little four-year-old Mathew exclaimed gleefully.

Suddenly the phone rang. Earnest reached over to pick it up. "Hello?"

"Earnest. This is Rocco."

"Hey. How are you?" Earnest asked, leaning forwards.

"Who is that?" Angelina whispered. "It's your dad," Earnest answered back.

"We have to meet up right away. We have to talk," Rocco said sounding anxious.

"What is it, Rocco?" Earnest asked, sensing his father-in-law's fretfulness.

"We can't discuss this over the phone. We have to talk in person. My driver will be there in half and hour. I'll see you then." Rocco hung up.

Earnest hung up the phone with a puzzled expression on his face.

"What's the matter? Is Papa okay?" Angelina asked, clearly worried.

"Something's up. He didn't give me any details over the phone. I'm going over there right now. His driver's coming to get me," Earnest said, walking towards the front closet to get his jacket.

Twenty minutes later a black sedan pulled up in front of the house. Earnest quickly kissed his wife's face with a promise to be right back and that everything would be alright, he rushed out the door.

Ψ

When Earnest got to the house, it was clear to see that his father-in-law was in a clear state of alarm. There was something very wrong going on. The moment that Rocco saw Earnest, he ushered him into the library.

Earnest took a seat. "So what's going on, Rocco?"

"I think I would prefer to wait until Abner got here so that I don't have to repeat the information twice. He'll be here shortly."

Within moments, Abner walked through the door. After some quick pleasantries, Rocco sat down across from them and got right into it.

"The FBI's been given some information on me, thanks to the Feds. This could put me away for life in combination with some other things that they've been itching to pinch me with," Rocco stated. He nervously smoothed his hand over his hair.

"Who told you about this?" Earnest asked.

"One of the lieutenants that I know in the department."

Abner leaned forward in his chair. "What have they dug up?"

"They're trying to get me from tax evasion. Now the FBI is going to try and bring that up and add on money laundering and extortion." Rocco put his face in his hands. "I'll be in jail for the rest of my life. I won't get to see my grandchildren grow up."

"Hold on, Rocco. Let's not think the worst. Abner and I are here to help you. Now. The FBI and the feds can bring up as many things as they want. The question is whether they will actually have enough information and proof for you to get charged with it," Earnest said, trying to calm Rocco down.

Rocco leaned back in his chair and let out a big sigh. "You're right, Earnest. It just seems too overwhelming."

"I know, but we have to try and not become overwhelmed," Abner said. "Now Rocco, tell us everything you know and whatever we don't know, we'll do our damndest to dig it up."

Ψ

For what seemed to be the hundredth time, Earnest glanced around the small Italian restaurant. Abner anxiously took a sip of his lemon water.

"McMillan said that he would be here at five," Earnest said shifting in his chair. "It's already 5:30. What's going on?"

Just after he finished his sentence, Captain McMillan walked through the doors of the restaurant. His brown beady eyes swept the restaurant and rested upon Abner and Earnest's table. He handed the host his trench coat and came walking over.

Abner and Earnest rose to shake his hand and all three of them took a seat. McMillan quickly waved the waiter over and ordered a drink. Earnest noted that he hadn't even bothered to offer a reason for his tardy arrival nor was their anything offered along the lines of an apology.

Earnest had met McMillan once at a city social event. He hadn't liked him one bit. He found the man to be too pompous and sure of himself. The man's obnoxiousness was shocking. His wife was a big boned blonde with large features and a horsey lower face. Throughout the night, McMillan was seen eying every attractive female that came within seeing distance, as his wife trailed pitifully behind him. When Earnest started to see him eying Angelina, they had promptly left the party with Earnest giving the excuse that he was experiencing nausea.

When Earnest had heard that McMillan was the man going to head the investigation and ultimately decide whether or not Rocco was to be nailed with the charges, Earnest felt sick to his stomach to think that he would have to see this man face to face again.

"I don't see why we had to meet up at this dumb Guinea place," McMillan said with a nervous chuckle.

"We assume that you have already spoken to Mr. Gionelli yesterday evening," Abner began, choosing to ignore the vulgar statement.

"If I hadn't spoken to him, do you think I would be meeting the two of you this afternoon?" he said with a smirk. "I have things to do you know."

Earnest felt like punching him in his puffy nose. The man was a true prick.

"Well, as you know," Abner continued undeterred, "there is an alleged claim that Mr. Gionelli has been involved in some money laundering and extortion—"

"Well, I would say that it is more a fact than alleged," McMillan cut in rudely. "Look gentlemen," he continued sliding up in his chair, "I didn't come here to review things that I already know."

"Well Mr. McMillan. Sometimes it's good to review information so that we can separate the truth from the make-believe. Don't you agree?" Earnest retorted, trying to remain calm. "And that truth is that you have no hard core evidence that Mr. Gionelli is directly involved in money laundering."

"Oh, yeah?" Mr. McMillan sneered. "His posse under him's doin' it, so that means that he's involved somewhere. We look hard enough and we'll find it. That's good enough. Besides, he was busted fifteen years ago for involvement in something like that."

Abner smiled coldly. "You have your facts mixed up, Sir. He was charged with possession of illegal arms. The extortion charges never stuck."

"Look here. I don't care what he was convicted with. We're gonna look and we're going to find his involvement in this money laundering and extortion scheme somewhere. No one can tell me any differently."

"Look, how much would it take to just smooth this whole thing over? We came here to work things out," Abner said calmly.

"What do you mean? Are you offering money?" McMillan asked, with bafflement.

"If it has to be. Whatever it would take to get you to just stop this investigation." Abner responded.

"No money in the world's going to get me to stop this investigation. We've gone too far to stop now," McMillan snapped. "And when the feds get a hold of this, which will be soon, there'll be no stopping them"

Earnest glanced at Abner. His face was expressionless. "You've been investigating this case for a few months, six months to be exact. You found nothing to directly link him to anything. What makes you think that you're going to find anything now?"

Pat McMillan's face slowly turned red with bafflement and rage. "How did you know that? How did you know that this investigation's been going on for six months?"

Earnest shrugged. "Lucky guess."

McMillan eyed them with malice. "They're a few companies that we haven't investigated yet. We're going for them next. Something will show up there, believe me."

Abner shrugged. "Okay. If you say so. What ever happened with the tax evasion charges?"

McMillan's face turned almost purple. "To think that I would tell you anything concerning that."

"All we're trying to point out is that Mr. Gionelli just wants to live a peaceful life and watch his grandchildren grow up. He doesn't want anything to ruin that so why would he get involved in things that would jeopardize that?"

"If he was trying to live a peaceful life, why would he be around those gangsters and hoodlum unless he's one of them himself…" McMillan scowled. "I know he's one of them, he's their leader. I'm not stupid."

Earnest and Abner exchanged glances of amusements. "We can see that you are a man of assumptions and hearsay. Fortunately for us and most unfortunately for you, facts and hardcore evidence are what matters when it come to the law."

McMillan looked as if he were about to explode. "I don't have to sit here and put up with this bullshit." He said, starting to rise from his chair.

"Whatever you wish, Sir. We'll be seeing you," Earnest said calmly. "We hope we haven't wasted too much of your time."

McMillan grunted at them and stalked away and out of the restaurant.

"Well I guess it's time for plan B," Earnest said and took a sip of his drink. He turned around to the waiter. "We'll have our coats now, Luigi."

Ψ

As Pat McMillan sat across from Alvin Yarley, the president of C&C Metal Productions, McMillan got more and more frustrated.

The investigation of this company was turning up nothing. McMillan and his men had already gone through all the business reports over the last five years and then the last fifteen years and they hadn't found a trace of anything that would suggest any business dealings with Rocco Gionelli.

"Do you mean to tell me that you have no dealings with Mr. Gionelli whatsoever?" McMillan asked the balding, middle-aged man sitting before him.

"No. I've had no concrete business dealings with Mr. Gionelli. He was thinking of buying some shares in our company at one point, but he declined to do so," Yarley said easily. "We had much discussion on it. It would have been nice for a man like Mr. Gionelli to have a part in our company."

McMillan shot forward in his chair at this comment. "Why would it be so nice for Mr. Gionelli to have been a part of your company?"

"Well, that's easy to answer. Mr. Gionelli's financial embankments have always been solid. Take for instance, that grand hotel chain of his, *Sunset Palace*. Everything he does flourishes. He's a very good businessman," Yarley said with a smile.

McMillan had had enough. He stood up abruptly.

"I think that would be all for the day. I might want to send one of my investigators over here again within a week's time."

"That would be fine. I would be delighted to help you in whatever way possible." Yarley answered back politely.

McMillan and his men walked out of his office. Five minutes later, there was a buzz on Yarley's intercom. Yarley walked over and pressed the button.

"All is clear, Mr. Yarley," a security officer's voice said through the voice box.

"Thank you Smyth," Yarley answered back.

Yarley looked through the blinds of his office window and got the backside view of the investigators vehicle just as it disappeared around the corner. Yarley walked over to his desk and dialed a number.

"How did everything go?" the voice asked the moment the phone was picked up.

"Everything went perfectly fine. Nothing was uncovered, of course. All your files and information have been taken away and stored in where they could never be found by them. McMillan said that he might be sending some more men over here in about a week. But that's nothing to worry about," Yarley answered.

"I want to thank you, Alvin. You have been so helpful. I really appreciate this."

"Not a problem. After all, where would my business be without your help Rocco?"

Almost anything could be bought for the right price.

Ψ

"Do you have to leave already?" asked the lithesome redhead lying on the bed.

Anthony shrugged into his jacket and smoothed back his black hair. "Yeah, I gotta go. I can't stay out all night."

"But it's only midnight. She really has the ball and chains on you, doesn't she?" the redhead complained.

Anthony was instantly angered by this statement. He turned on her in a flash.

"Look here. Nobody's snapping the whip at me. But I'm married and I gotta be smart about things. You knew this coming in. Don't pretend that you don't know the situation, Betty."

The redhead rolled her aquamarine eyes up in her head. "All right already. Don't have a cow. I know you're married and all...no strings attached, right? That was the deal. As long as you keep me living like this, I'll shut my can." She swept her hands over the expensive silk sheets and gestured at the expensive European furniture.

Anthony narrowed his dark eyes at her. "You don't make the conditions here. I do, you got that?" he said forcefully.

The titian haired beauty backed up. "Of course you do, luv. You're the boss. Why would I have it any other way? Now come on over here, my Italian stud. Let me wrap these long legs around you just one more time before you go back to that wall flower of yours."

Anthony's face reddened again. "Don't you dare talk about my wife, you understand? You know nothing about her," he said stepping back from the bed.

"I know that she has your heart," she said simply.

"And that's all you need to know and don't you forget it," Anthony spat.

She threw back her head—exposing a long white neck—and chuckled, and then she straightened up. "How can I forget? She has your heart and I have your body."

Anthony stood glowering at her.

"Come on. I'm sorry. I didn't mean anything bad. Please come here," she said as she outstretched her hand, "You can't go home all tense. Come here, let me relax you."

Anthony took her slender hand into his and allowed her to pull him to the bed—she was one thing that he couldn't resist.

He had been seeing Betty Ladrow for almost a year now. When he first met her, she was a sales girl at J.C.Penney.

While he was looking around, a soft, bell-like voice asked him, "Can I help you?"

He looked up and came eye to eye with a tall, slender redhead with a beautiful face and captivating aquamarine irises staring at him through hooded lids. Her eyelashes were long and curling, her eyes catlike in shape. And the rest was history, as they say.

In all the eleven years of Anthony's marriage to Rebecca, he had never cheated, until this point. Never before had he even considered being with another woman since he saw that young, stoically beautiful woman standing on her front stairs and crying as she read a letter from her dead love. And he fell head over heals in love with her when she looked up at him with those dark liquid pool eyes, so full of sorrow. He had comforted her then, at first she was hesitant to accepted, but she soon did.

And he was still in love with Rebecca.

And although he still enjoyed making love to his wife, a fiery passion burned for Betty. He knew he did not love Betty, he only lusted after her. Physically, she had him, but beyond that, it all belonged to Rebecca. Initially, he had never expected the affair to last as long as it did—almost a year now. But it did. He was sure that eventually he would grow tired of her, but that time had yet to come. She still made him hot with desire. What could he do? He was helpless and he had to give in.

Ψ

Rebecca had become an alcoholic, and she knew it. She was sure that Anthony knew it too.

Rebecca watched in alarm as she steadily began to depend more and more on alcohol. Rebecca had never been a drinker. In fact, the only time that she would drink anything with alcohol in it would be on Passover when she would drink the wine. Otherwise, alcohol had never touched her lips. She couldn't believe that she had come to this. She had gone from a good Jewish girl who was a good mother and a good wife to a person that she loathed and despised.

The alcohol in the house was bought by Anthony for himself and for guests. She had never given these a second glance. But one night, she had looked at the clock and saw that it was one o'clock in the morning and her husband still wasn't home. That was when the idea had come to her that Anthony was likely seeing another woman. And it was then that she pulled the bottle of liquor of the shelf and poured herself a glass. For months, she had been telling herself that it wasn't true. For the past year, there had been subtle changes in him that she dismissed.

But now she was sure of it, because people had seen him with this woman and had come back and told her.

Now tonight, it was two o'clock in the morning, and Anthony had yet to make an appearance. The strong urge to drink took over Rebecca. She decided, once again, to give in to the compulsion. She pulled down a glass tumbler and a bottle of red port wine, and filled the glass up with ice and poured herself a drink.. She swallowed down a mouthful of the bittersweet drink. She finished off the first glass and another and then another and another after that. By the time that Anthony got home, around three in the morning, Rebecca was more than half way thought the sizable bottle. She was slumped over at the dining room table in a semi-comatose condition.

Anthony rushed over to Rebecca and took the glass out of her hand, covered the bottle of port and put it back in the shelf that it came from.

"Rebecca, you've been drinking again, where are the girls?" Anthony commented in a frustrated sort of voice. He gently pulled her up with the determination to carry her to bed. Rebecca pulled back with as much force as she could muster.

"The girls are upstairs sleeping. I had to tell them that you were working late," she slurred.

"And that's exactly what I was doing," Anthony answered.

"Damn you, Anthony. You haven't been working. You've been out all night," Rebecca slurred. "She must be really good. Does she screw you good?"

Anthony grew red in the face hearing his wife talk in this unaccustomed manner. "Rebecca, you're drunk and you don't know what you're talking about. Come on, let's get you to bed."

"I'm not going to bed. I'm not ready." Rebecca attempted to rise. Anthony reached out to steady her. Rebecca broke away from his grip.

"Damn you, don't touch me Anthony. Not when you still have her on your hands," Rebecca screeched.

Just then, Rebecca tripped. It happened so quickly that Anthony didn't get a chance to stop it. She fell sideways on her face. Anthony gently pulled her up, she had a decent sized bruise on the side of her face, and it was getting bigger by the moment. Rebecca began to cry, tears streaked down her face. She relaxed into his arms.

Anthony led her to the bedroom. He sat her on the bed and went to get her an ice pack. By the time that he came back, she was fast asleep in bed. Anthony woke her up, knowing that it might not be such a good idea her sleeping in her extreme drunken state.

Anthony cradled her upped body in his arms. He put the icepack against her face.

Rebecca started to cry again. "Do you still love me?" she asked, her voice almost a whisper.

"Of course I do. I know I did since the time that I first saw you. I always will love you."

"Are you still *in* love with me?" she asked.

Anthony stroked back her wavy black hair from her face. Her hair fell in glossy, thick black waves. It was truly beautiful. He had always been fascinated by her hair. Her large brown eyes that were almond in shape stared up at him in a smooth creamy face with small pouty lips. Small wrinkles were beginning to appear at the corner of her eyes, but did nothing to subtract from her stunning looks. That serious, pensive, intense face that he had always loved.

"Yes. I'm in love with you. Only you," Anthony whispered.

"Then why are you with her?" Rebecca asked, slipping into sleep.

Anthony swallowed hard. "I'm not with anyone but you, Rebecca."

"Please stop lying to me. I know about her," she said softly before she dozed off to sleep.

Anthony decided to leave her be. Her leaned her back in the bed and pulled the covers up around her. He got undressed and slid in beside her. In her sleep, she turned over towards him and nestled onto his chest. He wrapped his arms around her and kissed her on the top of her head.

He had no answers for her.

Chapter Twenty-two

Feburary, 1954

When Abner had first heard about the idea, he had thought it was wild and inconceivable. His friend Lawrence Rice propositioned him.

"But that's fraud. To promote penny stocks as something else to shareholders," Abner said with alarm. "How could you even consider doing something like that?"

"Because of the money involved," Lawrence answered smoothly.

"What do you mean?"

"I mean that there's a lot of money involved. You can make a lot. A *whole* lot. I'm talking hundreds of thousands. Even millions," Lawrence responded. "We hype up the value of the penny stocks, get the people interested by making some calls. Get them to buy them up like hotcakes. Then we sell our shares at the right time. We get all the profit from that."

Abner pursed his lips. "It sounds easy enough. Why are you letting me in on this?"

Lawrence shook his head with a smile. "Because, number one, you have a percentage of ownership in my company ever since I took it public. And you are a good friend of mine, Abner. There is no one that I would rather work with concerning this other than you. So are you in?"

Abner thought for a while. He had never done anything of the sort before, "Won't we get caught?"

"Not if we play the game correctly. Only stupid, greedy people get caught. We have to do it carefully and in the right way."

After a minute of silence, Abner said, "I'm in."

Ψ

McMillan sat in court with a great deal of anticipation. He was waiting for the verdict to be said for the case *Gionelli vs. the city of*

Chicago. His investigators had managed to dig up a few things on Rocco Gionelli and subsequently bring charges against him.

The prosecuting lawyer, Mr. Bernard, continued to say that he had evidence to prove that money from Mr. Gionelli was filtered into a company called Brooks and Sons. The lawyer took out his folder and began to leaf through it, searching for the detrimental piece of evidence for the case.

Earnest at Abner sat on either side of Rocco. Rocco looked at them and wrote on a piece of paper. *Did it go through correctly?*

Earnest gave a slight nod.

Mr. Bernard began to grow more and more flustered as he continued to leaf back and forth through his files.

Judge Strickland furrowed his white brows. "Is there is problem Mr. Bernard?"

A thin film of sweat had formed on his forehead. "I can't seem to locate the information. I must have forgotten to put it in, although I am sure—"

"Are you telling me that you cannot find some evidence?" Judge Strickland asked, cutting to the chase.

"W-well I wouldn't say it was lost..." he stuttered nervously. "I'm sure it's back in my office. My assistant does all the filing. She might have forgotten to put it into this folder," he laughed nervously. "You know how flighty women can be at times."

Judge Strickland stared at him blankly.. "Really, because my wife and my daughter are one of the most grounded people I know. In fact, I have come across men that were more flighty than they," he responded, with a touch of nastiness.

"Y-y-yes, I'm sure..." Mr. Bernard said, shifting nervously on his feet. He looked over at the defense. All three of the men's faces were stoic, revealing no feeling. He scowled at them

McMillan's face grew red with rage. How could this be happening to him? He had given the evidence over to the prosecution team and they had lost it? The one thing that could have convicted a man whom he considered to be a lowlife gangster. McMillan, who was sitting behind the defense, stared at the back of their heads with murderous rage. He knew that things didn't just disappear like that. Unless, it has some help and he was certain where the help came from. Only trouble was that he couldn't prove it. As good as Mr. Gionelli was, he was sure that all the tracks had been covered up.

By the time it came to the closing statements, Bernard knew he had to do something drastic in order to get a retrial. Bernard knew that without the crutial missing evidence, an acquittal was likely to occur—the defense team had been well-prepared today and things were definitely going in their favor. But Bernard wasn't going down without a fight. He was determined to make sure that Rocco Gionelli ended up in prison where he belonged. He was determined to get the defense to motion for a mistrial.

Bernard cleared his throat and stood up when it came time for him to deliver his closing statement. He postioned himself in front of the jurors and stared each and everyone of them in the eyes.

"Ladies and gentlemen. Despite the misplacement of the most important evidence that I wanted to present to you today, evidence that would have left no doubt in your mind, the guilt of—"

Abner stood up. "Objection your honor. He's assuming facts not in evidence."

"Sustained," the judge responded. He gave Bernard a stern look. "Your closing statement is prejudicial against Mr. Gionelli. You are assuming facts that were not presented as evidence in this courtroom today. Jury, disregard what the council has just stated."

Bernard nodded and continued. "Mr. Gionelli is not new to money laundering accusations. In 1938, Mr. Gionelli was charged with money laundering, but—

Judge Strickland pounded his gavel. His face was a mask of disgust.

"Mr. Bernard, Mr. Hurst and Mr. Bernstein. I want to see you in my chambers. Now."

Ψ

Mr. Bernard stalked into his office, determined to rip into his assistant Wendy. He stomped over to her desk and stood in front of it. Wendy stood up and looked at him with pure horror written all over her face.

"Sir, I heard what happened. I'm sorry, I thought I—"

"Don't give me the 'I'm sorry bit,' you stupid woman. How could you leave out that piece of information?"

"Sir, when I gave you the file, you looked at it yourself and saw it in there. I put it there. This is not my fault."

"Of course it's your fault! I knew I shouldn't have hired a woman. I should have gone with my instinct and hired a man. All this would have never happened it I had had a man organizing my files. This is all your fault."

Wendy began to get angry at his statements, her hazel eyes flashing. "It could have happened to anyone, including a man. So don't give me that. Besides, as I said. The paper was in there when I gave you the file this morning. You saw it yourself. You just don't want to admit it because that means that you would have to take the blame. This had nothing to do with me and you know it."

Mr. Bernard's face puffed up in anger. "Get out, you stupid tramp. Get out! You have just ruined the biggest case of the year for me! You are fired! "

Wendy's jaw dropped to the floor. "You can't fire me!"

"I sure can and I just did. Pack your things together and get out this instant. You are no longer working for me. I will not have a smart mouthed female that is disorganized and scatter brained working here."

Wendy began to cry. "You know I need this job, Mr. Bernard. You know that I'm raising my children on my own. You know my husband just died eight months ago."

Mr. Bernard twisted his lips. "I don't give a shit. Get the fuck outta here," his professional tone was dropped in an instant revealing his true foul-mouthed manner.

Without another word, Wendy began to pack her things into boxes. She telephoned her oldest boy Alfie.

"Could you come over here and pick me up?" She asked her son, sobbing.

"Mom, what's the matter?"

"H-he fired me, Alfie. I can't talk here. Just come and get me, please. If you're busy I could wait."

"No Mom. I'll be there in an instant. I just got out of classes."

"Thank you, dear."

Ψ

Alfie walked right up into the office, rage written all over his face. "Where is that sonofabitch?" he spat furiously.

Wendy stood up from where she sat with alarm in her eyes. "Please, Alfie, let it be. Please. I'm begging you. I was thinking of quitting this job anyways. I can't work for a person like him."

"Yeah, but I know you wouldn't have quit without making sure that you had another job lined up," he said, his face red with fury.

"Let's just get out. We'll talk about it later. Here is not the place."

Soon they had the two boxes packed, but there were still some things that she had to get.

"We can carry those out in our hands. Let's just put these in the car and then come back up and get the rest," Alfie said as he picked up one of the boxes.

Wendy prepared to pick up the other box.

Alfie shook his head firmly. "Oh no, you're not picking that box up, Mom. It's too heavy. Can you go ask if someone, maybe the security, can bring it out for us?"

The minute they left the office, an office worker called one of the security officers. "Come up, and guard the door. Mr. Bernard said to not let Mrs. Zimmerman back into the office."

When they got down into the lobby area of the building, Wendy looked around for Garrett, a security officer. He was a pleasant man that she had taken to instantly. He had always been so nice to her, and she liked him immensely. He was a very good friend to her. She found him over on the side. He offered her a smile. His smooth, cocoa colored face regarded her with kindness. "What can I do for you, Miss. Wendy.

Wendy smiled. "Please, Mr. Garrett," she said jokingly, "how many times do I have to tell you to just call me plain ole' Wendy? I hate to ask you this, Garrett, but I was wondering if you could help bring down a box for me."

Garrett's smile faded off of his dark face. "What do you mean? Why you packing up for?"

"I got fired. I'm packing up my things. Please, I need a little help."

"I'm sorry, M- Wendy. I'll be much obliged to help you out."

"Thank you so much."

Garrett looked around nervously. "I think it's best if you come up there with me, Wendy."

"Of course," Wendy said, fully understanding. "We can go up there now, if that's okay."

"Let's go," Garrett said with a smile.

When they got to the front door of the office, there was a security guard standing there.

"Please. I'm just coming to get the rest of my things. Garrett is helping me." Wendy said to the guard.

"My orders are to not let you back into the office. Mr. Bernard said that he would send the rest of your things to you."

"Well, I would much rather get them now. I have some pictures in the box."

"Mr. Bernard said that he would send them to you," he repeated a little testily. His blue eyes boring into hers.

Garrett spoke up, "Come on, Jimmy. Can't you at least let her bring the box out? We won't come back no more."

"I have my orders," the guard said forcefully.

"Then can you bring the box out here in the hallway," Garrett said, "and we'll take it down."

Jimmy turned ferociously on him. "Take her back down, she's not allowed in here. And you sure as hell ain't either. Now don't do anything stupid, you do want to keep your job, don't you?"

Garrett stepped back in shock.

"Come on. Let's go, Garrett. I'll get my things when they send them. Come on," she said pulling on his wrist.

Jimmy noticed this and his face went red with anger. "What the hell is this? You can't be touching him like that! You know what? I'm gonna make sure you get fired for sure.. Just watch and see."

"Why are you carrying on like this, Jimmy? What did I ever do to you? You know my wife and son. I-"

"Get the hell out of my face now! You ain't gonna have a job tomorrow, Garrett. I guarantee it."

Wendy was filled with horror. "Please don't fire him. This was all my fault."

Jimmy said nothing more, but continued to glare at them balefully through slitted eyes.

They finally left. Wendy looked over at Garrett with sorrow on her face as they went down the stairs. Shock and bafflement were written all over his face

"I'm so sorry. I didn't mean for this to happen...oh God, I'm such a fool." She began to weep bitterly.

Garrett put an awkward hand on her shoulder. "Look, Wendy. It ain't you fault and you ain't no fool. I wanted to help. I knew it might cause some trouble, but I did it anyways."

"But your job...you've been here so long. Oh God!"

"Please, Wendy. I'll be all right. You just go on out to your son now and make sure they send you your things."

"Thank you so much, Garrett. I'll call later in the week. I would like if you and your family were to come over for supper one evening. You know, in all these years I haven't thought to ask you over for supper?"

Garrett smiled softly. "I would like that very much, Wendy. Thank you."

"No, I should be thanking you, Garrett," she said, her hazel-gray eyes soft.

Finally, they were in the lobby. Her son was waiting there with a worried expression on his face. He came over when he spotted his mother and Garrett.

"Mom, what took you so long? Are you okay?"

Wendy nodded quickly. "I'm fine. Alfie, where are your manners, you haven't even said hi to Mr. Jackson here."

Alfie blushed. "I'm sorry. How are you, Sir?" he said extending his hand.

"I'm fine, young man. And how are you?" Garrett responded as he shook Alfie's hand.

"Alright, I guess. What happened to the rest of the things? I thought you were going up there to get them?

"They won't let me back into the office."

"Well, they're going to let me in, or so help me God," Alfie said as he began to charge towards the stairs

"No Alfie, please. They said that they would send me my things."

Alfie looked at her quizzically. "Oh, yeah? Who's gonna come and bring them to you?" he said sarcastically.

Wendy knew that her son was right. Most likely, she wouldn't see her things again. But for the sake of peace, she said, "They'll send them. They promised."

"Promises mean nothing to these people Mom. You know that."

Ψ

Betty was waiting outside when he pulled up to the front of her workplace. But there was also a small, plain faced, dark haired girl standing there as well.

Betty came over to the car and gave him a kiss.

"Anthony, this is my friend Eunice. Would it be all right if we were to give her a lift downtown since it is along the way?"

"Oh gosh! A Bentley...," Betty's friend said in shock.

What else could Anthony say but yes without sounding like an asshole?

"Sure, no problem," he answered.

As soon as they were all inside the car, they drove off.

Once Eunice was deposited safely downtown, Betty made a grab at his crotch from the passenger seat..

"Betty, baby, I'm gonna crash if you keep that up," Anthony said softly, not really wanting her to stop. Her touch had sent an exciting shiver up his spine.

"Honey, there's no way I'm stopping now. When we get off the highway, find someplace to park."

"But it's broad daylight," Anthony pointed out.

"Who gives a fuck," was Betty's response.

"You know, you have a very filthy mouth," Anthony said, feeling quite turned on.

"Yeah? Le'me show you how I use it."

Ψ

Harold Lachney took the money out of the envelope and put into his safe. He smiled with mirth. His partner, Larry Bernard, who was an up and coming assistant district attorney like him, had no idea what had gone on.

After getting the files from Wendy, Bernard had given the file to Lachney to look over. He had looked over it all right. He slipped that piece of information right out of the file, hid it away, in his desk drawer, and locked it. He discreetly took it out later and burned it. Bernard had no idea that he took the evidence, neither would he ever in a million years suspect that his partner had anything to do with the disappearance of the vital piece of information. Bernard also had no idea that Lachney's grandnephew, Trevor, was married to Rocco Gionelli's second cousin Liza. So in a way, he was related the Gionelli's—although the relationship was distant through marriage.

By the time McMillan and his men went to recollect the evidence from Brooks and Sons, the company would have dissolved all the information—not totally, but anything even slightly incriminating would be cleaned up. Harold chuckled to himself as he closed back his safe and headed down the hallway to make himself a drink. McMillan must have his shorts in a knot over this.

It was too bad that Wendy had to be fired in the process. The poor woman was totally oblivious to what happened. Ah well. Wendy was an attractive woman with good looks and a sharp mind. She was sure to find another job. After all, it was her looks that first caused Bernard to hire her. He was after her for months, looking to get laid until she had brought her husband for an office party. After that point, Bernard had left her alone. He wanted no trouble with the tall, strong German with the ice blue eyes and stoic deportment. But after the husband died in a car accident, Bernard had resumed his pursual of her with a fervor. Wendy, now knowing that her job was precarious and she needed it more than ever, had accepted it. Harold was sure that Bernard had slept with her, although he wasn't one hundred percent sure. The man was a degenerate and underneath it all, Harold deeply disliked Bernard.

Lachney also found out that Bernard, with his customary tactlessness and occasional poor judgement, had goaded the defence to move for a mistrial. As a result of this, the retrial was barred from occurring as a precaution again double jeopardy.

Rocco was a free man. For now.

Rocco had given him a nice amount. Harold thought himself decent enough not to ask for *too* much money in payment for the deed. After all, they were family, in a way. But he did have to ask for money, after all, there was the risk involved and the fact that he would be losing the case and therefore, losing money.

Oh well,
Too bad.

Ψ

Wendy's parents, Gerta and Fredriche Strauss came over to America from Hamburg, Germany in 1901. Her brother, Bertram, was born first in 1906 and then, four years later she was born. From the beginning, her parents instilled in her and her brother the importance of hard work and education.

They were not impoverished growing up, but neither did they have a lot of money. The family owned a bakery, from which they made a comfortable living. But a lot of the profit went into rent, supplies, and other things. Each day, after school, her mother would help Wendy and her brother with their schoolwork.

Wendy and her brother were very close. So when Bertram contracted rheumatic fever and died at the age of sixteen, Wendy was inconsolable. The family buried Bertram in the small community church's graveyard.

When Wendy was seventeen, she had met Yohann Zimmermann, a German immigrant. He was tall and blond with a blandly handsome face and steely blue eyes that always stared with great intensity. He was eight years her senior at twenty-five and was currently getting his masters in physics. He wanted to be a physics professor.

The two had dated for some months when Yohann had said that he wanted to marry her. Wendy was in love with him, and him with her. He was going to ask for her father for her hand in marriage.

The father had agreed but said, not until Wendy was through with getting her degree in English. So Yohann waited. Finally, in the fall after the spring of Wendy's graduation, the two were married.

Alfie was born first and then her daughter Helga and then the last girl child, Edda. After Yohann got his master's, he had gotten a job teaching at the University of Chicago. And for years they had been a happy family until that day, eight months ago, when they had gotten the news that Yohann had been in a car accident and had been killed instantly. Wendy wasn't sure, at first, how she would go on without him. But for the sake of her children, she knew she had to do it. Her three children needed her now more than ever—seventeen-year-old Alfie, fourteen-year-old Helga and ten-year-old Edda.

She had never worked in all the years that she was married, but now that would have to change and she was so grateful that her parents had encouraged her to finish college and get a degree. With her English degree, the job search shouldn't be so grueling and she was right. She had gotten a job in a law firm as a secretary and after taking a training course, she advanced to the position of the approximate of being a legal assistant, which wasn't an easy task to accomplish for a woman.

But now she was alone, jobless and nowhere to turn. She considered getting her masters and going into teaching…but she didn't have the money to do that.

About two weeks after losing her job, Wendy was cooking in the kitchen, preparing a nice dinner—Garrett and his family were coming over.

Alfie came home from school and walked into the kitchen where his mother was cooking. He kissed her on the cheek and sat down at the kitchen table.

"Mom, I've been thinking. Maybe I should get a job to help out around here," Alfie said casually.

"Well, maybe a part time job. And that money will be pocket money for you. I don't want you thinking that you have to take on the responsibility of this household. You're far too young for that kind of pressure."

"But Mom, you still haven't found a job yet. We need money, but I know you won't admit it."

"I will admit, Alfie. We do need the money. But there is no way that you are going out there to work with the intention of supporting this family. You need to keep your grades up, Alfie. If you don't, you won't get into a good school or get a scholarship. That's very important and that is what you need to be worrying about, nothing else. A job will come. We have a little money from your father that we can survive on until a job comes. Don't worry."

But Wendy was terribly worried because, really, there wasn't a lot of money left after paying for the funeral and paying off the bills that Yohann had left behind.

They would have to survive. Somehow.

Ψ

It had been three months now, and Wendy was still out of a job. The bottom of their money pot was very apparent. In fact, she was sure that they wouldn't last more than another two weeks if she didn't find a job. She really didn't have a lot of people to turn to. She didn't want to ask her friends for any money and her parents, that had emotionally supported her for most of her life, were dead. Unless something turned up really soon, she would be stuck. Stuck like a rat.

Ψ

It had been three months, and things concerning Rocco's case had pretty much died down. McMillan and his men had been unsuccessful in their attempts to re- obtain the information. It was no longer at the company. They were currently trying to get some more damnable information to do him in. But Rocco was fully confident that there would be none for them to see. He had taken care of everything. McMillan and his men could search until they were blue in the face. They would never find anything.

As Rocco sat there at his desk, he thought that it was now time. He had just gotten off the phone. The host at his hotel in downtown Chicago had just recently retired and they were currently interviewing potential applicants.

He thought of Wendy. He had felt terrible that the single mother had lost her job in the process of the event that had taken place in order to secure his freedom. And he had promised himself that he would call her and offer her a job after things had died down a little. He had checked her work records and found her to be hardworking, accurate, and very efficient. He was sure that she would fill the position of hostess at his hotel very well. The only thing he had to figure out now was his method of approach. He couldn't very well just come up to her and say 'hi I'm the man that your boss tried to convict. I heard that you were out of a job and I was wondering if you would like to come work for me.' Or could he?

Rocco sighed and sat back in his plush leather chair. This was going to be a tough thing to tackle, but fortunately, he was a man that liked to be challenged. He would find a way.

The next night, after dinner, the phone rang in the Zimmermann household. Alfie rushed to pick up the phone.

"Hello?"

A female voice responded, "Hello. Is this Mr. Zimmermann?"

Alfie hesitated, "Well…no. I'm Alfie, the son. Can I help you?"

"May I speak to your father?" the pleasant female voice asked.

"Well, my father isn't here anymore. He passed away," Alfie said a little sadly.

The voice was properly sympathetic. "Oh, I'm sorry about your loss. May I speak to your mother then?"

"Of course," Alfie put his hand to the phone and called out for his mother. Wendy came to the phone and took it from her son.

"Hello, this is Mrs. Zimmermann speaking."

"Hello, Ma'am. I have called to say that you and your family have been randomly selected for a seven day stay at *The Sunset Palace* hotel. The one that is located in Reno, Nevada," the happy female voice chirped.

Wendy put her hand to her face. *The Sunset Palace* hotels were one of the most prestigious hotels in the country. Five star, all the way. She knew that famous actors, actresses, and sports legends had at one time or another spent time in one of those hotel chains. Including Judy Garland, one of her favorite actresses of all time.

"Is this some sort of joke?" She gasped breathlessly.

"No, Ma'am," the voice replied cheerfully.

"Oh gosh, how did I get chosen for this?" she asked, still not believing their luck.

"Well, it is sort of a random selection of sorts. It is a promotional offer. Lucky for you, you happened to be the one of the few that were chosen."

"So when do we arrive there?"

"Four first class tickets to Reno, Nevada, have already been mailed to you. They should arrive by tomorrow at the latest. They are booked for Sunday. You can leave at any time that day. But if Sunday's not okay for you, we can always change the—

"No. Sunday's perfect. We'll leave in the morning," Wendy said cutting her off.

"Well, there are morning flights at seven in the morning, at 8:45 and at ten. You can choose either one. When you get to the hotel, there will be a lot of activities and things for both you and your children. You will be filled in when you get there. You are sure to enjoy your stay. Congratulations, Mrs. Zimmermann. You have a nice day now."

"Oh, thank you!"

Alfie was standing nearby with a look of question on his face. "What is it Mom? What did they want?"

Wendy grabbed her son's hands and gushed, "We won a week's stay in Reno Nevada. And not only that, we get to stay in *The Sunset Palace* hotel!"

Alfie smiled. It was then that Alfie's two younger sisters came in through the door from outside. They saw the look of excitement on their mother and brother's faces as well as the energized talking.

"What's going on?" Helga asked, putting down her books. Edda trailed behind her with an anticipatory smile on her face. She too was curious to know what all the excitement was about.

"We won a trip to Reno Nevada and we get to stay in a five star hotel, to boot," Alfie responded, excitedly.

"That's amazing, Mom! What a swell way to start the summer vacation!" Helga exclaimed. "How did you win?"

"Well, apparently, it was a promotional offer. We were randomly selected. At least that's what the woman told me." Wendy answered.

Wendy couldn't believe their luck. Moment's ago things were looking bleak. A vacation was not going to give them money, but at least it would take their minds off of the financial problems at the present time. In three short days, they would be on their way to Reno, Nevada.

Ψ

Reno, Nevada was like nothing that Wendy had ever seen before. The bright flashing lights, the people, the glitter, the big hotels, and buildings were all captivating to her.

When they got to the hotel, Wendy gave her name. The man at the desk smiled warmly and told her that their suite was ready and waiting for them. Alfie and the girls looked wide-eyed and fascinated at the grand staircase, the hanging chandeliers and the richly decorated hallways and rooms.

"I heard that a lot of famous people come to this hotel," Helga said excitedly.

The young bellhop smiled. "You're right about that. Frank Sinatra stayed here a total of two times a year ago. Marilyn Monroe was here a few months ago. So was Joan Crawford. We even had Lucille Ball and Desi Arnez here once. Yep, we sure see our share of greats around here."

Alfie spotted a poster in the lobby area. It was advertising a fight between Rocky Marciano and Ezzard Charles. "Oh look Mom. There's going to be a fight here tomorrow night between Marciano and Charles. Ain't that amazing? I would love to see that."

"Yep, that fight tomorrow night's going to be something. We've had our sports celebrities here as well. Joe DiMaggio stayed here three years ago, back in the summer of 1951. Joe Lewis passed through here…a lot of people," he said happily.

"Wow," Alfie commented, totally impressed at this bit of information.

Finally they reached the elevator. Their suite was on the tenth floor. The young man brought their bags into their suite.

The four of them looked around, admiring the adjoining rooms. It was very nicely decorated. "This place is beautiful," Wendy commented, running her hand over the chiffon curtains.

"I'm glad you folks like it. It's one of the best suits in the place. If you look through that window over there, you can see the city. It's a wonderful view. It's going to be a hot day today, luckily, you two can cool off in our pool. There's a big hot tub as well."

"Yeah, I want to go to the pool!" Edda exclaimed.

Wendy walked towards her purse and pulled out her wallet. "Thank you so much, let me give you a tip."

"No, no, Mrs. Zimmermann. I don't need a tip. You just have a good time and enjoy your stay," the young man said with a smile and quickly exited the room before Wendy could protest.

Wendy shrugged and put the wallet back in her purse. "Okay, well. How about we go and grab some lunch?"

They all liked that idea.

They ate at a restaurant that they all agreed on. It was a casual restaurant with a very relaxed atmosphere.

After lunch, they went bowling together. Helga won, much to Alfie irritation.

"I told you that I hurt my wrist this week while playing tennis at school," Alfie complained, much affronted at his defeat.

"Sure, sure. Your wrist is fine, you're just looking for an excuse," Helga said stubbornly. "Face the facts, I'm a better bowler than you are."

Alfie smirked. "I can't believe I got creamed by a little girl."

Helga's face turned red with annoyance. "I'm not a little girl. I'm a young woman. Besides, females mature much earlier than males. So if you think about it, you and I are probably on the same mental level." Helga put her nose in the air. "In fact, I might even be thinking on a higher level than you."

Alfie snorted. "Don't count on it, little sis. Besides all this fuss and you only beat me by a few points."

"I'll call four strikes more than a few points," she responded, smartly.

Wendy decided that it was time to step in. "Okay, okay, you two that's enough. Well all played a good game, all right? Let's not argue over it."

That afternoon, Edda wanted to go down to the pool so all four of them changed into their bathing suits and went downstairs.

The pool was very large, very blue, and very refreshing looking. Wendy found herself a lounge chair and sat down.

"Mom, aren't you coming in the water?" Edda asked, from the pool.

"Maybe in a little while. For now, I just want to relax here," Wendy turned towards Alfie and Helga. "You two keep an eye on your sister."

While her children played in the pool, Wendy lay back in her chair and slid on her sunglasses. The sun was burning bright and hot in the sky, now was a good time to work on her tan.

As she lay, she felt a shadow come over her. She opened her eyes. Standing over her was a tanned handsome man that looked to be in his fifties. He had dark hair and eyes. He was dressed in a light button down shirt, crème linen pants, and sandals. He was smiling at her.

"Are you enjoying your stay, Ma'am?" the man asked, taking a seat beside her.

Wendy sat up in her chair and slid her shades to the top of her head. He had an accent. She smiled hesitantly. "As a matter of fact, I am. Do I know you?"

The handsome man smiled. "I'm the owner of this hotel. My name's Rocco," he extended his hand. Wendy grasped it.

"My name's Wendy, it's nice to meet you. And yes, I am enjoying my stay. Thank you so much."

Rocco smiled. "I'm sure a vacation is just what you needed," he responded.

"Yes, indeed it was."

Rocco looked towards the two girls and Alfie. "Those are your children?"

"Yes. Alfie's my oldest, he's seventeen and then there are my two girls, Helga who's 14, and Edda's 10."

"Very handsome children. I see that they take after their mother," Rocco said with a smile, the bright white of his teeth contrasted with the deep tan of his face.

"Thank you, Sir," Wendy responded, blushing deeply.

"Please, don't call me Sir," he laughed, "I feel like such an old man. Call me by my first name, Rocco."

Wendy paused, smile frozen on face. She had seen this man before, she just couldn't place it. And the name…so familiar.

"Have I met you before? I don't know... you seem so familiar to me. I know that probably sounds silly to you, but…"

"No, no. Not silly at all. I am the man of a thousand faces. Do you know how many people have said that I look like somebody else that they know? But you, my dear, have a face that is unforgettable."

Wendy blushed again and her heart fluttered in her heart. She felt like a schoolgirl. Why was this complete stranger having such an effect on her?

Rocco kept his smile. He couldn't tell her yet who he was, that she indeed might have seen him before in a newspaper three months ago when reporters had gotten a picture of him in court. But thanks to his connections, the story hadn't been widely publicized by the media. If it had, she would have recognized him immediately.

"Let me ask you, my dear, what are you doing tonight?"

"Well, nothing much. We were planning on sitting in and watching some movies."

"May I suggest something that may be a little more enjoyable?"

"Of course you may."

"How about going together to the fight tonight? I'm sure you and your children would enjoy it."

Wendy hesitated. "Well, we don't have tickets and I'm not sure that we could afford them. Besides, my daughters are too young, they wouldn't allow them in."

Rocco smiled and shook his head slowly. "Is that all that you're worried about? I can take care of all of those issues. I can get tickets for all of your children including the youngest ones and for you. They will all be allowed access."

Wendy's jaw dropped open. "Are you sure you can do that?"

"I am the owner of this hotel, aren't I?"

Wendy nodded and smiled. "Well yes, I guess you are."

"Well, how about I pick you all up around…say six? We can grab a quick bite to eat and then go to the fight."

"Well, that sounds wonderful, Rocco. I'm sure my children would like that as well, especially my son."

Rocco rose from his chair and tipped his hat. "Well, it was nice to meet you and I shall see you tonight." He held her hand and kissed it gently, and then he walked away.

Wendy stared after him, wondering exactly who this man was and why he was making such a big impression on her.

Ψ

"Oh my gosh, Mom, he's come for us in a limousine!" Helga exclaimed in excitement.

Alfie and Edda peeked through the blinds as well.

"Shucks Mom. She's right, it's a limo," Alfie said in amazement.

Wendy walked into the sitting area as she clipped her earring on. "You guys get from the window and listen for the door. Rocco should be coming up at any moment."

Three minutes later, there was a knock at the door. Alfie opened it. It was Rocco. They shook hands. Rocco smiled and asked them if they were ready.

"Mom's in the bathroom. She'll be out in minute," Alfie responded, impressed with the expensive clothing the Rocco was wearing.

"You look sharp, young man," Rocco said patting Alfie on the back. "You two young ladies look lovely as well."

Alfie smiled in appreciation. "Thank you, Sir.'

"Please call me Rocco. As I told your mother, calling me 'Sir' makes me feel like an old man," he said with a smile.

"Okay, I'm ready," Wendy called as she walked into the room. Rocco's eyes were fixed on her. He stared at her in open admiration.

Wendy wore a deep, golden yellow pencil skirt with a matching double-breasted suit jacket with a v neck and black pumps. Her wavy, shoulder length hair was pinned back and she wore a yellow hat.

"You look lovely, Wendy." Rocco came over and held out his arm.

Wendy grasped it with a smile and said, "Thank you. You look pretty sharp too. Well, shall we be on our way?"

"Yes, we shall," Rocco said holding the door open.

"Thank you Rocco," Helga said with a smile.

Ψ

The fight was awesome. The five of them had ringside seats and as a result, they were able to get a good view of all the action. All of them were getting so involved in the fight, including little Edda.

After Rocky Marciano K.Oed Ezzard Charles for the last time, the fight was over.

Rocco cheered loudly and clapped his hands. He looked over and smiled at Alfie. "They both put up a good fight, huh?" Rocco stated.

"Yeah, they sure did."

"I bet two grand on Rocky, I guess I hit pay dirt tonight."

"Yeah, I bet you did," Alfie responded, in wonderment. Two thousand dollars was quite a lot to throw around.

Rocco and the rest of them rose. He took out a pack of cigarettes, offered one to Helen, and took one out for himself. He lit Helen's for her and lit his own.

"What do you say we go get something to eat now? We'll go to *The Pimento*. You'll love it," Rocco said as they walked towards the limo.

"Oh gosh, I've heard about that restaurant. It's so famous. Do we have to dress up?" Wendy asked.

"All of you are dressed just fine for the restaurant," Rocco responded, as the chauffeur opened the limo doors for them.

The restaurant looked so nice from the front that Wendy was almost unsure of her attire, despite Rocco's assurances.

Rocco noted her hesitation. "I know what you're thinking, but don't worry because believe it or not, there are people in there that are more underdressed than you are. You might also be surprised at who those people might be," Rocco said with a smile.

All five of them walked into the restaurant. They were greeted immediately.

Alfie stared in wonderment at the tall woman teetering on stiletto heels. She was draped in diamonds and other jewelry. She was wearing a tight, gold dress, a mumu, and she held a thin cigarette in her hand with a gold cigarette holder. Alfie looked at the hand holding the cigarette. It was big and strong with various expensive gemstone rings on the fingers. Alfie studied the heavily made up face with its strong jaw line. His eyes slid down to the neck and that's when he saw the Adam's apple. He almost choked with shock. This was a man!

"Mr. Gionelli. Welcome! Welcome! Now who is this beautiful woman and these darling children that you have with you?" the being asked, with admiration.

Rocco gladly began the introductions. "Everyone, this is Frankel Hanesson—"

"Tiffany!" the being shrieked good naturally in correction. It had a heavy accent.

Rocco cleared his throat. "Excuse me, I mean Tiffany. H—She owns the restaurant here. Tiffany, this gorgeous woman by my side is Wendy Zimmermann and her three children. This here is Alfie, these two lovely young women are Edda and Helga."

"Nice to meet you!" Frankel-Tiffany said shaking their hands, "Please, follow me!" the being said with a flourish.

The being seated them at their tables and was off, leaving them with their waiter. The waiter left to get them refreshments and to give them time to order.

Alfie leaned over towards Rocco, the moment the waiter left. "I don't mean to be rude or anything, but was that a man? Dressed up like that?"

Rocco gave a lopsided grin. "Yes it was. Frankel is a bizarre character, but he has a good heart. Everyone in Reno knows who he is. He owns this restaurant as well as two others. He's become so famous, that people don't even look at him much as a man in a dress. That is a hard thing to do. I can't say I agree with what he does but I do respect him. He went through a lot to achieve what he has now."

"I could imagine he has," Wendy said with a nod.

The waiter came back. "Are you ready to order?"

"Yes, we are. I'll have the chicken fettuccine," Wendy responded.

"I'll have the salmon and the wild rice," Rocco said and closed his menu, handing it to the waiter.

"What are you three going to order?" Wendy asked her son and her daughters.

"I'll have the steak," Alfie said.

"I'll have the baked ziti. So will Edda."

As they ate, they got into conversation. Rocco asked them a lot of questions. He listened carefully and with interest and Helga told him about a club that she had joined at school. He listened and laughed as Edda told him about her weird math teacher at school. He asked Alfie if he planned to go to college. When he found out that Alfie did intend to go to college, he asked where he wanted to go and what he wanted to study.

"I think I want to write. I love writing."

Rocco took a mouthful of food. "What kind of writing. For papers?"

Alfie hesitated. "Well maybe to begin with. But I'm thinking more novels and maybe even screenwriting."

Rocco raised his eyebrows. "That's great. Writing is a very rewarding profession, when you work hard at it."

Alfie pushed the food around on his plate. "Yeah, that's what I was thinking."

During this time, Wendy had more or less been the observer at the table. She watched as Rocco communicated with ease with her three children and she saw how well they took to him. She couldn't help but think that she had met him before. She just had to think really hard.

Rocco noticed her gazing him. He smiled and placed his hand over hers "Are you okay, Wendy?"

Wendy smiled. "I'm fine. I'm just so happy and I'm having such a nice time," she responded.

Rocco and Wendy locked eyes.

"Can we order dessert now?" little Edda asked, as she polished off the last of her ziti. Rocco and Wendy tore their eyes off of each other.

Rocco smiled and then chuckled. "Of course we can. Tell me Edda, how do you fit all that food into that little body?"

Edda smiled proudly. "My Mom says I have hollow legs."

They all laughed at that.

When they left the restaurant, Rocco drove them back to the hotel. He walked them to their room. They all paused at the door.

"Come on, you guys, let's go in and get to bed," Alfie said hustling his sisters through the door.

"Mommy, are you coming?" Edda asked.

"She'll be in soon. Come on, quit breathing down her back." Alfie shut the door behind them, leaving Wendy and Rocco in the hallway.

Wendy nervously brushed her hair behind her ears and laughed. "My son is something else."

Rocco smiled, "He sure is. So are the rest of your children. You are lucky."

"Well, your children are all grown. That's good," Wendy said.

"Do you want to go out back on the main patio and talk for a while?" Rocco asked her.

"That would be nice," Wendy said smiling.

The moon was shining brightly in the dark velvety sky. A spattering of crystal stars twinkled in the ebony sheet that spread above.

There were a few other couples on the patio as well. They went to one end and sat on a chair.

"Why don't I get us some champagne?"

"That's sounds wonderful," Wendy responded.

Rocco came back with a small bottle of Moet and two flute, crystal glasses. He sat down beside her. He handed her a glass.

"Thank you," Wendy said as he poured it into her glass. Rocco then poured some into his glass.

Wendy took a sip. "I can't help but think that I know you." She studied his relatively smooth face and sparkling dark brown eyes. "I do know you. Oh gosh, aren't you Rocco Gionelli?"

Rocco took a long swallow and stared out at the sky before he answered. "That's right."

Wendy took a deep breath. "I mean Rocco Gionelli from the case, you were in court. I can't believe it. Maybe I've known all along underneath, but I just didn't want to make the connection."

Rocco said nothing. He swirled his glass of Moet.

"Do you know who I am?" Wendy asked.

Rocco nodded. "I was the one who got you to come here. It wasn't really a promotional offer. I wanted to talk to you and tell you how sorry I was."

"About what?" Wendy asked, confused.

"I'm sorry you lost your job when you have a family to provide for."

"What do you have to do with me losing my job at the law firm?" she asked.

"I'm just sorry that you did and I realized that you were a single mother and you needed the job. I felt terrible for you, so I wanted to give you and your family this vacation," he responded.

"So, this is a pity trip?" Wendy asked, feeling sick.

"No—no. I was looking at your work history and I want to offer you a job back in Chicago at my hotel."

"You've been snooping into my affairs? You've been spying on me?" Wendy said rising from her chair. "What sort of creepy man are you?"

Rocco rose too. "Please Wendy, let me explain—"

"There's nothing to explain. I'm going to go back to my room now. My children and I will be leaving tomorrow morning."

"Please, don't do this."

"Sorry, Rocco Gionelli, but I know your type. You think that you can control anyone and anything. I'm sorry, but you don't control the world and you definitely will not be controlling me."

"Please Wendy, that was not my intent. Let me at least walk you back to your room."

Wendy didn't say anything as he walked in step beside her.

"There is another thing Wendy…you are a wonderful woman. Stunning, intelligent, and full of life."

Wendy didn't answer. They finally got to the front door. Wendy turned to open the door. Rocco grasped her hand,

"Please, Wendy. Just listen to this. I was never a man to beat around the bush. I like you very much, do you hear me? I like your children a lot too. I can see myself being with a woman like you. Believe me, I wanted only good to come from this. I didn't know how to approach you about it. I didn't mean you any harm."

Wendy paused in mid air. She turned around and faced him, "What did you say?"

"I said I only wanted good to come of this."

"Before you said that."

"I said that I could see myself being with a woman like you," Rocco said with a hesitant smile.

Wendy stared at him expressionless. Her hazel-gray eyes burned into his brown eyes. Rocco shifted around on his feet and cleared his throat. He wished that she would say something.

"I don't know what to say," she said softly.

Rocco took a step closer to her. "Say that you can see yourself being with a guy like me."

"I don't like set-ups," she said slowly and took a step towards him as well.

"This is no set up," Rocco said, reaching out and drawing her to him.

Wendy folded into his arms. Rocco leaned in, kissed her lips softly, and then he leaned back and studied her face. Wendy slowly opened her eyes. She touched his face. Rocco put his hand over her hand.

"Goodnight," Wendy said and walked through the door.

Ψ

The next morning, Wendy was awakened by a knock at the door. She groggily rose from bed, put her robe around her, and went to open the door.

A grinning man in a uniform was standing there with a bunch of pink roses.

"Are you Wendy?"

"Yes I am," Wendy answered, quite taken back.

"Well then, Ma'am, these roses are for you," he began to bring the roses into the room. There had to be at least three dozen.

"Five dozen pink roses, hand delivered," the man said after he put down the last bunch.

"Oh my! Thank you," Wendy responded. She walked towards the roses and took a big whiff. Their sweet smell was beginning to permeate the room.

"No problem, Miss. Zimmermann. Somebody likes you a whole lot!" he said with a smile and a wink. Then he was gone.

Although she had a strong hunch about who sent her the flowers, Helen looked at the little card:

Good morning, you beautiful angel. You simply must meet me for brunch, bring the children. I will pick you all up around ten. Ps. I meant everything that I said last night, that was not the Moet talking! Your dearest, Rocco.

Pink roses were Helen's favorite flowers, but how did he know? Then she remember commenting on some of the lovely floral arrangements that were in the restaurant last night. She must have mentioned that pink roses were her favorite.

Helen got dressed in a sleeveless, white, flowered dress with a cinched in waist and wide billowing skirt that reached right bellow her knees.

"Mom, you look amazing," Alfie said.

"Thank you dear."

The four of them went downstairs to wait for Rocco in the lobby area of the hotel.

True to his word, Rocco was there promptly at ten thirty. They drove to nice, small, quaint breakfast nook called *Madison's*. They laughed, they talked, and they ate. Afterwards, they agreed that it was a nice day to go to the beach, but instead of going to the public beach, Rocco had something else in mind.

"This beach is private. I think you all would like it better," Rocco said to them

"You have a private beach here?" Edda asked, impressed.

Rocco smiled, "Yes, I do."

They set up an umbrella and a blanket. The kids went into the water. Rocco and Wendy laughed and watched as they played in the water. Alfie dunked an indignant Helga into the water. Helga spluttered furiously for a while, but then got her own by grabbing onto Alfie's legs underwater and pulling him down. Edda stood aside in the water and watched it all in amusement. It seemed that Helga and Alfie were forever in competition.

Rocco and Wendy sat down on the blanket. The large blue umbrella shielded them from the sun well. About 1000 feet away there was a house overlooking the water.

"That house is beautiful. Is it yours?" Wendy asked, squinting her eyes.

"It sure is. Perhaps you would like to have dinner with me tonight in my house? I will cook for you myself. I am quite the cook, I won't disappoint you."

Wendy grinned. "Shall I bring the children?"

Rocco shifted closer to her and held her hand," why don't we make it a dinner just for two, you and me."

Wendy smiled, "I think I like that idea very much. I'm sure Alfie wouldn't mind watching the girls.

Alfie stood up in the water and watched Rocco and his mother being involved in what looked to be a very intimate conversation. He was not upset.

Alfie supposed that normally, most offspring would feel offended if after eight months of one parent dying, the other parent went off and became attached romantically to someone else. But not Alfie. Alfie was a sensible boy and realized that his mother was a woman—a relatively young woman at that—and it would be good for her to have a man, to take care of her. Maybe if this thing between Rocco and his mother worked out, his beloved mother would never have to work again and risk coming across the likes of her former boss. Sure, Rocco was older than his mother, he wasn't sure by how much, but he was sure that it was by at least ten years, considering that is mother was 40. But what did that matter when Rocco was handsome, suave, and financially stable. Alfie shuddered when he thought back on the dreaded Larry Bernard and the control that he had over his mother's life and by extension, he and his sisters'. Soon anger began to bubble in the pit of his stomach. Pure hate and rage. If it were possible for him to have one minute alone with that man, he would strangle him to death. Why was it possible in the world for people like Bernard to survive and even thrive while innocent people suffered?

Well, hopefully things would look up from here on out. It definitely was a good start.

Wendy looked out to the water and noticed Alfie looking towards Rocco and her. He saw his mother looking, he quickly went over and dunked his little sister Edda. Edda and Helga then both attacked him, by jumping onto him and dragging him under the waves.

Alfie's probing expression was not lost on Wendy. She only hoped that he was not upset that she was beginning to have a relationship with Rocco. Wendy loved her children more than anything and if it was between her losing them and her being with Rocco, she would willingly give him up. It would be a pity though if that turned out to be the case. She sighed deeply.

"What is the matter, my dear?" Rocco asked, touching her face.

"I just hope that Alfie and the other kids are not upset about you and me."

"What would make you think that they are?"

"I don't know. Alfie was just watching us a moment ago," Wendy answered.

"I noticed. But he didn't look angry or upset to me," Rocco said with a shrug.

Wendy looked at Rocco's classic profile. Did anything pass by this man without him seeing? She doubted it.

"You don't think he looked upset?"

"Not at all. It seemed to me that he was in deep thought. Perhaps coming to a decision in his mind about what is taking place between the both of us. And I don't think that he is entirely negative towards it. He is a very thoughtful young man. It is only smart to consider things and look over situations before accepting them, don't you think?" Rocco asked, as he turned to face her.

"Yes, I suppose."

"I have no intentions of coming between you and your children. Believe me. If I sensed that the situation was not good, I would back off. But, fortunately, I have gotten no such feelings so far," Rocco said with a grin.

Wendy couldn't help but smile back.

He was so enchanting.

ψ

The night was calm and peaceful. The air was warm, yet not oppressively so. The moon shone silvery in the velvet sky.

When they got to the beach house, the air was cool. Wendy breathed in the salty-sweet air of the ocean. It tickled her nose.

The inside of the house was beautiful. Cream and red Persian rugs covered the highly glossed cherry wood floors. Plush chairs decorated the living room. Tiffany lamps and expensive vases and sculptures were all over.

"It's beautiful in here," Wendy said, looking around.

Rocco smiled at her, Wendy's heart fluttered. He was such a handsome man. She was amazed that there was not a trail of women following behind him…but then again, maybe there was. She wondered why he would choose her above other women that were more glamorous and maybe even more beautiful than she was. He could have any one of them, she was sure. Or maybe he did? She was having so many doubts.

"Are you all right?" Rocco asked, his smooth brow creased with worry.

Wendy attempted a smile. "I'm fine. I was just trying to guess what you cooked for dinner?"

Rocco shook his head playfully. "It's a surprise."

He led her to the dinning room. Wendy gasped in surprise. There were pink, red, and white candles all over the room. The table was beautifully set with fine bone china. Elegant hand woven placemats were set out and lovely crystal stem glasses were at each of the two places. Beautiful Italian opera music was playing softly in the background.

"Oh, it's so lovely…," Wendy gasped.

Rocco smiled and held the seat back for her. She sat down.

"Now you just relax and let me be at service to you. I shall now bring out the first-course—delicious minestrone soup."

Rocco went into the kitchen and brought out a silver tray with large white bowl on it and a liver ladle.

He ladled soup into her bowl and then into his. He gave her a piece of bread and took a piece for himself. "It's Italian bread."

"Umm, the soup looks good," Wendy commented inhaling its delicious odor.

"I certainly hope that you like it," Rocco responded, "and here is some wine to go with it…I am sure your taste buds will be properly roused."

Wendy took a spoonful of the soup. "This is amazing. I love it."

"Yes now, my dear, drink a sip of wine now."

And so Wendy did. "Ummm…" she said as she closed her eyes, "absolutely glorious!"

Rocco smiled. "I am glad that you like it," he said and took a spoonful of the soup. "Not bad, if I must say so myself."

Then Rocco brought out a fresh green salad

"A little bit of olive oil, a sprinkle of garlic…" Rocco began and then took a bite. He chewed, swallowed, and continued, "a splash of parmesan."

"The salad is delicious as well," Wendy watched as Rocco brought out another bottle of wine. "Another wine?"

"Yes, each course comes with its own special wine. The wine accentuates the taste if the food. Every food has a wine that it works best with," Rocco said softly as he poured the wine into her glass. Rocco's dark eyes locked with her's. "You can also say the same thing for people."

Wendy took up the glass and sipped the wine, her eyes did not leave his. It was sensual. The wine swept down her throat like a silken river that carried heat. Her insides warmed. Her face flushed with pleasure. Both Rocco and the wine were having a profound effect on her.

"You like?" Rocco asked, studying her face.

Wendy forced herself to squeeze out one single word, "Yes," she squeaked. She cleared her throat, embarrassed.

Rocco poured some wine into his glass and took a sip. His eyes closed as he swallowed the sweet liquid. Wendy watched his tongue move around in his closed mouth. His olive skin glowed in the soft lights of the dinning room. His black hair glimmered under the lights.

Wendy put her hand to her throat. She was having a little trouble breathing.

Rocco slowly opened his eyes and studied her. "Are you all right?" he softly asked.

"I'm fine," Wendy responded, softly.

Rocco smiled brightly. "Then shall we bring out the next course?"

"Yes, we shall."

After dessert, Rocco and Wendy sat by the fire. The night was chilly. Rocco put his arms around her and drew her near.

"Are you warm my dear?" he asked, rubbing her arms up and down.

"Yes, I am," Wendy said lazily.

Rocco looked at her in the face and raised her chin. He looked deep into her eyes. "Do you know how beautiful you are? How absolutely amazing you are? Your soul is so vibrant," he said softly as his dark eyes studied her.

Wendy touched his face. "So are you."

They leaned in and kissed. At first, the kiss was tentative and gentle. But very soon, their passions took over and the kisses became demanding and fiery.

Wendy drew back for a moment and with a breathy voice she said, "Please, I'm not this kind of woman."

Rocco gently pulled her back and kissed her all over her gave. Between each kiss he asked, "What kind of woman would that be?"

Rocco made his way down to her neck. Wendy arched her head backwards in pleasure.. "Flashy, quick, fast...," she sighed. "You know. That sort."

"Never. You are a gentle soul. But a soul should not be alone. You need someone to be with you. Not just tonight, but for a long time. And I want to be that man," he said as he slowly began unbuttoning her blouse.

"You do something to me, Rocco. You make me lose my senses," Wendy said and cried out as Rocco's lips connected with her collarbone.

"I want to make love to you, Wendy. Will you allow me to?" Rocco asked, drawing back slightly.

Wendy gently pushed his head back onto her shoulders. "Please don't stop," she whispered.

He pulled of her shirt. Wendy began to unbutton his shirt. She grew impatient with the last two buttons and just tore them off. She giggled softly. "I'm sorry."

"Don't worry, my dear," Rocco whispered.

Wendy ran her hand over his chest hair. His chest was strong and firm underneath. His stomach taunt and flat. A well kept 66.

Rocco unhooked her bra and gently leaned her back.

"Ah. You are so beautiful." He bent down and kissed her breasts. Her nipples perked up in response. He slid his thumbs over them and then his tongue.

Wendy leaned up and unhooked his buckle. She pulled his pants down. He stepped out of them and threw them aside. His sinewy legs were encased in boxer shorts, which Rocco soon abandoned as well.

Wendy sighed in pleasure. A well-endowed Rocco stood erect and ready.

Rocco smiled, his expression sultry. He pulled of her skirt and then her underwear. He gently kissed her all the way down to her stomach and stopped at the blond silken curls. Wendy sighed in anticipation.

Rocco opened her legs slightly. He ran his finger gently and slowly down the wet cleft. Wendy drew in a quick breath. He bent over and kissed her knees, then her inner thighs, all the way down to the juncture. Wendy opened her legs wider in arousal. She began to moan.

Rocco looked up at her and smiled softly. He gently slid a finger inside of her. She moaned and tried to reach for him.

"Please, I want you now," Wendy sighed.

"Oh no, not yet, my beautiful one."

Rocco buried his head in her silken curls. He lapped at her center, drinking her sweet nectar. Wendy held his head between her thighs, not willing to let him go.

Finally, he rose over her. "Are you ready?"

"Yes," Wendy whispered.

Her probed her opening with the head of his shaft before he slowly entered her. Wendy cried out in pleasure. He filled her up totally.

He began to slowly thrust in and out. He kissed her throat and her lips and her face as he did so. She moaned and clutched his muscled arms.

His pumping became more fervent and deeper. He called out her name gently. Wendy moved her hips in rhythm with his, hungrily meeting the thrusts of his sinewy hips. He burned deeper and deeper inside her a shockwave of pleasure began to shake her groin. She cried out and grabbed his hips. Intense spasms overtook her.

Wendy felt liquid warmth seeping into her passage from Rocco. Rocco let out a drawn out moan and collapsed onto her. He breathed heavily. Wendy ran her hands through his thick black and gray hair.

Rocco kissed her face.

Wendy whispered, "I love you."

The sun peeked through the gossamer curtains and onto Wendy's face. She groggily opened her eyes and rose up in the bed. Then looked to her side. The sheets were rumpled and pulled back.

At first, Wendy was a little confused as to where she was and then she remembered. And slowly, last night's events crept into her head. She looked at the clock that rested in the bedside table. It read nine o'clock in the morning.

Wendy threw back the covers and then, realizing she was naked, grabbed a red silk robe draped across the armchair on the other side of the bedroom.

Wendy walked out of the room and down the short flight of steps. As she walked down the hallway, from the kitchen she heard the sound of pots and pans and a rich baritone voice singing in Italian. Good food smells were also coming from the kitchen.

Rocco was at the stove mixing something in the frying pan. Like a sixth sense, he noticed her presence and turned around. He smiled at her. He came over and kissed her on the forehead and then on the lips.

"I am making breakfast for us…crepes with fruit filling and I have some fruit, coffee, and orange juice. Does that sound good?"

Wendy smiled hesitantly. "I should really be betting home now. I know that the kids must have woken up wondering where I was all night."

Rocco winked and smiled. "Already taken care of. I have called the hotel and someone will give them a message that you are fine and well."

Wendy relaxed a little. She sat down at the kitchen table. In that case, she would stay for breakfast. Although, she blushed a little as she thought that Alfie and possibly Helga would know what was going on.

Rocco finished making the crepes. Wendy helped him slice some fruit and put them on a platter. They sat down to eat.

"So, how are you feeling this morning Wendy?"

Wendy blushed. "I feel fine. And how are you feeling?"

Rocco grinned. "I feel fantastic, because I get to eat breakfast with the most beautiful woman in Reno."

Wendy blushed deeper, but did not respond. Wendy's mind flashed back to the love making of last night. It had been glorious. Her privates tingled just thinking about it. But then she swallowed hard with nervousness as she remembered what she had said to him as well—'I love you'. She had said it swept up in the moment. She really wasn't thinking. She really didn't mean that, or did she? For now, she would tell herself that it was on the spur of the moment thing until she was alone and she would have time to think about it. But since Rocco didn't bring it up, there was no point in her bringing it up.

"You never really answered me about my offer," Rocco said as he popped a red grape in his mouth.

"What are you talking about?"

"I'm talking about the job offer as hostess back at my hotel in Chicago. I think that you would fill the position well."

Wendy frowned. "Do you think so? I don't have experience in hotel work."

"Believe me. You would be just perfect. You have the character and the presence. And…I will pay you well," Rocco added with a smile, although he didn't know how long he really wanted her working for him. Eventually, if things went his way, it wouldn't even be appropriate. No wife of his was going to work for him.

Wendy thought about it for a minute and then answered. "I'll take the job, but I want you to consider something or rather, someone."

"What is it?"

"Well…when I got fired, because a friend of mine helped me, he also got fired. He's still out of a job just like I am. I would really appreciate it if you were to offer him a job if you have an opening. He's a really hard worker."

"Well, what does he do?" Rocco asked, leaning forward on his elbow.

"He worked in security. At the law firm. Please, think about it? He has a family to support. Right now, they are living off of what his wife earns as a launderer and, as you can imagine, it's not much."

Rocco thought in silence for a moment. "I can get him a job in security at the hotel…I have been looking for a watchman at the hotel. Can he work at night?"

"I'm sure he can! Oh he'll be so happy," Wendy beamed with joy.

"So, does that mean that you're going to come and work for me?" Rocco asked, with a smile.

Wendy got up from her chair and wrapped her arms around him. "You bet I will."

Rocco kissed her. "And you, my dear, I want to see a lot more of."

The next four days went by quickly. Everyday, Rocco would take them to do or see something new and exciting.

Finally, when the last day was approaching, Rocco said, "You know Wendy, now that you're working for me, you can stay on here a little longer if you would like."

Wendy smiled and held onto his arm. "I had a wonderful week. But to tell you the truth, I'm really excited about starting back work again. Plus, I can't wait to tell Garrett about his new job!"

Rocco kissed her soundly on the lips. "Fine. If you go back, I go back too!"

They went back home on the same plane and when they got to the airport back home in Chicago, Rocco's driver was waiting for them. Rocco dropped them off at home with a promise to telephone later on in the evening.

When they finished unpacking, they sat down in the kitchen table and were eating a lunch of soup and sandwiches.

"So tell me you three, do you like Mr. Gionelli?" Wendy asked, being careful to call him by his proper name.

"Yeah, I like him fine," Alfie said and took a bite of his sandwich. He chewed and then finished, "I know that you like him too, Mom."

Wendy blushed and smiled, "Y-yes. I do like him. A lot."

Helga smiled. "Rocco is so sophisticated and handsome. Mom, you should go for it."

"So you two wouldn't be upset…in light of your father and everything," Wendy asked, carefully.

"Well Mom, we feel terrible that Daddy's gone. And I still hurt a lot about it, but you should have someone…you shouldn't be alone, I don't think," Helga answered softly.

Suddenly, Edda who had been so quiet thus far, began to cry.

Wendy came out of her chair and wrapped her arms around your youngest child. "Oh, Edda, what is it dear? Please talk to us." Wendy stroked back her long blond hair.

"I miss Daddy," she said mournfully. "And I like Rocco, but I would much rather have Daddy back here with us all."

"Oh honey, we all want Daddy back," Wendy said and kissed her on the forehead. "I miss your father everyday, don't you think?"

"But if you marry Rocco, you might forget all about Daddy. Cindy Marshall at school told me that when her mommy married that new man, they threw out all the pictures of her daddy from the house. I don't think Daddy would like that. I think it would make him sad," she sobbed.

"First of all honey, no one said anything about marriage. I didn't say that Rocco and I were going to get married. Number two, I would never throw out the pictures of your father. Cindy's mom is divorced from her father, he didn't pass away, that's a completely different issue and situation."

Edda wiped her face with the back of her hand. "Okay. Just as long as you don't forget Daddy, because I can't forget him. He won't let me."

Wendy suddenly felt a chill run through her. What strange words to say, coming from such a small child!

Wendy was almost afraid to ask. "Edda what do you mean?"

Alfie and Helga watched their little sister carefully. They too were startled by the peculiar words and wanted to know their meaning.

Wendy repeated again. "Edda. What do you mean?"

Edda sniffled and wiped her nose. Wendy handed her a tissue. She took it.

"I don't want to say, then Daddy might go away."

Wendy felt prickling on her scalp and tightening in her chest, her heart began to pound dangerously fast. "But Daddy *is* gone, honey."

Edda shook her head and regarded her mother with her cool blue eyes. "No, Mommy, Daddy's still *here* in the house. I see him," she explained hesitantly.

Wendy was shocked and so were Alfie and Helga.

"But honey, Daddy's dead. So how can you see him?"

Edda shifted in her chair, uncomfortable with revealing herself. "I know, but he comes back to see me and to talk to me. Mostly at night is when I see him. Sometimes I'll be sleeping and he'll wake me up. Then he'll sit on my bed and we'll talk and stuff, just like we always used to."

Wendy didn't respond, she waited for Edda to continue, and so she did.

"Daddy said that he was not in the normal world anymore, but that most of the time, he was somewhere else. But he said that he would always come back to visit me, to make sure that I'm doing fine."

Wendy had tears in her eyes when she said the next thing. "Yes, honey, but why are you the only one that sees him? Why not me and why not your brother or your sister?"

Edda shrugged and paused to think about it, her forehead furrowed in concentration. "I think Daddy said that I see him better than anyone else. He said that I was more in tuned with where he was," Edda said, proud that she had remembered.

Wendy was thoroughly shaken. She looked at her hands as they shook before her face. Without another word, she slowly went back to her chair and plopped down.

Alfie and Helga were silent, and they regarded their little sister with a certain degree of shock and a slight bit of terror.

Edda sat in her chair and looked down at the food in her plate. Her face was flushed as she played with the ends of her sandwiches.

They all finished their meal in silence. No one knew what else to say, at the moment.

ψ

Dr. Halpern sat across from his desk and regarded the young girl with interest. He listened to what she told him about her daughter and how this girl was seeing her father at night and talking to him.

Helen shook her head. "I don't know. I think that this is an adjustment problem of some sort. I'm worried about her."

Dr. Halpern nodded his gray head. "I believe that you are right, to a certain degree. This is a coping mechanism. Even at her age, children can still be quite imaginative. I believe that she thinks up these meeting and these conversations with her father in order to assure herself.. That would, of course, explain why she's the only one seeing these apparitions."

Wendy nodded her head. She twisted her hands in her laps. She was so nervous and scared for her daughter. She felt as if the walls were closing in around her.

Dr. Halpern noticed her anxiety. "No need to get upset, Mrs. Zimmermann. This isn't something that cannot be fixed. After having therapy sessions with her, where we will work through the issues, she will be fine." The doctor took off his glasses and rubbed his eyes. "Believe me. I've tackled bigger issues in my thirty years of being in this practice."

"So when can I bring her?"

"I am totally booked for the next week, but I can have her the following Thursday, if you would like. I have a clear spot at...," he looked at his calendar, which was written all over, "one o'clock. Right after lunch. Shall we discuss the hourly fee?"

"I don't care how much it is. I just want you to fix my daughter."

Ψ

Ester poured Wendy a cup of tea and some for herself. She then placed the tray of almond cookies and cakes between them.

Wendy thanked her and took up a cookie. "I eat enough of these, I won't be able to fit through the door."

Ester's cinnamon brown face lit up in a smile. "Oh please, Wendy, you can gain twenty pounds and still look good."

Wendy laughed. "I don't even want to test if that's true." She took a bite of the cookie. "But anyways, I'm so glad that Garrett likes his job. I know that he's getting a good salary."

Ester nodded. "Oh yeah. A lot better than he ever got at that God forsaken law firm."

Wendy nodded and rolled her eyes. "Ester, I don't even want to remember the place exists."

Ester smiled in understanding. "So what about you? How is the job as hostess going for you down there at the hotel?"

Wendy beamed. "It's great, and I love the hours."

Ester gave a sly look. "And Mr. Gionelli…I'm a happily married woman, but he sure is a looker, ain't he? So debonair. Such a nice man."

Wendy blushed. "That he is."

Ester refilled her cup of tea. "What you need is a man like him to take care of you," Ester said with a firm nod of her head.

Wendy blushed. She wasn't quite ready to tell people about her and Rocco. Ever since they came back from Reno last week, they had been seeing each other. In fact, tonight, he was taking her to see a Broadway performance. *He certainly does spoil me*, she thought with pleasure.

"Hmmm…what are you smiling about?" Ester asked, suspiciously, her eyes slitting.

Wendy shook her head and took a sip of her tea. "Nothing at all, Ester."

Ester didn't look like she believed her, but she continued. "So, Edda's appointment is next week?"

Wendy sighed. "Yes. I'm so worried about her, Ester."

"Well, a parent's death is a hard thing to get through for a child," Ester said. "I remember when my mom died. I was only eight. It was so hard for me."

Wendy had never told Ester about the Edda claiming to see her father. She only told Ester that Ella was finding it difficult to deal with her father's death. The only person who knew all the details was the therapist. It was just too much for her. Wendy could only hope that things worked out okay.

Wendy glanced at her watch. She rose and took up another cookie and a piece of cake. "I gotta go back, Ester, lunch break is over. I'm so bad, I really shouldn't be carrying anything with me but these are so good that I can't resist You don't mind, do you?"

Ester swished her hand at Wendy. "Oh, please. Take as much as you want. In fact," Ester got up, got some plastic wrap, and covered the plate, "Take it with you. For the kids. I have a whole lot left over."

Wendy smile and gave her friend a quick kiss on the cheek. "Thank you Hun, I gotta leave now. But don't forget about dinner this Friday night at my house."

"Don't worry. I won't."

When Wendy walked outside to her car, she could feel the eyes of the neighborhood people boring into her. She was an anomaly in the black neighborhood. They hardly, if ever saw a white person passing through here. She would have thought the stares would have waned off, considering the amount of times that she and her children had been here, but they hadn't. Well, maybe it would take even more time for Ester's neighbors to get used to me, Wendy thought to herself. Ester always told her to 'pay them no mind'. And she really did try not to.

As she opened her car door, she saw and old man staring at her from his porch. She smiled at him and waved slightly. For a moment he looked quite taken aback, but then his face turned into a scowl. Wendy felt as if a knife had been jabbed into her. She got into her car, feeling quite embarrassed.

Wendy, not having American parents, felt that she didn't grow up with the same animosity that many of these American whites had against black people. Her parents had always taught her that everyone was a child of God, no matter what color he or she was.

She remembered, while she was around nine, her father had hired a black youth to work with him in the bakery. Because, most of the neighborhood was made up of recent immigrants, beyond curiosity, people hardly batted an eyelid and got quite used to it. But she remembered one evening, her father came home very upset and irate. He told them that an American woman had come into the bakery. She had seen the young black man, called Gary, at the front register, and had been horrified. She had screeched all sorts of obscenities, wondering why he would have a black working there in the front with the white customers. Wendy's father had had to calm her down and told her that if she did not wish to buy anything from the store, then don't. He had firmly told her that she was disrupting his business. Her father related, in German, how he saw the face of that young black man grow cold and stony and his eyes grow flat, almost as if he was removing his mind from the horrible situation. His father had grown sad about that and asked him if he wanted to take a break, maybe take a walk. The young man had simply responded, "I understand if you want to fire me, but please just tell me straight if that's what you want." Wendy's father was shocked. "I'm not firing you. You are a good worker and if I want to fire anyone, it would be my decision, not the decision of some woman that walks in the store and does not like what she sees. Now go and relax a little, take two of the buns in the back to eat, if you would like. No one should have to put up with such a thing in the morning. But I want you back here in thirty minutes. We have a lot of customers here today."

Her father had told the family about the incident that very night. "How can people be such a way? We have some Africans back in Germany. Particularly in the Rhineland. There are few problems. People are people, God is a God of variety and made us all different, but we are all people. No one better than the other. And people do not deserve to be treated bad because they are not the same as you."

Those words of her father had stuck with her throughout her life and despite the conditions surrounding her, she had always lived her life judging people for who thay were not what race they were. She and her husband had been sure to raise her children with the same morals. She was proud that her brain wasn't tainted by hate and the seperation that the American legacy of slavery had imprinted in its society.

ψ

Dr. Halpern peered down at the young girl that sat across from him. Currently, she was staring down in her lap, not saying a word.

"So how are you feeling today, Edda?"

Edda shrugged her narrow shoulders. "Fine, I guess."

"How is school going for you?"

"Okay, I guess."

"Do you like school?"

"School's okay. I don't like my math teacher though."

"Why not?"

Edda wrinkled her small nose. "He's weird. He laughs at his own jokes. And he slaps his desk so loudly with the ruler if he thinks we're keeping too much noise."

Dr. Halpern smiled. "Yes, he does sound a little odd. Do you do well in his class?"

"I do all right," she said a little uncomfortably.

"Well, I think you do more than okay. Your mother tells me that you do exceptionally well in your math and science classes. But not too good in English. Am I correct?"

Edda flushed. "Then why did you ask me if you already know?"

"I just wanted your perspective on things. That's really important to hear what you think."

"I don't think my math teacher likes girls very much. He told the class that girls were not smart in math like boys were. I told my dad what he said and he was very angry. He went to the school and spoke to the principal. I thought they were going to fire the math teacher, but they didn't. At least I don't have to see him next year. This fall, my math teacher is a woman."

"Are you happy about that?"

"Yes. At least she wouldn't say that girls are dumb in math, because she's a girl and she has to be smart in math in order to teach us."

"You're right, my dear. You too are evidence to prove that other teacher wrong, aren't you?"

Edda looked down again in embarrassment.

"Your father was a physics professor at the University of Chicago, wasn't he?"

Edda looked up and nodded, he blue eyes studying his face. She stared blankly for a moment before saying anything. "My daddy said that there are other places to this world that we're in."

Dr. Halpern peered at the young girl over his glasses. His expression unreadable.

"Pardon me?"

"My daddy said that there are other parts to where we are," she said, growing frustrated with the effort of trying to explain herself.

"Other places? Like dimensions?"

Edda nodded, her eyes lit up. "That's the word, 'dimensions'."

"Well yes, many people believe that there are other dimensions."

"Do you believe that there are?"

The doctor cleared his throat. "Well…I'm not sure. That's a tricky question. I don't know that it could really be proven."

"It can be proven," Edda said nodding her head, a serious expression on her face.

The tall, husky doctor, rested his thick hands on his rounded stomach and leaned back in his chair, all the while keeping his eyes on the child.

"How can it be proven?"

"Sometimes things and people 'bleed through," Edda said, her face very serious.

The doctor didn't know how to take this. "bleed through? Do you think you can explain that to me?"

Edda pursed her lips and tried to think. "Well…sometimes other things come to where we are in this world from another place, another dimension."

The doctor nodded his great big head, to Edda, he looked like a giant.

"You almost look like a 'bleed through' Edda said with a little smile

The doctor laughed at this, "Why do you say that?"

"Because you're so big and you look like a giant. Giants are from another place. But they don't hardly come through over here for us to see."

The doctor was truly baffled. He hadn't expected for the girl to come here talking about mythical creatures that were from another world. This certainly complicated things. But that was what kept his job interesting.

"So your father told you all these things?"

"Yes."

If the child's father had been telling her all these things, then things were definitely more complicated. That meant that she wasn't getting this from her imagination. Her father had actually implanted these incredible ideas into her head. He wondered if her mother knew about this.

"Do your other siblings know about such things?"

Edda shook her head. "My daddy only told me. He said that I was the type to be more in tune with things like that. He said the others would not believe him. He said something about "German practicality."

He slowly nodded his head and took more notes. This was interesting. Very interesting indeed.

"My daddy said that I had a special sense for things. And I can see and feel things that other people couldn't. He said that I had a gift that his mother had. He never got it though. He said that it must have skipped a generation."

The doctor's pen was moving furiously across his note pad. He reached into his desk and took out a small tape recorder. He thought that maybe he should tape these conversations to confirm the authenticity.

"Your mother tells me that you see your father, even though he has passed about a year ago?"

Edda nodded her head. "I can see him."

"Where do you see him?"

"Mostly in the house."

"Do you see him anywhere else?"

Edda pursed her lips. "Sometimes, he goes places with me. He says it's to protect me because some places aren't good for me to be in."

"Is your father here with you in this room?"

Edda's eyes flashed around the room within seconds, "No."

The doctor nodded. "Your mother said that at first you were hesitant to tell your mother that you were seeing your father, can you tell me why?"

Edda frowned. "I thought that he wouldn't like me telling anybody else. But I talked to him and he said that it was okay." She hesitated before she went on. "He said that it was okay that I come here too."

The doctor almost said that he was glad her father approved, but he didn't want to encourage this line of thinking.

The doctor glanced at the clock on the wall. It was five minutes past the hour. He would have kept on going if he hadn't had looked. He sighed and put his notebook and pen down. He had to have a talk with Wendy.

"Well, the time's up, Edda. Do you think that you can go out and call your mother?" he buzzed his secretary and told her to keep an eye on Edda who would be coming out shortly.

Wendy came into the room looking worried. "Well doctor, what do you say?"

The doctor took a deep breath. He picked up his note pad and then put it down again.

"Wendy, are you aware that your husband was teaching your daughter about…shall we say…spiritual things?"

Wendy looked confused. "What do you mean? My husband and I were Christians, so all my children know about church, the bible, and God."

"No. What I mean is about things like…giants and other such mythical creatures, other dimensions and spirits—things he called 'bleed throughs'?"

Wendy was truly baffled. "No, I had no idea. He never came to me with anything like that. My husband was a very realistic man. He was a physicist. He believed in atoms and the Theory of Relativity not in ghosts and fairies."

"Wendy, have you ever heard of a relatively new field in physics called Physics of the Paranormal?"

"Well…no…well, maybe I have heard something about it."

The doctor leaned back in his chair. "Well, although the history of paraphysics be found as early as eighteenth century, it is only pretty recently that it has become more accepted in academic circles. This is a group of people that combine use the laws of physics to try and explain and understand paranormal events. They try to prove that these…events are genuinely real."

Wendy bit down on her lower lip. She didn't know what to say. This was all too much for her. She had no idea that her husband was involved in things like this. She had always believed her husband to be a rational man. This new information had completely changed her view of him. Yohann Zimmermann had another side, a side that he hadn't revealed to them. A side that only her youngest child knew anything about. Wendy felt betrayed and hurt that her dead husband had not brought her into his confidences, that he had felt that he had to hide a piece of himself from her. She had believed they shared everything, she had been wrong.

Dr. Halpern saw her pain and felt sorry for her. "Wendy, I suggest that you do a little research. Look in at the university he used to teach at, speak to some of his colleagues. I am sure that they would have some information to give you."

Wendy nodded. She would just that, not only to get some sort of closure, but also to help her daughter.

Wendy rose from her chair, as did Dr. Halpern. They shook hands.

"Thank you Dr. Halpern. We will see you next week."

"Of course. You have a nice day now."

"The same to you."

A few moments after Wendy left, Dr. Halpern decided to review his notes and to listen over his tape.

Dr. Halpern picked up the tape and pressed Rewind and then Play. He covered his ears as a loud piercing noise issued from the speakers and filled the room. Dr. Halpern quickly pressed Stop and stared at the tape in bewilderment. What was that about? He pressed Fast Forward and then Play again. Instead of hearing his voice and the voice of Edda Zimmermann conversing, he heard something else all together, once again. For a split second, the sharp noise came back and then was replaced by a deep pulsing noise at first low in frequency and then very gradually increased.

"What the hell is this?" Dr. Halpern muttered. He wiped his upper lip, which was growing wet with perspiration.

He listened closer. The pulsing noise continued but he also heard a vibrating tone underneath. He turned the volume slightly higher. Now, on closer inspection, it sounded like a voice. But not a regular voice. It sounded like someone was speaking through a fan. He couldn't tell whether it was a man or a woman. At first, the words were unintelligible, but then he thought he heard the vibrating tone say his name. That thoroughly spooked Dr. Halpern. He quickly pushed down the Stop button. He then re-wound the tape and popped it out. He got out a leaf of paper and wrote a quick letter. He took out an envelope, put the letter and the small tape inside, and sealed the envelope. He wrote a mailing address on the envelope and then his return address. He put the envelop in the output box for his secretary to put into the mail later on today.

Someone else had to hear this and he knew just the person.

Chapter Twenty-three

Rebecca looked at the knife until it turned blurry before her eyes. Through the haze, the knife glinted and shone in the light of the kitchen. The silence of the house was like a deep ocean. There was not a soul around besides her.

Rebecca looked at the clock on the wall, it read six o'clock. This was around the time that Anthony left out the door when Rebecca knew he was spending his time with *her*. That slut, that home destroyer, that husband stealer.

Rebecca knew that it was the redheaded tramp's birthday today. She had done a considerable amount of snooping around and had uncovered some substantial information. Her husband would be taking her out. Supposedly, he would be arriving to pick *her* up at seven thirty. *Betty Ladrow*. What a name. A name for a slut, a prostitute, a trollop, a whore. Rebecca could feel her anger like hot blazing waves sweep over her from her head to her toes as she thought of these things.

But tonight, was the night.

Rebecca put on a pair of black colored women's slacks and a dark blue shirt. She pulled her black hair into a bun. She put on a large black hat and big dark shades. She looked in the mirror. Her identity was concealed. She slipped on a black trench coat. She put the large, sharp knife in the inside pocket of the coat. She slipped on black boots and left the house.

As Rebecca tore down the street in her brand new red Cadillac, her mind was totally centered on the upcoming task. As the needle on the car's odometer rose, Rebecca's mind began to drift. In fact, she was so spaced out, that she hardly noticed the blue lights that were flashing behind her. Rebecca let out a curse and pulled over to the side of the road.

The cop pulled over behind her and parked. He got out of his car. He walked his tall, bulky frame up to Rebecca's side window. Surprised to see her window up, he rapped loudly on it. A woman's face with large dark glasses quickly turned towards him. He frowned in further surprise.

With a start, Rebecca rolled down her window. She rapidly flipped off the glasses and gave him her most stunning smile, all white teeth and flushed rosy cheeks. "Can I help you officer?"

The police fixed her with his steel gray eyes, his lips a line of deep disapproval.

"You were speeding. You could have caused a serious accident."

Rebecca frowned. "Officer...?"

"Brandow," he offered snippily.

"Officer Brandow...I am so sorry. It's just that my mind is a thousand miles away...I have so much on my mind with my mother being sick and all. I was just on my way to visit her in the hospital."

The officer raised an eyebrow in disbelief. "Oh, really."

Rebecca nodded quickly. She attempted to conjure up some tears. She managed to squeeze out a few drops.

The officer didn't know what to think. This woman was an unbelievably good actor. He had seen her type before during his career as a highway patrol man. Many a woman had pulled the crying act on him before and it failed to affect him anymore.

He didn't bother to question her any further. "Well, Ma'am, next time you should be a little more careful. Think of this ticket as a deterrent. It might just save your life in the long run. Can I have your license and registration?"

Rebecca handed both to him. He studied them and handed them back to her.

The officer quickly scribbled out a ticket, tore it off his pad, and handed it to Rebecca who was, at the moment, shocked.

"But officer Brandow..."

"You have a nice day, Ma'am," he said before hurrying back to his car.

Rebecca watched as he pulled out from behind her and took off. Rebecca slammed the wheel of her car in anger. She wanted to explode. She wanted to kill everyone in sight. She took a deep breath and willed herself to calm down. She had to stay focused, she had to keep a clear mind. She couldn't let some dumb idiot officer who was obviously a moron, let her lose control. Rebecca sighed in relief as the last bit of her anger was pushed down successfully. Rebecca gave the ticket a cursory glance and stuffed in into her glove compartment. She didn't have time to worry about that nonsense. There were bigger fish to fry at the moment.

Rebecca took off down the highway on her way to her destination.

Ψ

At six o'clock, Betty decided that it was time to start getting ready. She knew that Anthony was coming to get her at seven thirty. She wanted all the time to get herself prepared. She wanted to look extra special tonight. She wanted Anthony to be swept away. She wanted Anthony to fall in love with her. She *needed* Anthony to fall in love with her.

She was in love with him. And not only that. She had some important news that she had to divulge to him. If anything was going to make him leave his wife and be with her, it was this bit of information.

She knew the rules of this game, and she had broken them. For a long time, it had ceased being a game for her. Her feelings had become serious. She hadn't dared tell Anthony because she knew the type of man that he was. He was not a man that liked surprises, neither was he the type to deviate from his course. But she also knew that he was a stand up guy. A guy that took care of his responsibilities and did whatever he needed to do without question. That thought gave her courage and strength.

Betty tied up her hair and tucked it into a shower cap. She stepped into the shower and turned on the faucet, she let her mind drift as the warm water washed over her body and soothed her.

Ψ

Luckily, getting into the building was not a problem. There was no heavy security. In fact, the only security that the occupants had was a door to buzz visitors in. But Rebecca had easily gotten in. She quickly stopped the door from closing after a resident had gone through, by sticking her foot in it. She slipped into the lobby area and quickly glanced up to see if the resident had seen her. She older woman continued on up the stairs without a glance backwards. Rebecca looked towards the elevator. She decided that was the way to go, rather than taking the stairs. She got in a pressed the button for the eighth floor.

It felt as if the elevator was going slow motion. Much to Rebecca's aggravation, the elevator stopped on the fifth floor. A short man with light brown hair got in. Oh, shit. This was no good. Rebecca didn't want anyone to get a look at her. Luckily, she had her sunglasses on.

The man smiled at her. "I know you're hot in all that black," the man commented. Rebecca didn't respond. The man was not to be put off. He continued on in his attempt at conversation.

"Nice sunglasses. What make are they? They look expensive."

Rage began to boil in Rebecca like a cauldron of hot soup. Her hand began to play with the lapels of her thin, black trenchcoat. She felt like just reaching in, pulling out the knife, and stabbing *him* to death. But once again, she quickly regained control. She hesitantly lowered her hand and stuck it in her pocket. The devil wasn't going to win tonight. He was trying to throw her off course.

The man chuckled. "It's only August and you got on that jacket like it's fall."

Rebecca's left eye began to twitch in annoyance. She felt the back of her head begin to quiver like a bowstring. Satan was after her tonight. Calm…calm…calm…

Finally, the elevator reached the eighth floor. She rushed out of the elevator as if it were on fire, leaving the man standing dazed. The doors closed behind her. The man was still in the elevator and on his way up. She breathed a sigh of relief. She searched the carpeted hallways. It was deserted. Just the way she wanted it.

Rebecca crept down the hallway, looking at the numbers on the doors as she passed. She stopped when she saw the door marked 806. She took a bobby pin out of her pocket. She picked the lock as quietly as possible. Finally, the door sprung open. *Cheap lock for a cheap whore,* Rebecca thought. She was delighted that she had come up with such a clever line.

She quietly stepped into the apartment. She could hear the sounds of a shower running. In the living room, the radio blared. Betty was nowhere in sight. She moved around the apartment, through the living room, the kitchen, and the small dining area. The apartment was well furnished. No doubt compliments of her husband. Rage almost overwhelmed her. She moved towards the hallway and that's when she heard the sound of a running shower. And over this, she could hear the sound of a female singing. Rebecca instantly bristled as she recognized the song to be one of her favorites. The Bitch was going to die. She quietly crept to the bathroom door and opened it slowly, it was not locked.

The bathroom was foggy and full of steam. She slowly walked to the shower. The singing continued.

Rebecca pulled the large knife from her jacket. The knife quickly formed a thin sheen on moisture on its metal blade. Rebecca dug the tip of her finger into the point and pushed until skin was punctured. She removed the knife. A bead of red remained. It was time. The time was now.

Rebecca flung back the shower curtain. A naked, startled Betty turned around, her aqua eyes harboring surprise, her face a mask of deep shock and unbelief. Rebecca raised the knife above her head and plunged into the left eye first.

Eyes were the window to the soul.

Betty's soul would rot in hell.

A blood-curdling scream arose from Betty, drowned out by the sound of the running water and the blaring radio in the living room.

Rebecca raised the knife again and plunged it into the right eye. She dug deep. She was doing what was needed. She could feel the Lord nodding. Telling her, it was all right. He understood. The red headed woman slipped to the floor of the shower, her hand gripping her face, blood slipping from between her fingers. Moans of agony, pleas of mercy, begging to stop.

Rebecca next plunged the knife into the shiny white shoulder, the neck, the head, then when the woman was sprawled out on her stomach, barely breathing, Rebecca turned her over and plunged the knife into her lower stomach, right above that triangle of red pubic hair. Again and again, she stabbed, recklessly and with abandon—her full breasts with the pale pink tips, the face, now staring at her with gouged out eyes. Things were blurring before Rebecca's eyes and she knew that it wasn't just the water because it wasn't only her seeing being affected, it was her head. She started to get confused. She lost her train of thought. One minute God was talking to her, and the next minute he had left her. The rushing noise in her ears was gone and was replaced by the steady down pouring of the water in the shower.

Rebecca stared down at the now still woman. Her blood poured down the drain of the shower, right along with the water. The woman's mouth was slightly open, her lower lip split in half.

Rebecca's dark hair hung down, soaking wet. It had become undone from the bun during the frenzy. She was soaking wet. The water ran into her eyes. She looked at her hands. They were covered with blood. The knife clattered to the floor of the shower as she released her grip on it. She slowly watched as the water swept the blood away. Rebecca quickly peeled off her jacket and tossed it outside of the shower. She peeled off her sweater and her trousers. She now stood only in her bra and underwear.

Instead of getting out of the shower and getting herself dried of, Rebecca dropped to her knees beside the body of the dead woman. She bowed her dark head as the water fell on her, like a cleansing wave.

The voice that had first called her and then had left was back again. It was speaking to her, telling her that it was time to pray.

Ψ

When Anthony pulled up into the parking lot of Betty apartment, he was feeling on top of the world. He felt a flash of guilt as he thought of his wife who was sitting at home, but he quickly banished the thought. As much as he loved his wife, he didn't like spending a lot of time around her anymore. The fact was, that she scared him a little. If she wasn't drinking, she was praying, in Hebrew. He couldn't understand what she was saying, and that frustrated him to no end. He knew a little Hebrew, just what he had learned nine years ago when he went to Judaism classes, but he had done that only to marry Rebecca.. Now he couldn't remember half of the things that he had learned, since he never used it. Rebecca, on the other hand, as of lately, had been fervently practicing her faith. More than she ever did. What scared him was that when she was worshiping, she would totally block everything out. Nothing else mattered to her, but what she was doing at the moment. And when she wasn't praying or drinking (which was rare) Rebecca could be seen wandering around the house with a dazed look on her face. She wasn't taking good care of their daughters Naomi and Eve, who were seven and five respectively and Rebecca had neglected all chores around the house. Anthony had remedied this by hiring a chef and they already had a cleaning woman that would come in. He replaced her with a full time maid. The children were also noticing a difference in their mother. Anthony didn't know what to do. Unfortunately, it hadn't even once occurred to him to ditch his mistress.

Anthony got out of his car with a bouquet of red roses. As he looked around the parking lot as he was walking, he noticed a red Cadillac that looked very much like his wife's car. Puzzled, he walked towards it to get a better look. He saw the little scratch by the fender identical to the one that Rebecca had gotten a week ago while backing out of a parking spot. He looked at the front and saw the praying beads hanging from the rearview mirror. Then quite reluctantly, he took a look at the license plate. Anthony swallowed hard in alarm. This was Rebecca's car, just as he suspected. But what was she doing here…

Anthony quickly rushed into the apartment building. He used the keys that Betty had given him to open the front doors. He rushed into the elevator and pressed the button for the eighth floor. When he got there, he hurried to Betty's apartment. Though the door was closed, he saw that it wasn't locked. He walked in and closed the door behind him.

A feeling of utter dread swept suddenly over Anthony as he surveyed the empty living room. The radio that he had bought Betty months ago was blearing loudly. He walked over and clicked it off. He listened closely. He could hear the sound of running water from the shower.

"Betty?" Anthony called out. There was no response. He continued to walk towards the hallway. The sound of running water became louder and louder.

"Betty?" Anthony called loudly again. Three was still no response from her. He felt panicky and he didn't know why. What was his wife's car doing parked out there? It couldn't be a coincidence. Rebecca didn't have any friends around here…why would she be parked out there? Furthermore, where was she?

He approached the bathroom. The hallway was foggy with steam. He saw that the bathroom door was opened. He looked in. The bathroom was filled with steam. Then the faint coppery smell of blood hit his nostril. *Oh God, let it not be what I think.* He thought that he could hear some muttering. The shower's doors were closed. Once again, he called out Betty's name.

Getting no response, he pulled back the sliding door and was shocked at the sight. Betty was obviously and clearly dead. Her skin was deathly pale, despite the hot water running over her. Her eyes were gouged out, and the ragged flesh of her eye sockets, stared back at him. Anthony, in a state of shock ran his eyes over the mutilated body as the steam coated his skin. There were wounds and cuts all over, only there wasn't any blood left. Just open, raw wounds. He stared at the flame red shoulder length hair that was spread out in a fan under the head of the dead body. Her bloodless lips were parted slightly.

Anthony's eyes finally slid over to his wife. His dear wife with the water running over her thick black hair, pasting it to her skull like a cap. Her hair running down her back like spilled oil. Rivulets of water running over her reddened body. She was kneeling over the body, muttering what he assumed to be prayers. She had the knife in her left hand and was currently slashing it into the palm of her right hand. Her blood ran down the drain. She didn't seem to be aware of what was going on, that he was there.

Anthony, breaking his shock, stepped into the shower. He grabbed the knife from Rebecca's hand and flung it into the corner of the shower. He pulled his wife up by the armpits. He lifted her out of the shower and carried her into the living room. He laid her down on the couch. Her face was a blank mask. Her eyes were flat and unreadable.

Anthony rushed back to the bathroom and once again stared at the body of Betty. He felt a lump come to his throat, but he quickly got a hold of his emotions. He turned off the water. Gingerly, he lifted the body out of the shower and laid it on the floor of the bathroom. He got a sheet out of the hallway closet and covered the body from head to foot.

He went back out into the living room and saw that his wife was still lying there and hadn't moved from her position. Then he heard her saying something. He came closer.

"God told me to do it. He told me to rise out of it all, out of my misery." She began to sob. "I was saving you from hell and me from hell..."

Anthony furrowed his brow, what was she talking about? He swallowed in nervousness. Now wasn't the time to try and interpret his wife cryptic words. He had to deal with the situation at hand. And quickly. He knew what he needed to do. There was no way that he could allow his wife to get nailed for this.

Anthony walked over to the phone and made a phone call. His call was answered on the first ring.

"Santino?" Anthony called into the phone. He was aware that he did not sound like himself.

"Who's askin'?"

"It's Anthony."

The voice instantly perked up and lost its suspicious edge, "How ya doin' Tony? You sounded really different there. What can I do for ya?"

"I need something cleaned up over here. Get a couple men over to the Carlstie Road Apartments."

"You got a body?" Santino asked, quickly

"Yeah. I need it taken care of and gotten rid of as discreetly as possible. I don't want this getting out." Anthony looked over towards his wife. "You think you can get some tranquilizers as well?"

"I kin' get ya anything you want."

"Good. Be low key about it, got it?"

"Perfectly," Santino responded. "You want we should come over now?"

"There's no time like the present, Santino."

After Anthony hung up he went back to the bathroom, stepped over the body and took up the wet clothes of what he assumed where Rebecca's. He looked in the cupboard under the sink and found some bandages. He walked back to the living room with them. He got a plastic bag from the kitchen, put them inside, and tied up the bag. He went back to his wife who was now sitting up on the couch and wringing her hands. He held her hands out. Rebecca pulled them back violently. Her blood was dripping down onto her lap.

"Please Rebecca, let me help you. You can't let your blood get on anything, you understand?"

Rebecca folded up her hands, refusing to be bandaged. He gave up and sat and waited for them. He took his trench coat off and gave it to Rebecca to wear.

A short, heavily muscled man in black trousers and a dark brown jacket came walking through the door. He was trailed by a taller, skinnier man with a pale pockmarked face carrying a small case and an even taller, beefy man with deep olive skin and startling green eyes followed after the both of them. The last man was carrying a cardboard box. He closed and locked the door behind them.

Anthony walked up to the short, muscled man first and shook his hand."Santino, I'm so glad you got here. Bernie, Riccardo. No one saw you guys?"

The man shook his head, "Not at all. Don't worry."

Bernie, the tall man with the pockmarked face, put down the case that he was carrying. "These are the tranquilizers. Pill and needle form. We brought both. We didn't know which kind ya wanted."

Anthony nodded. "That's good."

Riccardo, the tall beefy man looked startled as he caught sight of Rebecca sitting on the chair wearing a black jacket. "Ain't that your wife?" he asked, tentatively.

Anthony nodded. "I'll explain later. Right now, we gotta get this body outta here."

The three men followed Anthony into the bathroom. Their eyes instantly fastened on the sheet covered form lying on the floor.

"I'm assumin' that to be the body," Santino said gravely.

Anthony nodded. "You assume right."

The pockmarked face man, named Bernie, pulled the sheet down from the face. He flinched when he saw the eyeless face staring up at him.

"Ouch," Riccardo commented.

"It seems to me that half the jobs done for us. There ain't a spot of blood in her. Ya did that Tony?" Santino asked Anthony

Anthony shook his head.

Santino didn't inquire any further.

"Well, we gotta chop this here lady up and put her in the box. We'll bury her in canvas tarp. There ain't no way we can bring a whole body down just like that," Santino said.

"The bathroom is yours, gentlemen," Anthony said and stepped out.

Anthony went back out to his wife who still refused to be bandaged. He saw that her blood was now all over the couch. He looked over at the box of tranquilizers. He got out the pills.

"Rebecca honey, why don't you take a couple of pills for me. They'll make you feel better."

Rebecca looked up at him, her face blank. "I don't want pills."

"But they'll make you feel better, baby," Anthony yelled from the kitchen as he got a glass of water. He came back and offered both pill and water to his wife. She refused both.

Anthony sighed as he realized that he was going to have to do this the hard way. He pulled the needle from the box and sat beside his wife.

"Honey, I'm going to give you a little stick. You'll hardly feel it."

Rebecca shook her head and slid away from him on the couch.

Anthony moved closer to her. He hated to do this, but it was the only way. He held Rebecca down and pulled out her arm from under her. She began to cry and scream.

Riccardo came rushing into the living room. "She all right, Anthony?"

Anthony nodded. "Don't worry. I'm just trying to give her this shot. She wouldn't take the pills. Can you hold her arm out for me?"

Riccardo came over and held out her arm. "The tranquilizers ain't that strong, so she should be able to walk with some help."

With one hand, Anthony covered her mouth, with the other he stuck the needle in. Both men released her. Riccardo went back into the bathroom. Rebecca sprung up once released. She cursed at him and sank to the floor. Anthony lifted her up and put her on the couch.

Anthony called her name. Her eyes slowly opened. "I can hardly move. I'm so tired Tony."

Anthony pulled her into his arms. "Don't worry about a thing. I'm here. I'll always be here."

About half an hour later, Bernie came out carrying the large box. Santino gave it two pats. "She's in here. I guess we'd better be goin' now, Tone." He looked at Rebecca with sympathy. "She all right?"

Anthony nodded. "Yeah, she's fine."

"All right. We gonna go and deal with this now. We cleaned up the bathroom with bleach," Santino said

"One more thing, you guys. Burn this apartment. Start the fire on the couch. I don't want nobody finding my wife's blood on anything."

"Sure thing, Tony."

Ψ

Later that night Santino, Bernie, and a young, unconventionally pretty brassy brunette named Fran went back to the apartment. Santino doused the couch and the rest of the living room with gasoline. Bernie lit the match and flicked in on the couch. It went up in flames. It quickly traveled to the rest on the living room.

Santino turned to his cousin. "All right, Fran, you know what ta do. We'll be parked around da block."

Fran snapped her gum loudly. "Yeah I know. What, you think I'm stupid or somethin'?

Santino and Bernie made a quick, but discreet exit down the backstairs.

Franny watched for five more minutes to make sure that what needed to be burned was burned up and that Santino and Bernie were safely away, then she began to scream in horror.

A resident opened her door and poked her head out. "What's the matter dear?" Her face scrunched up as she smelled the smoke. "Is that smoke I smell?"

Fran said her lines. "Yeah, I came in to get my friend Betty and I see that her apartment is in flames! Luckily, she ain't here. We better make sure everyone gets out!" Fran said as she pulled the fire alarm.

With that, everyone on the floor rushed out of their apartment and down the stairs. Fran rushed down as well. She was met with a mob of people in the stairwell. She pushed her way past them, but couldn't get through.

"Get the hell outta my way, bastard," she screamed to one guy that copped a furtive feel on her behind.

Smoke was beginning to fill the stairwell. People were screaming and crying all around Fran. She could hear the sound of sirens in the distance. Fran continued to push past people. She made it down the first flight of stairs past all the panicking people. She couldn't get past the second landing at the moment. Suddenly, this impossibly tall man cornered her. His crazy black hair sticking out in tufts. His crazy blue eyes fixed on her.

"Andrea! It's me Ray. Don't you remember me?"

Fran attempted to move past him. "No. Who the hell are you?" The man was unmistakably a nut.

The man wasn't having it. He blocked her path, preventing escape. Everyone else around them was making their way down the stairs.

Fran stared at him, bewildered. "You idiot. My name ain't Andrea. Move outta my way. Can't you see the building's on fire? You wanna burn up?" She attempted once again to move past him. He barred the way. She tried to elbow him in the gut. He stood firm. He shoved her back and she toppled over. She hit the back of her head hard on the floor. The people running around her seemed to be going in slow motion. The smell of smoke was heavy now and it invaded her lungs with a vengeance. Slowly, her surroundings dimmed and she found herself in darkness.

Ψ

In the thunderbird parked down the block and around the corner from the burning building, Santino began to get worried. It was well past the time that he estimated it would take his cousin to get out of the building. Santino watched as two fire engines and two police cruisers zoomed past.

"I can't take sitting here anymore. I'm gettin' worried Bernie, I think that we should go check and see what's going on."

Bernie nodded in agreement. They stepped out of the car and began to make their way to the burning inferno.

Ψ

When Santino and Bernie got to the apartment, the building was totally engulfed in flames. Santino looked to the large group of people huddled together. Ambulances were coming in groups, taking people to the hospital.

Santino walked towards the crowd and began to search through it. When he couldn't see his cousin among the faces, he began to panic. He searched in the ambulances that were parked on the side. Fran wasn't in any one of them. Santino could feel his heart thumping in his chest. He knew that this would be a bad idea. Why didn't he listen to his gut instinct? He began to ask around, if anyone saw a small dark haired woman with brown eyes, young. All he got was blank stares in response. He roared in anger.

Bernie placed a hand on Santino's shoulder. "Calm down, Tino. We'll find her. She might even be in one of the ambulances that left already."

Santino shook his head. "She might be inside. I'm goin' in to get her."

Before Bernie could stop him, he made a rush towards the building.

A police officer stepped in front of him. "I'm sorry, Sir, but you can't go in."

"The hell I can't. My cousin's in there," Santino spat. He continued onward. The police grabbed his arm.

"I must insist, Sir. You cannot go in there. Please. Let the firemen do their job."

"Fuck you. They ain't doing their job well, cause I don't see my little cousin." He jerked himself out of the police's hands. Then another policeman came over.

Bernie walked over to where Santino was. "Come on, Tino, just wait a minute."

Santino turned on him, furious. "If that was ya family in there, wouldya be saying the same thing?"

"You're gonna get yourself inta trouble," Bernie warned.

Santino pushed past the police. They followed him and attempted to grab him. Santino turned around and punched one of the officers square in the face,

"I told ya not ta touch me!"

Soon, a group of officers were upon him. They wrestled him to the floor and cuffed him. They stuffed a cursing Santino into an awaiting police vehicle.

"Damn it," Bernie muttered to himself as he watched his friend being hauled off.

Ψ

The next day, Anthony and Bernie went down to the precinct to pay the bail and get Santino out.

Santino was sullen and silent.

"Are you okay?" Anthony asked, cautiously.

Santino turned his reddened, glazed eyes upon Anthony. "If your sister died, how would you feel?"

"I'm sorry, Tino. I really am. I'll do anything to make it up to you."

"I practically raised her, ya know. She came to live with my family right after she was born because my aunt couldn't keep her." Santino bowed his head and cried bitterly, like a child. Sobs racked his body and his large shoulders shook.

Anthony and Bernie embraced him in a hug. It was the least they could do.

Ψ

Now, Rebecca's isolation from the outside world was complete. After the incident, she was totally out of touch with reality. She did nothing but stay in the upstairs bedroom and pray. She only ate when Anthony brought something up and reminded her to. Anthony didn't even think that she realized what she did back in that apartment to Betty Ladrow. Luckily, he was able to cover it up. The police had it as a missing case, since there was no body uncovered. And after a while, he was no longer considered a suspect in her disappearance. Sometimes his heart grew sad when he thought about Betty no longer being in his life, but when he though about Rebecca not being in his life, it was unthinkable. He could life without Betty. He couldn't live without Rebecca. Because he loved his wife dearly, he had his mistress cut into pieces and buried somewhere out in the woods.

At first, the kids would try to come into the bedroom and talk to their mother. Rebecca would totally ignore them, either that or she would scream at them and tell them to get out. Eventually, hurt, the girls stayed away from their mother all together.

When their daughter Naomi discovered Rebecca in the bathroom with her wrists slit, but still barely breathing, Anthony decided that it was time to have her institutionalized. All his efforts and the psychotherapy was going nowhere. Eve was too young to really fully know what was going. Naomi understood, but even her understanding of the situation was limited.

Everyday, Anthony would visit Rebecca in her small room. She would look at him with vacant eyes, but wouldn't say a word. But

Anthony would still talk to her, even though he never got a response. Then when it was time to leave, he would kiss her on her forehead and tell her that he'll be back tomorrow. He wanted to bring the children, but he was afraid that it was too soon to do so.

Without Rebecca around, the house seemed deserted and his heart was heavy. He felt guilty that things had gone this far and that his two young daughters were now, more-or-less, motherless. And he felt horrible that his wife was no longer the woman that she used to be.

He wished that he could do things over and somehow make it right. But now it seemed as if it was too late.

Chapter Twenty-four

Abner was living large and he was loving every minute of it. He loved that he would take his famous wife, Dorothy Ashford, out to dinner almost every night, take her to plays, and other events. She was so cosmopolitan and she knew the best places to go and to see. Dorothy could speak four languages— English, German, French, and Italian. She also loved to travel. Abner made sure that they did more than enough of that. Every year, they would go to at least two different countries, that is if Abner's job allotted it.

Abner adored his wife. Although not what one would call gorgeous, she had a unique attractiveness about her that people noticed instantly with her deep red hair and her smoking gray eyes. She had just a splattering of freckles on her small upturned nose. Abner thought that was absolutely adorable. But not only that, Dorothy was absolutely intelligent and very perceptive. Her combination of book smarts and good common sense were very appealing to Abner. The woman had a surprising level of street smarts that no one would expect a woman of Dorothy's social standing to need. She always claimed, that if you traveled a lot, it was necessary and you would obtain it.

Dorothy was queen of their rambling estate that they called home. She was always holding fundraisers, dinners and other social events. She was the perfect hostess.

One evening, Abner came home and called out for Dorothy.

"I'm upstairs, in the rec-room," Dorothy called down the stairs.

Abner climbed the stairs. Dorothy was sitting on the couch. She was wearing gold, silk lounging pajamas. She held a long thin cigarette in her hand. She looked up when she saw him.

"Hello, darling," she said in her low throaty voice that Abner found so appealing.

Abner came over and gave her a kiss. "Hello beautiful. What are you up to?"

"I'm just glancing through this magazine." She flicked the cigarette ash in the ashtray and continued, "I'm trying to find something to wear to that charity ball next month."

Abner smiled. He didn't bother to point out that she had loads of clothes. It would have done no good.

Suddenly the phone rang. Dorothy reached over to answer it.

"Hello," she called into the receiver. She took a drag of her cigarette.

"Hi there, Dorothy. It's Lawrence."

Without another word, Dorothy handed the phone over to her husband. "Here, it's Lawrence," she said with an edge to her voice.

Abner knew that Dorothy didn't like Lawrence, for whatever reason.

"I'll take the call in the office."

Dorothy picked up the phone and told Lawrence this is short clipped words.

Once Abner was in the office and told Dorothy so, he picked up the phone. "Hey Lenny, What's up?"

"Nothing much, but your wife sure knows how to give a guy frostbite," he said good naturally. Lawrence wasn't easily offended.

Abner chuckled. "How are the stocks going?" he asked, as he lit a cigarette.

"They're going good, my friend. We're just about ready to sell this next round. I anticipate big bucks from this lot."

"Yeah, better be with all the promoting we've done," Abner said..

Lawrence laughed. "I assure you. The profit will be substantial. Abner, do you think we could meet sometime this week? I gotta touch base with you a little."

"Sure, not problem. When do you want to meet? I have Thursday open."

"Thursday's not a problem. What time can you get here at my office?"

"How bout we do lunch?" Abner suggested.

"A grand idea. We can meet at *Lenny's*."

"Alright. I'll see you then?"

"You bet."

After Abner hung up, he went back to where his wife was, still reading her magazine and smoking.

297

"I have to ask you, Dorothy, why do you hate Lawrence so much?" he asked, curiously.

Dorothy continued to leaf through the magazine. "It's not that I *hate* him, Abner, I just don't like him very much."

Abner laughed. "Well, why do you dislike him?"

Dorothy turned her silvery-gray eyes to him. "Well, I can't really put my finger on it. I just don't like him. There's something about him…I don't know. But he's your friend, darling."

"Okay. Enough about that. What about we go out to dinner tonight? I heard of a French restaurant that just opened down town. How does that sound to you?"

"Sounds great, Abner. I'm as hungry as a horse."

Abner smiled at her. Whatever Dorothy ate, it never showed. She stayed tall and svelte. Just like the first day he set eyes on her years ago. He loved her to death and he felt he would do anything for her.

She was the love of his life.

Ψ

"So Wendy, when are you going to marry me?" Rocco asked, as he stroked Helen's wavy hair with his hand. He reached for her left hand and fingered the diamond solitaire on her left ring finger. "I gave you this ring for a reason."

Wendy turned over on her back. The silk sheet slipped, exposing her right breast. Rocco smiled in pleasure.

"Rocco, you know that there's a lot going on right now—"

"You mean Edda."

"Yes, I mean Edda. I just can't go and get married now. I don't think that would be such a good idea."

Rocco sighed deeply. "Why do you think something is so wrong with your daughter?"

"Rocco, it's not normal that she's seeing these things. Her father has put a lot of things in her mind that I now have to get out."

"Who says that it's wrong?"

Wendy frowned at him. "Do you see spirits that talk to you?"

Rocco grinned. "I can't say I have. But I had a grandmother that did."

"Rocco, what are you talking about?"

"Well, I didn't want to mention this before, but my grandmother was sort of a...mystic. She claimed to see things and get messages. Many times, she would tell us things that were true, but we ourselves couldn't explain how she knew. I believe that there are indeed people that have unusual sensitivity to the spirit world. A sense that we lack. I think that instead of stifling it and calling it abnormal...I think that we should encourage Edda. She has a gift Wendy, and the sooner you realize it, the easier it will be."

Wendy shook her head. "I don't know about that, Rocco. I just don't like the whole business of it."

"That's because you don't know it, Wendy. When we don't know something, we tend to stay away from it and even fear it. Why don't you just listen to her, Wendy?"

Ψ

"I just wanted your approval before I brought him in to speak with Edda."

Wendy shrugged her shoulders. "Do you think it would help Dr. Halpern?"

The doctor pushed his glasses up on his nose. "I definitely think it would help to get an experienced perspective on this whole situation."

"Okay, I trust you, Dr. Halpern."

The doctor nodded and buzzed his secretary, "All right, Lilly, We are ready for Dr. Zolyar. You can send him in."

A short man with brown hair, looking to be in his mid forties, entered the room. His nervous brown eyes instantly fell on Wendy and quickly flicked off onto Dr. Halpern.

"Wendy, this is Dr. Zolyar. Dr. Zolyar, this is Wendy."

Wendy held the nervous man's damp hand in her's for a moment before letting go. The man offered her something along the lines of a smile. Wendy smiled back.

"Dr. Zolyar is the head of the department of Physics at the University of Chicago. He specializes in astrophysics and paranormal physics."

The short man cleared his throat. "Actually, my degree is in astrophysics. The paranormal is a field that I started to dabble in about two years ago. But I really started to seriously study this field only this past year."

Wendy said nothing. The man nervously glanced at the doctor and back at Wendy and then cautiously continued.

"I knew your late husband quite well. In fact, just before he…passed we were working on an investigation of sorts, shall I say."

Wendy looked puzzled. "What kind of investigation?"

"We were looking at the phenomena of hearing voices through electronic media such as radios and tape recorders. But not just any voices, Mrs. Zimmermann, voices from the other side."

"So when you say other side, you mean people that are dead?" Wendy asked.

Once again, Mr. Zolyar cleared his throat. "Do you have any water, Dr. Halpern?"

"Of course. I'll get my secretary to send some in."

"Mrs. Zimmermann," Dr. Zolyar took a deep breath before continuing, "We—at least your husband and I— harbor the belief that people do not really die, in the way that most people understand it. We believe that what we often call death is actually a passage into another world, let's say, another level of existence." Dr. Zolyar thanked the secretary as he took the Styrofoam cup of water. He took a gulp. "Me and some of my other colleagues believe that once a person has passed over to the other side, they often make an attempt to communicate with us—the people that they have left behind. Electronically, is just one of the many ways."

"This is all so much to take in," Wendy said, rubbing her temples. She was developing a headache.

"I understand. It is a lot of information to digest. If you would like, we can finish this conversation at a later time."

Wendy shook her head. "No, no. I want to hear it all now, if it is possible."

"Yes, of course. Now, Mrs. Zimmermann. I want you to listen to something." Dr. Zolyar played the tape. Wendy sat amazed as she listened to the high screeching noise, followed by the pulsating sounds and the wavery voice at the end.

"What was that exactly?" Wendy asked, alarmed.

Dr. Halpern took off his glasses and began to polish the lenses in the front of his button down shirt. "That is supposed to be a recording of the first session between your daughter and I. As you can hear…it sounds nothing like it. If you listen closely in the end it sounds as if my name is being said."

Dr. Halpern played the end again. Wendy motioned for him to play it again and so he did.

"Yes, it does sound like your name is being spoken, now that you mention it," Wendy said feeling quite surreal. "What does this all mean?"

"Well, we believe that someone was trying to communicate through the tape recorder." Dr. Zolyar said.

Wendy turned to Dr. Halpern. "Do you actually believe this?"

Dr. Halpern hesitated before answering. "We have some very unusual phenomena here. I am simply trying to look at it from all angles. One must be very thorough."

"Mrs. Zimmermann, I have a strong suspicion that…" Dr. Zolyar began.

"What?" Wendy asked, sharply.

"I have a strong suspicion that this might be your late husband."

Ψ

The minute that Wendy heard Dr. Zolyar say that the wavery voice on the tape might be her husband, she left. She walked straight out of the office without another word and paid no attention to their pleas for her to listen and she ignored the men as they called her name. She got into her car and just drove away.

She couldn't believe the accusations they were making. It was all so crazy and bizarre. She felt as if this really wasn't her life. That she had been put on another planet and had been forced to take on the life of some extraterrestrial being. But most of all, it felt like something made for the movies. A movie with a strange and bizarre plot line.

Wendy prepared dinner in silence and as she and the kids sat down to eat, they chatted away, all except her. She was deep in thought, and deeply disturbed. She didn't know what to make of anything. The kids didn't really seem to notice, all except Edda who kept stealing serendipitous glances at her.

Wendy climbed into bed and dialed up Rocco.

"I was waiting for your call, my *Cara*," Rocco whispered the moment he picked up the phone on the first ring.

Wendy laughed. "How did you know it was me?"

"I can sense you, my love. How are you tonight?"

Wendy sighed. "Not very well, I'm afraid."

"Let me guess. This has to do with Edda?"

"Of course. What doesn't have to do with Edda lately here," Wendy said and let out a big sigh.

"Did you meet with Edda's therapist today?"

"Yes, but not only him. A physicist, apparently my late husband's colleague, came as well. He studies the paranormal."

"Okay, what happened?"

"Well..." Wendy told Rocco about the tape and what the doctor was proposing. Rocco listened carefully, interjecting only to ask questions and for clarification.

"It just sounds so... over the top," Wendy said, aspirated.

"Well, don't give up on them so soon. They might be on to something."

"Don't tell me you believe them?"

"Well...I'm not saying that, I'm just saying that it's good to keep an open mind. You've got to listen closer to your daughter Wendy...you might be missing something."

$$\Psi$$

Wendy woke with a start. She looked at the clock on her bedside table. It was two thirty in the morning. She sat up in bed. She had such a weird feeling throughout herself that she could not explain. A slight tingling at the back of her neck and her heavy heartbeat made her uneasy and worried.

Wendy pulled the covers back and got out of bed. She stepped into the hallway. It was quiet. For some reason, she passed by her oldest son and daughter's rooms without looking in and went straight to Edda's room at the end of the hall. Her door was partway opened.

Wendy pushed the door open slowly. Much to Wendy's alarm, Edda was sitting on the edge of bed looking straight at her the moment she opened the door. It was almost as if...she was expecting her. Wendy swallowed hard and approached her daughter. She put her arms around her. Wendy saw the sad, far away look in her daughter's eyes, and was scared by it.

"Honey, what are you doing up so late?" Wendy asked, softly.

Her daughter didn't answer right away. "Daddy said he would call you."

Wendy felt a chill go through her. Surprisingly, there was anger as well.

"Honey, don't start this tonight. I just want you to go to bed, okay? No more talk of your father. You have school tomorrow."

Edda frowned.

Wendy gripped her arms. "Do you hear me, Edda?"

"Mein kleines Sonnenblume-Gesicht," Edda muttered.

Wendy froze, she couldn't believe her ears. "What did you say?"

"Mein kleines Sonnenblume-Gesicht. Haar wie die Sonne, Augen wie der stürmische Himmel," Edda said clearly.

Wendy clamped her hands over her mouth in shock and horror. She fell to her knees as the tears spilled out her eyes. There was no possible way that Edda could have known to say that. *My little sunflower face. Hair like the sun, eyes like the stormy sky.*

Helen's mind flashed back to that day, twenty-three years ago, when she and Yohann had first started seeing each other. They went for a walk in the park near her house. They walked arm in arm. They had sat on a rock near the river. Yohann had begun to skip rocks across its clear surface. Not long after, raindrops had begun to fall. Yohann had looked up at the sky, and then at her and in German he said. "Your eyes are somewhat gray now, almost the same color as the storm moving in. You have hair like the sun and eyes like the stormy sky." Wendy had smiled. She had thought it such an odd thing to say. She supposed that was why she had remembered it down through the years. As for the sunflower face, that was a nickname that he would often call her, but not in the presence of the children. How was it possible that Edda knew about what her husband had told her those many years ago? How was it possible that she could know the nickname that he had for her? Edda didn't even know how to speak German beyond the words hi and goodbye.

Wendy held on to her daughter's shoulders, her eyes full of tears. Her daughter gave her a scared look.

"How did you know to say that? How did you know? Who told you?" Wendy asked, desperately.

"Daddy told me," Edda said. "He wanted me to tell you. But I don't know what it means."

Wendy pulled her daughter into her arms and held her close. She kissed her on the head as the tears came down her face.

"Don't worry, darling. There's nothing to be afraid of, anymore. Mommy believes you now."

Chapter Twenty-five

Wendy was ecstatic on June 18 of 1955—the day of her wedding. There were so many guests that Wendy could barely believe it and there was a plethora of food to go along with it—there was caviar, there was salmon, there were quail eggs, there were clams, there was lobster …the list went on and on. There was also a lot of music and much to Wendy elation, Rocco had gotten Frank Sinatra to sing live at the reception. When Rocco and Wendy danced, Rocco was ever looking at her with such adoration and love in his eyes. She was so proud to be his wife and so proud that he was her husband.

After a passionate night of lovemaking, they left on a jet plane to the Canary Islands to honeymoon.

They were living pure bliss.

Ψ

Sometimes the shadows on the wall spoke to Rebecca and other times they didn't. When they refused to, Rebecca would close her eyes and ask God for another way of communication.

But when the shadows spoke to her, they would reveal a lot of things. They would tell her what the woman in the next room was doing, they would tell her what the aids in the hallway were talking about, and they would tell her what food would be served for the next meal. These shadows were very informative and accurate—at least in her mind they were.

But the shadows were also comforting. When Rebecca would feel as if her head were caving in from all the pressures such as the aid telling her to do this and that, the woman in the cafeteria with the watery blue eyes and razor cropped hair trying to grab the food off Rebecca's plate, the doctor in his blindingly white lab coat always asking questions, aggravating her, the shadows would remind her that she was God's messenger and enforcer. She was special and the only reason that she was here was for her test of faith.

Rebecca didn't like when the man with the darkish skin and the shiny black eyes and hair came to see her. Rebecca could tell the shadows didn't like him either, because when he would come, they would retreat and leave her all alone with him. He would always open his mouth and talk about nonsense and things that she didn't want to hear about like the family, house, the kids and then he would talk about how much he missed her and his eyes would get watery. Rebecca would never respond. She sat and stared straight ahead, thinking of more important things such as the shadows, God, and her mission in this place. The first few times that he visited, he used to try and touch her, but she wouldn't allow it. She would shrink from him as if he were diseased. And in her mind, he was. Some days, she would see maggots and beetles crawling from his nose and mouth. She would scream and scream until the nurse came and said that he had to go and that he could come back tomorrow. He would reluctantly leave, staring back at her with a penetrating gaze.

But then he started to bring these girls with him. One younger than the other. They would look at her strangely, almost as if they were afraid. She stared back at them, blankly, not saying a word. Eventually, the man stopped bringing them.

The shadows informed her that the visitors were evil and they were seeking to destroy her mission and her faith. And Rebecca believed.

Rebecca always listened when the shadows talked.

Ψ

Santino woke from his sleep with a start. His skin was clammy and wet with his sweat, his heart beating like an enraged tambourine player. His eyes looked speedily around the room.

There was no fire.

There was no pungent smell of burning flesh.

There were no terrible, desperate screams of terror and pain.

"Tino," his wife's sleepy, but miraculously still squeaky voice called from beside him. "Are you all right baby?

Was he all right? He didn't know. For yet another night since the death of his cousin, he had a nightmare that seemed so real and alive. It was hard to imagine that it had only been in his head. The nightmares all had the same theme but with some variation. But all ending the same. The blackened crispy corpse of his cousin Fran always being the end result.

Then Santino did something for the second time since the ordeal that he had never done since he was a boy at the age of sixteen as he had been forced to watch his own father being butchered to death by vicious thugs before his eyes.

Because the ordeal had been too much for him and he felt that if this went on for yet another moment more he would totally and utterly break into one million pieces on the inside—so badly wounded, only no one would see on the outside and no one would be able to reach him within.

He cried. Deep racking sobs that shook his shoulders
She would haunt him forever.

Ψ

Rocco looked at the man trembling before him. Rocco felt no pity. All he could think about was what, if anything, the detective had discovered while searching through the house. It wasn't as if he had anything out in the open. Now that there were young children in the house, he had to be careful. God forbid the two younger girls come across anything about their stepfather. And although Wendy was aware of some things, she didn't know everything and Rocco had no desire to have her know. As for his stepson Alfie, he was away at Florida State University studying Journalism and English so there wasn't really anything for him to be worried about there.

"Didn't I tell you not to let anyone on the premises like that unless I was here?" Rocco asked, between gritted teeth.

The man took off his uniform cap and held it in his hands. Rocco could see a thin sheen of sweat on his pale forehead. "I'm so sorry. He said he had a search warrant, so I let him in. I didn't know what else to do. He said it'll be best for me if I let him in."

"Did he actually show you the warrant?"

The man looked to the floor and hesitated, "W-well no, but—"

"But nothing!" Rocco yelled and slammed his fist on the desk. The sound echoed throughout the room. Luckily, Wendy was out downtown doing some shopping, so except for the workers, the house was empty.

The man jumped back, he looked at Rocco with fear in his brown eyes. "Sir, I've been working for you for five years no police had ever come threatening with a search warrant before, I didn't know what to do."

"Well, the first thing that you should have done was make him show it to you. Chances are, he didn't even have a search warrant. In fact, I bet my right arm that he didn't." Rocco looked at the thirtyish man contemptuously. "The man knew an idiot when he saw one. How long was he in here poking around?"

"I don't know…like forty, forty five minutes," the man answered in a low voice.

"Damn it!" Rocco hissed. That might have been enough time to find something. He bet that the detective had been watching, waiting until he was gone to come up to the house. The detective knew better than to come here when Rocco was home.

"That's it, you're fired," Rocco said simply.

The man panicked. "Now, now wait, Mr. Gionelli. I'm sorry about what happened, but if I refused to let him in, he could have put me in jail."

"That's why you should have asked him to show you the paper! Then all of this would have been avoided. If he had showed you a paper, there would have been nothing that you could do. But in your stupidity and carelessness, you didn't even ask him you show you one. If he had one you begin with, that would have been the first thing that he flashed in your face, but you know what? He didn't have a paper! Now get out of this house when you still can. I'll mail you your last check—consider me a fair man."

The terrified man didn't have to be told twice. He turned quickly and walked out of the house.

Alone once again, Rocco sat down in his chair to think. He had just fired his head security guy that kept watch over his house and who got in and out of the front gates of his house. He needed a replacement. Suddenly, he had an idea. He picked up the phone and dialed a number.

"Hello, is this Garrett?" Rocco called when a male answered the phone.

"Yes, this is him. Mr. Gionelli?" the man asked on the other end.

Rocco smiled. "That's right. Now, Garrett. I have a proposition for you."

"What's that, Sir?"

"Please, enough with the 'Sir'. Everybody wants to call me that," Rocco said jokingly. "I feel ancient."

Garrett laughed. "Sorry bout that. I didn't mean bad."

"I know that, Garrett. But listen. I need security man that monitors who goes in and out of my house and makes sure things are secure around here. I just fired my head man this morning for him doing something stupid and I still have the other guy that works underneath him, but he doesn't have enough experience to move up to this position. But I do know that you do. How about you become my private security man? Move you out of that hotel and into here. I promise you the pay will be substantially more that you're working for now. In fact, I think that you'll be very pleased."

Garrett was almost speechless. After a moment he said, "Are you serious?"

Rocco frowned. "It was only an offer, Garrett," he said taking the man's response for rejection, "You can stay at the hotel if you want, it's up to you. I'll give you some time to think about it though"

"Are you kidding, Mr. Gionelli? I don't need no time to think. You got you a new head security man, effective immediately."

Ψ

About two weeks into Garrett starting work at his house, Rocco was in his office thinking. Rocco needed someone to help him organize. He liked organization in his life, when things were too awry, he got aggravated. He did most of his work from home—phone calls, business deals, appointment setting, and other such things. Over the years, he had done it himself, but as of lately, it seemed to be too overwhelming. He needed some help in the office. He needed an assistant. Someone that he could depend on totally. He preferred a woman. Over the years, he realized that women tended to be more detailed oriented and organized than men. They often put their heart into their work as well. Then he remembered Garrett once again.

He went out to the hallway to speak one of his men keeping watch at his door.

"Carrey, please go and get me Garrett. I have to speak to him."

"Right away, Mr. Gionelli," the tall Irishman said with a nod. He disappeared down the stairs.

Soon Garrett was standing in his office, a worried expression on his face.

"Is something the matter, Mr. Gionelli?"

Rocco smiled. "Nothing terrible. How do you like working here?"

Garrett smiled. "I like it just fine. I thank you for givin' me this chance, Mr. Gionelli."

"I'm glad that you like it."

Garrett nodded and smiled, waiting for more.

"I just wanted to ask you a question. Your wife went to secretarial school didn't she?"

"Yes she did, Mr. Gionelli," Garrett answered wondering where this was leading.

"Why doesn't she have a job doing that?"

"Well, no one would hire her… for a job like that, Sir," Garrett said feeling a bit uncomfortable.

Rocco nodded his head understanding fully. "Well, Garrett here's the deal. I need some help, actually a lot of help, around here in the office. I've been doing things mostly myself, sometimes Wendy helps out…but I need someone that's constant and permanent. Do you think your wife would be interested? Don't worry, she'll be paid nicely."

Garrett's eyes opened wide in shock. "Would she ever!" he said with a smile.

Ψ

Later that night over the dinner table, Wendy smiled at her husband. She loved him so much. It had been a little over a year since they had been married.

"It seems that you're hiring the whole family," Wendy said with a laugh.

Rocco shrugged. "They've been handed a hard hand. I know how that feels. And I need the help, they need the opportunity. Garrett is a good man and so is his wife."

Wendy nodded. "They sure are."

Ψ

"The idiot just let me right through the gate the minute I told him that I had a search warrant," the young detective reported with glee.

Detective Lee was at a phone booth speaking to Patrick McMillan, his superior.

"Oh really, he didn't even ask to show the warrant?"

"Not at all. Not that I would have any warrant to show. All I did was show him my badge and he shook. He let me right in. The moron."

"Hah!" McMillan said derisively. He took a certain pleasure in getting over on people. "Did you find anything?"

"Well…" Lee enjoyed keeping people in suspense.

"Out with it," snapped McMillan, all too aware of Lee's sadistic nature.

Lee cleared his throat. "I found some paper work, looks like a list of names and amounts of money owed, and vig that's being paid weekly."

"A debt sheet," McMillan muttered. "Yeah, looks like our friend is into some serious loan sharking."

"Yeah. Not only that I found some paper work about tractor-trailers and shipments. There's a list of what truck is going out and what cargo is on it."

McMillan frowned. "Hmm…I wonder what that's about."

"Not only that. I found something else really strange…," Lee trailed off.

"What? What did you find? Quit playing with me Lee."

"Okay. I found a paper with 'O'Hare International Airport' written on it." Lee said mysteriously.

"Yeah, so what?" McMillan growled, growing impatient.

"Well, it was written down that on December 12, 1959 a plane leaves from the O'Hare International Airport to the New York International Airport."

"Yeah? So what's the big deal? He's taking a trip or something. That's about two or so years from now," McMillan snapped, as he thought that Lee was wasting his precious time.

"I don't think so. There were some names listed there as well." Lee said lightly.

"Look Lee, are you gonna be straight with me or do I have to kick your ass?"

Lee quickly continued. "There were names of some high society people like Marylyn Lake, the woman that owns that art museum downtown, Charlie Cohen, the real estate mogul..."

"Yeah, yeah, I know those people, who in Chicago doesn't? But what I wanna know is why their names are listed there." McMillan said, feeling that they were on to something but not knowing exactly what.

"What else you got?" McMillan asked, hurriedly.

"Well I spotted two illegal guns that he must have gotten off the black market or something."

"What kind of guns?"

"He has an M240 with a silencer and a sawed off shotgun. You and I both know that those are illegal in this state."

"Damn straight. There's no way he cold have gone an gotten those guns registered with his criminal record. He can't have those types of weapons!" McMillan growled indignantly. "And I am damn sure this evidence wouldn't hold up in court, considering how we came upon it. The lucky greaseball bastard."

"So, what are we gonna do, *Boss*?" Lee said emphasizing the last word of his sentence.

McMillan was silent for a moment. He was sure that Lee was mocking him at times.

"We wait."

Ψ

It was August 17, 1956. It was Winston's fifth birthday and Angelina and Earnest intended to go all out for their youngest son. They hired a clown, a magician, and ponies for the children to ride. Earnest and Angelina invited all the neighborhood kids, many of whom Winston played with, and also the kids from his class. Angelina and Earnest also invited family members and some of their friends.

"Angelina, honey, you have to let me pay for part of the expenses," Rocco told his daughter as she was making preparations.

Angelina shook her head. "No, Dad. Earnest and I have got it covered. I'm sure you've spent a small fortune on whatever you bought Winston. That's enough."

Rocco grinned at his daughter. "Nothing but the best for my grandson!"

On the day of the party, it was warm and the sun was shining brightly in the sky. Wendy and Rocco came over early. They were soon followed by Sal, his wife and children and Anthony and his two little girls.

"I didn't think it was a good idea to bring Rebecca," Anthony said in a small voice when Angelina gently inquired about her.

Angelina respected this and did not ask her twin brother any more questions.

"Well, I'm going to go and get Winston dressed before the rest of the guests arrive."

"I'll come up and help you, Angelina," Wendy offered.

Angelina smiled at her stepmother. "Of course. I would love that."

Rocco smiled. When he and Wendy had gotten married a year and two months ago, he had been worried that there would be friction. After all, there hadn't been anyone serious after their mother's death many years back. But he was happy to find out that his children got along well with Wendy...well to a certain extent. Anthony and Angelina were their usual happy and accepting selves—bless his twins— but his older son, in his customary fashion, was not clear in his feelings towards the marriage. He had expressed his congratulations and had been nothing but respectful towards Wendy, but with Sal, there was no telling. Sal was never the one to get overly emotional over anything. Poker faced Salvatore. Rocco had no idea where he got it from.

"So what do you want to wear today for your party Winston?" Angelina asked her little son once she got upstairs.

"You have you blue outfit or your green polo shirt with your shorts, pick one sweetheart."

"I wanna wear the shorts." Winston said jumping up and down.

Wendy smiled. She adored this little boy. "You made a good choice, honey. The weather's nice and warm outside."

Suddenly Angelina remembered that she had forgotten the pick up the party hats at the store from which she had ordered them.

"Darn, I almost forgot about the hats…I should have picked them up yesterday. I have to go and get them now."

"Go on ahead, Angelina. I'll finish dressing Winston," Wendy said with a smile. Winston was hugging Wendy's legs.

Angelina smiled, relived. "Thank you Wendy. I'll be back as soon as I can. It shouldn't take more than an hour to get there and back."

With that, Angelina left. Wendy quickly got Winston dressed and ready.

"You are a handsome young man. Look at you in that outfit," Wendy said as she combed her step-grandson's brown hair.

Angelina arrived home just before the other guests began arriving. Angelina stood at the door to greet them.

First, the kids were entertained and enthralled by a magician and his ingenious, imaginative tricks. Afterwards, the kids went on the ponies. The children excitedly waited in line, there were five ponies. The clowns entertained the waiting children by making animal shaped balloons and behaving silly.

Earnest watched in pleasure as his son laughed and shrieked with delight upon the pony. He looked over to his brother in law, Sal, who was standing nearby also watching the scene with a rare smile upon his face.

"Looks like they're having lots of fun," Earnest commented.

Sal looked over at him, his expression stoic—all traces of the previous smile gone, "Yeah. It looks like they are."

Earnest turned, once again to look at the children playing on the ponies.

"Winston might want this for every birthday now," Earnest said jokingly.

"Well, with all my father pays you, you can certainly afford it," Sal said in a low voice.

Earnest quickly turned his head to Sal and met his eyes. They stared in silence for about five seconds and then Sal broke into a small grin, yet another rare occurrence. Earnest followed suit, somewhat relieved. Throughout the whole time that Earnest had known Sal, he had always felt an undercurrent of animosity. Most of the time, he manage to convince himself that it was only his imagination and other times he told himself that was just the way Sal was. But he couldn't ever totally shake the feeling. It didn't help that Earnest clearly remembered the punch in the face he had received from Sal years ago after he had found out about Julia He was sure that Sal disliked him. Strongly.

Afterwards, the big cake was brought in and they sang happy birthday to Winston. Winston opened the presents in view of everyone. Angelina and Earnest thanked everyone, making sure that Winston did the same.

Then they all sat down to eat outside at the picnic tables that were set up. After a very noisy and messy afternoon lunch, Angelina was somewhat relieved to see the guests out the door, thanking them for their attendance.

Angelina was glad to note that all in all, the party was a success and she was glad that Winston and the other children enjoyed themselves immensely.

Next year, she decided, Winston's birthday party would be smaller. Much smaller.

Ψ

"I'm sorry, but you can't speak to him right now. Mr. Gionelli is in the middle of a meeting," Ester said in a polite, but firm tone of voice.

"But we need his okay on some decisions down at the hotel," the manager of the Chicago Sunset Palace said testily.

"I will inform Mr. Gionelli. I am sure that he hasn't forgotten about it. But as of right now, he cannot come to the phone. Now, please. He will call you as soon as possible. I am sure that he will before this day is through."

The manager, Mr. Carson, let out a huff and slammed down the phone. He was not used to not getting his way. Especially if his was being barred by some Negro women. He snorted, one nostril twisted in derision. Now this is why *they* begin to get all uppity and start giving trouble when put in any sort of decision-making positions like that. Carson believed that was why it was better to just give them the menial jobs, to keep them in their place. There was an order to the world and it had to stick that way or things would go all awry. He, of all people, knew this and that and as a result, he ran the hotel with a firm hand.

Carson looked over the list that he held in his hand. It all needed to be signed and approved by Mr. Gionelli himself. If he were dealing with any other person, he would almost just write off for the things himself. But he knew that wouldn't be the smartest course of action as far as Mr. Gionelli was concerned. The man would have his balls, if he did such a thing.

Carson sighed and sat back in his chair at his desk. Oh, how he hated to wait. But there was nothing else that he could do at the moment.

Ψ

Ester frowned and hung up the phone. *What a rude man*, she thought to herself. Oh, well. She didn't have time to focus on the ignorance of others. Her motto was to just leave them be.

She turned to her typewriter and sighed with a touch of delight. She still had to finish typing the two business letters for Mr. Gionelli. He needed them posted by tomorrow morning.

Ester turned to the coffee maker and saw that the coffee was just about finished. She got out the mugs, put them on the silver tray, and placed the tray and the coffee pot on the little service cart.

When Ester reached the study where Mr. Gionelli was holding his meeting, she knocked lightly. The door opened and a young man with a smooth, baby face opened the door wide for her.

Ester pushed the cart past him and succeeded at holding her smile for the five men that were seated.

Rocco smiled warmly at her.

"This is Ester, my assistant slash secretary," he said introducing her to the four other men that were sitting in the plush seats with expensive suits on. "Thank you Ester. You can just leave the tray over there. We'll help ourselves."

"Are you sure you don't want me to pour the coffee for you all?" Ester muttered, her eyes drifting around the room. One man that looked about fifty in a gray suit was staring at her with penetrating black eyes. A slight smile was on his lips. He was sitting back in the leather chair with ease, his hands rested on the arms of the chair. A gold ring with a large gemstone adorned his left pinky finger. Ester watched as it caught the light from overhead and gleamed.

"No, we'll help ourselves. But please, can look on my desk and you'll see a large brown envelope. Can you bring it in here for me?"

"Certainly, Mr. Gionelli."

Ester found the envelope and brought it back into the room. The young baby faced man opened the door and took the envelope, thanking her. Before the door closed, Ester caught a glimpse of the man in the gray suit. He as staring straight at her. Easter felt her stomach flop.

Once Ester left the room, the man in the gray suit, called Marco turned to Rocco. "So, that's your assistant?"

Rocco started pouring the steaming coffee into a mug. Finally, he said, "Yes, it is."

Then Marco gave a half smile. "Nice looking."

Rocco eyed him. He knew that Marco had always had a penchant for colored women. Newly divorced from his Italian-American wife, he was now on the prowl.

"She's married. She has an eleven year old son," Rocco stated pointedly.

Marco paused for a moment and then finally shrugged his broad shoulders, "So, what does that mean."

Ψ

From the time that they had met about two years ago, Edda and Michael had been friends. Then they quickly became best friends. They were practically inseparable. That was why when Edda came home from school to find Michael sitting at the kitchen table eating cookies, she smiled in greeting.

"Hey, Mike. I didn't know that you would be here so soon."

"Well, we got out early at my school because the teachers had to have a meeting. So my mom came and picked me up."

"Where's my mom?" Edda asked.

"She's outside in the garden, I think," Michael said sliding off his chair.

They both headed outside. Edda glanced over at Michael. His dark mahogany skin gleamed in the light of the kitchen. Although not overly, Edda had always been somewhat secretly intrigued by his smooth dark skin tone, which stood in contrast to her pale, almost white complexion. But that was the only difference between she and her best friend that she saw in her own mind. To her the difference in their skin color was just a conventional difference, like the difference between her mother eye color and her's—her mother's being hazel and her's being blue. Her mother and father had left her mind free from being bogged down with the strong stigma of race and all that it meant being black in the late nineteen fifties America. Wendy had decided it was best that Edda find out for herself and if she had any questions, she would ask.

But Edda had already seen that in society's eyes, there was a drastic difference between she and Michael. She remembered the day that she had been invited to a friend's house to play. She had asked the girl if a friend of her's could come over too. The girl had asked her mother, and gotten an okay. So Edda brought Michael along. When Edda had rang the doorbell and the woman opened her door and saw Michael standing alongside Edda she was baffled.

"Honey," the woman said addressing Edda. "Does your mother know that you're out walking around with him?" she had asked, pointing a seemingly accusing finger at Michael.

Edda stood confused for a moment at the seemingly strange question. "Yes."

The woman shook her head and rolled her eyes heavenwards, "Well, I almost forgot that your mother's a woman that married an *Eye*-talian," she said stressing the first syllable with apparent disgust.

Edda stood shocked not knowing what to say. This was the first time that she had encountered such behavior. Her parents had kept her well hidden from it.

"Well…I don't think it's best for him to come in here. You can come in Edda, but he can't," she said to her. Not once did she address the young black boy standing there on her porch. To her, he was invisible.

"W-well, why not?" Edda asked, not seeing the problem. Not getting the racial and ethnic anecdotes.

The woman stared at her strangely, as if Edda were from another planet and was visiting for the day.

The woman now spoke as if she were addressing a slow child. "He's a colored, Edda. We shouldn't mix with them. It may be okay with your mother, but that kinda thing doesn't go on around here."

Edda continued to stare, dumbfounded.

"Perhaps you can come back another time." The woman stared pointedly at Michael. "Alone," she finished.

The woman said goodbye and closed the door promptly in their faces.

Edda looked over to Michael. He was staring off to the side, his expression blank.

"Michael...I don't know what to say. That woman is crazy...I-I... we better get outta here."

Michael's head whipped around to face her. "No, I'd better get outta here. You heard the woman. I'll leave so that you can go ahead and play with Martha."

Edda looked at Michael. His facial expression was totally unreadable, but when she looked into his eyes, they were filled with unconcealed rage. The dark irises flashed with anger and high energy. The truth was in his eyes.

In a sense, Michael was testing her.

"Do you think I would do that?" Edda asked, softly, feeling hurt.

Michael stepped down from the porch and began to walk away. Edda followed and caught up with him.

"Michael, you didn't answer me. Do you think that I would do that to you? Do you think that I think the same way that she thinks?" Edda asked, growing upset.

Michael continued to walk, not responding to Edda's words.

Finally, in frustration, Edda reached out, grabbed Michael's arm, and stopped him. She stood in front of him.

"Do you really think I'm that bad? Have I ever done anything to make you think—"

"No," Michael answered quickly. His eyes burned into her's.

"Then why are you so angry at me?" Edda asked him, gently.

"Because that's how it begins. I used to have a few friends, when I was younger, that were white. But then, pretty soon when we got older...they stopped playing with me. Just like that. I never really got an explanation from them for it. They would just shrug their shoulders and mutter something about being different. It would happen like that all the time. So then, I decided that I would just be friends with people that were black like me. That is, until my parents started working for your step-dad. That was when you and I became closer. Now I think that maybe, you're gonna start to feel the same way."

Edda shook her head. "Michael. I will never stop being your friend. I don't care what anybody says. I would still be your friend. I hope that you'll still be mine. I'm sorry about what went on back there. If Martha can't accept you, then I can't accept her. You're my best friend."

Michael let out a small smile for the first time since the occurrence. "Yeah, I still wanna be your friend. Your best friend, I mean."

Edda smiled and held out her hand. Michael gripped it in his.

Together, they walked back to her house.

Ψ

Anthony stepped into the J.C.Penney, picked out the tie that he wanted, and stepped out. He had an unexpected company meeting in about a half hour. The building developers that were using his contracting firm to build had called for a meeting all of a sudden. Anthony had agreed to it. Anything for one of their most important clients.

Anthony had just begun to get into his car when he heard a woman's voice calling out his name.

Anthony turned around to see who it was. He saw a diminutive, brown haired woman rushing up to him. Her face was so familiar to him, but he couldn't place it at the moment.

He stopped and the woman came up to him.

"Don't you remember me? I'm Eunice."

Anthony looked her over, trying to remember anything. He wished women weren't so fond of playing guessing games.

Then it struck him. Full force.

Eunice. Betty's friend. The one that he had given a lift to over a year ago and met a couple of times after that.

Anthony forced a smile that he hoped looked genuine. "Hi, how are you?"

Eunice looked at him and frowned. "I'm doing fine."

Anthony nodded his head. There was an akward pause and then Eunice comtinued. "Well...no one's been able to find Betty. At first, we just assumed that she had died in her apartment building when it burned to the ground, but her body didn't turn up. So we're thinking that she ran off somewhere. You don't happen to have a clue as to where she is, do you?"

"I was just about to ask you that," Anthony said, holding up the act nicely. "I haven't seen her for months. I'm worried about her." He made his face into a mask of fret and concern.

Eunice nodded. "Her parents reported her missing. Unfortunately, they haven't come up with anything. It's such a shame."

"It is," Anthony said with a frown. His mind flashed back to Betty's ravaged corpse, lying on the floor of the shower. Pale, bloodless lips parted in a silent scream. He suppressed a shudder.

"Look, why don't we go out for dinner tonight? We can talk some more," Anthony said quickly. He was surprised at what had just come out of his mouth. It was a purely impulsive move.

The plain girl's eyes lit up in pleasure. "I would love to."

"Shall I come pick you up? Or do you want to meet? I know a nice French place."

"Can you pick me up?" she asked, quickly.

Anthony nodded and gave her his best smile. She wrote down her address and phone number on a slip of paper and handed it to him. He took it and put it in his pocket. They said their goodbyes and parted ways.

Anthony still couldn't believe that he had asked her to dinner. Then he thought that it wasn't such a bad idea. He could find out what she knew about the situation and…he could steer all suspicions away from him.

Dinner was a good move.

Ψ

The restaurant was small and quaint, giving it an intimate atmosphere. The instant they got to the door, they were seated in one of the front side tables—the best seats in the whole house.

Anthony was a little surprised at how Eunice looked. As plain as she usually was, tonight, she looked quite attractive in her lavender colored outfit. Her brown hair looked silky and soft and was swept up into a chignon. Her makeup was flawless. Her cheeks were flushed with obvious pleasure. Pearl drop earrings adorned her small ears.

Too bad she wasn't his type. She was too short, too mousy, and too boring for his tastes.

After they had ordered, they began light conversation.

"So, where you born, in Chicago?" Anthony asked her, attempting to draw her in.

"No. I was born in Minnesota. I actually grew up on a farm," Eunice flushed deeply with embarrassment. She couldn't believe that she had told him that she grew up on a farm. He probably thought that she was some hick or something.

Anthony smiled, appealingly. A country girl. It shouldn't be hard to charm her at all.

"That must have been nice, growing up in the country. Away from all the squalor of the urban life," Anthony commented.

Eunice smiled, clearly enchanted with the handsome, swarthy gentleman sitting before her.

They chatted throughout the meal. Finally, Anthony decided that it was time to get down to business.

"So, do you have any leads on where Betty might be?" Anthony asked, wiping his mouth with the linen napkin.

Eunice shook her head. "We have no clue. The police have no leads. No nothing."

"Oh," Anthony commented, putting on his best sad face.

Eunice reached her hand across the table and touched his. "Don't worry. We'll find her. I know how much you cared for her."

Anthony nodded, his eyes pointed downwards.

Eunice looked like she was about to say something and then stopped.

"What is it?" Anthony asked, softly. "You were about to say something."

Eunice gave him a steady look and began. "Oh, I could imagine how terrible you feel considering her condition."

"What do you mean? Her condition?" Anthony said, growing nervous.

"Well…Betty was pregnant. I thought she told you," Eunice said with shock. She was sure that he was aware of that.

Anthony felt as if a fist had curled around his gut and clamped down hard. He swallowed hard with much difficulty.

"She never told me," Anthony squeaked.

Eunice came around the table and put a thin arm around him. "I'm so sorry, Anthony. I thought you were aware."

"W-was the baby mine? I mean, I don't know…," he asked, already knowing the answer to the question. He was the only one that Betty was seeing.

Eunice nodded her head vigorously. "Betty wasn't sleeping with anyone else. I would have known. Plus, she told me it was yours. Betty wouldn't lie about something like that."

Anthony shook his head. It was all too much to take in. Not only was his mistress dead, so was his unborn child. If he had known she was pregnant…things would have turned out differently.

After they had finished eating, Anthony drove her to her small apartment building. He stopped in front of it to let her out. His mind was so foggy that he could barely remember driving there.

Eunice looked over at him and saw the utter despair in his eyes and profound sadness in his face. Now, it was genuine.

"Do you want to come up for some coffee? Relax for little while? Perhaps you shouldn't go home in this condition…you might get into an accident or something."

Anthony nodded his head. What she said made sense.

He parked the car and they got out. Eunice gripped his arm and led him towards the building and up the stairs to her flat. She was so small, but he felt the strength radiating from her to him.

The apartment was small, but cozy and nicely furnished. A large rug covered the hardwood floor. A dark blue couch and a matching armchair was in the living room. Polished wooden end tables stood with lamps on them.

Eunice flushed, her cheeks growing bright red. Anthony noticed with pleasure. He liked when she blushed, for some reason. It made her look attractive to him.

"I know the apartment isn't much, but I don't have the time or the money to look or a new place. I'm working on getting my masters now."

"Oh really? In what field?" Anthony asked, curious.

"Psychology," she answered.

"Wow, that's interesting. I bet you're a really good student," he said just so he could see her blush again. And sure enough, she did. He found that his heart fluttered in his chest.

Eunice went off into the kitchen to make coffee. Anthony looked around the living room. There were a lot of photos. On the coffee table, there was a picture of Eunice in a long coat, snow was on the ground. A sixtyish man, whom Anthony presumed to be her father, had his arm around her. They were both grinning widely. In another picture, a pretty young woman that looked to be around fifteen or sixteen was sitting on a horse, waving at the camera.

Finally, Eunice came in the living room carrying the coffee and the two mugs. She got two coasters out and poured the coffee into the mugs.

"Is that your father?" Anthony asked her.

Eunice nodded, a smile on her small lips. "Yes. That's me and him on the farm. That was taken last year a day before Christmas. I went home to visit." Eunice turned to the other picture on the table, the one with the girl riding the horse. "That's my little sister Melinda. She's sixteen, still in school. She wants to be an agriculturalist."

Anthony smiled and nodded. He took a sip of the coffee. He looked at the small woman sitting before him. He watched the muscles and the small bones move in Eunice's thin neck as she talked. He looked at her slender wrists, so tiny and dainty. He looked at her doll-sized stocking encased, feet. Her face, looked soft and serene in the low lights of the room. Anthony felt a stirring inside him. He wanted her.

Eunice continued to chat, Anthony heard hardly a word of it. He got up slowly and stood over her. Her talking ceased. He gently took the coffee cup out of her hand and placed on the table. She continued to stare on in silence, waiting to see what would happen next. Anthony stared into her brown eyes the whole time.

Anthony took her hand and gently raised her from her seat. She allowed him to gently pull her to him. He wrapped his arms around her. She too wore a look of desire in her face. He cupped her small face in his hands and kissed her gently on the lips.

"I want you so much," Anthony whispered. Oh, he wanted her so bad. Not only because it had been months since he made love, but for other reasons as well that he couldn't quite determine at the present moment.

She led him to the bedroom. A double bed stood in the middle. He laid her down and gently began peeling off her clothes. He handled her as if she was a piece of glass that would break and in a way, he felt that she was with her pale, luminous skin and small bones.

Her small hands began to pull at the buttons of his shirt. She undid them quickly and hesitantly touched his belt buckle.

"Go on," Anthony urged, his voice choked.

Eunice opened up his pants and Anthony helped her pull them off. Anthony guided her hands to his manhood. She held him in her hands, a look of rapture on her face.

Anthony laid her back on the bed. He kissed her small breasts. They were so small, that he was able to put a whole one in his mouth. He sucked her pointed nipples, then made his way down her stomach and to the tangle of light brown hair between her thighs. Her parted her skinny thighs and inhaled her musky scent. Eunice moaned with pleasure as his tongue found her center and expertly moved over her wet folds and her swollen nub of flesh.

"I want to…try," Eunice said softly, her face flushed.

Anthony lay back on the bed. Her small mouth kissed his full lips. Her small hands explored his muscled stomach and then his swollen penis. She moved her lips down and took him into her mouth. Anthony sighed in pleasure. He ran his fingers through her glossy brown hair, undoing the chignon. He pulled her up, wanting her to ride him.

"Please. First you on top," Eunice said shyly.

Anthony turned her on the bed and straddled her, pushing her knees wide apart. He ran the tip of his penis up and down her crevice. Eunice moaned and shifted her slim hips in response.

When he slid inside of her, to his delight, he found that she was extremely tight. As he pushed deeper into her, he met with some resistance. He frowned, puzzled.

"Keep going," Eunice said, her face screwed. He pushed her hips towards him.

Anthony prudently continued. He pushed and pushed, finally the barrier gave way, and he dipped into the deep recessed of her tunnel.

Eunice groaned in pain and pleasure. She gripped him between her legs.

Anthony thrust slowly at first, nibbling her ears as he did so. Then he began to ride her with a furious passion. Eunice cried out in pleasure. The headboard slammed against the wall, causing a great racket.

Finally Anthony came. He cried out as the fiery liquid spilled from his loins and into her channel. He came some more when she came soon after and her already tight muscles, tightened even more, squeezing his manhood.

Finally, they collapsed, their sweaty limbs intertwined.

Eunice rested her head under the nook of his arm.

"I was a virgin," she said softly.

Anthony chuckled, and stroked her hair. "Yeah, I figured that."

Eunice snuggled into him. "It was okay, though?"

Anthony kissed her on her broad forehead. "It was . Wow. A 26-year-old virgin. Didn't think those existed anymore."

Eunice smiled softly. "My father was pretty strict when it came to me and my sister. He's a very religious man that sticks to the rules. We were raised that way."

"So why me?" Anthony asked her.

Eunice turned her face towards him and shrugged. "I don't know... there's something about you."

Anthony chuckled. "Sure."

"No. I mean it. Before, it just didn't feel right to sleep with any other man. But tonight...it felt so right. I didn't feel guilty about feeling the way I did."

Anthony said nothing for a moment, then, "What about your mother?"

"What?"

"I mean, you didn't say much about her."

"My mother died when I was twelve, my little sister was two. My father raised us both alone. I love him, he was a good father. Always did the best for us."

"Well, he raised a very decent person. You're a wonderful woman."

Eunice blushed. She wasn't used to complements. "Thank you."

"I'm just telling the truth."

Ψ

"I think that it's about time to sell the company," Lawrence said.

"What do you mean?" Abner asked, as he sipped his scotch. His friend was always coming up with something.

"I mean we sell the company so that we could make even more profit," Lawrence said with a canny grin.

"We promised the stockholders profits by the end of this year," Abner stated.

Lawrence rolled his eyes, "That's the problem. That's why we're going to sell the company."

"How are we going to do that without anyone noticing? Besides, your company hasn't existed for five years," Abner said grumpily as he thought about all the money he had invested two years ago in his friend's non-existing company.

"Hey, and I got away with it thus far, haven't I?"

"How did you?" Abner asked, curiously.

"Well, I assumed another legitimate company's name, charged expenses using their account, canceled the orders, got the money back then gave just enough profit to the stockholders to allay their suspicions and I, of course, pocketed the rest. And then there were the false statements."

"Yeah, barely enough, you kept saying that the company would pick up soon and that soon the money would really start coming in," Abner said huffily.

"Hey, hey," Lawrence said with a smile, "Don't get grouchy, I'm more than returning the money that you put in, aren't I?"

Abner reluctantly agreed.

"Here's a way that we can indeed sell the company and it'll be safe," Lawrence said smugly.

"Oh really? How's that?" Abner snorted, not really believing him.

"Well, we sell the company under another company's name. Get the buyer believing that it is a faction of a larger company. And of course, we do not give out our real names."

Abner looked out the window behind Lawrence's chair. He mulled over his friend's words for a moment. "What company would we use?"

Lawrence nodded and took out a folder from his briefcase. "Well, in actuality, we can use any company that is legitimate. I have a company in mind though. Emerson & Mills Shipping Corporation. This company has been laying low over the past nine or ten years. It's stocks are in the ground. Hardly anyone is paying attention to it, it has a low profile, which makes it good for us to use. Apparently, the man that owns the company is going into retirement and wants the company off his hands. What we can do for the prospective buyer is to type up false reports on the company and it's 'success' by showing profits over the years etc., etc. Really, all of that would be the only thing that would be false. Everything else we use, will be real, direct information from the company."

"So when we find these buyers, what do we do then?" Abner asked, thinking that this was not so bad of an idea.

"We hire a couple of guys, give 'em a small cut of the profit. They go, meet with buyers, pretending that they are the owners. I can rent an office. They would use that for the meeting. The company gets sold, the men we hire disappear, and no one knows we have anything to do with anything. We get the money. End of story."

"Well, what about your company name? And what about your name?" Won't people come looking for you?"

"What about my company name? It's non-existing. And my name's not connected to any company. The only person they know is Harvey Stretck."

"Who's Harvey Stretck?"

"He doesn't exist."

Chapter Twenty-six

Spring, 1957...

"Come Alfie, it's bright and sunny outside. Let's go to the beach," Penny wheedled, wrinkling her nose.

Alfie glanced up from his books and looked at the copper haired young woman standing before him with hands on hips. "My report is due on Monday."

"Right! You've got the whole weekend to work on it! Alfie, when have you ever not done your work? You've been on the Dean's list every semester!"

"Yeah, two and a half years down. We still have three more semesters left." Alfie said jokingly.

Penny snatched the book out of his grasp.

"Hey!" Alfie protested.

"We'll go to the beach for a few hours, that's all. Then you can come back here and stick your nose back into your books." The girl scrunched up her face. "You never like to have fun, you take no risks!"

Alfie laughed. "Hanging around you is risk enough."

"Oh please," Penny huffed, she stuffed her hands into her crème chinos. Not once had Alfie ever seen her wearing a dress or a skirt. All she ever wore were pants.

"All right, all right. I'll come to the beach," Alfie said closing his books.

Penny jumped up and down. "Fantastic! I have the towel, the umbrella and everything packed. Come on, let's cut out!"

Alfie grinned as he looked for his swimming trunks. "So you just assumed that I would agree to come along, did you."

"I knew you were going to come. You know as well as I do that you need a break."

Alfie nodded his head. "You're right. I do need a break."

After changing, Alfie and Penny walked out to the parking lot behind the dorm.

"So are we taking your car or mine?" Penny asked.

"I'll drive," Alfie responded. "No problem."

They hopped into his shiny dark red 1957 Jaguar XK-140.

A cute girl with blond curls sauntered by, giving Alfie an inviting smile and a saucy wink.

Penny rolled her eyes heavenward. "These girls are so obvious. Anything for a guy with hot wheels."

Alfie pouted. "Thanks, and I thought it was my good looks that got them," he joked.

Penny leaned over to him and fluttered her eyelids rapidly, she stroked his arm.

"Hi! My name is Litza, I like walks on the beach, I have one brain cell, but I look really good on your arm!"

Alfie cracked up. Penny was a riot. "That doesn't sound so bad!" Alfie said teasingly.

"Please. If I ever start behaving like that, I give you full permission to shoot me in my head. Death is better than living like that."

Alfie laughed, and started the engine. Good ole Penny.

"This car is a really cool rag top," Penny said patting the dashboard.

Alfie grinned, "Thanks," Alfie responded. "You've been saying that ever since you set eyes on it."

"So has everyone on this campus!" Penny said, her amber eyes flashing with excitement, "This is truly a babe magnet."

Alfie laughed then said jokingly, "The only babe I have is you."

Penny stuck out her tongue at him as they sped down the highway. "I resent being referred to as a *babe*. And as much as I hate to disappoint you, our relationship is strictly platonic. A friend/friend basis"

Alfie put on an exaggerated frown. "So I guess a marriage proposal is out of the question. My pledges of undying love are unreciprocated."

Penny laughed, and punched him in the arm.

"Hey!" Alfie exclaimed, losing control of the wheel for a moment.

Penny let out a peel of laughter. "Marriage is for squares. I want to be single forever!" She squealed, her copper ponytail billowing in the wind.

Alfie smiled. Penny certainly was like no one he had ever met before. They had been tight since they met in freshman American literature class almost three years ago. He just thought of her as one of the boys. In fact, he usually didn't see her hanging out with a bunch of girls, although he had seen her with a few. But mostly, she hung out with the guys. She always told them that she got along better with men, women were too catty for her taste. And it made perfect sense considering she grew up around two older brothers and one younger one.

"Marlon and Carl are meeting us over by the lifeguard station," Penny said with a grin.

Alfie grinned. "All right, cool!"

After they parked the car and got their things, Penny and Alfie headed over to the lifeguard station. Marlon was already there, exuding confidence as he stood casually leaning against the railing. He pushed himself up when he saw them, his bright blue eyes glimmering and his perfect white teeth bared in a smile. His thick brown curls wavered in the slight breeze.

"Hey you two, right on time. I knew you'd be able to get him to come, Penny." Marlon said, smiling broadly, his dimples very apparent.

Alfie chuckled. "I see that this was planned, huh."

Marlon put a long, well toned arm around Alfie's broad shoulder. "You see, friends can anticipate your needs. We sensed that you needed some sun," Marlon pinched him on the arm.

"Hey!" Alfie said rubbing the red mark on his arm furiously.

"See! You're too pale! Time for a tan."

"I'm not pale," Alfie protested.

"Listen. If, I can pinch you and see red, you're too pale for Miami Beach."

Alfie laughed, "Oh, okay. I get the message. Where's Carl?"

"He should be here any minute," Marlon said locking eyes with Penny.

They exchanged looks.

Alfie, totally oblivious said, "Come on. Why don't we set up the blanket when we're waiting."

"Uhh, let's wait here for a while longer," Penny said distractedly.

"And why don't you turn west," Marlon said as he gripped Alfie's shoulders, turning him around. "So you can get a look at that fabulous sunset."

Alfie gave them a strange look. "You two sure are getting on strangely."

Soon Alfie heard the sound of people singing behind him. He recognized it to be 'Happy Birthday'.

"Surprise, buddy!" Marlon shouted as Alfie turned around.

Alfie smiled. A group of his friends were singing happy birthday to him. Carl was in the front carrying a big cake with a giant grin on his face. Carl's girlfriend Bridgett was beside him, singing along.

"Wow, you guys really surprised me."

"What, you thought that we would forget all about your birthday?" Wanda, a dark haired girl with soft brown eyes and a pout said.

"Not on your life, buddy," grinned Ritchie with his pale blond crew cut hair.

"Come on, make a wish and blow out the candles," said Murielle, a small, curvy redhead.

So Alfie did.

After settling on the blanket, they cut the cake and began eating.

Later on in the evening, they were joined by more friends.

"Hey, isn't that Mikey over there?" Murielle pointed out.

"Yeah and Quincy, Eric, Peter, Rebecca, Jessica…" Alfie said, trailing off.

Mikey and the others finally reached them. He and Eric were carrying a giant cooler.

"Hi there, birthday boy," Jessica said with a wink of her sea green eyes.

Alfie blushed. "Hi Jessica, how are you?"

Jessica was wearing a red apron swimsuit. Her curves were quite apparent. She came over and sat beside Alfie.

"I'm doing great now that I'm here," Jessica said, holding his arm.

Penny slowly shook her head. Jessica, one of the prettiest girls on campus, had it bad for Alfie. Surprisingly, Penny felt a flash of possessiveness that left as quickly as it came.

"Now, the party begins!" said a guy named Ned. "We have a cooler full of beer! Birthday boy gets the first sip!"

Ned took out a can, opened it, and handed it to Alfie. Without thinking about it, Alfie took a long guzzle. All seventeen of them cheered.

Players of the Game

"Come on. I brought my radio," Rebecca said. "Let's blast some tunes!"

Jessica pulled Alfie to his feet. "Let's dance!"

Soon everyone was dancing, except for Penny who sat on the blanket in her blue culottes.

Quincy came beside Penny. "Come on and dance with me. You're sitting there while everyone's up and partying!"

Penny laughed. "You know I'm not one to dance."

"Well, tonight you are!" Quincy said pulling her up.

Within the hour, the party was in full swing. There was drinking, dancing and talking.

"Come on, let's go swimming!" slurred a drunk Ritchie.

Marlon laughed. "You're too drunk to go swimming! Sit down, buddy."

"Pass me another cigarette," Penny said, her legs exhausted from dancing. When she got it she asked, "Paige, can I have a light?"

"Sure thing, Penny," the pretty brunette said.

Penny took a deep drag of the menthol and stared off into the clear night sky.

Pretty soon, it was time to head back. Alfie as well as half the other people, were as drunk as fishes. Penny took Alfie's car keys.

"Whadya take them for?" Alfie asked, his blue eyes clouded. He had one arm wrapped around Jessica's waist who was equally as drunk.

"I'm driving, since I'm sober," Penny said firmly.

"All right. Jessica's coming along," Alfie slurred. The two of them began to stagger in the general direction of the car.

Soon the others began to scatter as well, as they called out goodbyes. Penny hopped into the driver's side first. Since the car was a two-seater, Jessica jammed herself in the middle, with Alfie on the passenger side.

Jessica and Alfie began to make out big time.

Penny rolled her eyes. "Oh, come on you guys."

They paid her no attention. Penny continued to drive back to the university.

"Do you want me to drop you off at your dorm?" Penny asked Jessica, once they got on campus.

"No, sweetie. Take me to Alfie's place," she said and laid a sloppy kiss on Alfie's cheek,

"I'm going to crash there for the night."

Penny's stomach flopped. "Okay. If you say so." Penny looked at Alfie to see if he would protest. He said nothing.

Penny helped them up to Alfie's room and saw them in. As she closed the door behind her, she felt an unfamiliar stab of jealousy. She was shocked and amazed that she was feeling that way. She didn't think of Alfie as anything more than a friend. She didn't want a relationship of that sort with him. She didn't want a relationship like that with anyone, at the moment. She was determined to be a famous anthropologist. She dreamed traveling the world, discovering new artifacts and seeing her articles showing up in famous journals No one would stand in the way.

Penny got into her own car and drove to her dorm. Before she got ready for bed, she called her parents in Minneapolis and then her oldest brother in New York. She chatted with them for a while before climbing into bed. As she lay in bed, her mind kept drifting off to Alfie and Jessica. She was imagining what they were doing right now, at this moment, then she quickly stopped herself. *What are you thinking, you crazy woman.* Penny thought to herself. She pushed all thoughts of Alfie and the blond from of her mind and began to do something that always made her fall asleep, as mundane as it sounded to most.

She counted sheep.

Ψ

"Do you think you can hook me up with her?" Quincy asked Alfie, as they sat in the booth at *Tipsy's*.

Alfie chuckled. "Come on, Quincy, I don't think she would go for it." He took a sip of his malt. To him, it tasted especially delicious today.

Quincy nodded his head, his lips in a straight line, his attractive face stoic. His light brown eyes stared straight into Alfie's. "I know, I know. But I thought that maybe, you know, since you're so close to her…you can talk to her for me."

Alfie shrugged his shoulders. "I could try. I can't promise you anything though. I didn't know you thought of her like that. She's just like one of the guys, you know?"

Quincy blushed. "I can't help what I feel. She's cute though, ain't she?"

Alfie shrugged. "Yeah, I guess," he responded, not really thinking about her in that way. To Alfie, Penny looked like a kid sister with her ginger hair and crazy freckles.

"And she's smart. Not like these dumb ass girls that are worried about hair, clothes and shopping. I like that she can sit down and watch the game with us, you know?" Quincy said softly.

"Man, you really have it bad, don't you," Alfie said, amazed.

Quincy turned even redder. "Yeah, I guess I do."

Alfie shook his head. "I don't know, buddy, She's not really the type," he said trying to discourage him for reasons that were beyond his own understanding.

Quincy frowned. "What are you trying to tell me. Does she like women or something? She a dyke?"

Alfie shot him a sharp look. "Of course not. I just mean that she's very focused on school and stuff."

Quincy leaned back and put his arm on the back of the chair. He grinned. "Yeah, well so am I."

Alfie laughed. "In a pig's eye. You get your C's and that occasional B and that's all good for you."

"I could be a serious student. She could help me," he said with a leer.

Alfie sighed. He had a bad feeling that this was going to backfire. Hooking friends up with other friends was not top on his list of the smartest things to do. But he decided to agree with it anyways. Quincy looked so hopeful.

"Fine. I'll talk to her. Just give me the rest of this week to do it."

Quincy smiled broadly. "Thanks bud. You're the best."

Alfie looked at his friend's smiling face and felt a pang of regret mixed, surprisingly, with a touch of resentment, and finally a grain of amusement.

Poor man, Alfie thought to himself.

Penny was going to crush him.

Ψ

Alfie looked up from the book that he was reading. He glanced at Penny who was sitting across from him. She was totally absorbed in the anthropology textbook that she was reading.

Alfie started to read again, but after a minute, he looked back up at Penny. She was still reading intently. Her teeth lightly chewing her bottom lip in concentration. Her amber eyes slitted and catlike as she read, totally focused.

"What's the matter, Alf?" Penny muttered without looking up.

Alfie turned red with embarrassment. "What do you mean?"

Penny sighed, put the textbook down, and pushed it slowly away. "Well, let's see…within the last five minutes, you must have looked at me one hundred times. At least. I'm not blind, you know." She favored him with a slight smile. "Now come on. Out with it, Zimmermann."

All week, Alfie had been trying to come up with a way to tell Penny about Quincy's 'crush,' on her. And every day this week, Quincy had been badgering him, asking him if he had talked to her and if not, then when would he.

Alfie sighed and closed his book. "Why don't we take a break. Let's go down to the café and grab something to eat."

Penny shook her head, her copper bangs shaking. "No, first, you tell me what's going on and then we get something to eat. You've been getting on weird this whole week."

Alfie nodded and swallowed hard. "Okay, I'm gonna just be straight with you. Somebody really, really, likes you and wanted me to tell you."

Penny gave him a lopsided grin. "Don't toy with me, Zimmermann. What are you talking about?"

Alfie cleared his throat. "Here's the thing…Quincy likes you. A lot."

Penny giggled, "You've got to be kidding me. Q?"

Alfie nodded, "Yeah."

Penny began to laugh uncontrollably. People at the other tables in the library looked over at them with amused and curious expressions.

Alfie reached across the table and covered her hand. "Calm down."

"So why couldn't he tell me himself?" Penny asked, between giggles, not fully believing him.

"Because of this. This is exactly why he didn't want to tell you himself. He's a little…afraid of you. Of how you would react."

Penny shook her head, a smile on her face.

"So, will you talk to him?" Alfie asked.

Penny sat still for a moment, a thoughtful expression on her face then finally answered with a shrug, "Sure. But I'll have you know this goes against everything that I stand for."

A beat, and then Alfie said, "Whatever."

Ψ

Quincy was exactly where Penny told him to meet her. She stood at a distance, unbeknownst to him, and watched him standing there, in front of the university center. He was really tall—about 6'4"—dwarfing her 5'5" frame, athletically built with a nice tan. His caramel colored hair was slicked back on the sides. He wore dark blue cuffed Levi's and a checkered red and blue sweater. Black loafers were on his feet. *He was always a nice dresser.* Penny thought to herself.

Penny walked up to him and smiled. "Hey, Q. Alfie said you wanted to talk to me, so let's talk," she said, not giving him the opportunity to beat around the bush.

Quincy smiled. "Boy, you sure like to get right to the point. You hold no punches, I like that."

Penny held her smile as butterflies floated in her stomach. She had never felt this way around Quincy before, because she had only thought of him as a friend, but now this. She was feeling so nervous, she just wanted to get this over with.

Quincy put a gentle hand on her arm. "Why don't we go grab a bite to eat. What do you feel like?"

"Well, how about we check out the new pizza parlor that just opened?" Penny offered. She was so hungry. She hadn't eaten since this morning.

"Sure thing," he said with a smile.

When they reached his shiny red and white Buick Roadmaster, he quickly went over to her side to open the door for her. Flustered, she mumbled, "Thanks," and climbed in. He closed the door behind her. She turned to the driver's side and pulled up the lock on the door. Quincy looked pleased at this. He thanked her as he opened the door and climbed in.

"So, we're off. Let's burn some rubber," he said, grinning mischievously.

Penny couldn't help but laugh. He was adorable. Gosh, she never thought that she would think of Quincy as being adorable.

When they reached the restaurant, they ordered a large pepperoni pizza and a pitcher of Coke. Penny hoped that she could eat. Now that she was here, she realized that the fluttering in her stomach might not make any room for food.

Quincy smiled at her from across the table, his warm brown eyes filled with delight.

Penny blushed deeply. She couldn't remember a guy ever looking at her like that before. It left her feeling embarrassed, but she also felt a warm feeling.

Penny decided not to expose her weakness with her words. "So, what's the deal, Q? Alfie says you have…this thing for me. Was he joking or what?"

Quincy grinned even harder. This girl was something else. It would be a challenge winning her over and her liked that. "Do you think he was pulling your leg?"

Penny shrugged and took a sip of her drink. She waited for him to say something else.

Quincy studied the young woman sitting before him. She had wide, slanted amber eyes that were so appealing. Her small, snub nose with a small splattering of freckles was set above small pouty lips. An other small splattering of freckles adorned her high, sharp cheekbones. She had big beautiful white teeth that stuck out just a touch at the front. All in all, Quincy found her adorable. She had a unique look to her that he found hard to resist. Unfortunately, when he had first met her freshman year, their relationship had gone the way of a friendship, not romantic as he had wanted it. Plus, she had made it clear that they were nothing more than friends. But the more he got to know her, the more appealing she had become to him. He loved her carefree attitude and her sense of adventure. So different from many of the uptight girls that roamed the campus. He knew that he could have more than a chance with any of the girls on campus, from the most prettiest to the most homely, but she was the one that he wanted. She had him hooked. And for years, he had been biding, waiting for his opportunity. Last week, he had grown impatient and thought to himself that it was now or never.

"You're so cute," Quincy blurted out before he could stop himself.

Penny blushed and took a bite of her pizza. She chewed and swallowed. "Stop kidding me. I never had a guy say that to me before."

"Maybe, because you push them away," Quincy suggested, wiping greasy fingers on a napkin.

"I don't push guys away, I'm friends with you and practically every guy on this campus."

"Yeah, but you would never allow a relationship to go any further than that. You ward them off."

Penny snorted. "When have you ever seen me fighting off guys with a stick?"

Quincy laughed. "Well…you're not exactly inviting. Guys know your reputation."

"Oh? And what reputation is that?" Penny asked, archly.

"You know…tomboyish. Kinda standoffish when you wanna be."

Penny shrugged her shoulders and took a sip of her coke. "So, I'm a tomboy. What do you want me for?"

Quincy blushed. "Well, I think you're really attractive…you're even pretty."

Penny snorted with derision. "Pretty? Don't insult my intelligence."

Quincy frowned, his normally smooth brow furrowed. "You're not good at taking compliments at all," he said miserably.

Penny decided to give him a break. She really was giving him a hard time. She guessed that he was right…she did push any chance of romance away. But it was because she was so sure about what she was going to do with her life and she didn't want anything to stand in the way of that.

"Okay. You say I'm pretty. In what way?"

"Well, in an offbeat kinda way, you have an attractive quality."

"Offbeat? I don't know how good that sounds," Penny said, teasing him.

Quincy gave her a half smile. "What? You wanna look like everyone else? You look different…in a good way of course. A very good way, if you ask me."

When Penny smiled at him, her expression totally uninhibited, Quincy felt his heart flutter in his chest. He smiled back.

"So…what do you think about me?" Quincy asked, nervously.

Penny smiled softly, she had never seen Quincy so ruffled. She was shocked and amazed that she was having that kind of affect on a guy. A good-looking one, at that.

"Well, I think that you're a nice guy and all. You're fine looking, you're fun to hang around and stuff…"

Quincy's face fell. "But you would never date me."

Penny stared at him. "I didn't say that. You never even let me finish—"

"So, you would date me?" Quincy asked, eagerly.

Penny reluctantly nodded her head. "We can go out on a date. Why don't we start with that then we'll see where it goes. Q, you gotta know that I'm very focused on my work and I can't let anyone get in the way of that."

Quincy shook his head vigorously. "I know that. I promise, that I will never distract you or get in your way. I wouldn't do that to you."

Penny nodded approvingly. "Well…okay. But we'll see."

Quincy gave her a lopsided grin. "So how am I doing so far?"

Penny laughed. "You're doing just fine."

Quincy smiled and looked at his watch. "Well we'd better get you home. I'm sure you've got some studying to do." He placed the money for the bill and the tip on the table.

"I could pay my half," Penny said, speaking up.

Quincy shook his head. "No way! Now that we're dating, I pay."

"I agreed to go out on *one* date," Penny reminded.

"Well, believe me. We'll be going out on a lot more following," Quincy said assuredly.

Penny snorted. "So sure of yourself!," she cracked.

Quincy grinned. "Don't I know it! We match."

Penny nodded. "Yeah," she said standing up.

Quincy held out his arm. Penny hesitated.

"Don't worry, I don't bite," Quincy said slyly.

Penny laughed. "But what if I wanted you to?" she said jokingly. The words were out of her mouth before she realized what she was saying. She flushed hard and bright. "I-I didn't mean for that to come out like—"

Quincy smiled at her. "I have a feeling I would do pretty much anything you want."

Penny, still blushing terribly, wrapped her arm through his. She felt the ropey muscles underneath and felt a warm feeling at the bottom of her stomach.

That night, Penny slept like a baby.

Ψ

Alfie was surprised at how quickly Penny had taken to Quincy. They were seen all over campus together. Within a month or two, it seemed as if they had grown attached at the hip—one couldn't be seen without the other. People talked about the blossoming relationship with wonderment and surprise. Penny, the self-proclaimed tomboy had found a man! And not just any man, Quincy Roberts! One of the most popular guys on campus. They seemed like such an unlikely pair. So opposite.

With a pang of regret, Alfie noticed how much he missed Penny. Sure, they were still friends and all, but she wasn't around him nearly as much as before. Pre-Quincy, Penny and Alfie used to hang around like that, almost like conjoined twins. But now it was the two of them—Penny and Q. And man, the way they looked at each other. When the group of them would go out to lunch, Penny and Q would be in their own little word. They would exchange knowing looks and intimate touches on the hands and arms. And last night, when the gang went out to eat on Carl's birthday, he felt a stab of jealousy seeing Quincy's arm possessively hold the small of Penny's back.

Alfie wasn't used to seeing Penny having a relationship with a guy, and he definitely wasn't the only one that registered shock when news of Penny and Q's relationship began to circulate. There were jealous and frustrated girls that took it as a personal snub that Quincy had passed them over to go out with what they considered a 'boyish' girl.

"She's such a boy. Plus she looks like someone's little sister. Now, I'm a real woman. Quincy should be with someone like me!" Janet, a popular gorgeous blond had said to her best friend Francine.

Francine had merely shrugged and said, "She's a nice person. I think she deserves him." As she said this, she thought about how bitchy her friend could be at times.

Janet looked at her in shock and frowned. "You must be kidding me. You know, sometimes I think that you say silly things like that just to irk me."

You thought right. Francine thought to herself.

Ψ

Since his good friend Penny was basking in the glow of a pleasing relationship, Alfie decided that he too should become involved. And he knew exactly the person.

Jessica Bailey. After that night in his dorm, she had called him non-stop. At first, he would return her calls, but eventually, he stopped. Then he began to avoid her on campus. He knew that she wanted a relationship. But frankly, to him all it had been was a night of sex, which he now regretted. He was drunk and hadn't been thinking clearly at all. Before, the night of his 21st birthday, he had managed to hold her at arms length, but now, since that steamy night, it was becoming an arduous task. He hadn't had the desire to carry it further. But now, he thought, perhaps he should. After all, any guy would be happy to have Jessica for himself.

Shouldn't he be happy as well? He decided that he should.

Much to Jessica's delight, Alfie began to call her. He asked her out on a date, and then another date. Pretty soon, they were the hot couple on campus and just as widely talked about at Q and Penny.

"I'm glad that you finally found someone," Penny had told him one night as they studied for their Western Civ II test in his dorm. "I think that you and Jessica look great together."

Alfie forced a smile. "Thanks." He went back to studying.

"Well, aren't you glad that I'm in a relationship too? You've teased me about that since we met," Penny said lightly.

Alfie shrugged. "Yeah, I guess. I'm glad that you're happy. You are happy, right?"

Penny's eyes instantly lit up. "Ooo. I feel like such a girl when I think of him! He makes me so happy...I never thought that I would get into a relationship and then, to top it off, with Q of all people."

Alfie felt a wave of jealously sweep over him. What the hell was happening to him?

"Yeah, well, that's just great," Alfie said curtly. He clamped his lips together and looked back down at his book, refusing to say another word.

Penny stared at him, perplexed.

Ψ

Penny and Quincy had been dating for six months. But they felt just as they had at the beginning. The passion had not died down.

As they sat in a darkened movie theater one evening, Quincy noticed that Penny was distracted. He frowned, he didn't like to see her worried.

"What's the mater, Baby?" He whispered, pulling her closer to him.

Penny leaned her head against his chest. "Nothing."

"Don't tell me nothing's wrong. I know something's the matter," he gently chided. "After the movie, we'll talk."

After the movie, they found a small coffee shop and went in.

"Well?" Quincy prodded after they had ordered their coffee.

"Well what?" Penny said, giving him her customary hard time.

"Well, what's the matter?" he asked, patiently, now used to her demeanor.

Penny paused for a while, taking in the details of the coffee shop. "I'm a little worried about Alfie."

Quincy gave her look. "Why in God's name are you worried about Alfie?"

Penny shrugged. "He doesn't talk to me like he used to."

Quincy frowned. "How so?"

"Well, it's just that we were such good friends before…and I feel as if something is missing now. When I try to talk to him , it always seems as if there's something at the back of his mind that he's thinking about."

They paused as the waitress brought them their mugs of coffee. She was an attractive brunette that flashed Quincy a coy smile before walking away. Penny smirked. She was used to things like that now. After all, Quincy was a good-looking guy. She was just glad that whenever a woman threw herself at him, he paid them no mind. Well at least not that she was aware of.

"I think the waitress has the hots for you," Penny bantered. She enjoyed teasing him for some reason. Maybe because he was such a good sport.

"I could care less," Quincy said, fully meaning it.

"She's cute," Penny stated matter-of-factly.

"You're cuter," Quincy snapped back.

Penny rolled her eyes. "Yeah right. You must be blind."

"Blinded by your beauty," he answered back, unperturbed.

Penny snorted, one of her most favorite noises of amusement. "You are a real cornball."

"But I'm your cornball, right?" he said, baby browns fixed on her in a silent appeal.

"Yeah. For now," Penny said, feeling especially insecure tonight.

Quincy looked at her, confused. "What's that supposed to mean?" he smiled slightly, "Someone cuter eyeballing you now?"

Penny frowned ruefully. "Get real! Newsflash: I look like Pippi Longstocking. Who would eyeball me?"

"I would. In fact, I enjoy looking at you," Quincy said honestly.

"I think you need to get your vision checked," Penny said miserably, feeling the sting of tears in her eyes. "Soon you'll find someone really foxy to be with." Unable to hold back, the tears started flowing down her face.

Quincy's face was a mask of horror and worry. He came around beside her and wrapped her thin body in his strong arms. "What's the matter baby? What's wrong tonight?"

Penny continued to cry, the soft cotton of his shirt catching her tears. She hoped that she wasn't ruining his shirt. Then she realized that it was the shirt that she had bought him when she went back home to Minneapolis during the summer. For some reason that made her cry harder. The sobs shook her thin shoulders.

Quincy was now frantic with worry. In an alarmed voice he said, "Please talk to me, baby."

Penny continued to sob, but soon gain control of herself. She began sniffling and wiping at the wet spot at his shoulders.

"Oh gosh, I think I've ruined your shirt," she said wretchedly.

Ψ

After the coffee shop incident, Quincy started treating Penny like glass. He obviously didn't want a repeat of what happened.

He probably thinks I'm nuts, thought Penny. She decided to ask him if this was the case.

"Do you think of me differently now?" Penny asked him one day as they were sitting out on a picnic table eating lunch between classes.

"What do you mean?" He asked, puzzled.

"I mean…ever since I broke down in the coffee shop a week ago, you've been treating me…differently."

"Maybe so," Quincy said simply.

"Oh gosh. If you want to break up, just tell me," Penny said fretfully.

"Are you kidding me? I don't want to break up with you. I think that last week, you revealed a side of yourself that you rarely show."

"What do you mean?"

"Well…vulnerability. You know, you always seemed so sure of yourself and tough. That was the way I was used to seeing you. And honestly, when I heard you saying the nonsense you said and crying the way you did…I hardly knew what to do."

"Oh great,' Penny muttered.

"But in a way, I was relieved…that you…exposed yourself that way to me. I mean…I feel kinda closer to you," Quincy said with a blush.

"Oh really?" Penny mumbled

"Really. And at the same time, I don't ever want to see you that way again…It kinda hurt me when you said all those things about yourself."

"What things?" Penny asked, wanting him to say it.

"I mean…you saying that you were just a phase for me, that I would find some other foxy girl…you don't really think that's true do you?"

Penny shrugged and bit into her sandwich. She chewed staring off into the sky.

"Well, it's not true. You're gorgeous, absolutely beautiful and I'm so happy that we're together," Quincy said softly.

"Oh, yeah? Tell me more," Penny said with a playful smile.

"Yeah. And I've been meaning to tell you something for the past two weeks," Quincy added, playing with the crust of his sandwich.

"What?" Penny asked, curiously.

"Well..."

"Come on, out with it!" Penny cajoled.

"Well...I love you."

Penny nearly choked on her juice.

Quincy frowned, not expecting that sort of reaction. "I'm sorry if you think that was the wrong thing to say. I should have shut my trap," he said, obviously hurt.

Penny shook her head. "No, no," she came around the table and sat beside him and leaned against his arm. Quincy pulled her closer.

"You know...you don't have to say it back or anything. I just wanted you to know how I feel," Quincy said, relieved he had finally gotten his feelings off of his chest.

"But I want to say it back. I think I love you too, Q," Penny said.

And they kissed.

Chapter Twenty-seven

"Oh, what's the matter, Alfie, why can't you come with me to the party that my sorority's holding?" Jessica whined.

Alfie shook his head. "Because that's not my kinda scene."

Jessica pouted. She was currently in Alfie's apartment dressed only in her panties and a bra. It was a Sunday afternoon, and they were lounging around doing nothing in particular. She was gorgeous, but for some reason, Alfie wasn't aroused at the moment.

"I go to all your stupid events. Why can't you come to this one?"

"Oh come on. You hated sitting through that lunch two weeks ago. You kept fidgeting and asking me if it was gonna end soon. You behaved like a little kid," he complained.

"What do you want from me? It was boring! I hated it!" Shrieked Jessica.

"Yeah, that's right. Quit holding back, tell me your true feelings!" Alfie yelled, feeling enraged.

Jessica quickly pulled on her skirt and her blouse. She ran a hand through her blond waves. After she had put on her shoes, she turned to him.

"I'm not staying here anymore to argue with you. I have better things to do," she said icily.

"Great. By all means, start doing them!" Alfie said gruffly.

The door slammed hard behind Jessica. Afterwards, the room was plunged in silence. Alfie sat in his armchair and sighed deeply.

It seemed that all he and Jessica ever did was to argue. And in his heart of hearts, he knew that it was mostly his fault. He just didn't feel for Jessica the same way that she felt for him. They weren't exactly compatible. But it seemed that Jessica didn't notice it or refused to acknowledge it.

His mind thought back to all the events that both Penny and him had attended as friends. Both of them would always enjoy it. The plays, the museum, the cultural events, the fundraisers...all things that he and

Penny had in common but that Jessica abhorred. He missed that. They didn't see each other half as much as they used to.

He also knew that he wasn't treating Penny fairly, but it seemed that he couldn't help it. Every time he talked with her, his stomach would get heavy with regret. And sometimes, he felt a touch of annoyance towards her. Sometimes, actually more often now than before, he regretted hooking his two friends up. Alfie had watched as Penny and Quincy got closer and closer. He could tell that they were truly in love. He wondered if they were sleeping together. The thought sent a jab of jealously through him. What was he getting jealous for? She wasn't his girl, never was.

He wished he could change that.

ψ

Alfie thanked God that winter break was now upon them. The break is well deserved, he thought to himself as he thought about his tumultuous school year. He was glad to be going home to Illinois.

"Am I going to meet your parents?" Jessica asked Alfie, blue eyes looking innocent.

"They're not coming up here. I'm going home," Alfie responded.

"Well, what about I come to you for part of the winter vacation? After Christmas, we have two weeks left." Jessica said, "I could come up there. Or, you can come over to Pennsylvania. My parents really like you."

Sometimes, Alfie couldn't believe that he was still with Jessica. Despite their arguments, she had latched on to him and refused to relinquish her grasp. Alfie, not really up for the fight, considering his mild depression over the Quincy-Penny situation, had passively allowed the relationship to continue.

"We'll see," he said distractedly. He just wanted to shut her up.

"Well, I'll be expecting your call," Jessica said firmly.

Well, don't hold your breath. Alfie thought bitterly.

ψ

Wendy and Rocco waited for Alfie in the airport. Wendy was so nervous, her palms were sweating.

Rocco put an arm around his wife's shoulders. "What are you so worried about?"

Wendy shrugged her shoulders and gripped his hand. "I don't know. I haven't seen him for months, since summer time."

Rocco kissed her on the cheek. "Don't worry, he's still the same Alfie."

Wendy nodded her head. "I know. I know."

"Oh, I think that's him," Rocco said pointing ahead.

Wendy smiled when she set eyes on her son. He was alarmingly handsome. His blond hair was greased back, in the current popular fashion of the youth. His bright blue eyes stood out from the deeply tanned face. His tall athletic frame walked with confidence through the crowd. His eyes lit up when he spotted his mother and his step-dad.

"Hey!" Rocco said hugging him and giving him a slap on the back. "You look good, like you've been getting a lot of sun? You definitely don't look like a Chicago native."

Alfie smiled.

Wendy saw that the smile didn't quite reach his eyes. *Something's wrong with my son and I'm going to find out what it is.*

The driver waited for them with the Mercedes. They all got in and made their way home.

The moment Alfie was through the door, Edda and Helga threw themselves into their older brother's arms.

Alfie hugged them back, truly happy to see them. Every time he saw them, he was amazed at how fast his little sisters were growing up. Edda was now thirteen and Helga was seventeen, graduating from high school next spring. And they were both so beautiful. Dresden dolls. He felt a fierce protectiveness towards them.

Behind his sisters stood, his stepsister Angelina and his two step brothers Anthony and Sal. There was also Garrett and Ester. They greeted him warmly, Alfie also was happy to see them.

"You're growing up so fast, young man!" Ester said, embracing him in a hug.

Alfie laughed and pecked her on the cheek. "I think it's because of all the sun in Florida," Alfie said jokingly.

They all laughed.

Later that night, when Rocco and Wendy were in bed, Wendy thought to bring up the subject that had been secretly disturbing her since Alfie came yesterday morning.

"Have you noticed anything different about Alfie?" Wendy asked her husband.

"What do you mean?" Rocco asked, putting down the book that he was reading.

"Well…I don't know. He looks a little listless sometimes. A little sad," Wendy answered.

Rocco pursed his lips in concentration. "You think so?"

"Yeah! I don't know…but I don't think that I'm imagining things. I just feel that something is bothering him."

"Do you want me to ask him?" Rocco offered.

Wendy hesitated and then said, "Maybe it would be better if you did. He might feel more comfortable speaking with a man."

"Okay. I'll speak to him tomorrow."

Ψ

The next day Wendy and the girls went out to go shopping, leaving Rocco and Alfie alone.

Alfie stood in the living room, looking out the window. Rocco observed this, now he definitely got the sense that something was the matter with his stepson.

Rocco came beside him and put a hand on his shoulders. "What do you say we go out and do something? It's such a nice day."

"It's cold outside," Alfie mumbled, his mind somewhere else.

Rocco frowned and thought for a while. Suddenly an idea hit him.

"Have you ever gone ice fishing?" Rocco asked him.

Alfie shook his head. "Why?"

"Well…I was thinking that maybe we could go. We could round up a few guys and go on the lake. It's the perfect time of the year to go."

Alfie shrugged his shoulders. "Okay."

"Come on, it'll be fun. We can talk, reminisce, drink some hot cocoa, eat cookies…it's be fun—just the guys. Do you have anyone in mind that you want to take along?"

Alfie shook his head. None of his friends were around for the holidays. But he wouldn't mind if Anthony came along. He was a cool guy.

"How about Anthony?" Alfie suggested.

"Sure! Sounds good! Me and my two sons out on an outing together," Rocco said, pleased with the idea. "We'll leave today and come back tomorrow morning, how does that sound?"

For the first time in a while, Alfie felt a touch of happiness.

Ψ

By the time the three men reached the cabin by Lake Michigan, Alfie could barely feel his feet. That was how cold it was.

"Isn't it great out here?" Rocco exclaimed, his breath coming out in clouds.

"It's as cold as a witch's teat," Anthony said, rubbing his arms.

"Damn straight," Alfie agreed.

"Oh, come on boys. When was the last time that we ever spent time together like this?" Rocco asked.

"And why wasn't Sal summoned to come up here as well?" Anthony asked his dad, despondently.

Rocco laughed. "Come on—you know your brother, he's just not the type for this. There had to be a reason you agreed to come up here, Anthony."

"Well, anything to get my away from work and home for a while, I guess," Anthony commented.

"Yeah, I'm glad that you found a babysitter for the girls," Rocco said with a smile. He patted his son on the back.

"Hey, this might actually be fun," Alfie said, taking in the snowy view around him.

"That's the spirit!" Rocco exclaimed.

The cabin, although not large, was roomy enough. There were three bedrooms, a living room, a bathroom, and a kitchen.

"Come on," Rocco said excitedly, "Let's go get some firewood."

"Me and Alfie will chop the wood. You get something for us to eat, Dad. I'm so hungry, I think that if I come across a bear out there, I'll tackle it and eat it," Anthony said with a laugh.

Alfie laughed. "I'm right behind you on that one. But I think I'll go after something a little smaller, less risk involved."

Anthony nodded his head, smiling at his stepbrother, "True, true."

They got the axe and headed outside. Behind the cabin, there was a bunch of logs. A tree stump stood nearby

Alfie carried a log to the tree truck and placed it on top. After motioning for Alfie to step back, Anthony raised the axe and chopped the wood.

"So how's school doing?" Anthony asked, taking the heavy log from Alfie's gloved hands.

"S'alright," Alfie responded, not getting into details.

"How's that girlfriend of yours? What's her name…Jessica?"

"Yeah. She's all right."

"You don't sound too enthused."

"That's because I'm not," Alfie responded, hefting another log.

"Why's that?"

"We're just so different. We like different things. I can't stand the things she likes to do and she can't stand what I like to do. We argue all the time. We hardly get along."

"All that? Then why are you still with her?" Anthony asked, swinging the ax again.

"I just don't…have the motivation to get out of the relationship right now. I mean, I just can't be bothered."

"Well then, there's no one that you think you might like to go out with instead?" Anthony asked.

"Well…there is someone…," Alfie said, suddenly red in the face.

Anthony laughed when he saw his stepbrother's reddened face. "Awww…whoever it is, you really got it for them! I can tell."

"It's Penny."

"Penny? You mean that read headed sprite that you introduced us to when we went up there last year?"

Alfie nodded his head.

"I thought you guys were just friends."

Alfie picked up an armful of chopped wood. Anthony did the same. They made their way back to the house. They put the wood in a corner and went back out again.

"Well, I thought we were, but then I started getting weird feelings."

"Weird feeling?"

"Well…I kinda hooked her up with a friend of mine…but he was also friends with her, only not really close. He liked her and asked me to speak to her for him. So I did. And now they're together and they look as happy as ever," Alfie said bitterly.

"Hooking friends up with other friends? Bad news, buddy." Anthony said assuredly.

"Don't I know it. I went against my gut instinct."

"*Always* trust your gut instinct," Anthony said with a raised finger.

That afternoon, they decided to go out on the lake.

"We need a area where the ice is at about four inches thick. I know the perfect place." said Rocco

They walked across the ice in their rubber-soled boots. Rocco lead the way. Finally, Rocco stopped. Alfie and Anthony followed suit.

"Here's the place. We can pitch the shack right here," Rocco said as he set down the gear.

After the shelter was set up, they went in and drilled a hole in the ice, right under the middle roof point of the tent.

Alfie pulled out the lines and hooks and handed each to Anthony and Rocco. The three men put the bait on the end of the hook. They each took a seat around the ice and waited to see what they would catch.

After several minutes had gone by without a tug on any of the three lines, Alfie began to grow impatient.

"Nothing yet," Alfie said, pulling on the fingers of his gloves.

Rocco smiled. "We have to give it time, son. This is a very good opportunity for us to talk."

Alfie shrugged. "What do you want to talk about?"

"Well…we haven't seen you in a while, Alfie. How about you tell us about school." Rocco said.

"Nothing really interesting to tell."

"Well…how are you classes going?" Rocco asked, good naturally.

"They're going fine. I'm taking some upper division electives early, so that I don't have to scrabble to take them next year."

"That's good. It's always smart to be ahead of schedule." Rocco said with a nod.

Anthony gave a start. His fishing line began to bob and pull. "I think I've got something'!"

Anthony pulled his line up. A squirming salmon was on the end. Anthony pulled the fish onto the ice. It flopped wildly.

Alfie and Rocco laughed. "Put in the bucket!" Alfie exclaimed.

Anthony quickly put the squirming fish into the big bucket. They listened as it flopped around inside, its solid body hitting the hard plastic sides, creating a dull thumping sound.

"Ummm…we'll cook that one for dinner, I have the perfect salmon recipe," Rocco said with a smile.

"You and your cooking, Dad," Anthony said, amused.

"Back to you and school…" Rocco began.

Alfie groaned. Anthony laughed.

"Oh, come on. I'm sure there're a lot of interesting things going on down there." Rocco said.

Alfie glanced at Anthony. Anthony gave him a lopsided grin.

"Hey, I saw that look." Rocco said accusingly. "Want to let old Rocco in on the secret?"

"Well…just a little relationship problem," Alfie said.

"What's the matter? If you don't mind me asking. We're all men here, huh? We can be honest with one another." Rocco declared.

Alfie and Anthony laughed suddenly and didn't stop until the tears came running down their faces.

Rocco stared at his sons, bemused. "What's so funny?"

Alfie attempted to gain some control. One thing about Rocco, he was a really cool guy that took jokes well. He had thick skin and was a good sport. He could also be extremely hilarious as well. Alfie had a nice, easy relationship with him.

Anthony spoke first. "It's just the way that you said it…I don't know."

"It sounded like you were on the pulpit preaching," Alfie said, wiping away a few tears.

Rocco grinned like a silly boy. "I'm glad that I make you two laugh so much…I can feel the love," Rocco said sarcastically, which made them laugh even more.

"Okay, okay. Let me tell you," Alfie said, glancing at the hole in the ice. The water looked so gray. "Well…you know that for the past six or so months, I have been dating Jessica."

"Oh, yes. Lovely girl," Rocco commented.

"Yeah, but she doesn't suit me. We don't suit each other."

"Not only that, he has eyes for another," Anthony said, putting in his two cents.

Alfie rolled his eyes at his stepbrother. "Thanks for blabbing everything out. Let's talk about you for a moment, why don't we," Alfie said, cornering him.

"Nothing really interesting to talk about," Anthony said easily

Alfie laughed loudly. "Using my lines, are you?"

Anthony grinned and looked away.

Rocco joined in with Alfie. "These past months you have been positively glowing. Could it be because of…Eunice? A lovely romance, my boy. But you must remember that you are a married man."

Anthony frowned. "Yeah, I'm married to a woman that doesn't even know who I am and that shrinks away whenever I get too close to her," he said bitterly.

"She can't help that, Anthony. She's sick," Rocco reminded.

"Yeah, I know," Anthony responded. "But I really do care about Eunice, you know? I can't really help that."

Alfie laughed. "Who'd a thought it. She really doesn't seem to be your type at all."

Anthony shrugged his shoulders. "It was pretty unexpected, she and I. But when you have feelings, you can't deny them. You find love in the most unexpected places. But of course you know that, Alfie. There's more to your story, go ahead," Anthony said with a wave of his hand.

Alfie grinned, then continued. "The girl that I have eyes for is Penny."

"Who's Penny?" Rocco asked, confused.

"Dad. Don't you remember the girl that I introduced you all to when you all first came down to my school? You saw her the last time we went up there too, this past March."

"Oh…that girl with the orangey-brown hair? And all those freckles?"

"Yeah, that's her," Alfie responded, with a nod.

Rocco grinned. "I thought the two of you were just friends."

"Yeah, well…we were. But now…"

"You want it to be more," Rocco finished for him.

"That's right. The only problem is that…she's dating someone else and they're really close."

"Is she in love with him?" Anthony asked.

"I don't know…It looks so," Alfie said, hating to admit it. He felt the familiar sadness of the past months, sweep through him.

"Do you love Penny?" Rocco asked.

Alfie hesitated before he answered. "I don't know. I think that I do. But I know that I have really strong feelings for her. I wish that it were me with her instead of my friend. But the thing is, I was the one that got them together in the first place, so really have no room to talk. If you really think about it."

"Does Jessica know how you feel?" Rocco asked.

Alfie let out a mirthful chuckle. "She wouldn't notice anything like that. All she's concerned about is herself. She's very self-centered, although she claims to love me."

"Have you ever told her that you love her?" asked Anthony.

"Who, Jessica or Penny?"

"Jessica."

"Never. I know she wants me to though."

"Well don't. If you do, you'll really be trapped then," Anthony said with conviction.

"I feel trapped already."

"You're too young to feel that way. Do what you have to do. You have only God and yourself to answer to in the end," Rocco said simply.

Ψ

When Alfie got went back to school, he promptly dumped Jessica. And of course, she was not pleased. After switching from begging to crying, Jessica saw that Alfie was not going to be moved. Finally, the anger came. In burning waves. Jessica was a woman scorned and she vowed that she was not going to go down without a fight. If she couldn't have him, no one would.

"I can't believe Jessica and Alfie have broken up," Janet said gleefully to Francine as they sat eating their lunch.

"I heard that he dumped her." Francine took a big bite of her tuna salad sandwich and chewed sulkily. Tuna fish wasn't her most favorite meal, but she was attempting to eat healthy.

Janet's wide violet eyes opened even wider with shock, "She's telling everyone that she dumped *him*."

"Which is a lie," Francine said simply.

"Whatever. Hmmm...that means Zimmermann is up for grabs," Janet said craftily.

"I don't know about that," Francine said as she smoothed down a strand of unruly dark hair.

Janet fixed her best friend with an imposing look. "What's that supposed to mean?"

"Well...it doesn't exactly seem like he's looking," Francine pointed out.

"When it comes to me," Janet said with a bat of her long eyelashes, "every guy's looking to get a piece of the pie."

And I'm sure that every guy on this campus has gotten a taste. Francine said to herself. She supposed that she shouldn't be thinking such things about her best friend, but it was merely the truth. Francine was never one for idealism. But she wouldn't dare say such a thing like that to Janet out loud. Janet had a very volatile temper.

"I'm going to seduce him at that party that his fraternity is having this weekend you just watch, I'll have him eating out of my hand... Francine!"

"Hmmmmm?" Francine said rolling her eyes back to her friend's pretty face. She had been daydreaming about food from *The Stack Shack*—pretending that her tuna salad sandwich was a double cheeseburger, her carrot sticks were steak fries, and her organic fruit juice was one of their delicious malted shakes.

Her diet wasn't going well.

"Did you hear what I said?" asked Janet in a crotchety tone.

"What did you say?" Francine said blinking her dark eyes.

"Forget it. You're impossible," Janet mumbled to her plump friend.

Ψ

Every eye was on Janet Gilmore when she entered. It was very plain to see why. Besides being incredibly gorgeous, Janet was done up to within an inch of her life—her hair was immaculate, the top half of her outfit hugged her curves to perfection, leaving nothing to the imagination. And her makeup was flawless. Lustful stares from the males were cast her way as well as envious glances from many of the ladies. This made Janet even bolder.

A dark haired guy with yearning eyes came sweeping over. "Would you like to dance?" he asked, hopefully.

"Maybe later," Janet said as she caught sight of Alfie, who was at the moment surrounded by friends.

Janet moved on, leaving the young man standing awkwardly. Gracious, Janet was not.

"Hello," Janet singsonged as she approached the group. The group of young men smiled admiringly at her, except for Alfie who gave her a wan smile.

"Hey cutie, how are you doing tonight?" Jed asked, his face a mask of desire. He wouldn't mind hooking up with her tonight.

"I'm fine. And how are you all?" she asked, trying to be polite.

They all began to talk to her, all except for Alfie. He stood aside and listened to the friendly banter, smiling slightly. All attempts of Janet drawing him in, were useless. Janet decided to try another method. A more direct method.

"Come on, sweetie, let's dance!" Janet whooped, grabbing Alfie's hand before he knew what was happening.

"I don't know, I—"

"Come on! This is a party!" Janet called before tugging him helplessly along.

Ψ

Penny eyeballed the blond couple from out of the corner of her eye. Janet and Alfie were dancing up a storm. At first, Alfie had seemed reluctant, but he was certainly all in it now.

"Hey, do you want some more to drink?" Quincy asked.

Penny diverted her attention back to her boyfriend. She smiled, exposing her bright, white teeth. "I would love some more fruit drink."

Quincy went off to get them refreshments.

Penny went back to looking at Alfie and Janet.

"Seems like he wants to plug every blonde on campus," Penny muttered to herself.

"What did you say?" Quincy was back with the drinks.

"Oh, nothing. I was just looking at the dress that Patricia was wearing," Penny lied. "She looks like a tart."

Quincy grinned. "And you, I must say, that you look perfect in yours. I've been waiting forever to see you in a dress."

"This old rag?" Penny said jokingly as she plucked at the material of her dress.

"I never saw a rag that looked *that* good."

Ψ

Jessica watched angrily from across the room at the dancing duo. It certainly didn't take Alfie long to find somebody else. That showed how much he cared for her—not at all. This just wasn't fair.

This was the first time that Jessica had ever been dumped.

She didn't like it in the least. She would have her revenge.

Ψ

Francine watched Janet flouncing herself on the dance floor and felt the distinct feeling of disgust.

She watched Janet's skirt billow up around her thighs as she spun around, exposing her panties. She saw Alfie blanch. She watched as Janet wiggled her full breasts right in his stunned, reddened face. She watched Janet turn around and rub her behind across Alfie's crotch. His eyes bugged out at this.

Alfie.

She wished that she could take his place.

Ψ

"I've had enough, Janet. I think I'm going to go have a seat," Alfie said begging off from dancing the next song.

"Then I'll sit down with you," Janet quickly said.

"You don't have to do that."

"I know, but I want to. You know, we've never really had a real conversation in all the years that we're been at this school?"

"Yeah, I guess we haven't," Alfie muttered, wondering where this was leading. Who was he kidding. He knew exactly what Janet was pulling. Only, he wasn't going for it.

Once seated, Janet made her move. Eager hands began to creep up his pant leg.

Alfie jumped. "What are you doing?" he said, scooting away from her.

"Doing what I know you want," Janet breathed, her mouth close to his ear.

"But it's *not* what I want," Alfie said firmly. He brushed her hands off.

"Of course it's what you want. Do you know how many guys would be happy to be in your place?" Janet asked, attempting to slide a hand under his shirt.

"Then, get one of them!" Alfie exclaimed. He was not going to get rid of her quickly. She was a very persistent girl.

Ψ

From the dance floor, Penny watched Alfie and Janet sitting on the couch. She saw them touching up on each other…well not really Alfie, but soon he would be. Penny felt a tinge of anger. Janet was such a slut. She hated her. She loathed both her and her chubby, sneaky looking sidekick Francine. For the life of her, she couldn't see why Janet was so popular. Sure, she was pretty, but was that all that counted? It obviously did, Penny noted sadly. It also helped that Janet put out for almost every guy that asked.

"Babe, are you okay?" Quincy asked her, for what must have been the twentieth time that night. *I must really look distracted*, Penny thought to herself. Better pull it together.

"Yeah, I'm fine. Why wouldn't I be?" Penny said, touching his cheek.

This was the man she loved. This was the man that she cared about and wanted to be with.

What Alfie did, was his own business, and had nothing to do with her.

"Honey, I was thinking…" Penny began

"What?" Quincy asked.

"Why don't we go upstairs to your room? Let's get away from this party," Penny said softly. "It's dying down anyways."

"So, our party was lame, huh," Quincy laughed. "I'm sure my brothers would be pleased to here that."

"No, no, honey. It's good. But…I want to be alone with you."

Understanding dawned on Quincy. He smiled softly. "Are you… sure?"

"I'm very sure. Will you go up and wait for me? I want to run back to my dorm and get something," she said thinking about the pink, unused diaphragm that she had sitting in the bathroom drawer at home.

"Okay…I love you Penny," Quincy said gently.

"I do too," Penny said and gave him a kiss. "I'll be back in like ten minutes." She weaved her way through the thinning crowd and out the front door.

Ψ

A rejected Janet watched curiously, as Quincy made his way up the stairs towards the bedrooms.

Hmmm…what was he doing up there? She wondered to herself. She glanced around the room. Penny was nowhere in sight. She must have left. Maybe to get something. Possibly…

Little Penny wasn't so little after all.

If what Janet was thinking was right, little Penny and Quinsy were about to embark upon a little rendezvous. Why else would Quincy go upstairs at this time? Why else would Penny leave so quickly? No doubt, she would be back. But when Penny came back…she wouldn't like what she was going to find.

Janet smiled to herself. If she couldn't get Alfie, Quincy was the perfect substitute. She would have him.

After about five minutes, Janet went up the stairs when she was sure that no one was watching.

Jessica's eyes followed Janet all the way up.

Ψ

Quincy was so excited that he didn't know what to do with himself when he got to his room.

Tonight was the night.

He had wanted Penny ever since they began dating and even before that. But he had been patient. He knew that she was a virgin, and he didn't want to force her into doing anything that she would regret. He loved her too much. But tonight, when she had said those words to him, his heart fluttered with pleasure in his chest.

He would be so gently with her.

He would give her all the pleasure and enjoyment that she deserved.

Their love would guide them.

Quincy put on one of the *Righteous Brother's* records. It was one of his favorites as well as Penny's, he knew.

He got out some clean sheets from his closet and changed his bed. It wouldn't do to make love on week-old sheets. Everything had to be nice and fresh for Penny.

Oh, I'll take a shower. Quincy thought with a smile. Clean sheets, clean guy to match.

After the shower, Quincy slipped into a pair of his best boxers.

Quincy had just slipped under the covers when the door to his room swung open. His smile turned to a look of shock when he saw who it was.

"A man like you shouldn't be up here all by your lonesome," Julie drawled, high emotion causing her faint Georgian accent to come strongly through.

She closed the door behind her.

Ψ

Penny stuffed the container with the diaphragm into the black pocketbook that she borrowed from her roommate. She hated purses, but what was she supposed to do, carry it around in the open? Not likely.

She paused by the bureau and thought if she should bring something to wear. But she didn't really have anything that fit to be called sexy. Most of her pajamas were boyish. Previously, she had no use for anything frilly, lacy, or silky. Those things didn't suit her. But now, she wished that she had something like that to wear for Quincy. Oh well. There was nothing that she could do about that now.

Penny rushed out the door to head back to the man she loved.

Ψ

As Jessica was wondering what Janet was up to, going upstairs like that, she caught sight of Alfie walking by. He went to stand amongst a group of friends. It wasn't long before they were laughing and merrymaking. Jessica was pissed. He was supposed to be moping around because they weren't together anymore. He was supposed to be telling her that he had made a serious mistake and ask her to take him back..

Jessica walked up to him. She was instantly greeted by the group. She smiled kindly. She stood beside Alfie and whispered in his ear, "We need to talk."

Alfie tried to keep a normal face, "What about?" he asked, through gritted teeth.

"Something very important that I think you should hear."

Alfie stared at her in wonderment. "Okay fine."

"Let's go somewhere else to talk. What I have to say is too personal," Jessica said.

"We can go upstairs," Alfie offered warily. He wondered what she was trying to pull. Couldn't people just leave him in peace?

Ψ

"What the hell are you doing here?" Quincy asked, totally shocked. He hadn't thought to lock the door behind him.

"I'm taking what's rightfully mine," Janet cooed, all pouting lips and heaving chest. She took a step towards the bed.

"Look, you need to get out of here. Where do you get off just coming here to my room?" Quincy asked, angrily.

"I get off on a lot of things. Want me to show you?" Janet said demurely. She took another step closer.

"No!" Quincy exclaimed, "I do not! Now get outta here before Penny comes here and sees you here. She might think something's going on," Quincy said rising from his bed.

"Ummm…something could be going on if you'd like," Janet said, getting an eyeful of muscled chest and strong sinewy legs.

Quincy walked towards the door to open it.

That was when Janet struck. She jumped on his back and held on tightly.

Quincy yelled and they both fell backwards on the bed. They thrashed around for a moment. Quincy pushed her away, but she simply jumped on him again. She was surprisingly strong. Julie climbed on top of his chest, grasping him between her knees. His arms were pinned beneath him, making it next to impossible to get her off.

"Get off me!" Quincy called, horrified.

Instead, Julie quickly pulled the front of her dress down, exposing her breasts. Quincy attempted to shove her off, but she held on.

Julie leaned over and kissed him full on the lips, gripping his swinging head.

It was at that moment that Penny walked in. She looked on in shock and amazement. She didn't know what to say.

Quincy moved from underneath Julie now that her grip was loosened. "It's not what you think," he said in a firm tone of voice.

Janet looked boldly at Penny, a smirk on her face.

Penny's eyes took in the bare breasts and exposed red panties. She saw the red lipstick smeared on Quentin's lips, which were now twisted in dismay.

"She jumped on me, I tried to get off her, but she wouldn't let go—"

Penny ran from the room.

Ψ

"I'm pregnant," Jessica said, attempting to force tears from her eyes.

"You've got to be kidding me," Alfie said with a befuddled expression.

"I am. I just thought you should know." Jessica paused. "I went to the doctor last week. That's when I found out."

Alfie couldn't believe his ears. How could this be happening to him?

Before he could think or say anything further, they heard the sound of running feet and a voice, whom he recognized as Quincy, desperately calling out Penny's name.

Alfie and Jessica opened the door to investigate.

"You damn bastard. How could you do this to me?" Penny screamed to Quincy at one end of the hallway.

"Penny, you gotta listen to me. She came into my room when I was waiting for you! I didn't tell her to come in," Quincy cried out.

"Oh, yeah? So she just came into your room by chance? Why your room? Why would she leave the party?" Penny snapped, not believing him. She was trembling like a leaf. Her face was red and her eyes were flashing.

"I don't know!" Quincy cried out miserably. Everything was working against him. He glanced backward at Janet who was lingering by his bedroom doorway at the other end of the hallway. He gave her an evil glare. This was all her fault.

"What's going on?" Alfie asked, taken back.

Penny turned to look at Alfie. "I saw him making out with that… that slut over there! Can you believe it? We were going to make love! He couldn't even wait a minute!"

Quincy's face was red as a beet. His brow was creased in distress. "Please baby, listen to me. Do you think I would do that knowing you were coming back at any moment? How stupid would that be?"

"Well, who said you were smart?" Penny spitefully shot back.

Quincy turned to Alfie, appealingly. "You gotta talk to her, Alfie. She won't listen. Janet opened my door. When I head the door opening, I thought it was Penny. I swear that I didn't invite her up," Quincy turned back to Penny, "I love you. I wouldn't disrespect you like that."

Alfie's stomach flopped. This was his chance. This was his opportunity to drive a wedge between the two of them.

He didn't know who did what, but he knew what side he would take.

Then he could have Penny for himself.

Alfie assumed a pitying face. "Quincy, I was surprised you had lasted this long."

Quincy stared at Alfie blankly. "What?"

"I mean…all the women you had. It seemed that every two weeks, you were with a new one. The longest relationship I ever saw you in lasted three months. That's a bad track record."

Quincy swallowed hard, his eye watery. "That was before. Don't bring that up."

Alfie continued, on a roll and unable to stop. "And remember, Gina, that one girl you managed to keep for three months…you went on ahead and cheated on her. You never could keep it in your pants, could you. And now, you've hurt poor Penny. How could you?"

"You stinking mother-fucker!" screamed an enraged Quincy, "You just want Penny for yourself!" he said, finally getting the deal. Quincy lunged at him so fast that Alfie didn't know what hit him. Quincy delivered a stiff uppercut to the underside of Alfie's jaw. It sent him reeling. Alfie returned the shot, Quincy blocked. But when Alfie punched him in the stomach, Quincy doubled over in pain.

Alfie lunged at Quincy, knocking him to the floor. The two scuffled viciously on the floor, Quincy, at one point getting the upper hand and sending a series of punches into Alfie's face.

Somewhere in the background, they heard screaming and yells to stop. At one point, Quincy could feel a light hand in his back, but he paid it no attention.

After a while, there was a bunch of people in the corridor. A bunch of guys pulled the two young men apart. Both were bloodied and had ripped shirts. They glared each other down.

Eric, their head fraternity brother, stood in the middle with a look of shock on his face. His round face was frantic. "Come on, what's all this about you two?"

"This bastard is trying to get me into trouble with Penny," Quincy snarled.

"I'm just telling the truth!" Alfie shot back.

"What you're saying has nothing to do with the situation at hand and you know that!"

"Okay, okay, stop, stop," Eric said raising his hands. "Let's try to get this solved and figured out."

Jessica looked into the crowd and saw Francine standing there, with a sneer on her round face. Francine looked over at Janet who was now standing closer by. Janet and Francine exchanged looks.

"Well, I was up here waiting for Penny. Then she comes in," he said pointing a finger at Janet, "and jumps my bones, practically! I didn't tell her to come in and I was trying to get her out."

Jessica decided that she'd better chime in. Alfie wasn't going to win here tonight.

"When I was downstairs, I saw Julie looking at Quincy as he snuck up the stairs. She had this sneaky look on her face, like she was up to no good. Then she followed him up. She did it without him knowing," Jessica said scoffingly.

Alfie scowled Jessica. "Oh please."

"It's the truth!" snapped Jessica.

Penny, who at the moment was at lost for words, looked back and forth between Jessica and Alfie who were currently staring each other down, viciously.

"Jessica's right," a voice said. Everyone turned and looked at the person from which it came. Francine.

Janet looked at her best friend, stupid expression fixed on face. Francine gave her a disgusted look.

"Janet came up here when she saw that Penny had left and Quincy was going upstairs. She figured that they were…meeting so she decided to go up there and put a wrench in the works."

"Shut up, Francine!" screamed Julie.

"No, I'm not shutting up," Francine shot back. "Why can't you just leave people be? Do you have to attempt to break up *every* relationship?" Francine said dejectedly. *And why can't you see I want you?* Francine said to herself.

Janet glowered at her.

"Penny…ah we have to talk," Alfie said giving her a beseeching look.

"There's nothing to talk about," Penny snapped in Alfie's direction as she, came towards a miserable looking Quincy.

"I'm sorry, baby. I didn't know what was going on, I just assumed," Penny said, holding his hand.

Quincy gave her a stiff smile. That was the best that he could do at the moment considering the pain in his face. "It's okay. I love you."

There was a chorus of "Awwww!" and everyone clapped

Francine and Jessica joined in.

Alfie and Janet did not.

Ψ

The last semester of school couldn't have been more miserable for Alfie.

His love was with another man and his discovery that his ex-girlfriend was lying to him and really wasn't pregnant after all…were all accumulated burdens on Alfie's back. And to add insult to injury he found out that after graduation, Penny and Quincy were both going away to England. Their anthropology internship was offering them both a temporary job there.

And Alfie was all alone. Mostly, by choice, but partially as a result of Jessica scaring the girls away from him. And frankly, he could care less. The other girls that came his way just didn't do anything for him. And he had no desire to be back into a meaningless relationship like the one that he had with Jessica.

Alfie and Penny were not talking at all. As for Quincy, he hated Alfie with a passion for trying to take Penny away from him. They kept a far distance from him, which was kinda hard to do considering they were pretty much in the same circle of friends.

"You guys have gotta stop this," Ritchie told Alfie at one point. "Why can't you guys just put it in the past?"

Alfie had shrugged and said, "Some things are easier said than done."

"Come on, you two. Can't you just forgive Alfie? I know that was a really fucked up move that he made, but I know he's sorry. I mean look at him, he's pathetic." Marlon said to Quincy and Penny one day.

"Yeah, it was really fucked up and that's why I have nothing to do with him anymore," Penny had retorted.

So that was that.

Just before graduation, Alfie discovered that he and Penny were valedictorians of the school. They would have to go up and make a speech together.

Alfie wasn't relishing the thought.

"How the hell am I going to go up there and give a speech with that miserable man?" Penny fumed one afternoon to Quincy. "Maybe I'll pretend I'm sick."

"Come on, Penny, you gotta so it. You deserve to be up there. You can't let him have all the limelight," Quincy said.

Penny couldn't agree more.

Ψ

"Let's just do the speech and get it over with," Penny snapped in a businesslike manner.

Alfie nodded absently. They had met in the library in an open area. Not their usual studying spot. To both, that was just another thing of the past.

Once they were finished, Penny jumped up from her seat, ready to pack up and leave.

Alfie jumped up too. "Wait a minute, Penny. Can we just talk for a moment?"

"We've done all the talking that needs to be done. I'm exhausted and I'm going back to my dorm."

"Do you want a ride back?" Alfie asked, desperately.

"I can walk, I have feet," Penny snapped.

"But, it's kinda dark out there," Alfie intoned.

"Oh please, don't give me a hard time," Penny said with a snort.

So he didn't. He left her alone.

Ψ

The day of the graduation, the sun was shining brightly and the weather was warm.

Alfie could feel his back sweating underneath the graduation gown and his button up shirt.

Not to mention, he was as nervous as ever. They had all gotten their diplomas and now it was time for his and Penny's speech.

Penny nodded at Alfie. They made their way to the stage.

Alfie stared at the sea of faces and instantly felt a fluttering in his stomach. He wasn't used to making speeches to such a large amount of people. He thought he spotted his family in the crowd, but he wasn't sure. He wished that he could see their faces.

Penny began saying her part. Alfie listened for a while, but his mind began to wonder. He wondered how many people were sitting out there today…

Suddenly, he felt a sharp elbow dig into his ribcage. It was Penny. He cleared his throat before he began.

Alfie droned on. He was hardly into what he was saying. He paused after the funny parts, giving the crowd room to laugh and then continued on. The flashing of cameras was all over the place. Finally, he was done and he breathed in relief.

Everyone was standing around, talking excitedly.

"Mom, Dad, I gotta go pull of these stockings. I'm about to melt," Penny said to her parents. "I'll be right back. Wait for me here."

Alfie noticed Penny leaving to go towards the school building.

"Ah…Mom, Rocco, I'll be right back."

"Where are you going?" Wendy asked, alarmed.

"I gotta talk to somebody. It's really important."

Alfie left before they could say another word.

Alfie followed Penny into the empty building. She was moving towards the bathroom further down.

"Penny!" Alfie called.

She turned around. Her face was shocked when she saw who it was. Then she frowned.

"What do you want?" she said.

"I want to talk to you," Alfie said calmly.

"I don't think that we really have anything to talk about," Penny said crisply.

"Really? Because I think we do," Alfie responded, a little sadly.

Penny stared at him, her lips in a straight line. Her eyes unreadable. She waited for him to continue.

"I want to apologize for what happened four months ago at the party. I behaved like a total donkey's ass. You didn't deserve that."

"Then why did you do it? Penny asked, challengingly.

Alfie looked down at his feet.

"Well! Why did you do it? You want me to be alone, stay miserable for the rest of my life?" Penny screeched. "What do you want from me?"

"I want you." Alfie took a step forward. "I've always wanted you, but I just didn't realize it. I-I love you, Penny," said Alfie softly. His palms were face up in appeal. His eyes were filled with genuine pain.

Penny stared at him, her face still hard. But her eyes were filled with unshed tears.

"I should have never hooked you and Quincy up. That was the biggest mistake that I made in my entire life," he said quietly. "I missed you. I missed hanging around you, I missed being your friend…and most I missed what could—should have been…"

"Oh, Alfie!" Penny cried, the tears flowing down her face, "I loved you too, but you never saw it. You were too busy flirting with the other girls. Too busy with your clubs and your meetings and your work. I never thought you wanted me...I thought I was too plain...I don't know." Penny wiped her eyes with the back of her hand.

"You're beautiful Penny, and don't you think otherwise for a moment. I'm sorry, I didn't know what I had until I lost it. But you and I...we're both here now. And we both have these feelings. I want to be with you, Penny. I love your laugh, I love your smile! I like the way your eyes light up when you tell a joke! I even love that little snort that you do. Oh gosh, he doesn't know you like I do, Penny!" Alfie cried, his face a mask of agony. A lump was in his throat. His stomach was wrenched with hurt. If he lost her now...oh God, what would he do?

Penny shook her head, tears still flowing. "But it's too late, Alfie."

Alfie shook his head hard and continued to walk towards her. "No, no. Don't say that. It's never too late for love."

"It's too late for us, Alfie," Penny said, trying to control her tears but not succeeding. "I love you, but it can't be."

"Do you love him?" Alfie asked, in a choked voice, referring to Quincy.

Penny looked at the floor and nodded her head despondently.

There was a silence between them for a while as they realized all that was lost with that confession.

"More than me?" Alfie asked, softly in a strangled tone.

Penny raised her head and looked at him. "No," she answered him softly.

"Do you love me more?"

"Oh, Alfie! Don't ask me to answer that!" Penny sobbed.

"Just answer it, please. If we can't be together, at least give me this," Alfie said, tears falling down his face. He hoped that no one would come in and see them. This was a moment that couldn't be broken.

"I don't know! It's so different between the two of you. With Quincy, I feel calmness and security. With you, Alfie, I feel this pain, a sort of despondency mixed with the love, restlessness...but I feel so strongly for you, Alfie! Oh, I can't explain it at all! Oh, if I could only do it all again!"

Alfie came up to her and grasped her small hands within his large ones. He swallowed hard. "Would you choose me then?"

She looked up at him, sorrowfully, wet amber eyes. "I can't answer that,," she whispered. "I don't want to."

"If you won't be with me. Kiss me this one time. Kiss me goodbye, will you?" Alfie said sadly.

And so they did.

Never had they felt more pain in their lives.

Chapter Twenty-eight

Two years later (1959, Chicago Illinois)

McMillan was sitting at his desk, daydreaming, when two of his detectives came in, with a file in hand.

"We got another complaint from an investor concerning the Harvey Stretck scam," Irving Bronson said, waving around the file, "The man who made the police report said that he was trying to get in touch with Harvey Stretck. Apparently, the investor hadn't gotten a company report in a while. He tried to call the given office number, and he discovered that it was now disconnected."

"Great," McMillan barked. "Have you been able to locate this Harvey Stretck guy?"

Detective Lee spoke up, "Well...we've been searching, but so far we have no leads. We're not even sure that this person exists."

"Chances are, he doesn't. That sounds like a made-up name. There's also a chance that he does. Keep looking. I'm going to crack this case if it's the last thing I do."

Ψ

Harvey Stretck scratched his balls as he watched the delectable brunette parading across the small television screen.

He smirked. Boy, would he like to get a piece of that. Too bad it was just a movie.

He got up to get a beer from his beat up refrigerator. Suddenly feeling hungry, he went back into the fridge and picked up a loaf of bread and some cold cuts. Before he put them on the counter, he watched as a troop of roaches made their way across the linoleum surface. With his left thumb, he crushed the last roach to make it across. He chuckled in amusement.

With sandwich and beer in hand, he made his way back to the broken down couch that sat in the middle of his trailer in front of the small black and white screen TV. He devoured his meal with glassy eyes fixed to the screen.

Harvey Stretck lived alone in his trailer and he loved it. He had no one to answer to, no one to tell him what to do. The only person that he had to look after was himself.

He had been married once, a long while ago. But after a few months, he saw that the married life didn't suit him, so he packed up and left one night without a word. Sometimes he wondered how his ex-wife was doing. But most of the time, he didn't give her a thought. He was only glad that no kids came of it.

He made his living selling car parts. It wasn't much of a living, but it kept him alive with roof over his head and food to eat, which was enough for him.

He didn't need anyone but himself.

Ψ

"Please, I swear I didn't do anything. You gotta believe me," the man said as he writhed in his chair. The ropes were cutting into his wrist and his ankles. He stared up at Anthony and Santino beseechingly.

The man, Emanuel Fitore, was nothing more than a snitch. He had given up information on Anthony about a year ago and as a result, Anthony had served six months in prison. Not so long a sentence in comparison to the five years that he should have gotten, but thank God, Earnest and Abner had fished him out. After six months, he had gotten out on parole.

But now, Emanuel had to pay.

Because Emanuel had opened his mouth about Anthony, the young man had only gotten probation as a result of the plea bargain.

"You opened your hole about my dealings in the prostitution ring," Anthony yelled.

"I-I didn't do it," he muttered, lying through his teeth.

Santino punched Emanuel square in the face. The man flew back in his chair from the impact. Emanuel spat up blood and three teeth.

Anthony pulled out his pistol and put it right to the man's forehead.

"Oh God!" the man gurgled.

"God can't save you now," Anthony said before he fired off two successive shots.

Emanuel slumped dead in his chair. His eyes were wide opened, the back of his head blown apart.

"Come on, let's get rid of him," Anthony said to Santino and Riccardo.

Santino looked at the dead man in the chair.

He only wished that it had been Anthony instead.

Ψ

After the company was sold, Lawrence and Abner made a big profit. Now they had more money than ever. Now, they were pretty much out of the game. The office where the supposed Harvey Stretck used was shut down and vacant. There would be no more company reports.

Lawrence was sure that once the shareholders discovered that there were no longer getting reports and that the made-up Harvey Stretck was nowhere to be found, they would contact the authorities. Which was why Lawrence made every effort to clear any tracks that could possibly lead back to him and Abner.

Abner thought about what would happen if Dorothy were to ever find out about what he was doing. She would leave him for sure. He couldn't bare the thought of not having his wife and their small infant daughter, Estelle, in his life.

Later on that evening, Abner came home to find Dorothy looking through her closet and pulling out different outfits.

"Jane and Kirk want to go out for dinner tonight," Dorothy said referring to her best friend and her husband.

"Sounds like a good idea," Abner said cheerfully.

"We're not sure where we want to go yet," Dorothy said, trying on a pair of diamond studs. She turned around and faced Abner. "What do you think?"

"Lovely. That would go perfectly with that outfit," Abner said referring to the cream pantsuit lying on the bed.

"Honey, you'd better get ready. They're coming to pick us up in about forty minutes or so," Dorothy said.

After they were dressed, they went outside to wait, since it was such a nice day. Soon, they saw their friends' black Rolls Royce driving up.

"So where are we gonna go to eat?" Kirk turned around and asked, once they were out of the house's driveway.

They thought for a while and finally Jane came up with an idea. "There's a new restaurant that opened downtown. Nellie was telling me about it. She and her husband went there and she said it was delicious. She said that I should try it. Let's all go!"

"Do we need a reservation?" asked Dorothy

"I don't think so…but let me call just in case," Jane said.

So they drove back to the house.

Jane called up the number. She asked for a reservation for a party of four. She left it in her name, Jane Adams.

When they got to the restaurant, the waiter asked their name. They gave Jane Adams.

"And what about the rest of you? May I have your names as well," the young man asked.

The four of them exchanged looks.

"I'm Kirk Adams, I'm her husband," he said indicating Jane.

The young man turned to Dorothy. "And you?"

"I'm Dorothy Ashford-Bernstein," she said easily.

The young man raised his eyebrows, "Bernstein?"

"Yes. She's my wife. My name is Abner Bernstein," Abner said stiffly.

The young man looked between Abner and Dorothy like he was unsure of how to proceed.

"Well are we going to be seated or not?" asked Jane, impatiently. "Come on. We do have a reservation."

The young man licked his lips nervously. "Well, you see…umm."

"What is it?" Kirk asked, exasperated.

"Well, we usually don't accept…Jews in here. You see, this restaurant is associated with the Springlife Country Club. Mr. and Mr. Adams can come in as well as Mrs. Ashford, but we cannot allow…Mr. Bernstein."

There was a vulgar silence after these words were said. Kirk and Jane flicked their eyes at Abner, obviously quite embarrassed at the current situation. Dorothy's face was slowly turning red. She stared straight at the young man with her lips clamped together in a straight line.

Abner felt his guts clench. Now here, of all places, he was to be embarrassed in front of friends and his wife.

"Are you suggesting that I leave my husband outside while the rest of us go in to eat?" Dorothy asked, between clenched teeth.

The young man turned red in the face, "No, no. I-

"Do you realize who I am?" Dorothy asked, haughtily.

"N-no," the young man stuttered miserably. Today, so far, was going terrible for him. Earlier on, he had gotten into a fight with his girlfriend who was now threatening to leave him and now this.

"Have you ever heard of Ashford studios?" she asked, primly.

"Y-yes. Of course. Who hasn't?" the young man responded, quick to appease.

"Well, my father owns them. My father gives a lot of financial contributions to various establishments. My father is very well known and well liked. Have you any idea the trouble that I could cause for this place?" Dorothy said, trying to keep her voice calm.

The young man's face was filled with astonishment, "W-w-well, I had no idea it was you, I mean, I didn't make the connection—

"Well, now you've got it. So you'd better let us in. How dear you insult us like this with your pettiness!" Dorothy said firmly.

"M-Ma'am, I didn't make up the rules. I'm sorry, I'm just doing my job."

"Go and get your manager, I wish to speak to him," Dorothy snapped with irritation.

The manager, a tall thin man in an immaculate suit came gliding towards them. He held a bright smile on his face.

"Hello, my name is Mr. Harroway. Mrs. Ashford, I—

"Mrs. Ashford-Bernstein," Dorothy stiffly corrected.

"Yes, I mean Mrs. Ashford-Bernstein. I'm sorry about all of them. Harry didn't realize who you were. You four can come right in, of course, because of you, we will make an exception. You'll have the best seats in the house, please. You're meals will be on us."

"An exception?" Jane repeated, not quite getting it.

"Well, we don't really allow Jews in here. We are actually associated with the Springlife Country Club."

"Yes, the young man at the door told us all that," Abner said impatiently. At the moment, he felt like such an inconvenience. What a way to make people feel. What right did they have?

"You know what? I've lost my appetite," Dorothy snapped. "If you two wish to stay and eat, Abner and I will just catch a cab."

"No, no. We'll leave as well. There are plenty of good restaurants downtown. We can choose from any one of them," Kirk quickly said.

"But, please do stay," Mr. Harroway said, looking nervous. He knew that he had said something wrong.

"It's quite all right. We like to be comfortable when we eat. I'm afraid that we won't all feel comfortable if we stay here," Jane said.

And with that, the four of them turned on their heels and left the restaurant.

Ψ

"We found him. Harvey Stretck. He lives in southern Illinois in a small town called Carterville," Lee told McMillan one afternoon after another lengthy search.

"Carterville? That's a small town. Humm. Interesting. Wouldn't think that a big time scam artist would be in such a small hick's area," McMillan said with a chuckle.

"Well, we've seen odder things before, haven't we?" Lee responded. "By the way. Do you want me to look some more into that business with Gionelli and the plane?"

"What are you talking about?" McMillan murmured, looking over some reports.

"Well, the O'Hare International Airport thing. With all those important names listed—"

"Oh, right, right. One thing at a time. Let's get this nailed first, then we'll nail that bastard," McMillan growled.

Lee sneered. "Good idea, Boss."

McMillan nodded. "Well are we gonna go get some men over there to bring him in for questioning?"

"Sure thing," Lee said with a nod.

"Good. I've already called the jurisdiction down there. I want you and Bronson to head up the team. Bring two other officers from the county with you. That should be enough. We don't want to scare him."

"Right Boss," Lee singsonged.

"Quit with the mockery, will ya?" McMillan snapped.

Lee made his way to the door.

Ψ

"So, do you think that you could help me?" the man asked Earnest over the phone.

"Well, why don't we set up an appointment and discuss a few things," Earnest suggested.

"Okay, that's sounds good," the anxious man responded.

They set up a time and date before they said goodbye and got off the phone.

"You wouldn't believe who just called," Earnest told Abner as he walked into his office.

"Who was it?" Abner asked, curiously.

"That was Leslie Emerson. The owner of Emerson & Mills shipping Corporation."

Abner felt his stomach flop. He forced himself to remain natural. "Oh really?"

"He wants us to represent him," Earnest said excitedly.

"But there are no leads on who stole his company's name, right?" Abner asked, in way trying to comfort himself.

"That's right. Not yet. But when they find whoever did it, he wants to prosecute them to the fullest extent. He's extremely upset about this. He was looking to sell his company and quietly retire. But now, his name's been run through the mud because of all this.

"I could imagine," Abner stated, trying to keep the uneasiness from his voice. "So are we going to take it?"

"Why don't we just wait and see. I set up a meeting for Thursday this week. He'll be coming in to the office," Earnest said.

That Thursday, Leslie Emerson was at the office at exactly at ten in the morning. The secretary seated him and offered him a cup of coffee.

Soon, Abner and Earnest called him into their joint office.

Earnest thought that he looked exactly as he did in the newspapers. He looked old, but could have looked worse for a man soon entering his seventieth year. He had combed back grey hair, brown eyes, jowls, and a heavily creased forehead. He wore a pair of pants and a button down shirt. On his face, he wore an expression of anxiety and worry.

"No, no. Things definitely were not supposed to work out this way," he said before anything.

"I understand," Earnest said soothingly.

"I wanted to just sell the company and go into retirement. Afterwards, I wanted to move to Michigan to be near my daughter and her family. But now all this. This put a kink in my chain," he muttered. He scratched the side of his face, an obvious nervous habit. "I'm to old for all this stress now."

"Well, that's what we're here for. To make sure that you get the justice that you deserve. We'll take care of all your rights," Earnest said again. "So why don't you tell us what happened from your point of view?"

"Well, basically, I was looking through some stocks and I find out that a subsidiary of Emerson and Mills has just been sold to these two guys…I can't remember their names right now. But I'm like, I don't know anything about this! Secondly, they're aren't any subsidiaries of Emerson and Mills and I damn sure didn't sell my company yet, what's going on?"

"Continue, Sir," Earnest said as he jotted down some notes.

"So I get to looking around and pretty soon, these two guys are complaining that there ain't no company. That the company didn't exist. Before I could decide what to do, I got some detective knocking on my door, asking me about all this. So I tell him that I'm as clueless as everyone else. I never did sell my company, I don't know what's going on. Now my good name is sullied. I'm a suspect in this whole thing. They think I worked this scam with somebody else," the old man said with vehemence.

Earnest glanced over at Abner. He had been strangely silent throughout the whole thing. Earnest raised an eyebrow at Abner. Abner gave him a slight shrug in return.

By the time the Leslie Emerson left, Earnest had filled up four pages of notes.

"Well, we certainly have a lot to research, don't we?" Earnest said cheerfully.

"We're taking the case?" Abner asked.

Earnest shot him a look. "Well, I assumed that we would. Why wouldn't we?"

Abner shrugged his shoulders. "I don't know it's such a good idea."

Earnest chuckled. "This company fraud situation is a very big thing. It's all over the news and everything else. This could do nothing but good if we get involved. We would make an even bigger name for ourselves," Earnest responded, as he thought that his friend was behaving very strangely. He was surprised that Abner wasn't jumping at this opportunity.

"I guess you're right," Abner said vaguely.

Ψ

"The man lives in a trailer," Bronson said, pointing out the obvious.

"Well, you never know. It could be just a cover. Plus. We gotta follow the orders," Lee responded. He turned to the two officers. "You two ready?"

The first officer nodded his head a bit reluctantly. "He's a bit nasty, so we should watch out. You never know what he's gonna do."

"Yeah, he got into quite a few bar fights and scuffles with people around here. So he's a bit of a cowboy. We gotta be a little careful," said the other officer.

Lee snorted. "Bar fights? That's your usual small town nonsense. I've seen much worse than that in the big city, boys. That doesn't scare me at all. Now come on. Let's get going."

When Harvey Stretck heard the knock on his door that Friday at eleven thirty A.M. he was just about getting up.

The knocks got louder and more urgent with each passing second.

"All right, I'm comin', I'm comin'," Harvey yelled out. He held his head in pain as he walked to the door. He was suffering from a major hangover.

Harvey looked through the peephole. He was surprised to see four men standing on his front stairs. They were obviously from the police department. Two were in suits and two were in police uniforms. He recognized the two officers to be from the precinct not far away. But the other two suits, he didn't recognize in the faintest. *What the heck was going on?* he asked himself.

He opened the door slowly and stood bewildered as the man in the gray suit flashed a badge at him and said his name was Detective Lee. The other suit called himself Detective Bronson.

"Dave, Bradley," Harvey said grimly acknowledging the two officers. They nodded their head in response and continued to stare directly at him with dour expressions on their faces. "What's the matter?" Harvey asked, confused.

"Mr. Stretck we would like for you come down to the police station for questioning," Lee said smoothly.

"Oh? And why's that?" Harvey asked, forcefully. He learned long ago not to show fear, especially not to police.

"Well, it's concerning a case that been going on. We'll explain more once we get down to the station, Sir."

"How 'bout you explain now," Harvey said firmly.

"We would much rather explain once we get there," Lee said, staring up at the disheveled looking man. He resisted the urge to cover his nose. The man had some serious B.O. issues.

"How's bout' I say no," Harvey said, sneering at them. His mouth under the bushy mustache was twisted in derision.

"Well, it would be better for you if you do," Lee said trying to inch his way through the door.

"You got a warrant, *Detective Lee?*" he said spitting out the name as if though it were poisonous. He attempted to bar the entrance by blocking the doorway with his skinny shoulders.

"Actually, we do," Detective Bronson chirped in.

"Yeah? Le'me see it," snarled Harvey Stretck.

They pulled out the paper. Harvey's dark beady eyes ran over it, reading each and every word. Finally, he reluctantly looked up.

"Well, I can't fuck with that, kin I."

Ψ

Alfie loved his job as a reporter at the *Chicago Informant*. Most of the times, it was extremely interesting especially when he did research for stories. He met a lot of new and interesting people and went to a lot new and interesting places.

He also enjoyed working for his boss, John Welsh, who was quite the character. John Welsh was the editor-in-chief at the *Chicago Informant*. So when on Monday John told Alfie to meet him in his office after lunch, he looked forward to it with a great deal of anticipation.

"Alfie. I have something that I want you to do for me," he said sliding off his thick bottle glasses and cleaning them with a tissue. "I think you'll like it."

"What's that, Mr. Welsh?" Alfie asked, as he tried to avoid looking at the bald spot that sat exactly on top of Mr. Welsh's head. Alfie knew that Mr. Welsh was somewhat sensitive about his balding head. Most often, Mr. Welsh would make an attempt at a comb over, but some days, like today, he just didn't bother.

"Well, I want you to try and get an interview with that Leslie Emerson fellow," said Mr. Welsh.

"You mean the guy from Emerson and Mills?" Alfie asked, with growing excitement.

"That's the one."

"But I heard that he wasn't taking any interviews," Alfie responded.

"I know. But if anyone could do it, you could. That's why I called you of all people, in here to take this on. You get this interview, I see great things in the future for you here," Mr. Welsh said with squinted eyes. He was talking to the picture on the wall which was right beside Alfie's head.

"I'm over here, Sir," Alfie said.

Mr. Welsh moved his head in the right direction until he was staring right in Alfie's face. "I'd better put back on my glasses. I'm practically blind without them," he mumbled. He slid them back on his face and gave Alfie a sudden smile. "Well. Are you going to take it?"

"Yes. I'll do my best, Sir."

Ψ

"Hey, Alfie, you're early!" Angelina exclaimed when she saw her stepbrother standing on her front steps with a bottle of red wine in his hands.

Alfie grinned. "I know, but I had some stuff to do around here already, so after I was done, I decided to just come instead of going all the way back home again," Alfie said as he kissed her on the cheek

"Please, that's not a problem. I hardly get to see you anymore! You're so busy with work," Angelina said as she ushered him in. She took the bottle of wine from his hands. "Kids! Your Uncle Alfie's here!" Angelina exclaimed.

Seventeen-year-old Antonia, twelve-year-old Dwight, eleven-year-old Matthew and nine-year-old Winston came hurrying up to Alfie.

"Hey, Uncle Alfie, how are you doing?" Antonia's lovely hazel eyes were lit up with happiness.

Alfie greeted each and every one of them, "My, my Antonia aren't you just a beauty now! Dwight, you're growing well! Mathew, how are your football practices going? Winston, you're getting bigger and bigger every time I see you! Soon, you'll be taller than I am!"

Winston smiled at his words. "Do you think so, Uncle?"

"I think so!" Alfie said patting him on the back and giving him a hug.

"I'd better go check on the chicken, I don't want it to burn. Alfie, make yourself comfortable, Earnest will be home soon," Angelina said before rushing off towards the kitchen.

"Come on, Uncle Alfie, I wanna show you my new model planes!" Winston said pulling on Alfie's hand.

"Sure thing, buddy."

Earnest pulled into his driveway and parked his car. He headed to the house, whistling along the way.

"Hey, Angie," Earnest said going into the kitchen. He kissed Angelina on the cheek. She turned around in surprise.

"Oh darling, I didn't see you come in. Alfie's here. I think he's upstairs with the kids."

"Whatever you're making smells good. What is it?" Earnest said, lifting the lid off a pot.

"*Galletto con le Mandorle*," Angelina said.

"Ah, Chicken with almonds," Earnest said inhaling deeply.

"And *Caponata di magazine*," Angelina added.

"Umm...that sounds delicious...and what about dessert?" Earnest said mischievously.

Angelina gave him a mock frown. "You keep pestering me, there'll be no dessert." Angelina turned to Greta, their helper. "Greta, please start setting the table. I'll take care of the rest of things in here."

"Which dishes would you like me to use, Mrs. Hurst."

"Use the white ones with the pale yellow flowers. I think those would be lovely. Also, use the yellow linen napkins and the straw placemats."

"Very good, Mrs. Hurst," Greta said and left.

"Don't torture me like that," Earnest said with a smile. "I must have my dessert," Earnest said, feeling on her backside.

"My, my. Aren't you in a great mood," Angelina commented. "I mean, you're extra chipper today," Angelina said swatting his hands away.

"Well, I got a new client today," Earnest said.

"Really? That's great," Angelina said stirring the food in the pot.

"I mean not just any client. I have Leslie Emerson from Emerson and Mills."

Angelina stared at him in shock. "Seriously? That's wonderful! This definitely calls for a celebration."

"For sure. If our names weren't out there before, they'll definitely be out there after this."

"That's a definite."

"Well, my lovely wife, I'm going to go and say hi to Alfie," he said kissing her on the cheek.

"I'll call you all once dinner is ready."

Earnest made his way upstairs. Alfie and his three boys were in the upstairs rec-room watching television.

"Hey, Dad! You're home!" Dwight called out. The other boys came over and gave him a hug.

Alfie came over and shook his hand. "How are you doing Earnest?"

"I'm doing great, Alfie. How's that job of yours going?" he asked, as he gave his brother in law a hug.

"Just fine. I got a new interview. You'll never guess who it's with."

"Who?" Earnest asked, sitting down on the couch.

"Leslie Emerson."

"Leslie Emerson?" Earnest smiled. "I have him as a client. Did you interview him yet?"

"Well, the truth is that he's not really keen on taking interviews. No one has been able to get him to take one as yet."

"Oh?"

"Yeah…hey…do you think you can help me since he's your client and all?"

"I don't know about that, Alfie…"

"Please. I'll promise him that it won't be all glitzy," Alfie said pleadingly. "It'll be very factual and informative."

"Well…he has been getting bad publicity since all of this had went down. Maybe if you take the approach of telling his side of the story. Maybe try and help him clean up his reputation. Maybe then, he'll do it."

"Sure, that's a great idea. So you think you can propose an idea like that to him?" Alfie asked, hopefully.

"I think I can. But it'll be up to him to decide whether or not he wants to do it. Maybe you can come in and speak to him as well. I don't want to push it too much though if he doesn't like the idea."

"I understand. I don't want you to lose your client."

"Well, just see how it goes. I'm meeting with him again on Friday."

"That's great! I'm off work then."

"Well then, why don't you come into the office around ten thirty?"

"I will!"

Ψ

The moment Leslie Emerson came into the office, Earnest called him right in.

"How are you feeling this morning Mr. Emerson?" Earnest asked him after giving him a firm handshake. The two men sat down.

"I'm doing all right, except for the fact that my prospective buyers want nothing to do with my company and one of them was previously really interested. I was almost sure he was going to buy. It seems like I'll have this company on my hands for longer than I thought. This is such a burden to me," the man said miserably.

Earnest thought in silence for a moment before going on. "I have a proposition for you. Now you can take it or leave it, but actually it might help you."

Leslie leaned forward with interest. "What are you suggesting?"

"I know that you've gotten a lot of bad press. I personally know someone that works for the *Chicago Informant*. It's my brother in law. What about he'll be the one to help you get back on track?"

Leslie rubbed his jaw in contemplation. "I'm listening."

"Okay. I actually took it upon myself to invite him in today to speak to you. He can give the public your side of the story. Let the people know that you were the victim. That you have been wronged. He can give them the truth. And I'm sure that afterwards, you will be able to continue with your retirement plans because you'll get someone to buy your company."

Leslie smiled slightly. "I think that it might not be such a bad idea. To tell you the truth, I had been shying away from the media and interviews during this. But maybe, it's about time to speak up."

"No only that, it would be on your own terms. This is going to help you, not hurt you."

"Why don't you bring him in? I think I would like to talk to him."

Earnest buzzed his secretary and told her to bring Alfie in. Alfie came in through the door. Earnest introduced them.

"It's nice to meet you, Sir," said Alfie giving him a handshake.

"Likewise. Now. Can you tell me how you can help me?"

"Sir, the problem is that you've gotten some very bad publicity. What is also a problem is that you've been totally silent on the issue. This silence in the face of accusations has most likely caused people to loose confidence in you."

"Okay, continue," Leslie said, listening closely.

"Well, what I want to do for you is to write your story for the public. This will help dispel the doubts that people have about you. I guarantee that by the time that I'm done, you will have your name back," Alfie said with confidence.

"Hmmm…I like the sound of that. So this is a sort of campaign for me?"

"If that's the way you want to see it, I'll be your head publicist."

Ψ

For the next few weeks, Alfie did nothing but research. He did research on the Company of Emerson and Mills, he did research on the backgrounds of Leslie Emerson and Eric Mills, the two co-founders of the company. After finding all he wanted in the written word and public documentation, he decided to do interviews to delve deeper. The first person he interviewed was Emerson. Then he interviewed friends and family members including his daughter Emily. Unfortunately, Eric Mills passed away seven years ago. Finally, he was ready to do his first article.

In total, the article took about a week to write. Finally, he was ready to have Mr. Welsh inspect it.

Alfie stood nervously before Mr. Welsh as his eyes read each line. Every so often he would slowly nod his head or he would glance up at Alfie, his face expressionless. Finally, done with reading, he put the article down and sat back in his chair, wordlessly.

"Well, what do you think?" Alfie asked trying to keep his voice steady.

"I think this is a fantastic article. You took Mr. Emeron and wrote his side of the story. The research is thorough and your sources are excellent. I would be happy to put it in the *Chicago Informant*. All we need to do is get my new freelance editor to look it over for grammar and such." Mr. Welsh leaned forward. "Did you see the new freelance editor? We hired a woman. And I must say, her last name 'Fox' suits her well."

"Really? A woman other than a secretary working *here*?" Alfie repeated with mock amazement.

Mr. Welsh shrugged his shoulders. "Well, her credentials were extremely good and we really didn't have much of a choice. The candidates were few and very lacking in experience and skills."

"Oh, okay."

"Well, just you take that article right on down to Miss. Fox. She shares an office downstairs."

Alfie was ecstatic. "Thank you, Sir, thank you. This by no means is the first article I want to do on Leslie Emerson, in fact, I have some more ideas."

Mr. Welsh raised his eyebrow. "Oh?"

"Yes, of course if you don't mind," Alfie added quickly.

Mr. Welsh took of his glasses. "I'm turning this into your project, Alfie. You can write as many articles as you want, keeping in mind to watch all developments on this. Of course, I would have to review each article and decide if it goes in or not."

"Of course, Sir."

"Keep up the good work, Alfie."

"I will, Sir."

Alfie left Mr. Welsh's office and went in search for Miss. Fox. He came to a room more like a cubbyhole than an office. A slender young woman with golden brown hair was sitting leaning over her desk. She was totally focused on what she was reading. Alfie cleared his throat. She looked up at him with clear green eyes. She smiled.

Alfie, disarmed at her stunningly pretty face, was at lost for words at the moment.

"Can I help you?" she asked, smile still firmly in place.

"You're Miss. Fox?"

"Please, call me Laura"

"Uh, yes. I have an article for you to edit," Alfie said handing it over to her. She took it and glanced quickly at it before saying," I'll have it done by Friday."

"I-I was hoping to get it in this week," Alfie protested.

"Well, I have a lot of articles to read, uh…"

"Alfie"

"Alfie. It's the best I could do," she said pleasantly. "Now, if you'll excuse me, I have so much work to do. I'll have it to you on Friday morning."

"Great," Alfie said dispassionately.

Ψ

Rebecca woke up sweating and gasping. She raised a shaking hand to her throat to feel if the rotting hand was still grasping her.

There was no hand there. It was not the dream that had wakened her. It was the Shadows that had waken her. It was time for the message. It was time to go to the mirror.

For the four or more years that Rebecca had been in the institution, she had refused to look at any mirrors and had avoided them because somehow in her mind, she had come to think of them as the gateway to hell. The way they could capture action for action everything one did. How they can put forth detail for detail everything that lay before them. Rebecca began to think that if she looked too hard at them, one day, she would see something that should not be there. If she looked too hard at herself, something terrible would come forth from the mirror and grasp her, pulling her into a dark and evil place.

But a few days ago, she had requested the mirror, to the surprise of the orderlies. At first, they had been hesitant to bring it in. In fact, they had refused to. Rebecca had complained to the man with the black hair and eyes that came to visit. He had insisted the they give her a mirror. Anthony thought that it would be okay, considering that she hadn't made any attempts at taking her life since she came in. They reluctantly agreed.

They had brought the mirror in and placed it against the far wall, so that she didn't necessarily have to see it's reflective surface unless she stood directly opposite it.

The Shadows had told her that it was time. It was time for the divine message being sent to her from God. The Shadows had told her that they would be waiting for her, beyond the reflective surface, to give her a message. They told her that she had no reason to fear the mirror. It was a gateway to better existence and not to hell as she thought. When The Shadows told Rebecca this, she had instantly requested a mirror put in her room under the pretense that she wanted it to groom herself.

Who was she to deny a message from God?

Until tonight, Rebecca had not looked at it. But now, at one in the morning, The Shadows had wakened her.

Rebecca got up and ran over to the mirror hanging on the otherwise featureless wall. Rebecca stared for a while in wonder, her reflection captivating her for the moment. Her pale gaunt reflection stared back. Her eyes looked like black holes in her face. Her face, once blushing and glowing was pinched and drawn. Creases flowed from the corners of her mouth like tiny rivers. Her forehead was lined as well.

Then finally, the mirror's surface stirred. Rebecca smiled in welcome knowing instantly that it was the Shadows.

At first, the change in the mirror's appearance had been so subtle, like tiny, far spaced raindrops disturbing the still surface of a pond. But soon, the silver surface dissolved and was replaced by black inkiness that swirled and frothed like a river during a storm.

Rebecca gasped and took a step back. Suddenly, it felt so evil. It didn't feel right. What was pleasantly akin to spring droplets on a mirrored surface had turned into a seething mess intent on sucking her into itself.

Suddenly, Rebecca smelled the strong odor of burning sulfur. The pungent odor was so strong that she could see wisps of the fumes in the air. And as it burned her nose and her eyes, she knew that it was the mark of a demon.

This was no sign from God. The mirror was pulling her in. Rebecca fell to the floor with a shriek. She attempted to grab the linoleum surface with her palms, but the force was too strong. Her palms dragged across the floor with a squeaking noise.

The Shadows had deceived her. They had been tricking her all along, making her believe that they were her friends, her companions, and her fellow messengers. But they were evil and had only demonic intentions, all along. Now they were tired of their little game and had come to destroy her.

"God help me!" Rebecca cried out. Or so she thought she did, but it was barely audible to her ears. It seemed as if the mirror was a vacuum sucking in everything, including sound.

When the mirror had dragged her to a position right in front of it, she plunged her fists into the murky surface to no avail.

"Ahhh! God help me!" She called. Why wasn't he here? She needed his protection. But then she next realized that if the shadows had deceived her, then perhaps God had as well.

She had nothing to live for then.

Rebecca relaxed her body allowing the demonic mirror to draw her in. Then total darkness clouded her vision.

So this is the end, she thought.

Ψ

"We found her right here, in front of the mirror," the young orderly told Anthony. "The nurse heard glass shattering and figured out that it came from this room. The nurse came in and found her on the floor," the young man said pointing at the area. "We called 911, by the time the paramedics got here, she was already gone. The police came here and made a report. The glass was shattered and apparently, she had taken a shard of glass and had slashed her throat and her wrists with it…I'm sorry. I can't find a better way to say it," the young man said, clearly flustered.

"It's okay," Anthony assured the young man.

"The mortician already has her down at the morgue. Sorry, but when there are deaths, we try to get them out at soon as possible. We don't want any of the residents to accidentally see anything."

"That's understandable," Anthony said, peering around

The room had been cleaned and was now spotless. And the broken mirror had been disposed of. It looked like it did over four years ago when they had first brought Rebecca to this room. Untouched. All evidence that anyone was in this room had been erased.

Anthony swallowed a lump in his throat, but did not cry. His heart was heavy with loss and he felt an empty space inside of him.

When they had called him and told him that Rebecca was dead, he had been stunned, but not surprised. He had prepared himself for something like this. Rebecca had been deeply disturbed and he knew that it was only a matter of time.

"Why don't we go into the waiting room? The doctor wants speak to you."

Anthony soberly followed the dark haired man out into the waiting room painted a pale green. Anthony sat in a plastic blue chair. He shivered.

Finally, the psychiatrist came along. He was a short balding man with round spectacles and bushy eyebrows. Dr. Osbourne. He had been Rebecca's primary physician in this place.

"Hello, Mr. Gionelli." The two men shook hands. "I'm sorry about what happened. It is a true tragedy."

Anthony nodded and looked away. "She didn't deserve this."

"Of course not. Please, let's sit down. I just want to talk about what I feel occurred last night."

"Please, go on."

"Well, the autopsy report, of course, hasn't come in yet. But we think that she died between twelve and two in the morning. When they checked on her at twelve, she was asleep in her bed."

"I see."

"I believe that she suffered from a psychotic episode. As you know already, she frequently suffered from delusions and hallucinations. We believe that she was having one or both of these psychotic symptoms which pushed her to her death."

Anthony looked down and nodded. He suddenly felt so weak and tired. All the strength had seeped out of him. The green walls seemed to be closing in on him.

Anthony shakily rose to his feet. "I think…I should go home and rest…I feel very tired."

The doctor gave him a look of concern and put a gentle hand on Anthony's shoulder. "I understand. Please, go home and rest. You have my number if you need me. Call me, please don't hesitate to do so. The autopsy report should be here by tomorrow. You'll get news of that. The coroner and the police will be in contact with you."

"Thank you doctor."

Ψ

Eunice sat in the kitchen, wringing her hands as she waited for Anthony to return. Finally, she heard the door rattle. Anthony came in, a grave expression on his face.

Eunice hurried up to him and led him to the couch. "I'm so sorry, Anthony. Are you okay?"

Anthony raised his eyes to meet her's. "I'm just so tired. I think I'm going to go to bed."

"You don't want to talk?" Eunice asked, full of concern.

"No. Not now."

"Well, you can go in and sleep on my bed," Eunice said.

Anthony hesitated. "A-a-are you coming?"

Eunice looked at the man she loved and gave him a painful smile. "Of course I am, darling. I would never leave you alone."

The following month, they were married.

Ψ

After doing some more investigating, it was realized that Harvey Stretck was completely innocent of the charges. He just happened to be unlucky enough to have a name that the perpetuators made up. McMillan released Harvey back into society, now very intent on capturing the correct impostures. Leslie Emerson's name was also cleared with the help of Abner and Earnest.

"Those bastards have alluded us far enough. It's time that we get the son-of-a-bitches and lock them up in jail," McMillan said.

After exhausting every pointless lead, on the morning of October 2, 1959, they found something worthwhile. McMillan hooked onto it.

"Well, boss, we found something," Lee pompously said as he strode into McMillan's office.

"What?" McMillan barked, pushing aside his mug of coffee.

"Well…we looked over the list of shareholders that the supposed Harvey Stretck had. We looked into each person and we found that everyone involved has filed a complaint, all, that is, but one person. I think that's worth looking into."

McMillan sat up in his chair, "Do you care to tell me this person's name?" he asked, sarcastically.

"Abner. Abner Bernstein. Apparently, he was a shareholder in the fake company since 1953. That's six years. You would think he would be indignant enough to make a complaint, but he hasn't. I find that odd. We have people that have invested in the company for less than a year and are really angry at the situation."

"Abner Bernstein, you said?"

"Yes, Sir."

"Hmmm…ain't that one of Gionelli's attorneys?"

"I believe it is, Sir," Lee responded.

"I'm *positive* that it is," snarled McMillan. "I want somebody to go and bring him in for questioning," McMillan said.

"Me, Sir?"

"Yeah, you and Bronson go on ahead. Tell him if he doesn't come in, we'll subpoena him."

"Sure thing," Less said before exiting his office.

As Lee walked down the hallway and made his way back to his desk, he wondered if McMillan was capable of speaking in a normal tone voice.

He doubted it.

Ψ

"There. Now you're all fresh and clean," Abner said as he lifted his six-month-old daughter from her bathwater. She gurgled and waved her little arms.

"Now, we have to dry you and put a nice little dress on. See, Daddy can do what Mommy does too," Abner said with a smile. He kissed his daughter on the cheek.

Abner carried her into the room and placed her on the changing table. He dried her off, powdered her, and then put a diaper on her. He was prepared to put an outfit on her, just as the doorbell rang.

The housekeeper came up to the nursery with a nervous expression on her face. "The police are here. They say they want to speak with you," she said in her heavily accented Spanish.

"Okay. Can you finish dressing Estelle please?" Abner said, trying to remain calm.

"Yes, of course," the housekeeper said walking up to the changing table

Abner walked downstairs. Two men, whom he assumed were detectives, and a uniformed officer were sitting in his living room. They looked out of place on the plush furniture.

"Can I help you?" Abner asked, as he approached them.

One of the detectives, the skinnier one, jumped up and held out his badge. "I'm Detective Lee and this is my partner Detective Bronson."

"How do you do," Abner said shaking their hands. At the present moment, he was so glad that Dorothy wasn't home. He was also happy that she wasn't expected back for hours to come.

"We're fine. And what about you, Mr. Bernstein?"

"I'm fine," Abner muttered, a bit startled that they had said his name.

"We have an investigation going on concerning the Harvey Stretck scandal and the Emerson and Mill's scam. We're interviewing all the people that had invested in fake Harvey Stretck company. Your name was one of them. We just want to ask a couple of routine questions. Do you mind coming down to the station so we can question you there?"

"Can you do it here?" Abner asked, trying to sound casual. "I'm looking after my daughter right now."

"Can you drop her off at the friend's or relative's house for just an hour?" Bronson asked.

"Well...I can't rightly think of anyone that can take her at the moment," responded Abner.

"Well then, perhaps you'd better bring her with us," Lee quipped.

"Ah...wait. My housekeeper's here. She can take care of my daughter until I get back. Let me go and tell her," Abner said somberly as he headed towards the stairs.

When they got to the station, they began questioning immediately. First, they asked routine questions like age, employment, where he was from, etc. But then they began to ask about the company situation.

"So how do you make your money?" Lee asked.

"I'm an attorney in the Chicago area," Abner responded, calmly.

"So how many years have you had stock in Harvey Stretck's company?" Lee asked.

"About six years."

"As I'm sure, you are aware of the whole sham. We found something very interesting, while we were looking over the complaint reports. Everyone of the investors had made some form of complain against the fake company, but you have't. Why is that so?"

Abner swallowed hard. He was never one to cope well under a lot of pressure. He tried to keep himself together, telling himself, that they had no way to link him with anything.

"Well, I was planning on making a report. I just hadn't gotten around to it."

"It's been almost a year, Mr. Bernstein."

"I know, I-I...I have a lot going on. I'm a lawyer, there're a lot of cases on my plate right now."

"But surely one would find time to report something as important as that?" Lee said in a friendly manner.

"Well, I didn't. It wasn't top on my list of things to do. I naturally assumed that my name would be included in those complaints. You mean to tell me that every single one of those investors filed a report?"

"Yes. All have come forward, or at least made themselves known. And if they hadn't they're either dead or no longer in the country. There were only a few of those cases."

Abner shrugged his shoulders. "Maybe I should have made a report. But is it against the law that I didn't?" Abner asked, smartly.

Lee leaned back in his chair and stared at the curly, sandy, haired fellow sitting before him. The man was hiding something. Of that, he was sure and would bet his life on it. Abner Bernstein was involved in this thing somehow, someway and he was going to find out. Not tonight, though. Best to let him think he was safe.

"No, Sir, it's not against the law at all."

"Then can I leave?"

"Of course you can, Mr. Bernstein. You have a nice evening, now. If we need you, we.ll be in contact."

Abner nodded his head, got up and walked out of the room without another word.

Ψ

The next morning, Patrick McMillan was on the phone to the D.A.'s office. After a few minutes, McMillan was passed through to the D.A., Thomas Hunter.

"Mr. Hunter, I have a strong suspect for the Harvey Stretck and the Pederson and Mills case. I really think that it would be a good idea to have some surveillance on this individual."

There was a pause and then, "What information have you got?"

"Well, first of all the person that I am asking to have surveillance on is Abner Bernstein. He was a shareholder in Harvey Stretck's fake company. Bernstein is the only shareholder on the list that hasn't filed a report with the authorities. We find this extremely odd. Also, he was taken in for questioning by one of my detectives. His behavior, according to Detective Lee, was highly suspicious. I would also like a phone tap."

The D.A. mulled over this for a while before giving him an answer. "Well, it sounds like you have a chance at surveillance. Of course, I'll have to go to the judge on it and get it okayed in court. I'll call today and see when I can set up a court date. I'll tell you by this week.Oh, and McMillan."

"Yeah?"

"You do know that this is an FBI case, right?" the DA firmly asked.

"Well, I was hoping—"

"This is fraud and larceny on a large scale. It has to go the feds. You know that as well as I do."

"Yes, I do." McMillan said with a sigh.

"Good. As of now, you and your men are officialy off this case."

Suddenly, McMillan remembered something. "Also, I want to ask you about another situation that I want to look into."

"What's that?"

"Well, I have a possible crime that I think is going to take place. A year or so back, my detective searched the house of a known criminal and we came up with some very interesting information. We saw the name of a flight and names of some important people that we know are going to be on that plane. We think that this man is planning a heist of some sort."

"Who's the man?" the D.A. asked.

"Rocco Gionelli."

"Did it actually say anything along the lines of a high jacking?"

"Weeell… no it didn't but—"

"May I ask how you came upon this information? Did you have a search warrant?"

"N-no I didn't."

"Then, there's nothing that can be done. You know as well as I do that any information that is obtained without a search warrant will be thrown out of court. You have to have a search warrant."

"Yeah, I know. I was just asking," McMillan said nodding his head.

"Excellent. So, I'll give you a call later this week.."

"All right," McMillan said. "I'll hear from you then."

After McMillan and Thomas Hunter got off the phone, McMillan reached into his bottom desk drawer, pulled out a small bottle of Scotch, and got a paper cup.

He poured the scotch into the cup, raised it high in the air, and took a gulp with a gleeful expression on his face.

It was cause for celebration.

Ψ

"Who's that guy that's been with him this whole week?"the middle aged man called Agent Ayers asked his younger companion.

Players of the Game

The younger man called Agent Fisk, shrugged his shoulders. "I'm sure the men that are in the restaurant with them will pick up on a name."

And sure enough, by the end of the day they discovered that the tall, brown haired man with blue eyes was called Lawrence Rice.

That evening, they listened into, on the tapped phone line, to a conversation that Abner and Lawrence were having.

Lawrence*: don't worry. They can threaten all they want. They have no evidence that we had anything to do with this Harvey Stretck thing.*

Abner*: But they brought me in for questioning.*

Lawrence*: and your answer is that you know nothing. If there's no evidence, they've got nothing. Just because you didn't make a complaint isn't grounds for them to throw you in jail.*

Abner*: I'm just so nervous about this whole thing.*

Lawrence*: No need to be. We got out money from the deal and we got away scot clean. We're in the clear, Abner. Soon this will all die down and things will get back to normal. They'll never know it was us.*

Abner: *How did they get my name? I thought you destroyed everything.*

Lawrence*: But I did. I don't know. Maybe they got it from one of the shareholders or something.*

"I think it's time to get a couple of arrest warrents, don't you think Ayers?" Agent Fisk said with a smirk on his face.

"My friend, I think you're right," answered Agent Ayers.

Ψ

Both Abner and Lawrence were arrested and taken in to be booked. They were then placed in cell. After about an hour of sitting in cell, Abner had been summoned by one of the officers and was led into a room where A middle aged man in a black suit with graying hair and a young man in a brown suit were waiting. Lawrence, on the other hand, spent the night in jail afterwich, there had been an arraignment for Lawrence were it was determined, much to the dismay of Lawrence and his high-priced lawyer, that he would not be released on bail, because he was considered to be a flight risk. He also plead not guilty. He was then transferred to the county jail to await trial.

Abner Bernstein sat nervously across from and the middle aged man called Ayers and the assistant ADA, Donald Lorry. Both men had introduced themselves to Abner when he entered. Ayers silently stared at Abner, allowing the other man to grow more and more unsettled. Ayers enjoyed having the edge on people. Especially hot shot people like Bernstein who was a successful lawyer and married to the daughter of a famous movie studio owner.

"We found a lot of things out since you were last down here, Bernstein," Agent Ayers said easily.

Abner swallowed visibly. "What do you mean?"

"I mean, we found a lot of things that could put you away in jail for a good long time. You'll be at least seventy before you see the light of day again"

Abner was silent. He stared at Lorry, who only stared back at him blankly. Abner then stared at Ayers, waiting for him to continue.

"We know you were the one that's involved in this stock market scam. We know that for sure," Ayers said easily.

Abner frowned. "I didn't do anything."

"You and Lawrence Rice were in on this thing together."

"That's not true," Abner said. He was visibly shocked from the mention of that name.

"I've got all the evidence. The best thing you can do for yourself is to come clean."

"I don't know anything."

"Don't lie. You'd better open up and speak on some things…we might be able to work things out," Said the man in the brown suit, speaking at last.

"I want to see the evidence."

Ayers nodded and then pressed Play on the tape recorder. The room filled up with the taped conversation between Abner and Lawrence from the tapped phone line. As Abner sat there and listened, he got paler and paler. His lips clenched into a thin line.

"You didn't have a warrant for this, so it won't hold up," Abner said, clutching at straws.

Ayers gave him a sick smile. "We sure did. You wanna see it?"

Abner nodded, trying to be brave.

Ayers handed it to him. Abner looked it over, his face getting ever more pale. He shoved it back across the table at McMillan.

"Believe me now?" Ayers asked, mockingly.

Abner gave him a frightened look, and then he looked down at the table, his lips clamped together.

Ayers leaned forwards towards Abner. "Mr. Bernstein, think about your wife, your daughter…don't you want to see them again? Don't you want to see your daughter grow up? See her wedding? Think of all the shame and embarrassment this will cause. You'll never live it down."

Abner was silent for a moment, his eyes never leaving the table. Then finally, he looked up. "What do you want to know?"

"First of all, I want to know who Lawrence Rice is. Let's begin with that. What part does he play in all this?" asked the young assistant district attorney.

"You have to promise me that if I tell you these things…you can keep me out of jail," Abner said in a shaky voice.

Ayers smirked. The man was a real wuss. A person like Bernstein wouldn't last a night in jail.

The young lawyer cleared his throat and said, "You'll be totally cleared, but you have to give up what you know on Lawrence Rice and this whole scheme that you two had going on."

Abner nodded quickly. "Okay. I can do that."

"We're not finished yet, Mr. Bernstein. We also want information on Rocco Gionelli. We have a lot of questions to ask you about him. I want you to answer the questions honestly. This is the only way that I can offer you this deal. Either you go along with it, or you spend many, many years in jail," the assistant DA said grimly.

Abner's eyes bulged open in surprise. "What does Rocco have to do with this?"

Ayers smirked. Detective Lee—who was Agent Ayers' cousin—and Captain McMillan had informed him of the Gionelli situation. The FBI had been after Gionelli for years. Lee and McMillan had told Ayers, much to his delight, that Bernstein would have information on Gionelli. After hearing this, the feds had went to the DA to work out a deal. The DA, who also desperately wanted to see Gionelli behind bars, had agreed to it. "He has a lot to do with this. It's about catching the bad guys and putting them away. Rocco's like a worm. He's escaped us for years. But now, I'm going to catch him and put him where he belongs. You give him up, you walk free. He'll never know it was you that told."

"But he's my client…I can't."

"Jail time, or talk, Bernstein," Lorry snapped. "The choice is yours. Abner swallowed hard, "What do you want to know first?"

"Let's start with Lawrence," said Lorry smoothly.

Ψ

Agent Ayers was on the phone to the D.A.

"I think I've got what I need for that Gionelli case," Ayers said as he puffed on his cigar.

"What have you got?"

"I got a sworn statement from Abner Bernstein about what was going on with the plane situation amogst many other things. It's robbery, just as I thought."

"Tell me more."

"Well, according to Bernstein, Gionelli plans to have some of his men on the flight. They're going to pay off a few flight attendants and the co-pilot to get them to the cargo area and steal a shipment of money and jewelry that will be on board, once the plane lands."

"Oh Gosh, this is serious."

"Very. I think it's best to catch them in the act. What do you think? Is surveillance feasible?"

"Very."

Ψ

December 12th was a cold and blustery day in Chicago. The snow came in great flakes and the sky was gray.

"We've got six men on the plane, Sir," Agent Ayers said to his superior over the phone over the phone.

"Okay. They're all sitting separate from each other?"

"Yes, Sir, no one would think they are anyone other than passengers riding the plane. They don't look the least bit suspicious."

"Good. I'll keep in touch."

Agent Ayers hung up the phone and quickly boarded the plane with his partner, Agent Fisk. For the first time in his life, Fisk was flying first class. He took a seat beside a mustached man that continually tried to start conversation with him once the plane was in flight. Fisk kept his response minimal, aside from an occasional nod, a smile, and answers of yes or no, Fisk was silent. The older man, seeing that he wasn't getting much talk from Fisk, turned to the passenger to the left of him and attempted to start with him. Fisk was relieved. He casually looked around the cabin. His eyes easily swept over the passengers and three of his six men who were scattered all over the seats. The other three were sitting in the coach accommodations.

For the first half hour, things were pretty low-key and uninteresting. Fisk began to browse through a newspaper. After about forty minutes of reading, Fisk saw something a little suspicious.

One tall, dark haired man sitting across the isle from him raised a hand, motioning for the stewardess. The stewardess, a small blonde, smiled and came to his seat.

"Is it okay to get up to use the bathrooms now? This is the first time I've been on a plane. I'm not so sure about how things work around here," the man said quite loudly and let out an embarrassed chuckle.

The stewardess smiled broadly at him. "Of course, Sir. The plane is no longer ascending. Would you like me to show you to the bathrooms?"

"Yes, please, would you?"

Fisk noticed a man to the left of him steal a glance at the dark haired man and the stewardess. The man shot his eye quickly back down to the magazine that he was reading.

Fisk looked towards Carter, one of his men. He stared back and Fisk. Fisk gave a slight nod and continued to read the newspaper. After about thirty seconds, Carter got up and discreetly followed after the stewardess and the dark haired man.

Fisk looked to the left of him. The man that had been reading the magazine was staring straight at him. Fisk gave him a confused look. The man seemed to relax and went back to reading the magazine. Fisk let out a silent sigh of relief.

"Imagine, a guy that doesn't know how to find the bathroom by himself on a plane. Jeeze, some people are really strange," the man beside him said jovially.

"Yeah," Fisk mumbled, "real strange."

Ψ

Three men, having been caught in the cargo area with hands on the precious money and priceless jewelry, were apprehended and sent off to the police station when they landed in Queens, New York. Three flight attendants and the co-pilot were also taken in for questioning.

"There was a guy sitting to the left of me in the next row over. I got a feeling that he was involved in it too. The only thing is, I can't arrest him. He didn't actually do anything. Only thing I could hope for is that one of the three men rat him out," Fisk and Ayers had first called their superior the moment that they arrived at the police station in Queens. Afterwards, they called McMillan to give him a briefing. Although McMillan was no longer on the case, he had begged Ayers and Fisk to let him know what was going on. Since Ayers had known McMillan for so many years, and throughout they had each done favors for each other, he agreed to it. McMillan was the person that they were currently speaking to.

"Yeah. But what I really want is for one of them rat Gionelli out. He's the only one that I care about. I want to crush him like a tin can. You gotta do everything in your power to get one of those scumbags to confess that he was the one to orchestrate this whole damned thing," McMillan said with vehemence.

"You know I'll do everything that I can—we want him too. The other two men didn't cough up a thing about Gionelli. Five hours of questioning for each one of them. It's tiring. But at least their asses will be shipped back to Chicago to due time."

"Well, you got another guy, right?""

"Yes. We got one more guy. We're hoping he breaks down...I got a feeling he will. I gotta go."

"Okay. I'll speak to you later."

Ayers stared at the dark haired man that he had gotten up to use the bathroom on the plane. The man's face was an unreadable mask. His black eyes glittered in his face and seemed to bore through Agent Ayers face.

Ayers sat across from him and opened the file. "Vincenzo Espozito?"

The young man continued to stare at Ayers not saying a word. Ayers smirked at him and leaned back in his chair. Fisk stood behind Vincenzo—his face grim.

"So, where you from, *Vinny?*" Ayers said and noticed with pleasure that the man winced at the nickname that Ayers took the liberty of giving him, and it was said as if it were an obscenity. The man continued to say nothing.

"I asked you a question, Mac. Where the hell are you from?"

"Chicago," the man spat, his dark eyes flashing with rage.

"Hmmm. A Chicago native. So I guess you think you're one of those hot shot gagsters or something," Fisk said, twirling a pencil between his fingers. He took a seat beside Agent Ayers.

"You two don't know a damn thing about me," the man muttered.

"Yeah, well, let's share and tell," Ayers said leaning forward. "It's the perfect time to do so. So…as you've already probably guessed, I'm an FBI agent. Now your turn. What do you do for a living?"

"I'm a bartender," Vincenzo quickly said.

"Oh, okay. You make a lot of money doing that?" Ayers asked.

"I make enough," he answered stiffly.

"So then, why would you wanna steal something that ain't yours if you got enough to live by?" asked Ayers.

The man clenched his teeth. His powerful jawbones moved under his lightly tanned skin. Good, I'm pissing him off some more, Ayers though with glee.

"Where do you bartend at?" Fisk asked, pencil pointed at the man sitting across from him.

"At a club," Vincenzo said, drumming his fingers on the formica top of the table.

"What's the name of the club?" Ayers asked, calmly.

"I don't know…I move around a lot to different places," the man said hastily.

"Well surely you remember the name of at least one of the clubs you've worked in during your whole life," Ayers said easily.

"Nah, I don't. I got a bad memory," the man said with a mocking glint in his eyes.

"Well, maybe I could help you…could one of the clubs be located on Iverson Avenue? Kinda placed back from the street, a little hard to notice," Fisk slowly.

The man's face grew pale. His lips tightened into a straight line.

"Does that sound familiar to you Vinny boy?" Ayers asked with a sneer.

"I don't know what you're talking about," he said, his eyes focused on a spot above Ayers' head.

"Well, we have reason to believe that you frequent there," Ayers said.

"Whatever you think, it ain't true."

"Who owns the club Vinny?"

Vincenzo Espozito stiffened in his seat. "I don't know. But this ain't got nothing to do with what I'm in here for."

Ayers gave him a smile. But this smile wasn't warm and friendly. It was the smile of an animal about to eat its prey. "Oh, but it does, Vinny boy. It does. Do you know why?"

Vincenzo stared at him, face blank. He did not answer.

"Because the same person that owns that club had something to do with the setting up of this plan, didn't he?"

Vincenzo sat as still as a statue.

"Rocco Gionelli. Does that name sound familiar?" Ayers asked.

"I ain't ever heard that name in my life. I don't know who the hell you're talking about, boss," the man said with a sneer.

Fisk nodded his head slowly. "I got some things I want you to look at." Fisk opened a manila envelope and took out a smaller white envelope. He pushed it across to Vincenzo. Vincenzo stared at the white envelope with a blank expression.

"Open it up, Vinny boy. See what's inside," Fisk commanded.

Vincenzo reached out for the envelope and with pleasure, Ayers noticed that Vincenzo's hands were shaking slightly. He opened it and took out the stack of glossy black and white pictures. He grimaced when he saw what they were.

Ayers pushed back his chair and stood up. He came around the table and stood beside Vincenzo who was still seated. "Why don't you spread those pictures out here on the table so we can get a good look at them." Ayers placed a hand on the man's shoulder. Vincenzo stiffened. Vincenzo attempted to do what was asked as his hands shook even more.

"Well, it looks like you have a case of the shakes. I'll do it for ya." Ayers plucked the pictures from Vincenzo's hands and laid them out on the plastic surface of the table.

In every one of the pictures, Vincenzo Espozito could be seen. In many of them, he was either coming out or going into the club that Fisk had previously described. In about a third of them, he was unmistakably with Rocco Gionelli.

"So. What do you have to say?" Ayers said in the low tone of voice with his face only inches away from Vincenzo's.

Vincenzo looked down. He tucked his hands in his lap now that they were shaking uncontrollably. A thin sheen of sweat covered his forehead.

Ayers smiled to himself. Vincenzo was right where he wanted him. Ayers was going to get him to break. Unlike the other's, this man had a weakness and a reasonably attainable breaking point. He wondered why Rocco would use a man like him.

"You might as well give it up. Your other partners in crime have already confessed that Rocco was involved. They told me that he was the one that set this thing up. Because of it, they're getting a lesser sentence," Ayers lied. "You don't want to rot the rest of your days away in jail, do you?"

Vincenzo looked off at the wall in front of him with a blank expression.

"Vinny, I know that you're not a bartender. I know you take illegal bets for Gionelli. I know you sell things on the black market. You don't want me to peg you for those too, do you? If I did, you wouldn't see the light of day again. So. Was Gionelli behind it or not?"

Vincenzo shifted in his seat, very uncomfortable. "The others said it was him?"

"That's right," answered Ayers

"I want my lawyer. I ain't saying anything else."

Ψ

Abner looked at the front page of the newspaper and saw a picture of Lawrence Rice in the courtroom during his trial. He flipped to the second page of the newspaper and saw a picture of Rocco Gionelli being led out of his large house in handcuffs—his face staring defiantly ahead. Abner breathed a sigh of relief as he put down the paper.

But he knew he wasn't out of the woods yet, not by a long shot. He was still quite a bit nervous about ratting on his client, Rocco Gionelli, but considering the circumstances, he had no choice in the matter. It was either himself or Rocco. Naturally, he had chosen himself— he had a family to worry about. But Abner tried to comfort himself by saying that there was no way that Gionelli or his family could find out. It could have been anyone that told on Rocco. Why would anyone suspect that his own lawyer was the one to do it? The thought eased his mind greatly.

"Gosh, Abner, I don't know what we can do about Rocco. I'm trying to look for loopholes, but I don't see anything that I can use to get him off. Maybe we can get him a little less time…but that doesn't look to promising either," Earnest told Abner one Monday morning when they were in their office.

"Yeah, it looks pretty hopeless," Abner muttered. The last thing he wanted was for Rocco to get off and be let free. There was more of a chance that Rocco would find Abner out.

Earnest gave Abner a cockeyed stare. "You know Abner, you've been getting on really weird these past few months. Especially since we got Leslie as a client. Are you doing okay? We hardly ever get the chance to really talk with all the work going on."

"Things are going great," Abner said quickly. He forced a smile. "Estelle stood up the other day. Dorothy was so happy. She took a picture of it."

"That's great. You have to give me a copy of it," Earnest said with a smile.

"I sure will," Abner answered.

Ψ

Feburary, 1960

"Rocco Gionelli, you have lived a life of crime for many years and have managed to allude the law by clever tactics and two very smart lawyers. This time, you're going to be held accountable for your actions. You are hereby sentenced to twenty years to life in prison for conspiracy to robbery in the first degree, possession of illegal weaponry, and possession of counterfeit money and loan sharking. You will be eligible for parole after thirteen years. That is all. Court adjourned." The Judge banged the gavel down hard.

There was a cry behind them. Earnest turned around. Wendy was crying horribly, her faced buried in the shoulder of her son. Angelina wiped at falling tears, Anthony put an arm around her his eyes watery. Sal stared straight ahead like a statue, his face grim. "I'm going to find the bastard that did this," Sal muttered to himself.

"Rocco, remember you're up for parole in thirteen years," Winston said.

Rocco smiled painfully and nodded. "You guys did all that you could. I could have gotten like fifty years minimum if it wasn't for you two. Thank you for what you've done." Rocco shook their hands.

Abner was riddled with guilt.

Chapter Twenty-nine

May, 1960

"Oh gosh, I think my water just broke!" Eunice said in alarm. She flung her magazine aside.

Anthony jumped up from the deck, his face filled with panic. "That's impossible! You're due in a month!"

"Oh gosh Anthony…something's happening. There's no denying it!" Eunice said clutching her side. "Oh God, I'm having contractions. Quick Anthony, do something!" she screamed.

Even screaming, to Anthony, Eunice looked beautiful. Pregnancy had given her a glow that made her look extra attractive.

Anthony helped her up from the chair. "We're going to the hospital."

They arrived at the hospital and were told by a surly attendant to wait.

"But we think something's the matter…she's not supposed to have the baby yet. She's a month early!"

"Okay. A doctor will be down right away. We're paging one right this moment."

Anthony looked back at his wife who was sitting on one of the plastic chairs, her face wet with sweat and distorted with pain. Suddenly, blood began to run down her legs and formed a small pool at her feet.

"My God! Look at her, she's bleeding!" Anthony yelled.

An orderly came and placed Eunice in a wheelchair.

"Hi, I'm Dr. Greene," a short, curly haired, bespectacled man said to Anthony and shook his hand.

"I'm Anthony Gi—" Anthony stopped short. The last thing he wanted was curious people inquiring about his infamous last name.

"What was that?"

"Just call me Anthony, please," Anthony responded.

"Okay. Walk with us. We're going to examine your wife, but chances are, we're going to have to take your wife into the O.R. to do a C-section ."

"Is she going to be all right?" Anthony asked.

"We'll do everything that we can, Sir."

The examination comfirmed the doctor's suspicions. Eunice needed a C-section immediately. When they got to the O.R, Anthony followed the doctor to the door.

"I'm sorry, you have to stay out here and wait, Anthony. We'll tell you when you can come in."

"Okay," Anthony said softly. His heart dropped to his stomach. He sat down in the waiting room. He stood up and went to the pay phone to call Angelina.

"We're at General Hospital. Eunice is having the baby."

"Really? She's early, isn't she?" Angelina asked, surprised.

"Yeah, she is," Anthony said sadly. He swallowed the lump in his throat.

"Anthony, what's the matter."

"I think something's wrong—" Anthony choked on his words. "I think something's wrong with Eunice and the baby. They have her in the O.R."

"Oh gosh, I'll be right down there as soon as I can." Angelina said.

Angelina was there in twenty minutes. They hugged and kissed each other and sat down.

"So, did the doctor come and talk to you yet?" Angelina asked.

"No, not yet. I'm still waiting."

After about forty minutes, the doctor came out. The front of his smock covered in blood. His face was grim. Anthony and Angelina stood up.

"Is my wife okay?" Anthony asked, shakily.

The doctor cleared his throat and said, "Why don't we sit down and talk. Who is this?" he asked, indicating Angelina.

"This is my twin sister. What happened? Can I see her? I want to see her." Anthony said in a strangled voice.

"Please, Anthony, sit down."

They sat down across from each other. The doctor turned sad eyes upon Anthony.

"I'm sorry, I don't know how to tell you this."

"What? What is it? Just tell me, please."

"We did a C-section, but the baby was still born. Apparently, he died in the womb."

Anthony held his face in his hands for a while then he looked up, his eyes filled with unshed tears. "It was a boy?"

"Yes, it was," the doctor said softly.

"Can I see Eunice?"

The doctor shifted in his seat. "She lost a lot of blood."

"Can I see her?" Anthony repeated.

"I—I'm sorry. Eunice passed away...there was nothing that we could do for her. The blood loss was too much."

Angelina wrapped her arms around her brother. Anthony leaned on her shoulders and cried. Angelina leaned her head against his and cried as well.

"I'm terribly sorry," the doctor said sincerely. He awkwardly cleared his throat and shifted in his seat.

Anthony lifted his tear streaked face from his sister's shoulder and looked at the doctor. "Can I please see her?" he asked, in a strangled tone of voice.

"Umm...Yes. Of course. If you want to. Come this way." The doctor slowly rose to his feet and waited for them too to arise. He led them out into the hallway and down to the O.R.

The moment they entered the O.R., the smell of blood assaulted his nostrils. He walked up to the small table beside the gunnery. A small, blue-white baby, covered inblood lay motionless. Anthony touched the small hand and held it. He began to cry anew. Angelina came up beside him and put her arm around his waist.

"This is my baby...my son," Anthony said mournfully. "We were going to name him after me."

Anthony turned to the still female form laying on the gurney. He put a hand to his mouth as he walked towards it.

There, lay his beautiful wife. Her delicate lids were closed and a look of serenity was on her face, as though she were only sleeping. One pale arm was out from under the blue sheet and lay on top. Anthony gently ran his fingers from the top of her arm to her hand. He held it and kissed the open palm. He held it against his face and cried, deep racking sobs shook his body. Tears flowed down his face.

"Oh Eunice, my love, my wife. My angel. I loved you so much, our love was so…different. Our feelings were one of a kind. How can I ever have someone like you again?"

Ψ

"Hello. What are you doing here, waiting for the bus?" A deep tenor voice asked. Ester looked to her side. There was no one there. Then she looked ahead of her and her heart started to beat wildly in her chest when she saw who it was. It was Marco Arnone. He was in a beautiful, glossy black Cadillac. One of Rocco's "business associates." The man in the gray suit that had watched her so closely almost four years ago in Rocco's office when they had seen each other for the first time. And here he was. She knew she recognized that voice from somewhere. Why was her heart beating like this? She could also feel butterflies in her stomach.

"W—well, my car's in the shop for the day, so I'm getting the bus."

"Well, why don't I give you a ride home?" Marco asked, with a smile.

"Umm…I don't want to put you out of your way. It's not far to go. All I gotta do is catch this one bus."

"Please, I insist. It will definitely not put me out of my way."

Ester glanced around her, she felt so guilty all of a sudden. "Okay."

Marco got out of the car and held the door open for her. Ester smiled thinly and sat inside the car. He got in after her. He drove her home.

And so, it had begun like that. Over the next months Ester would meet secretly with Marco. He would take her to five star hotels, take her out to eat, buy her expensive things that Ester carefully kept hidden from her husband Garrett.

"You gotta marry me," Marco told her one day while they were in bed.

"You've got to be crazy. I'm married already, Marco. Besides…what would people say? You're…white and I'm a black."

"I don't give a damn what people say. Do I strike you as the type that cares? Besides, it ain't illegal or nothing in this state. Listen to me talking about 'legality.' Divorce him, Hun. I can do more for ya."

"Garrett does a lot for me…I thought there was an understanding in all this…"

"Yeah, but I got feelings for you, honey. I love you."

"Please don't make this difficult Marco."

"Tell me you don't love me and I'll leave you alone. Look me in the face and say that you don't."

Ester looked away. She was silent.

"I rest my case," Marco said.

"Whatever the case may be. I'm not divorcing Garrett, Marco."

Ψ

Chicago, Illinois, spring, 1963

"Guess what, Edda, I joined CORE!" Michael excitedly told Edda one day after classes were out.

"Michael, are you crazy? Didn't you hear about that bus that they set fire to down in South Carolina? They could have been killed. I don't want anything to happen to you," Edda said, her face frowning.

"But, there were also times when they were not attacked," Michael pointed out. He waved to a group of friends that passed by.

Edda rolled her eyes at that statement.

"We're part of the SNCC. We do sit ins and a whole bunch of other things." Edda paused and turned to him. "Michael, you know I'm all for this. I want to do everything…but just not that. Hell, I'll march and all, but to be trapped in a bus that's on fire? What a way to die!" Edda exclaimed. She continued walking. Michael followed.

"Look, there are colleges that are not integrated like our Loyola University here. That's just not right. Come on, Edda. There's going to be a ride this weekend. You gotta come with me. Please."

Edda paused and shrugged her shoulders. "Fine. I'm not going to let you go down there by yourself, but I have to tell you…I have a bad feeling about it."

"Oh come on. You and your 'feelings' Edda." Michael gave her a quick hug. "Thanks Edda. I'll meet you after classes? We'll talk more about it."

"Sure Michael," Edda said distractedly as Michael walked off into the building. Edda had caught sight of Peter Downing.

Peter Downing was not top on her list of favorite people. In fact, Edda couldn't stand the guy. He was popular and good looking and had on more that one occasion made his interests towards her known, but she wanted none of that.

Edda tried to turn in the other direction to avoid being spotted, but that didn't work. He noticed her right away and came rushing up to her. Edda exhaled deeply.

"Hey, Edda. How are you doing?" he asked, with a smile. He fell in step beside her.

Fine until you just came along. Edda said to herself, but aloud she said, "I'm great."

"Good, Good. There's a party tonight, and I was wondering...would you like to come?"

"No, it's okay. I have some stuff to do later on," Edda said breezily.

Peter paused and said, "Hold on a minute."

Edda stopped and looked up at him. "What?"

"You know, I don't get you. You've got to be the prettiest girl on this campus, you're smart. You could have so much going for you. But you live like a hermit and besides your little crazy organizations which are filled with misfits that probably couldn't fit in anywhere else, you have no social life. But there's not one guy on this campus that wouldn't jump at the chance to take you out. It seems like the only friend you have is that black kid Michael. But even he's more social than you are."

Edda slitted her eyes at him. "You don't know a damn thing about me, yet you have me all summed up in one paragraph. Kindly, go fuck yourself," Edda walked off.

"My, my, my. The lady's got a mouth like a sailor," Peter called heartily after her. "Talk to you later, sweet cakes!"

Edda rolled her eyes to herself. Peter was incorrigible.

That Friday, Edda and Michael went home.

"I feel terrible for my mother. You know how broken up she was after Rocco went to jail. It's been two years now, though. I'm glad she's doing a lot better. I have to try and spend some more time with her."

"Yeah. She is doing a lot better. Did you tell your mom that I'm coming?" Michael asked.

Edda flicked her hand at him. "Nah. She probably assumed it already. I'm sure your mom's over there anyways."

"She is. I called her earlier," Michael said with a smile.

"Well okay then. You know my home's like your home."

"My house is your house too. Although it's the size of a cardboard box compared to your giant castle."

"Michael, your parent's house is very nice and you know that."

"Sure, but who can compare with yours?" Michael said, and tugged at her pony tail.

"Oh stop it before you drive us into a ditch," Edda said laughing.

Michael drove his Firebird into the driveway of the house. The speaker was on the passenger side of the car, so Edda poked her head out the window, pressed the button, and spoke into the speaker.

"Uncle Garrett? Kindly open this gate and let Michael and I through. By the way, we have about thirty more people with us. They're spending the weekend," Edda joked.

A chuckle came through the speaker. "Please, girl. I can see you right here in the camera. Come on through the gate, you two."

The gate slowly swung open backwards. Michael drove the car right up to the house. Wendy and Ester were standing on the porch with smiles on their faces.

All four of them embraced.

"How are you all doing?" Wendy asked, wiping at a spot on Michael shirt.

"We're great, Mom. Where's Uncle Garrett? We heard him over the speaker."

"I'm over here, girly. I got a job to do. I can't just be letting everyone in through the gate!" Garrett said coming up behind them.

Edda smiled and gave him a hug. "Hi Uncle."

"Hi pretty. You all home for the weekend?" Garrett asked, giving his son a big hug.

"Yeah...but we have somewhere to go tomorrow. We probably won't be back until Saturday night," Edda said nervously.

"Where are you two going?" Ester asked, as they walked into the house.

"Nowhere important," Michael said quickly.

Wendy pulled out a plate of cookies from the fridge and placed them on the table. She got out a pitcher of juice. They all sat down around the table to eat, laughing and joking.

"So, when's Alfie coming home from Thailand?"

"We're not sure. He just arrived yesterday afternoon," Wendy said and took a sip of juice.

"Yeah, he called me last night," Edda said, taking a bite of the oatmeal raisin cookies. "Ummm…these cookies are soft and nice. Who made them?"

"You have to credit Ester with those…she's a fabulous baker," Wendy said, putting an arm around her friend.

"Oh please, you know you're good too. You got your main courses down, honey," Ester said with a smile.

They laughed.

"Speaking of that, I'm going to get started on dinner," Wendy said standing up.

"I'll help," Ester said firmly

"No, no. Why don't you all go out to the pool and relax? It's certainly hot enough to go swimming. This is one of the hottest Mays that I've ever encountered. You know what? We'll have dinner out on the deck. It's beautiful outside. What about that?"

"Sounds good," Michael said with a smile.

"It sure does, let's go get dinner started," Ester said with a smile. "And I'm helping, no ifs, ands, or buts about it."

After dinner, Michael and Ester went home. Wendy and Edda were in the house alone.

"Did Helga tell you? She got into a medical school in New York," Wendy said happily.

"Yes she told me. She also said that she thinks she'll be the only woman in the class. She's really brave, isn't she Mom? I admire her."

"Yes. Sometimes we have to be brave to accomplish things we want and to make changes," Wendy said softly.

Edda nodded her head and looked down for a moment. She looked back up at her mother. "Mom…Michael and I are planning to go on a freedom ride tomorrow. The bus is stopping in Georgia and Alabama."

Wendy frowned. "Have you two any idea how dangerous that is?"

Edda nodded. "I know Mom. But as you said…sometimes we have to take chances, right? I think civil rights for human beings is worth taking risks for."

Wendy stared at her daughter and let out a big sigh. "You're young and brave Edda. Use it to your advantage while it lasts. A beautiful, smart young woman like you has a world of possibilities before her. I won't try to stop you, but I'm torn. I fear for your safety, but at the same time I know the great importance in all this. Just you and Michael be safe, please."

"We will Mom. Michael won't let anything happen to me, neither would I to him."

Wendy smiled with tears in her eyes. She placed a hand on her daughter's blonde head. "I know that honey. I know that with all my heart."

Ψ

Edda and Michael got there early. By the time they were ready to leave, there were five other white students besides Edda and seven other black students besides Michael.

"Are you ready to go my friends!" called the driver of the bus, who was a young Japanese man, with long flowing hair, called Haru.

They all cheered and then they were on their way.

They made rest stops along the way. Things were not bad for the first few stops. The most they got were some stares. But as they got into the South, things got considerably worse. They decided that they wouldn't stop until they got to Georgia.

Edda was terrified. But she didn't tell anyone else. She looked over at Michael who was sitting beside her. He wore a determined look on his dark face. Then she looked out of the window. People on the streets were stopping to stare at the bus. The expressions on people's face were first shocked and then angry. A few of them began to pelt rocks at the bus.

"Get away from the Window Edda," Michael called. He pulled her over.

A stone shattered a bus window behind where they were seated.

"Come on, comrades, we're almost there in Stonewall," called Haru.

The people on the bus began to sing freedom songs. Michael pulled Edda into his arms. Edda leaned on his shoulder. They sang along.

They pulled into the Greyhound station in Stonewall. A groups of white people were standing there with angry looks on their faces.

"Fucking niggers and nigger-lovin' white trash. Come on out so we kin beat you," shouted a ruddy faced, middle aged man with steely blue eyes.

"Oh look, we got us a gook too. God damned Jap! Let's git the yellow bastard first," shouted another red faced woman.

Edda turned frightened eyes to Michael. "Do we have to get out?"

"I don't know about you, but I have to pee like a race horse," Michael said quietly.

Edda swallowed hard. *Come on girl, this isn't the time to chicken out.* Edda told herself, trying to be brave.

"Come on," Michael said holding out his hand. Edda nodded her head and grasped it.

Michael and Edda followed the rest of them down the stairs of the bus.

The groups of white Southerners stood in silent amazement as they all poured out of the bus. They all headed towards the rest rooms.

"Come on Edda," whispered a tall red headed girl called Carrie. "Fran, and bunch of the other girls, and I are going into the bathroom. Come with us," she said holding her hand.

The seven girls, three white and four black, all held hands and walked together, one behind the other, to the bathroom.

For a while, the crowd let them pass. But as soon as they reached the door, two young women stepped in front of the door with there hands crossed over their chest. "You all can't come in here. No niggers or nigger lovers allowed."

The girl at the head of the line, a startlingly attractive brunette, gently tried to get around the two angry women. But they shoved her back. She stumbled and almost fell, but Wanda, a beautiful girl with deep mahogany skin, held her up.

Then there was a ruckus behind them. Edda turned around quickly. One of the people from the angry crowd had punched Michael right in the stomach.

Edda shoved her way back to him, cursing, and screaming as she did so.

"Get away from him! You evil bastards. You all belong in hell!" Edda screamed. She grabbed at the back of the young man now attempting to attack Michael again.

"Get off me, you little nigger lover," he growled. He turned around, and flung Edda to the concrete. She cried in pain as she felt her wrist snap underneath the weight of her body.

"You white bastard," Michael yelled and punched the guy straight in the face. The man tumbled to the ground. Michael's eyes were wild with fury.

The crowd went wild.

The others helped Edda to her feet and brought her onto the bus. The others quickly jumped onto the bus as well. Haru closed the doors before anybody from the crowd could attempt to get on. He pulled off from the curb and shot out of the station. Rocks and other objects rained on the bus. A few people tried to run after the bus, but soon gave up.

"Are you okay?" Michael asked Edda who was holding her arm.

"I think it's broken," said Bernard, a young white man with brown curls.

"Let's get her to a hospital," Cried Haru from the driver's seat.

They had only been to one of their stops and already something serious had happened.

Ψ

When Michael and Edda returned, Wendy and Ester ran up to them, terror all over their faces.

"My God! We were so worried about you! Are you two okay?" asked Wendy. "Oh gosh, your arm's broken Edda."

Edda gave her a lopsided grin. "Yeah, I know. It doesn't hurt so bad now."

Ester was crying as she wrapped her arms around her son. "I don't want you two to ever do something like that again, you hear?"

"Mom…I had to," Michael said softly. "I can't say that I won't do anything like it again."

"You all were on the news when you were in Alabama. We were watching it," Wendy said, attempting to smile, "We were so proud of you."

"We sure were, but terrified," Ester said, wiping her eyes.

Ψ

Alfie nervously glanced at his watch and let out a sigh.

He was nervous and with good reason. He was meeting Penny and Quincy at a café called *The Kulap Cafe* in Bangkok. Unbeknownst to him until he arrived in Thailand, Penny and Quincy were the ones who found the ancient artifact. So it was them whom he was going to interview for the paper. Ever since getting those series of articles concerning Leslie Emerson and his company almost four years ago, he had become the lead reporter at the *Chicago Informant*. So far, he had enjoyed traveling to Thailand, but he wondered if it was all going to change this afternoon.

When Alfie saw Penny coming in, his heart leapt to his throat. She was striking. Her copper colored hair, brownish as he had remembered it, was now more coppery red because of the sun and it was swept up into a pony tail. She wore a sleeveless cream shirt. Her long tanned thighs stretched out of khaki colored shorts. Brown leather sandals adorned her feet. She carried a canvas bag over one shoulder. She looked around nervously. Quincy was nowhere to be seen.

Alfie stood up and waved to her. She gave him a toothy smile and started walking towards his table. When she reached there, they embraced and reluctantly let go of each other and sat down.

"Where's Quincy?" Alfie asked, looking behind her head.

"Well, we have a couple of projects to finish. He stayed behind to work on them, so I came by myself," she said quickly.

Alfie nodded. He knew why Quincy didn't come. It was because Quincy hated his guts. Alfie could hardly blame him.

"So how are you doing, Penny?" Alfie asked, as he felt all the old feeling for her come back with a rush.

"I'm doing fine. Quincy and I have fun. We love our job and all the traveling. It's what we both always wanted to do."

"We have so much to talk about," Alfie said softly.

Penny blushed. There was a moment of silence as they sipped at their mango juice.

"Yeah, well, I have the artifact right here. I had to beg them to let me take it with me. I have to hand it over by this evening." Penny pulled it from the canvas bag and placed it on the table. It was a small statue made out of stone. The workmanship was amazing.

"It's beautiful," Alfie said, amazed.

"I know. So glad we found it."

"So shall we begin the interview?" Alfie asked.

The interview took about an hour to complete, but finally they were done.

"So, do you want to go get something to eat? Some traditional Thai food would be nice," Alfie said standing up and stretching.

Penny blushed. "I don't know about that, Alfie."

"Come on Penny. It's totally innocent. We're both hungry, aren't we?" he said with a smile.

"Well, Quincy is expecting me back...I don't want him to worry."

"We won't be long. We'll eat and then I'll see you home. Come on, I go back tomorrow. When am I gonna get to see you again? We've been such good friends."

Penny sighed, "Okay. Let's go eat. I know the perfect restaurant."

They traveled further into central Bangkok and finally came to the restaurant that Penny was talking about.

"It looks nice," Alfie said.

"Nice, but casual. I just about pass for what's appropriate dress in there. You, on the other hand, are more than fine," Penny said with a smile.

A young, petite, oriental woman seated them and gave them menus.

"Hmmm...I think we should order the duck. It's really good here."

"Where's that on the menu?"

"It's called *Khao na phet*. That's roast duck over rice," Penny said pointing it out.

"What's this?" Alfie asked, pointing to another item on the menu. "I could be ordering dog for all I know."

"That's *Khao phat*, which translates as fried rice with some sort of meat like beef, shrimp, pork, or chicken."

"Hmm. That sounds good too…so you know what? I'm going to let you order for the both of us," Alfie said closing his menu.

Penny laughed. "I'm not going to order for you. What do you want to eat?"

"Well, let's try the duck with the rice. Are there any appetizer like items here?"

"We can have some soup. *Tom yam kung.*"

"Okay. What kind of soup is that?" Alfie asked.

"Well…it's spicy made with lemon juice, lemon grass, and shrimp."

"It sounds good. We'll order it. That and the duck and rice. What about something to drink?"

"Well…let's see," Penny said examining the drink menu. She suddenly put it down. "You know what? We'll have some *Mehkong.*"

"What's that?" Alfie asked.

"You've been here…two days and you don't know what Mehkong is yet?" Penny asked, teasing him.

Alfie smiled. There was the playful Penny that he was used to. "No, I haven't had the pleasure. I guess you'll be the one to introduce it to me."

"Well, Mehkong is a rice whisky. It's very popular over here. It's sweet and strong. It tastes kinda like rum. I think you'll like it," Penny said with a smile.

The pretty waitress came back over, took their order, and left just as quickly as she came.

"Do you know how much I miss you Penny?" Alfie said, fixing her with his eyes.

Penny looked away.

"Penny, did you hear what I said?" Alfie asked, softly.

"Alfie, I'm married."

"Do you miss me too? There's not a day that does by that I don't think about you."

Penny turned her amber, slanted, cat eyes to him. They glowed in the soft candle light.

"I think about you all the time, Alfie. What could have been...what will never be...I do miss you."

Eventually the food came. They ate, talked, and laughed, recounting events and old stories. Finally when they were finished eating, they paid the check and walked out of the restaurant. They stood outside, the sun could barely be seen above the horizon. It was dusk.

Alfie pulled Penny to him.

"Alfie, what are you doing, we can't—"

"We can. If we both want to. Penny, come back to my room," Alfie whispered, his lips close to her ears.

"I can't. What am I supposed to tell Quincy?" Penny said softly.

"Nothing. Tell him you got lost. Anything. We'll worry about that in the morning," Alfie said quietly.

"I can't stay until morning," Penny said and accepted Alfie's passionate kiss.

"Then stay as long as you can, I go back tomorrow," Alfie said between kisses

They went back to his suite.

Ψ

Lee was miserable. Ever since getting dismissed from his job on a suspicion that he was taking monetary bribes, he'd done nothing but mope around, watch television and eat. His sedentary lifestyle was also taking a toll on his health. He had gained ten pounds in a month. This made him even more depressed. The only thing that Lee went out for was to buy food and the bare essentials of life. With a feeling of doom, he waited out the investigation of the bribes that would determine his fate. Although, he suspected that he would only get probation if anything at all. Funny that McMillan never got caught, Lee often thought angrily to himself.

That day, seeing that he needed more toilet paper, Lee went down to the corner store. He bought the toilet paper, as well as three Milky Way bars, and left the store. When he got to his front porch, he saw a man standing there. When the man turned around and stared at Lee, Lee knew that the man had been waiting for him.

"Who the hell are you?" asked Lee, reaching for his keys. He was sorry that he had left his gun in the house.

"Mr. Lee. Why don't we step inside. I want to have a few words with you," the man said, his face unreadable.

"First of all, who the hell are you?" Lee asked, nastily, not in the mood for any crap.

"Why don't we step inside first. It's not good laying our business out here on the front steps, don't you think?"

"I don't know you, I don't trust you," Lee said succinctly.

"I'm not here to hurt you in any kind of way. I think you'll like what I have to say, considering you've been out of a job for a month now."

Lee gave him an amused look. "So you know everything about me, huh."

"I know enough," the man said vaguely.

"All right. Come on in. It's hot as hell out here," Lee said unlocking the door.

Lee followed the man into the house. "You can sit down where you want. Do you want anything to drink? I got some ice tea in the fridge I think."

"That's fine Mr. Lee. Why don't I get straight to the point."

"Why don't you tell me your name first," answered Lee.

"My name is Salvatore Gionelli," the man said, his face still stoic.

"You got the same last name as…hold on. You're Rocco Gionelli's son?"

"Yes I am. My point is that I found out that you were one of the detectives on the case concerning my father," Salvatore said.

"Look, you ain't coming here to kill me, are you?" Lee said getting up from his seat.

Sal shook his head, "Relax. Nothing like that. I'm just here willing to pay for some information. I'm willing to pay quite a bit. Information that I feel you have."

Lee squinted at him. "Well, you should know that the FBI was the one actually dealing with the case…but my cousin, Andy Ayers, is an agent and he was the one that was heading the investigation. He might have told me somethings…what do you want to know?"

"I want to know who squealed on my father, that's all."

"How much you gonna pay me for that?" Lee asked, feeling greedy.

"How much do you want?"

Lee thought for a moment. "How about three thousand."

"Okay." Sal answered immediately.

He answered too quickly, thought Lee. "Can I raise that price?"

"To what?" Sal asked, patiently.

"How about five thousand?"

"Fine," Sal said after a moment of silence. "I just hope you give me the right information. I wouldn't like to be misled."

"Don't worry. I know exactly who it was," Lee said with confidence.

"Oh, do you?"

"I sure do. Because my cousin, Agent Ayers was there during the confession. He and his partner were doing the interrogation. He told me all about it, although he swore me to secrecy."

"Well, who was it?" Sal asked, picking at a piece of lint on his jacket.

"Someone you never would guess…" continued Lee, falling into his old habit of stringing people along and keeping them in suspense.

Sal stared at Lee dead in the eyes. Lee almost gasped aloud at the deadly look in the other man's eyes. It was clear that this was not a man to be tampered with. This was hardly a McMillan type. Lee decided it would be best to get right to the point. The man, Sal, didn't say a word, but he certainly got his point across. If looks could kill.

"It was one of your father's lawyers," he said quickly.

Sal tensed at this. "Which one? Earnest Hurst?"

Lee thought for a moment and shook his head. "It was the guy with the curly, light brown hair. What was his name. A real Jew name… ahh… Abner or something like that."

Sal's eyes lit up, but his face remained relatively expressionless. "Abner Bernstein?"

"Yeah, that's it."

A beat and then, "Can I use your phone?"

"Sure, go ahead. I'll be in the bathroom."

Lee went upstairs to use the bathroom. Then he went into his room for awhile and stared at the double bed that he now slept in alone.

God he missed Irene.

Finally, Lee came back down the stairs. Now there were two men standing in his living room. One of them held an envelope.

"Here's your money. You can count it if you want," Sal said.

Lee took the envelope from the other man. He opened it and peered inside to make sure it was money in there. Green bills stared back at him. He smiled and closed the envelope.

"I'm sure that it's all here. You look like a man of your word."

Sal nodded, but said nothing.

"By the way," Lee started, deciding to throw a little bit in about McMillan, a man that he now begrudged for getting him fired, "McMillan's been after your father for years. He hates his guts."

"Oh, really," Sal said thoughtfully.

"Is there anything else I can help you gentlemen with?"

Sal shook his head. "Nothing else. Thank you for the information."

"Thank *you* for the money," Lee responded, as he saw the men out.

Ψ

"This car's been sitting here for over two weeks. Every time we patrol this area, we see it. No one's come to get it," the young dark haired officer said to his older partner.

"Come on, let's go check it out. We'll run the plates, maybe we can trace it to whoever it belongs to," the older man said as he got out of the black and white police vehicle.

The two officers made their way over to the blue Chrysler sitting on the side of the low-traffic road.

The younger officer sniffed the air as they got closer. "You smell that?"

The older officer paused, took a sniff, and continued walking. "Yeah, I smell it," he said grimly.

By the time they reached the car, the smell was overpowering. Both officers knew what the smell was—especially the older cop with his many years of experience—it was the smell of death.

"The car doesn't have any plates," the younger officer one muttered.

The car doors easily opened, since they were left unlocked. The two men gave the interior a cursory glance.

"Let's pop the trunk," the older officer said with a nod. "This time, put on your gloves. There might be fingerprints on the car we can pick up. We don't want to smudge them."

The young officer jumped back in shock and disgust once the trunk was opened. His eyes bugged out in horror at the sight before him.

The older officer stayed put—the only change in his demeanor being the squinting of his eyes.

There were two corpses stuffed into the trunk, back to back. Both were bloated and had skin that looked purplish in color. Both corpses had their wrists bound together with duct tape behind their backs and long strips of duct tape were wraped around their heads, covering their mouths.

Despite the odor, the older officer bent over to get a look at the faces. He let out a small sound of surprise.

"What?" the younger officer asked from behind him.

"This looks like Captain McMillan," the older officer answered. A beat, and then, "the other one looks to be Detective Lee. The both of them had been missing for weeks. I guess now we know where they are."

"Oh, shit," said the younger.

Ψ

Abner yawned and quickly turned his attention fully back onto the road. It was late and he was exhausted. All he wanted to do was to get home and crawl into bed. Unfortunately, his wife Dorothy and his daughter Estelle weren't going to be home tonight. They were visiting Dorothy's parents. Abner promised to join her tomorrow morning. He couldn't leave any earlier because of work.

Abner opened the door himself because he knew his butler was probably asleep and he didn't want to disturb him.

Abner closed the door behind him and went straight up the steps to his bedroom, undoing his tie and unbuttoning his shirt as he went along.

Abner undressed the rest of the way in the dark, not bothering to turn on the bedroom lights. He was going right to sleep, anyway.

Abner, with his eyes half closed, slid into bed. He shifted over and turned around into a more comfortable position and his body hit something solid. Abner, shifted back, startled.

"What the hell?" Abner muttered to himself in the darkness. He turned on the light. He now noticed a form wrapped up in a blanket lying on the bed. He had been so tired, that he hadn't noticed it.

Abner felt a trickle of dread. He felt as if his blood was freezing, at this moment, right in his veins. Abner turned on the light, pulled back the blanket, and came face to face with a very bloody and a very dead butler, his butler Milo Garcia. The dead man's eyes stared glassily back at him.

Abner yelled and jumped back from the bed. He began to panic. What was he to do? Wait, calm down. Call the police. That's what you do. Abner went straight to the nearest phone and picked it up. But it was dead. There was no dial tone. Abner slowly put the receiver back onto its cradle. There was something wrong here. Something seriously wrong. He had to get out of this house and get out of it now.

Abner slowly looked around and started towards the stairs. He was on the second step when he felt the barrel of the gun at the back of his head.

Then a male voice said, "Step back up the stairs and come into the bedroom."

Abner raised his hands in the air and stepped up the stairs backwards.

"Come on, now. To the bedroom. Don't make any sudden moves or I'll shoot you right here, right now."

"Here, I'll give you all the money that I have in the house. Just take it. I have jewelry too—"

"I don't want your fucking money. Just shut your mouth and sit down there on the bed!"

Abner turned around and sat down on the bed. His heart was beating like a drum. Sweat was pouring down his back and sweat was shining on his forehead. Abner studied the man standing before him. He was a tall man with tanned skin, close cut brown hair and brown eyes. The man had a mean slash of a mouth and stared unwaveringly at Abner with a lot of malice.

"What do you want then?" Abner asked.

"You've done a lot of wrong, Mr. Bernstein," the man said instead of answering the question. "You have to pay for that. Selfishness is never a good idea."

"What are you talking about?" Abner asked.

"You know what you did. You ratted on Rocco. You gave up all his information. Thanks to you, he'll never make it out."

"We're trying to get another hearing—"

"Bull—shit," The man said enunciating each part of the word.

Abner began to cry now. "I had too. They were going to put me away. I have a wife and a daughter that I have to raise."

"You could have talked to Mr. Gionelli. He probably would have been able to help you. But you decided to go the other way and rat out on him. Now you're going to pay. Me, Antonio Capone, is going to take you out."

"Why did you have to kill Milo?" Abner asked, distressed.

"He got in the way," the man said easily.

Abner cried and begged for his life to no avail. Fifteen minutes later, he was laid in bed beside his faithful butler of six years.

They both had matching bullet holes through the head.

Ψ

Teresa let herself into the house using her spare keys. She knew that Mr. and Mrs. Bernstein were not going to be home. She glanced at her watch. Mr. Bernstein should have left for Mrs. Bernstein's parent's house over an hour ago. It was ten o'clock in the morning.

Teresa cleaned the entire downstairs before deciding to stop for a break. She got some juice out of the fridge, poured herself a glass, drank it, and then continued cleaning. She sang a Cuban Salsa number aloud, twisting her hips a little as she carried her cleaning supplied up the stairs. As was customary, she was going to start with the Bernsteins' bedroom. The door was closed. Teresa pushed the door open and once her eyes took in the grisly scene before her, her song stopped short in her throat.

She let out a blood curdling scream.

Ψ

"Okay, you wait here. We'll bring him right in," the prison guard said to Earnest.

Earnest nodded and sat at the Formica table. He glanced at the clock on the wall, it was ten past four in the afternoon.

Earnest watched as Lawrence Rice was ushered in through the door. He had handcuffs and shackled on his ankles. Once he was seated, the prison guard locked the shackles onto the leg of the chair and took off the hand cuffs. The prison guard stood up and looked at Earnest.

"When you're done in here, you can knock on the glass on the door. We'll come in and bring him back to his cell."

Earnest nodded. "Thank you."

The prison guard nodded and left, locking the door behind him. Earnest and Lawrence were in the room alone.

Lawrence gave him a wry grin. "They have me locked down like an animal."

Earnest gave him an apologetic smile. "That's prison life, I guess."

"Yeah," Lawrence said bitterly. "So, what did you come here for?"

"I came here to talk about Abner Bernstein."

At the mention of that name, Lawrence's face twisted with disgust. "That bastard. He ratted on me, just to save his ass."

"What do you mean?" Abner asked, confused.

Lawrence leaned in towards Earnest and wagged a finger at him to come closer.

"I wasn't the only one in on this thing. He was in on it as well. I wasn't allowed to mention Abner at all during the trail and otherwise. They told me that if I did, I'll be tacking on some more years to my sentence. They didn't want any leaks—to the media or otherwise. Now here I am, rotting away in prison, while he's out there, walking around, scott free, because he gave up all the information on me. But I figured that he had to give up more than just the details of our scheme to keep out of jail, and I was right."

Abner's face went pale. "I don't believe you. I don't believe that Abner would get involved with something like that."

"Well then, you're a damned fool if you don't. So you can get the hell outta here and leave me alone," Lawrence said nastily. He was about to raise his arm for the guard when Earnest reached over and touched his arm.

"Please. I'm sorry. I'll listen to what you have to say," Earnest said pleadingly.

Lawrence slowly lowered his arm, keeping his blue eyes fixed on Earnest as he did so. "I'm here on a favor for you. Don't you forget it."

"Please, continue. I'm glad that you granted me this."

Lawrence grunted and looked away.

"First of all, who told you that Abner told on you?"

"I can't reveal my sources, but bread will make a person open up like a whore in a hotel."

Earnest cringed at the vulgar analogy, but continued. "Do you know who might have wanted to kill Abner?"

"I wanted to. But unfortunately, someone got to him first." Lawrence let out a cackle.

Earnest ignored this comment. "Do you have any idea who would have wanted to kill him?"

"Besides me? I don't know," Lawrence said shrugging his broad shoulders. Lawrence's face darkened. "And it wasn't me that did it. Nor did I hire anyone to do it, if you know what I mean."

Earnest nodded. Somehow, he believed him. "Is there anything else?"

Lawrence squinted and leaned forward in the chair. "I know that he gave me up to keep his ass out of jail. But I wasn't the only one that he gave up," Lawrence said mysteriously.

Earnest felt his blood go cold. "Who else did he tell on?"

Lawrence stared Earnest right in the eye. "I don't know, he wouldn't give me any names. But it wasn't a pauper, from what I gather. And he has some clout, whoever it is. He might've been the one to wipe of Earnest. Any idea who it might be?"

Earnest tried to keep the fear out of his voice. "If I did, do you think I would be here?"

Earnest prayed that it wasn't who he thought it was.

Ψ

Angelina rang the doorbell and waited. After about a minute, she heard someone fiddling with the latches and unlocking the door. The door swung open. Dorothy, her face blotchy, her eyes red and swollen, her red hair a messy halo, stared despondently at her Angelina. She was still in her pajamas.

"Oh honey," Angelina cried, running to hug her friend. Dorothy wrapped her arms around her short friend and sobbed into her raven hair. Then she began to ball loudly, her eye flooding and spilling tears.

Angelina eased forward, nudging them into the house. She turned slightly and closed the door. She led Dorothy to the couch. They sat down.

"Where are your parents, are they still here?" Angelina asked, patting Dorothy's pale hand.

Dorothy shook her head. "No, they left this morning. They took Estelle with them. I think it was a good idea. They wanted to stay longer, but…I needed time alone."

Angelina frowned. "I hope I'm not disturbing you. Would you like me to leave? Don't worry, I won't take offence."

Dorothy shook her head and grasped Angelina's hand. "No, no. Please stay." Her voice was like sandpaper. She looked skeletal, about ten pounds less than her usual thin form. Two weeks, and she was shrinking. Angelina was scared for her friend. Angelina wished she knew who killed poor Abner, forcing him to leave behind a wife and a baby daughter. And not only that. With the death of Abner, a more disturbing thing began to surface, and was now running rampant throughout the media. There was a rumor going around that Abner was involved in the great stockmarket scam, with the now infamous Lawrence Rice.

Dorothy as well as her family, were devastated.

"Why don't you stay with me and Earnest?" Angelina said suddenly, "Just for a while. You shouldn't be here by yourself."

"That's what my parents said. They wanted me to stay with them, but I think I'll stay here alone for a while. I need quite time. I need time to think."

Angelina nodded. "I understand perfectly. Would you at least come over for dinner?"

"Well, I really don't have much of an appetite. Thank you though. I think I'll stay here."

Angelina nodded. They talked for a while and finally, an hour later, Angelina got up to leave.

At the door, Angelina asked, "Do the police have any leads?"

"None. None at all. But they're still looking."

Suddenly there was a knock at the door. Angelina turned around and opened it. A man with a notepad stood there. He was wearing a suit.

"Ma'am," he said looking at Dorothy, "I'm from the *Voice of Illinois* and I was wondering if you could—"

Dorothy slammed the door in his face and let out a loud noise of frustration and anger. "Those dammed reporters! They don't ever stop. I tell you, they have no mercy!" Dorothy began to cry again.

Angelina hugged her. "Come on. Why don't we get you upstairs? I think you need a nap."

Dorothy allowed Angelina to lead her upstairs. When Angelina started to go towards the bedroom that Abner and she shared together, Dorothy pulled back and gasped.

"I can't go back in there. Ever. I'll sleep in another room. One of the guest bedrooms," Dorothy said somberly.

Angelina tucked Dorothy in bed and smoothed back Dorothy's hair softly with the palm of her hand. "You might get hungry later. If you do, that invitation for dinner at my house still stands."

Dorothy closed her eyelids and nodded her head slightly.

Angelina softly shut the door behind her and started down the stairs. She went out the front door and made sure that she locked the door securely behind her. For a moment, she felt fear as she considered the possibility that the person who killed Abner might still be lurking around. A flash of worry towards Dorothy went through her. She looked around, there was no one.

"Can I talk to you for a moment?"

Angelina turned around quickly, shocked at the voice. It was the reporter that had knocked at the door. He stood before her, his stupid face grinning broadly.

"Get away from me and you get away from my friend," Angelina said huffily. She continued walking towards her car.

The reported followed. "How has Miss Ashford been holding up?"

"Get away from me!" Angelina yelled, not slowing her pace.

"Is it true that Mr. Bernstein was involved in fraud and took a plea bargain—"

The reported didn't get the chance to finish his sentence because he was cut off by a sharp punch to the jaw administered by Angelina with her small fist.

The man stopped and howled in pain. He held his jaw between his hands. Angry brown eyes flashed at her. Angelina shook her hand out and continued walking to her car. Angelina could hardly believe she had just done that. She had never punched anyone in her life. More publicity was the last thing her family needed. She could see the headlines now: "Mafia princess punches reporter in the face."

She hoped he didn't sue.

Ψ

Rocco smiled broadly when he saw Earnest. His chains jingled as he came towards his son-in-law to give him a hug. He scowled in annoyance.

"Come on, come, on, take this off. I'm an old man. Where am I going to go?" Rocco said in his accented English.

"Sorry Rocco," the prison guard said nervously. He sprung forward to take off the confinements. "It's procedure."

"Fuck procedure," Rocco growled.

Earnest was a little startled at Rocco's language. The man rarely cursed. In all Earnest's years of knowing Rocco, he could only remember a handful of times that he had heard he father-in-law curse aloud.

Rocco embraced Earnest and kissed him on the cheek. Earnest forced a smile. If his father-in-law had anything to do with Abner's death, Earnest certainly couldn't tell by looking at him. The man was totally at ease and was in good spirits.

The two men sat down across from each other.

"So how are my grandchildren?" Rocco asked, with a smile. His face, quite smooth for a man about to enter his seventy fourth year, was bright and warm.

Earnest shifted in his seat, unsure of how to react to Rocco. "They're fine. Matthew just got onto the little league baseball team."

Rocco slapped his knees with a smile. "I knew he would get in. he's got skill, Earnest. He'll be the next Joe DiMaggio. I can feel it."

Earnest nodded and gave a thin smile. This was turning out to be harder than he thought it would be.

"Angelina was over at Dot's house last week. Dot's not doing so great. She's really crushed about this whole thing."

Rocco's smile wavered. Something flashed in his eyes but was quickly gone before Earnest could read or recognize it. "I'm sorry she's hurting so much," Rocco said finally

"Yeah so am I. Especially when it could have been avoided. Senseless killing is never easy to get over, don't you think?" Earnest asked, steadily.

Rocco frowned. "Earnest, is there something you want to talk about?"

"We're talking now, aren't we?" Earnest responded, in a calm tone.

"Is there something on your mind, I mean."

"Yes. As a matter of fact there is."

"Well, why didn't you talk about it from the get go? It's not good to keep things bottled up," Rocco said simply.

"Well, it's never easy thinking that your wife's father might have murdered a dear and close friend."

"What are you talking about, Earnest?" Rocco asked, frowning.

"You want me to put it simply? I'll put it simply. Maybe you might decide to get me knocked off too, if God wills it, let it be. I believe you had Abner murdered. I know that he was involved in the stock scam. He gave information on you to keep him out of jail. That is what I believe. Who else could it have been? Who else does he know with a rap sheet that's as long as the Mississippi River? Who else does he know who would do a contract killing like the one done on him?"

Rocco's usually full lips were drawn into a thin straight line. His dark eyes were luminous and penetrating. Two dark inky pools. Earnest forced himself to look Rocco straight in the eyes.

"Who said it was a contract killing?" Rocco said in a low tone of voice.

"The way he was killed, Rocco. Execution style. It's just too much to be a coincidence. He was killed for a reason."

Rocco stared at him, but said nothing.

"What I want to know is, how could you do that to him when he has a baby? He will never get to see Estelle grow up. He will never get to see her get married. He will never get to see his grandchildren. All of the things you were given the privilege to see with all your three children. And then there's Dorothy. She loved him so much, Rocco. I doubt that she'll ever get over his death."

Rocco continued to stare, not saying anything.

"Why don't you just admit it!"

"Because there's nothing to admit," Rocco said cool as a cucumber. "I never ordered a hit on him."

Earnest stood up quickly and gestured to the guard. "You're lying, Rocco. I know you ordered that hit. You murdered my best friend."

The guard opened the room. Earnest pushed past the guards and stalked away.

This was more than Earnest could take.

Ψ

When Rocco had first found out that Sal was the person to order the hit on Abner, he had been furious. His son hadn't bothered to consult him, deliberately doing the killing behind Rocco's back. Rocco hadn't even known that Abner had been the one to snitch on him until after Abner was dead. Had he known what Sal had planned, he would have persuaded him not to do it. Now, Rocco was mad that Abner had told on him, but at the same time, he couldn't really blame him for it. Abner had gotten into trouble with the law, and he had been trying to save his family and himself by giving out information. It wasn't the smartest thing to do and maybe, if Rocco hadn't been sent to jail he would have done what his son Sal had done, but the fact was that he was already behind bars when he first found out about Abner's ratting so what would killing the man change? What's done is done. Besides. He was an old man. He had lived his life. He had seen his children married and had seen his grandchildren. He would be eighty in six years. He was precariously close to the end of the road. Abner, on the other hand, was relatively young, still had half his life to live, still had to be a father to his daughter, had to see her get married, have children…all this Abner would never see.

But really, now that Rocco was in jail and was most surely going to die in there, Sal had taken over. Rocco has stepped into retirement. Sal was the one making all the shots now. Sal was the cheese. A position that Rocco was sure Sal had desired from his father for as long as Sal knew what the 'family business' was.

Rocco was too old to fight anymore. He missed his children, he missed his grandchildren, but most of all, he missed his lovely wife, Wendy. At least he had made good provisions for her. She would live very well for the remainder of her days. She had been the loving and loyal person that he had always loved throughout this whole ordeal. She came to see him every week and she brought him things. They would sit and talk for hours, holding hands and laughing. But he wouldn't blame her if she were to ask for a divorce. He loved her enough to grant her one. And if she decided to get married again, she was only fifty-five after all, she would still be given a portion of his money. But she would be most wise if she were to wait for him to die. She would get a great deal more, Rocco often mused to himself. He was sure, that indeed, death was just around the corner. Indeed, every day, it seemed to be staring him in the face.

Ψ

When her husband came in through the door that evening, Angelina instantly knew something was wrong. His face was drawn, his forehead was furrowed, and the lines around the corners of his mouth were more pronounced. His lips were drawn into a straight line. His eyes were fiery.

Angelina helped him out of his coat and followed him into the living room.

"Honey, what's the matter? You look upset."

"Where are the children?" Earnest asked, instead.

"They're not home yet," Angelina said. "So let's talk."

"I'll tell you what's the matter," Earnest said, flashing her a look. "Your father's a cold blooded murderer. That's what."

Angelina stepped back as if she was slapped. She blinked and stared at him with her mouth slightly hanging open. An expression of shock was all over her face.

"Earnest, what are you talking about? What happened?"

"Your father killed my best friend! Your father killed our children's godfather. That's what. He ordered a hit on Abner, Angie," Earnest hissed.

Angelina's eyes filled with tears. "Did my father tell you this?"

"No. But I know it, Angie. I know it in here," Earnest said pointing his chest. "Most of all, I feel it in my gut. There are just too many things that point to him."

Angelina began to sob. "How could you say that, Earnest. My father wouldn't do that."

"But he did."

"Damn you, Earnest! Take it back! Don't you dare—"

"Dare what, Angie!" Earnest said stepping closer to her. "I suppose your father will kill me off next."

Angelina smacked him in the face. The sharp noise resonated throughout the room. They stood and stared at each other for a while. Earnest looked slightly shocked. He rubbed his cheek.

"I see you like to smack and hit people," Earnest said calmly walking towards the stairs. Angelina followed.

"I didn't mean to—"

"You have quick hands," Earnest said ascending the stairs. He walked towards their bedroom.

"No, no I don't!" yelled Angelina. "What are you doing?" she asked, when she saw Earnest pull a suitcase down from the shelf.

"You were in the papers, don't you know. You punched a reporter in the face," Earnest continued as he began to pack clothes into the suitcase.

Angelina gritted her teeth. "He was harassing me! I told him to go away and he wouldn't. He was right outside of Dot's house!"

"You're like your father! You're crazy!" Earnest screamed. "How do you think that makes me look? Me, a well known, respected lawyer with seniority, having a wife that punches people in the face. You're forty-two, for God's sakes! You're not a child anymore Angelina. But I guess that's the result of one being pampered her whole life!"

"You talk as if you weren't born with a silver spoon in your mouth!" Angelina screamed. "Your family and their Southern aristocracy. To think that the lily white, protestant bloodline is now marred with wop blood!" screamed Angelina

Earnest turned around on her with anger in his green eyes. "Don't you dear put me on that lowdown level, Angelina. Not when it's not true."

"But it is, Earnest. Your parents hated me!"

"But my mother loved you, did she not? Maybe not at the beginning, but she came around. You can't deny that. Besides, what my parents or anyone else feels about you is not the issue at the moment."

"But isn't it? It has to do with this when it comes to you pointing fingers at my father and dehumanizing him. My father has never made you feel anything other than welcome into my family. He loves you, Earnest. He always talks about you."

"More than your brother Sal, no doubt. Because around me, he doesn't talk at all. I think he despises me. In fact, I know it. He was against me from the beginning." Earnest let out a mirthful laugh. "I am an inheritance from his father. That is the only reason he didn't cast me away as the family lawyer the moment Rocco was put in jail. But I'm sure he'll replace me soon. He couldn't do it quick enough for me! In fact, I'll break the ties myself. Save him from having to do the whole messy business of it." Earnest closed the now filled suitcase and zippered it up.

"Where are you going Earnest?" Angelina asked, anxiously. "Why are you packing?"

Earnest turned to her, his eyes sad and full of overwhelming emotion. He stepped towards her, until he was mare inches away from her body. But he did not touch her.

"What am I supposed to do? I can't go back to my practice now that Abner's gone...he was a part of it. A part of me. And the way he was killed...I can't bear to look at the place anymore," Abner said turning his face away.

Angelina reached up and touched his face. He cringed at her touch. She lowered her arm. Her face full of grief. "Do you hate me that much Earnest?"

Earnest was silent. He continued to look off to the side, but Angelina could see his eyes filling with tears.

"Then set up somewhere else. We can look for a new office together."

Earnest shook his head. He was still looking away from her. "I don't think I want to practice law anymore—at least not now, at this moment. At the very least, I need a break. But I think my days of litigation and trials are over. The ranch is there in Texas. I think I want to go there for a while and relax...to think things through. Get my life together."

Angelina wiped at her tears. "But this is where we live...how can we leave and move to Texas? That's almost like a completely different world! It would be so hard for the kids to adjust...and what about our friends...and my family. My brother. I don't want to leave Anthony or my father."

"Your father's in jail. Your brother is a grown man." Earnest said dryly. He looked at her now, his face filled with bitter mirth. "I tell you. I wonder if you care for me, your own husband, as much as you care for the two of them. You behave as if you cannot survive without them."

"I don't know...oh, Earnest. I don't know!"

Earnest pursed his lips and closed the second suitcase. He lifted one and headed out of the room and down the stairs. Angelina followed.

"Did you hear me? I don't know!" Angelina cried. She was gasping in hysteria as she attempted to catch up with him.

"Well, perhaps I should go down there by myself. Sort my mind out. Get back on track. Afterwards...you and the kids come down or...maybe I'll come back up here. Which ever way," Earnest sighed. "Angelina, I think we need some time apart. We need room. This has been too much. Just too much that we don't agree on...too much that I can't live with. And these are things that are too big to ignore."

Angelina looked at him in the face, her eyes beseeching. "Are you leaving me Earnest?"

Earnest looked away. "I didn't say that. I just think we need some time apart. Please, you must understand. I'll stay to say goodbye to the kids. I would never force you to explain it to them by yourself. That wouldn't be fair."

Angelina cried silently, glanced at the floor, raised her head and looked at Earnest again. She nodded her head. Earnest held out his arms. Angelina fell into them. They held each other for a while.

"Do you still love me Earnest?" Angelina mumbled into the front of his shirt.

"I'll always love you."

Chapter Thirty

October, 1964

"So, what time are we going to meet them?" Anthony asked Sal, as he took a sip of lemonade. He pursed his lips. "This lemonade is a little too sour," Anthony said putting it on the table beside him.

"Tell that to Margarite. She's the one that made it. Besides, Marie likes it like that," Sal said with a little smile.

Anthony bugged his eyes out and then smiled. "And risk your housekeeper's wrath? I don't think so."

"Okay. So you, Riccardo, and Bernie are going to meet Chavez and two of his men at the warehouse at exactly one A.M. We'll send men out to watch the warehouse for about two day before the meeting. We will use seven men in all. They'll watch in shifts. They'll look around, search out the area to make sure Chavez isn't up to anything. Now, on the actual day of the meeting, five men will stay outside to take out Chavez's other men waiting in the car, right after Chavez enters the warehouse, right before the exchange. I know he'll have men waiting outside in a car, despite the fact that he claims it'll only be the three of them. He'll have them for backup. Now. You're going to have the money. The moment you hand them the money, and Chavez gives you the gun shipment, the two of our men who will be hiding in the rafters, will shoot Chavez and the other two dead. When our men outside hear the gun shots, they'll come busting in to help. So we'll have the guns *and* our money in the end."

"Will Riccardo, Bernie, and I have a piece on us?"

Sal shook his head. "No. Chavez's three other men will shake you and the other two down to make sure you don't. They said that you can return the favor."

"So the three of them are not supposed to have any guns on them either."

"Correct, but…"

"But what?"

"There's always a chance that they will have guns...somewhere in the warehouse nearby. That's why we're sending men ahead to search the area out."

Anthony nodded his head. "This is going to be tricky, huh."

Sal gave him a lopsided grin. "Yeah. I guess it will. I could send somebody else in your place and you would still get a good cut of the money. But you said you wanted to go."

"And I do," Anthony said.

Ψ

Anthony, Bernie, and Riccardo stood before the short, Argentinean man and his two side kicks. The two sides greeted each other half heartedly. Then they patted each other down.

"Wait. Let me check your truck and you can check mine as well," Chavez said indicating the small shipment truck that Anthony had driven into the warehouse in order to receive the guns.

"Sure. Go right on ahead," Anthony said. Riccardo and Bernie checked the cargo area of Chavez's truck. They looked at the crate in the back.

"Those are the guns," Chavez said flatly.

After being satisfied that there wasn't a gun on anyone, they got right down to business.

"You got the money?" Chavez asked, in heavy accent. His pale, pasty skin looked gray under the lights of the warehouse. The two, taller men stood beside him looking menacing.

Anthony nodded and opened the suitcase. Chavez looked in and nodded approvingly. One of Chavez's men walked up to a medium sized crate, crowbarred it open, and gestured for Anthony to step forward and look. The crate was filled with various guns—all black-market.

"One hundred and nineteen guns in all. Twenty Uzi's, ten Carbine rifles, ten magnums, nine Beretta pistols, ten M60 machine guns, twenty M16's, ten High Standards, fifteen Stens, and fifteen AK-47's."

"Good. Then it's all here. Shall we make the transaction gentlemen?"

Chavez nodded, his face bland. Anthony stepped forward and handed the suitcase to Chavez. The men transferred the crate of guns from Chavez's truck into Anthony's.

"Well, it was nice doing business with you gentlemen," Anthony said.

Suddenly, there was a succession of three shots. Chavez screamed and fell forward, clutching his middle. One of the men was hit in the head and the chest. He toppled over as well, a look of surprise on his face. The other man pulled a pistol from the back of his pants. He made a shot towards the rafters. It was so dark up there, that they were more or less invisible to him. A man fell from the rafters, yelling all the way down until he hit the concrete floor. Then he was silent.

"How the hell did he get a gun?" Anthony said before he and his other two men dove for cover. The man, now desperate, turned to Anthony and made a shot at him. Anthony was hit hard in the shoulder and fell to the ground, his teeth gritted in pain. Riccardo and Bernie carried Anthony behind some boxes to hide.

Before the man could make another shot, suddenly, three other men came in through the warehouse and pumped bullets in the man. He crashed to the floor with his other companions.

The man from the rafters came down to join the others. They checked to see if the man that fell was still alive. He was dead.

"Shit. Sergio's dead," one of them said after checking for a pulse and finding none.

They went to check Chavez and his two other men. They were dead as well.

"Come on. Let's get Anthony to a hospital. Luckily, he's not too bad," Riccardo said.

"Two of the guys brought the car around. So we can take him right out and they'll take you to the hospital," one of the men said.

"Okay. The last three men that came in here will stay behind and take care of the bodies," Anthony said gritting his teeth in pain. "Bernie and Riccardo. I want you two to stay behind as well to get the truck with the guns, and the money, outta here," Anthony said, barely above a whisper.

When Anthony was safely in the back of the car, two of his men were already in the passenger and driver's seats. As they were driving to the hospital, Anthony asked them a question.

"So, was there a car with Chavez's men outside for backup?"

The man in the passenger side called, Fred, nodded his head. "There sure was Tony. Four of 'em. But we took them out. They hardly knew what hit them. We used a suppressor."

Anthony cringed as a flash of pain overtook him.

"You all right?" Fred asked, nervously

"Yeah," Anthony said. "Mario. Just get us to the hospital as soon as you can. But don't drive too fast. We don't want no cops stopping us."

"Sure thing," Mario said as he glanced in the rearview mirror.

$$\Psi$$

August, 1965

The funeral was dignified and elegant—just as Rocco would have wanted it. There was a big turnout—Rocco was a popular man well liked in life, despite what he was. Family, friends, employees, all came to show their respect to him.

"He didn't even show up," Angelina murmured to her older brother. "I thought he would be here."

"Who? Earnest?" Sal asked her, with his eyes focused on the front of the church.

"That's right," Angelina answered. "Dad cared a lot about him. Dad would have given Earnest his right arm if he asked for it." Angelina sighed and wiped the tears from her face with the back of her hands. "Gosh. I don't know how much more of this I can take. I feel as if I'm losing everyone in my life. First Earnest runs away from me, then Winston, my own son, doesn't want to be around me and then my father dies."

Sal put an arm around his little sister's shoulders. "It's going to be okay, Angelina. Things will work out."

"I hope so," Angelina said despondently.

At the wake, Angelina greeted all the guests and then disappeared upstairs. She was definitely not in the mood to play hostess. Let Marie and her brothers do it.

Angelina went into the upstairs guest bedroom and closed the door. She sat on the bed and stared at the phone. She took a deep breath and picked it up. She dialed her husband's number in Texas.

Earnest picked up on the third ring.

"Hello?" He sounded out of breath.

"Hey," Angelina responded.

The voice chilled considerably. "Hi. How are you feeling?"

"How do you think I feel. I just came back from my father's funeral," Angelina said sharply.

There was a silence. Angelina continued.

"Why didn't you come? I thought you said you would."

"I decided that it would have been a bad idea. Besides, how could I, considering. It would have been too uncomfortable for all of us there."

Angelina felt a flash of anger. "I can't believe you're still pursuing that train of thought. You need to give it up, Earnest."

"If I didn't still believe, do you think I'll be miles away from you?"

Angelina was silent. Earnest cleared his throat.

"How are the children doing?" Earnest asked, changing the subject.

"They're fine. Right now, they're downstairs." There was a pause and then Angelina hesitantly asked, "How's Winston?"

"He's okay. Look, I tried to get him to fly out but—"

"I understand," Angelina said cutting him off gently. There was a another pause and then, "Earnest, I've been thinking. Maybe we should…I think we've been dragging this along and I don't know anymore. We need to do something. It isn't right to have the kids in limbo like this. This is why Winston is behaving this way, I think. Although, I don't know why it's only him reacting this strongly. The others…"

"Yes. I agree," Earnest said a little sadly.

"Should we…I mean…do you see us working this out?"

Earnest exhaled a deep breath. "Honestly, I can't go back to that life, Angelina. I love it down here. It's simplicity. No pressures, no absolute time schedule…I enjoy running this ranch. I never thought that I would. I never thought I would enjoy having a life like this, but I do, Angelina. I don't want to be around those things anymore, Angelina. It all seems so dreary and meaningless now. Unless you can come down here and be with me…I don't see another way. I just can't go back to that life."

Angelina wiped at a fallen tear. "I can't leave my family, Earnest. I'm sorry. I grew up here and I've lived here all my life. I can't uproot.

And I can't accept the way you feel about my father and the rest of my family."

Earnest sighed. "Then I guess this is it. I'm glad that were able to talk amicably. I'll send over the divorce papers."

Angelina sniffed and nodded. "Yes. Just send them over and I'll sign them."

"Well, I'd better be getting back, Angelina. I have a lot to do. I'm sorry about your hurt."

"But you're not sorry my father's dead."

Earnest didn't answer. There was no need to.

Ψ

"Michael and I have decided to move in together," Edda announced to Wendy one afternoon during lunch. It was a hot August afternoon. They were sitting out on the deck having lunch together. Just the two of them.

Wendy's fork paused halfway between her plate and her mouth. She looked at her daughter with eyebrows raised.

"Honey, are you sure about this?"

Edda nodded. "Very sure. Michael and I were meant to be, Mom. We love each other."

Wendy brought the forkful of food the rest of the way to her mouth. She chewed slowly and swallowed with a little difficulty.

"Michael's a wonderful man," Wendy said carefully.

"You're preaching to the choir, Mom," said Edda cheerfully. Her bright blue eyes were flashing with happiness.

Wendy smiled at her daughter. Michael certainly had an effect on her, and she couldn't blame her daughter for loving him. Not only had Michael matured into an incredibly handsome young man, he was also incredibly bright with a good heart and a sense of humor. But he was also extremely intense, and sometimes that threw Wendy off kilter. It was the only thing that made Wendy a little uncomfortable about him.

"Edda, I'm not holding any punches. This relationship is not easy as it is, considering. Are you sure that you won't be complicating things by moving in together?"

Edda shook her head. "Why would it Mom? We were meant to be together. I can feel it. I've had dreams."

"You two are so young…has he asked you to marry him?"

"Not yet. There's too much going on to think about marriage right now." Edda said in a serious tone of voice as she picked at her salad.

Wendy looked at her daughter solemnly and thought how beautiful she was with her piercing blue eyes, bright blond hair and beautifully sculpted cheekbones. She was a sight to behold. It was true that her daughter was only 22, but she had the mind of a woman twice her age, it seemed. Her daughter had always seemed to be above her years in thinking and outlook.

"So, have you two decided who will be moving in with whom?"

"We're going to get an entirely new place to live. An apartment near the campus."

"So are you excited about starting classes in a month?"

"I sure am. Pretty soon, I'll have a master's in English literature and Michael with have his masters in anthropology specializing in African and Oriental cultures. Can you believe that? He even wants to continue learning Hindi. Mom, you should hear him speak it. It's amazing."

"I'm so proud of you two. I can still remember when you two were eleven years old. The years go by so fast," Wendy thought wistfully. She sipped her grape juice.

"So what are you doing this weekend?" Wendy asked her daughter.

"We're going to a war protest rally that they're holding on campus," Edda answered easily.

Wendy stared at her daughter, speechless for a moment. "You know, you never cease to amaze me."

Edda smiled. "Really Mom? I would think you'd be used to it by now."

Ψ

They met in a restaurant in the city. Penny got there first. When Alfie walked in, he was shocked to see a toddler sitting on Penny's lap at the table. Alfie could see the toddler's golden blond hair that curled softly on her head. The toddler was playing with the table cloth, while Penny tried to distract her by making funny faces and singing softly to her.

Alfie walked up to the table and gave Penny a smile.

"Hi." he kissed her quickly on the cheek. He turned his eyes to the little girl sitting on her mother's lap.

"I'm assuming that this is Marsha."

Penny smiled nervously. "Yes, it is."

"She's adorable. I know Quincy must be really proud," Alfie said pleasantly.

Penny smiled, a little less brightly this time. "He is."

"I didn't know you were bringing her," Alfie said shifting in his seat. "I thought this was going to be a meeting between only the two of us. I'm sure little Marsha would have been happy to stay with her daddy."

Penny moved uncomfortably. "Well, actually, Quincy's at the conference. Apparently, no women are allowed. It's like an 'all boys's club'. We didn't know it until we got here. Can you believe it? After all the work that I've done. I had to stay behind in the hotel. I had no one to keep her with, so I brought her along."

Alfie smiled, "Oh. okay. Well that's fine. Me and children get along pretty well," he said touching the little soft hand of the pretty girl. Marsha turned her amber eyes to Alfie.

"Oh, she's got eyes like you," Alfie said, studying the small child.

"That's right," Penny said softly.

Alfie frowned slightly and looked at the child's curling light blond hair, so unlike Penny's copper hair and Quincy's brown hair, but an exact match to his. Alfie examined the child's full eyebrows and her small, narrow, straight, nose—quite different from Penny's own cute snubbed one and Quincy gently arched one. It looked like his own nose. In fact, the child looked very much like him.

Alfie looked up at Penny with questions in his eyes and confusion in his face. Penny stared back, not saying anything.

"She has your eyes and face shape, but that's about it," Alfie said in quiet contemplation.

Penny nodded and looked down.

"And she looks nothing like Quincy," Alfie added softly.

"I know," Penny muttered.

"In fact, she looks a lot like me." Alfie reached across the table and touched Penny's hand. "Penny, is this my child?"

Penny stared blankly at him for a while and then nodded quickly. She flushed and looked down. "I didn't want to tell you."

"Quincy doesn't know, does he."

Penny shook her head. "He thinks she's his. He always says that she looks like his mother. His mother's a blond with mostly Scandinavian ancestry."

Alfie sat back and let out a sigh. "What are we going to do?"

"Nothing. Just go on living our lives," Penny said firmly. "What we did was a mistake. I should have never slept with you."

"But I love you."

Penny shook her head. "It doesn't matter. What matters is that Quincy can never know. He's my husband and I do love him, Alfie. He's very good to me."

"But, she's my child. What if I want to be part of her life?"

Penny hesitated and said, "I could send you pictures, write you letters about her…things like that. But that's it." A pause and then, "I swear, if you ruin my marriage Alfie…I'll never forgive you for it."

Alfie looked at his daughter again and then back up at Penny.

"Fine. If that's the way you want it."

Ψ

March, 1966

Ester slipped into the house as quietly as she could. As she crept up the stairs, she berated herself over and over again. What was she doing? A married, middle aged woman over fifty, sneaking around with another man.

Ester and Marco had been seeing each other for about six years now. It was a long, drawn out affair that Ester had expected to end a long time ago. But it hadn't. Marco was in it for the long haul and never lost any interest in her. In fact, it seemed, that he loved her more than ever. A love that appeared to grow with every year that they were together.

Ester had been discreet about it, making sure that Garret and Michael never found out about it. The only person that knew anything was Wendy. And that had been an accident. What happened was that Marco and Ester had been out for dinner—Ester had recommended a small, but neat little Caribbean restaurant—and they had eaten there. Ester had thought it would be okay, considering it was in a black community and nowhere near anyone that she knew. Of course it had been a bit of a surprise for the people in the restaurant when Ester and Marco had walked in, but the dinner had been pleasant. After they had finished eating, they left and got into the car. Ester had asked him to stop at a store before he dropped her off, so they did. Marco insisted on waiting outside the car for her, if he didn't go into the store. He wanted to make sure she got in and out okay. When Ester came out, she was heading back towards the car, and was quite close to both Marco and the car, just when she heard a familiar voice call her name. Ester turned around, horrified to see that it was Wendy. Ester, trying to remain calm, had turned around and spoke to Wendy, pretending that she had come to the store by bus. Wendy had told her to come and get a lift home with her. Ester had begged off saying, she had some other things to do and wasn't ready to go home as yet. When they finally said goodbye, Ester began to walk towards the bus stop, playing the role. Then when Wendy was out of sight, Marco had picked her up there in his car, his face grim. Ester knew that he hated running around in secret. But there wasn't anything that Ester could do about it. She had a family to think about. He had to accept it…or leave.

Whenever Ester thought about Marco and asked herself whether she loved him or not, she decided that she did. But the fact was that she couldn't give him what he so desperately wanted, which was for her to divorce her husband.

The next day, Wendy had invited her over. As they were having refreshments out on the patio, Wendy had asked Ester if she had seen Marco standing outside a car in the parking lot of the store where they had met, yesterday. In her mind, Ester remembered that Wendy would know who Marco was. After all, he was one of Rocco's 'business associates' that had frequented the house. Ester said she didn't see Marco. After some other subtle questions, Wendy had asked her straight out if she was seeing Marco. Ester couldn't continue lying to her friend. She admitted to it, but swore Wendy to secrecy. Wendy, although sounding quite disappointed, reluctantly agreed to keep her secret.

But lately, it was becoming more and more apparent that Marco wasn't willing, any longer, to be the man on the side. He wanted Ester to bring their relationship in the forefront, divorce Garret, and marry him. They would often have long arguments about it, where Ester would threaten to never see him again, and then he would acquiesce, halfheartedly, to her decision.

"Come on. Why don't we go to California next weekend, it'll be fun," Marco said to her one day as they were driving around.

Ester looked at him strangely. "California? All the way out there?"

"Yeah. I have a beach house just outside of L.A. with an ocean front view. We can stay there. Also, I own a restaurant down there. I haven't been down to check on it in person for quite a while. We'll have fun. We can stay for the weekend. So what do you say?"

"What am I supposed to tell my husband? I can't just pick up and leave. He'll be wondering where I was."

"Tell him that you're visiting family. You have family down there, don't you?"

"Well…I do have a cousin. But I barely speak to her."

"Well, strike up an imaginary relationship with her and tell him that you're going down to visit her."

"What if he wants to come along?"

"Tell him that your cousin wouldn't be comfortable around him and that she needed to speak to you in private. She's having problems, women problems. I don't know. Just tell him anything."

Ester thought about this for a while. She thought of the sand between her feet, a beautiful spacious beach house, and the salty air. She thought of a whole weekend with Marco, with whom was never a dull moment, which was more than she could say for Garret who was beginning to slow down considerably since he started having heart problems.. She decided to tell her husband that she was going to Virginia instead. Her mother lived there and Garrett didn't like her too much and would be happy to stay behind.

"Okay. Let's do it," Ester said with a smile.

Ψ

Alfie looked at the letter addressed to him from Nairobi, Kenya. It was from Penny. He sat on his bed and began reading. He was so absorbed in Penny's descriptions of the Savanna and the natives and the culture that he didn't hear a key turning in the door of his condo. But he did notice when the door to his bedroom was flung open and Laura poked her smiling face through the door. She came into the room, wearing a wool micro mini skirt, as was the fashion at the time, a sweater, and oxfords. Her golden brown hair was pulled back into a pony tail. She looked lovely.

Alfie quickly stuck the letter behind his back and gave her a smile.

"Come on, Alf. What are you hiding there from me?" Laura asked, playfully. She approached the bed. Alfie's eyes slid down to her long, shapely legs. They were beautiful.

Not long after meeting each other seven years ago, when Alfie was a reporter and Laura was a freelance editor at the *Chicago Informant*, they expressed interest in each other and started a relationship. They had been together ever since. But sometimes it came to Alfie's mind that Laura had only shown interest in him after his successful string of reports on Leslie Emerson's company had put his name into the limelight and made him one of the most popular people in the media. Afterwhich, he resigned from the *Chicago Informant* and started his own currents events magazine called, *On the Spot News*. That Laura was an opportunist, was a thought that he tried to brush off whenever it came to mind.

"Nothing at all, my dear. I'm just reading a letter from a friend," Alfie said easily. "But enough of that. Come over here, I've missed you so much," Alfie said stretching out his arms towards her.

Laura grinned mischievously, "Really? How much do you miss me."

"Come over here and let me show you, beautiful."

Laura smugly came over and hopped into bed with him. She wrapped her arms around him. "Sleeping with the editor-in-chief of his own magazine certainly has its perks."

Alfie smiled and kissed her on the top of her head. "I think the sex is the best perk of all," Alfie said jokingly.

"Mmmm...so do I," Laura said leaning back to stare Alfie straight in the face. She kissed him on the lips and wrapped her slender arms around his neck.

"I think I'm the luckiest man in the world," Alfie said when they came up for air.

"Is that why you haven't asked me to marry you yet?" Laura said jokingly.

Alfie tensed at this. Laura noticed and let out a small laugh. "Alfie, you take me too seriously. I was just joking."

Alfie forced a smile and then let his face get serious. "You know I care about you, right?"

Laura nodded with a smile. "I know. But just so that I can get reminded a little more…why don't you show me?"

Alfie smiled, fully. "Gladly, Miss. Fox."

Ψ

When Michael came in from his classes at four P.M., he found Edda sitting at the kitchen table studying. He came over and kissed her on the forehead. Edda looked up and smiled. She wrapped her arms around his neck and kissed him deeply on his lips. Michael slipped a hand under her blouse and cupped her left breast. Edda gently pulled back.

"My, my. Don't you have an appetite," Edda said in a husky voice. She ran her hand through Michael's thick afro. It was soft and wooly to the touch. She slid her hands down to cup the sides of his smooth, mahogany skin. She ran a finger over his mustache. "It's growing in nicely."

"I'm trying. I think that maybe it's time to grow a beard as well."

Edda nodded and smiled, intrigued.

Michael smiled and stood up. He smoothed down his colorful Dashiki. "Speaking of appetite…I smell something cooking and it smells good."

"It's curry rice and lentils," Edda said proudly.

Michael raised his eyebrows, impressed. "Well, you're certainly becoming the exotic cook. I love it when you come home first because that means that I get to taste some of that nice foreign food."

"Thank you. I'm so glad that we became vegetarian, Michael. That lecture that we went to last December really opened my eyes. The way they slaughter those animals is cruel and evil."

Michael nodded his head solemnly. "It is. We're still going to that meeting in California this weekend, right?"

"We'd better! I have my clothes packed and everything."

Michael smiled. "We're going to learn more about yoga and meditation. That's really important for our spirituality."

Edda nodded. "Hearing you talk about those Eastern religions really has me interested in them. They seem to be so at peace and spiritual," Edda said dishing out the food onto two plates. "So unlike the West with all its problems."

Michael nodded as he sat down at the table. "I've learned a lot considering it's my course of study. Christianity is oppressive and racists. Christians were the ones that brought slaves over here and kept them shackled mentally and physically for all these years."

Edda nodded her blond head. "You're right Michael. We need a revolution."

"It's coming my dear, it is coming," Michael said a little fiercely.

They ate there dinner and continued to discuss the exciting weekend ahead of them.

Ψ

"So, where's Santino? I thought he said that he was coming with us tonight," Anthony said, as he, Bernie and Riccardo walked toward the club.

"Nah. He said he had something to do," Bernie responded, with a shrug of his shoulders.

Suddenly, a figure emerged from the shadows and approached Anthony and his friends. It was a young, teenaged black girl. Her face was all done up in garish make up. Her hair gently coiffed, fell slightly past her earlobes. She wore an impossibly short mini skirt and a tight top that exposed the top of her small bosom. Her big brown eyes stared coyly at the men. Her full lips were upturned in a cheeky smile.

"How ya'll doing?" she asked, in a syrupy voice.

The three men stared at her, taken aback at the sight of her. They exchanged glances.

Bernie half smiled and said, "We're doin' good. What about you?"

The girl batted thick, false eyelashes at them. "I was doing good. And then I saw you three and now I'm doing even better."

Anthony stared at the girl uncomfortably. It was clear that she was a prostitute, but she was so young. She looked no older than sixteen, despite the overdone make-up. Anthony had seen his share of hookers and escorts in his life, after all, it was part of his business. But he had never employed one under the age of seventeen or eighteen.

"Come on, you all. Let's go," Anthony said urging them on. He wanted no part of this.

"She's cute, ain't she. Nice looking little chocolate thing," said Bernie, his eyes looking at her lustfully.

"Yeah, but what's she doing around here?" Riccardo wondered aloud as they continued walking.

The girl hung behind, watching them as they entered the club, a smirk fixed firmly on her pretty face.

About three hours later, the three men came back out of the club and headed towards the car. As they walked down the block, they saw the same girl leaning up against a lamp post, staring boldly at them.

Riccardo leered. "Looky here, she's back."

Anthony gave Ricardo a thin smile and looked towards the girl who was staring straight at him.

"What do you want, little girl," Anthony asked, wishing she would get outta here. "This ain't a good place to be."

"Really? Because the business is real good around here," she retorted and gave him a saucy grin.

Bernie let out a chuckle. "I say we take her with us." He then addressed the girl. "Would you like to have a little fun with us?"

Anthony gave his friend a sharp look. "She's a kid. She can't be anymore than sixteen, while we are a bunch of men in our forties and thirties. I don't think so."

"Hah!" the girl said loudly. "Shows how much you know. I'm eighteen," she said lying through her teeth.

The conversation was cut short by the loud sound of bullets spraying from a passing car. The few people that were on the block ducked or ran for cover. Bernie and Riccardo plunged to the ground. Anthony instinctively ran to the girl and pulled her to the floor, but not before Anthony felt a slug hit him in the chest. Anthony let out a cry of pain. The girl was screaming her head off. Four men, carrying guns, ran out of the club, hopped into their car and followed the speeding car around a corner and out of sight. The sound of bullets being exchanged could be heard in the distance.

"Shit! Tony got hit," Bernie said crawling towards Anthony who was lying on the floor with a bright red stain on the front of his shirt. Riccardo came towards him as well.

"Let's get him into the car," Riccardo said anxiously. "Kid, why don't you take a hike?" he said turning to the teenaged girl. The girl gave him a nasty look and stood up on her skinny legs.

"Is he going to be all right?" she asked, pointing at Anthony.

"Not if we don't get him to the hospital right now," Bernie said, putting Anthony into the back seat of the car. "You didn't get hurt, did ya kid?"

The girl shook her head.

Bernie and Riccardo climbed into the car and slammed the door shut. The girl stood in the sidewalk looking at them as they pulled off.

As Anthony lay in the car, he watched the girl's face until they pulled off and she could no longer be seen.

Ψ

"Well, the men from the club caught up with the men that did the drive by," Sal related to Anthony who was lying in the hospital bed. Anthony had come out of surgery the day before and was on the road to recovery.

Sal continued. "They found out that the men that did the drive by were part of Chavez's crew. Apparently, Chavez's cousin, Juan Santiago, sent them after you. Avenging his cousin's death, I suppose."

"Plus the fact that we screwed them over," Anthony said. A beat and then, "why did they wait this long to get back at us? I mean, that incident happened two years ago."

Sal frowned. "I don't know, Maybe they were waiting to catch us off guard. They probably wanted to make us think that everything had died down."

Anthony tried to sit up. Sal put a firm hand on his brother's shoulder. "Take it easy, Anthony. Don't make any sudden moves and hurt yourself."

Anthony waved his older brother off. "I'm fine. I just wanna sit up. I'm tired of lying on my back all day."

Sal helped his younger brother sit up in the bed. They continued their conversation.

"How did they know I was at the club? There wasn't no one following us or anything. We checked."

Sal shrugged his shoulders. "Lucky guess?"

Anthony shook his head grimly. "Not likely. But I don't know. Maybe they were passing by and they saw us or something and decided to shoot."

"It's possible," Sal said. "But from now on, you're going to have some body guards with you where ever you go. I don't want to hear no complaints about it either," Sal said stubbornly.

"Yeah, and what about you? They gotta be after you too."

Sal nodded. "That's why I bring men with me wherever I go."

"I got Riccardo and Bernie," Anthony protested.

"Bodyguards, they are not," Sal retorted. "A lot of good they did."

"They got me to the hospital," Anthony responded.

Sal sighed. "Anyways, we're trying to get this sorted out as soon as we can. I think that we're going to have to have a sit down."

"I think, that would be best," Anthony said looking down at his bandaged chest.

Ψ

Dominick Mancini was an imposing figure to behold. At six foot five and weighing about 250 with a broad chest and arms like steel, he was intimidating to most people that saw him for the first time. Sal, as were most people that first met Dominick, was at first put on guard by the mare size of him. But as Sal got to know Dominick, he found him to be a pleasant man, fair and with a good amount of human compassion which was very unlike his father, Francesco Mancini, who had passed away about six years ago. Dominick had taken over from his father as the *don*. Sal, taking his father's place as underboss, was a mere step below Dominick in rank. Dominick was the only man that Sal answered to.

Dom stood, gave Sal and Anthony hugs when they came into the room, and then they sat down. They chatted a while, making small talk, but soon they got down to business.

"Well, we can't have people taking shots at Anthony here," Dominick said flicking his eyes at Anthony. "We gotta do something and do it quick. What do you suggest?"

"I was thinking that maybe we should have a chat with them. See if we can talk it out with Santiago. Tell him let's cut our losses and end it at this point. We don't want this war to drag on for an extended period of time. We've got too much going on as it is," Sal said.

Dom nodded his head slowly. "You're right. We'll arrange a meeting with him. We'll even offer to go over to him to talk. I doubt he has enough trust towards us to come to us to meet. We'll try it this way first, but if it doesn't work, he has to go, we have no other choice, even if it starts an all and out war between us and the Argentineans."

Ψ

Juan's black eyes followed Sal, Anthony, and two of their men as they walked into the room.

"Why don't you take a seat gentlemen," Juan said gesturing at the soft-looking leather seats that were in front of him.

Anthony glanced at the three men standing behind Juan Santiago. All of them had machine guns and wore dark glasses. They stared straight ahead, unmoving, as if they were statues.

Sal and Anthony exchanged looks and sat down on the leather seats. They were surprisingly comfortable. Anthony half expected a bed of nails to be underneath.

"Do you want a cigar? They are Cuban. The very best."

Sal shook his head. "No thank you."

"Then, perhaps you want something to drink? Some wine? Scotch? Port? Gin?"

Anthony sighed. "I'll have a small glass of port."

Juan beckoned a short skinny man in a suit standing to the side. "*Hace una bebida por Senor Gionelli. Port. Yo tambien. Dame vino blanco.*"

Sal shot a look at Juan Santiago.

Juan raised his hands before him. "Ernesto does not understand a word of English. All I told him was to make a drink for your brother. That is all. I swear it. And I asked him to bring me some wine."

Sal nodded, although still doubtful.

Anthony wasn't sure that he wanted the drink anymore.

"Well, anyway. Shall we get down to business gentlemen?"

"Yes. Let's. I don't like the fact that you sent your men to shoot at my brother in the street like he was a piece of trash," Sal said in a controlled voice.

Juan gave him a grin. "Well, let us not forget that you mowed my cousin down like an animal two years ago. How do you think I felt about that?"

"That was two years ago. We didn't do anything to you since then. We wanted to just let that pass—"

Juan chuckled. "You have got to be joking. Let it pass? My cousin is dead, Senor Gionelli. Dead from a deal that he thought was legitimate. But you and your men screwed him over! You deceived us!"

"Okay. We did. But I think that it would be in your best interest to just end things right now. We don't want to take this to another level, do we. That could bring on all sorts of problems," Sal said pinning the South American man down with his eyes.

Juan frowned. The man came back holding a silver tray with two drinks on them. Juan took up the goblet with the light liquid. He took a sip. The man came over to Anthony and held out the tray to him. Anthony looked at the glass with the dark maroon liquid inside and then at the small man carrying the tray. The man's face was expressionless.

Juan watched Anthony with a slightly amused expression.

Anthony reached out and took the drink from the tray. He nodded his head and muttered a thanks.

Juan continued. "What I want to know is if you are threatening me."

Sal gave him a shrug. "I am merely telling you what this could result in. I can't have you threatening my brother's life. We'll have to fight back, no? But it doesn't have to end up that way. We can stop it now. Put it behind us. We can strike up a truce and then maybe in the future we can have business dealings."

Juan stared at Sal as if, at that very moment, Sal had sprouted another head on his shoulder. "After what you did to Chavez? I do not think so. There is no way we can trust you." Juan rose in his seat. The man with the tray came beside him. Juan placed the half filled goblet on the tray. "I think this meeting is over, *senores*."

"Do I have your promise that you stop this continual attempt on my brother's life?" Sal asked, not willing to walk out without a deal.

Juan clenched his jaws, seemed to think about something, and then relaxed. "Fine. I will not make anymore attempts on your brother's life. You have my word."

Sal and Anthony stood up. The three men shook hands. They had a deal.

Ψ

When Anthony went back to the club three weeks later, he spotted the young black girl he and his friends had seen three weeks ago as he was coming out and heading to his car. But this time, he was alone. No friends, no bodyguards no nothing. Despite what Sal said, he didn't want to be followed around and watched like a hawk, so he had dismissed his bodyguards for the night before venturing out.

The girl was talking to someone. Anthony paused and looked on, unbeknownst to the girl and the other person. The girl (he didn't even know her name) was in the alleyway between the building adjoining the club and the next one. She wasn't alone. She was talking to a person hidden in the shadows of the alleyway and the night. On the other hand, she was illuminated by the low lights from the sides of the buildings. Her face looked panicked and troubled. By the looks of it, it was a heated discussion. A deep male voice could be heard yelling at her. The girl's high voice talked back with snap responses.

Suddenly, Anthony saw a well dressed black male that looked to be about medium in height and weight but way larger than the girl, step forwards, and smack the girl right in the face. The smack resonated through the air as did the girl's scream of pain. This was followed by a closed fist pounding by the man on the face of the girl. The man gripped the girl's upper arms and flung her against the brick wall.

Anthony, seeing enough, advanced forward. He pulled out his pistol and held it to the side of his right thigh as he walked. The man, hearing footsteps, looked up as did the teenaged girl. Her bruised face was streaked with tears, but Anthony saw a look of recognition in her eyes. She remembered his face.

Anthony pointed the gun straight at the man and released the safety. Anthony's dark eyes bore into the other man's startled and then angry face.

"Let go of her," Anthony said calmly. "Don't make me have to shoot you."

The man sneered at him, let go of the girl, and took a step towards Anthony.

"Who the fuck is you? A cop or somethin'," the man barked. Anthony noticed one of his hands moving, slowly sneaking down to the pocket of his pants.

"Hey. Raise your hands in the air. You move your hand again, I'll blow your brains out. And no. I ain't no cop. I'm something a lot worse than that," Anthony said ominously.

The pretty teenager looked back and forth between the two men with terror on her face. She was frozen with fear. She didn't know what to do.

"Look man, this ain't any of your business. Why don't you just walk on," the man said angrily.

Anthony glanced over at the girl. "Go around the corner and wait in the club. Tell the man at the door that Anthony sent you. His name's Roberto."

The girl stood still. She looked at the black man with fear.

"Don't fuckin' listen to him, man. You stay right where you are," the man snapped.

"Fuck that. Go on into the club. It's two buildings down from this alleyway. Don't worry. He ain't gonna do a thing," Anthony spat.

"That's my hoe! She goes where I tell her to go, you fuckin' Puerto Rican bastard," the man snarled.

Anthony chuckled at his mistaken ethnicity. "I ain't no Puerto. I'm Italian. Sicilian to be exact."

The man nailed Anthony with his black eyes. "Look man. Whatchew want? I'm just handling business!"

"Well, lemme tell you something buddy. That girl ain't gonna be part of any business that you're going to handle from this point on. And don't you forget it. Because if you do, it's gonna cost you big time," Anthony said matter-of-factly.

Now why don't you just get the hell outta here? And let me tell you something….what the hell is your name anyways, motherfucker?" Anthony asked the man, with disgust.

"Ain't none of your business," the man snarled.

"You really askin' for trouble, aint' ya? Just tell me your name and if I find out you lied to me—"

"William," the man spat angrily.

"Okay. Willie. I hope that we don't have to meet again. Because that wouldn't be good for your health. Now scram!" Anthony said.

With one last withering look, the man in the tailor cut suit turned around and began to swiftly walk down the alleyway. Anthony watched him until he disappeared around the corner.

Anthony headed back to the club and found the girl standing at the door arguing with Roberto. When Roberto saw Anthony he looked up with flashing eyes.

"This here kid's tryna say that you told her to come inta here. Can you believe it? She musta overheard someone calling our names. I seen her around here a few times selling her little ass." Roberto said with a smirk.

Anthony shook his head. "I told her to come here."

The girl threw Roberto a disgusted look. "I told you so! Don'tcha feel fuckin' stupid!"

Anthony and Roberto looked at the girl with shock. She had a filthy mouth for one so young. The streets had definitely hardened her.

"Sorry Tony. I didn't know...this ain't exactly a good place to be letting kids into, especially not no little girl."

Anthony gave him a slight smile. "No problem. At least she stayed here, even if she was bickering with you. Some guy in the alleyway was beating on her. I couldn't just stand there and watch it."

Roberto frowned. "Of course not."

Anthony turned to the girl. "Come on. I know you're hungry. Let's go getcha something to eat.

The girl didn't have to be told twice.

The two of them stopped by a little roadside diner. Once they were seated, Anthony told her to order whatever she wanted.

The girl ordered a bacon cheeseburger, French fries, onion rings, a milkshake, and cheesecake. Anthony was shocked at the amount of food that she ordered. She must have not eaten in a while. Anthony eyed her bony arms and small narrow face. It looked that way.

Anthony grinned. "Is that order for the both of us?"

The girl looked down, shamefaced. "You said I could order what I want."

Anthony nodded his head. "I was only joking with you. That's fine. You can order whatever you want and if you want more after that, you can get it."

The girl nodded. Then her eyes grew dark. "What do you want? Nobody don't just take a girl like me to get free meals off of them."

Anthony shook his head slowly. This girl was really jaded. But could he blame her?

"I don't want anything. I'm just trying to help you out. That's all. I don't want nothing in return…except for a few things."

The girl's dark eyes flicked up to him. "What?"

"First, I want to know your name."

"Bessie. Bessie Woods," the girl drawled.

"Second, where are you from originally? Because you don't sound like a Chicago native."

"I'm from Georgia. Atlanta," the girl answered eyeing the waitress who was placing the food on the table.

"Third. How old are you?"

"Fifteen. I turn sixteen in a few months," she answered quickly.

"The last time we saw each other, you said that you were eighteen," Anthony said trying to restrain a smile.

The girl bit into her hamburger and shrugged. "Okay, so I lied."

"Do you have a place to stay?"

Bessie put down the hamburger with some reluctance and looked at Anthony, her face solemn. "I lived with *him*."

"By *him* you mean the man with you in the alleyway?"

She nodded curtly and stuffed a bunch of fries into her mouth. "He's my pimp," she said reluctantly. "He takes care of me."

"But he also beats you," Anthony protested.

"I don't have anyone else," she said a little sadly. "When I came up here from Georgia, he took me in. I know he's going to throw me out though."

"Don't worry about that," Anthony said. "Where are your parents?"

The girl's face turned blank. "They're dead."

"I'm sorry."

"They died in a fire. Them and my little brother. But I wasn't there. I was at my friend's house."

"I'm sorry," Anthony repeated.

"I wish I had died in there with them," she said frankly.

"No you don't," Anthony said sipping his coffee.

"Yes I do."

Ψ

"This place is amazing!" Edda said looking around at the retreat. Each couple or family was given their own cabin which overlooked a crystal clear lake. There was a large, modern sized building that contained a cafeteria where they would eat, bathrooms, and other rooms. The meetings would be held there.

"I would hope so. I certainly paid enough for it," Michael responded, giving Edda a kiss on the cheek. "Are you okay?"

"I'm fantastic!" Edda said climbing out of the car. "Let's get our stuff." Edda headed to the trunk and started pulling out their bags. Michael joined her.

A tall, gangly man with bright, shoulder length, red hair and an abundance of freckles started towards them. He wore frayed bell bottoms and a Grateful Dead tee-shirt. Worn leather sandals adorned his feet. Beside him walked a short, chubby, young woman with impossibly long, wild brown hair. She wore a sleeveless, flowered dress that was light and summery. Unlike her companion, she was barefooted. In her arms, she carried a young child that looked to be a little over a year old. The child was only a diapers and nothing else. Then both of them gave Edda and Michael a wide smile.

"Welcome to Better Lives retreat." He shook Michael's hand and then Edda's. "I hope you two have a wonderful weekend with us. My name's Tim. This is my partner Tina and our little son Dylan." Tina shook their hands as well, smiling.

"My name's Edda, and this is my boyfriend Michael," Edda said and shook their hands. Michael followed suit.

Edda noticed that they didn't bat an eyelid when she said that Michael was her boyfriend. They stood, completely unfazed.

"I'm so glad that you can have us here," Michael said with a smile.

"We're glad that you two came," Tina said. "We as one human race need to come together in harmony and peace. That is the atmosphere that we are hoping to achieve here. If we don't come together, we will all go to our destruction."

Michael and Edda nodded in agreement.

"Shall we show you your accommodations?" Tina offered kindly.

"Of course," Edda said with a smile.

Ψ

Ester looked out at the ocean from the window and smiled. She was loving every minute being here with Marco. And what scared her, was that she was bearly thinking about Garret..

"I can see that you're enjoying yourself," Marco said coming up behind her. He handed her a glass of wine. Ester accepted it and smiled.

"I love it here. I haven't been to the beach since I was a child," Ester said with a smile and took a sip.

Marco put down his glass of wine and took Ester's and put her glass on the table as well. "I was thinking, maybe we can take out a picnic lunch on the sand and eat under the moonlight. It's a beautiful night out there."

Ester smiled, liking the idea. "Yeah that sounds like a great idea, but…"

"But what?" asked Marco.

"Do…they have to come along with us?" asked Ester, pointing her chin at Marco's two, ever present, bodyguards who were currently standing outside the living room door.

Marco shook his head. "No. They stay here. Don't worry, I'll tell them."

They built a small fire, right out there on the beach. They spread out a blanket and began to eat.

"It's so beautiful out here. Look at the stars," Ester said, pointing up into the night air.

"Yeah, I know. Most of the times, the sky is clear out here. I guess because it's away from the city and all the pollution," Marco said with a smile.

They ate and talked, having a good time as they did so. Afterwards, they sat by the fire sipping white wine.

"What would you think if I said I wanted to make love to you," Marco said looking deep into Ester's eyes.

Ester smile softly. "I would say, let's go back in and do it then."

Marco moved closer to her and kissed her deeply. Then he pulled back a little and stared at her in the face as he held her hand.

"What if I were to say I want to make love to you right here. By the water, under the stars?"

Ester looked a little surprised at first and then wrapped her arms around Marco.

"I would ask you, what are you waiting for?"

And so they did.

Ψ

"Oh Gosh, do you think that Tina and Tim would approve of us going to this restaurant? I think it's considered consumerism, don't you think?" Edda said glancing down at the emerald green dress that she was wearing. She flushed guiltily.

Michael chuckled. "They probably won't approve of us going to a fancy, establishment restaurant like this one, but, hey. We need a night out, don't you think?"

Edda nodded and ran a finger through her blond hair, which she was currently growing out. "We'll eat vegetarian. No meat. They have a vegetarian menu here, I think," Edda said.

"They should. This is L.A. after all," Michael said with a smile.

They were seated at a table and given their menus.

"Hmmm...I think I'll order some pasta with tomato sauce and spices. I'll tell them to leave out the meat," Edda said.

Michael looked at the roasted chicken with longing. "Gosh, do you know how tempted I am to order meat? All of a sudden too. Okay. Let me just order some wild rice and vegetables," Michael said and put down the menu. "Should we order some wine?"

"Sure. What about a bottle of Spanish wine?"

"Sounds good," Michael said with a smile.

They talked for a while before the food came. Halfway through the meal, Michael looked behind Edda and suddenly his face froze and his eyes got round.

Edda gave her boyfriend a queer look. "What's the matter?"

Michael slouched down in his chair and looked down at his half eaten food. "Don't look now, but I think I just saw my mother walk in with some guy."

"What?!" Edda exclaimed. "What's she doing all the way in California? Is she with your dad?"

Michael shook his head. "No. Some white guy. Oh, gosh. What the hell is going on?"

Edda turned around to look, no longer able to contain her curiosity. She turned back around in a flash, her face red. "Oh Gosh. That *is* your mother. And the guy she's with…he looks familiar. But I can't place his face."

Michael peered at the man who was now laughing because of something that his mother said. A flash of recognition went through him but it went as quickly as it came. He was clueless as to who the man was. Maybe he might have seen the man once before?

"Let's get out of here before they see us," Edda said putting her fork down.

Michael's eyes slitted. "Are you kidding? I want to know what she's doing up here when she told my father that she was going to be in Virginia visiting my grandmother. I also want to know who's that guy she's laughing and talking with."

"Yeah. The two of them look very familiar with each other," Edda said, admitting the truth.

Michael got up from the table.

"Michael. Are you sure you want to do this here?" Edda asked, uncertainly.

"I sure do. I want to know now. Not later."

"Do you want me to come with you?"

"Sure. If you want," Michael said.

Edda wiped her mouth and put down her napkin. "All right. Let's go," she said as she stood up.

The two of them walked up to the table where Ester was sitting. The couple didn't even notice them until they were right beside them.

"Hey Mom," Michael called in a controlled voice.

Ester looked up at her son with a look of pure alarm. She glanced back at Marco, who had a shocked look on his face. She looked again at her son and forced a smile.

"Hello, Michael, Edda. What are you two doing here?"

"I think I should be asking you that. Especially since my father thinks that you're somewhere in Virginia right now. How did you end up here in California?"

Ester shifted uncomfortably in her seat. She looked at Marco. He stared on, not saying a word.

"W-w-well, the thing is that…I decided to stop here on my way back home…uhhh…"

"Who's this guy?" Michael asked, with disgust as he pointed at his mother's dinner companion.

"This is Marco. I…met him over here. We decided to go to dinner together since we were both alone."

Michael looked at the man's face. His eyes were flashing with anger, apparently, at what his mother just said. That was why it was clear to Michael she was lying.

"Don't bull shit me Mom. You guys know each other good. Not for just one or two days either. We've been watching you all for a while at our tables and you didn't even notice us."

Michael could see his mother's face slowly get a reddish tint to the brown skin. She was embarrassed.

Finally, the man spoke. Before that, he looked like he was getting ready to burst.

"Come on Ester. He's a grown man. He ain't no idiot. Why don't you just tell him the truth."

"What truth?" Ester said playing dumb. "I just told him."

Suddenly, recognition dawned on Edda like a ton of bricks. This was one of her step-father's friends. She remembered seeing him at the house a few times before Rocco passed away. She let out a small gasp.

Michael turned to Edda, his eyes still blazing. "Are you all right?"

"Yeah. Aren't you my step-father's friend? I saw you by the house before," Edda said tentatively.

Marco nodded, no longer willing to hold back. "Yes. That's right. I'm Marco Arnone," he glanced hesitantly at Ester who was begging him with her eyes to shut up.

Two big guys came over to the table. Their faces grim. "Are you all right you two? We were trying to decide whether or not to come over."

Marco nodded and waved them away. "Everything fine. We're just talking. This is Ester's son and his girlfriend."

The two men retreated as quickly as they came.

Michael stared after the two men with a bemused look and turned back to Marco. "So, you two been seeing each other?"

Marco glanced at Ester and then looked back at him. "Why don't you ask your mother?"

Michael turned to his mother who looked like she was ready to sink into the ground and die. She had the look of a scared deer caught in the headlights.

"Mother?" Michael said with a sneer. "Care to elaborate?"

Ester sighed and leaned her elbows on the table. "Yes. Me and Marco have been seeing each other for quite a while now—"

"Six years," Marco cut in.

"You've been having an affair behind Dad's back for six years?" Michael asked, incredulously.

Ester nodded. "Yes. I'm sorry Michael. I never wanted you to find out...not like this at least."

"So what, are you leaving Dad now? This would kill him, Mom!" Michael yelled. People at the tables beside them turned to look.

"Why don't we take this outside," Marco said calmly.

"Yeah, why don't we!" Michael said angrily.

All four of them left the restaurant and went outside. Edda noticed that the two men in the black suits came outside as well, but discreetly kept their distance.

"Dad is sick, he has heart problems, and this is what you do to him? Are you trying to kill him?" shrieked Michael. "Why did you do this?"

Edda put a hand on Michael's shoulder trying to calm him down.

"Michael, your father's been so sick these past years...I don't know. I wanted to live a little more...we can't do what we used to do—"

"I don't want to hear it!" Michael yelled loudly.

People coming out of the restaurant stood to stare.

Marco grew uncomfortable. "Come on, come on. Not in the street. Why don't we go back to my house. We can talk it out there."

"I'm not going anywhere with you two," Michael yelled.

"Okay, okay," Marco said trying to placate him. "You don't have to."

"You're damned right I don't. But I'll tell you what has to happen," Michael hissed.

Ester, who was crying by now, looked at her son's face in terror. "What?"

"You and this guy's gotta end it. Or I swear to God, I'll go and tell Dad. End it now, Mom."

Ester sobbed and nodded slowly. She attempted to touch her son. Michael backed away from her as if she was diseased.

Michael grabbed Edda's hand and turned around without another word. They walked towards their car, got in and sped off, leaving Ester and Marco standing with morose expressions.

Ψ

Michael and Edda rode back from California in mostly silence. Along the way, they stopped at two hotels for the nights and stopped in diners to eat. Finally, they reached home. As they were taking out their bags, Edda said, "Well, we learned a lot this weekend, didn't we."

Michael gave her a queer look and said, "More than I ever wanted to learn." He turned around and lugged a bag towards the apartment.

"Oh Michael, I was talking about the retreat not…your mother."

Michael glanced back at her, his eyes sad.

That night they lay in bed, side by side, staring up at the ceiling. They were silent and untouching.

"She better end it with that guy. I don't want to have to tell my father," Michael said, speaking at last.

Edda rolled onto her side and touched Michael's strong chest. "She will Michael. She loves your father…you know that. She'll come around. Just watch and see."

Ψ

Marco ate dinner alone in his dinning room. He had told his body guards to go out and get something to eat, or do something for a few hours. He wanted to be alone. Alone with his thoughts, alone with his misery. He thought about last night, when Ester had come over and with tears in her eyes, she had told him that she would no longer be seeing him. She didn't want her family to be at risk, she didn't want to lose her son. He had calmly listened to her and then Marco had done something completely out of character for him. He had pleaded with her and tried to reason with her for at least an hour to no avail. Never in his life, before Ester, had he ever begged a woman, not even his ex-wife. He was used to having willing and available women all around him, ready to accommodate him at the snap of his fingers. Smooth operator, was what they called him. And he had lived up to that name in the fullest, that is, until he had started seeing Ester. She had been the only woman, so far in his life, that had been able to slow down his fast lifestyle with various women. In fact, she had sent it to a complete standstill. Not even his ex-wife had been able to slow him down in that department. He had screwed around on her without so much as a second thought. And he knew that he had hurt her. Deeply. And now, for the first time, he felt empathy towards his wife and understood the pain she had felt as a result of him.

He wanted Ester. There was never a woman that he had wanted as much as he wanted her. Without her, his life was dull, meaningless, and routine. For six years, she had put a refreshing spark into his life. And now she was gone. And the thought of having to go back to the way he was, before she was around, was unthinkable for Marco. He couldn't accept it. He wouldn't accept it.

Marco knew what he had to do.

Ψ

"I'm coming, I'm coming," Garret yelled as he slowly approached the door. He reluctantly tore his eyes away from the movie that he was watching on the television.

Where was Ester? Didn't she hear the doorbell ringing? Then he remembered she had gone out for some groceries at the supermarket.

He walked up to the door and looked through the peephole. He was surprised to see a man standing at the door. A white man. He frowned as he thought that the man looked a little familiar. Then he recognized that it was one of Rocco's friends that used to come by the house quite often. He remembered many a time letting him in through the gates when he used to do security at Rocco's estate.

Garrett opened the door and gave the man a slight smile.

"Mr. Arnone. What are you doing here?" Garrett asked, a little confused.

"Do you mind if I come in?" Marco asked, politely.

"Sure. Come on in and take a seat." Garrett closed the door behind him and led him into the living room. Marco sat down on the couch. Garrett sat in his armchair.

"Well, what's going on?" Garrett asked, kindly.

"Ummm...we need to talk," Marco said nervously.

"Sure. But what about?"

"This is about Ester," Marco said.

Garrett face turned grim. "What's the matter, is she alright? Is she hurt? She just went out to the store..."

"Oh, she's fine," Marco said calming him down. "But...I need to tell you something."

"What is it?" Garrett asked, curiously.

"Well...your wife and I have been seeing each other," Marco said deciding instantly that the direct approach was best.

"What do you mean?" Garrett asked, puzzled.

"I mean...your wife and I had been having an affair, Mr. Jackson."

Garrett stared at the man sitting across from him with an expression of shock, and then anger.

"What do you mean? How long has this been going on? You bastard. You must have made her—"

"I didn't make her do anything, Mr. Jackson. She and I were together by her own free will." Marco paused.

"How long has this been going on?" Garrett repeated.

"Six years."

Garrett buried his face in his hands for a moment and then looked up. "I don't understand."

"Your wife ended it with me last week. She said that she couldn't see me any longer and I know it was because of your son Michael. You see...he saw us together and he more-or-less told her to end it or he was going to tell you. But I decided to just come here and tell you myself. You see, I want to be with Ester. I love her and I never loved a woman in my life as much as I love her. I'm not willing to give her up just yet."

Garrett suddenly grabbed his chest and slumped over in obvious pain. Marco, panicked, rushed over to Garrett. "Are you all right?"

Garret jerked away from him. "Get away from me," he whispered and then fell to the floor. At that very moment, Ester came back through the door with a bunch of bags in her hands. Her eyes grew wide as she took in the scene before her. She looked at her husband on the floor and then looked at Marco.

"What are you doing here? What did you do to him?" she asked, frantically.

Marco shook his head and glanced at the writhing form on the floor. "Nothing! I came here to talk to him and then he just clutched his chest and fell to the floor." Marco leaned over and felt for a pulse.

"He's still alive," Marco announced.

"I'm calling an ambulance," Ester said rushing to the phone.

Ψ

Dr. Stevens pulled off his mask and sighed.

"Time of death, three fifty P.M." said Dr. Stevens as he peeled off his gloves and threw them into the waste bin. "I'm going to go and tell his wife and son."

Ester sat impatiently in the waiting room beside Michael and got up as she saw the doctor approaching her. She read the expression on the doctor's face and knew instantly that the news wasn't good. She began to sob.

Michael, fighting back his own tears while simultaneously casting angry glances at his mother, walked up to the doctor and said, "He's dead, isn't he?"

The doctor nodded his head sadly. "I'm sorry to say that he is."

Chapter Thirty-one

January, 1967

"Michael, don't you think you should at least tell her goodbye?" Edda asked, touching her slightly swollen stomach.

Michael shook his head as he stuffed another article of clothing into the suitcase. "Hell no. She and that damn bastard Marco killed my father. Can you believe that my mother had to nerve to marry Marco four months later? My father's not even cold in the ground yet. Hell no. I ain't got nothing to do with neither of them."

"But…don't you want your mother to see our baby when it's born?"

Michael stopped and gave Edda a penetrating stare. "Not on my life."

Edda's heart dropped into her stomach.

It seemed that Michael would never forgive his mother for what happened. In fact, it appeared that Michael hated both Marco and his mother.

Michael and Edda had decided to move to California. They were transferring to UCLA in order to finish their last year for their masters. They decided to go to California, because Tim and Tina had invited them to live at a commune. Edda and Michael, at this point, fully believing that the much of the world and in particular, this country, were an evil establishment, were totally ready to denounce it all in favor of a more simple existence.

"My mother said that she'll be down as soon as possible to visit us," Edda told Michael.

"Yeah, that's great," Michael said distractedly.

Michael could hardly wait for them to get to California. If he had to spend another day in Chicago, he felt that he was going to commit an act of violence. Most likely against Marco. But this would be completely against the lifestyle that he and Edda were attempting to follow.

"I would like for our son to know *both* of his grandmothers, Michael. You know, maybe you should just put it behind you."

Michael paused from his packing and looked at her. "Did you say a boy?"

Edda smiled hesitantly. "That's what I feel it is. In fact, I know it will be."

Michael nodded with a grin. Usually, if Edda said that something was going to happen, it turned out to be true. For many years, Michael had been fascinated with Edda's sensitivity for the spiritual world and her knack for predicting things.

"Well that's great. I guess we should start looking for boy names," Michael said as he pulled another suitcase from the closet.

Ψ

Penny had come home early from visiting her and Quincy's publisher. After five bestseller archeology books, based on their adventures and finds from around the world, Penny and Quincy were now working on writing a college textbook.

When Penny came through the door, she was surprised to find it silent. The living room was empty. She called out Quincy's name, but there was no response.

She climbed the stairs to their bedroom. The door was closed, which was strange. As she stood still before it, she thought she could hear some muffled sounds coming from behind it. She frowned and swung the door open.

Penny gasped in shock when she took in the sight before her. There was her husband, lying naked and spread eagle on the king sized bed as a voluptuous young brunette crouched over him, riding his cock like a stallion. Her head was thrown back and sighs and moans of ecstasy issued forth from her lips. Quincy's eyes were squeezed shut. He grasped the brunette's waist with one hand and rubbed her rounded behind with the other.

"You fucking bastard!" screamed Penny.

Both the girl and Quincy turned startled eyes to Penny. Quincy's face took on an expression of surprise mixed with distress. The girl jumped off of Quincy and tried to cover herself with the sheets. Her face turned as white as the sheet wrapped around her.

"P-Penny, what are you doing back so early? I thought that—"

"You're not the one that's going to ask questions here. How could you? How could you do this behind my back? I'm over there seeing about our book and you're over here…screwing some dumb slut!"

"I'm no slut!" the young woman retorted. She pouted out her full lips and her hazel eyes filled with tears. Penny ignored her.

"Get her the fuck out of here! Now! before I wreck this place!" screamed Penny.

The girl immediately began pulling on her clothes. Quincy slipped on his boxers. Penny eyed his body. It was still as lean and strong as the day that they got married. She flicked her eyes away.

"I hardly see how you could complain," muttered Quincy.

Penny's head snapped in her husband's direction when she heard this. The girl slipped out the door and closed it behind her. Penny could hear her going down the stairs and out the front door.

"What? What are you talking about?" Penny demanded.

Quincy turned to Penny with anger. "You know exactly what I'm talking about! You think I don't know about you and Alfie! I know that you fucked him when we were in Thailand two years ago! Don't you dare deny it. And the sad thing is that you thought I was stupid enough to believe that you got lost and spent the night in a hotel until daylight."

"If you didn't believe me, then why didn't you say anything?" Penny asked, as her heart beat wildly in her chest.

"Because—" Quincy stopped short and swallowed. "Because at first I wanted to believe you…I tried to tell myself that you were telling the truth…but when Marsha was born…I knew that you did sleep with him. Come on Penny, the girl is a carbon copy of Alfie."

"But you always say that she looks like your mother—"

"I knew she wasn't mine, Penny. I know it. But I didn't want to say anything to you…I didn't want to lose you, not yet. I was waiting for you to tell me. But you didn't. So I realized that you were attempting to play me for a fool and try to pass her off for my child. I wanted you to confess to me, Penny. I would have forgiven you. I would have loved you…and continued loving Marsha. But I saw that you wanted to deceive me. So I got angry. I thought that if you cared so little about me that you could sleep with someone else and have a child by him, and to add insult to injury, try to pass the child off as mine, I could be just as callous as you. I decided to sleep with other women," Quincy said as he buttoned up his shirt.

Penny sat down on the bed feeling exhausted. "So you weren't sleeping around on me from the beginning."

Quincy shook his head, grimly. "Sorry to disappoint you, but I wasn't. But I have been doing it for the past year."

"How many has there been?" Penny asked, needlessly.

Quincy shrugged. "Fifteen…twenty. Something like that."

"You were *really* angry then," Penny said wryly.

Quincy nodded. "I said I was."

"And that's why you stopped making love to me," Penny continued.

Quincy nodded quickly.

Penny shook her head numbly. "So I guess this is the end…of us. But Quincy, sleeping with other women wasn't the answer. Besides Alfie, I've never been with anyone else."

Quincy came and sat beside her. He put a hand on her knee. "I'm sorry, Penny. It was stupid of me. But I do love you Penny. I don't want to lose you. If we can promise each other…promise that we won't see anyone else anymore…you have to say you'll never see Alfie again. Ever. I don't want you communicating with him."

"But Marsha's his child. He wants to hear about her. It's only fair."

Quincy shook his head. "No way. No letters, no meetings, no nothing."

Penny looked at Quincy's toffee colored eyes. Her amber eyes began to fill up with tears. "I can't do that, Quincy. I couldn't do that to him. It wouldn't be right. Marsha's his daughter and no matter how she came about, he has the right to know about her. It's the least that we could do."

Quincy shot up from the bed, angry. "But Marsha is *my* child. I've been the one raising her! I'm the one that she calls Daddy! Not him!"

Penny sobbed. "I know, I know!" Penny cried. "I can't take his daughter from him—"

"But you can take my daughter from me!" Quincy yelled. He walked towards the door.

"Hold on Quincy, wait!" Penny cried, trying to hold him back.

Quincy shoved her hands away and turned to face her, his face red with rage. "I was always in competition with him! I thought that once we were married…that you would forget about him. But you didn't. You still love him, Penny. You do and there's nothing that you can say to convince me otherwise. I want to have all of you Penny! I don't want to have to share you with that man or anyone else! God, I hate him! The persistent devil that he is," Quincy said before dashing out of the room.

Penny followed after him, trying to plead with him, all the way until he left out the door, and hopped into his small, dark blue Porsche sports car. Penny watched with tears in her eyes as he sped away out of sight.

Penny slowly went back into the house and lay down on the couch. She cried and cried until she drifted off into a deep sleep.

Penny jumped out of her sleep at the sound of a doorbell ringing. She slowly sat up from the couch and glanced that her watch. It was six P.M. She had been asleep for four hours. Who could be knocking at the door? Not Quincy. He had a key.

Penny walked up to the door and peeked through the peep hole. She was surprised to see two officers standing there. Their faces were grim. One reached out and rang the doorbell again. Penny unlatched the door and opened it.

Penny poked her head out the door. "Can I help you?" Penny asked.

One officer pulled of his cap and stepped forward. "Mrs. Penny Hawkins?" Penny nodded her head in acknowledgement. The officer continued. "May we come in for a moment? We want to speak to you."

Penny frowned. "What is it?"

"Please, Mrs. Hawkins. May we come in?" the other officer asked, and took his cap off as well.

Penny stepped aside and let them in. They sat, perching on the edge of her couch, looking very uncomfortable.

"Well? What is it?" Penny asked, nervously, sensing that something wasn't right.

"Well…it's about your husband."

"What? What about my husband? Is he all right?"

"I'm sorry to tell you, but, Mr. Hawkins was driving fast and skidded on the road when he reached a corner…his car broke through the railing and fell off the cliff…he hit the rocks below. I'm sorry. He died."

Penny passed out before they could say anything more.

Ψ

Penny's eyes opened wide when she saw Alfie suddenly appear and take a seat beside her at the funeral service.

"Alfie! What are you doing here," Penny whispered. But she was happy to see him.

Alfie glanced around and turned to look at her. "I thought I should come. I wanted to make sure that you were okay."

Penny frowned and looked over at her parents. Her mother was holding Marsha in her lap. Both her mother and her father were looking curiously at them. Alfie waved to them. Penny's mother reluctantly waved back. Her father didn't, but continued to stare. Then Penny looked at Quincy's parents who were shooting daggers at Alfie and her. Penny blushed and turned quickly away.

"I don't think your parents want me here and Quincy's parents sure as hell don't. If they could kill me with their looks, they would."

"They're surprised that you're here."

"I can tell."

"What about Laura? Does she know that you're here?"

Alfie was still for a while and then nodded. "She didn't look exactly thrilled…but there was no way I wasn't coming."

Penny nodded.

After the funeral service of her dead husband, Penny walked outside beside her parents and her daughter who was being held by Penny's mom. Alfie had disappeared into the crowd. Penny's eye's sought him out. Finally, she saw him walking away from the church, to his car, Penny assumed.

Penny turned to her parents. "I'll be right back."

Penny's mother frowned. "But Penny, the limousine—"

"Wait for me inside the limo. I'll be right back." Penny kissed her daughter on the forehead and then went towards Alfie.

"Alfie!" Penny called out.

Alfie turned around and walked towards her with a slight smile on his face.

"Aren't you coming to the wake?" Penny asked him, desperately wishing that he would say yes.

Alfie shook his head. "Nah. I couldn't do that."

Penny nodded and looked away. She understood.

"I have to ask you something though. Do your parents know that Marsha's really my child?" Alfie said quietly.

Penny looked around. There was no one within earshot. "No. Not yet. I decided that I would tell them after the funeral."

Alfie clamped his lips together and nodded. He looked up at the sky for a moment and then back down at her. "When am I going to get to see you?"

"Alfie, I don't know…this is kinda hard…"

Alfie nodded. "I know. I understand."

Penny nodded. There was an awkward silence and then Penny said, "I'll call you."

"I'll be waiting for it," Alfie said before he turned and walked away.

Ψ

Laura sat on the couch and watched television, but her mind was a thousand miles away. She had been upset when Alfie had told her that he was going to Quincy's funeral. But she tried not to show it, knowing that it would only make Alfie withdraw from her. Laura knew that Alfie was going there to see Penny. Earlier, just after Alfie had left to go to the funeral, Laura had done a little snooping around. She felt guilty, at first, for doing it knowing that Alfie treasured his privacy, but when she found the stack of letters and pictures in a shoebox at the back of the closet underneath a pile of things that they didn't use, Laura knew that there was something going on. Laura read through each letter and felt all the emotions, deep love, and feeling that were expressed from this woman to Alfie. Laura then looked at the pictures of the little girl that a brassy haired woman carried in her thin arms. Laura had felt a flash of jealousy. There was Penny— the established, well known archeologist. Penny, the one that Alfie called his 'buddy'. The letters didn't sound like letters that buddies would write. They sounded like letters between two people that loved each other. Laura wondered who the baby was. She guessed that it was Quincy and Penny's baby. But as Laura read more and more into the letters, she came across another startling fact. It sounded as if the little blond toddler in the picture was Alfie's child. Laura was amazed. The child didn't belong to Penny's equally well known husband Quincy, the child belonged to Alfie. But it appeared as if Quincy was unaware of it. Laura felt a flash of anger and hurt. Alfie didn't tell her anything about having a child. How much more was there to this man?

Alfie slipped in through the door and headed straight to the bedroom. Laura followed.

"So how was the funeral?" Laura asked, calmly.

Alfie barely glanced at her. "It was okay. I mean, it *was* a funeral."

"Luckily Penny had you there to support her," Laura said casually.

Alfie looked at her a moment, before shrugging out of his black suit jacket. "Yeah. I mean, she was crushed. After all, it was her husband, she loved him."

"I don't think that he was the only one that she loved," Laura quipped.

"What do you mean?"

"You know what I mean." Laura tried to gain control of herself. She took a deep breath. "I know that you and Penny are more than friends. And…you have a child! How could you do this to me, Alfie? Why are you hiding things from me?"

Alfie's face turned as red as a beet. "You've been snooping! You went through my things?"

Laura said nothing. She had tears in her eyes.

"How could you go through my things? You know I hate things like that."

"What about lying to me."

"I never once lied to you, Laura. Not once. I've been honest with you Laura."

"Is that why you've never asked me to marry you? Because of her?"

Alfie said nothing.

"You never planned on marrying me, did you. You never even loved me! I was just something with which you could keep warm at night!"

"Now Laura—"

"Ha! And here I was thinking like an idiot that maybe you were just afraid of the ultimate commitment! But that's not the case at all, is it Alfie. You are very committed to your dear Penny, aren't you? And to think that I wasted all these years with you." Laura sighed and plopped into a chair beside the bed. She turned to Alfie, her demeanor now quite calm. "I'm 34, Alfie. Two years older than you are. I'm not getting any younger. I need someone that can be committed to me. Someone that I can have a family with, grow old with. That's what I want."

Alfie looked to the floor. "I can't give that to you, Laura."

Laura nodded. "I know. I can see that now. Goodbye Alfie. I want you out of this condo by tonight. And you can leave your keys on the coffee table," Laura said as she stood up.

"Where are you going?" Alfie asked.

"Anywhere but here," was Laura's response.

Ψ

October, 1967

"Now, repeat after me. I, Alfie."

"I Alfie," Alfie said as he looked deep into Penny's cat-like eyes

"Do take thee, Penelope."

"Do take thee, Penelope."

"To be my lawful wedded wife," the pastor said.

Alfie repeated.

"And I do promise and covenant, before God and these witnesses to live together with thee after God's own ordinance in the hold state of matrimony. To have thee, hold thee, love thee, and honor thee…"

After the vows were exchanged, the bride and the groom placed the golden rings on each other's fingers.

"I now pronounce you husband and wife. You may now kiss the bride."

Alfie, with a big smile, pulled Penny close to him and kissed her full on the lips. There were some whoops, cheers, and then thunderous clapping. Penny came up from the kiss, blushing and smiling. Her eyes were sparkling brightly with happiness. Penny couldn't remember feeling this happy. Alfie couldn't remember feeling this joyous. Penny's father came up and gave them their little girl Marsha. Alfie took his daughter into his arms and kissed her plump rosy cheeks. He then put his other arm around Penny, his new wife.

"Gosh, they look so happy," said Edda to her mother.

"Well, it's about time," Anthony whispered to his twin sister Angelina. "I thought they would never tie the knot."

"Oh please. This was a long time coming," Sal said overhearing his brother's comment. Sal smiled.

"I'm so sorry that Rocco isn't here to see this," Marco said to Ester with a smile.

"I know. The wedding is so beautiful," Ester responded to her husband, as she twisted her neck to look for her son Michael. She finally spotted him on the other side of the isles. He was standing beside Edda. Edda with her swelling stomach. According to Wendy, Edda was due anytime. Yet, Michael and Edda still weren't married. Wendy had said that they didn't believe in marriage. They told her it was just a certificate and they didn't need that to validate their love. This troubled Ester, but she hadn't said anything in response. Michael didn't glance over at her once. Ester felt her heart drop. Michael was still mad at her.

Marco noticed his wife's distress and knew why. He put an arm around Ester's shoulders and pulled her close. Ester smiled up at him, feeling comforted by his strength. Ester loved him so much. It was a love so different from the love that she had shared with Garret, but it wasn't any less strong.

Wendy stared at her son, his new wife, and her granddaughter and felt a swelling of joy and pride.

They were meant to be.

Ψ

December, 1967

"The girls are coming home from college, Angelina. I was thinking about going up to the cabin for the weekend? Isn't Winston coming down from Texas State University?" Anthony asked his sister, sitting across the table from him. Angelina and Anthony were out for lunch together.

Angelina smiled. "He sure is. My youngest boy is in his last year of college. Gosh, it was just the other day that I was changing his diapers. Matthew's coming as well. He has the weekend off from his job."

"How's law school going for him?" Anthony asked.

"He's doing great. So far, so good. He's smart like his father. I know he'll be just as good a lawyer as Earnest was."

Anthony noticeably bristled at the mention of Earnest's name.

Angelina leaned across the table and put a hand over her twins own. "Anthony, Earnest and I aren't mad at each other anymore. We're not together anymore, but we're friends. We've gotten over it all. Don't be mad at Earnest."

Anthony shifted in his seat. "I'm not."

Angelina grinned. "Well, you can fool me."

"So what do you say? Should we go?" Anthony asked.

"It sounds like a good idea," Angelina said with a smile.

Ψ

When Santino got off the phone with Anthony he sat still for a moment and thought.

Anthony had called him from his cabin by Lake Michigan. According to what he said, Anthony, one of his daughters, Angelina and two of her sons, were up there spending the weekend. Anthony had invited him to come up for the day tomorrow.

Santino made a snap decision.

He picked up the phone and dialed a number.

"Juan. This is Santino. I think I got something for you."

Ψ

Santino arrived at the cabin around two o'clock in the afternoon. He had his wife's nephew Richard drop him off a short distance from the cabin.

"Do you want me to come get you later?" Richard asked his uncle.

"Nah, it's all right. I'll get a ride," said Santino quickly.

Richard shrugged. "Whatever you want. But thanks for letting me keep your car for the weekend."

"No problem. Have fun with it. Just don't go crashing it or nothin'." Santino slammed the door shut. Richard gave him a quick wave and took off.

"Great, you're just in time for lunch," Angelina said cheerfully as she gave Santino a peck on the cheek.

Santino grinned, "At two in the afternoon?"

Anthony laughed. "We have late lunches around here. We were out all morning ice skating on the lake."

"Well, I'm not sorry about missing that. I can't ice skate to save my life," Santino said jokingly.

They all sat and ate. Winston talked about the consulting job that he had waiting for him when he graduated. Eve spoke about college and how her first semester at the University of Chicago had went. Matthew talked about his job a little Then they talked about everything else. Lunch was fun and enjoyable.

"You know what would be good? Some port or brandy to drink before we go to bed. That would hit the spot right about now," Santino said cheerfully.

Angelina looked around at the group with a smile. "You know what? You're right. But we don't have any here."

"Well, when I was coming up here, I saw a beverage shop in town. Me and Anthony can go and get a bottle or two," Santino suggested. He turned to Anthony. "What do you think?"

Anthony shrugged his shoulders and smiled. "Sounds good. We'll get going right now."

"I hope you all don't mind us younger folk partaking of the alcohol as well," Winston drawled with a smile. His accent was strongly southern, considering the many years that he had lived in Texas. All traces of his city accent were gone. Sometimes Anthony was a little bemused that this southern sounding young man was a part of his blood. It seemed so incongruous to him. What were also incongruous was Winston's bright green eyes and his golden brown hair, features similar to his father's. Although the shape of his mouth and ears matched his mother as well as his skin, which was darker than Earnest's, although not exactly olive like his mother's. Sometimes Anthony forgot that Winston was half Sicilian.

"Of course not. You guys are adults. We'll all drink together," Angelina responded, with a smile.

Santino thought for a while and then spoke. "Anthony. Why don't you go and warm up the car? I'll go get some money, it's up in my room. I'll pay for the drinks." Santino headed towards the stairs.

Anthony smiled thinly at Santino. Just like Santino to offer to pay. "No, I'll pay for the drinks. We can go out to the car together. I have my money on me." Anthony wanted to leave now and get back soon.

Santino froze in his tracks. He tried to calm his beating heart. He cleared his throat. "Nah. My treat. You all invited me up here. The least I could do is buy the drinks. Now come on. I'll get my money. Wait in the car for me Tony. Get it warmed up, huh?" Santino said forcing a chuckle.

"Well, my car doesn't need too much warming up," Anthony said carefully.

"All cars need to be warmed up in this weather," Santino said with a smile.

Anthony watched in contemplation as Santino started to climb the stairs. His behavior was very unusual. Why was Santino insisting that Anthony go out first to warm up the car? He decided to ask a question.

"Hey, Tino!" Anthony called out. Santino turned around midway in his ascent.

"I'll come up with you too. I'll tell Winston to go warm up the car for us. I gotta get something." Anthony turned to Winston. "You wanna come Winston?"

Winston brightened at the idea. "Sure thing!"

"All right. Sit still for a minute though, son," Anthony said to his nephew.

Anthony turned back to Santino and saw a panicked expression pass over his face for a second and then it disappeared. That was when Anthony knew, beyond a shadow of a doubt, that something was wrong. Santino was up to something.

"Why don't just the both of us go, Tony. So we can chat," Santino said quickly.

Suspicions confirmed, Anthony turned and looked at his sister, his daughter, and his nephews. They were sitting down looking on with confusion on their faces. They looked back and forth between Anthony and Santino. They knew something was up, but they just didn't know what.

"Why don't you all go into the other room and watch some television?" Anthony said calmly to his family members.

Winston frowned. "I thought I was coming along?"

"Umm…in a minute. I gotta talk to Tino for a while," Anthony turned to Santino and stared him dead in the eyes. "We got something really important to discuss."

That comment drew another look of panic from deep within Santino's eyes. Bravely, he gave Anthony a lop sided smile once the group was out of the room.

"What's the matter, partner?" Santino asked, with forced brightness.

"Why do you want me to go out there and turn on that car before you?" Anthony asked, calmly.

"Because I gotta go get my money. The car's gotta warm up first. It's pretty cold out there, ya know," Santino said keeping the smile on his face.

"Yeah, maybe so. But when I told Winston to go out there and warm up the car, you got panicked at that."

Santino shifted on the stairs. "Nah. I gotta talk to you about something…I don't think you want your nephew hearing any of it," Santino said with a chuckle.

Anthony stared at him with a grim expression. "Go on out and get into the car first, Santino. You warm it up for us."

Santino tried to remain calm. "Ummm…you know what? It's getting kinda late. Maybe the store isn't open anymore."

"Stores like that stay open way past 8:30 at night," Anthony said glancing at the clock.

"Yeah, but…"

"But nothing. Go turn the car on Santino. Turn it on now," Anthony said between gritted teeth.

"I don't want to go anymore, Tony," Santino said nervously.

"I do. Now go on!" Anthony yelled.

Angelina peeked around the corned of the door. "Are you two okay in here?" She asked, her face worried.

"Go back in the other room, Angie. We're fine."

Angie's head disappeared again.

"Come on. Let's go," Anthony said grimly.

Santino came down the stairs hesitantly.

"Come on, come on!" Anthony yelled, grabbing Santino's jacket by the lapels and pushing him towards the door.

"Anthony, what's gotten inta ya?" Santino asked, his eyes wild. "Why are ya doing this."

"Just go!" Anthony yelled. "Go turn the fucking car on now!"

Anthony handed him the keys to his car and hurried Santino out the door.

"Anthony, I don't know what you think...but you gotta stop this. Come on, we're friends."

"Then be a pal and warm up my car," Anthony said harshly. Anthony stood on the porch. "Go on. Get into the car."

Santino walked up to the car then paused to look back at Anthony.

"Open the fucking door, Tino. Get in and turn on the car." Anthony instructed. He pulled a gun from the back pocket of his pants and pointed it at Santino.

Santino opened the door slowly with the keys. His face was grave. He swung the door open and looked back at Anthony. He looked like he was about to slide into the car until he tried to make a run for it towards the adjoining woods.

Now Anthony knew for sure that Santino must have planted a bomb on his car. He would now make Santino suffer the same end that he had planned for him. Anthony shot at him. The shot hit Santino in the left leg and he went down onto the ground. Anthony rushed up to him and dragged him up. He felt him for a gun. There was none.

"You're going to get into the car," Anthony said pulling him to his feet.

"No Anthony," Santino sobbed, "I can't get into that car. Don't make me. Take me to the hospital, Tony. Please. I'm bleeding like crazy."

"I'll take you to the hospital, once you warm up the car. We gotta warm up the car before we go anywhere, ain't that what you told me? Funny, you didn't come in yours. We would have had another car to drive," Anthony said pushing Santino into the front seat. "But I guess that's the way you planned it."

"Oh, God! Don't Anthony."

"Start the car, or I'll blow your head off," Anthony said simply.

Anthony closed the car door and rushed back to the porch.

Santino gave him one last beseeching look before he turned the key in the ignition of the black Mercedes.

The car went up in flames, which was accompanied by a loud exploding sound. Bits of the car flew into the air and landed to the cold ground with a scraping metal sound.

Anthony stared on grimly. He had been right.

Angelina and the kids came rushing out. They looked at the car engulfed in flames. They had shock written all over their faces.

"What the hell happened?" Eve asked, staring on with amazement in her dark eyes.

Anthony turned to them. "The car blew up."

"Where's Santino?" Angelina asked. But it looked like she already knew the answer.

"He's in there," Anthony said shrugging towards the car's remains.

Ψ

Sal and Anthony discovered that Santino had been in contact with Santiago and had been helping him in his efforts to destroy The Family, Anthony in particular.

At first they had been puzzled about him turning on them, but then they found out, through his wife, that he had held a grudge against Anthony for years. The reason for the grudge, according to his wife, was because he blamed Anthony for his cousin Fran's death in the apartment fire since Anthony had been the one to order them to burn down the apartment.

After a little more persuasion, his wife told them about Santino's vivid nightmares and how he would wake up sweating and screaming. He would mutter to his wife that Fran was in his nightmares calling out to him, reaching for him through a blazing inferno.

Anthony and Sal had concluded that Santino had been a very troubled man.

Ψ

The following day, Juan Santiago was found dead in his condominium—all ten of his fingers were cut off and missing as were both of his eyeballs. He was set in his chair behind his heavy oak desk, his fingerless hands folded on the desktop as if he were conducting a deal from beyond the grave. His face was frozen in a strange macabre grin. The detectives soon noticed that not *all* of fingers were missing. Two of his detached fingers, the index fingers, were inserted pretty far up his nostrils—something that the detectives found to be quite amusing. A top hat covered the gleaming top of his skull underneath, from which most of his scalp was scraped. Tuffs of bloody dark hair and scalp hung down onto his chilling face.

He was wearing his best suit—uncreased and perfectly fitting.

He was wearing his best shoes—they were shined up and laced to perfection.

But he didn't know it.

Ψ

The next week, there was a special delivery for Mrs. Santiago. A small pink box with a red bow was delivered to her by a smiling postman. She kindly accepted the package and took it inside. Curious, she undid the ribbon and opened the box in the middle of her gleaming, large kitchen.

She screamed when she saw what was inside.

She dropped the box to the floor.

Six fingers and two thumbs rolled out onto the floor.

Chapter Thirty-two

February, 1968

    Anthony pulled into the parking lot of the modern styled apartment buildings and felt a vague sense of déjà vu.

    Years ago, he had been visiting a young woman at her apartment as he was doing to today, only to find her dead. But Anthony shook his head of those thoughts telling himself that, years ago, he had been visiting his mistress. He wasn't visiting a young woman that was his mistress, he was visiting a 17 year old girl who had needed help almost two years ago, and he had given her that. Perhaps more than most would give, but...what could he say? He felt sorry for the kid.

    Anthony heard the thumping of loud music as he approached the door. When he was directly in front of the door, he recognized the singing artist to be the Supremes. Anthony knocked on the door.

    "Is that you Anthony?" a young woman's voice called out.

    "It is."

    "Come on in then," the voice answered back.

    Anthony took out his key and opened the door. Bessie and another young girl with tawny skin and black shiny shoulder length hair were sitting on the plush carpeted floor laughing and talking as they listened to the music. Bessie turned her large dark eyes to Anthony and smiled. Her friend looked curiously at him.

    "Anthony, this is Molina. She works with me at the supermarket."

    The girl smiled at him and said hi. Anthony shook her hand and greeted her as well.

    "Do you want anything to drink or eat?" Bessie asked, standing up on her legs, which, rather than being bony as they were two years ago, were now slender and well shaped. She had a small waist and gently curving hips. Her breasts were small and pert.

    "Yeah, get me something to drink...fruit juice or something," Anthony   stood up."I'm going to use the bathroom. I'll be back."

When Anthony came out of the bathroom he heard a clear alto voice singing along to the song that was playing. Anthony paused and listened closer. Whoever was singing, Bessie or Molina, had a beautiful, strong, voice. He continued walking and entered the living room quietly. Bessie was standing in the middle of the carpeted floor, holding a hair brush and singing into it like she was on stage. It was Bessie whose voice was so clear and lovely. Molina was sitting down, smiling as she listened to her friend sing.

Anthony smiled. "Bessie. I didn't know you could sing like that."

Bessie turned to Anthony and stopped singing. She smiled shyly. "I'm alright, I guess."

"You're more than all right. You're fantastic. I've never heard of voice like yours…gosh. You are amazing."

Bessie, thoroughly embarrassed now went to the kitchen and brought back a glass of cranberry juice and handed it to Anthony who was sitting on the couch.

"You know what. With a voice like that, you can get a record deal," said Molina. She had a strong Latin accent.

Bessie smiled quickly. "I don't think so."

Anthony nodded. "She's right, Bessie. In fact. I think that I have a couple of people on mind that wouldn't mind listening to you. They would sign you to their label in an instant."

"I don't know," Bessie said mournfully.

"Believe me, kid. When I hear something good. I know it. And you, my dear, are good," Anthony said. His mind was already formulating a plan.

Ψ

"This rice is delicious," Tina said with a smile. "Edda, I must tell you. You are a wonderful cook."

Edda smiled at her friend's praise.

Edda and Michael had been living in the commune in Southern California for almost a year now and they were loving every minute of it. The simplicity and calmness of the environment was soothing to them as was the high spirituality and sense of unity.

Here at the Starlight Unison commune, they grew their own vegetables and fruits, they grew their own grain, baked their own bread, and they made the majority of their food from scratch. They were almost totally self-sufficient.

"I'm so glad that we found the true path, Hare Krishna. Thanks to our leader Srila Prabhupada," Michael said with great reverence.

Tim nodded. As the rest of them, he was dressed the flowing saffron robes with beads draped around his neck. His long red hair was twisted in dreds and he wore a scruffy beard and mustache.

"You know what? We need to get the full experience of this. We need to go back to the roots of India so that we can be more immersed. There are too many distractions here," Tina said as she took a bite of the rice and vegetables.

"The headquarters of our movement, International Society of Krishna Consciousness, are in Mayapur India. I think it would be a good idea to go there for a while and get a true sense of it. India is such a spiritual country," Edda said with a nod.

Michael and Edda had gotten married in accordance to the religion and it's philosophies on sex and marriage. They had invited some family members to the whole unusual affair. Alfie and Penny looked shocked to see bald headed followers shaking rattles and thumping drums at the ceremony as they chanted 'Hare Krishna.' Alfie tentatively held four year old Marsha on his lap, while Penny rubbed her swelling stomach (she was eight months pregnant). Ester had refused to come because she thought the idea of Michael and Edda being in what she called a 'cult' was wrong. So by extension Marco, didn't come either. But who was she to talk, Michael had pointed out. Besides, he had only pity, not anger, for his mother and her lack of enlightenment. Wendy had come and tried to look blasé about the whole thing. She was mostly just happy that the two were finally getting married considering that they now had a baby boy, Benjamin. Anthony and Sal had also come, although they thought this spiritual enlightenment thing going on with Edda and Michael was a bunch of crock. Sal had sat through the whole affair wide-eyed while Anthony had been amazed and somewhat intrigued.

"You know what? I think that we should *live* in India for a while. There are a lot of others like us there," said Tina.

They all agreed.

The next week, when Edda calmly told her mother that she and Michael were moving to India to live, she had been shocked. Edda and Michael were there in Chicago visiting for the week.

"What do you mean you're moving to India!" Wendy had exclaimed.

"Because it is the perfect environment for us. America is too superficial. The Indians are so down to earth. Besides, we will learn more while over there."

Wendy looked at her strangely. "You know, Edda. There is an extreme to everything. Don't you think Michael and you are going too far with this thing?"

"No. I want our son to live in a spiritual environment like India. It is where we belong."

Wendy just shook her head slowly. She could barely believe her ears. She was afraid that her daughter and her son-in-law were going off their rockers. Not only that, they wanted to drag her grandson Benny into it. That she did not like. That evening, she called her step-son Anthony.

"Please, you've got to talk to them, Tony. She and Michael are intent on moving to India with Benny! Can you believe it? Someone has to talk some sense into them."

"I'll try Wendy," Anthony answered, feeling that he wouldn't have much success either.

Anthony came over the next day. He was glad to see that both his step-sister and his brother-in-law Michael were there.

"I don't know that moving to India is a very good idea," Anthony told them.

"Why not?" Michael had answered with a challenging look in his eyes.

"Because, I'm not sure that it's the best environment for my nephew, Benny. That's why. You two gotta think about your kid. It's not only about the two of you," Anthony had shot back.

"Benny will be in a wonderful environment. He will be away from the materialism and the violence of the west," Edda had answered calmly.

"And you don't think that there's any violence in India? Please. Those people are probably more lax with it," Anthony pointed out.

Michael shook his head, which was now totally shaved bald. All his facial hair was gone as well. His handsome features were quite prominent. "Not where we're going. There will be nothing but peace."

"That's a load of crap," Anthony spat out, getting more and more pissed off by the minute. "What about Wendy, Edda. Don't you care about how much you hurt her?"

Edda looked at him with her clear blue eyes. "Mom will understand eventually. Everyone would, including you."

Anthony gave his step-sister a strange look. She was totally gone. He wondered if they were using drugs, but then decided no. He had done a little research and found out that it was against their religion to do any type of drugs. They were merely brainwashed.

"We're going and there's nothing that anyone can do about it," Michael succinctly said.

The next week, true to their word, they had left for India.

Ψ

The man was about ten years younger than her and attractive. He had dark olive skin and dark blue eyes. He had chiseled cheekbones and full lips that covered a set of straight white teeth. His nose was gently arched and his jawbones strong and square. He told Angelina that he was from the Greek Dodecanese Island of Leros. He spoke fluent Greek, and his accent was charming.

Angelina had met him in an unusual place—while waiting in line at the bank. It was a Monday morning and the line was going extremely slowly. He was standing behind her and had struck up a conversation with her.

"I do not think that we will be out of here before noon," he had said to her as he glanced at his gold Rolex watch.

Angelina, not noticing him before, had turned around to see who was talking to her. She saw a pair of deep blue eyes staring back at her. He was incredibly handsome and there was such intelligence in his face. His firm jaw line spoke of self-dignity and pride. His steady stare showed great acumen and deep thinking. Angelina was instantly attracted. She was sure that she had seen a spark of attraction in his eyes as well.

"Yes. It's usually like this on Monday mornings," Angelina had responded, trying to keep her voice casual. Her back had broken out into a sweat. Luckily she was wearing a suit jacket over her blouse.

"Well, I certainly hope they don't take forever." He looked her over, taking in her full breasts and her curvy hips. He held out his large hand. "My name is Damaris Brettos."

Angelina took his hand. She felt shivers at his touch. "My name's Angelina," she had said, purposefully leaving out her last name.

They had dated for two weeks. On the third week, Angelina and he had made love.

And Angelina had loved it. He was a phenomenal lover. In bed, Demaris was passionate and experimental, which reminded her of Earnest. But Damaris was ten times as intense and had her doing things that she had never done before. Up until now, she hadn't had anyone else to compare Earnest's lovemaking with. She was enjoying every minute of this affair with this younger man that showered her with affection and attention. He was constantly telling her how beautiful she was. Constantly giving her kisses and touches…leaving her weak with desire.

"You gotta be careful with this guy, Angie. He looks kinda sneaky to me," Sal had told his little sister.

Angelina had stared disdainfully at him. "You just don't want to see me with any men. I have a life to live just like you do, Salvatore. I'm a grown woman. Don't *you* tell me what to do."

When Damaris had begun asking her for monetary loans, Angelina had handed the money to him blindly and without the slightest worry.

"I will pay you back every cent!" he would declare each and every time she would place a check into his enthusiastic hands. "When my business soars, and it will very soon, I will pay you back double. And you will have everything you want! I will buy you diamonds, jewels, and furs."

Angelina believed him. She never told anyone about the loans. She knew that they would be quick to judge him and her. Damaris and she had something special. She didn't expect anyone to understand.

"Let us go away for the weekend…Let's go to Greece. I want you to see my homeland. You will love it. And don't worry. I will pay for it all."

Angelina had happily agreed to the trip. She had told Anthony that she was going away for a few days and would be back. When he had questioned her more, she had hesitantly revealed that she was going to Greece with Damaris.

"What, are you crazy? You've known the guy for only a few months," Anthony had exclaimed, amazed at his sister's naivety.

Angelina shrugged.

"And who's paying for all this?" he asked, eagerly waiting for the answer that he wanted to hear.

"He is," Angelina responded, with satisfaction. "He's paying for everything."

Much to Angelina's relief, that had shut her twin brother up. She wondered where he found all the time to be up in her business between managing the young, up and coming singer Bessie Woods, taking care of two of the hotels that he owned, and everything else that he did.

Two days before they departed, Damaris picked Angelina up in his Mercedes.

"So where are we going?" Angelina asked, once they pulled off.

Damaris smiled at her as he drove down the road. "We are going shopping! I am sure that you need some clothes for our little trip. And do not worry. I will pay for everything. I will spare no expense when it comes to you, my dear."

Angelina smiled. So they had gone to all the department stores and the boutiques and Angelina had bought outfit after outfit and bathing suit after bathing suit.

"Come, come, try this on," Damaris said holding up a deep, wine colored bikini.

Angelina blushed. "I can't wear that…it's so small." Angelina chuckled nervously. "Besides, I think I'm a little to old for that."

Damaris flicked his wrist at her. "Oh please. You look ten years younger than you are. What are you talking about? And you have a beautiful body."

"It's just that I've never worn anything like this…"

"Well, there is a first time for everything," Damaris said holding the bikini out to her.

Angelina took it and disappeared into the changing room.

Angelina took off her clothes and slipped on the small bikini. She looked at herself in the mirror and almost gasped aloud. She looked wonderful in it. Her lush body filled out the bathing suit very well.

Her full breasts were prominent, almost wantonly so, in the bra top. Her waist was small and her stomach flat. Her hips flared out smoothly. She turned around and examined her still pert behind. Over the years, she had not lost a bit of her shape. She looked positively sexy.

"Do you have it on yet?" Damaris called eagerly.

Angelina stepped out of the room for him to see. His eyes twinkled at the sight of her. He took her in greedily with his eyes.

"My God, you look amazing. Like a siren. A temptress."

Angelina blushed. "You don't think it's too much, do you?"

Damaris instantly shook his head. "Not at all. I must buy this one for you. I will enjoy walking on the beaches with you in this. Such a beautiful woman is all mine?" he said with amazement.

The next day, Angelina happily related the past day's shopping spree and all that Damaris had bought for her.

"Well, at least he was the one buying," Anthony said a little grudgingly.

The next day, Angelina and Damaris left for the Mediterranean.

Ψ

"Oh my gosh, Sal, come here! Quick! Isn't that Angelina's boyfriend on television?" Squealed Marie as she stood in front of the television set in the living room.

Sal came rushing in. It was the four o'clock news with a report. And sure enough, there was Damaris on the screen, looking shocked and upset, talking to a news reporter. Tears were coming down his face.

"I couldn't find her! I tried to get to her, but...she was gone by the time I went to get her!" Damaris said to the short, black, news reporter and then he buried his face into his hands.

The coffee colored man made a frown and asked, "so it was just the two of you?"

"Yes, we were on vacation here. We were staying at a villa by the sea. I rented a boat for us to sail in for the evening, we were drinking quite a lot…especially Angelina. I should have told her to slow down with the drinking, but she was having so much fun. The winds got a little rough and she fell in, just like that. She was drunk! I kept telling her to stay away from the edge."

Suddenly the phone rang. Marie rushed to pick it up.

"Hello?" Anthony's despondent voice called into the receiver.

"Anthony! Are you watching the news?" Marie asked.

"Yes—yes. T-they called me—" Anthony broke down into tears before he could finish his sentence.

"What is it Anthony, did they find her?" Marie asked with worry. But it was no use. Marie's brother-in-law was crying hysterically over the phone.

"Who is that?" Sal asked his wife after tearing his worried eyes away from the television screen.

"It's Anthony! He's crying, I don know…" Marie said with a sob.

Marie and Sal turned their eyes back to the television in time to see a man come up to the news reporter and whisper something in his ears. The news reporter nodded his head and turned back to Damaris.

"I was just told that Angelina's body was found…

Sal's face went into a frown and his eyes filled up with tears. He hunched over on the couch. My God, how could this be happening! His little sister, gone. It had to be a mistake…

Marie, forgetting for the moment that Anthony was on the other line, put the phone down, and came up beside her husband. Tears were also in her eyes. She hugged her brother. "I'm so sorry, Sal. I'm so sorry."

Ψ

When Anthony heard the news of his twin's death, he went into hibernation for months and refused to speak or see anyone.

"Anthony, I'm sorry about your sister, but if you want to continue being my manager, you have to be there! I can't do everything by myself!" exclaimed Bessie.

Anthony knew she was right.

Ψ

The medical examiner, Eddie Mitchell, gave Earnest, Sal, Anthony, Wendy, and Earnest the straight facts. The four of them had come down together. Earnest and Winston had flown in from Texas.

"Well, it does appear that Angelina did die from drowning, but... well, here's the thing. We drew some blood from the cadaver and we found a high concentration of diazepam or better known as Valium. The first thing I did was to call her doctor, who happens to be a close and personal friend of mine. He told me, off the record, that she did have a prescription for Valium for sleep problems. Were any of you aware of that?"

All four of them exchanged looks. Finally Anthony spoke. "She never told us that."

Eddie sighed. "Well, apparently she was having problems sleeping. Her doctor prescribed them. If taken correctly and in the proper dosage, they do what they're supposed to do. But as I just said...she had three times the amount that she should have consumed. An over dose of Valium could result in impaired motor coordination, impaired reflexes, impaired balance, dizziness...and even coma. And if taken with alcohol, these symptoms become even more pronounced and we did find alcohol in her system." The medical examiner nervously cleared his throat. "Did Angelina ever have any...suicidal tendencies?"

Sal scowled. "No, she did not."

Eddie nodded quickly. "I didn't think so. Besides, even if she did, why would she choose, of all times, to kill herself while on vacation with a man that she cared about? It sounds too ludicrous. So...um...I've reported all this to the police. There's going to be an investigation. Apparently, she was also seeing a psychologist. The police are going to get her records from there. Since this is an ongoing investigation, you folks aren't really supposed to know all the details. Please keep what I told you today to yourself."

Wendy nodded in appreciation. "Thank you. We will."

"So, do you think that Damaris, had something to do with her death? Do you think he spiked her food or drink?" Anthony asked.

The medical examiner cleared his throat. "I'm not really at liberty to discuss that..."

"If I were to give you five grand, would you talk?" Sal asked.

The Eddie Mitchell looked at him as if her were a Martian. "My job could be on the line here, if I give out too much information during an investigation."

"Well, you gave us some information already…and we're not going to say a word to anyone else," Earnest said somberly.

The medical examiner looked around at the group standing before him. "Please keep your money. But you have to promise me that what I say will not go beyond these four walls," he said earnestly.

All four of them nodded.

"Okay. Well, about two hours before she died, she had an alcoholic beverage. Now, her blood alcohol level wasn't very high so we can't safely attribute her death to her falling off the boat in a drunken haze, as Damaris claims. But…I find it highly probable that Valium had been crushed up and mixed in the alcohol…and it is highly likely that she became uncoordinated then… she could have fallen…or she could have even gone into a coma…it was quite a lot of Valium."
"Do you think that my sister was murdered?" Sal asked, softly.

Eddie hesitated and said, "It's looking more and more likely. She was drugged and I don't think that she drugged herself," the medical examiner told them. Eddie rose to his feet and headed towards the door.

"Well, that's about all I have for today, but I'll keep you folks in the loop. I will definitely keep in touch."

Anthony nodded. "Thank you. Thank you so much. We won't forget this."

Eddie smiled slightly. "I'm just doing my job."

Ψ

Angelina's death was no longer being considered an accident. It was now considered a homicide. But by the time the police went to get Damaris, their main suspect, for questioning, he was gone without a trace. After months and months of searching, he still wasn't found. The FBI was baffled at Damaris' total and absolute disappearance. All the FBI discovered was that his name, Damaris Brettos, was just an alias and wasn't his birth name, but they had no idea what his birth name was. Anthony and Sal also did an extensive search, using their connections, and only came to dead ends. As a last resort, Earnest hired private detectives to try and find Damaris. The PI also turned up with nothing after an exhaustive search.

It was as if Damaris Brettos never existed.

Ψ

"Oh my God, I can't believe I got signed to MCA records!" Bessie said hugging Anthony.

Anthony smiled. Holding her at arms length he said, "We're going out to celebrate…This is amazing. But I always knew that you would be signed. You have a wonderful voice. Did you see how entranced Harry Layman was when he heard you?"

Bessie frowned. "Wait. Who was that again?"

"That was the white guy with the mustache and the beard. He's the Record Label A&R."

"Oh okay," Bessie said nodding her head. "But you're still going to stay as my manager, right?"

Anthony shrugged. "If you want me to. I have a certain amount of experience, but I'm not going to lie to you. I ain't no professional."

Bessie chuckled. "Yeah, I want you to manage me. You'll learn, right?"

Anthony smiled. "Right."

They went out to eat and Anthony drove her home. He stopped in front of her apartment, Bessie didn't get out.

"What's wrong?" Anthony asked her.

Bessie turned and faced him. "Would you come in with me?"

"You mean walk you to the door? Sure! I don't know where my manners are at."

Bessie shook her head. "No, I mean…would you come in for a while?"

Anthony stared at her blankly.

"Would you come in for the night?" Bessie asked, softly.

Bessie leaned forwards and kissed Anthony on the lips. Anthony felt a rush of heat, but quickly contained himself. Anthony pushed her gently away.

"Bessie…I can't. I don't want you to think that this is what I ultimately wanted…that you owe me…I wanted to help you."

"I know."

"You're just a girl…I'm in my forties."

"So what? You're the nicest man I've met."

"You're young yet. You'll meet plenty of guys that are nicer than I am," Anthony said with a chuckle. "I think of you…as a daughter. You know what I'm saying?"

"But I'm almost eighteen. I'll be eighteen in a month."

"Yeah, but—"

Bessie leaned over to him and kissed him deeply again. This time, Anthony didn't push her away. He touched her smooth shoulders, ran his hands softly down her slender arms, and finally held her small waist. Bessie leaned back a little to look him in the eyes.

"Are you coming up?" she asked, softly as she slid out of the car.

Anthony turned off the car and followed right after her.

Ψ

Bessie's life, almost instantly, began to be filled with appointments, contracts, recordings, and publicity appearances. It was such a whirlwind, but she was enjoying every minute of it. She was happy to have Anthony with her every step of the way. Bessie was truly in awe of him. She looked to him as both a lover and supporter. He was almost like a father to her in the way of making sure she had everything that she needed, and taking care of her. But she also felt a strong sexual attraction to him, she knew that he felt the same way towards her and their passionate sex life showed it. He may have been in his forties, but he looked at least ten years younger and he was incredibly handsome and attractive. Her feelings were very ambivalent. At times, she was sure that she was in love with him, but sometimes she would try to convince herself otherwise.

Chapter Thirty-three

1971, Chicago Illinois

On the morning of her twentieth birthday, on July 15th, Bessie woke up with extreme nausea. She hopped out of her queen sized bed, covered with linen sheets, and rushed into the adjoining bathroom. Before she closed the door, she saw that Anthony was still sleeping soundly in bed and hadn't stirred.

Bessie stuck her head into the porcelain bowl and threw up. For five minutes straight, she was throwing up. She thought she would never stop. Tears came to her eyes. After ten minutes she was still in the bathroom. She heard a knock.

"Bessie, are you all right in there?"

Bessie moaned in response. Anthony opened the door and poked his head in. When he saw Bessie on the floor, he came in and squatted beside her.

"What's the matter?" Anthony asked, putting an arm around her.

Bessie slowly shook her head. "I don't know. I feel so sick…I woke up like this!"

Anthony frowned and then a spark of realization came into his eyes. "Oh gosh…do you think that you're…pregnant?"

"I don't know! Maybe. I hope not now!" Bessie exclaimed.

"But I thought that you had that IUD thing put in…" Anthony said, trailing off.

"I do! I don't know what's happening!"

"Let's not panic. We could be mistaken…"

But they were not mistaken. The next week, the doctor told Bessie that she was pregnant.

"But I thought that with the IUD it was impossible to get pregnant!" Bessie had wailed.

"Well, my dear, you happen to be in the lucky, small, percentage that got pregnant with the IUD inserted," the doctor had responded cheerfully.

"Yeah, lucky," Bessie had muttered.

Ψ

Edda sat on the soft cushion and swept back her long blond hair that trailed past her waist. She rested her hands on her swollen stomach. She was due in a month. She nodded to Michael to let in their next visitor.

A brown skinned woman with a long jet black braid came in. She was dressed in a green Sari. She carried a small child that looked to be fast asleep in her arms. She spoke in Gujarati, one of the local tongues.

"I need to know, will my husband return from Pakistan safely?"

Edda gestured for her to put her head forward. She woman did so. Edda placed her hands on the woman's temples and closed her eyes.

In her mind, Edda saw a young man in an Indian army uniform, carrying a gun. He spoke rapidly to a comrade and then there was an explosion. Then she saw the young widow carrying a child and grieving at the funeral. Edda quickly sat back and opened her eyes.

The woman noticed the disturbed expression on Edda's face and asked her, "what is it? Is my husband going to be okay?"

Edda's blue eyes filled with tears. "I'm sorry," she muttered in Gujurati. "He won't."

The woman nodded her head as her eyes filled with tears. "I didn't think so. I'm so sorry. That is all I wanted to learn. Thank you Wide Eyes. I will leave now."

"Do you want to know how?" Edda asked, softly. She took the woman's hand.

The woman shook her head and stood up. The woman left a gift by the door, before she quickly slipped out.

Edda looked at her four-year-old son playing in the corner with Michael and she felt truly blessed.

Months after Michael and Edda had moved to India in 1967, they had accepted Hinduism as their main religion. Tina and Tim had moved to Odessa, while Michael and Edda had remained in the North. Soon, the locals began to take notice of Edda's extra sensory perception and her uncanny ability to tell the future. She was also able to speak with the spirits of their dead ancestors and give them messages. They began to believe that she was a prophet blessed by the gods. Edda, although reluctant at first, would receive gifts in return for her predictions and communications. And if the person had nothing to give, Edda would help them all the same.

Edda came over and joined her son and husband and tried to look happy.

She would be disturbed by this last revelation to the young wife for the rest of the night.

She accepted no more clients for the day.

Ψ

April, 1972

Leonardo Gionelli was born on April 17, 1972.

Anthony held his small son with amazement. "Why don't you move in with me."

"No," Bessie responded.

"Why not?" Anthony asked with a frown. It was a strange stand of morals, considering everthing.

"Well…I know it sounds crazy, but we're not married, so I prefer to have my own place."

"Well, let's get married then," Anthony said.

Bessie chuckled. "I don't think so. What kind of proposal is that?"

Anthony made a face at her and looked down with pride at his son. He had always wanted a son and he had finally gotten one. He put his finger in the small delicate hand. The baby instantly gripped the finger and gurgled. The small dark eyes stared up at Anthony. Anthony felt a swelling of pride.

As he looked at his son, he remembered the words of his brother months earlier, "I can't believe you're having a kid with a girl that's over twenty years younger than you! But I gotta give it to you…you were always a lady's man."

"Make sure no one gets through those doors but the doctors and the nurses," Anthony said to the bodyguards.

The press and the media as well as avid fans of Bessie Wood were screaming by the hospital doors down below. Some fans had managed to squeeze past security and get into the hospital. As did some people from the press, but they never made it to the third floor where Bessie was.

It wasn't everyday that a hospital delivered the baby of a big star.

Chapter Thirty-four

Los Angeles, California, July, 1990

Colors swirled and swirled around in the atmosphere that surrounded her. Anna looked around her and saw nothing but shades of blue, green and orange...she felt as if she was floating in space. There was nothing and no one beside her, but the iridescence and the seeming endless silence. Space, slightly cool, but not cold. Neither was it too warm. It was just perfect. Something compelled Anna to look up, and so she did. A big bright globe of pulsing, white light was above her, yet strangely, its light never reached down to where she was. In fact, if she hadn't had looked up, she wouldn't have known that the light was there. Then she heard a whisper...soft and insistent. She was sure that it was her name being called...Anna, Anna, Anna...

"Anna! Can you hear me?" a voice frantically asked.

Anna fully opened her eyes. And although her sight was considerably cloudy, she took in the bright, white walls that surrounded her. She pulled up her right arm to wipe at her eyes and saw that an IV was attached to it. For a moment, she stared at it confused and realized that it was confining her from raising the arm any further. She lowered it and instead used her left hand.

Anna looked at the woman standing by her bed. For a moment, she couldn't think who it could be, but then it hit her with a force. It was her mother.

"Oh, Gosh, Anna. You're awake! I'm so happy. Oh gosh!"

Anna's mom leaned over and embraced her.

"I'm going to get the doctor!" her mother exclaimed before rushing out the door.

Candace came back with a dour looking, middle-aged man. Two nurses were with him as well. He came over to Anna's bedside.

"How are you feeling?" he asked, checking her pulse.

"I'm fine," Anna said softly.

The doctor got out a small light and placed it before Anna's eyes. After a moment he said, "Please follow the light with your eyes as I move it."

And so Anna did. The doctor nodded approvingly and put the light back into the pocket of his white lab coat. He examined her further. Anna sat patiently through it before asking a question.

"Uhhh...what's going on? Am I in the hospital?" Anna asked, confused as to why she was here.

"Yes, honey. You are," her mother said with sadness in her eyes.

"How did I get here? What happened?" Anna asked, trying to sit up. "How long have I been here?"

'Well, you've been in a coma for a little over three months now," the doctor answered.

Candace placed a firm hand on her daughter's shoulder, compelling her not to raise herself any further.

"I don't want you to exert yourself, Anna. We have to keep you in observation for a few days before we discharge you," the doctor said firmly. "I'll be back later to check on you. If you need anything, call a nurse." The doctor left with the two nurses trailing behind him.

Anna repeated her question once the doctor and the nurses left.

"You, Jackie and Winston got into a car accident," answered Candace.

Anna rubbed her forehead with her left hand. She flinched at her own touch. She felt soar all over.

"Oh Gosh! Are they okay?"

Candace gave her a smile. "Jackie's fine..." Candace's face darkened at her next words. "So is Winston."

"You don't look too happy about that, I mean Winston being okay."

"How could you say something like that?" Candace asked, managing to look properly affronted. "I wouldn't wish death on anyone."

"But what happened?" Anna asked.

"What do you mean?" her mother responded.

"I mean...what happened in the accident?" Anna asked, impatiently. What else could her mother think she was referring to?

"Well...Jackie, Winston and you were driving. I don't know where. According to you *husband*, you three were going to the mall. Apparently, somebody ran the car off the road. At least that's what the witnesses are saying," Candace said softly.

Anna's heart began to beat heavily in her chest. "We were run off the road? What for? Was that somebody's idea of a sick joke or something?"

Candace sighed. "One of the witnesses got the tag number of the perp. Well, it traced back to someone. An old woman that lives in the valley and had had her car reported stolen a few days before. So, at this moment, the cops don't know who's behind this."

Anna frowned. She was deeply disturbed by this revelation. She closed her eyes and a dull aching went through her head. "I have a major headache."

"I'll call the nurse," Candace said frantically.

"Mom, calm down. It's only a headache."

Candace looked at her daughter disapprovingly. "One can never tell in a condition like yours." Candace rang the button.

A short, African-American nurse with caramel skin, came bustling in. She smiled at both of the ladies.

"Anna says she has a headache," Candace began.

"Let me give you some Tylenol. The headache is most likely due to the concussion you had," the nurse said kindly. She turned towards the door. "I'll be back with the Tylenol in a jiffy."

True to her word, the nurse was back in less than a minute. She handed Anna the two pills and a paper cup of water.

"Swallow those. And if you need anything else later on, just call one of the nurses."

"Thank you," Anna said as she put the pills in her mouth. She washed them down with the cup of water.

There was a slight knock at the door. Anna looked at her mother. Candace shrugged her shoulders, headed to the door, and opened it.

Standing there was Winston with baby Jackie in his hands. Tall and incredibly handsome as always, he stood nervously in the doorway. He gave his mother-in-law a hesitant smile and looked over at Anna. Anna stared back at him, her face expressionless. She glanced at her mother who was wearing a look of displeasure.

Winston stepped inside the room and walked up to Anna's bedside. Anna smiled at her baby and reached her arms out towards her. Winston placed the baby in her mother's arms. Anna kissed the one-year-old's plump cheek and placed her on her lap.

Winston leaned over and kissed Anna on the forehead. Candace's frown deepened.

"How are you feeling?" Winston asked, gently as he touched her face. He stared intently into her eyes. His green eyes were filled with concern and worry.

Anna glanced at her mother. Her mother stared back at her.

"I'm all right...just getting some headaches," Anna responded. Jackie gurgled on her lap and reached a small hand up to touch Anna's face. Anna smiled.

"Well, the doctor says that he wants to keep you in for observation. If everything is fine, you might be able to come home later on this week."

"You weren't hurt badly?" Anna asked her husband.

Winston smiled slightly and touched the bandage on his head. "Besides this here gash, I'm fine. Jackie has only a few minor abrasions. Other than that...we're both great. Unfortunately, you took the brunt of it," Winston said, his face transforming into a frown.

Anna nodded and looked again at her mother who was now wearing a curious expression.

Something was rotten in the state of Denmark.

Ψ

"Are you sure that you're going to be okay?" Winston asked Anna as he looked worriedly at her.

Anna, finally home from the hospital, was lying in bed experiencing another one of her frequent and terrible migraines. CAT scans, MRIs, and other tests revealed no foreseeable damage, they could find no organic cause to link it to, but ever since the accident, Anna had been having extremely debilitating migraines. Tylenol and aspirin were doing nothing to help, so the doctor began prescribing codeine for her. Fortunately, the codeine was working. Within minutes, Anna's headache would ease after taking it.

"I'm going to be fine," Anna told her husband. "I have Mae to help me with the baby. Plus the cook that you hired—I have all the help that I need, Winston."

Winston nodded. "I know that this business trip is important, but...I'm still worried about you. I'll be gone for quite a while...but I need to be there to oversee the new project to make sure everything goes smoothly."

"I'll be fine, Winston. Don't worry about me," Anna said with a small smile.

There was a knock at the bedroom door. Winston said to come in. It was their driver, a Pakistani man called Ali.

"It is nine o'clock, Sir. We had better be going," Ali said in his clipped accent.

Winston nodded. "Are all my bags in the car?"

"Yes, Sir," he responded.

"I'll be right out, then," Winston responded.

Ali nodded and left the room

Winston turned back to his wife. "Take it easy, Anna." He kissed her on the lips. "If you need me, call me. You know the number to my room at the hotel I'm staying in New York."

Anna nodded. "I do. So don't worry."

Winston smiled. "I love you. And I'll see you in three weeks."

Anna smiled and forced the dreaded words out of her mouth. "I love you too."

Ψ

"It's about time that bastard gets on his way," Ramón said cattily to Anna over the phone.

Anna chuckled. "You're so mean."

Ramón let out a little gasp, "Me? Mean? I'm simply honest, darling. He's a bastard and you know it. We all know it. Don't we, Hector," Ramón said to Hector who was sitting beside him on the couch. Hector smiled at his partner with a mischievous grin.

Anna laughed. Much to her surprise months ago, Hector and Ramón had started a relationship. At first, Ramón had been hesitant to do so, considering that he had AIDS. But before anything, Ramón had been completely honest with Hector, letting him know about his status and what impact that would have on any sex life. In fact, Ramón had told Hector that he couldn't, *wouldn't*, have sex, protection or no protection, afraid that he would infect another person. Hector had agreed and told him that just being around him, hugging him, holding his hand, and touching him, was enough for him. He didn't care that they couldn't have sex. Ramón had been surprised at this and told him that he understood if he were to look for sex elsewhere. But, during the year that they had been together, not once had Hector been with anyone. He was content with Ramón and loved him deeply. Ramón felt the same way towards Hector and often wished that he had met Hector before he contracted AIDS. This was a man that he could have spent the rest of his life with. But whatever time Ramón had left in this world, he was happily spending it with Hector. Six months ago, they had moved in together.

"Come on. We are going out tonight—"

Anna cut Ramón off. "I have a terrible headache. I can't even think of going anywhere tonight. Forget that," Anna said evasively.

Ramón caught on like a cat at a fish market. "You're up to something, aren't you!" Ramón exclaimed.

"What are you talking about?" Anna responded, a little pissed that her friend was sharp when it came to sneakiness.

"There's something you're not telling us…hummm…what are you doing?"

"I'm lying in bed tonight and trying to get some rest, that's all…"

"You are fibbing! I know when my Anna fibs!" Ramón shrieked.

"Oh for God sake, Ramón. You're imagining things!"

Anna heard a rustle and then she heard the voice of her long-time best friend, Hector, on the phone.

"What are you up to?" he asked, right away.

"Look, I don't need the two of you bitches ganging up on me. My head is hurting like a motherfucker."

"I'm a bitch?! Thanks so much for the complement…she called us bitches, Ramón!" Hector said to Ramón in the background. Anna heard giggling. "All right. We'll let you get away tonight. But tomorrow night…we won't let you slip away so easily!"

Anna laughed. "Okay. Tomorrow night, all right? I'll take an extra dose of codeine."

Hector tut-tutted. "Don't you know that stuff is addictive? Anyways, I'll talk to you tomorrow."

"All right, bye-bye. Luv ya," Anna said with a smile in her voice.

"Love you too, hon," Hector said before hanging up.

When Anna hung up the phone, she reached for her bottle of codeine and gulped down one pill. She felt instant calm and euphoria. After that, she hopped out of bed and went down the large hall way and into her husband's office. She tried the door, afraid that she would find it locked. But it wasn't. The door swung open and Anna stepped inside.

She headed to the big cherry wood desk that stood at the back of the room and stared at the drawers in either side of it. She felt a sudden flash of guilt at what she was thinking. For the most part, Anna had stayed out of her husband's affairs and she could count on one hand the number of times that she had been in this office over the three years that she had been married to him. She was thinking that her husband knew more than he was saying concering the situation of them getting run of the road four months ago.. And although her mother hadn't said anything, Anna sensed that her mother suspected something as well. Anna didn't know what she was looking for or what she would find, but…for her own peace of mind, she had to know.

Anna tried to open the top, right hand drawer. It opened with ease. She searched through it but could only see regular office supplies like staples, line paper, paper clips, and pens. She closed that drawer and went into the second one underneath it. There was some paper work and folders. She looked over ever document, finding nothing of interest. She closed that drawer growing slightly disappointed. Maybe there was nothing here. But she had been so sure….

Anna went to the last drawer in the column. The drawer was locked. She felt a trickle of trepidation. There had to be a reason as to why all the other drawers were open but he had locked this one.

Anna pulled a bobby pin out of her head and attempted to pick the lock. It wouldn't budge. Anna wasn't even sure if she was picking it right. She futilely pulled at the drawer again. She knew she couldn't break the lock because if she did, Winston would know for sure what she had been up to.

There has to be a key somewhere, Anna thought to herself as she rose to her feet from off her knees. Anna's eyes roved all over the room to search for the most likely hiding place. Anna's eyes settled upon his collection of books. Hiding a key behind them was a likely possibility.

Anna pulled every book down from the shelf. There was no key. She replaced each and every book to the position that she had found it. She searched under the rugs, looked in the filing cabinets, checked the wall under the Van Gogh painting and under the giant, perfectly intact, trilobite fossil that he dug up ten years ago in Utah. It had been a struggle sliding the large fossil aside, but she had managed. She made sure that she had pushed it back into position after—Winston had a keen eye for detail.

After about an hour of searching, Anna still couldn't find the key. She had searched every nook and cranny in the room. By the end, her curiosity about the contents of the drawer had grown so strong that she had to restrain herself from breaking the lock. She was sure that whatever was in the desk drawer would give her the answers that she was seeking. Was it possible that Winston had taken the key with him? Anna didn't know. She guessed it was possible…but it was more likely that he had it in its usual hiding spot, wherever that was.

The next day, after downing two codeine pills (she had taken three more earlier on), she called Hector and Ramón. She knew that they would be home from work by now.

"Celeste wants to know when you can come back to work. You know, you've been missing in action coming four months now," Ramón said. Anna could hear him chewing over the phone. He was obviously eating something.

"Are you having dinner?" Anna asked, feeling especially tranquil.

"No, just a snack. But I am cooking. Do you want to come over? I'm cooking up a Brazilian treat. I'm making some *moqueta, acaraje*…," Ramón trailed off.

Anna cringed as a flash of pain went through her head. Damn. The pills were wearing off again and she had just taken two about an hour ago. Cordless phone still in the crook between her shoulder and neck, she pulled open her bedside table and took out her bottle of codeine.

"Girl, how many of those pills have you taken today?" Ramón asked.

"What pills?" Anna asked, innocently.

"I can hear the rattling of the pills in the bottle, Anna, I'm not deaf," Ramón quipped. Then Ramón said "Oh, shit!"

"What?" Anna asked.

"I almost burned the stew. I had to turn off the stove and take the pot off," Ramón said mournfully. "So are you coming over or not?" he whined.

"Yeah, I'll be over," Anna said. "Set a place for me."

Ψ

"That food was delicious," Anna said to Ramón. "You are an amazing cook."

"Thank you, I know," Ramón said with pleasure. He took compliments very well.

"So, are you going to tell us what you were up to yesterday night?" Hector asked.

Anna silently damned his good memory, but then reconsidered. "Well...I've been doing some investigation."

"What about?" Hector asked, and took a sip of his drink.

"Well...the accident. I just have this feeling that Winston knows more than he's telling me...more than he telling anyone," Anna said and took a bitefull of food.

"Hmmm...I won't be surprised," Ramón said offhandedly. "The man is treacherous. When he went after you, he knew what he was doing. Young and naïve. So he could mold you."

Anna felt stung. "Well, I'm going to show him that he can't keep on fooling me," Anna shot back. "I'm no idiot."

"No darling, you aren't. As Ramón said...you're—you *were* just simply naïve," Hector said. Then he leaned forward. "We want in on this. What can me and Ramón do to help?"

Anna looked at the two men's expectant faces. "Okay. Here's the thing. Yesterday, I was looking for a key for one of the drawers in Winston's desk. I turned the office upside down. Then I looked around the house too. I found nothing. I have to find that key. Maybe your guys could help me find it?"

"I have a better idea. Why don't we just pick the lock?" Ramón said.

"I tried that. It didn't work," Anna responded.

"*You* know how to pick a lock?" Hector asked her, incredulous.

"Let me have a go at it. I'm a pro," Ramón said.

"Okay. Let's go over now," Anna said.

"But what about dessert?" Ramón protested.
"We could bring it along," responded Anna.

Ψ

In the office, Ramón attempted to pick the lock. After about half an hour of trying, he realized that it was no cheap lock. It wasn't budging.

"Now what?" Anna exclaimed and plopped down in her chair.

"I don't know," Ramón said sitting on the rug beside the desk.

Hector sat in the leather chair and picked at the cake that he was eating. Several crumbs dropped onto the floor.

"My God, Hector. You're getting crumbs everywhere!" Ramón said shrilly as he frantically plucked at the crumbs on the floor underneath the chair. He poked Hector on the arm. "Get up!" he exclaimed.

Hector reluctantly stood up and stooped down to help Ramón clear up the crumbs.

Anna spotted more crumbs by the door, in fact, Hector had left a trail. She sighed in aggravation. "Hector, you are such a messy eater."

"I am not," Hector said huffily, feeling attacked.

"I'm going to have to get the vacuum," Anna said getting up. Anna came back with the vacuum.

"There're still crumbs near the desk," Ramón complained.

"Somebody move the damn chair then. It's in the way," Anna said a touch snippily. "If Winston spots *one* crumb in here, we'll be toast."

Hector grasped the chair, lifted it, and laid it on the top of the desk. "There. It's out of the way now."

Ramón stared that the bottom of the chair with a curious expression on his face.

"What's the matter with you?" Anna asked.

"There's a small slit in the bottom of the chair," Ramón stepped forwards and stuck a finger in the slit. A moment later, he pulled out a silver key.

"Oh gosh. That's gotta be it!" Anna said excitedly. She took the key from Ramón's hand and kissed him on the cheek. "Thank you so much!"

"No problem. I have a knack for these things," Ramón said with a smile.

"You wouldn't have seen it if I hadn't made a mess on the floor," Hector said, determined to have a small part of the glory.

"I'm sure I would have. It was only a matter of time," Ramón said filled with self-confidence.

"Or perhaps not. You didn't even think…"

Anna ignored them both as she placed the key in the lock. She pulled the drawer open. There was a large manila envelop on top of the pile. She pulled it out and took out the rest of the stuff underneath as Hector and Ramón looked on. At the bottom, there was a black and white headshot picture of a woman. Anna took it out and looked at it.

"I wonder's who *that* is," Ramón commented about the dark haired woman with the wide smile.

"Do you know who it is?" Hector asked Anna.

Anna shook her head and frowned.

"Whoever it is, she looks a little like Winston, around the mouth… do you suppose that it's a relative? She looks Spanish," Ramón said quietly.

Hector squinted at the picture and shook his head. "Nah. Not Spanish. She looks Italian. Southern Italian. Maybe Sicilian. You can see it in her face."

Anna shook her head and stared at the smiling woman. She looked to be in her mid thirties. She wasn't conventionally pretty, but she did have an attractiveness about her that was wholesome and catching. Anna wondered if this was a picture of a woman that Winston was seeing.

Everyone was thinking the same thing, neither Ramón nor Hector brought up the obvious question out of good taste.

"Turn the picture around. Maybe there's writing on the back," Hector said.

Anna flipped the picture over. It had the year 1953 on it. She relaxed with relief. Because it was only a headshot. Before, she couldn't really tell that it was an old picture. Plus, the woman's hair wasn't in any distinctive style of the period. It was loose, the dark waves hanging down her shoulders.

"Maybe it's his mother," suggested Ramón.

"I don't know," Anna answered.

"Of course you don't know. That man's been keeping secrets galore from you," said Ramón with a touch of annoyance.

"All right, let's look at the rest of the stuff," Hector said glancing at the pile of papers and envelopes.

Ramón reached for the large manila envelope and dumped the contents on the desktop.

"Ramón!" exclaimed Anna, amazed at his rashness.

"What?" Ramón said sheepishly. "We can't stand around forever."

The first thing that caught their attention was the pictures. A man that looked to be in his fifties, with dark olive skin, salt and pepper hair, and a tall, muscular frame, was in every one. One picture was of him on a balcony overlooking the sea, another was of him getting into the back of a black Rolls Royce, and another was of him kissing a beautiful, shapely, dark-haired teenaged girl that looked to be around fifteen.

"Hmmm...whoever this is he is certainly robbing the cradle," Ramón commented. There were others as well, all having the common theme of him. But it also appeared that he was unaware that these pictures were being taken of him. They looked like surveillance pictures.

"Who the heck is this dreamboat," Hector asked, obviously in awe of the older handsome man.

Ramón gave him a nasty look. Hector saw it and grinned. "I can look, can't I? But I don't touch.."

Ramón turned his eyes back to the picture. Anna looked through the papers. They were photocopies of documents. One was of a passport. It appeared to belong to the man in the picture. The man was about thirty years younger in the passport picture, but the face was still obviously his. The name identified him as Adar Antoun. His birth date was January, 19, 1936, his birthplace, Damascus, Syria.

"Hmmm...," Hector said examining another photocopied document. "Here's a driver's license. It's was issued in America in 1968."

Anna took the paper from Hector and looked at it. The same man looked to be in his early thirties, about ten years older than his passport picture. Only thing was that on this document, he had a different name. The license said Damaris Brettos. The birth date was a little different as well. It read June, 17, 1934.

"Hummm. Greek name," Hector commented. "Thing is, he doesn't look Greek to me. He doesn't have the features."

"These are all one and the same person. Obviously, some of these papers are false. Question is, which ones?" Ramón said, looking through the other papers.

"Well, I'm thinking that the more recent one is false. The driver's license. I think that maybe the passport is the right information, considering that he looked so young there," Hector said. "Plus. He doesn't look Greek, although most people wouldn't question it because of the inexperience. But he does look Middle Eastern."

Anna took up one of the pictures where the man was standing on his patio. It almost looked as if he were staring directly into the lens of the camera. His dark blue eyes were staring straight ahead, his sharp jawbones slightly tensed as if he were thinking of something. *Who are you?* Anna silently asked the picture.

"You know what? I know who might be able to help us," Anna said.

"Who?" Ramón asked, poking through the other papers on the desk.

"Winston's father. Are you two up for a trip to Texas?"

Ramón placed a disbelieving hand against his chest. "Are you nuts? Texas? Just like that?"

"Winston's coming back in three weeks. I gotta go sooner than later, I don't have a lot of time. I really want to find this out, you know. Me and my daughter's lives are in the balance here," Anna said earnestly.

Hector grunted and stood up. "Well, since you put it that way...I guess we can go this weekend."

Ψ

That evening, Anna had made sure to call ahead and tell Winston's father, Earnest, about her and some friend's being in town for the weekend.

"Sure thing, Anna. Come on down. In fact, if you like, you all can stay with me. I have no problem at all," the old man said jovially.

At 77, Earnest Hurst looked about a decade younger with his youthful face, his clear green eyes, his erect posture, and ropey arms and legs.

Earnest came to the airport to meet them. They drove back to his ranch and he had his housekeeper show them their rooms.

"This place is gigantic," Ramón said in complete awe.

Anna nodded. "I know. There are six bedrooms in all."

"He lives here by himself?" Ramón asked, amazed

"Well, besides his staff," Anna responded.

That evening at dinner, Anna brought up the reason for their trip. She told her father-in-law about the pictures and the documents that she found. She was careful not to say where she found them and hoped that he wouldn't ask.

"Well, let's take a look at them after dinner," Earnest said, curious about it all.

Anna brought out the envelope that she had crammed all the pictures and the documents in. Anna at last showed him the framed photograph. When Earnest saw it, the color drained from his face.

"What's the matter?" Anna asked, afraid for him. "You know who this is, don't you, Earnest."

Earnest nodded stiffly. "This is Winston's mother. Angelina. My wife...My ex...," his voice trailed off. His face took on a blank look.

Anna came beside Earnest and rested a hand on his shoulder. "Are you okay?" Anna asked, worriedly.

"I'm fine. What else is there that you have to show me?" Earnest asked, hollowly.

Anna looked at him. She wondered why Earnest didn't keep any pictures of Angelina in the house. Not once, before the discovery of this picture, had she ever seen Winston's mother before. She decided to ask these and other questions later.

Anna took out the surveillance pictures and the documents. Earnest frowned, confused as he looked at the glossy, colored photographs of the fiftyish man. He looked over the different documents and his face turned into a look of shock when he saw the license and other picture ID. He stared at the photocopied picture in amazement. And then his eyes darkened.

"I know who this is," he said softly. "Where did you get this from? Tell me!"

Anna was taken aback at the emotion. "Who is it?"

"This is the man that murdered Angelina...this is the man that the police have never been able to find! I'll know that face anywhere. Where did you get these pictures from? It is very important that I know."

Anna's heart beat in her chest. She wasn't expecting a reaction like this. And what was this about Angelina being killed? Winston's mother was killed?

"How was Angelina killed?" Anna asked.

"I'm not answering anything else until you tell me where you got these from," Earnest said stubbornly.

Anna cleared her throat and decided to come clean ... partially. "I found them in the house. In a drawer. I didn't know what they were. I thought that you would be able to help me."

This answer seemed to have calmed Earnest down a little. Earnest sat back in his chair and studied the picture with the man and the young teenaged girl.

"Who's that girl?" Hector asked Earnest. "Do you know?"

Earnest looked at the back of the picture. "It says Lupe Santiago..." he muttered.

"Yeah, but do you know who that is?" Anna asked.

Earnest looked at her blankly. "I don't know."

"Earnest. Please help me! I'm so afraid. Jackie and me were run off the road and I want to know why. We could have been killed! There's something that Winston isn't telling me!"

Earnest let out a deep breath. "I don't know much. All I know is that he is the man that killed Angelina. As for the name Santiago? It sounds very familiar. I think that Angelina's family was having trouble with them...beyond that I don't know much more. After I moved to Texas, I stayed out of all of that. All of that gangland business. Whatever I know, I got from Winston."

Anna leaned forward and looked Earnest in the eyes. "Be honest with me. Do you think that the accident that I was in is a result of Winston being involved with...the Santiagos? Was it an attempted and intentional hit on Winston and us for revenge?"

Earnest looked at her, but did not answer.

"Please! You have to tell me! Your granddaughter could have been killed! Think of the baby," Anna exclaimed.

Earnest looked down to the floor. He nodded his head slightly. "I don't know all the details, but it's possible. It's very possible. About six months ago, Winston mention something about people getting what they deserved...I really didn't pay much attention to it. My heart tells me that he did whatever he did and that now they're looking to get back at him."

"So, why is there a picture of the man that murdered Angelina and a Santiago together? Whoever the Santiagos are, they must have ties to this man…or had."

Earnest nodded. "Apparently, but how, I don't know. I'm telling you. I was out of the Gionelli affairs when I picked up and left Chicago. Angelina and I got divorced. All I knew about her family afterwards is what my children told me."

"Gionelli? That name sounds familiar."

"Perhaps. But it's Winston's mother's family name. Back in 1960, Rocco Gionelli, Angelina's father, was charged for orchestrating the famous attempted plane heist of 59'. Thing is, the thing wasn't carried through. The perps got caught before they could get away with any valuables on the plane. At that time, I was his lawyer. I couldn't save him this time though. Rocco ended up with a lengthy prison sentence. He died in jail. You must have heard about it."

Hector nodded his head. "Yeah, that was really big. I heard about it when I was a child. I knew I recognized that name somewhere."

Earnest nodded. "The Gionelli family was or is …involved in organized crime. Rocco, my father-in-law, was a big boss. A higher up. I was his lawyer…along with another friend of mine…," Earnest said distractedly.

"So why did you leave Chicago?" Anna asked.

Earnest shook his head. "Rocco was carried to jail, so I was no longer in business as far as he was concerned. Plus there were other circumstances that I don't care to discuss."

"Italian…" Angelina muttered. "He never told me that he was Italian."

"Yes. My wife was Sicilian, so he's only half Italian," Earnest chuckled. "I'm not."

"Is that why he's fluent in Italian?" Anna asked.

"Well, growing up, Angelina would speak to them in Italian so all of my children were pretty fluent in it. Winston took language classes in school though, that helped." Earnest answered.

"Why was he keeping all of this from me?" Anna asked. "He never told me this…"

523

"Well…when his mother and I were first divorced, he was estranged from her for a little while. But he came around. I feel that Winston didn't tell you anything because he didn't want you to find out who his family was…the name Gionelli is pretty well known and associated with crime. I myself don't like to talk about Angelina…," he smiled painfully. "I feel guilty. Even after all these years. If I had stayed with her…this would have never happened. You know. I never stopped loving her…I love her so much…I always have." Earnest rose to his knees. "If you all would excuse me, I'm very tired. I'm going to retire for the night…I'm exhausted," he said with great sadness. With that, he turned and left the three of them there.

Anna quickly stood up and called Earnest's name. He turned around questioningly. He looked so vulnerable now, so different from the strong, confident man that Earnest usually showed himself to be.

"Please…don't tell Winston that I was here this weekend…please," Anna asked, pleadingly.

Earnest stared at her for a moment and nodded his head solemnly. "Don't worry I won't. I am a man of many secrets. Secrets that will go with me to my grave," Earnest said with a haunted expression. "Now. If you will excuse me," Earnest said turning around and continuing his journey down the hallway and up the stairs.

"What do we do now?" Anna asked her friends, fretfully.

"What we need to do is to find out more on this Santiago family and how they are tied to the Gionelli's," Hector said.

"Yeah, but I don't think that we're going to find anything else more from him," Ramón said, referring to Anna's father-in-law.

Anna nodded. "You're both right. We should probably leave tomorrow."

Ψ

That night before they left, Anna heard the sobbing sound that she heard whenever she came to the ranch. Without Winston here to stop her, she decided that she was going to find out what it was once and for all.

Anna got out of hall and crept down the hallway. The crying grew more pronounced. Anna finally came in front of the door that she had come to over two years ago. The crying could be heard coming from behind it.

Anna tried the lock. She was surprised when the door clicked open. She heard a startled gasp.

There was Earnest, sitting on a chair in front of what looked to shrine for Angelina. In fact, the whole room appeared to be dedicated to her. Pictures upon pictures of the woman decorated the walls. *I didn't see any pictures of her because they were all in this room,* Anna thought to herself. The biggest picture of them all, which seemed to take up half the wall, was surrounded by candles and gold jewelry, as if someone was making offerings to a god. Earnest turned around and stared at Anna with a startled expression. His eyes were watery and his cheeks were wet. It was clear that it had been him crying. He said nothing.

Anna stepped into the room.

"NO! NO!" protested Earnest. "You must come in on your knees. Leave your shoes at the door!"

Anna gave him an odd look, but did as he said. She came up beside the chair that Earnest was sitting on. "What is all this?" she asked him.

Earnest turned and looked at the giant picture in front of him. "I built this room soon after Angelina died. I want to keep her alive…she comes here, you know, to speak to me. She loves this room."

Anna struggled to keep her sentiments under check. "Why do you come here at night?"

"Because…this is the time she comes. The time that I grieve. During the day, she is not here," Earnest buried his face in his hands. "I never wanted you to find out about this but since you have, I might as well tell you all this. Winston discovered this room years ago and he was not happy about it. He threatened to tear it down. I wouldn't let him."

"I'm….sorry," Anna said, not knowing what else to say.

But Earnest was no longer paying attention to her. His watery green eyes had turned back to the picture.

Anna quietly exited the room.

The next morning, Anna, Hector and Ramón left and went back home.

Ψ

In her mind, the information that Anna had was enough for her to want to divorce Winston. It was clear that he was a very dangerous man involved with very dangerous people and situations. But she knew she had to play it cool and find more information on the Santiago's. She decided that since his home office held no clues, that maybe his office at work would hold something. At the moment, she couldn't think how she would gain access to the office, but she knew she had to do something quickly...before Winston came home.

Then Anna got the idea to hire a PI to find some information on the Santiago's. After about two weeks, Greg Fenner, came back to Anna with some interesting information.

"Please come in, Greg," Anna said when she opened the door. The tall, African-American man was slender with a medium brown complexion. He smiled and breezed past her.

"Do you want something to drink?" Anna asked him. "Please take a seat."

The man sat down. He crossed his long legs in front of him. "No, I'm fine, but thank you."

Anna sat down across from him. "So, what have you found?"

"Well," Greg said as he opened his briefcase and took out a thick file. "Well, let's start with the Santiago's. From the name Lupe Santiago, I found other relatives..." Greg cleared his throat. "The Santiago's...are involved in quite a lot of criminal activity. let's see...I have a Juan Santiago. He's the grandfather of Lupe, the girl in the pictures. He was killed about twenty years ago. But when he was alive, he was involved in drug trafficking, black market trafficking and trading...he had a criminal record a mile long. I also dug up the name Chavez Morales. He was Juan Santiago's cousin. Apparently, the two grew up together in Argentina and were very close."

"So who killed Juan?" Anna asked, as she twisted off the cap of a bottle of water.

"Well, the killer was never found. I doubt they looked very hard anyways. One less criminal out of society. The authorities probably thought that whoever did it did them a justice. But they should probably stop to think that the murderers might be a great deal worse than the man that was killed," Greg said with a rueful look. "Anyways. Juan Santiago's son, Ferdie Santiago apparently wanted to stay out of the life. He has a clean record, went to medical school. He's a well known plastic surgeon. Has a successful practice in Pasadena. Have you heard of him? Ferdie Santiago?"

Anna shook her head no.

"Well, anyways, he's married to a rich, Cuban socialite from Miami, Teresa Burgos. Lupe is their only child. She's fifteen. Soon to be sixteen in a few months. She's a bit of a renegade. Apparently, she's gotten arrested about three times for shoplifting and once for destruction of property...but apparently the charges were dismissed. Probably has to do with her family's influence," Greg cleared his throat. "I know I said I didn't want anything to drink before, but—"

"No problem! Would you like some water?" Anna asked, before he could say anything else.

"Yes. Some water would be nice, thank you so much, Mrs. Hurst."

"Soon to be Miss. Senghor," Anna sniffed.

Greg shifted in his seat and scratched the tip of his nose. "Yes, of course."

Anna smiled endearingly and went to the kitchen to get a bottle of Evian. She spotted Alice, her maid, hovering nearby.

"Alice, could you fill two glasses with ice and some EVIAN water?"

Alice smiled, "Of course. I'll bring it right in."

Anna thanked her and bustled back to the living room.

Greg discreetly watched Anna as she came back into the room. She was quite a looker with her long legs and smooth brown skin. Plus, she had the cutest face. He felt an instant attraction. He wondered if she would go out with a guy like him. After all, she did just say that she was soon to be ex-Mrs. Hurst.

"Alice will bring the water soon. She's getting us some ice," Anna said sitting down.

"Alice?"

"That's my maid. Anyways, what about that man...ahh...the one with the fake papers."

"Yes. You mean Adar Antoun. Well, your father-in-law was right about him. He was the guy that they were looking to investigate back in 1968 for the killing of your husband's mother. But he had disappeared.

Adar was his real name. Demaris Brettos was an alias that he used when coming into this country from Syria. He's never been convicted for anything, although he had been suspected in a few murders, that is before Angelina Gionelli's, but they were never able to nail him with anything. Angelina Gionelli's murder was the first sure thing they would have been able to get him for. But he disappeared. Apparently, he went back to his real name, he went back to live in Syria. But he had come back to America about three years ago."

"I notice that you're using a lot of past tense when you talk about him. Is he no longer alive?" Anna asked him.

Greg nodded his head. "He was killed. About six months ago. Thrown of the balcony of his condo in Venice Beach. Apparently, he had been tortured first, though. All of his fingers were cut off and missing, well, not all of them were missing. Two of the fingers were found stuck up the nose of the corpse. The corpse was also scalped and the eyeballs removed. The condition that Antoun's corpse was left in was very similar to the way that Juan Santiago's was in years ago. Both were scalped, both had the eyeballs removed, both had their digits cut off…both had two fingers stuffed up the nostrils."

"Well, apparently Antoun has a connection to the Santiago's…

"Yes, he does. It's clear that he at least knows Lupe and by extension, I will assume that he knows at least her parents as well. Although how they know each other, I am not quite clear about. But let's make a few shots in the dark that might not be too far off mark. I found something else as well. Chavez turned up missing back in the early 60's around 1963. We don't know the exact reasons, but we can assume that it was probably an underground deal gone bad. Let's say he was killed and the body was gotten rid of. Now who did he make this botched deal with? Let us assume that it was with a Gionelli or something attached to them or someone underneath them. Now. People in that kind of life are pretty closed mouthed…but thankfully I have my connections. Apparently, after the disappearance of Chavez, some attempts were made on Anthony Gionelli's life."

"Who's Anthony?"

"Well, that's your husband's uncle. Angelina's twin brother."

"Oh…go on."

"Well, Anthony and some others must have had something to do with Chavez's disappearance and the Santiago's were getting revenge. Let's assume that the Gionelli's struck back and killed Juan Santiago. Then let's assume that Antoun was 'hired', Greg said making bunny ears with his fingers, "by the Santiago's to kill off Angelina to get revenge… someone found Antoun years later to get back at him…" Greg trailed off for a moment, looked away, and then looked back at Anna.

Do you remember that story in the paper a few months ago? Well, it would have been out before you got into your accident…Lupe Santiago was kidnapped. It was all over the papers. Her father and her mother refused to say anything to the public about it, which I find strange. Apparently, the authorities found it strange as well and they did investigate the parents and their family, but they didn't find any evidence that the family knew more than they were saying. But anyways, one day she was released, just like that, and sent back home…but with a missing kidney."

"Oh, Gosh!" Anna exclaimed. "Why did they take out her kidney?"

Greg shrugged and took a sip of his water. "Maybe just for spite…or maybe to sell it on the black market. Both? Lupe Santiago has a rare blood type. AB-. Only about one percent of the population has that blood type. An organ from her would sell very high in the black-market to someone that desperately needs it."

"My God!" Anna exclaimed.

"They haven't found who kidnapped the girl and they have no leads. The girl claims that she was blindfolded the whole time and she has no idea what any of them look like. It's all very strange, but there are no leads. This seems to be a family vendetta between the two parties. One does something, the other retaliates, the other gets them back, and it goes on and on."

Anna's heart beat wildly in her chest. Winston. He had to do something with all this. She felt the blood in her veins turn to ice. My God. She was in the middle of something so dangerous. She and her baby. How could Winston do something like this? Anna was afraid to mention her husband, but she knew that Greg was thinking the same thing.

"Will you, umm…"

"This information is strictly for you only. It's not going anywhere else. I just hope that you used it wisely," Greg said answering the question in her head.

Anna nodded and looked down to the ground. "Thank you so much," she muttered.

Greg got up and put a hand on her shoulder. Anna looked up and stared him in his brown eyes.

"Look. If you need me for anything…call me. Even if you want to talk. I want to help you."

"I-I-I have to get away from him…my husband."

Greg nodded. "I know. Sooner rather than later would be best."

"It's that bad…" Anna said.

"Honestly, Anna…I fear for you and your daughter's safety."

Ψ

A course of action. That was what was needed. Anna had to figure something out and fast. In all her life, Anna never thought that she would ever be in the middle of something like this, but it was here and she had to deal with it. No time to sit back in amazement and wonder, no time to think about where she went wrong, no time to think about what she should have done, no time to think if there were any clues that were foreshadowing this situation…no time. Time was clearly in the lacking here, a precious commodity that she couldn't take advantage of.

The next day, she decided to send Greg on another assignment. The moment that Winston came back into town, she wanted Greg to follow him and find out if he was cheating on her. That would be good ground for divorce. She needed to be armed with as much information as she could get to make things turn out in her favor. She also had to make sure that she got full custody of her daughter.

The day that Winston came home, Anna went through all the motions. She pushed down her fear and pretended that she was extremely happy to see him, she made sure that his favorite dishes were made and then she made glorious love to him on their moonlit, kingsized, bed.

"Wow," Winston whispered when they were finished. "That was amazing…so beautiful."

Anna forced herself to stare him in his eyes. "Yes. Yes, it was."

Ψ

'I can't find a thing. It's been two weeks now and they're no signs," Greg said to Anna.

They met in a park. They were sitting down on a park bench in an area where there weren't any people besides the occasional passersby.

"So, he's not having an affair?" Anna asked, incredulous.

"Not from what I could see. But I'll keep looking."

Anna nodded, crestfallen.

"Hey," Greg said softly, "Don't worry. It'll be all right."

"Easier said than done," Anna said with a sigh.

Ψ

"Hector…do you still have those pictures that you took of me two years ago…when Winston hit me," Anna asked Hector.

Hector's brown eyes flicked quickly to Anna's face. His eyes narrowed suspiciously.

"Yes, I still have them…Why?"

Anna cleared her throat and looked around her living room. She had invited Hector over. Of course, Winston wasn't home at the time.

"I might need them…so that I have more than enough reason to divorce Winston."

Hector perked up at the word divorce. "I'll give them to Ramón to bring to you tomorrow at work."

"Thank you Hector."

"My pleasure," Hector purred.

Ψ

Two weeks later, Anna got a call from Greg.

"I found something," he told her over the phone. "We should meet up. Not good having conversations over the phone."

"Should we meet at our usual place? "

"Yes. I'll see you in half an hour."

"Great."

Ψ

Anna stared at the glossy, colored, photographs. Her mouth was in a straight line and her forehead was wrinkled.

"So, I guess this is what I was looking for," Anna said and swallowed the big lump in her throat.

"I'm sorry Anna…that you have to see this," Greg said sympathetically. "I wasn't able to make an I.D. of the woman as of yet. Maybe you'll recognize her"

"It's okay. I'm fine." Anna stared at the burnish-brown colored woman that Winston was embracing and kissing in a parking lot. Anna couldn't see the woman's face in the first photograph. Anna looked at the second photograph and gasped. She dropped the pile to the ground.

Greg put a hand on her arm, alarmed. "What is it?"

"Oh—my—God," Anna muttered, shaking terribly.

"Anna, please, talk to me…I know that this is not good, but then you were looking for something like this…"

"That's my sister. My older sister, Tessa," Anna muttered and burst into tears.

"What?" Greg asked, confused.

"My husband is having an affair with my sister!" Anna screamed.

Greg was shocked. He didn't know what to say.

Ψ

The next few days and weeks, grinded past. To Anna, every minute was stretched out and pronounced, like she was living underwater. As if thought she was living under a dark cloud.

Anna spoke to her lawyer, turned over all the pictures of the beatings of the cheating…

Anna went to work and went through the day like a zombie, only to return home and work some more.

Winston spent more and more time away from home, claiming that it was work related, but Anna knew better. She found it amazing that her sister had the nerve to still call her and behave that everything was okay. Since the pictures, Anna would hang up the phone right away if she heard her sister's voice on the other end. Anna felt an intense hate towards Tessa. The Bitch. She was always such a whore. But never did Anna think that she would sleep with her own husband. She wondered how long the affair had been going on.

Finally, Anna couldn't take it anymore. She had to confront Winston and move out. She had to tell him that a divorce was underway.

"Are you sure that you want to give them to him? I could send somebody to deliver them, you know." Anna's lawyer, Brinn Steel, a tall Asian woman with short cropped hair told her. Brinn, who had been born in China, had been adopted by two Americans at the age of one.

Anna shook her head. "I'll be fine. I want to give them to him. I have to confront him eventually."

"But this man is very volatile. Anna. I've seen the pictures…they're horrible! No way am I going to allow that to happen to you again. You need to move out and *then* I'll get someone to deliver the divorce papers."

"Please, Quinn. Just give them to me. I'll be fine."

Quinn eyed her client and gave a curt nod. "If that's what you want…"

"That's what I want," Anna said taking up the papers.

Ψ

Luckily, the next Monday, Anna had a day off. She packed up her things and Jackie's things drove over to Hector and Ramón's house. They helped her unpack her things.

"Girl, I'm so glad that you're staying over here! It's going to be so fun," Ramón chirped happily.

Anna tried to smile.

"Ramón. She's going through a divorce. This isn't a slumber party," Hector said disapprovingly to his partner.

Ramón scowled at him and covered his mouth as he coughed. The dry cough shook his shoulders and resonated around the room. Anna and Hector stared at him worriedly.

Ramón flicked a hand at them. "I went to the doctor today, Anna. I have an upper respiratory infection. She gave me some antibiotics to take. I just started them today. I'll be fine."

Anna nodded, worried still. Was it just her, or did Ramón look a little thinner as well?

"So when are we going to deliver the papers to *Mr. Hurst*?" Ramón said with disgust.

"We can go this evening. We'll come with you, of course."

"That goes without saying," exclaimed Ramón, "We would never let you go by yourself."

Anna smiled and looked at the both of them. Lovers, not fighters. Ramón with his curly, black, hair and his clear milk chocolate skin and his slender body. Hector, although he was strong and had sinewy muscles, wasn't one for fighting either. But she knew that he would for her. So would Ramón, as weak as he was. Ramón. Poor Ramón. He was sick and he was dying, but one would ever know listening to him. He had enough energy and happiness for a million people. He was a fighter in spirit if not in the body. She felt a heaviness in her chest as a sudden bout of deep sadness overtook her. Why is this happening to us? Anna asked herself.

Hector and Ramón came to Anna's side the moment they saw the first tear drop from her eyes.

"It's okay. He can't do anything to you, Anna," Ramón said, thinking that she was crying out of fear.

Hector nodded in agreement.

At that moment, Jackie cried in her crib. Loud, desperate cried that wrenched at Anna's heart.

Anna nodded and wiped her eyes. "Let's go."

Ψ

Winston crushed the pen in the palm of his hand and cursed as the black ink seeped all over his hands. He threw the pen in the waste basket and got up to walk to the bathroom to wash his hands

He was so mad. He was more than mad. He was furious. Anna was divorcing him. If she thought that she was going to get away that easily, she had another thing coming. And if she thought that she was going to take his daughter away from him, she was mistaken.

"I want you to trace every private call made in and out of this house from the time that I left for my business trip two months ago up till now," Winston told the man on the phone. The man was a police officer.

After Winston hung up, he went to his mini bar and poured himself a drink.

Anna had no idea who she was up against.

Ψ

"I'm fine. I'm fine," Anna muttered as she unsteadily got to her feet. "Can you hand me my purse Ramón?"

Ramón shook his head. "Anna. No more of those pills. You've got to stop it. You depend too much on them. Look at what they're doing to you!"

Anna cut her eyes at him. "I had a raging headache. What do you want me to do?"

"You didn't look like you had a headache," Ramón retorted.

"Anna? Why don't you go home early. Relax," Celeste said sympathetically to Anna. She knew what Anna was going through, having been through three divorces herself.

"Okay. Okay, thanks."

When Hector and Ramón came home that evening, they found Anna passed out in bed with a glass of scotch on the nigh table and a bottle of codeine clutched in her right hand.

They called an ambulance.

When Anna woke up, a woman was sitting by her bedside. The women smiled at Anna.

"Dr. Fulton?" Anna asked, groggily.

"Yep, at your service," the woman smiled.

Anna sighed deeply and ran a hand through her hair. "What's going on?"

"Anna, you're addicted to codeine, to pain killers. I know that I was the one to prescribe them to you, but perhaps we should look into some other alternatives. Your friends told me that you were going through a divorce and everything and that you were in a car accident a few months ago…perhaps I can suggest a psych consult. Maybe you need someone to talk to…"

"Yeah, and I've been having terrible headaches ever since," Anna snapped. "That's why I take the codeine. And I don't need a shrink."

"Do you have the headaches every day?"

Anna hesitated. "No. But at least two times a week."

"It seems to me that you take the pills way more than that," Dr. Fulton said.

"Fuck off," Anna snapped. "I don't need this from you. I want to get out of here."

"Not yet, Mrs. Hurst."

"Don't call me that.'

"I'm sorry. Anna. Is that okay?"

Anna stared daggers at her doctor and didn't answer her. Instead she asked, "where's my baby?"

"Well...your husband has her now."

Anna's stomach dropped. "No! I don't want him to have her!"

"Well, Anna, considering that you were in the hospital during this time...he has the right to her. Although, I must say, your two...friends made quite a noise about it."

Anna sneered at her. "Just leave me alone. I'm not speaking to you anymore."

"You have to speak to me eventually," the woman warned.

"Screw you," Anna said succinctly.

"Please don't talk like that. I don't understand what's gotten into you! Please, let me help you."

"Then get out," Anna screamed. "Get out of my room right now!"

The baffled woman hurried out. She was soon replaced by Hector and Ramón. Much to Anna's surprise, her sister came in a moment after them.

"Anna! I was so worried about you—"

"Get the hell out of here! You have a lot of nerve coming here!" Anna yelled.

Tessa stared at her sister with shock. "What do you mean? I'm your sister, I wanted to see how you were doing!"

"Why don't you go see how your boyfriend Winston is doing? But I'm divorcing him, so soon, you can have him."

Tessa's pretty brown eyes got as wide as saucers. "What! I—"

"Get out of my room, Cunt!" screamed Anna.

Tessa made a quick exit.

Ramón threw an amused look at Anna. "My, my. You certainly told her."

Hector chuckled.

Chapter Thirty-five

At the custody hearing...January, 1991

The judge, a middle aged dark skinned, black man with graying hair, pronounced his verdict as he looked around the courtroom. He looked at the tall, powerful, and dignified Winston who was sitting calmly between his two topnotch lawyers, and Anna, who was wearing a forlorn face, slouched over, and sitting beside her lawyer, a tall Asian woman. He looked off into the crowd. Anna's mother and father were there, holding hands. Her two friends, the two gay men, were sitting beside the parents with a look of trepidation on each of their faces. And then way, way in the back, away from all the others, was Anna's sister. She wore a look of anguish on her face. For a moment, the judge felt a pang of regret, but then steeled himself for the verdict that he was about to make. He cleared his throat and began.

"A divorce is never stable for a child, even for one as young as Jacqueline Hurst. My job is to look at what I am given, the evidence, and decide which course of action is best. Baby Jackie either lives with her mother or her father. In most cases, by default, the child would go with his or her mother. But sometimes, there are circumstances that prevent such a clear cut decision as that. Such as we have seen here in this courtroom over the past weeks. Based on the evidence given, I can see, as could the rest of the court, that Anna Senghor is clearly not in the condition to take care of a child right now. She has a serious addiction to painkillers, she doesn't have a place to live, and at the moment she is living with friends...it just seems to not be a very suitable environment for a child. On the other hand, Winston is a stable person, a provider. He may have made mistakes in his past...with Anna...but Anna is not the one that this is about. It's about Jackie and how well she would be taken care of. Winston has proven himself to be a very good father when it comes to his daughter. So I rule that permanent custody be given to Winston Hurst. Anna Senghor will be allowed supervised visitation, once a week, for one hour. That is my ruling," Judge McCarthy said pounding his gavel down. "Court adjourned."

Chapter Thirty-six

July, 1991

"Gosh, I'm so glad that we took this vacation together," Pamela said to Anna as she slipped her sunglasses onto her face.

Anna stared at her attractive, Filipina friend and smiled. "Yeah. I'm glad too. I need it."

Pamela smiled, a row of white teeth standing out against a café au late background. "You *definitely* deserve it."

"It's just too bad that Hector and Ramón couldn't come," Anna said with a touch of sadness. Ramón, who was really sick now, wasn't in any condition to go on a trip. And Hector, not wanting to leave Ramón alone, declined the invitation.

This past year has certainly been a nightmare for her between her difficult divorce from Winston, the loss of her daughter and rehab for her addiction to pain killers. Two months ago, she had completed her rehab. Anna had bought a small house using some money from her divorce settlement (which was *very* good indeed). A month ago, when Winston had brought Jackie over for her visit, he had seen a bunch of paper work that Anna was filling out to petition for custody of her child. Anna had tried to snatch it up, but it was too late. Winston had already seen. Winston had turned to her with a look of amusement mixed with anger.

"You'll never get custody of Jackie. I promise you that," Winston had said.

Anna eyed him nervously. "Don't threaten me, Winston," Anna muttered.

"I'm not threatening you, Anna. I'm simply telling you the truth. You can fill out as many forms as you want and go to court as often as you feel and you still won't have her. You might as well save yourself the embarrassment," Winston said had and turned on his heels.

"Hey. I managed to get the supervised visitation changed to unsupervised, didn't I?" Anna had shot back at him.

Winston turned slowly around. "Don't be so smug because you might not have even this privilege for long. In fact, you'd better tresure this time while you have it. In the future, you might not be able to see your daughter at all."

Anna's breath caught in her throat. She couldn't believe what he saying. "You fucking bastard. Get out of my house," Anna hissed.

Winston had merely smiled at her and said "I'll be back to pick her up at five on the dot. Make sure she's here."

Anna slammed the door shut after him and stared at her sweating hands. They were shaking uncontrollably.

But now, Anna tried to push those unpleasant things out of her mind as she stared up into the clear, blue, Belizean sky.

"We should have went to Jamaica, Barbados or something so I can get one of those cute chocolate men," Pamela said with a smile.

"Yeah, But I've always wanted to go to Belize…," Anna said.

"Oh yeah. You don't like black men very much," Pamela said off handedly as she patted her shiny black hair.

Anna turned her head to her friend. "What? Just because I married a white man doesn't mean that I don't like Black men. I happen to like them a lot, thank you very much!" Anna said huffily. The nerve of Pamela to say such a thing. Sometimes Pamela's mouth was too much.

"Okay, okay. Don't get so defensive," Pamela said with a chuckle. "Anyways, there might be some Black Latino men to get into over here…

Anna shut out the voice of her man crazed friend and tried to focus on relaxing.

Later on that evening, Anna and Pamela went into Belize city to do some shopping in the market. Anna and Pamela bought souvenirs for friends and family back home as well as clothes and accessories. Finally, they stopped by an outdoor restaurant to get something to eat. As they were sitting down and eating, they noticed a young woman, in traditional Mayan dress, pulling a small child by the hand that looked to be around two years old. Both woman and child were tattered and grungy looking. The woman held out a hand to passersby asking for some money.

"I'm going to give them some money," Anna said rising from her seat.

Before Pamela could comment, Anna was already on her way over there. She stood in front of the woman, smiled, and dropped some money into her clay jar. The young woman smiled and said thank-you. Anna was a little taken aback that she was able to speak English being that she appeared to be indigenous.

"So you can speak English?" Anna asked her.

The woman nodded and smiled. "Yes. Yes I can. I learn to speak because it easier to talk with people in city. Many visitors speak English."

"So who's this cute little girl?" Anna asked about the small, caramel colored little child.

The young woman frowned slightly and glanced at the young child.

"This my little niece. My sister die when she born. I now look after her myself," the young woman said sadly.

"By yourself? You don't look any older than sixteen!" Anna exclaimed incredulously.

"I eighteen. No more family. Just she and me," the young woman said a little gruffly. "I no know if I can care for her much longer. I want to take her to orphanage. She stay with me, she starve. Is Catholic orphanage, do not know Mayan way, but she will have food and bed. Besides, her father was Mestizo and a Catholic, so not so bad anyways."

Anna looked back and forth between the young woman and the adorable little girl with the thick black curtain of hair.

Suddenly Anna got an idea. It seem crazy at first, but as she listened to the woman talk some more and the thought grew and grew in her head, she got more and more excited about it. Finally, she couldn't keep it to herself anymore.

"Anna! I thought you were never coming back," Pamela said whiningly as she came up behind the group of three. She broke Anna's thoughts.

Anna turned around to her friend and gave her a smile. She introduced all of them. Then the thought came back into Anna's head and she decided to just say it.

"Look…what's your name?"

"Izanami," she answered. "The girl's name is Meena."

"Meena? That doesn't sound like a Mayan name…"

"No. My sister worked for a foreign woman in her house. As maid. Woman was from Asia, I think. But she had skin like us. Meena was the woman name."

"Oh okay," Anna said. She looked at Pamela who was just standing silently by, listening to the conversation. Anna finally mustered the courage to say what she wanted to say.

"What if I were to say I would like to…adopt Meena." Anna glanced at Pamela. Her face was totally shocked and her mouth was hung open in amazement.

"Anna, you can't be serio—"

Anna cut her off mid-sentence. "Please, Pamela. If I wanted your opinion I would ask for it."

Pamela shut her mouth.

"Adopt?" The young woman repeated.

Anna stepped closer to her and held her hand. "Yes. Adopt. I will give her a home, food, clothes, toys, education…she's have everything she wants and needs. I'll be like a surrogate mother for her. And I promise to send pictures of her to you, you can come and visit her…"

"You American. Right?"

"Yes. I am,"

The young woman pursed her lips in thought and looked at the little girl. She turned back to Anna. "America is good place. Many opportunities. I can come see her if I want?"

Anna nodded her head quickly. "Any time you want to see her, you can. I'll even pay for the flight."

The young woman nodded, clearly interested in her offer. She wasn't about to pass an opportunity like this. Her niece would be in America and get education, be successful even, and be looked after by a kind woman. She thought of the alternative. Keeping Meena here where she will most likely be married off to an old man because no one else in the group would want her because she wasn't a pure Mayan, she would slave away for him, bear many kids and most likely die early and in poverty…

"Okay. How can this be done?" the young woman asked.

Ψ

December, 1991

Since the divorce, one of the good things that happened was that Anna was able to go to work with freedom, without Winston breathing down her back. She was also working on her masters. one afternoon, while Anna was working, she had gotten a call in her office while she was in the middle of reviewing some reports.

"Who is it, I'm busy," Anna asked, pissed that she was being disturbed.

"She says that she's your sister...Kati?"

Anna, excited, grabbed the phone out of her co-worker's hands. "Hello?" she called expectantly.

"Anna? Is that you?" a voice asked, plaintively.

"Yes, It's me. Is that you Kati?"

"It's me." Then silence.

"Where are you?" Anna asked, excitedly.

"I'm here. In LA."

Kati told her the street where she was.

"Don't move from where you are. I'm coming to get you." Anna slammed down the phone and hopped up from her chair. Her sister was back!

"You do know that we have a presentation this afternoon after lunch, I hope you'll be back by then," her co-worker Gwendolyn whined as she nervously pulled at her thin blond hair.

Anna, barely paying her any attention, waved her off and was on her way.

Her sister was exactly where she had said she was, standing on the corner. But she wasn't alone. She held a toddler in one arm while a small boy around four years old, grasped onto her other hand.

Anna stopped her Mercedes convertible directly in front of her sister and was a little shocked at her appearance. She looked so tired and bothered. Other than that, she had grown into an exceptionally pretty young woman.

"These are my kids," Kati said shortly, before helping them into the car. She buckled them into the back seat and then climbed into the passenger side.

"You need a car seat for them."

Kati eyed her wearily. "I don't have a car seat."

Anna looked back at them. They were gorgeous children both with copper red-brown skin, big brown eyes, and silky, wavy black hair.

"We should call Mom and Dad. They'll be glad that you're back," Anna suggested.

"No!" Kati protested. "All they'll do is pester me. Later," she said settling back into the leather seat of the car.

Anna drove them directly to her house. "I guess you can stay here until you get settled and everything," Anna said as she showed her sister around.

"You have a nice house," Kati said, sounding a little jealous.

"Thank you," Anna said. She looked at her watch. She still had two hours before the presentation.

"So, are you going to tell me what happened to you?"

Kati plopped down on the couch. Anna looked at her, just noticing how spaced-out her eyes looked. They were the eyes of the druggies that she often saw on the streets of downtown L.A. She hoped that she wasn't on coke or anything.

"I ran away with Romel, we shacked up for five years, and I had his children," she said summing it all up in one sentence.

Anna looked at her, amazed at her flippant attitude. Her sister surely was a piece of work—always had been. But maybe this was the drugs talking.

"Are you on drugs?" Anna asked.

"No!" Kati snapped. "Are you?" she retorted.

"Ok, no need to get all angry with me. I was just asking," Anna said, offended at her sister's vicious behavior.

"Why did you come back?" Anna asked, casually.

"You woulda liked it if I stayed down there, huh," Kati commented, her eyes slitted in suspicion.

Anna ignored this weird question. "Is Romel here too?"

"No, he's not," Kati said curtly. "He beat me too much. So I left his ass down there."

"Oh," Anna commented, feeling sorry for her. Sensing that her sister wasn't willing to share anymore about her five year long escapade in Mexico, she turned to the children who were sitting on the couch in silence. Anna found that very strange.

"Why are they so quiet?"

"I dunno," Kati said and shrugged her shoulders. "You got any water?"

"What are their names?"

"Maria and Brian. Maria's one and a half, Brian's four," she snapped, agitated at being asked so many questions.

"Hello," Anna said, reaching out to the children. The little boy tentatively got up from the couch and came over to her. She placed him on her lap. The little girl crawled over to her mother, ignoring Anna completely.

"They can't speak no English."

And neither can you. Anna thought, noting her sister's messed up way of speaking. How did it get to that?

"*Va a su tia,*" Kati told the little girl. She looked up at Anna with shiny dark eyes, and frowned, Her black, wavy hair was in two pony tails. Anna reached out and touched the baby's hair. It was so soft and silky.

"*Brian, canto's anos tienes?*" Kati asked her little boy.

The little boy looked up at Anna from her lap and thrust up four grubby fingers. "*Cuatro!*" the little boy exclaimed smiling brightly. Anna smiled. At least the kids seemed to be smart.

"I tried to teach them English, but with all that Spanish all over the place, I just give up," Kati said shrugging. "I learned pretty good Spanish. Thought I'd never hear English again."

Anna nodded. Her sister had always been quick at picking up languages. Before Kati left, she had been taking Spanish in school. Beyond a few words, Anna didn't know Spanish. She had been learning French in school. Her father had told her that it would be more useful, since French was the main language of Senegal. Anna shook her head. But they were in America, not Senegal. Her French was pretty much useless. So much for that.

After getting them settled, Anna returned to work. She counted herself fortunate for getting the job that she had. She now worked in at a well-known record label called *Entourage Productions* as a staff publicist after resigning from *DJ Play*. One day she hoped to have her own label.

Players of the Game

Her best friend Hector had recommended her for this job and the next day they were calling her in for an interview. Good old Hector. She was fortunate to have met him.

Not according to plan, Anna had had Brian and Maria almost from the time that her sister turned up in LA from Mexico.

After Kati had settled down with her two young children in her sister's home, she wasn't too eager to go out and search for a job. In fact, Kati spent the first two weeks in front of the television watching cable movies and talk shows, while Brian ran wild around the house and Maria was creeping and crawling about with no supervision from Kati. In fact, Anna came home one day to find Maria about to play with a kitchen knife that had fallen on the floor. Anna quickly snatched it from her reach and put it on the counter. She picked up her little niece in one arm and picked up the knife in the other. She walked angrily into the living room to find her sister sitting dazed out as usual in front of the television.

"Do you realize that your daughter was about to play with this knife?" Anna yelled, jabbing it in the air.

Kati continued to watch the television, unaware of Anna's scolding.

"KATI! I'm talking to you."

Kati reluctantly dragged her glassy eyes from the television. "Huh?" she asked, reluctantly.

Anna threw her arms up in the air in defeat. Her sister was really working her nerves.

"It's high time that you get a job," Anna said, feeling that it was a good a time as any to tell her sister to get it together.

"I'll tell you what. Tomorrow, you are going to go through the papers and look in the want ads and you are going to find a job. I don't want any more excuses. You're just sitting around here, eating and watching television. Look at you," Anna said gesturing at her sister's slumped over on the couch. "You look like a bum. You've got kids to support, so snap out of it."

Kati frowned. "I was gonna look for a job, I just needed a little time to adjust," she whined, feeling offended at her sister's criticism.

"Yeah? Well, you got them to think about," Anna said pointing at Maria and Brian, who was following his mother's example by sitting on the couch in front of the television. And he was only four!

"Tomorrow you look for a job. I mean it."

"All right!" Kati said testily, feeling quite harassed.

True to her word, Kati had gotten up the next morning and began looking through the want ads.

"They all want experience," Kati complained to her sister

Anna took the newspaper from her sister's hands and scanned the paper with a sharp eye. She dropped the paper back on the table and pointed to a want add.

"That one doesn't require any experience."

Kati wrinkled her nose in disgust. "It's dishwashing."

"So what. It's a start," Anna said, not putting up with any excuses.

"Can't you get me a job where you work at?" Kati wheedled.

"Definitely not!" Anna proclaimed. The last thing she needed was her sister messing up at work. Then Anna would be out of a job. Rule one: never work with family members. It always turned out to be a mess in the end.

"Why not?" Her sister mumbled miserably.

"Look, just go down there and try and get this job. It's a start. It says to come right in for an interview."

"I don't know how to get there," Kati said trying to put off the inevitable.

"Well, I'll give you a ride," Anna responded sweetly, refusing to giver her a means of escape.

Anna dropped her off in front of the small restaurant named *A Taste of Sicily*.

It looked nice and quaint. Anna crossed her fingers hoping her sister would be able to get the job.

"Coudja come with me to the door?" Kati pleaded after taking in the proper atmosphere of the establishment.

Anna sighed. Anything to get her sister off of her couch and into the workforce.

"Okay, but I can't take the interview with you," Anna said once they reached the door. "You have to go in by yourself," she said giving her sister a slight shove in the right direction

Kati looked at her like a wounded puppy. Anna scowled. Kati, seeing that she was getting nowhere, walked in through the swinging doors of the restaurant.

Anna sighed in relief.

A month later, with a little help from Anna, Kati found her own place and moved out with the two kids.

Ψ

April, 1992

Anna was so excited that she could barely contain herself. Today was the day that she would be taking Meena, her little girl, home. She would meet Meena and two members of the Belizean agency at the airport, and take her home. Six long months of petitions, forms to fill out, going though the Belizean government as well as the American one, all the formalities. Finally, it was over and she would have the little girl with the dark liquid pools for eyes.

Muhammad and Candace came along with Anna to the airport. At first, they had been a reticent about Anna adopting a child, considering what she had just gone through, but Anna refused to back down. She wanted this little girl and she wouldn't let anyone talk her out of it.

When Anna held Meena, who was soon to be three, in the airport, she was moved to tears. The little girl stared at her in wonder—her eyes taking everything in.

At home, Anna had a bedroom painted and furnished for a little princess. There were toys and stuffed animals all over the place. When Anna had brought Meena into the room, Anna and her parents watched as the little girl wondered around, touching everything with her little hands. She looked back at her new family and smiled.

Anna and her parents smiled back in relief.

Everything was going to be all right.

Ψ

When Winston had heard that Anna had gone and adopted a little girl from Belize, he had been at first amazed and then furious. How could she just go and make a decision like that on a whim? Also, he wondered how she had been allowed to keep the child considering her history of addiction. But then, she had been out of rehab for some months now and it wasn't recreational drugs. It was a pain reliever given to her by her doctor. Damn her! He wanted her to be miserable without him. The nerve of her to go and divorce him. Winston had found out that she had been talking to a private investigator, Greg Fenner. He wasn't exactly sure all that she had found out, but she had to know something and it had to be pretty important because she had the guts to divorce him. She had also shamed him in court, showing pictures of injuries that he had supposedly given her. Luckily, she wasn't able to bring up any police reports. He had taken care of that. Winston had watched in glee when her face fell and she shook her head, "No," when asked if she was able to produce any police reports. But she had been able to produce hospital reports. There were also pictures of him cheating with her older sister Tessa. (Not that he regretted that. Tessa was a nice piece of ass and he intended to continue sleeping with her.) Not only that, she had gotten a very good settlement, thanks to that damn bitch lawyer of her's, Brinn Steel. Thanks to Steel, and the communal property law in California, Anna had gotten the house in Long Beach and the luxury condo in Palm Springs. She also got one of the Rolls Royce's, one of the BMW's and a Mercedes convertible. He found out that she had kept only the Mercedes and sold the other two for a good price. How dare she sell his cars! Not only that. She had also gotten thirty of his one hundred and eighty million, and a monthly alimony of ten thousand which wasn't to stop until she got remarried. So in other words, she could screw as many people as she wanted, but still get his money as long as she didn't marry any one of them. This had infuriated Winston to no end. He damn well should have made her sign prenuptial agreement. He also found out that since the divorce, Anna had been seeing this Greg quite frequently. The little pisser was probably living off the money that he was providing for Anna. That fact did nothing but anger him some more. Pain. He had to cause her pain. It wasn't right that she wasn't living in misery since divorcing him. She was living in luxury and happiness. The bitch.

But not for long.

Ψ

For what had to be the hundredth time, Anna looked out the window to see if she could spot her sister's blue Honda. And just like five minutes ago, it was nowhere to be found.

Anna was taking care of Maria and Brian while Kati was at work—well at least that's where she said she was. But it was now long past the time that she should have returned home.

"Where mama?" Brian asked Anna, as he tugged at her jeans. He was beginning to pick up on some English since coming to America.

Anna smiled at her nephew and picked him up. She gave him a kiss on his soft cheek. "She'll be home soon. Don't worry."

When seven rolled around, Anna put Meena, Maria, and Brian to bed. Then eight, nine, and then finally ten rolled around without her sister Kati making an appearance, Anna began to panic. She called her parent's house. Her father answered on the second ring.

"Hi Dad," Anna greeted.

"Hello, Anna. How are you?" her father responded, cheerfully.

"Ummm...I was wondering. Did you hear from Kati by any chance?" Anna asked.

There was a pause on the other end and then her father answered, "no. Why? What is the matter?"

"Well, Dad, she's not home from work yet. I'm starting to get worried. She should have been home like five hours ago."

"Did you call the restaurant where she works?" her father asked.

"Yes, and they told me that she left a long time ago. Around the time that she usually leaves," Anna said anxiously.

"Well...Anna you know how your sister is," her father began wearily, "She does what she wants. There's no telling where she is."

"But Dad, she usually calls if she's going to be late to pick up the kids," Anna explained.

"Really? She's never called your mother and I when she was going to be late picking up the kids," her father grumbled.

Anna ignored this statement, not willing to cause any friction. "Dad, should I call the police?"

"No, no. Your sister's probably met some guy on the street and is out with him now," Muhammad said testily. "Just wait a few more hours and if you don't hear anything then, call the police. Call us if you hear anything."

"Okay, I will," Anna said recognizing this to be a dismissal. Her father was clearly unconcerned.

After hanging up with her father, Anna sat on the couch and switched on the television. Soon after, the phone rang shrilly. Anna ran to pick it up.

"Hello?" Anna called breathlessly into the receiver

"Hey, Anna," a male's voice cheerfully called. It was Greg.

"Oh, hi," Anna responded. She was disappointed that it wasn't Kati.

"Wow, you sure know how to make a guy feel good," Greg chuckled.

Anna laughed. "I'm sorry Greg. It's just that, at this point, I was hoping that it was my sister calling. She should have been here to pick up her kids almost six hours ago. But she's still not here and I haven't heard from her. I'm worried."

"Do you want me to come over and wait with you?" Greg asked, concerned.

"No...I don't want to drag you out at this time of the night."

"I'll be right over. Talk to you then," he said and hung up before Anna could even respond.

Within an hour Greg had arrived. Anna opened the door for him and gave him a lingering kiss on the lips.

"Mmmm...that just made my day," Greg said with a smile when the kiss was done.

Anna smiled thinly. They sat down on the couch and relaxed. For three hours, they watched television as they anxiously awaited a phone call or the sound of a car in the driveway. There was neither. Finally, at about one in the morning, they drifted to sleep.

Anna woke up to the sun streaming through her window. She looked beside her. Greg was fast asleep. One arm was wrapped around her. She carefully disengaged herself and slipped up the stairs. She looked at the upstairs grandfather clock. It was seven in the morning. She went into her daughter, Meena's bedroom to check on her. She was fast asleep under the covers. She then checked on her niece and her nephew in the other bedrooms. They too were fast asleep.

Suddenly, the fact hit her that her sister still wasn't here. But she might have called...

Anna went into her bedroom and checked that answering machine. There was a new message. Her heart began to beat quickly as she pressed play.

"Anna. This is Kati…umm…I was wondering if you can come and pick me up. I'm down at the station…I need bail….two thousand dollars…"

Kati was in jail? Anna couldn't believe it. According to the answering service, Kati have called at four in the morning. Soon after she and Greg had drifted off to sleep. The phone hadn't woken either one of them.

When Anna came back downstairs, she shook Greg awake.

"Kati's in jail! I have to go bail her out," Anna said, slipping on a pair of old sneakers. She was still in the jeans and tee shirt that she was wearing yesterday.

"What? In jail?" Greg asked, shocked. "I'm coming with you."

"What about the kids? I can't bring them to the station with us. Anna thought for a moment and then came up with an answer. "I'll call the babysitter and see if she could come over."

Anna called Shiree, a seventeen year old Trinidadian girl that lived a few blocks away. Shiree said that she would be right over.

Once Shiree arrived, Anna and Greg left in his Acura Legend. Luckily, it was a Saturday morning, so there wasn't a lot of traffic. Anna and Greg pulled into the Wachovia bank so that Anna could withdraw the money.

When they arrived at the police station, Anna paid the bail in cash. Kati was released into their custody.

"So what did she do?" Anna asked.

"She was caught, with this other guy, snorting cocaine. They were up in his apartment. We were at his apartment because he had a warrant for his arrest for another matter," the detective said leaning back in his chair.

Anna shook her head and looked at her sister who was staring at the ground. Anna felt like strangling her. How could Kati do this?

"She's got a court hearing in thirty days," the detective continued. She's gotta be there or she'll be arrested and put in jail immediately."

Anna glanced at Greg. He wore a frown and his usually unlined brow was furrowed.

"Don't worry. She'll be there and I'll be watching her," Anna said gruffly.

Anna didn't say a word to Kati as they walked out of the building to the car.

"Anna, I'm sorry. I—"

Anna spun around to her sister, anger all over her face. "Don't say a word to me. You have no respect, Kati. None. For yourself or for others. You don't give a damn about anyone but yourself. Actually, I don't think that you even care about yourself. I've been covering for you ever since we were kids. But I'm not covering for you anymore. I've had it with you."

They reached the car and the three of them climbed in. Greg, still looking somber, started the car and pulled away.

"Please Anna. I swear. I'll pay you back every cent," Kati said as she sobbed from the backseat.

Anna turned around in her seat to look at her sister. "Spear me the histrionics. What I want from you is to shape up. You're not a child anymore. You're a grown woman. You have children and responsibilities. I can't carry you for the rest of your life."

Kati sat back and looked down. She didn't say anything else for the rest of the ride.

Greg dropped Kati and Anna home and promised to give Anna a call later before he pulled away.

They somberly walked into the house down to the basement playroom where Shiree was playing with the three children.

"Shiree, do you mind taking the kids to the park? I have a few things that I have to discuss with my sister. I don't want them hearing anything."

"No problem, Miss Senghor," Shiree said with her pretty brown face beaming. Once Shiree and the kids had left, Anna turned to her sister.

"What were you doing sniffing coke?" Anna asked. She started to make some coffee.

Kati sat down at the kitchen table and shrugged her shoulders.

"Is that all you can do? Shrug your shoulders? What drugs do you take besides coke?"

Kati shrugged and said, "Sometimes I smoke weed. I've done crystal meth a few times…"

Anna plopped down into a chair beside her. "Are you taking any drugs intravenously?"

Kati shook her head. "No."

"But that doesn't make it okay, none the less," Anna said. But she was relieved at the fact that her sister wasn't using needles, considering the high infection risk.

"So who was this guy that you were with?"

"Some guy that I met in the bar," Kati answered.

"You go off with some guy that you just met to do drugs? Kati. You are making all the wrong decisions."

Kati didn't say anything for a while and then she said. "Well, I'm not the only one. If you didn't make any mistakes you would have your daughter now, wouldn't you."

Anna looked at her sister, stung. "Don't go there, Kati. That was a cheap shot and it has nothing to do with the trouble that you're in now. I'm not even going to go into the obvious. Now. Instead of throwing you out of my house for you impertinence, I'm going to overlook it and allow you to stay because you are my sister. And I love you. Whether you believe it or not." Anna drained the last of her coffee from her mug.

"Now. I'm going to go upstairs and get one of the bedrooms ready for you. I think it will be best if you stay here until the court hearing." With that, Anna walked out of the kitchen and headed up the stairs.

She made it out of the room just before the tears started to flow down her face.

Ψ

When Kati went to court a month later. Because this was Kati's first offence, the judge decided not to give her any jail time. Instead, she was given six months probation plus 150 hours of community service. She was also ordered into rehab for 90 days. Both Kati and Anna were relived that there was no prison sentence.

Kati went off to rehab and in the meanwhile, Anna's parents took in Brian and Maria, their two grandchildren. When they left, the house felt a little empty now that it was only Anna and Meena once again. But on the other hand, Anna was happy to be alone with her new daughter.

Because of everything that had been happening, Anna hadn't been able to bond with her daughter the way that she wanted to. And bond, they did over the next three months.

Ψ

Anna stared at her friend in the hospital bed. He looked like a concentration camp victim. All the muscle from his arms was wasted away and they looked like dried out sticks. His face was a mare skull covered with blotchy skin. His eyes balls were sunk into his socket and were dull and lacking in life. The rest of his body was also skeletal in appearance. Sometimes it was painful for Kati to even look at him. Often, when she would visit him, she would feel as if a fist was tightening around her throat.

At the beginning, Ramón had started using AZT. And although Ramón's viral load became low as a result of taking the drug, he suffered bad side effects. He then started on the newly developed drug didanosine and stopped taking AZT. But, after about a year and a half, didanosine just wasn't working for Ramón anymore. For a few years, didanosine was effective in stopping the viral load of the HIV virus, but now the HIV had become resistant to the powerful drug. A month ago, the doctor had informed Ramón that his CD4 cell count was below 200. Pretty soon, Ramón had to be admitted to the hospital. But Hector and Anna would visit him every day. Hector would sit by Ramón's bedside, hold his hand, wipe his brow, feed him, help him use the bathroom, etc. Hector was totally devoted to him.

Two weeks after being admitted to the hospital, on June 12, 1992, Ramón quietly passed away in his sleep.

A week later, a new, more effective drug, Zalcitabine, was approved by the FDA to be used in combination with AZT.

"If only he had hanged on a little longer…one more week…he would have had more months, even years…," Hector cried quietly to Anna at the funeral as he twisted the ring on his finger that Ramón had given him three months after they began dating. Ramón, in his casket, was wearing an identical one. "Oh God Anna! I'm going to miss him so much!"

Anna put an arm around him as she wiped her tears away.

"So will I, Hector."

After the funeral, Hector held a wake at the condo that he and Ramón had shared for the past two years.

Poor Hector looked like a zombie as he greeted his guests and attempted to play host. Anna was glad that she was there to help him. He couldn't have done it by himself.

When the wake was over and all the guests had left, Hector wandered, like a ghost, around the condo touching this and that, looking and staring with wide round eyes. Anna watching him, cautiously.

Finally, he came back into the living room where Anna was. He turned his eyes to her and after a silent moment he asked, "what am I to do with all of these things? His things are all over this place…"

"Well, you might want to keep some things for keepsakes—"

"I have what I want already," he said quickly, cutting her off. "But what about the rest?" Then he flopped down onto the plush, coffee colored couch that Ramón, with his good taste, had chosen out at the furniture store when he and Hector had first moved in here. Then, Hector began to cry. At first quietly, and then he began to sob painfully. Anna, her heart broken at the sound, came over beside him and wrapped her arm around his broad shoulders.

"I'll help you, Hector. You're not in this alone. I'm here, remember?" Anna said quietly.

Hector continued to cry into his hands.

"Ramón's family might want some of his things…"

Hector looked up at her and sniffled as he wiped his eyes. "Well… most of his family's back in Rio de Janeiro…" Hector's face got stony all of a sudden and his lips clamped. "His father didn't mind taking the checks that Ramón sent to him every month, the father didn't mind leaching off his success! But he wouldn't accept Ramón back into his house once he found out that he was gay. He wouldn't even speak to Ramón. I know that used to hurt him so much…like my father hurts me…and his mother, she's been dead for years…only one of his siblings lives up here in the States. Maribella. Remember her? The caramel complexioned girl with the cornrows sitting beside us at the funeral? She didn't come to the wake though… Oh what am I talking about! Of course you know her. You've met her before…today."

Anna nodded. "Well let's call her, okay? I'm sure she'll love to have some of his things," Anna said soothingly.

So they called Maribella and asked her if she wanted to come over and look to see if she wanted anything.

One the third ring, Maribella had picked up. Hector put her on speaker phone so that he and Anna could both talk to her.

Surprisingly, to Anna and Hector, she sounded a little nervous as she declined the offer.

"Why not, Mari? You've always admired Ramón's things. I would have thought that you would have wanted to take some…to remind you of him at least," Hector had told her over the phone.

"I prefer not to take anything…thank you though for asking—"

"But why?" Hector protested over the phone, "Why not?" he demanded. Anna placed a calming hand on his shoulder.

Maribella was silent on the other side and for a minute, Hector and Anna thought that she had hung up.

"Are you still there, Maribella?" Anna asked.

"Yes," was the tentative reply.

"What is it, Maribella. We don't understand. Why don't you just be honest with us?" Anna said calmly.

"I don't want those things in my place…I feel that they will bring bad luck," she said so softly that they barely heard her.

Hector and Anna exchanged looks.

"What?" Hector yelped.

"Calm, Hector," Anna intoned.

"What do you mean bad luck?" Hector asked, with a false singsong voice.

Maribella sighed and said, "I love my brother dearly. But I don't want things from a dead person that had AIDS. It will bring bad luck…I don't want that in my house."

"Was it bad luck to take his money too?!" Hector shrieked, losing all control and abandoning the forced pleasant front.

I'm sure you still have some of that six grand that he put into your account three weeks ago to pay for your classes! Will that bring a curse on you too?"

Maribella was at a lost for words.

"And I'm sure that you'll be there for the reading of his will next week to take whatever valuables that he left to you! God! That man would have walked through fire for you! His little sister did no wrong!

But you can't have the Monet, do you hear me! You can't! Ramón and I bought that in Germany last year!" Hector said, totally flipping out. Once again he began to cry.

For a while, there was only the sound of Hector crying. Anna was sure that Maribella had hung up. But she hadn't.

"I have to go now…I'll be seeing you," Maribella said quietly before hanging up.

Soon the loud sound of the dial tone was piercing their ears. Hector pressed the speaker button again to hang up. He looked miserably at Anna and said

"Anna, can you spend the night? I don't think I can be in here alone. Not so soon."

"Of course. Just let me go and get Meena from the babysitters. I'll pack our bag and come right over."

Hector looked relieved. "Thank you. You can have the extra bedroom. While I'll sleep on the couch."

"Why don't you sleep in your room?" Anna asked.

"I can't. Every hour of the night, I'll be expecting to feel Ramón's body beside me. I can't bear that he's not here!" Then Hector, for the hundredth time that day, began to cry again.

Anna nodded, understanding. She comforted Hector for a while before leaving to go and get her daughter. She promised Hector her return.

Life was no cup of tea.

Ψ

Winston silently sold his independent oil company, "Hurst Industries," and its two subsidiaries to a rival company, "Lumis Petrol". Winston's company ended up being worth many times the amount that he had first put into it over a decade ago. He was pleased with the offer, and accepted it. He then created an offshore account in Dominica and wired the money there.

Winston then quickly and silently sold his estate. He also sold his apartment in New York and his summer cottage by the lake. He sold his yacht, his speedboat, and his sailboat. He also sold all his cars—his Rolls Royce, his Porsche 911, his Bentley, and his Maserati Spyder. As for his furnishings and knick-knacks, he decided on what he would take with him and what he would not. The things that he wouldn't or couldn't take with him, he sold. All the money from the estate and the selling of his things, he also wired into the same offshore account in Dominica.

Winston then inconspicuously tied up any other loose ends that he needed to take care of.

Finally, on the day before he and Jackie's departure, he was nervous and anxious. He was just hoping that everything was set up the way that he had planned.

"Don't worry. The minute you get here, everything will be given to you. It's all waiting for you over here," the man told him discreetly over the phone.

"Good. I am certainly paying you enough," Winston said gruffly. He looked around and saw no one. It was midnight and he was talking at a payphone a good distance away from where he and baby Jackie were staying.

"Yes, yes. And everything is taken care of. The only thing you have to do is to get here. I will see you tomorrow," the man said soothingly.

After hanging up, Winston felt a little better. Everything was going to be okay. Everything will go according to plan, he kept telling himself. He needed it to. It had to.

After all, it was too late to turn back now.

Ψ

Bright and early, Anna swung by Winston's house to pick up Jackie. She, Hector, Meena, and Jackie were going down to the beach house on Long Beach for the weekend. Anna had come up with the idea and then thought to invite Hector, who was still in mourning and hardly went out to see the light of day.

"You need to get out, Hector. It's not good isolating yourself the way you are. It's not healthy. I know that Ramón wouldn't have wanted you to do that," Anna had told him two days before.

Reluctantly, Hector had agreed to go. And by the next day, to Anna's delight, he was getting so caught up in the preparations for their trip down to the the beach house, that he hardly even thought of grieving.

Players of the Game

The first thing Anna noticed that seemed a bit strange was that she didn't see any of Winston's cars in the outside driveway. Instead, of seeing the usual bright red Maserati that Winston often drove, she saw a blue BMW in front. Winston didn't have a car like that. At first Anna thought that maybe she had taken a wrong turn and was not at Winston's house, but then she looked at everything else, and it looked the same. She was at the right house.

Confused now, Anna slowly got out of her Mercedes convertible and locked the door behind her. She walked up to the front door and knocked. After a moment a short, blond haired woman answered the door.

"Can I help you?" the woman asked, nervously, her eyes darting behind and around Anna.

Anna looked at the woman dumfounded. "Who are you?"

"Who are *you*." The woman responded.

Anna, quickly deciding that this was probably one of Winston's little tarts, shook her head and said. "Look. I'm here to pick up my daughter. Please tell Winston that I'm here," Anna said snappishly.

The woman stared Anna down, taking in the designer clothes and the expensive sandals that adorned Anna's perfectly manicured feet. She looked back at Anna's face with a look of question.

"Look. I don't have time for you to stand here and stare at me and decide if I'm here to rob the house or not! I'm Winston's ex-wife and that is my red Mercedes sitting out there in the driveway which I am going to use to drive to my Beach house in Long Beach tomorrow! Just bring me my daughter!"

The woman, caught off guard by all that was being said, stared for a moment before opening her mouth to utter any words. "There is no Winston living here, lady. I live here with my husband and our little boy. We just moved in about a week ago."

Anna thought that she was hearing things. For a moment, she thought she heard sirens go off, but realized that it was only in her head. "What?" Anna managed to utter.

"I don't know why you're here. But I don't know any Winston. He might have been the man that sold us the house, but we weren't given that information. We just moved here, and we don't want any trouble so please. Just leave," the woman pleaded as she stepped behind the door and closed it in her face.

Anna took a deep breath and knocked on the door again. The woman opened it a crack and poked her head around the door.

"What?" the woman whined

"Can you please tell me what's going on? Quick the game playing. I don't care if you're seeing him or anything. That's none of my business. I just want to see Jackie. This is my weekend to see her. I only get one weekend a month."

The woman gave her a queer look and said, "Look. For the last time. I don't know who Winston is. Please don't come back here. You're making me nervous." And with that, the door was shut in Anna's face again.

Anna waited a moment and knocked on the door again. This time the blond woman stuck her head out of the upstairs window.

"If you don't leave, I'm going to call the police," the woman threatened.

Anna was too dazed to have an angry response. She drifted to her car and slowly started down the road.

"Hey! Hey! Anna!" a woman called out.

Anna looked around and saw a woman rushing out onto her front lawn in spike heels and a blue dress suit. The woman flagged her car down. Anna recognized the woman to be Mrs. Silverman, one of her former neighbors that lived across the street from Winston.

Anna pulled the car over in front of her house. The woman came up to the car, out of breath. Her plump face was flushed and her hair, expertly dyed to a deep black, was short and well styled. She gave Anna a tentative smiled, her blue eyes sparkling.

"Anna, darling. I haven't seen you in a while! Come on in for something to drink. I never thought I would see you around here again!"

Anna got out of her car and followed the matronly woman into the large house.

"Hilda? Do get us some lemonade and bring it out to the patio. We'll take our refreshments out there," Mrs. Silverman told a tall, morose looking blond woman.

"Come, come. Do sit down."

Anna did as she was told and sat down in the cushioned patio chair. "What did you mean you never thought that you would see me around here? I come to pick Jackie up once a week."

Mrs. Silverman fixed her with a stare and said, "Why, of course. But I mean, after Winston moved out. I mean. I didn't even know he moved out until I saw that cheap blond and her husband who's twenty years her senior, moving in. He was very silent about it. I had just assumed that you knew about it...," Mrs. Silverman said trailing off. She eyed Anna, eagerly awaiting a response.

Mrs. Silverman was the neighborhood busybody. Insatiably curious and nosey. If anyone knew about anyone in the neighborhood, and beyond, it would be her. But Anna sincerely liked her because she was real and she was kind hearted. And she knew that Mrs. Silverman liked her too, dubbing Anna as one of the only sincere people around here. That is, when Anna used to live around here.

Anna couldn't believe her ears. "What do you mean he moved out?"

Mrs. Silverman looked shocked. "You mean you didn't know?"

Anna shook her head slowly.

The older woman frowned. "Oh dear. This is quite a predicament, isn't it?"

Yes. Yes it was.

Ψ

Aldo Nicolini looked out his window and out at the seacoast and breathed a sigh of relief. He looked down at his daughter, Alessia, who was playing with her toys on the carpeted floor. He smiled.

"We made it, my dear," he said softly to his daughter. "We're going to be just fine, you and I."

Ψ

Months and months of searching led to only dead ends. Anna, enlisting the help of Greg, was frustrated that he came up with almost nothing.

"I don't know," Greg said shaking his head. "He's covered up really good. Not a trace did he leave. He could be anywhere by now."

Anna felt as if she was on an edge about to fall over. But she knew that she had to get a grip. She couldn't afford to lose control. Any wrong moves, and she would lose Meena. She had a lot to consider.

"I can't believe that he would just do something like this," Pamela said to Hector and Anna as they were sitting out on the patio making phone calls one afternoon.

Hector shot Pamela a look. "If it's a surprise to you, then you really don't know the man."

Since Ramón's death, Hector sold the condo and bought a nice, spacious house (six bedrooms) on the other side of town, only about ten minutes drive away from Anna's house, much to Anna's pleasure. Hector claimed that he couldn't bear walking around the condo that he and Ramón once shared. Anna did notice that he seemed less depressed since the move. She tried to keep him occupied, they spent a lot of time at each other's houses.

"No one knows anything. Winston was really secretive about everything that he did. Plus he knows a lot of people—more than I could ever imagine. I don't know if I'll ever find my daughter," Anna said sadly. She tried not to cry.

Hector and Pam each put a comforting arm around their friend.

"Don't worry, we'll find Jackie," Hector said.

They were words of comfort from a true friend, but how true were they?

Ψ

September 1993

"Don't play with that Meena!" screeched Hector as he snatched the dangerous object out of her reach just in the nick of time. He breathed a sigh of relief. Children. They were not his expertise.

It was a Friday afternoon and Hector was spending the weekend over at Anna's house. Currently, Anna was on her way to pick up Kati and her two kids. They were all going down to Palm Springs later on.

"Daddy!" Meena cried out.

"No, *not* Daddy. *Uncle. Uncle* Hector. Remember that," Hector said anxiously. The mare thoughts of parenthood sent his head reeling. He didn't know how Anna did it. She was a natural mother.

"Uncle!" the girl cried.

"That's right, honey. Uncle," Hector said lifting her into his arms. He couldn't believe that in a month, Meena would be four years old.

Suddenly, Hector heard the phone ring. He rushed to pick it up. "Hello?"

"Hector? There's a problem over here at Kati's place," Anna said.

"What's the matter?" Hector asked, worriedly.

"Well. I came over here and I saw that the kids were alone. Now the lady next door tells me that they've been here for two days without Kati. She doesn't have a clue where Kati is. She said that she let the kids sleep over in her apartment last night. She didn't want to call Child Services on Kati yet. I came just before she was going to." Anna let out a big sigh. "She's screwing up again."

Hector shook his head. Kati was up to her tricks again. Was that girl ever going to straighten up?

"Okay. I'll come right over," Hector said.

"No, no. Stay where you are. I'll just bring the kids home. My sister will have to get them at my house later on."

Later on that evening, just as they were about to leave for the condo in Palm Springs, Anna heard the phone ring. She rushed to pick it up.

"Anna, it's me," a low voice said. It was Kati.

"Where the hell have you been for the past two days?" Anna asked. Her sister sounded like she was high.

"I went out...I forgot about the kids...I'm sorry," Kati said in a spaced out voice.

"God damn it, Kati. You're high! I can't believe you! You left your kids alone for two days! You left a six year old and a four year old home alone! How could you?"

Kati was silent on the other end. "I'm sorry. Can I come and get them now?"

"Have you forgotten that we're going down to the condo this weekend? We're already packed to go. We don't have time to wait for you," Anna said harshly.

"I'll be over soon. Please," Kati pleaded.

"I'm sorry, Kati. I can't trust your word. We're leaving now. Just go home and sleep it off, okay?"

Kati slammed the phone down in Anna's ear. Anna shrugged, determined not to let Kati manipulate her any further.

Anna grabbed her bag from off the chair and headed outside. Hector was just closing the trunk of his black Range Rover when he spotted Anna. He came up to her.

"Hey. So what's happening with your sister?"

"We're leaving right now. We're not going to let her spoil the weekend."

"Good. The kids are all buckled in," Hector said as he slipped on a pair of Ray-Ban sunglasses. He slid behind the driving wheel.

"Wonderful. Then let's hit the road," Anna said as she climbed into the brand new, 1994 Range Rover SUV.

Ψ

Anna looked across the desk at the dumpy looking Gyanese woman. The Indian Gyanese woman stared right back at her.

"You do understand what I am saying, right?" The case manager said calmly.

"Yes, of course," Anna said calmly. But inside she was fuming at her sister.

"The children have to be taken out of her custody. We like to look for family that can take the child in, of course. In this case, we have a court order to remove the two children from your sister's custody. Your sister's neighbor told us that she saw your sister doing crystal meth in front of them. Obviously, she has relapsed from the rehab that she was in. Also, she told us about the incident that happened two weeks ago when she left the children home alone for two days."

"Well, we'll take them," Candace spoke up from beside Kati. Muhammad nodded his gray head in agreement.

Anna shook her head. "No. Mom, Dad, you two are too old to be taking on young children like this. I'll take them. I'll be their guardian."

"At this point, your sister no longer has parental rights over them. Guardianship will be assigned to you, if that's what you wish Miss. Senghor."

Anna nodded her head. "That's what I want."

Ψ

June, 1994

Once again, Kati had taken off into the streets without a word to anyone. Anna noted that it had been a month now since she had last seen her sister. Since getting custody of Brian and Maria eight months ago, Kati had come to see them less and less and half the time when she would come, she would be high off drugs, so Anna wouldn't allow her to see Maria and Brian. In and out of their lives, Kati played the illusive mother until bit by bit her presence dwindled to almost nothing.

But there wasn't anything that Anna could do for someone that didn't want to help themself.

Chapter Thirty-seven

Present day, Beverly Hills, California

"Come on! Come on! Hit that ball into the sky!" yelled Coach Peters from the sideline.

The bat hit the ball with a loud crack and went sailing into the air.

"That's right Brian!" a teammate cried from the sidelines.

Brian, dropped the bat and sprinted to first base.

The opposing team in the outfield went after the ball. One attempted to catch it in his mitt, but he missed.

Brian ran to the second base.

Another person in the outfield grabbed the ball from the grass and started running back towards Brian.

Brian sprinted to the third base.

"Go all the way for the home run!" yelled Coach Peters.

Brian ran to the home base and was safe.

There were loud cheers from the audience and they stood up to applause. Teammates came up to Brian and lifted him up on their shoulders. Brian beamed with happiness.

Coach Peters came up to the group of his players with a bright smile on his face. He congratulated them all on their good work.

"If you'll let Brian off your shoulders, I'd like to speak to him."

The young men let Brian down. Brian walked over to the coach and smiled.

"What's up Coach?"

Coach Peters put an arm around Brian's shoulders and led him off to the side where it was less crowded. They sat on one of the benches. Coach Peters turned to face Brian.

"Son. There's only a select few that I could tell this to because talent like yours only comes by once in a blue moon."

Brian looked at the coach's dark eyes and his smooth, unlined, cocoa brown skin. "What is it Coach?"

"Well, Brian. Have you ever thought of going professional—getting into the minor leagues, at first?"

Brian was a little taken back at this question. The Coach had never approached him on the subject before.

"Well, no," Brian responded.

"Well Brian, you certainly have a chance to make it into professional baseball. Now I know that there's only a slim chance for the people that try out to make it in, but it couldn't hurt for you to try out. And let me tell you. I think you've got a real chance at it. More than anyone on this team, but please don't repeat that."

Brian nodded slowly as he took in the words. Major league baseball? He had never thought of it.

"Well, I'm going to college in the fall," Brian said hesitantly.

"Hey. And that's good. I'm just telling you that you should try out. Soon a scout will be making the rounds. I recommend that you come out and show him what you got."

Ψ

"Okay. Now just relax your face a little more. Give me a ethereal look. Open those eyes, honey!"

Meena tried to do as her photographer was instructing her.

"Good! You look fantastic, doll! Utterly beautiful! Now let's get some shots with the wind blowing." The photographer—a tall, lanky, black man with shoulder length, relaxed, hair and a peanut butter brown complexion—turned to his assistant, who was a small Hispanic man. "Turn that fan on!" he screeched.

"Okay," Fernando said hurriedly as he began to rush over to the large, high-powered, fan. He wondered why Yaasa had to yell all the time. But he didn't dare confront the famous photographer—he was notoriously bitchy.

"Now turn your face a little, darling. Let's get that lovely profile! Great. Now face forward again, stretch out, but look natural! Fantastic! Well, that's all for today!" Yaasa said standing back.

Fernando turned off the fan before Yaasa could tell him, saving his boss the pleasure of an argument.

"Well girl," Yaasa said walking up to Meena. "You did great today. How's your contract with *Twilight Essence Perfumes* going?"

Meena smiled. "It's going great. All we have to do is to work out some technicalities and that will be it."

"Ah! So young and already making a name for yourself! Who would believe it at fifteen, right Fernando?"

"Yes, yes," Fernando responded, quickly.

"Do you need a lift? I can call you a cab and don't worry. You wouldn't have to pay for it."

"No, I'm fine. My mom's picking me up today. My cousin Maria has a gymnastics match."

"Oh, that's just fantastic! Wish her luck for me!"

"I will, Yaasa. I'll see you next week."

"Absolutely! Have a fabulous weekend, doll!"

Meena and Yaasa exchanged air kisses.

"Bye Fernando," Meena called to him.

"O-oh, bye…" he responded, clearly flustered. A bright red color spread in his cheeks.

Meena was exhausted. She was happy to see her mother's silver Mercedes 500 waiting outside the studio when she got outside.

"So how was it today?" Anna asked, cheerfully

"It was interesting. I'm glad that I had Yaasa. He's good. He's gets me to take really good pictures."

"Great. I saw your picture on the cover on Teen People, you looked amazing, honey!" Anna exclaimed happily to her daughter.

"Thanks Mom. Are we going straight to the competition?"

"Yes. Brian's going to meet us there once he gets out of baseball practice. Hector and Comete are dropping Maria there, so they'll be there as well. Oh Gosh, I'm so happy that Maria's team is in the regionals now," Anna said happily.

"Yeah. That's because she's really good, Mom."

"She is," Anna responded, cheerfully.

When Anna and Meena walked into the large gym, they noticed that the spectator seats in the seating section were quickly being filled. They spotted Maria warming up with her team in one corner of the gym. Maria looked up and saw Anna and Meena looking towards her. They smiled and waved at each other. Anna and Meena looked around the crowd and saw that Hector and Comete were already there. They went over to where they were to sit down beside them.

"Thanks for coming, you two," Anna said giving them each a kiss on the cheek.

"I wouldn't miss this for the word. Two sporting events in one week. I feel like an athlete!" Comete exclaimed.

A moment later, Brian walked in. Anna and Meena waved him down. He came over to sit beside them.

By the end of the completion, Maria's team had raked up the highest points out of the four teams. They were about five points above the team in second place. They had made it to the state finals.

"You know what? This calls for celebration," Hector said once the competition was over. "Let's go out to eat! It's on me."

"That's right. Maria, you did fabulously," Comete said giving Maria's arm a gentle squeeze.

"Thank you Comete," Maria said beaming.

"So where are we going to go?" Meena asked.

"Well, what do we feel like having?" Anna asked.

"Whatever Maria wants, Maria will get," Hector said. "Oh. And this is a bit of a celebration for Meena as well, who is about to finalize her contract with *Twilight Essence* Perfumes!" Hector added hurriedly.

"I know. Let's go to *Muy Fuego*," Maria said indicating one of the trendiest hot spots in L.A.

"I love your thinking, girl," Comete said with a smile. "But we must get in before nine, or they'll be asking for ID's from you kiddies."

And celebrate they did.

Ψ

"Man, what if I didn't get accepted?" Brian said as he uneasily eyed the unopened white envelope.

"Then you have your other choices to fall back onto," Anna assured him. "But you haven't even opened the letter yet."

"I'll open it for you," Maria said attempting to snatch the letter from her brother's fingers.

Brian held it away from her and scowled. "I could open it by myself, thank you."

Brian took a deep breath and began to open the letter. Once it was opened, he took the folded letter from out of the envelope. He glanced up at Anna and Maria. They stared back at him, waiting.

Brian slowly unfolded the letter and started reading out loud from the top line. He forced himself not to read ahead.

"Thank you for your interest in UCLA. We are happy to inform you that you have been accepted for admission into the fall class of—"

"Oh my gosh! You made it!" Anna screamed excitedly. She jumped up from her seat and hugged her nephew. Maria joined them as well.

"I'm proud of you , big bro. Nice job," Maria said smiling.

Brian was beaming from ear to ear. He had gotten accepted into the college of his first choice. The minute he got there, he would try out for the baseball team. He was sure that he could get in.

Things were really looking good.

Ψ

Anna rang the doorbell of the gigantic house once she was let in through the gates. A second later, the door was opened and a pretty, smiling, Latina led her into the house.

"Mr. Damon is out on the deck, near the pool," the woman said in her heavily accented Spanish.

Sure enough, there was Walter Damon, the recording company mogul, owner and CEO of *Entourage Productions,* sitting outside by the pool.

For a man nearing his seventieth birthday, he looked well. His charcoal gray hair was still thick and full. His skin had a healthy, natural tan and his blue eyes were sparkling and youthful. His body was also in good shape—strong and lean.

When he spotted Anna coming through the sliding doors of the deck, he waved to her and motioned for her to come and take a seat. He was on the phone talking at the moment.

"Butchers, I 'ave to go now. Me guest is 'ere. Yeah, I'll talk to yer later."

Walter Damon quickly hung up the phone and gave Anna a big smile with his perfectly white teeth.

"how r yeh doing, love?" he asked, in his strong London cockney.

"I'm great," Anna said, giving him a peck on the cheek.

"Don't get dis old geezer all excited, now. A young beau'y like yer."

Anna laughed and patted him on the hand. "You're not so bad yourself."

"Would yer like a drink?"

"Sure. What about a Perrier?"

"Certainly, darlin' ".He motioned for his butler, who was standing nearby and told him to get some refreshments.

"Wod yer like a fag?" Walter said lighting a cigarette up.

Anna chuckled. "You know I don't smoke."

"Cor blimey. It was worf a 'ry . Nuff said, yeah? But considerin', I do not fink yer should start," he said as he took a deep drag. He smiled at Anna. "I guess yer wonderin' why I called yer up 'ere. A tad curious, I bet.

"Well, actually I am wondering."

"Well… 'ere's the thing, me love, I'm dying."

"What?!" Anna asked, shocked.

"Yep, my dear," he looked at the cigarette that he was holding in his hands. "Dis 'ere stick's fullin' up me lungs wiv cancer. They say I 'ave six months left, and then I'll be pushin' up daisies," Walter let out a whooping laugh that quickly turned into a coughing fit. Anna patted him on the back. He waved her away.

"I'm allright, luv."

"But you're still smoking," Anna said, upset.

"So what, eh darlin'? I'm going to die anyway, didn't yer 'ear me? . Might as well enjoy meself on the flamin' trip dahn."

Anna couldn't believe this. This man, sitting before her, a man that she had admired and cared about was going to die and he was taking it so lightly like someone had told him that he was going on a cruise.

"Walter. I can't believe this," Anna said beginning to cry.

Walter jumped up from his chair and came around to where Anna sat. He put a tan arm around her shoulders, "There, there, Anna. Chin up. No tear fer me please. I've accepted it."

Anna wiped her eyes and stared down at the table top.

"Now, now. I've 'ad a solid scarper. I've clocked things most people don't clock in three lifetimes.. Time fer me to settle dahn, anyhow …" he said trailing off.

Anna looked up at him. "I just can't believe this. You have to try and fight this, Walter. Are you going through treatment?"

Walter shook his head. "Nah, end stage cancer. I don't wan't to spend the rest of the time I 'ave vomitin' in the toilet and as Tom and Dick as a dog."

"Tom and Dick?" Anna repeated, confused.

"Sick. Sick as a dog," clarified Walter.

Anna nodded slowly.

Walter sat back across from Anna.

"Now 'ere's the real issue. I 'ave a problem, me dear. What's to 'ave dis company when I'm gawn?"

"What about Eva?" Anna said referring to his ex wife.

Walter scrunched his face up in disgust. "I know yer're jokin', right? she 'wod scarper the place into the ground, she 'wod. Beside, why 'wod I want to give 'er me company fer? I give dat leech enough from me settlement now dat I'm alive. I'm not givin' 'er anythin' when I'm brown bread."

"Brown bread?" Anna repeated in question.

"Dead, me dear. Dat's what I mean."

Anna nodded.

Walter continued. "I'm not leavin' me company to Tina, Leah, or Patricia either," he said listing off the long list of past wives.

Anna laughed. "Okay."

"Thank God I don't 'ave any kids, bleedin' maggots dat they are," he continued.

Anna shook her head in amazement. The man said whatever was on his mind.

Anna frowned and shrugged her shoulders. "I don't know then, Walter." Anna paused. "Why don't you sell the company then?" Anna suggested tentatively.

"An' then give the money to who? I'll be in the bloomin' same predicament. Wot about yer 'ave it?" Walter said quickly.

"Huh?" Anna said, confused.

"Wot about I leave the company to yer, when I take off. I can't fink of anyone who would scarper it better. Yer've a mind fer business. Yer've brought me label *Eden's Apple* to top place since yer took over years ago. I want yer to 'ave the company. Will yer 'ave it?"

Anna couldn't believe her ears. "I-I-don't know."

"What do yer mean, yer don't know, eh darlin? I'm offerin' yer a first rate company dat's one of the bleedin' most successful in dis country 'ow could yer refuse?"

"I…okay. I'll take it," Anna said, still quite dazed.

Walter smiled broadly. "Solid then. No going backsies, either." Walter leaned closer to her. "And don't worry. I will talk to me business people. They'll show yer all the ropes. Yer know 'alf of it already, and dat's the most important 'alf."

Anna smiled, even though on the inside, she felt like crying.

Ψ

"Walter has lung cancer," Anna said to Hector as they sat by the street side café sipping lattes

"What? Do you mean Walter Damon?" Hector asked, intrigued.

"Yes, that's him. He told me yesterday. He has six months to live and he said that he wants me to have the company when he's gone. He doesn't have any family to give it to and he doesn't want to sell it."

"Anna, that's amazing!" Hector said excitedly. "My God! You're well off as it is, but you'll be rolling in dough when it's all said and done!"

"Well, this isn't only about money, Hector."

"Of course it isn't darling. My father's a top notch developer and real estate magnate. I know what money's *all* about, my dear. I'm just waiting for the chance to get it all."

Anna laughed. "Hector you're horrible."

Hector pouted. "The man hates me. What do you want from me?"

Anna shook her head. "You're a successful events planner, the best in L.A. What more could you want? Plus, your father doesn't hate you. He just doesn't understand you."

"Correction. He *doesn't* want to understand me. He's afraid to try!"

Ψ

In spring, of next year (March, to be precise) in the second semester of Brian's freshman year at UCLA, Brian discovered that the baseball scouts were coming that summer, just as Coach Peters had said. Brian was trying to decide whether he should go to try out or not. He had chosen a business major and was doing great, coasting through his classes as he had done in high school. Anna was amazed at his scholastic abilities.

"With all the partying you do, it's a wonder how you keep up a 3.8 GPA" Anna would often say, shaking her head. "But you promise to ease up on all the merry making?"

"Sure thing, Auntie," Brian would say. But he never would. How could he? College life was too exciting and pass up. Girls, parties, and booze…ahh. He was living *the* life and loving every minute of it.

Brian looked up from an assignment he was typing on the computer when he heard the door to his room open. His roommate and new friend, Freddy Huang, came in and plopped on his bed on his side of the room. He flung his book bag to the ground.

"What's up, amigo," Freddy said before turning around in his bed to face the wall.

"What's up Freddy. Where you coming from?"

"Bio lab. I decided to take it for an election this semester. I thought that I might as well get my science elective out of the way as soon as I can. I don't understand why we have to take a science elective when we're not even science majors. I'm in accounting, man," he said wearily. He rolled around and faced Brian. "You going to the party this weekend at Stephanie's house? She's promising it to be the party of the year," Freddy said smiling wickedly.

Brian hesitated. The bad thing about Freddy was that he was as much a party animal as Brian was. Together, they had found that they had the ability to get into some serious trouble. Besides, he wanted to spend this weekend practicing. The tryouts were this summer, and he was determined to go. But he couldn't tell Anna. She would have a fit if she thought that he was thinking of giving up college for a career in sports.

"I don't know…I wanted to practice some baseball this weekend, make sure my game is tight. I think I'm gonna try out for baseball when we get out on summer vacation. I want to make sure I'm ready for that," Brian said.

"What do you mean? You're already on the baseball team," Freddy said, perplexed.

Players of the Game

"I mean, professional baseball. My coach from high school said that I should try out."

Freddy sat in silence, thinking, then he said, "Well, amigo, you are good. Maybe you should. Man. It's all easy from there on, if you get in. If you make it, you'll get paid millions just to smack a ball around with a stick."

Ψ

After finals, Brian packed up and prepared to go home for the summer. He had no intention of staying on campus a moment longer than he needed to.

While at home, Brian remained silent about his intentions to try out the upcoming weekend.

That Saturday, Brian got ready to leave for tryouts.

"Where are you going?" Anna asked him, when she saw him leaving the house with his baseball shoes.

"Umm, me and a bunch of guys are going to play a game," Brian said quickly. He flushed and felt his face turn hot. He really hated lying to his aunt.

"All right. I'll see you later then," Anna said giving him a quick kiss on the cheek.

Brian came back from the tryouts that Saturday evening feeling nervous excitement. Lucky for him, the house was empty. Anna must have gone out. His sister and his cousin were probably with friends.

The recruiter had been extreamly impressed and pleased with Brian's performance and had told him that if he wanted, he could have a place on a class A minor league team, the California Suns. The recuiter was sure that within in a few years, the California Suns's "parent" major league team, the L.A Suns, would take Brian onto their team since he was such a phenomenal player. Brian could hardly believe it. Unbeknownst to him, the scout had watched his college team play on several occasions and had seen him play as well. They liked what they saw and though that he stood out from the other players.

But the stark realization hit him that Anna knew nothing about this. She would never agree to it. But, then again, he was almost 19 and he could make these decisions by himself.

Brian was still lying in bed thinking about it at three in the morning, which was around the time that he heard someone come into the house.

He got up from bed and stood by the stairs. He saw his cousin making her way up the stairs. She didn't see him overlooking her until she was halfway up.

"Does Aunty know that you went out tonight?" Brian asked her. "What are you doing back so late?"

Meena scowled at him. "Why are you asking me so many questions? I just want to go to sleep." Her expression softened. "Please don't tell Mom."

Brian shook his head, backed off, and went back into his room. He would forget what he saw tonight. He had too much on his mind to be bothered with arguing with his cousin.

Ψ

Walter Damon passed quietly in his sleep. And as he promised, the company was passed on to Anna. Some of the executives were not very happy with Damon's choice for successor, but they had to live with it. Or find another job, which Anna made very clear from the beginning.

Almost from the start, Andrew Wilkinson, the Chairman of the Board of Directors, didn't approve of Anna. Rumor was, that he was upset that Walter Damon didn't leave the company to him after all the long years that he put in as his head man. He was also saying that perhaps, Anna had been sleeping with Walter Damon, so that's why he left the company in her ownership, which was far from the truth. But at every meeting that Anna would have with the board, ever so subtly, he would shoot holes in all of Anna's ideas and undermine her choices.

"I think that at Eden's Apple, we need to have a more rounded representation of the different types of music. Most of the artists that Eden's Apple carries are pop, R&B, and rap artists. We have a few alternatives and like two punk groups that are under that label. We need to do some more recruitment in that genre of artists," Anna told her board of directors. "So what do you think?"

"I agree," said Sandra Beedle, the only other woman on the board. "We need more diversity."

Andrew Wilkinson rolled his eyes slightly. "Well, we are one of the top music companies out there and our label Eden's Apple is doing quite good…I think we have all of those other types of artists at out other label Krystel Klare. Many, if not most of the artists over there are alternative and alternative rock. One label's mainly urban, the other's mainly alternative. A nice divide. So it really all evens out," he said smugly.

"No it really all doesn't," Anna said, mimicking him. "Division makes room for conquering."

Andrew Wilkinson chuckled, "We're not talking about a war here, Miss. Senghor."

"But isn't it, in way? We're trying to make it to *the* top, from being *one* of the top," Anna said addressing the room. "And to do that, we have to fight, and fight hard." Anna was not going to let this man take over. "Some of us might be satisfied with mediocrity," Anna said pointedly looking at Wilkinson, "but others of us want perfection. I like to think myself to be in the latter category."

The board was giving her their undivided attention.

"We want to be able to attract all genres to both record labels. Not just one type. Eden's Apple is known as an urban label while Krystel Klare is known as a Rock/Punk/Alternative. That, in my opinion, needs to change. We don't want the two labels to be pigeon holed. We need and aggressive recruitment of artists other than urban at Eden's Apple and recruitment of urban artists at Krystel Klayre. That way, both labels will attract more artists, no matter what their genre," Anna said calmly. "We also need to work on getting more artists, period."

"So, how do you suggest we do this?" Trevor Reynolds, another board member asked.

"Well," Anna began, making eye contact with all eleven of them, "most of our artist have come to us in the traditional way. Word of mouth, demo's being sent, etc. I think that we should do something a little more interesting and a little more hands on."

I was thinking that instead of them coming to us, we go to them. Why don't we do showcases across state? Let's get out of California and look for those talents that are in the Midwest, the South, and the East Coast, whatever. Maybe we can even have on in Canada. Do you know that 40% of our artists are from California? And 22% are from adjoining sates? That means that 62% are close to home and only 38% are not. We need to stretch out some more."

The board members nodded their heads in agreement. There were even some statements like "good idea," and "she's got a point there."

Andrew Wilkinson was the only one lacking in excitement at the proposal. At the moment, his eyes were narrowed into two little slits. "Do you have any idea what all that would cost us?" Andrew said coldly, slicing through everyone's happiness. He looked around at the others, completely ignoring Anna. "That would cost us, millions to do. Traditionally, we have done just fine getting our artists the way that we usually do. I don't see any need to change our methods and adopt something new and have it blow up in our faces."

All eleven faces were staring at him. Anna's stomach was bubbling with rage, but she said nothing.

Andrew continued, content that he had their full attention. "Let's say that we do this idea that Miss. Senghor is proposing. We go to several states, have tryouts and such, but then we don't get as much talent as we need. Let's say, the vast majority of the people trying out…how shall I put it, simply…suck. Let's say that seventy percent of them are terrible. Then what? We've wasted a bunch of money and came up with almost nothing in the end for our efforts. Millions down the drain for a few good artists. Where's the profit in that? I see only a liability."

"But that's the worst case scenario," Anna shot back.

"Don't we have to consider the worst case scenario?" Wilkinson said back with a roll of his eyes as if Anna didn't know what she was talking about.

Anna ignored him and continued. "Our labels are popular labels and many people are waiting to get heard out there. So there will be many people coming to get a chance. And I think that Mr. Wilkinson is being a little melodramatic in his estimation of the vast majority "sucking" as he so articulately put it."

There were a few laughs. Anna waited and then continued. "There are going to be as many talented as there are bad, in my opinion, or even more. And even if they aren't, I feel that it is worth the risk. We don't need to spend millions on showcases. We can easily implement a very cost effective sort of method for it. This is not going to be "American Idol" with camera equipment, props and such. It will be much simpler than that. What do you think Mr. Benson?"

Audrey Benson, The chief financial officer, nodded his head slowly. "It can be done on a budget. If we keep it simple and cut down on a lot of glitz and sparkle, we won't lose a lot of money. Even if we come up short in the end."

"Mr. Benson. Can you work out a plan using a budget?" Anna asked him. "I'll let you decide what would be the appropriate amount of money."

"Sure I can. Just tell me when you want it done, Miss. Senghor."

"Good. Now we'll pass this information down to the departments."

Ψ

"That man gets me so mad. I'm sure he would be happy if I cleaning the toilets here instead of making important decisions. Remember how mad he was when I became president of the Eden's Apple? If I was white, maybe he wouldn't mind as much."

"With Wilkinson, I feel that it's more about an ego thing, than it is about race and politics. If Damon was going to give the company up, Wilkinson was expecting it to go to him. I mean, after all, he was Damon's right hand man. I think he took it as sort of a personal insult that the company was left to you instead. But you can't let him try to control your life. It was you that Walter left the company to. Not him. Don't let him get you down," Franklin told her one afternoon while the two of them sat in her large office, eating takeout for lunch.

"I know, but he undermines everything that I say, like I'm some idiot. I have a MBA and a degree in communications. I graduated in the top ten percent of my class. I'm no idiot."

"Of course you aren't," Franklin said with a shake of his head. "You're brilliant."

"I just feel like getting rid of Wilkinson. Do you think I should? Replace him?" Anna said to Franklin as she took a bite of Lo Mien.

"Well, you might have to put up a bit of a fight getting rid of him. But it's your company. You can do what you want with it. You do have the final say so."

"But what should I *do*?"

"Maybe you should have a little talk with him. See where that leaves you," Franklin answered.

Chapter Thirty-eight

Caleb Jefferson stood out on his balcony overlooking the city of L.A. His dark, nimble, fingers held the expensive Cuban cigar to his full lips as he took a deep drag. He exhaled and watched the wisps of white smoke disappear into the velvet night air.

He felt on top of the world. And in a way, he was.

On the surface, Caleb Jefferson looked like your typical, successful, businessman. Seventeen years ago, Caleb Jefferson had come up with the most perfect idea. And this idea had made him millions.

Caleb Jefferson grew up in St. Louis Missouri. He and his younger brother and younger sister grew up in a small, neat three bedroom house in a middle class, African-American neighborhood. His mother worked as a receptionist for small insurance company and his father was a truck driver, on the road much of the time. His brother, his sister, and him went to the neighborhood public school located a few blocks away from their house.

As a senior in high school, Caleb was an avid sports player as was his brother, who was younger than him by two years. Caleb liked football, while his brother, Darrell, liked baseball.

Once day, Caleb had come home from school, ready to head off to play football, when he found that his favorite tee-shirt was missing. He looked all over his room and turned over everything to no avail. It was gone.

When his brother came in from school, he asked him if he knew where his shirt was. His brother gave him a guilty look and avoided eyes contact. That was when Caleb knew that his brother had done something awful with it.

"Aww, man. What did you do to my shirt?" Caleb asked his younger brother.

"I took it with me to baseball practice yesterday…I got a stain on it."

Caleb groaned and held his head. "Why'd you do that for?"

"You said it was a lucky shirt…my team could use some luck."

"*My* lucky shirt. Not yours!" Caleb answered back. "Where's my shirt?"

Caleb followed Darrell into the basement, where there was a load of laundry that had just been taken out. Darrell sifted through these and held up the shirt. Despite it just being washed, it had a big green and brown stain on the front of it.

"Aww…man! Don't you know how careful I am with this shirt?"

Mikey looked appropriately shamefaced.

"There's gotta be a way to clean this shit off," Caleb said hopping up the basement stairs, two at a time.

And Caleb, desperate as ever, tried everything. He went into the kitchen, combined different things from vinegar to sugar to Pine-sol. He went through hours of this. It was something to do, he thought. Plus. His shirt couldn't get anymore ruined if he tried.

Finally, he came across a combination that when he put it on the shirt, and left it there for about a minute and then washed it off, the stain was completely gone. It was as if it was never there. For a minute, he thought that maybe he was imagining things, maybe the stain was somewhere else, and he was just looking in the wrong area. But the stain was nowhere to be found on the shirt. Growing excited now, Caleb got a dirty pair of white sock from his hamper and put the solution on it. He left it on for a minute and then washed it off. His sock was white as snow as if it just came out of the package. Caleb quickly wrote down the ingredients of the solution before he forgot.

"What are you doing with all this stuff out in the kitchen?"

Caleb turned around. His mother, Brenda, was standing at the kitchen door with her hands on her hips.

"Mom, you won't believe this, but I found something that totally cleans stains away!"

Brenda gave her son a disbelieving look. "Excuse me?"

"Come look."

Brenda walked over to where he was standing. Caleb took out the other dirty white sock to the pair and put the solution on it. "Now I have to leave it on for a minute," he said excitedly.

His mother raised her eyebrows at him.

"Trust me, Mom."

After a minute, Caleb washed the sock. It was crisp white. His mother couldn't believe her eyes.

"This is amazing, Caleb. How did you come up with it?"

Caleb shrugged. "I just started mixing things together, trying to save the shirt that Darrell ruined and I came up with this."

"What's inside of it?"

"That's my secret," Caleb said excitedly.

"This thing could sell, baby," Brenda said with a smile

Caleb was never one to trust anyone. He knew that there were people out there just waiting to prey on naïve people and steal their ideas. So he decided that he would market his product to the public by himself—with the help of his brother as well. But he knew he needed money to do something independently. So he and his brother did what the many of kids from the "bad" side of town were doing—they started selling drugs. But they kept it secret. After about two months of penny-ante drug dealing, Caleb decided that if they wanted some real money to launch this thing, he needed to start selling the bigger stuff. And they did just that.The transition to the larger drug deals went pretty smoothly. After about a year of him and his brother selling, they made enough to start their own company selling his special product. Within five years, the company was a great success.But this didn't stop Caleband his brother Darrell from continuing their drug dealing. Within three years, Caleb and Darrell were also successful on the streets, quickly rising to the top as the biggest drug dealers in town having the majority of the territory. It was like living a double life. One above ground, and one underground. Both were kept very seperate—one didn't interfere with the other. Caleb was very careful to keep it that way. Caleb knew that if anything concerning his underground life became exposed to his legitimate world—which included his cleaning business and his public life—he would be finished.

There was a sudden knock at the door. Caleb turned around and looked at his two body guards. They looked back at him and shrugged.

"See who it is," Caleb ordered.

The taller of the two looked through the peephole and turned back to Caleb. "It's that woman…I forget her name. The crack head the brown skinned one—"

Caleb knew exactly who he was talking about. "Let her in," he ordered.

The body guard opened the door and let her in. The brown skinned woman, once so pretty, now had a drawn face, blotchy skin and was generally unhealthy looking. Her skinny arms and legs poked out from her clothing.

"Kati," Caleb said and exhaled a long line of smoke, "I've been waiting for you."

Ψ

"But the men and the ladies aren't the only hot tiiings in Tahiti, so is the food! And today, ladies and gentlemen, we are cooking in Tahiti in Bora Bora! Our destination for the week," Comete said with a big smile. He turned to the tall, Tahitian man standing beside him. "This is my guest, Nunui. He's going to teach us how to make a Tahitian feast. So, what are we going to start with, Nunui?"

"Well, the first dish that we're going to make is Poisson cru. Now this is a popular dish that is made from fish."

"Raw fish, am I correct?" Comete said frowning slightly.

Nunui smiled. "Yes. But believe me. It's nothing like sushi or sashimi."

"Thank God!" Comete exclaimed. The audience laughed.

Nunui laughed heartily. "First we're going marinate this fish with some lemon juice in this sauce pan."

Nanui added the fish and the lemon juice to the saucepan and stirred it. "Now, we let it marinate."

When the marinating was complete, Nanui took up some coconut milk. "Now, we soak it in coconut milk."

When the dish was complete, Nanui told Comete to try it.

"Okay, I'll try it. But I want someone from the audience to try it first!" Comete exclaimed. Again, the audience laughed. Comete was quite the character. Never squeamish about putting his welfare before his audience's when it came to tasting food.

Comete chose a woman from the front row to come up on stage. "Okay darling. Take a taste!"

The woman happily took a spoonful. Her eyes bugged out in pleasure as she chewed. "It's absolutely delicious!" She exclaimed once she finally swallowed.

"Let me taste a little of that, girlfriend," Comete said opening his mouth.

The woman laughed and put a forkful in his mouth.

Comete took a bite and smiled as he chewed. "This tastes like ambrosia for the gods!" Comete exclaimed.

The audience applauded. Oh, how they loved their Traveling Chef. Comete certainly had a large, faithful following.

The large Tahitian man laughed and got some for himself. He tasted it and smiled. "Good as always," he said cheerfully.

"Okay," Comete said turning to the camera. "When we come back from break, Nunui is going to teach us how to make amura! Stay tuned, we will be back in a flash!"

Ψ

As it turned out, the showcase ended up being a success. Not only did the artists that the two labels already had and the labels themselves gain more publicity, Entourage Productions signed on a new bunch of promising, talented, artists to both labels. In the end, both of the labels had almost equal representations of artists from both urban and alternative genres.

Anna was extremely pleased. Their records sales had gone up more than fifty percent and the profit was astounding. Wilkinson was forced to eat his own words and he admitted it openly.

"I must say, Anna. You were right and I was wrong," he told her one day during a private meeting between the two of them.

"So, does this mean that you'll cut me some slack?" Anna said with a quirky smile.

Wilkinson laughed. "I've really been a pain in the ass, haven't I. To be honest, I was a bit upset that the company was not left to me."

"I know. Word travels fast around here. I also heard that you were saying that I had been sleeping with Walter Damon."

Wilkinson nervously cleared his throat. "Well, um. Perhaps people exaggerated it a tad."

Anna shook her head. "It's not true."

"I didn't think so. I just wanted to feel better about you getting chosen over me," Wilkinson said honestly. "I've been a real drag, haven't I?"

"To the point that I was considering replacing you."

Wilkinson frowned and shrugged. "I couldn't blame you. Are you still considering it?"

"No. I just don't want any bad vibes between it. It's not productive."

Wilkinson nodded and extended his hand. "Here's to future success?"

Anna grasped his hand and shook it. "Most definitely."

Ψ

"Auntie. I'm thinking of giving up school. I'm going to play for the California Suns."

No, no. That wasn't the right way to tell her.

"Mom. I'll be making a bunch of money, right away. It would take me years and years to make anything close to that amount if I get my degree."

Brian was rehearsing what he would say to Anna. He had already signed the contract this past summer and was due to play soon. It had been months since then, but he hadn't told Anna anything.

That weekend, in September, Brian came home for the weekend. He decided to drive. That would give him a lot of time to think

"My long lost nephew is home for the weekend," Anna said happily. "How's school going?" she asked him, when she opened the door.

Brian tried to smile. "It's doing all right."

"Well, I got the cook to make your favorite meal...Meena! Maria! Brian's here."

Brian smiled and hugged his cousin and his sister when they came bustling into the room. They were both in their bathing suits.

"Come on Brian. We were just about to go swimming, come with us," Meena said excitedly.

Brian shook his head. "I think I'll stay inside. It's too hot."

"Duh, that's why we're swimming..." Maria said rolling her eyes.

Brian shrugged. "I'll stay here."

"Suit yourself," Meena said and the two of them walked off towards the sliding backdoor and out to the pool.

Anna gave Brian a strange look. "You love swimming. That's always the first thing you do when you come home—you take a dip in the pool."

"Yeah well, I thought that we could talk," Brian said taking a seat on the leather sofa.

"Well, what about we go on the deck so we can get some fresh air?" Anna said. "I'll get Marcia to bring some refreshments."

They went out to the patio and sat down. Marcia, their newly hired housekeeper, brought out a pitcher of pink lemonade.

"Now. You want to tell me what's on your mind?" Anna asked, pouring herself and Brian and glass.

"Well, remember I told you that the baseball recruiter for the California Sun's was coming around?"

"Yes, I remember you mentioning that," Anna said carefully.

"Well…here's the thing. I went and I tried out."

Anna gave him a sharp look. "What for?"

"Well…I wanted to see if I had what it takes to make it."

"And?" Anna asked, waiting for the other shoe to drop.

"And…I did. They offered me a place on the team. They said that I was really good."

Anna sighed. "Brian, I know you're good. Don't you think I do? But you know important school is. It's always good to have a degree to fall back on. You can always accept their offer once you graduate."

"It doesn't work that way, Auntie. I would have to try out again. And who's to say that they would accept me again?"

Anna took a sip of her lemonade and looked out at the pool were Meena and Maria were busy ducking each other into the water. Anna noticed that Meena's friend, Xander, who lived only two blocks away, had ambled his way into the backyard and was currently peeling off his tee-shirt to hop into the pool. Both Meena and Maria were splashing him. He caught sight of Anna and waved. Anna waved back and then turned to Brian once again.

"Look. You know how important an education is. Believe me. You'll thank me in the long run."

"I've already signed the contract."

Anna coughed up the juice that she swallowed, making a big mess on the front of her cream, Donna Karen halter top. "What?" she chocked out.

"I signed the contract. I've joined the team, Auntie."

Anna heard a shrill scream and then a loud splash. She looked out at the pool. There were now five people in it. Another girl and boy had joined the festivities. Anna squinted, trying to see who they were. Christina and Edward. Two more of Meena and Maria's friends. They said, "hi," and waved from the pool.

"What, is this turning into a pool party?" Anna screeched.

The bodies in the pool froze and stared at her uncomprehendingly. Anna turned back to Brian and the splashing commenced again. "How could you do that? Go behind my back and do such a thing! You didn't even get a lawyer to look over the contract or anything. They could have screwed you over!"

"I didn't need a lawyer. They said so."

Anna let out a sound of frustration. The teenagers in the pool glanced over in their direction. "That's what they all say!" Anna exclaimed.

Brian looked down into the cup of pink liquid. Anna certainly wasn't taking this well.

Anna let out a loud breath and slid down in her chair. "You're about to turn nineteen in three months. You're grown. What can I do?"

Brian shrugged his shoulders.

"So, now you have to leave school."

Brian shifted uncomfortably in his seat. He was silent for a moment and then said, "Not necessarily. But most likely."

"I wish you had said something to me before doing this. You've given me such a shock."

"I'm sorry," Brian said beseechingly. His big brown eyes looked pleadingly at her.

Anna shook her head and held it as if she were about to pass out. "Do you have a copy of the contract?"

Brian nodded his head. "Yeah. I brought it with me."

"Bring it to me. I'll look it over and see if it looks all right."

Ψ

Meena stood on the scale for the second time that day. 125 pounds. The same weight as yesterday. She had lost exactly five since starting her modeling career about a year ago. Her goal weight was 120. At least she hadn't gained anything from last night's fiasco.

Self-control, for her, was not the easiest thing to do. Just yesterday, after eating a grapefruit for breakfast and a salad for lunch, she had had three slices of thick-crust, pepperoni pizza and a tall glass of coke to finish the day. Of course, she hadn't planned on having the pizza and the soda, but...she saw Maria and Brian eating it (they had ordered take out) and she had to have a slice...and then another...and then another. It was sooo good!

But today, she promised herself, she would fast for two days to make up for all those calories that she ate the day before. No food for her! She would just drink water and diet soda and diet juice and work out all day.

She had to get down to 120 by any means possible

Chapter Thirty-nine

"I hope you take me somewhere real good this year, Caleb. You took me to Jamaica two years in a row. I'm tired of Jamaica. I want to go to Fiji or something," Tiara said as she painted her long fingernails a shocking shade of pink.

"All right. we'll go to Fiji this year," Caleb said trying to placate his demanding wife.

"Good. You know I'm gonna need a whole new wardrobe for the trip."

"Yeah, yeah, of course. Don't you always?"

Tiara gave Caleb a sharp look. Her dark eyes boring into his. "Yeah, and so what? You do want me looking good, don't you? You don't want some trashy looking woman on your arms, do you?"

"Honey, you could put on a garbage bag and carry it off it you wanted to," Caleb said honestly. It was true. Tiara was a gorgeous, milk chocolate skinned woman with a beautiful, sultry face and a body to die for. Tiara was a former model and she looked it.

Tiara smiled, happy at the compliment, but then quickly frowned when she saw her husband getting up. "Where you going?"

"I got some business to conduct. I'll be back in an hour—two hours tops."

Tiara twisted up her lips at him. "Which is it. One hour or two hours?"

"Two hours."

"Fine," Tiara said sucking her teeth.

Caleb left out the door.

Ψ

Kati was so nervous seeing him standing there. Caleb exuded a kind of presence that screamed "not to be tampered with." Kati tried to be careful not to, but sometime the drugs called to her...

"Did you make the shipment?"

Kati nodded her head, earnestly. "I did it. The packs were transported and taken care of."

Caleb stared at her for a while and watched as she moved from foot to foot and twitched and sniffled. He thought that she looked like a dog.

Throughout his years as a drug dealer, Caleb had met his share of drug fiends and desperados. Kati just happened to be one of them. After some time of being her supplier, he began to realize that she had some smarts, despite her drug addiction. So he began to use her to make some transports. Also, the fact that she was a woman was a big plus—she was less likely to be a suspect for carrying drugs.

"I guess you want your payment," Caleb said with a cold smile.

Kati nodded, her head bouncing up and down. "Please. Yes."

Caleb reached into his pocket and pulled out the small bag of white powder. He grinned and dangled it in front of her. He got a sense of satisfaction when he saw her eyes light up and the thin line of sweat that instantly formed on the tip of her nose.

"You want this?"

Kati nodded, eagerly. "I do."

Caleb threw it at her feet. She instantly dropped to her knees to retrieve it. She opened the bag and took out a little on her finger. She held it up to her nose and snorted it up. She closed her eyes in satisfaction and opened them slowly.

"T-thanks," she said as she closed the bag and put it in the back pocket of her jeans.

Caleb merely looked at her and said, "Don't use it all up at once. I don't want you scratching at my door later."

Ψ

Hector sighed and looked at the end results. He turned to his assistant Tanya and asked, "What do you think?"

"Absolutely fantastic! Should we bring Mr. and Mrs. Timmons in? We can't keep them waiting."

"Of course, my child. Bring them in!" Hector exclaimed.

When Mr. And Mrs. Timmons walked through the door, Hector saw such a look of enrapture and pleasure on their faces, so he knew that it was a job well done. He congratulated himself silently.

It was the Timmons' thirtieth wedding anniversary. They wanted to have a celebration that would be remembers, so naturally, they came to Hector for help.

"Absolutely perfect!," Mrs. Timmons exclaimed. "This is exactly what I wanted."

"I'm so glad that you like it," Hector said happily. "I have everything planned. The band will be here at seven on the dot and we booked the best catering service there is, Prime Time." Hector rested a hand on Mr. Timmons back. "Come on, you two. Let's take a seat and let me show you the agenda."

Ψ

Kati looked at package of drugs that she was smuggling into Toronto, Canada. It was worth about one grand. She wondered if anyone would notice if she took a little bit of the cocaine off, like maybe two ounces. She decided that wouldn't be the best decision. Then she came up with an idea. After the drugs were delivered and she had the money, she would tell Caleb that she was robbed and all the money from the drug sale was taken. Kati needed the money more than anything. She couldn't remember the last time that she had a decent meal, and most of all, she needed it to feed her cocaine and meth habit.

After the delivery was made and Kati got the money, she went back across the border and made the long trip back home to LA. She went to the supermarket and bought a cartful of food. Enough to last her for months—spending close to five hundred in groceries. She went to another dealer and got about two-hundred dollars worth of cocaine. After all that, went to one of her junkie friends, Jaime, that lived in the same dilapidated building as her. He was a tall, Columbian man with incredible strength.

"I need you to beat on me a little," Kati told him.

"What? What are you talking about?" he asked, confused.

"Come on. You heard me. I need you to hit me, beat me up. I need to have bruises on my body, especially my face," Kati told him.

He gave her a weird look and shook his head. "Nah, man. I ain't getting in no trouble for you, woman."

"You won't get into any trouble. And…I'll pay you. One hundred. How does that sound?"

Jaime thought it over for a minute and gave her a quick nod. "As long as there's no cops or nothing fishy involved, I'll do it."

"Don't worry there isn't."

The next day, when Kati went to meet Caleb, he noticed the bruises right away. "What the hell happened to you?"

Kati wept. Her shoulders trembled.

"What? What happened?" he asked, impatiently.

"I-I-I delivered the drugs, and…"

"And what?"

"I got robbed. Somebody beat me up and robbed me. I-I ain't got the money," Kati mumbled miserably.

Caleb stared at her. "You mean they took my money? Who the hell took it?"

"I don't know…it was a bunch of guys…I didn't see their faces. They were wearing hoodies and ski masks.

Caleb cursed and threw up his hands. "You better be telling me the truth. You better not be lying to me."

Kati shook her head. "No, no. I'm not lying. I swear to you."

"Fuck. Ah well, it's only one thousand. But don't let it happen again. And just for losing the shit, I ain't giving you a damned thing in payment."

Ψ

Tiara came in through the door and gave Caleb a kiss on the cheek.

"Hello honey."

"Hey baby," Caleb said glancing up from the television. He noticed the grocery bags in his wife's hands. "What you got there?"

"I bought some steak and potatoes—all your favorites. I want to cook for you this weekend."

"Wow! Where's my wife and what have you done with her?"

Tiara walked up to Caleb and wrapped her arms around his neck. "I'm right here baby and I ain't going anywhere."

They leaned in and kissed. Tiara pulled back. "But all that's for later. I'm gonna cook now."

Although Tiara rarely did, Caleb knew that Tiara could cook. Most of the time, their chef cooked for them.

"Honey, I saw the funniest thing today while I was at the supermarket shopping today," Tiara said, tying on an apron.

"What's that?"

"Well, there was this little woman that looked like a straight crack head. She was buying up the store!" Tiara laughed, "like there was going to be a flood or something! Her cart was overflowing with food. She had to have like five hundred dollars worth of groceries in that cart…honey what's the matter?"

Caleb's face had taken on a shocked appearance. That had to be Kati. Buying 500 dollars worth of groceries? With what? His money, no doubt.

"What is it?" Tiara asked, getting worried.

"No, nothing. My mind was somewhere else. I had just remembered something from work. So, this girl, you say she looked like a crack head? Real skinny? Black woman?"

"Yeah, that's right. It almost sounds like you know her!" Tiara said with a giggle.

Ψ

When Caleb looked back on things, he discovered that there were many other instances, in the past, where he thought that Kati could have robbed him. For such a savvy business man he was ashamed and angry that he could have not seen the signs. He wanted revenge and he wanted it bad. At first, he thought of just getting rid of Kati, killing her and dumping her body in the river until one night when he was over at her run down apartment.

He and some of his men had come over to confront her about the stolen money. When she let them in, he saw that she was as high as a kite.

"She won't even try to find me. My own sister," Kati was muttering as she looked at the news paper.

"What the hell are you talking about?" Caleb had snapped. He was ready to blow the bitch's head off.

"My sister has all that money…," Kati started sobbing. "I thought she loved me…she has my kids and everything…she's left me in the dirt…," Kati moaned.

Caleb's ears perked up. "What? Your sister has money?"

Kati continued to stare down at the newspaper in her hands. Caleb walked over and snatched it away from her.

There on the front page was a picture of a pretty black woman in a pants suit. She was standing beside an old white guy in an expensive suit. He read the headline. "Anna Senghor, owner of Entourage Productions, holds a country wide talent search."

Caleb looked up at Kati and then looked at the smiling, brown-faced, woman in the paper, then back up at Kati again. They both had the same eyes. Also, there features were similar, although Anna Senghor was slightly darker in complexion and her face was healthy looking, as opposed to Kati's.

"This your sister?" Caleb asked.

Kati continued staring into space.

"This is your sister, huh?"

Kati stared on, totally spaced out.

Caleb didn't need an answer. In his head, he was already starting to formulate a plan.

Ψ

When Anna came home that day, she noticed a man standing out in front of her gate, just as she went through them. She stared at him suspiciously. His face was impassive and emotionless.

"Can I help you?" Anna asked, gripping the pepper spray on her key chain.

It was only then that the man smiled, if it could be called that. It was a cold, humorless smile that chilled Anna to the bones.

He stepped forward, sighed, and looked around at the property, his hands wrapped around the black rails.

"Nice house you've got here, Anna. Really beautiful."

"Look. Who are you?" Anna asked, fazed that he knew her name.

"Who am I? I'm a person with whom you have a lot to discuss," he said breezily.

Anna studied the man standing before her. He had a nice looking face with sharply defined jawbones and big, dark eyes. His skin was a smooth, milk chocolate color. His face was completely hairless except for a thin, well trimmed mustache just above his full, sensual, lips.

His hair was closely cut. He wore a well cut Brooks Brothers suit and expensive looking leather shoes that were polished to a shine.

Anna looked back up at his face and once again asked, "What do you want?"

"I think that maybe we should go inside and talk. It's a hot day. I wouldn't mind having something to drink."

Anna was nonplussed at his audacity. "Sorry, but I don't think so," Anna said, preparing to turn around and leave him standing there.

"I believe that it would be in your best interest," he said calmly.

"Oh really. Here's what I think. I think It would be in *your* best interest to leave because I'm about to call the police."

The man smiled and tut-tutted her. He slowly shook his head. "Now. You do that and you're definitely asking for trouble. For you and especially for your little sister Kati."

Anna felt her stab of panic course through her. "What?" she said in a strangled voice. "Where is she? We haven't seen her for years…"

"I think you heard me. Now. Why don't we go inside and discuss this like two reasonable adults."

Anna opened the gate and let him through.

"We can go out back on the patio. I don't want you in the house," Anna said disdainfully.

The man merely smiled and said, "Whatever suits you best."

Anna paused in her tracks and faced him. "What would suit me best is for you to get the hell out of here. But I see that's not to be."

The man nodded slightly. They walked out to the patio and sat down.

"Do you mind if I have something to drink?" the man asked.

"Who are you?"

"I really can't talk much more with this parched throat. Can you get me something to drink?" he asked, sweetly. But his eyes were mocking. He leaned back in the chair and crossed his legs.

Anna felt sick to her stomach. This couldn't be happening to her. Not when everything was going to well. Kati. What had she done now?

Anna stood up and went towards the house. She saw Marcia in the backroom tidying up.

Anna walked past her and went into pantry. She pulled out a bottle of Evian water.

"Do you need anything Miss. Senghor?" Marcia asked.

"No, thank you. I found what I needed."

Anna was about to walk back outside before she thought of something. She turned back to Marcia and said.

"Marcia. Me and a man are out on the patio. I want you to keep an eye on us from the kitchen. If you see anything suspicious, I will signal you and I want you to call the police."

Marcia stared at her with worry in her dark eyes. "Is everything okay?"

"I don't know just yet. But please. Do as I said."

"Yes Ma'am."

Anna walked back outside with the bottle of water. She handed it to the man and sat down.

The man took his time opening it and then he took a large sip.

"Hmmm. The water's a little tepid. I like my water ice cold."

"Look. I don't give a damn how you like your water. You'd better tell me who you are."

The man smiled again, displaying two rows of bright white teeth that had received hundreds of dollars in dental work.

"Okay. My name is Caleb Jefferson."

"Wait. Your name sounds familiar…"

"I own *Never Was There*, you know, the cleaning company. We make cleaning products."

Anna nodded grimly. "I've heard of it."

"Who hasn't?" the man said cockily.

"Let's get to the point, Mr. Jefferson. What is it with my sister?"

"I'm going to be straight with you. Your sister robbed me blind and then she lied about it. On several occasions. It was only just of lately that I got a gist of it."

Anna continued to stare at him with every effort focused on trying to keep her expression unreadable.

Caleb continued. "Now. The moment that I realized all this…my instant reaction was to go over and shoot her head off. After all, one less coke head in the world is mostly a benefit. But then I found out that you were her sister, Miss Owner of Entourage Productions. And I thought, she was more useful to me alive than dead."

Anna took in a sharp breath. Her stomach was jumping up and down inside of her. Her heart beat wildly in her chest.

"Anna!"

Anna knew who the voice belonged to even before she turned around. When she turned around she saw Hector and Comete standing there smiling.

"Where were you. We tried to call you, but we got no answer! Even your house keeper Marcia was nowhere to be found so we saw ourselves eeen…" Comete's voice trailed off. He looked back and forth between Anna and Caleb.

"Well, Well! What have we here…are we intruding?" Hector asked, smartly.

Anna looked at Caleb. He was taking small sips at his bottle of water, all the while keeping his dark eyes trained on her.

"Um. Well…,"Anna began nervously.

"Well Anna, I'd better be going. I have so much to do," Caleb said rising to his feet. "But we'll continue this conversation tomorrow?" he said in a kind voice that belied their earlier discussion. He stared at her with intensity.

"Yes," Anna managed to say. "Of course."

"No need to get up. I can see myself out," Caleb turned to Hector and Comete. He smiled at them and the pointed at Comete.

"Wait…are you Comete The Traveling Chef?

Comete smiled, "That ees me!"

"Wow. I love your show. My little sister watches you religiously. She was there in the audience in Tahiti."

"Wow. that ezzz something. I am always glad to hear from de fans. Did she enjoy herself?"

"She loved it! She loves you!" Caleb said laughing with his arms outstretched towards him. "Anyways. Nice meeting you. I really have to get out of here."

Caleb disappeared around to the front of the house. After a minute or so, Anna heard the distant sound of a car engine starting and tires driving down the road.

It was then that Anna breathed easier.

"Well, who was that hunky guy! Anna, you catch them like fly tape," Hector said jokingly.

They saw the horrified expression on Anna's face, and the despair in her dark eyes. Their smiles were instantly erased and replaced by pensive expressions. They came up to her and stood on either side of her.

"My God Anna, you look like you have just spokeen with *o diabo*, what de hell ezzz the matter?" Comete demanded.

Anna cried even harder. "I think I just have," she sobbed.

Ψ

"So, Miss. Senghor, people are quite perplexed at your sudden step down from your position at Entourage Productions," commented the pretty, perky, Hispanic news reporter.

"Now. I want to make it clear that I have only passed on ownership of the company. I haven't resigned from it all together. I am assuming my former role of president at *Eden's Apple*. Also, I will stay on as a board member I feel that the position of ownership is too much for me to handle at the moment. I don't think that at the time of my promotion that I had enough experience to run such a large industry. It's a lot of work for a single person to take on."

A tall, lanky Asian man stood up next. "People are wondering why if you didn't feel that you had the experience to assume ownership, you didn't just pass the company on to the next person in charge, Andrew Wilkinson. Or maybe even take the company public—"

"It's my company and I will do as I wish," Anna responded, stubbornly. "Caleb Jefferson will be the majority shareholder in this company—"

"So it *is* going public," the Asian man shot back.

"No. Not exactly. The rest of the stock will be owned by a small group of select people."

"Who are these people?" asked a small, black woman.

"Look, those are all the questions that I will be answering. You can direct all other questions to Mr. Jefferson."

"If he was here, we would!" exclaimed an effeminate looking man in a pink tie.

After that, Anna made a quick exit from the press conference. The crowd of reporters was starting to get rowdy. She had no desire to be caught in the middle of it all. She was so tired and depressed that she just wanted to go home and sleep.

She felt as if her life were spiraling down into a black hole.

Before Anna got into her car, she heard a man's voice calling her name. It was Andrew Wilkinson. Anna stopped and waited for him to catch up with her.

"Wait Anna, I wanted to speak to you—"

"You don't have to worry, Andrew. You're position is still there as it is at the company," Anna assured him wearily.

Andrew Wilkinson shook his head with one jerky motion. "No. That's not what I wanted to talk about."

Anna frowned, glanced around, looked back at him, and waited.

"What was all that bullshit in there, Anna, about you not having enough experience and all that to run a company?"

"Look. It's true. You were probably right when at first you thought that I shouldn't be running the company.

Wilkinson shook his head again. "I was wrong. You know what you're doing Anna, you're damn good at it *and* you know it. Let's stop the pretense. Now what's really going on?"

"Caleb Jefferson is a well-seasoned business owner. He'll be wonderful for the position," Anna said quickly.

"Yeah, but what does he know about the music industry? What expertise does he have in that? Nothing! He might run the company into the ground!"

"He won't because you'll be there to help him," Anna said calmly. "And so will I," she added reluctantly.

Andrew gave her a piercing look. "There's something more to all this, isn't there. Caleb Jefferson just drops in from the clouds!"

Anna started to turn back to her car. "I have to go, Andrew—"

Andrew placed a hand on her arm. "Anna, wait. If you thought the responsibly was too much, which is a bunch of crock, you could have come to me…we could have discussed some options. Options that were far less drastic than this road that you're talking."

"It's too late now Andrew. The forms are already signed," Anna said dryly.

"We might be able to contest it! Maybe get out of it. Let our lawyers look for some loopholes—"

"I don't think so," Anna snapped.

"You're not stupid Anna. A move like this is uncharacteristic of you—"

"Bye Andrew, I gotta go." Anna opened her car door and hopped in. She slammed the door after her and started the engine.

Andrew knocked on the car window. "There's something more going on! I know it! I'm going to find out!" he yelled as she pulled away.

"Yeah, sure you will," Anna muttered to herself as she drove off.

Chapter Forty

Hector had developed a deep distaste for hospitals. With their cold hallways, eerie corners and hidden rooms. The smell of death seemed to lurk all over. The sharp smells of disinfectant and medicine turned Hector's stomach. The sound of beeping machines and humming equipment gave him the chills.

But most of all, hospital reminded him of Ramón and the last weeks he spent on this earth.

Hector swallowed hard and tried to remain brave, but already he could feel the fear growing inside of him. He studied the elevator's numbers as they blinked from floor to floor. One…Two…"

"Sir, are you okay?" asked a young kindly nurse he was sharing the elevator with.

Hector forced a smile. "I'm fine. Just a little queasy."

The nurse smiled, nodded, and turned back around.

Finally, the elevator reached the floor that his father was on.

He had begged Anna to come with him, but Anna had refused, telling him that he needed to speak with his father alone. He didn't ask Comete to come. He was sure that Comete would have agreed to come—only out of love for Hector. But bringing him to his father would have been asking for trouble.

His father was staunchly opposed homosexuality. Ironic, Hector thought. Considering that the ancient Greeks were once well known for their homosexual liaisons.

Hector stood a while in front of the door to his father's room. He tried to muster all his strength and courage before going in.

Demetrius Minatos looked up when he saw his son walk in through the door. His face, now thinner because of his illness, made his black eyes look even larger and more intimidating.

Demetrius was suffering from cancer. At first it was just prostate cancer. But then he had surgery, after which, most unfortunately, it spread to his liver and his colon. At the moment, he was in the hospital for treatment.

Demetrius was a dying man. The doctor estimated that if things kept up the way they were going, he would be dead within one year. But his illness hadn't made him any less formidable. He still managed to put a spark of fear into Hector. Quite honestly, the man was intimidating.

"Son, you are here," he pointed to the seat beside his bed. "Please take a seat. We have much to discuss."

Hector hesitantly sat down. He looked at his father nervously and waited for him to talk.

"Hector, I really don't think that I will live to see the end of this year," he said suddenly as he stared straight ahead. He cleared his throat and turned around to face Hector.

"You don't know that. Doctors have been wrong before. The treatment might turn things around," Hector said uneasily.

Demetrius shook his head and the coughed loudly, his broad shoulders shaking as he did so.

"Are you okay?" Hector asked, with alarm.

"I am fine," Demetrius said and took in a deep breath. "Anyway, as I was saying, I know in my heart, that I will not see the end of this year. Trust me."

"How can you be so sure!" Hector cried dispassionately.

"I had a dream," Demetrius said quietly. "It was very clear in its meaning."

"But Dad—"

"But the dream is not what I want to talk about," Hector's father quickly cut in. "I want to talk about you and the direction that your life is going."

"What do you mean?" Hector asked, warily.

"Hector, you are almost forty. Yet you have no marriage, no children…is that the way you want to live?"

Hector shook his head. "Dad. Not this conversation again. We've had it time and time again and it always leads to nothing. This is the way I am, Dad. I can't change."

"No. you don't *want* to change. You are holed up with a man that you've been living with for years and that is it. There is more to life than that, Hector. So much more…"

Hector slowly rose from his chair. "Look. I don't believe that you brought me here to discuss this. It's a mundane subject that has been totally exhausted. I don't want to discuss this any further."

Players of the Game

Demetrius raised an arm towards his son. "You are my first born. And despite what you may believe…I want you to be happy. You cannot be happy living like this—"

"How dare you judge me. I *am* happy, Dad. The happiest that I've been in my life. And yes. I do love Comete. And if you would just give him a chance, you would love him too. But you'll never do that, will you. You're going to remain stubborn to your death," Hector said sadly. "What a sad way to go, Father. Wouldn't it be nice to die without all that load on your shoulders?"

"Yes Hector, it would. That is why I have a proposal for you. No, wait. I would more so call it an ultimatum," Demetrius said easily.

Hector sank back down in his seat, his eyes fixed on his father.

"What are you talking about?" Hector asked mechanically.

"I want you to find a woman. A wonderful woman, like how I found your mother, get married and have children," Demetrius said quickly.

Hector looked at his father, dumbfounded. "You're kidding me, right?"

"No. I am not," Demetrius said looking him straight in the eyes.

"Dad. I'm sorry, but that's not going to happen. That's not me. A woman? I'm with Comete. The thought of me being with a woman…is inconceivable. And a child? I can't take care of a child…"

"Of course you can. You would make a wonderful father. You just don't know it," Demetrius said. "And as for a woman…I am sure that if you find the right one—"

"Absolutely not, Dad. I wouldn't even consider it."

"Really?" Demetrius said casually. "What if I were to tell you that you receiving your part of the fortune, as first born son, is contingent on you doing precisely that?"

Hector felt his blood turn cold in his veins. "What?" he croaked.

"I am telling you, Hector, that you will not receive a dime from me unless you are in a relationship with a woman. And not just any relationship. A marriage. I will not sponsor your live of homosexual decadence with my money," Demetrius said in clipped sentences.

"You aren't serious, are you?" Hector asked.

Demetrius nodded. "I am."

"You are a bigoted, self-righteous, man and I have nothing more to say to you."

Hector stood up and walked right out of the room without another word.

Ψ

"Okay, that's all for today ladies! You all be in the hotel lobby tomorrow morning at seven o'clock sharp! No one be late, or you'll get left behind!" said Antoinette Bontecoe, the woman who designed their clothing for today's fashion shoot.

Meena sighed and let down her dark hair, which had just recently been cut into a shoulder length style. She was so glad that the photo shoot was over for today. She just wanted to go back to her room, have a shower, climb into bed, and watch movies for the rest of the night.

"I know what you're thinking…and it's not going to happen!" exclaimed a soft voice behind Meena.

Meena turned around. It was her friend Hannah.

"No sleeping in for you. We are going to find Cathy and hit the city tonight!" Hannah exclaimed with flashing hazel eyes. She grasped Meena's hand and led her into the group of chattering young women.

"We'd better hurry outside before our ride leaves us," Meena said desperately.

"Oh please. We can always get a cab. I've never been to Miami before and neither have you. This is an opportune time!" Hannah said as she flipped her long, bone straight blond hair over her tanned shoulders. "Oh look, there she is," Hannah said excitedly. "Cathy!"

Cathy, a gorgeous, black Latina from Cuba came walking over when she caught sight of them. "Hey you all! Ohhh! I'm ready to hit the clubs, girlfriends!" she said swaying her hips back and forth.

"That's what I'm talking about!" Hannah said excitedly.

"How am I going to get into any clubs? Hello, I'm only sixteen."

"A minor inconvenience," Cathy said slyly. "I got you a fake ID You forget that Miami is my territory, *mis lindas*. We are going to have a blast tonight!"

Ψ

When Meena stepped into the club, it was unlike anything that she had ever seen before. The music was loud and pounding, women in skimpy clothing were dancing with men all over the place. Some of the dancing was so suggestive that Meena got a little embarrassed just staring at it.

"Whooo! This is the shit!" Hannah exclaimed as she wiggled her butt to the beat. She was wearing a short skirt, a scanty halter top and heeled sandals. She wore gold, chandelier earring that just swept the tops of her shoulders.

Cathy wasn't dressed any less revealing. She wore short shorts, a top that barely covered her breasts and a pair of slinky, stiletto sandals. Her dark, copper- brown skin glowed under the undulating lights. Her long halo of kinky hair was out lose and flowed down past her shoulders.

Meena, opting for a little less exposure, was wearing some skin tight, flare jeans, a black, low cut top, and some stiletto pumps. She wore a silver necklace and matching dangling earrings.

Almost right away they were invited to have drinks by various men in the club. Instead, the three of them took a seat in the corner to relax for a while.

They finally accepted some drinks from three good looking, Latino men that stood by the bar.

"Should we let them come over?" Meena asked, anxiously as she fingered the flute of champagne.

"Yes. We accepted the drinks, didn't we?" Cathy answered and she motioned for them to come over.

"Wow, you three are some really gorgeous girls," one of them said. He had café, au late skin and black, shiny hair styled with gel.

"Thank you," Hannah said batting her eyes.

One of them fixed his eyes on Meena and smiled. "*Hola, mamacita. De donde eres?*"

Meena gave him a blank look in return.

The young handsome man's face took on a look of confusion. "You don't speak Spanish?"

Meena shook her head, embarrassed.

"Oh. You look Hispanic."

"Well…I am."

The young man smiled at her. "What are you, Puerto Rican? A lot of them don't teach their American born offspring the native tongue. No offence."

"None taken. I'm not Puerto Rican. I was born in Belize. But I was adopted. My mom's not Hispanic."

"Oh, okay. I'm sorry. I hope you aren't offended. I think you're gorgeous. By the way, my name's Manuel, and yours?"

"Meena," she answered back.

"And what about you, sexy," one of the men said addressing Cathy.

"*Mi llamo es Cathy. Soy Cubana, mi amigo,*" she said smoothly in Spanish. "Yeah, I'm that cocoa brown Latina!" Cathy said with a proud smile.

The man raised his eyebrows. "*De Claro! Ah, una morena. Que bonita! Muchas morenos en algunos partes de Venezuala, mi pais. Que parte de Cuba es usted?*"

"La Habana," Cathy answered. "*Como te llamas?*"

"Matteo."

"Can we *please* speak English here?" Hannah moaned.

"Definitely, pretty," the last one of the handsome young men said. "My name's Pablo. Where are you from?"

"California," Hannah said with a smile. "Where are you from?"

"Cuba," he answered.

After about fifteen minutes of talking, they got up to dance. Then they went to sit back down.

"You are a fantastic dancer!" exclaimed Manuel to Meena.

"Thank you," Meena said with a smile.

"Hey. We got some…stuff if you want it," Matteo said suddenly.

"What stuff?" Meena asked.

"Do you have coke?" Hannah asked, quickly.

Mateo's eyes lit up. "That's what I'm talking about. You guys want some?"

"Yeah, give me a hit," Hannah said smoothly.

Meena looked at her alarmed. "Are you crazy? Coke?"

Cathy gave her an odd look. "Do you mean to tell me that you've never had any before?"

Meena looked at her, horrified. "No!"

Matteo put out a line of white powder on the countertop of the table. Hannah rolled a ten dollar bill into a tube, put one end of the tube to her nose and the other end to the powder and snorted up the whole line. She sat back and closed her eyes. She let out a sigh.

Meena couldn't believe what she was seeing. "Hannah! What are you doing?"

Hannah didn't respond.

Cathy looked at Meena. "Do you want some?"

"I don't think so," Meena huffed.

"Come on. We don't do it all the time…just sometimes. Do you remember when you said that you were trying to lose those last five pounds?"

"Cathy!" Meena said embarrassed that she had mentioned it in front of their male companions.

"Sorry. I'm just saying. We use it to help keep the weight off. It helps us stay skinny. Plus…the high is *fantastico*!" Cathy exclaimed.

Meena looked at the line of powder before Pablo. He quickly snuffed it up his nose.

"I don't know about this…"

"Come on. Just try it. You'll like it. It does wonders for the waistline." Hannah said, finally speaking.

Matteo put a line of powder in front of her and handed her a rolled up piece of paper.

Meena looked at all of them. They looked back at her, waiting.

Meena thought about Brian and Maria's mother who was all strung out on drugs. Well, I can control it. Unlike her. Meena thought to herself. Plus, she wanted so desperately to lose the last five pounds…

Meena snuffed up the line and laid her head back.

Not bad…not bad at all…

Ψ

Anna wondered how far Caleb Jefferson was going to take this charade. That afternoon, she had come out of the board meeting fuming. The gall of the man! He had made changes to the company that Anna didn't totaly approve of and not only that, he also wanted to throw a shindig in his name, for the new takeover. To introduce, the newly renovated company to the public. As far as Anna was concerned, there was not a thing to celebrate about. And not only that, after the meeting, Caleb had pulled her aside and asked her—no—*told* her, that she would be the one to host the party. He gave her a monetary amount to work with. She had two weeks to plan it. He was certainly rubbing her face into it. Luckily she had Hector and Comete to help her out.

God damn him!

"That guy's a fucking joke," fumed Andrew Wilkinson to Anna. It was the end of the day, and they were walking to their cars in the parking lot. "It's almost as if he's trying to be spiteful or something," Wilkinson said giving Anna a suspicious glare.

Ψ

After about a week of preparations, they were three fourths of the way through. Lucky for Anna, Hector, and Comete had agreed to help, although they were not happy about it.

"I mean, what's this guy trying to pull, Anna. He's a sick man," Hector said to her.

Didn't she know it.

It was promising to be a very big party with a lot of guests. Important guests. Many important artists from their two labels, actors, actresses, politicians, and other high profile people would be rubbing shoulders at the soiree. Anna knew that if she didn't make this party successful, she would be shamed. She was sure of it. Caleb wouldn't pass of the chance to do it. If a disaster ensued, he would be sure to announce that she had been the one to put the thing together. Her failure would spread like wildfire throughout the public. It was embarrassing enough that she gave up the company without a good explanation. This would just be the icing on the cake…Anna shuddered at the thought. A lot was riding on this. She had to prove herself to Caleb. She would never give him the pleasure of her not succeeding.

Comete and Hector were well aware of the situation that their friend was in and they guaranteed to make it the most outstanding event that they had done all year.

Comete planned the menu and organized his cooking team together. They planned to start cooking the morning of the party.

Hector and his workers put together the decorations, the seating, the entertainment, etc.

Anna threw herself into the arrangements on both ends, crossed her fingers, and hoped that all would work out.

Ψ

"I must say, this destination of the week has been the best by far!" Gunnar Clarke said with an impish grin as he toasted Comete.

Comete smiled. "You're only saying that because the destination was England, you Brits and your arrogance!" Comete said with a chuckle. Gunnar, his producer, had been with him since the premier of his show ten years ago. It was pleasant and comforting to have him fly along with him in his private plane to the various destinations. And today, as they had done so many times before, they were flying home to LA.

"I certainly hope he picks up some speed! I have a gigantic feast to cook the day after tomorrow. I need all the rest that I could get. Plus, there are some things that I have to start to prepare tonight." Comete divulged to his flying companions.

"Why don't you just catch some shut eye on the plane?" said Bruno Kafe, his camera man, who was a small man originally from Kenya.

"I could never sleep on a plane. You know that. I'm too nervous to."

"It's true, he never does. Not once in the ten years that I have known him have I ever seen him sleep on the plane," Gunnar said with a shake of his blond head.

Comete leaned back and put on his headphones to listen to some Mozart. Classical music always relaxed him. As the music was playing he thought about Hector—the love of his life. He felt as if he could be with that man forever. Not once, in all the years that they had been together, had he ever felt the desire to stray and he never had. He had no need to. Hector was everything that he had been looking in his life. Then he thought about that day a few weeks ago when Hector had come back from visiting his father in the hospital. He had looked upset, but he refused to talk about it. Then Comete thought about Anna. And for a moment, he felt a flash of anger because of what she was going through. That damned man Caleb Jefferson. Anna had secretly divulged to Hector and Comete the true reason that she had given the company to the worm of a man. She had sworn them to secrecy. Comete didn't have a problem keeping secrets. And neither did Hector. He just wished that there was some way that he could help her. But then he thought he could help her—by cooking the best damn food that he could for tomorrow night. He would not let his friend down. He loved her dearly.

"Jesus Christ. What is all that thrashing around about?" Gunnar yelled from beside Comete.

Comete took off his headphones, feeling the turbulence as well.

Comete walked up to the cabin and came into the cockpit.

"What's going on?"

The pilot turned around and faced Comete. "We're getting some unpredicted strong winds."

"You mean you couldn't look at the weather before flying?" he asked his pilot.

"I did! I always do! It wasn't supposed to be windy like this. I would have never taken off in such a condition.."

Comete sat down. "Well, you can control the plane, can't you?"

"I'm trying. Please. Let me concentrate, Mr. Azevedo," he said desperately. "I believe that we're caught in a wind shear. I'm trying to keep the plan at a level altitude."

A thin sheen of sweat was beginning to form on the pilot's forehead.

Comete reluctantly shut his mouth and refrained from further questions. He took a seat behind the pilot.

"Oh God! The plane is going down!" Comete exclaimed, jumping from his seat.

The pilot wiped his brow. "I know. We're having a microburst. Please, calm down. The wind is so strong. I'm attempting to land the plane. I'm calling for help in the landing!"

Despite the instruction coming over the intercom, the plane continued to plunge downwards at a startling speed.

"What's all this then! Are we about to take a nose dive?" Gunnar asked, frantically bursting into the cockpit.

"I'm trying to regain control...hello? Hello? Oh, shit! I can't hear them anymore!"

"The boys back there are about to piss in their pants," the Brit continued, running a nervous hand through his frosted blond hair.

"Oh my God!" the pilot and Comete exclaimed in unison just before the plane nose-dived into the dense forest below.

When the plane hit the ground, the blackness surrounding Comete was absolute and final.

He didn't feel a thing.

Only, he didn't know it.

Ψ

"Yes. Okay," Hector said hollowly over the phone. He replaced the receiver on the cradle and just stared at the wall.

It had to be some mistake.

Comete. The love of his life. Killed in a plane crash. Would you come down to talk? They asked him. We found some of his organic material, but we're still trying to piece him together, they told him as gently as possible. They didn't tell him to come and identify the body, because whatever they found was beyond identification. Yes, I'll come to talk…

Hector felt the pressure, like a large fist, first start in his stomach, and slowly rise to his throat. He flopped back on the bed and stared at the ceiling. This had to be a dream. Just close your eyes, Hector. Then the dream would go away. Somewhere in the distance, he could hear the doorbell ringing and then there was pounding on the front door of his house.

"Hector?!"

He heard a voice call out. He didn't move. He concentrated on the swirling patterns of the plaster on the ceiling.

Finally, he heard the jangling of keys and the door opening downstairs. Next he heard the pounding of footsteps coming up the stairs.

Anna and Pamela appeared in the room.

"We heard on the news, Hector," Pamela said, with tears in her eyes.

They came over to where Hector laid, afraid of the condition that he looked to be in. Afraid that maybe he had taken something in an attempt to end his life.

Anna sat on the bed beside him. "You didn't take anything, did you?"

Hector continued to stare at the ceiling.

"I'm calling the ambulance," Anna said frantically. She began to reach for the phone.

"I have to go down there…they're still trying to gather his remains…" Hector said huskily.

Anna let out a big sigh. "I know, honey. We'll go down together. Remember. We're all in it together."

"I should have been on that plane with him," Hector said in a flat tone. "Everyone dies and leaves me behind. That is the great mistake. Maybe I'm cursed."

"No, no it's not Hector," Anna said, smoothing down his dark curls. "You were meant to be alive. And you are *not* cursed. I don't want to hear you say anything like that again."

"Yes. Stay alive to grieve and clean up the pieces of my shattered life each and every time." Hector slowly rose into a sitting position. "I didn't even get to say goodbye. it's all so final and sudden."

Anna could see that he was struggling to hold back the tears.

"It's okay, Hector. Just cry. You can cry," Pamela said rubbing his back.

And so he did.

Ψ

"I'm sure you could understand why at this moment I don't feel like putting together a party," Anna said calmly. "One of my closest friends has died. I have more important things to worry about."

Caleb stared at her without an once of compassion. "So, you expect me to call off the party tomorrow after everyone has been invited?"

Anna couldn't believe how cold he was. "Yes. I do. Otherwise, get someone else to do it. All you need to do is to find someone to cook the food. I already have a menu that my friend made before…the accident. They can use it or not. As for everything else, it is already taken care off."

"I'm sorry. But that's not going to happen. You have to be the one to do this."

"Why?" Anna pleaded. "I don't understand. Why are you continuing to do this to me? You have control of the company and everything. What else do you want?"

Caleb ignored her questions. He gave her a rueful smile and leaned forward. "This is a very important event. There is no way that you're going to mess it up for me. Do you understand? You are *going* to find someone else to cater the party and you're *going* to host it. Because if you don't I'll see to it that you regret it."

Chapter Forty-one

Anna had managed to find a caterer, although she knew that it could never compare to what Comete would have done. Anna tried not to allow herself to focus on Comete because every time she did, her mind would go off track and things wouldn't get done. But oh how she missed him. Today, he and his team would have been cooking, laughing and joking here in her kitchen. It would have been fun. Comete always made things fun. He just had that way about him.

Hector had been staying over at her house since that fateful afternoon. Most of the time, he would mope around the house or stay upstairs in the bedroom that he was currently sleeping in.

Hector was a man that hardly drank. But she noticed that he was taking to the bottle with an increased frequency and this troubled her. She hadn't seen him get stone cold drunk before, maybe just a little tipsy, but she feared that it would soon reach that point.

"Meena, have you chosen what you're going to wear to the party tonight?" Anna asked her daughter, as she was coming out of her room.

Meena quickly turned to her. "Ummm...I don't think I can make it."

"What do you mean?" Anna asked. Meena, as of lately, was beginning to worry her. Since she had come back from Miami, she had been acting suspiciously. She also started to spend more and more time in her room. Anna wasn't so sure that she liked the idea of Meena hanging around the two older girls Hannah and Cathy. Anna was also noticing that Meena was losing even more weight. As if she wasn't small enough as it were. She was beginning to regret allowing Meena to pursue modeling.

"Well...there's going to be a party for the models tonight... Antoinette Bontecoe is hosting it. I think it would be a good idea if I went. Some important people in the fashion and modeling world go to these things...It helps to make contacts."

"Why didn't you tell me about this before?" Anna asked.

Meena shrugged her shoulders. "I didn't know you positively expected me to go to your get together tonight."

Anna sighed. "All right. But I hope this isn't some crazy party—"

"No, Mom, it's not," Meena said hurriedly. She ran a shaky hand through her shoulder length hair.

Anna felt a stab of foreboding and was momentarily taken aback by it. Now where had that come from?

"Okay. By Mom. Hannah and I are going out to shop for an outfit," Meena called, rushing down the stairs.

"Okay," Anna answered.

Meena hurried outside to wait for Hannah. She was worried that her mother would sense that she was using drugs. She had also started smoking a little weed. Just for recreational purposes. It was no big deal.

Meena spotted her cousin coming in from gymnastics practice. She was dressed in track pants and a tank top. Maria was such a tom boy, Meena thought regrettably to herself. It was too bad, because Maria was pretty and she had a fantastic shape. If she wanted to, she could have guys lined up from the door of the house to down the block.

"Hey, Maria," Meena called.

"Hey. What are you doing?" Maria asked, putting down her small duffle bag.

"I'm waiting for Hannah. We're about to go shopping for something to wear tonight."

"To Auntie's party?" Maria asked, shielding her eye from the sun with her hands.

"No. I'm going to another party instead. Mostly for the models that I work with. But other people are going to be there."

"Oh," Maria said with a frown. "I though that Auntie wanted us at her thing tonight."

"Well, I can't go," Meena snapped.

Maria's frown grew deeper.

"I'm sorry. I didn't mean to be short with you. I'm just saying.... say! Do you want to come with us tonight? I'm sure that Hannah can get you an invite."

Maria looked surprised at the question. "I don't know. Anna's expecting me."

"Come on. Do you always have to do what Mom says?" Meena asked, slightly aggravated.

They both turned around to the blear of a horn. It was Hannah, driving her small BMW.

"Are you coming?" Meena asked Maria.

Maria thought for a minute and then said, "Fine. I'll come."

Ψ

"Are you going to come to the party tonight?" Anna asked Hector, who was currently sitting in the living room with a bag of potato chips. His eyes were glued to the television and the beginnings of a beard could be seen on his face. Never in all the years that Anna had known him, had she ever seen Hector with a beard—she was worried.

"Anna, you know better than to ask me that. Of course I'm not," Hector said without even looking her way.

Anna sighed and left the room.

Ψ

Brian looked at himself in the mirror for what must have been the hundredth time tonight. He looked good. Damned good in his Versace suit. He was so excited about going to the party that his aunt was having. A bunch of famous people would be there. Including famous artists.

Brian hoped that Nadina Zeen would be there.

She was one of his most favorite singers.

Ψ

Duke decided that this was one party that he was going to bale out early on. Not that it was horrible…it was just that there were no honeys for him to hit on. He wanted a party filled with willing and available girls for him to fraternize with. All the females here were either taken, too old, or had their noses too far up in the air to notice anyone but themselves.

Anyway, his friend gave him an invite to another party tonight that sounded like it was tending more towards his taste. His friend had promised that the place would be filled with lots of hot women and beautiful models.

He would definitely put in an appearance.

Ψ

When Brian saw Nadina, he was greatly disappointed to see that she was accompanied by a man. Although the man did look a little…swishy. But what man in Hollywood didn't look slightly so? Even if they weren't actually gay? Few, was the answer. He couldn't believe that he had actually thought of going up to her and striking up a conversation. Who was he kidding? He was just a kid in her eyes. A nineteen year old kid. He felt his cheeks flush. What a crazy idea. He was glad that he hadn't had the opportunity to follow through.

Ψ

"Who is that man standing over there?" Nadina asked her escort, Raul, a famous, Hollywood hairdresser who was a close and dear friend to her.

"I don't know girlfriend, but I wouldn't mind getting to know him!" said the smooth faced Uruguayan, excited by the stranger's dark, handsome looks.

Quite Suddenly, a short plump woman, whom they both recognized to be the senator's wife, swept in beside them and said, "I couldn't help overhearing you two as I passed by. I do believe that the young man in question is Anna Senghor's nephew. I believe that he plays pro baseball for the California Suns."

Nadina smiled like a Cheshire cat. "Thank you for the information, Mrs. White."

"Not a problem, my dears. Now. If you'll excuse me…" she said as she moved onwards and away.

"Hmmm…I hope he's not on that side of the fence, because I definitely want to know him by the end of the night," Nadina said forcefully.

"He's got to be like ten years younger than you," said her escort a little cattily.

Nadine sniffed at him. "So what. Do you think I care? As long as he's legal. Nadine cannot afford to go to jail. Besides. I know that's not a problem for you. You like them young."

Raul's buttery brown face took on a decidedly crimson undertone.

Satisfied on the affect that her little retort had on her friend, Nadine patted down her hair and turned to Raul. "How do I look?"

"Absolutely smashing, darling. As always," Raul admitted. "You go get him. And if he's my kind of guy, throw him over here to me."

Nadine started walking towards him.

Ψ

Brian wore a look of shock as he spotted Nadina walking in his general direction. But she couldn't be coming to me, Brian thought nervously. Her cinnamon brown skin glowed under the lights of the dining hall. Her slim, curvy body seemed to float on air.

She was gorgeous.

He wanted her. Badly.

"Hello there," the goddess said the moment she reached him. "I couldn't help noticing you from over there. My name is Nadina," she said and extended her hand.

Brian grasped it and quite unexpectedly, planted a small kiss on it. Nadine flushed with pleasure at the gesture.

"My name's Brian."

"My, my. And you're a gentleman. Are you *always* a gentleman, Brian?"

Brian felt an instant tightening in his groin.

It was lust at first sight.

Ψ

The moment that Duke arrived at the model's party, he was instantly mobbed by a group of young woman.

"Oh gosh! Can I have your autograph?"

"Oh, you're so cute in person. I could barely see you from the seat that I had at your concert last year…"

Duke was pleased with the attention. The girls surrounding him were gorgeous, but his eyes searched around the room for an even better prospect.

Then he spotted her.

She was standing amongst three other, beautiful girls, whom he assumed were models. One was a blond haired white girl with such a deep tan that if it wasn't for the blond hair, from the back, he would have thought that she was Latina or maybe even black. One other girl was black with a puff of long black hair. The other one was most certainly Latina with shiny black hair and smooth mocha skin. He didn't think that the one girl that he had his eyes on was a model. She was a little too short to be one. She was a caramel color with long wavy hair. Her waist was impossibly small and she had small, perky breasts. Her legs were strong and well muscled. She had a pert little ass.

Nice. Real nice.

"Hold up. I gotta go for a second. I'll be back," Duke said, waving the fans away.

They hesitatingly stepped back from him.

"Hey lovely."

Maria turned around and saw herself staring into the brown eyes of the famous rapper, Duke.

"H-hi," Maria said nervously. He was so cute! He was actually talking to her!

Maria glanced at her cousin. Meena cut her eyes at Maria. She was jealous that it wasn't her on the receiving end of Duke attention.

"Do you mind if I were to ask you to sit down so we can talk a little? You look like a really interesting girl. Besides being damn fine, of course."

Maria blushed.

"Is it an open bar?" Duke asked her, as he glanced over at the bar.

"Yeah, I think so," Maria answered, "but I can't drink I'm only—"

Maria felt a foot stomp down hard on her toes. It was Meena. She gave Maria a warning look.

"Let's go get us something to drink," Duke said.

"Okay," Maria said, to fascinated to say much else.

Ψ

"She's been talking to him all night," Hannah said bitterly.

Cathy leaned over close to Hannah ears.

"Come on. Don't spoil it here with these guys! They've got a shitload of money!" Cathy whispered referring to the two, tall, good-looking Arab guys that had befriended them and were now sitting down with them.

Meena was already cozied up with one of them, high out of her mind on coke.

Cathy and Hannah were halfway there.

Finally, Maria came up to their group with a smile on her face.

"So where's Duke?" Hannah asked, and giggled. The coke was starting to take affect.

"He had to leave. But he gave me his phone number. He made me promise to call him." Maria looked at them suspiciously. "Are you guys okay?"

"Why don't you have a drink?" one of the guys said to Maria.

"Who are you?" Maria asked.

"This is Yusef," Meena said, patting the guy that had his arm wrapped around her. "And that is Kalil," she said pointing at the one that had offered Maria a drink.

Maria sat down, a little uneasily, but accepted the drink.

The more and more that she drank, she noticed that the room was swirling around her.

"You guys. What's in this drink?" Maria slurred.

"Alcohol," Yusef said and giggled. "What else do you think? You cannot hold you liquor," he said in his clipped accent.

Maria shook her head. She must have been *really* was bad at holding her alcohol because at this point, after one half a glass, she could hardly see straight.

"I can't hold my liquor either!" Hannah exclaimed and kissed Kalil full on the lips. She slumped into his arms and chuckled. He chuckled as well after taking a quick peek at his friend.

Meena was leaned back against Yusef. She wasn't saying anything and was quite still.

Later on that night, when the party was still swinging, Yusef and Kalil helped the girls to their feet. Two girls leaned up against each of them.

"Where we going?" Hannah asked, wearily from behind closed lids.

"Don't worry. Just follow us. Everything will be fine," Kalil said soothingly. He glanced over at Yusef. They exchanged looks and continued on to the door, trying to be as inconspicuous as possible.

No one saw them leave.

Ψ

"Anna, I don't think that it's smart that you drive home tonight," said Franklin.

Anna stared at him through bleary eyes.

"What do you mean?" she said and hiccupped. She giggled and almost fell, but Franklin caught her. She leaned heavily against him.

"Well, you're drunk as a fish. There's no way you can get behind that wheel."

Anna looked up into his face. "I can handle my own, big boy."

Franklin chuckled. "Man, you really are drunk."

"Are you coming on to me," Anna slurred.

Franklin just sighed and shook his head. "Come on. I'll get someone to drive your car home. We're taking my car."

"Lovely," Anna said.

"You know Anna…you can't let this whole thing get you down."

"That's easy for you to say," Anna said airily.

"Why am I trying to reason with a drunk woman?" Franklin asked himself aloud.

When they reached the house, Franklin walked her to the door.

"I can see myself in. Thank you very much," Anna said touching his face. "Do you want to come in…fool around a little."

"You've got some serious beer goggles, Anna," Franklin said chuckling. "Besides. I don't think my wife would approve."

"Okay, suit yourself," Anna said breezily and she almost tripped over the threshold. for the hundredth time that night, Franklin held her up.

"I'll see you up the stairs, thought," Franklin said. "Wouldn't want you to tumble down."

"No, no. My friend is here anyways. He can help me," Anna said.

Franklin gave her a funny look. "Are you sure?"

"Anna?" a voice called from upstairs. "Is that you?"

"See?" Anna said to Franklin.

"Ah…a friend, friend…"

"No. Just a friend. He's gay."

"Oh, I see," Franklin said nodding.

Franklin shook his head and stepped back. "All right. I'll see you then. Okay? Sleep it off."

"Anna? Whoever it is I've got a gun, you know!" the voice from upstairs warned sternly.

After a swift wave, Franklin quickly stepped back and closed the door behind him.

Anna struggled towards the steps. She hiccupped and giggled to herself.

"Hector! You gotta help me up these steps. I don't think I kin' make it."

Hector appeared at the top of the staircase. He looked down at her.

"I don't know if I could get down those stairs...I'll try," Hector said with a chuckle.

Hector slowly made his way down the stairs and when he reached her he chuckled and threw up his hands

"If you haven't noticed Anna, I'm drunk," he said. Then his face turned serious.

"I sat up in that room and drank the night away."

"And if *you* haven't noticed, Hector, I'm drunk too," Anna responded.

They both looked at each other for a moment and started giggling. Soon the giggles turned into belly laughs, and they leaned against each other for support.

Anna buried her face in his chest. "Ah, Hector. I love you."

Hector leaned his chin against the top of her head. "I love you too, Hun."

Anna leaned back and looked up into Hector's face. For a long moment, they studied each other, as they held each other close.

Anna took in his honey colored eyes, his dark, almost black curls. His well defined jawbones, which were at this point covered with a short beard. She studied his arched, Roman nose that had a slight, appealing bump on the ridge...and suddenly she felt a flash of desire that started in her stomach and traveled down into her groin.

Hector studied her as well. He took in her smooth, cocoa skin, her long thin neck. Her big brown eyes, and her full lips. He felt a twisting in his gut and his chest grew heavy. Hector was shocked at his response and backed up a little. It couldn't be desire...he was gay! He loved men! It was only a handful of times, but he remembered throughout the twenty years that he had known Anna, he had once in a blue moon felt a feeling a similar. He had always interpreted it as just being the deep love that he had for her because of their friendship...but now he wasn't so sure. Because right at this moment...he was experiencing those feeling again, only now they were much stronger.

Hector stepped back even further and wiped his face with his hands. He sat down on the stairs and looked at the wall with an expression of bewilderment.

"What?" Anna asked.

"Whoa...I dunno. I think I'm really drunk...," Hector said slowly.

Anna sat down beside him and slumped against the railings of the stairs.

Once again, Hector turned to Anna and looked at her pretty face. He reached out a tentative hand, and touched her soft cheek. Anna stared at him, unmoving.

Hector ran a finger down the side of her neck. It was so soft. He had always wandered what it felt like...wait what the hell was he talking about? He didn't know...but, he was feeling something.

Anna sat still, and her breathing quickened.

Hector leaned in and kissed her full on the lips. Anna kissed him back. The kissing turned frantic and they began to grope and pull at each other's clothes.

"What are we doing?" Anna said between each kiss and caress.

"I don't know Anna! Tell me to stop it now!" cried Hector, but he made no move to cease his actions.

"I can't," Anna said breathlessly.

"Let's go upstairs!" groaned Hector, eager to devour her.

They ran up the stairs, giggling all the while. They stumbled into Anna's bedroom and into the king-size bed that Anna slept in alone.

"Ummm...I don't know what to do...," Hector said between breaths and he slowly eased down the zipper at the back of Anna's dress. "I've never done it with a woman before. Seriously. "

"You're good, you're doing good...," Anna said breathlessly. She began to slide off his tee shirt. Once the shirt was off, she moaned as she looked at his muscled chest. Dark hair covered it. She kissed his collarbone and reached for his pants.

"Ahh...Anna..." He peeled down her dress to her waist and stared in wonder at her high, full breasts.

Hector reached out a hesitant hand to touch her breasts. At first, he lightly ran his hand down the upper part of her cleavage, which caused Anna to moan. Encouraged, he touched her nipples and started to make circles on them. He lightly pinched them.

"You have...nice breasts," he said and flushed.

Anna smiled and leaned in to kiss him. He held her face between his hands. Anna reached down and slid down his boxers. He took off the rest of the way and flung them to the corner of the room.

"You're a good kisser," Anna muttered like a school girl.

"I never thought a woman could make me hot," Hector said and began sucking on her nipples. They felt so good to him! As he was doing so, Anna attempted to reach down and grasp his manhood. Not being able to reach, she moved down, releasing herself from Hector's eager lips. She grasped his member between the palms of her hands.

"Oh, Hector...you're so large," Anna said breathlessly.

"Ummm...," Hector groaned.

Anna continued to play with him until he was ready to explode.

"Let me be inside of you, Anna...lay back. I think," Hector whispered, flooded with desire.

Anna lay back on the bed. Hector drank her all in with his eyes. He ran his hand over her flat stomach and down to the silky trimmed hairs of her pubic area. Anna moaned.

"You're waist is so small," he said in awe as he gripped it briefly.

Hector smiled and ran his hand down the slippery cleft between her thighs. Like a child, discovering something for the first time, his face was in deep concentration and wonderment.

"It's so wet...and soft...really smooth," Hector said softly as he explored her farther. He gently slid a long finger inside of her. Anna moaned and writhed on her back.

"Come, Hector...," Anna said stretching out her arms to him. She opened her legs.

Hector awkwardly, but eagerly positioned himself between them.

"Do I just..."

Anna nodded her head. She reached down and guided the tip of his swollen member into her channel. Hector slid it the rest of the way in, holding himself up on his elbows. Anna moaned, and held his back.

"Oh, it's so…soft…and tight. It's like dipping myself into warm pudding…," Hector gasped.

Anna wrapped her legs around his slim waist.

Hector slowly began to thrust back and forth inside of her. Anna moaned and rubbed her hands up and down his back. "Yes, yes," Anna cried.

Hector, establishing a nice rhythm, moved faster and plunged deeper. He groaned in pleasure.

"Oh Anna! I can't believe this!" he exclaimed in delight.

"Hector…" Anna groaned, feeling the pressure of an orgasm build in her stomach.

Hector climaxed first and was quickly followed by Anna. Their sighs and groans of pleasure filled the dark room.

Hector collapsed on top of her, his penis still inside her.

Anna rubbed his broad back and felt all the muscles. She kissed his damp neck and ran her fingers through his dark, silky curls.

Hector kissed her forehead and pulled out of her. He rolled over on his back.

Anna snuggled up to him and rested her face on his chest.

Hector turned his face to her in the dark.

"You have the most beautiful eyes," he said to her before drifting off to sleep.

Chapter Forty-two

Brian woke and sat up. He looked around him and saw that he was in an unfamiliar setting and he was in a strange bed. Then he remembered. He quickly looked beside him. There was Nadina, sound asleep with the covers wrapped around her. The pretty features of her face were relaxed in slumber.

Brian felt a glow of pleasure. Last night had been amazing. Nadina had not been the first female that he had been with, but he felt that she had been the first *woman*. Real woman. The three girls that he had slept with before had been exactly that: girls that had no idea how to make love to a man.

Nadina not only loved to receive pleasure, she knew how to give it, and give it well.

Brian lay back in bed again next to Nadina. In her sleep, she swung an arm onto his chest and snuggled up to him.

Brian planned on keeping her around for a long time. He couldn't let her get away.

Ψ

Meena woke up with a pounding headache and blurry eyesight. She rubbed her eyes, and everything around her became clear. She was in a room with cement walls and no windows. She looked down at herself. She was wearing a light blue outfit that resembled a hospital gown. She looked around for the clothes that she had been wearing before. They were nowhere to be found. She was on a mattress on the floor. She was sharing the mattress with a blond girl sleeping in the fetal position. She was wearing the same thing that Meena was wearing. It was Hannah. On the far wall, opposite them, there was another mattress. There laid Maria and Cathy. They too were dressed identically and were in deep sleep.

"Where are we?" Meena asked herself, beginning to panic. She reached over and shook Hannah awake. Hannah groaned, rolled over, but remained asleep.

"Hannah!" Meena hissed and shook her again. Hannah slowly awaked. She fixed her hazel-green eyes upon Meena with a confused expression and sat up slowly.

"Where the hell are we?" Hannah groggily asked.

"I don't know!" Meena responded.

Maria and Cathy began to stir on the mattress across the room. They were soon awake and looking around with confusion.

"What the hell happened last night?" Cathy asked no one in particular.

None of them could give an answer.

Suddenly, they heard a metal door open. One of the men from last night, Yusef came in through the door. His face was stern.

"What the fuck is going on?" Hannah yelled at him. "Where are we?"

In two strides, Yusef was in front of Hannah. He swung a hand back and slapped her hard in the face. She screamed and hit the mattress where she stayed sobbing.

Meena jumped to her feet. "What are you doing?"

Maria and Cathy started to get up to go to Hannah. Yusef turned on them and gave them a venomous look.

"Stay where you are," he hissed.

Maria and Cathy froze where they were.

He turned to Meena, who was beginning to sit back down.

"That's right. No move from you either or else you'll see."

Hannah was sitting up now, holding her reddened cheek. Tears were streaming down her face.

"Fucking whores! All of you!" he screamed crazily.

Three more Arab looking men than came into the room. One of them being Kalil from last night.

Each man walked up to a girl and pulled her to her feet.

"Get up. It's time to go," one said coldly.

"Where are we going?" Maria asked, frantically.

The man gripping Maria shook her viciously. "You'll see when you get there. No more questions!" he screamed.

The four of them were hustled down a dark hallway and out a backdoor and into an ally. It was night. Meena wondered how long they had been in that room.

There was a black van with dark tinted windows waiting there for them. The back door of the van was opened and they were thrown inside.

"Please, please. Just let us go!" Sobbed Hannah.

"Shut the fuck up. Not another word from you," one of the men threatened and climbed into the back with them. He tied up each of their hands and ankles. He also gagged them, so they couldn't speak.

"If any of you get hysterical…" The man opened a black box that he had been holding and pulled out a large needle. He held it in front them. "I'll have to sedate you."

The four young woman exchanged horrified looks, but remained quiet.

As they were traveling in the van to an unknown destination, Maria felt her stomach begin to rumble with hunger. Her throat was also parched with thirst. But she was too afraid to say anything.

Finally, after an hour of traveling, they stopped the van. The four girls were unbound and were given something to eat and drink. Burgers and fries. Bottled water.

Meena watched Hannah scarf down the hamburger—Hannah was a vegetarian.

Finally, they were off again. And after about another hour and a half, they stopped once again. The man in the back with them opened the back door. The three other men in the front of the van came to the back and dragged them out of the van.

Meena's tried to adjust her vision to the night. She looked in amazement at the small jet plane before them. Meena was filled with fear. She stood frozen in one spot.

They were pushed towards the plane. But they realized that Meena wasn't moving. She was standing in one place and staring at them defiantly.

"Help!" Meena screamed once before one of the men swiftly moved towards her and slammed a fist into the side of her head. Meena heard the scream of the other three girls, which were quickly cut off when she went out cold.

They lifted Meena onto the jet and ushered the rest of the young woman on as well.

The girls, no longer bound, because there was nowhere for them to run while they were in the air, huddled together. They huddled around Meena's unconscious body as they stroked her hair and begged for her to wake up.

"She is fine," Yusef snapped sharply. "She will wake up soon."

"How do you know!?" Cathy exclaimed boldly.

"Because it would be stupid of me to destroy the merchandise," he responded with an evil leer.

Chilled, Maria looked out one of the small windows of the jet. The houses and the buildings on the ground below them looked like little toys and got smaller and smaller until they completely disappeared and were replaced by white fluffy clouds.

$$\Psi$$

Two days after Anna and Hector's lovemaking, they were still nervous and jumpy around each other. Neither had brought up the events of that night and tried, unsuccessfully, to pretend that it had never happened.

Besides, they had bigger fish to fry.

Maria and Meena had not come home after the night of the party. And as the next day went on...they were still missing. Hector and Anna also discovered that Cathy and Hannah were missing as well from two sets of anxious parents that had called her asking if their daughters were over at their house.

Missing reports were filed on all four girls. Anna was frantic with worry and her nerves were in shreds. She feared a mental breakdown.

Hector shared similar feelings.

Detective Muller, a medium sized man with a shiny bald head and dark brown skin, went into the club that had hosted the party two nights ago. His intent was to find out if anyone there had seen anything.

Muller flashed his badge at the lanky, white, young man behind the bar and asked him if he could speak with him for a moment. The young man shrugged and led him to a table.

"You work as bartender here?" Muller asked him.

The young man nodded, "Yep."

"Here's the thing. Four girls are missing. They were at the party held here Friday night. This was the last place they were seen. After that, they were seen no more." Muller reached into his pocket and pulled out four pictures.

"Have you seen these young women?"

The young man studied the pictures and quickly nodded his head. "I sure did. They came in here around eight o'clock. They were hanging out in a group together."

"Did you see them with anyone else?"

The young man thought for a moment before answering. His brow was furrowed in concentration. Then his eyes lit up. "Later on in the night, they were sitting with two guys at that table in the corner."

"Do you remember what the men looked like?"

"Well…they were looked Arab or something. Tall…dark eyes…tan skin…black hair…ummm…that's all I remember."

"Did you notice anything strange going on between them at the table?"

"Umm…no. I didn't. They were just laughing and having a good time. At least, that what it looked like."

"Did you see when they left?"

"No, I didn't."

"When did you realize they were gone?"

"Well, towards the end when people were leaving. Half of the people were gone already. I really wasn't keeping an eye on them or anything."

"Did you have a guest list by any chance?"

"I think there was…but I don't have that. The bouncer, Romel, would have had it because he was admitting the people in."

"So it was an invite only."

"Exactly."

"Do you have surveillance on this place?"

"Yes, but the owner would have to give that to you. He's not here today."

"That's okay. I'll contact him myself."

"And the bouncer. Do you know where I could reach him?"

"Yeah. I have a telephone number." The young man gave it to him. Muller took it up and slipped into his pocket. Muller pulled a card out of another pocket and handed it to the man.

"That's about all the questions I have for you today. That's my card in case you remember anything else you can call me."

The young man nodded and pocketed the car.

Muller quietly slipped out of the club.

Ψ

"I don't got the guest list anymore. You'll have to go to the people who hosted the party—Antoinette Bontecoe and her husband, Leon Binot," said the tall, well muscled Latino man to the detective.

"All right. You didn't happen to notice two Arab guys at the party, did you?"

The large man thought for a moment and shrugged his shoulders. "There were so many people there, that I can't remember any particulars like that."

"Okay. Here's my card in case you remember anything at all."

Ψ

Muller reviewed the surveillance tapes. But they were quite blurry and didn't give much detail. There was a hazy image of the group of six at a table, laughing and talking. But he couldn't see any of their faces very well. He thought that the four girls were behaving a little sluggishly, in fact, one of the girls, who looked like Meena Senghor, was leaned back against one of the men's arms and not really moving. After a while, he saw all of them get up, or rather, the two men got up and sort of pulled up the other four girls. The group of six were seen walking carefully to the door, weaving through the wild crowd, and slipping out the entrance.

Muller was hoping that there was a bouncer there when they left out the door, and there was, only the bouncer wasn't paying any attention to them. He was occupied with trying to disengage a fight that had developed just outside of the entrance of the club.

The surveillance cameras outside, picked them up getting into a black BMW and pulling off. The license plate of the car was a little blurry. He was able to blow up the image and see it better. Unlike the faces of the men, he was able to get a pretty good view of the numbers. He copied the plate numbers down.

Muller took out the guest list that he had gotten from the hosts and studied it. There were no names that stuck to him. The bartender at the club had told him that the men looked Arab. But there were no male Arab names on the list. There was a female's name that sounded Arab, Imani Benanou, but he had been told that was one of the models. He doubted strongly that she had anything to do with the girl's disappearance.

Muller looked up the plate numbers on his computer. It was soon discovered that they were registered to an Ahmad Majiid.

Muller then attempted to look up the address and the phone number of Ahmad Majiid. He found neither. Then he tried to find a social security number, a bank account, anything, in the name of Ahman Majiid. There was none.

Muller leaned back from the computer, perplexed.

He had reached his first dead end.

Ψ

For the fourth time that week, Anna woke up with extreme nausea that sent her rushing to the bathroom to throw up.

Not only that, she felt totally drained and the smell of food made her sick to her stomach. But it wasn't only the smell of food. It almost any smell that caused her stomach to turn.

On this particular morning, after throwing some tea and a slice of dry toast, Anna slowly got back into bed. She was relieved that it was the weekend and she didn't have to go to work. Today, by far, was the worst that she had ever felt this week. She was sure that even if she did have work today, she wouldn't have been able to make it in.

As she lay there in bed, a thought hit her forcefully and suddenly. She had felt exactly this way, sixteen years ago, when she had been pregnant with Jackie. Just the thought of Jackie brought a lump to her throat. No. No. She couldn't think of her now. It was too painful. Then she thought about her missing girls. Just the thought made her close her eyes and it brought on a pounding headache. The police were doing all they could, she reminded herself. All they could. But It wasn't enough. It had been a month since their disappearance, and there was next to nothing to go on. She feared repeat of the what happened with Jackie. Only this time, she had no idea who could have done this to them. Her first thought had been Caleb, but she had talked to him and was quite sure that he had nothing to do with it.

Anna held her head and moaned. *She was pregnant. She was positive that this was the case.*

The friendship between Anna and Hector had never been the same since that night of passion. They more-or-less avoided each other and they had never discussed it. Anna was hurt and wished that they had never done what they had. But it *had* happened, and there was nothing that she could do about it. And now, she was pregnant. Definitely from Hector because she hadn't slept with anyone since that night with him. They had slept together without protection and had been too drunk to consider possible consequences of their actions.

She was pregnant with her gay, best friend's baby.

Even saying it aloud to herself made it sound ridiculous. There was only one way to deal with this.

She would go to the doctor, and make sure that she was absolutely, certainly, pregnant.

After that, she would arrange for an abortion.

Ψ

"Please, you gotta come with me to the doctor, Pam," Anna begged her friend.

"You don't have to beg me. If you want me, I'm there," Pam said seriously. "Do you mind me asking what the problem is?"

Anna looked her friend's almond shaped eyes and then looked down at the table between them.

"I think I'm pregnant. I just want to make certain," Anna muttered.

Pamela looked shocked. She leaned forward, close to Anna. "What? By who? I didn't know you have a guy in your life."

"Well, it was a one night stand...umm...that's all," Anna said nervously.

Pamela frowned. "You? *You* had a one night stand?" Pamela asked, thinking that it wasn't like her friend to do that.

Anna nodded her head. "Look. I don't want to talk about it."

Pamela nodded. "Whatever you want. We'll go together, okay?"

"The appointment's tomorrow."

"Saturday. That's fine with me," Pamela responded, and held Anna's hand across the table.

Ψ

Anna and Pamela sat in the waiting room of the doctor's office awaiting their name to be called.

Anna watched the people coming in and she wondered what they were coming in for. She wondered if any of them were coming in to get pregnancy tests like her or if they were coming in for the flu, or for a regular checkup. She let her mind drift, as she imagined.

"Are you okay?" Pamela asked her, breaking into her thoughts.

"I'm okay," Anna said softly.

"We'll get through this, don't worry," Pamela reassured her.

A young black woman with brown skin and short hair dyed an auburn color, walked into the office and sat down across from Anna and Pamela.

Anna studied the girl. She looked somewhat familiar, but she couldn't place her. The young woman smiled kindly at her. Anna smiled back.

"Gosh, Dr. Mead's office is always overflowing with patients, isn't it?" the young woman commented with a smile.

"Yes. He's a good doctor," Anna said softly as she smiled. She remembered how she met Dr. Mead, years ago as a patient in the hospital after Winston had beaten her. Anna shook her head of those thoughts. She couldn't think of that now. But it was hard. Her life was full of bad memories and bad events.

Anna held her stomach as a rush of nausea hit her. Pamela gripped her hand.

"It's okay. don't worry. The morning sickness isn't forever."

"You don't know how right that is," Anna said, fixing her friend with a look that said she didn't want to discuss it any farther.

The young woman overheard their conversation. "I'm actually here to refill on birth control pills. It's so much easier...you know, don't have to worry about getting pregnant."

Anna glared at the young woman. The girl's face turned a reddish brown. She picked up a magazine and stuck her nose into it without another word.

Anna instantly felt bad for her reaction. The girl wasn't trying to offend her. She was just offering advice. She thought of telling the girl sorry, but just then, the receptionist called her name. It was her turn to go in.

Anna exchanged a look of anxiety with her friend and then rose and followed the woman back to the examining room.

Ψ

As Tanya went home, with her birth control tucked securely away in her purse, she thought about the woman sitting across from her with her Asian friend. The feeling that she knew her face had been nagging her since she left the doctors.

Then it hit her. That was Anna. Her boss's friend. The woman that owned…or rather…used to own the record company.

Hmmm…by the way that she and her friend were speaking, it was clear that she was pregnant. And foolishly, she had offered some advice on birth control…she knew that sometime the next generation up from her were not always up to date on things like the newest types of birth control. But the woman had not appreciated her advice. Not that Anna looked a day over thirty…but Tanya knew, from media news, that Anna was nearing her 39th birthday.

Well, that was certainly an interesting piece of information. Tanya wondered who Anna Senghor was sleeping with.

Ψ

Hector leaned into his desk and took out the newspaper that had Anna's picture on the second page. It was about the press conference that Anna had had weeks ago, discussing her step down from ownership.

For the second time that week, he read the article. He didn't know why he was reading it. But in the back of his mind, he knew that he just wanted to look at her picture. He hadn't seen Anna for about two weeks now. He missed her, but he was afraid. He had thought that the feelings that he had towards her would disappear with the alcohol, but they hadn't. He felt something for her, and he was too afraid to try and discover what that was. Because he knew that it was coming from an alien part of him. A part that he never knew existed. He almost wished that he had never slept with her…only for the reason that their friendship was now on the rocks. He couldn't deny the fact that night of lovemaking had been memorable for him and wasn't sure that he would take it back if he could.

Hector stared at the picture of Anna until his eyes got blurry.

Suddenly his office door was swung open. Hector jumped up in his seat.

It was Tanya. She wore a grumpy looking expression on her cute face.

"What is the matter? You scared me half to death!" Hector exclaimed, trying to calm his racing heart. He stuffed the newspaper into his desk, but not before Tanya's quick eyes had gotten a glance.

"I saw her in the doctor's office the other day," Tanya said casually.

"What are you talking about?" Hector muttered, his cheeks turning a fire engine red.

"I mean Anna Senghor. Your friend. Yesterday, she was at the doctor's office. We were waiting in the waiting room together. She looked familiar to me, but I couldn't place her at the time. It wasn't until I was coming home that it hit me who she was."

Hector sat up in his chair, and attempted a casual pose. "What was she doing there?" he asked.

Tanya shrugged and began to play with the stapler on Hector's desk.

Hector tried to remain calm. He gently took the stapler out of her hands, and replaced it on the desk top, away from her. He cleared his throat.

"Well, I talked to her. She was with a friend, I think. Some Asian woman..." Tanya didn't mention that Anna and the friend had been discussing morning sickness. She didn't want to start any rumors. She had gotten into enough trouble doing that in the past.

Hector, by now, was alarmed. Was Anna sick? He was worried, and then he began to feel guilty. They hadn't talked for so long...

"Anyways. The guy, Henry Mill's on the phone screaming my ear off, he says that he didn't want that country band that we had booked for his..."

Hector was no longer listening to Tanya. His mind was a thousand miles away.

This evening, he would go and see her.

Ψ

"Okay, okay," Hector said trying to calm the ranting man on the phone. "I'll come over right away and fix it. Yes. This evening. Don't worry. We won't use that band again. Yes. Thank you Mr. Mill."

Hector placed the phone down.

He had to take care of Mr. Mill. So there would be no going over to Anna's tonight.

But he would definitely see her tomorrow.

Ψ

"Are you sure that you don't want me to come with you?" Pamela said.

Anna shook her head. "You're at work. I don't want you to get into trouble. By the time it's over with, you'll be out of work. You can pick me up then, if it's okay with you."

"Of course, Anna. You don't think I would make you go home by yourself after such a procedure, do you?"

"I know," Anna said with a smile. "Thank you."

After hanging up, Anna pick up her car keys and headed out to her car.

She touched her stomach once she was behind the car wheel and said softly. "Sorry. It's just not the right time nor the right circumstances."

Then she drove off.

Ψ

Once leaving Pamela's workplace, Hector frantically rushed to his Maserati. Once he got out onto the highway, he cursed the long line of traffic and banged the wheel with his fist.

Pamela had reluctantly told him why Anna had been in the doctor's office that day. After reviewing in his mind what Pam had said about "an Asian woman", Hector had quickly realized that it had to be Pamela. The next morning, before heading to his office, he had stopped by Pam's workplace to talk to her.

Anna was pregnant. With his child.

The thought gave him a funny feeling and he thought that he was about to faint right there in the car. But he got a grip on himself and concentrated on what he had to do.

He had to stop her from getting that abortion.

Ψ

Anna looked around the office in the abortion clinic from behind her large black sunglasses and her long, brown, wig with bangs that half covered her face. She didn't want to be recognized by anyone.

After about twenty minuets of sitting in the office, she heard someone come through the glass doors. She kept her face straight ahead. Everyone in the office was staring towards the door at whoever it was… so Anna reluctantly looked over as well.

It was Hector!

His handsome face was frantic and had a this sheen of sweat covering it. His dark curls were pasted to his forehead as his brown eyes scanned the room. His eyes passed over Anna twice during the times that he swept the room. Then he got a confused look on his face. He reluctantly entered the office and perched on the edge of one of the chairs as he looked over at the receptionist desk. He clearly wanted to go up there, but was reluctant to do so.

Oh God! What was Hector doing here? She didn't want him to recognize her. She picked up a magazine and brought it up to her face.

Hector went up to the front desk.

"Hello. I'm looking for an Anna Senghor. Did she go back already?" he asked the robust, pale, woman behind the desk.

The woman checked over the list.

"No. She hasn't gone back yet."

Hector breathed a sigh of relief and once again, his light brown eyes swept over the office. *Where was she?*

"I don't see her in the office…"

"Look, Mister, Who are you?" the heavy woman asked, sternly.

"I'm—I'm her friend."

The woman scanned the office and pointed her pen at a black woman wearing large shades and long brown hair.

"There she is. You don't recognize your own friend?"

Hector didn't respond. Instead he rushed over to where Anna was sitting and squatted down in front of her.

Anna slowly lowered the magazine, realizing that she was discovered. She cast an angry look at the woman who pointed her out.

Anna pulled the glasses off her face. "What is it Hector?" she asked, impatiently.

"Please. Can we talk about this? Let's go get something to eat," Hector said grasping her hand with desperation.

"No we cannot talk about it. I have an appointment." Anna sad stiffly.

"Yeah. To kill my baby," Hector said trying to remain calm.

"You don't have to worry about it," Anna muttered.

"Yes I do!" Hector exclaimed loudly. Several heads turned in their direction.

"Would you shut up!" Anna hissed.

"If you don't come outside and talk with me, I'll make a scene right here in this office," Hector promised.

Anna angrily stood up and walked outside of the clinic.

"What do you want?" she hissed, turning on him ferociously once they were out on the sidewalk.

"I want you not to get that abortion…I want you to keep our child."

Anna laughed hysterically. And for a moment, Hector was afraid that she had lost her mind.

"What? Keep my gay best friend's baby? What, are you nuts? With everything that I have going on, I don't need another complication like this one."

"Anna, but you wouldn't be raising him alone—"

"I don't give a fuck! I have enough problems…I don't need to be a single mother to a baby that I gave birth to by a man that doesn't even like women!"

Hector threw his hands up into the air. "That's what I thought! That I didn't like women. But I like you, Anna. And something more…I don't know what to think anymore! That night. That night with you… did something to me Anna. I wanted you. I wanted to do it again. I can't get you out of my mind!"

"You certainly have a way of showing it," Anna mumbled. "We haven't seen each other in over two weeks."

"I was afraid, Anna," Hector said stepping closer to her. "But. I'm not afraid anymore. If there was ever a woman that I wanted to be with, it was you. Not another one. I'm tired Anna. I'm tired of looking for that one guy who's going to be everything to me and then finding him only to have him be taken away from me...either that or he cheats on me." Hector held her hand in his large ones. "I don't want to look anymore, Anna. You. Me. We're nearing middle age. We don't have a lot of time left to have a child. You've been my best friend for years...we've been so close. I think...that we should try this out, Anna. I think that we should give us a chance."

Anna studied his earnest face, looking for a hint of doubt. There was none.

Anna stepped closer to him and wrapped her arms around his neck. She buried her face into his chest. He smelled faintly of Acqua Di Gio Giogio Armani Cologne. Hector squeezed her close and kissed the top of her head. He ran his hands down her back and rested them around her waist. He chuckled and stepped back.

"That's some getup you have on," he said with a smile, his dimples showing.

Anna felt a flutter in her chest as she looked at him. Hector. Her man. Her gay best friend, becomes her man. He was so good-looking. He had the good, dark looks that were an instant attraction to almost anyone with blood running through their veins.

Anna smiled and tugged on her wig. "I was trying to be inconspicuous."

"Believe me. You looked anything but," Hector said touching her face. He leaned over and kissed her tentatively, gently, and then withdrew.

"You don't know how different it feels to kiss a woman," Hector said with a smile.

"Bad difference?" Anna asked, as they walked towards their cars.

"No, not bad," Hector said, trying to come up with the right words. "But it is different. The lips, the aura. I don't know how to explain it any better," Hector said with a shrug.

"Okay. You drive back to your house and I'll follow," Hector told Anna.

"Are you always going to be so demanding from now on?" Anna asked, jokingly.

Hector smiled softly. "That's my child in that stomach and…it's my woman that's carrying it. I can't be too careful. I wouldn't want to lose either one."

Ψ

To Meena, the nights and the days seemed to stretch on together without a break. Her life in the windowless, dark, quarters of the harem was oppressive and stifling. The rich velvets, the dark silks, and satins of the furnishings caused a feeling of claustrophobia and panic. Sometimes Meena looked around her, and came short of having a panic attack.

It had been two months that she spent here, in Saudi Arabia. Two months of living hell. The only things that kept her sanity was her cousin Maria and her two friends Hannah and Cathy. But the four of them were not the only ones housed here. There were ten others. Most of them from other countries and lands. With different customs and different languages. One or two were from Russia, one from Germany, another from Kenya, one from Ethiopia, one from Nepal, another from India, one from Thailand, one from the Philippines , and one from Spain. But all brought here for the same reason. To be sex slaves to a rich member of the royal family known to them as ʿAbd al-Latif—Servant of the Gentle. This was ludicrous to think about, considering his treatment of them.

Upon first arrival—right after they were purchased by him—they were given invasive physical examinations, an extensive battery of tests, and lab work were carried out on them—obviously to make sure that they were healthy.

Night after night, Meena would hear screams, moans, and pleas coming from one of the rooms as the prince settled in with his victim for the night. Every night was a different room. Every night was a different woman. And before, Meena would stay awake in fear, as she listened to the heartbreaking pleas of the young women as they begged their master to be merciful to them. But he never would. With

Players of the Game

trepidation, Meena awaited her time, as did the rest of the girls, she was sure.

The first night that he had come to her, it had been a nightmare. The moment he entered the room, he had commanded her to take of her clothes. Meena, coming to think of the long, black, ibayah as a sort of protection to hide behind, had refused.

Then he was instantly upon her. Her tore all of her clothes off, pushed her upon the bed and forced her legs open. He had stripped down naked and lay on top of her, his face leering and menacing.

Then he had pushed himself into her without warning. He grunted on top of her, as he tried to force his member through her tightness. Then he began to hump away, while all the while, Meena screamed beneath him. She clawed at his face and bit him in his shoulders. She had gotten a cuff in the face in response, so she stopped.

A couple of times a week, it would happen this way. She was now at the point that she would just be waiting for his appearance

She finally just gave up.

A few weeks later, she found out that she was pregnant.

She was totally helpless.

Ψ

A month ago, Anna had decided to go back to her old private investigator and old flame, Greg Fenner. He had been more than happy to do the investigation.

Greg had not really taken to Hector presence, but he remained polite, so it really didn't matter.

Five months later, Greg had come up with a lot of information, but no definite place that he could pinpoint to where the girls were.

The police were still doing their investigation, but they had come up with even less.

Both the police and Greg feared that they were no longer in the country. In fact, they believed that it was a strong possibly and were now looking at other countries such as South America and Canada as possible places.

"Do you think they're further than that?" Hector had asked Greg one afternoon when he was over at the house sharing information with Hector and Anna.

"Further than across the boarders?" Greg thought for a moment and then said. "It's possible." Greg shifted in his seat, growing uncomfortable.

"What is it, Greg, there's something else, isn't there," Anna said, holding her stomach which was now swelling from the baby—actually *babies*, to be exact. A week ago Hector and Anna had discovered that they were going to have twins. Two days after that, Hector had presented Anna with a five carat diamond ring and asked her to marry him. She had happily agreed.

"Well...I've been doing a little fishing around and found a guy that knew one of the men, Kalil Sadif, that were in the club. At first, he refused to talk to me. But after flashing a little green, he opened right up. I also promised him that I won't contact the police. He said that years ago, he used to be...a trafficker."

"A trafficker? What do you mean? Drugs?" Hector asked, with a furrowed brow.

Greg shook his head. "No. I mean a...sex trafficker. This means, he would find girls, mostly American because he operated here, and smuggle them to other countries. There, he would sell them to 'pimps' who ran brothels."

Anna gasped. She felt her throat close up and she began to panic. Hector was instantly at her side.

"Come on Anna. Let's get you upstairs. You need to relax. I don't want you hearing any more of this!" Hector exclaimed.

"I can't...I have to know...,"Anna gasped.

"Let me speak to Greg and I'll tell you later. Okay? I promise," Hector said leading up the stairs. He glanced back at Greg who looked worried.

Once Anna was safely upstairs, Hector came back downstairs.

"Is she okay?" Greg asked.

"She's fine. She's resting. I just don't want her getting upset. It's not good for her," Hector said.

"Of course not," Greg said.

"So what else can you tell me?" Hector asked.

"Well...I'm looking into the possibility...that this could have happened to the girls although the man denied that his friend wouldn't have anything to do with that. Apparently Kalil Sadif was an engineer student at MIT. He graduated four years ago. All his family lived in Saudi Arabia."

"So, do you think that's where they might be?" Hector asked, nervously. "Do you know the name of the other man in the club that night?"

"Yes to the first question and no to the second question."

Hector nodded slowly. In his mind, the wheels were turning.

Chapter Forty-three

"Hector, that's a crazy idea and I refuse to let you do it," Anna said firmly.

"Well, how else are we going to get Meena and Maria back?" Hector asked her, earnestly. "If we don't do this, we might never see them again. Saudi Arabia's no playground."

Anna sighed and looked down into her lap. Hector held her face and tipped it up until she was staring him in his eyes.

"I'm worried, Hector. What if something happens to you…and then you'll *all* be gone. What will happen then?"

"Nothing's going to happen to me, Anna. Trust me. I can speak the language, and I can act the culture. I've been to my mother's country Bahrain, many times. I lived in Saudi Arabia for a year when I was fourteen. I still remember what it was like." Hector paused. "I spoke to Brian about it. He wanted to come. But I told him no."

"Oh, no. Not Brian too," Anna said worriedly.

Hector touched her hand. "Don't worry. I told him no, Anna. He's not coming with me."

Anna breathed a sigh of relief and asked, "Why did you live in Saudi Arabia?"

"My father's business," Hector answered. His father. He thought of him now and remembered the joy on his face when he told him that Anna was pregnant and it was his child that she was carrying. His father had been even happier when he found out that she was carrying twin boys and that they were engaged. Never in a million years would Hector have thought that his life would turn out like this. It was surreal.

"How long are you going to be there?" Anna asked. She was aware that she was whining, but she couldn't help it. But she knew there was no other way. She had to see her daughter and niece again.

"I don't know. Greg is coming with me. We're hoping that it wouldn't take that long to locate them."

"Greg's going too?" Anna asked, in wonder

Hector nodded.

Anna sighed and smiled slightly. "Okay. I just want you and the girls to come back safely. Please."

Hector smiled. "I don't plan on coming back any other way."

Ψ

Visitors, unless native, were not readily welcomed into the Kingdom of Saudi Arabia. Particularly not Americans and non-Muslims. Hector made certain that both he and Greg got exit visas. Using his mother's family's connections, he was able to get permission to enter the country and he was also able to obtain exit visas. For if they didn't have one, they wouldn't make it out.

Luckily, Hector could more or less blend in. He had a somewhat Arabic appearance, thanks to his mother's half of the gene pool. Also, he new the language and he knew the customs.

Greg, although quite new to the experience, learned quickly, taking cues from Hector. If he didn't open his mouth, most people mistook him to be a from the southern part of the Arabian Peninsula, from a country like Yemen or Oman. Once, he was even mistaken for being from upper Egypt.

On their first night in the Kingdom, they spent the night in a hotel. But Hector thought that it would be a better idea if they were to rent accommodations.

They found a nice, medium sized villa in Riyadh that rented out for a monthly fee of about 7,000 in American dollars. After settling in they reviewed their methods and options.

Despite their hope, they knew it wasn't going to be easy.

Within the next few weeks they carefully and discreetly made inquiries. From once city and town to another, they went where they were directed by some to go. They went where their guts led them.

Little, by little, they compiled bits and pieces of information.

They would disguise themselves as Saudi businessmen, wearing the traditional robe and headdress. They wore leather sandals upon there feet. The sun was hot and the weather dry.

Because of the closed nature of the Saudis, when it came to anything sexual, Hector had to be extremely careful and delicate when making inquiries. He also had to go to the right areas and to the right people. But Hector and Greg quickly learned than money, large sums of it mostly from Hector's pocket, drew information from people that wouldn't otherwise talk. Having money gave them instant status in Saudi Arabia. Hector, because of his knowledge of the Arabic language, would do the talking, while Greg would stand stoically by, wearing a no-nonsense look on his deep caramel face that seemed to be carved out of marble.

They were quite a team.

That night, after another day of questioning and payoffs, Hector called Anna.

"Hector, I miss you so much," was the first thing that Anna said once he was on the phone. It had been just over a month since they had last seen each other.

"I miss you too," Hector said wistful. Man, did he miss her.

"How are you feeling?" Hector asked.

"Tired, but other than that, I'm fine."

"I hope that you're not still working, Anna. I thought we agreed that before I left, you would stop," Hector said gently. He knew that Anna had a strong mind of her own and did as she wanted. He didn't want to push her. He knew that was the quickest way to make her withdraw.

"One more month, Hector," Anna said with a smile.

Hector laughed. "Sure. You'll be working until your water breaks. Like you did with...Jackie. I just know it." Hector said shaking his head.

"Your mom's over here all the time. She's so sweet. Always has been. So your sister...she has a new boyfriend. Steven's his name. I think."

"Ah, a new boyfriend. What else is new?" Hector quipped. His little sister went through men like water.

Hector updated her on what he and Greg had found out and what else they were planning to do for the next two days.

When he got off the phone with Anna, promising to call tomorrow night. And as usual, he called his father and chatted with him for a while.

Finally, he climbed into bed. He needed all the sleep that he could get.

Tomorrow would be a busy day.

Ψ

"Did you eat yet?" Maria asked her cousin, sitting beside her on the large, sandy colored, velvet, cushion.

Meena looked up at her cousin quickly and then lowered her eyes. "No. I'm not hungry."

"You've got to eat, Meena," Maria whispered. Whispering, that's all any of them ever did. Not that they were required too…they just did it naturally. The surroundings affected them so.

Meena looked across the room at the Indian girl. Her belly was swollen with child. She was feeding herself grapes.

Soon, Meena thought, she would be like that.

Cathy slunk up beside them. She wore a bright red, flowing skirt and a matching top. Gold hoops hung from her ears and bangles were on her wrists.

Unlike Meena, Cathy opted to dress in provocative clothes and bright flashy colors. She once told them that it was to ward of the depressiveness of their surroundings. They didn't have to wear the ibayah when in the harem and amongst women. The only time that they were required to wear the ibayah and their veil, was when the male servant came in with their food three times a day, but Meena still wore her ibayah at all times, except when she went to sleep. Meena didn't understand Cathy's reasoning. The bright, provocative, clothing did nothing to cheer her up.

The prince had taken a special liking to Cathy, for some reason. Once the most vocal person in the groups when it came to badmouthing their oppressor, Cathy no longer spoke badly of him. Meena also noticed that she was seeing more and more jewelry on Cathy every time she saw her.

"Hey. Did you see Hannah?" Cathy asked, sitting down beside them

Meena and Maria shook their heads.

They hadn't seen Hannah for two days now and they were getting worried.

The next day, through the grapevine, they had discovered that the prince had sold her off to one of his friends that had taken and interest to her after one night.

So Hannah was shipped off to another compound, to another palace.

Another oppressor, an other abuser, another nightmare.

It was quite possible that they might never see her again.

The time stretched on forever. Their lives seemed like one big, everlasting, eternal night.

Ψ

Eight months. Eight long, hot, months had passed and Hector and Greg were still not home yet. It also seemed that they were not any closer than they had been a month ago to getting to the girls.

Anna, had given birth to their two twin boys. Hector and Anna named them Sebastian and Theodore. Anna insisted that she was doing fine. Hector was very tempted to go back home, but he knew he couldn't. Not after coming so far. He was disappointed that he missed the birth of his twin boys, but he accepted it.

Hector's father, though very sick now, was still alive and holding on. One night, he tearfully admitted that he was hanging on to see the wedding of his firstborn son.

His younger brother's wife, Heather, gave birth to their second child a week after Anna had. A girl they named Brianna.

And next week he would be turning 39. A year away from forty. Middle aged, but he didn't feel it. He felt like he did when he was in his late twenties. Sometimes he could hardly believe that he was almost forty. The years had certainly gone by fast.

Hector and Greg were now practically as close as brothers. After having been through all those months together in a strange land, they hadn't much choice.

From a very reluctant source, Hector and Greg had discovered the names of three men, two from Egypt and one from Syria, that were masters in the trade sex trafficking. Hector hoped that he could find them, which he wasn't having much success in doing. Once found, he hoped to question them and hoped that they had some information concerning the four girls.

That night, Hector had spoken to his mother and she divulged some information to him.

"I spoke my brother, your uncle Kareem. He has a friend, Hamed Sariyah. Copy the name down. He's staying in Riyadh. He has agreed to speak to you and Greg. Often, when he goes on business trips to Saudi

Arabia…he uses some of the services of local 'pimps'. It was very hard, but my brother has managed to convince him to talk to you two. But you must promise…to keep the information to yourself."

Hector nodded, "I give my word."

"Okay. But you must tell *him* that. Here's his number. You can call him and set up a meeting. Call before ten in the morning."

Hector copied the name and number down. He shared the information with Greg.

"This might be the big break that we've been looking for," Greg said excitedly before they went off to bed.

They certainly hoped so.

Ψ

The man watched the house, long after the lights were out. In the shadows, in his car, he reported on his cell phone, back to his friend.

Time to go home and rest for a few hours. He would, once his friend came to replace him on the watch.

Americans had always intrigued him. These two were no exception. He wondered what they would come up with next.

Ψ

The next morning Hector called the number at nine o'clock in the morning. A man answered the phone.

Hector greeted him in Arabic and told him who he was. The man was silent for a moment and then asked him to meet him in his hotel room at noon. He gave Hector the directions.

Hector readily agreed and recognized this to be the custom. Most businesses in Saudi Arabia opened from around 7:00 or 8:00 a.m. until noon, took a long break until 3:30 or 4:00 p.m. and began working again until they closed around 7:00 p.m.

Hector said goodbye to the man and hung up.

He turned to Greg and smiled.

"We have a meeting."

Ψ

The hotel that Hamed Sariyah was staying in was large and luxurious. Hector was sure that the cost for staying her each night was expensive.

When they reached the suite, they knocked on the door. A slender, dignified looking man with olive skin and a pencil thin mustache opened the door and stepped back to let them in.

The man came right up to Greg and Hector and shook their hands with a nod and a greeting.

"*Salaam alaykum*," said Hector and Greg before each of them shook his hand. Both Greg and Hector made sure to shake with their right hands. The left, was considered unclean.

He returned the greeting.

By now, Greg was so used to the customs of Saudi Arabia that the close proximity that Hamed Sariyah stood next to him, didn't make him step back. Greg had also picked up many words and phrases throughout the eight months of being in Saudi Arabia to the point that he could get by in terms of conversation. But he was, by no means, close to being as fluent as Hector, who had grown up speaking the language.

After removing their shoes, the men sat down. Hamed offered them coffee and some small, almond cakes that were incredibly sweet. Hector and Greg accepted. For a while, the three men sipped the coffee and nibbled the cakes silently.

Greg consciously kept the soles of his feet firmly on the ground. He knew the offense taken from exposed soles.

Hector waited for Hamed to speak first, out of respect. After all, he was his uncle's friend and was an elder.

"What is it that you want to know?" Hamed asked, in perfect, but accented English.

"*Amo* Hamed," Hector began, referring to the older man as uncle. "My friend and I are in a dire situation here. We wish to find four girls that we know, for certain now, that had been taken into this country, kidnapped from their homes in America."

The older man listened in silence. His eyes went back and forth between Greg and Hector, sizing them up.

"We were informed that you might have knowledge of…traders in the area. Please, if you may, can you give us the names of those people

Players of the Game

and where they are. I swear to Allah. None of this will leave this room, what is said here," Hector said.

The Bahraini man looked at the both of them in silence for a moment and then looked down to pick up his cup of coffee. He took a sip from it as Greg and Hector patiently waited for him to continue.

"I will help you. Now that you have sworn by Allah that you and your friend will keep quiet. Also, because you are the nephew of a dear friend of mine, your uncle. He had requested this from me, as a personal favor. I am willing to grant it."

Hector breathed a silent sigh of relief. As did Greg.

"There are two men…that I deal with. They go simply by the names Aban and Faris. Now all I usually do is call them and they give me a selection of girls…"

Hector felt sick to his stomach as he listened to this man's confessions. He tried not to show it though.

"Now. I know that they'll only see you if you are interested in doing business. I return to Bahrain in a few days, *Inshallah*. I can possibly set up a meeting with them. But you must make it clear to them that you want to do business with them."

"By any chance. Are they from Egypt or Syria?" Greg asked, speaking for the first time.

The Arab man's dark eyes flashed to his. "Yes. How did you know?"

"Well, previously we were looking into three likely prospects. Would you mind looking at the third name? The other two names match," Greg said taking the list out of the pocket of his thobe. He handed it to Hamel.

Hamed's sharp eyes looked it over. He then handed it back to Greg.

"I don't recognize the third name. But the other two might know him. Would you two like for me to arrange a meeting?"

Hector and Greg waited patiently as Hamel made arrangements with the 'pimps' over the phone. After a quick goodby, Hamel hung up the phone and turned to the two men.

"It is set up. They will meet with you tonight."

Ψ

When Hector and Greg had left, Hamel Sariyah made a phone call.

"Hello, Jabbar? This is Hamed. I need you to do me a favor…"

Ψ

"Okay. You know the drill. We're from Yemen. We're here on business and we want some entertainment for the night," Hector said to Greg.

Greg nodded his head. "I know enough Arabic to make it believable."

Hector and Greg rented a Mercedes. Donned in full Saudi attire, they arrived at the meeting place.

They approached a small house with stucco siding. Greg knocked on the door and glanced around. It was night and there was hardly a soul around.

A bronze skinned man stuck his bald head out the door and stared at them

"*Salaam alaykum*," Greg greeted with a nod.

"Malik and Omar?" the man asked, in Arabic. Hector nodded.

The man waved them into the door. They stepped past him and entered the small house. He seated them.

In rapid fire Arabic, he asked them where they were from, what they were doing in Saudi Arabia, and who lead them here.

Hector answered all these questions, knowing that it was a test. Even the quick Arabic that the man had initially used with them was a test to see if they were true Arabs who totally understood and used the language. Luckily, Hector was.

The man asked them what kind of woman they were looking for. Greg, roughly understood what he was saying and muttered a single sentence in description. The man nodded and asked Hector.

"My friend and I were also interested in some girls that my friend recommended. I cannot give you his name, but he said that he was with some girls…four that came in together, all friends."

The man looked at him quizzically. "What were there names?" he asked, in Arabic.

"Meena. Maria. Cathy. Hannah. One of them has long, blond hair. All of them pretty, models," Hector said, in put-on excitement. He spoke earnestly as if he were really interested in a night of passion with the mentioned ladies.

The man rubbed his chin and continued to study them.

"We want two for each of us," Hector said with a cackle.

"I know of whom you speak," the man said. "Unfortunately, they are no longer with me. They haven't been with me for many months… about eight months to be exact."

Hector felt his stomach drop in disappointment.

"Where can I find them?" Hector asked.

"I am sorry. They are no longer on the market. They belong exclusively to a member of the royal family," the man said with a sickening smile.

And before Hector and Greg knew it, there was the sound of the safety on a gun clicking behind them. Hector and Greg turned around. There was a man standing behind them with a gun. When they turned around again, the man in front of them, who they had been talking to, slipped a hand beneath his shirt and pulled out a gun as well.

"Who the hell are you two?" the man asked in Arabic. "And no lies or I shall shoot your heads off."

Hector and Greg slowly raised their arms.

"Fine, but you'd better hurry up and kill us before they come," Greg told the man in Arabic.

"Your Arabic is terrible," the man in front of them spat to Greg. "Who are the 'they' you are speaking of?" he asked.

Hector flashed his eyes to the door. The man on the other side of them glanced uneasily on the door.

"Well…you'll see," Hector responded.

"Don't you know that we've been watching the two of you almost from the moment that you came into Saudi Arabia?" the baldheaded man told them. "I bet you didn't even know that."

For the second time, Greg's eyes flashed to the door. Both men looked at the door nervously.

"Go stand outside and watch for anyone," commanded the bald headed man to his companion. "And you two. Move together in front of me. No sudden moves."

The other man went and stood outside, closing the door behind him. Hector and Greg moved as directed.

The bald man continued to watch Hector and Greg, with the gun on them.

"Now, who the hell are you?" he screamed, waving the gun at them.

Hector swallowed hard.

"I know that you've been here, poking around and asking questions. Don't you know that the two of you have stuck out like sore thumbs because of your questions?"

"Did Hamed set us up? Did he tell you about us?" Hector asked.

The bald man only grinned.

Hector again glanced at the door. The bald man was growing flustered. He studied the door and called out the other man's name.

"Faris!" He heard no answer. "Faris! Are you alright out there?"

Again, there was no answer from the friend.

Hector and Greg exchanged questioning looks.

The bald man, called Aban, was clearly worried now. He wiped at his sweating brow. The striped, button-down shirt that he wore had wet spots all over it—he was sweating profusely.

"Sit down over there!" Aban screeched to them. They sat down on the wooden chairs.

Aban backed up towards the door, keeping his eyes on them.

Greg fingered his key to the house that he and Hector rented. It was in his hand. Suddenly, he got an idea. A way that he could get to the gun strapped to his leg...

Greg threw the key to the wall just as Aban turned his head to open the door. He quickly rushed to where he had heard the key drop.

Greg quickly lifted his thobe and took out his pistol. He trained the gun on the Arab man in the corner.

"Drop the gun, Aban. Drop in now," Greg said.

Aban didn't move. He sneered at him

Hector pulled out the gun that he had hidden in his headdress. He trained it on Aban as well.

Aban, shocked that two guns were now pointing at him, dropped his gun to the floor.

"Get down to the floor. Kneel," Greg said in broken Arabic.

The man slid to his knees and put his hands behind his head. Greg rushed up to him and took the gun from the floor. He put the safety on and slipped it in his pocket. He pulled the man up to his knees and led him over to the wooden chair. He pushed him down into the chair. The bald man glared menacingly at Greg.

Greg turned to Hector. "Watch him. I'm gonna go see what happened to our friend out there."

Hector nodded.

Greg slowly crept out the door, keeping the gun cocked and ready. There was no one outside the door as far as the single light showed. He went outside the boundaries of the rays that the single bulb put forth. The night was dark and hard to see through. He continued on down the alleyway. Suddenly, his foot his something solid. He almost tripped, but steadied himself. He looked down.

It was a body. He kicked at it. It didn't move. He couldn't see the face, so he grabbed the ankles and pulled the body into the low lights. He turned the body over

It was the body of Faris lying in a pool of blood. There was a bullet hole through the side of his neck and another hole through his chest.

He was very dead.

But question was, who had done it?

Inside, none of the men had heard the sound of a gunshot. Whoever did it, had a suppressor on the gun.

Greg quickly looked around him. There was not another soul save for a couple of skinny, mangy, dogs that hunched past. He frowned in confusion. He grabbed the dead man's ankles and slowly backed up, dragging the body with him. He pulled the body into the house then shut and locked the door behind him.

Greg looked at Aban. His face had turned three shades lighter. He stared at his dead friend in shock. His mouth was wide open. He looked at Greg.

"You killed him!"

Greg shook his head. "I didn't, but somebody did."

Hector raised his eyebrows in amazement. He was very surprised. He was still holding his gun at Aban.

"No. I don't know who did it," Greg answered before Hector could ask him.

The man in the wooden chair gave Greg a dirty look and pointed the soles of his feet at him.

Greg only laughed. "You can do that as much as you want. You're still going to have to answer my questions."

"Never!" the bald man spat.

Greg pointed his gun at the man's head. "Either you speak, or you end up like your friend over there," he said pointing with his head.

Aban's lips tightened in anger.

"Now. You're going to tell us what happened to those girls," Hector said carefully. "Tell us, and maybe you have a chance at staying alive."

"We sold them to the Prince ꜥAbd al-Latif. They're now in his harem," he spat out. "You two would never get in there." He stared at them scornfully. "A harem is like a fortress."

"Never get in?" Greg said with a raised eyebrow, "Is that a challenge?"

Chapter Forty-four

No matter how much she tried, Meena couldn't touch her baby that was just three days old. The very sight of the child, a pretty, dark olive skinned girl, made her stomach twist.

"Did you name her yet Meena?" asked Maria softly that evening.

Meena looked at her cousin as if she were crazy. "No. I don't want anything to do with her...I don't want her."

Maria said nothing. Understanding.

"Wait. I have a name for her. Afya," Meena had muttered.

"What does that mean?" Maria asked.

"Shadows," Meena said silently. "Which is exactly how my life has been in this hell hole," Meena said mournfully.

Maria said nothing. Thankfully, she had not the bad luck of getting pregnant that first month in the harem, because soon after, they had found an Australian doctor that smuggled birth control to them. But unfortunately, it had been too late for Meena who had become pregnant within weeks of arrival.

"Mujib is here. Put on your veils," said Carla, the Filipina girl.

Meena and Maria quickly donned their veils.

Mujib, the manservant from Bangladesh, came in with a tall woman donned from head to toe in a veil.

"This is Suha. She will be the servant here for a few days when I go back home to visit my uncle," Mujib said arrogantly.

The young woman said nothing. Mujib gave a curt nod and left. Before he left tomorrow morning, he intended to get a piece of Maria for one last time until he saw her again next week. At first, she had been resistant. But soon, realizing that she had no choice, she gave herself to him.

Of all the girls, she enticed him the most.

Ψ

Greg was sweating profusely under the black ibayah that he was wearing. He cursed frustratingly in his head. Out of the two men, Greg was smaller, so he had been elected to wear the women's traditional dress. This damn thing was nothing like a thobe which was nice and cool. This getup was hot and sweltering.

He and Hector had paid Mujib off handsomely to give them access to the harem. He had readily agreed because of the American dollars and the chance at taking a small vacation back home. He left word with the cook and other staff that his cousin was replacing him for a few days. No one batted an eyelid when he said this. No one particularly cared. He was safe.

The young women went back to lounging around, chatting, and eating. They hardly paid him any attention.

Greg stayed in the harem for the next two days without revealing himself to anyone. He made sure he kept very quite and very much to himself. He needed some time to get a feel of how things worked around the place, in order to ensure that their escape would be successful.

Finally, when the end of the third day came around, Greg knew it was time for them to make their move. Ready or not, Hector would be waiting for them on this very night. Besides, the young manservant would be coming back tomorrow morning.

Greg spotted Maria and Meena. But not Hannah and Cathy.

Greg walked up to Maria and Meena. He nodded at them and greeted them in Arabic in his most womanly sounding voice.

They greeted him back.

"You know, you don't have to wear that veil and head covering in here. It's only the women here. You've been wearing it for three days straight."

Greg shook his head and said that he wanted to, in his best Arabic.

Greg gestured for them to follow in into one of the bedrooms.

"I have to speak to you for a moment," he told them.

The two girls exchanged looks, but followed him. Once the three of them were in the bedroom, Greg shut and locked the door behind him.

Meena and Maria only stared on, perplexed.

Greg spoke in his own voice, in English.

"Meena. Maria. I'm here to help you. Please. Be very quiet. I'm with Hector. I know Anna. My name's Greg."

Meena and Maria stared, doubtfully, at what they thought to be a woman.

Finally, Greg took off the veil and the head covering.

Meena and Maria gasped at what they now saw was a man.

"Believe me now?" he asked, with a slight smile.

Meena and Maria stared at him in wonder. "I can't believe it!" they whispered excitedly.

"Believe it. We leave tonight. Where are Hannah and Cathy?" he asked them.

"We don't know where Hannah is. All we know is that she got sold off to some cousin of the prince," Meena answered.

Suddenly, they heard the cry of a baby wailing. It was Afya.

"Whose baby is that?" Greg asked, curiously.

Meena gave Maria a warning look.

They shrugged their shoulders. "One of the girls," Meena said.

"So those little girls have babies for the prince?" he asked, shocked.

Meena and Maria uneasily nodded their heads.

"What about Cathy?" Greg asked, starting to put back on his head coverings and veil.

"She's with the prince…he's seemed to have taken a liking to her," Maria said with disgust.

"Is she going to be back tonight because we can't leave any later than that. With or without her, we'll have to leave," he said.

"She should be back tonight," Maria answered.

"What about Hannah?" Meena asked.

"Do you have any idea where she might be?" Greg asked.

Maria and Meena exchanged looks and shook their heads, dejectedly.

"We have no idea," Maria said finally.

Greg frowned. "Then there's nothing that I can do. The longer we stay in this country after tonight, the thinner our chances are of ever getting out."

Ψ

By eleven o'clock that night, Greg was nervous and ready to leave, despite the fact that Cathy was nowhere to be found.

"We have to leave here in like half an hour. With or without her. Hector's waiting for us."

Finally, at the very last minute, Cathy appeared. Humming to herself as she swept into the living room.

Maria and Meena pulled her into a bedroom and locked the door.

"What the hell's going on?" Cathy asked.

"We have a way out of here. But we have to leave tonight," Maria whispered excitedly.

Cathy gave them a queer look. "What about your baby, Meena?"

"I can't take her with me. I don't want her, anyways. Anything that reminds me of that man...Cathy, you'd better not mention her."

"To who?" Cathy asked.

"Greg. The guy who's helping us get out. He's with Hector and Anna," Maria said impatiently. "Now come on. We gotta get out of here."

Cathy looked hesitant to make any moves. "I've gotten so used to this place," she said finally.

"You can't be serious, Cathy," Meena hissed. She grabbed her friend's wrist. "You're coming. Like it or not."

Cathy allowed herself to be dragged along. Suddenly, she pulled herself back.

"Wait. I have to get my jewelry!" Cathy exclaimed.

"Forget the—"

"No. I want it," she said stubbornly.

They waited impatiently as she collected her jewelry. She placed all of her necklaces and her bangles on her at once.

"Those damned things are keeping so much noise! You're going to wake everybody up!" hissed Maria.

Cathy curled her lip at her.

The three girls snuck out to the courtyard, where Greg was waiting in his flowing ibyah and veil.

"Come on. We have to go a little ways on foot. Then Hector will be waiting there with the car," Greg continued.

They escaped from the high walls of the compounds and through the large iron gates.

As they walked, Greg whispered instructions to them.

"Now. When we get into the car, I'm going to pretend to be... Hector's wife," Greg said awkwardly.

The girls stifled a laugh. But Greg caught on.

"Don't laugh. It ain't funny," he said in a voice that he hoped sounded stern, but really didn't.

"And you three, will be the daughters. Hector's going to play... daddy. Now come on," Greg said hurriedly as he tried to cover his embarrassment.

Finally, they made it into a back alleyway. There was a black Mercedes with darkly tinted windows waiting. Hector stepped out of the car, wearing a crisp white thobe and full headdress.

Maria and Meena ran up to him and all three embraced in a long hug.

"I thought I would never see you again," wept Meena. Maria was crying too. Cathy and Greg stood awkwardly by and watched.

"Come on. We have to hurry," Greg said, cutting their reunion short.

"Where's Hannah?" Hector asked.

"She was sold off to some royal cousin. They haven't a clue where she is," Greg responded.

Hector frowned. "Well, we have to leave tonight. If we don't who knows when we'll have another opportunity."

There was nothing else they could do, but leave without Hannah.

"So, here's what's going to happen. Greg and I paid a Turkish pilot to take us into Jordan. From there, we'll get a flight to Israel. Then from there, into America," Hector said to them as he drove.

"Don't we need passports?" Maria commented as they drove.

"Yes. I have you girls' passports. I even have Hannah's. I got it from your parents. Now. It's no fun driving across Saudi Arabia. We have to head north, which will take a couple of hours. Now, the trick is to drive carefully. The people here are animals on the road," Hector told them.

About half an hour into their driving, they were rear ended on one of the main roads.

"Shit!" Hector cursed. He turned to the rest of them. "Stay in the car and don't say a word."

Hector got out of the car and slammed the door. The three of them watched as Hector argued with a short pudgy man, in the car behind, in loud, rapid Arabic.

Hector strode back to the car and got in. He slammed the door shut.

"Now we have to wait here until the damn traffic police get here. The bastard says that I slammed on the breaks. Not true."

Finally, the traffic police arrived. Both cars drove with the police to the station to make a report. The other car was found at fault while Hector was issued a permit to get his car repaired. This week, he was to look into estimates to fix the damage and get back to them.

Hector thanked them and took the permit. But he had no intention of waiting around for that. The car was still drivable, so they would continue.

After fifteen minutes, they reached a roadblock. A checkpoint where the police would make sure all documentation of a car's occupants were in order.

"Okay. I'll do all the talking. The rest of you, don't say anything," Hector warned them.

The police, dressed in uniform asked Hector something in Arabic. Hector answered back and gestured at Greg, his 'wife' and then at the three young women in the back, his 'children'.

The police looked at all of them, glancing from person to person. He said something rapidly to Hector. Hector nodded and reached into the glove compartment, pulling out papers. He handed them to the police. The police looked them over and handed them back.

The man snapped a command. Hector snapped back at him in rapid fire Arabic. The man's face grew red. Hector said spoke again. This time a little gentler. Hector handed him another piece of paper. Hector stepped out of the car and walked to the trunk of the car, which couldn't be opened because of the damage from the accident. They watched Hector point at it and say something. The police man huffed and walked back to front of the car.

"Get out of the car," he snapped in Arabic to the occupants of the car.

They glanced at Hector. He nodded slightly.

Greg, Meena, Maria, and Cathy piled out of the car.

The Saudi police turned and walked into his booth, while a woman, with only her dark eyes exposed, walked up to Meena first, and patted her down. Satisfied, she moved onto Maria and then lastly Greg.

Greg tensed up as the woman's hands moved over him. He stepped back. The woman officer's eyes snapped to Greg's in suspicion.

"What is your name?" the woman asked Greg.

"Suha," Greg answered, softly.

The woman stared at him hard for a moment and then turned away. The male officer came back out and handed Hector the papers. He gave them permission to go on.

"My gosh. All of that?" Meena asked, amazed.

Hector nodded his head. "And that's only our first checkpoint."

Ψ

When Mujib came back the next morning, he quickly went out into the courtyard and overturned the loose stone in the corner. He pulled out the pile of American dollars and counted them eagerly.

He had been paid very well. His lips would remain sealed concerning the girls' disappearances.

Although the trip was very short, he had enjoyed his stay in Bangladesh. Before that, he hadn't seen his family in almost two years. If anyone came to him about the woman Suha, he would deny it. He would be believed above a group of women. Women were known liars. They couldn't help but deceive.

Ψ

About forty minutes from where they were supposed to meet the Turkish man, they stopped to eat in the car. They pulled off onto the side of a deserted side road.

The first gunshot nearly caused Maria to choke on the food. "What was that?" she cried frantically.

Another gunshot shattered the side view mirror.

"Get down!" yelled Greg.

All but Hector and Greg remained at seat level.

Greg took the gun from the holder wrapped on his left leg. Hector pulled his gun from his thobe.

They slowly got out of the car and gasped at who they saw.

It was Aban and another man. Both were wearing a glare.

"Drop the guns, bastards."

They did.

Aban stared at the fully robed figure that was Greg. He didn't quite know what to make of it. But Aban had a sneaking suspicious about who it was.

"Take the damn head scarf and veil off," he yelled.

Greg took off the veil.

Aban and the other man laughed.

"How funny. Dressed as a woman. It is a shame that you will have to die here in the dessert so shamefully. Make the rest of them get out of the car."

Meena, Cathy, and Maria climbed out with their hands up in the air.

"Start walking!" Aban yelled.

The five of them started walking with two guns pointed at them.

"Where are we going?" Hector asked, in Arabic.

"No questions! Just shut up and do as I say."

"I suggest that you let them go," a voice called out.

Aban and the other man turned around and so did Hector and the others. There behind them was a tall man dressed in an all black thobe and headdress. His handsome, smooth, tan colored face wore an expression of perfect tranquility. He carried a large machine gun in his hands. Standing beside him, was another shorter, pudgier man that sported a full beard and mustache. He too held a machine gun. On the other side of the tall, handsome Arab, there was a tall, dark, chocolate colored man. He wore a thin mustache, and had dignified features set upon a long narrow face. He too was dressed in a full black colored thobe and had a gun.

"Who the hell are you?" asked Aban in Arabic.

"Don't worry about that. Just drop the gun," the cocoa colored man snapped quickly in Arabic.

The two men dropped the guns and raised their hands.

The short pudgy man and the tall handsome man, quickly walked up to Aban and his companion.

The black man stayed put and gave the group a slight smile.

"Do not worry. You are safe," he said in Arabic.

"Who are you?" Asked Greg, looking quite ridiculous in the ibyah, now that his face was exposed.

"My name is Jabbar Suaad. I am a friend of Hamed Sariyah."

Hector looked at him in shock and amazement. "Huh?"

"Hamed told me that he had had a meeting with you and your... friend over here. He told me that you were the nephew of one of his closest friends. He was worried that the men that he directed you to would do something wrong.Knowing how dangerous they were, he called me for...some reinforcement."

"Wait. Were you the one who shot the guy outside the house?" Greg asked, amazed.

Jabbar smiled and pointed at the pudgy man holding a gun against Aban's back. "Actually it was Ishmael over there that shot the bullet, but yes. That was us. We had been watching you all since you left to go to meet that animal over there."

"We thought that Hamed had set us up," Hector said with a small smile.

The dark man's handsome face transformed into an even broader smile. "That is far from the case. He wanted you and the other's safety ensured. He is a good man, Hamed."

"Thank you so much," Greg said. "We appreciate what you've done."

"Think nothing of it. But now, we must bid you farewell. You should be quite safe from here on out." Jabbar turned to Greg and smirked. "Perhaps you should change into a thobe now. There is no need for the dress up."

Greg face turned hot with embarrassment. The others laughed.

Their three guardian angels had left with Abad and his companion. What they were going to do with the two men, Hector didn't even care to know. But one things was definite. They wouldn't be bothering them anymore.

The weary group of five made it to the Turkish man who welcomed them onto his small plane.

The first thing they noticed was the crucifix that hung just outside the cockpit.

"You're a Christian?" Hector asked, in English.

The Turkish man turned around and smiled. "I am."

And then they were off.

At last their ordeal was over.

Epilogue

Hector and Anna were married not long after his return to American soil. Hector's father was alive and happy to see his oldest son married. He held his six month old twin grandsons in his arms during the ceremony.

Afterwards they went on their honey moon in Trinidad. They spent their days having fun and their nights making love.

Two days later, Demetrius Minatos passed peacefully away in his sleep. He was 71.

He left Hector his share of the inheritance. This was a very hefty sum, indeed.

In good faith, Kati admitted herself to drug rehab. She ran away about two weeks into it, unable to comply with the rigorous regiment. She reunited with her old druggie friends, but stayed clear of Caleb.

She no longer wanted anything to do with him.

Outside of Maria and Cathy, Meena was the only one at home who knew about the baby that she had in Saudi Arabia. It would forever remain her secret. She went back to modeling with a vengeance and became an instant success, shooting to the top in the fashion and modeling world. But the mare thought of being with a man, disgusted her, so she remained single as she fought off any arduous suitors that came her way.

At night, she suffered from nightmares. And during the day, from time to time, from acute anxiety attacks.

She smoked weed to calm her down and did coke a few times a week. But sometimes it helped stem the nightmares too.

Cathy, seeming to forget the year spent in a Saudi harem, went right back to her partying ways. And in the fashion world, just like Meena, she was the very top. One of the most sought after models. Once night, on a dare, she married a Polish count that she had met at a party. A week later, she divorced him after hooking up with a Nigerian businessman.

One man was never enough.

No one knew what became of Hannah after being whisked away to live in the mansion of Prince ʿAbd al-Latif's wealthy cousin. All attempts to contact her and inquire after her were futile. In fact, they were not even sure exactly where she was.

It was a sad situation.

Duke, hearing about Maria's ordeal in Arabia, found himself all the more attracted to Maria. He got into contact with her, and a sizzling relationship ensued. Pretty soon, Maria was in love and Duke was in lust. They eloped in Las Vegas soon after.

Delvair, Duke's gay discoverer and agent, was very jealous indeed. He had always harbored a secret crush on the young rapper.

Brian continued his affair with Nadina Zeen. It was a hot and fiery romance that made the headlines of every tabloid and magazine.

Brian proposed to Nadina a total of five times. And a total of five times, Nadina turned him down.

Marriage wasn't for everyone, particularly not for Nadina Zeen.

Pamela went on vacation in Tobago and found her dream chocolate hunk. They were soon married and settled down in California to live. Within a few months, she was pregnant with their first child.

Caleb reined supreme at Entourage Productions and felt proud about his business accomplishments. Unfortunately for him, his wife Tiara, not getting enough attention from her overworked husband, left him and ran away with one of his body guards whom she had taken a fancy to.

In his lifetime, Caleb had learned that the world was like a game board and all people were executors, in the game of life. Some players were good at what they did, making all the right moves and choices, and others were not. Some players reached their objectives while others fell short. Nevertheless, he decided, that we were all, Players of the Game.

Printed in the United States
100411LV00003B/2/P